OATH KEEPERS MC
HYBRID COLLECTION

INTERNATIONAL BESTSELLING AUTHOR
SAPPHIRE KNIGHT

Hybrid Collection

PRINCESS
Copyright © 2016 by Sapphire Knight

Cover Design by CT Cover Creations
Editing by Mitzi Carroll

This book is a work of fiction. The names, characters, places, and incidents are products of the writer's imagination or have been used fictitiously and are not to be construed as real. Any resemblance to persons, living or dead, actual events, locales or organizations is entirely coincidental.

All rights reserved. With the exception of quotes used in reviews, this book may not be reproduced or used in whole or in part by any means existing without written permission from the author.

The author acknowledges the trademarked status and trademark owners of various products referenced in this work of fiction, which have been used without permission. The publication/use of these trademarks is not authorized, associated with, or sponsored by the trademark owners.

WARNING

This novel includes graphic language and adult situations. It may be offensive to some readers and includes situations that may be hotspots for certain individuals. This book is intended for adults 18 and older. This work is fictional. The story is meant to entertain the reader and may not always be completely accurate. Any reproduction of these works without Author Sapphire Knight's written consent is pirating and will be punished to the fullest extent.

AN
OATH KEEPERS MC
NOVEL
Princess
INTERNATIONAL BESTSELLING AUTHOR
SAPPHIRE KNIGHT

Hybrid Collection

DEDICATED TO

My serial readers.
Thank you for sticking with me!
If you've read all my previous books,
I hope this one knocks your socks off.

Sapphire Knight

MC - Motorcycle Club
Ol' Lady - Significant Other
Chapel - Where Church is Held
Clubhouse/ Compound – MC home base
Church - MC 'Meeting'

Oath Keepers/Widow Makers hybrid charter:
Viking – President (Prez),
Heir to the Widow Makers MC, previous NOMAD
Blaze – Vikings cousin and Princesses security, previous Widow Maker
Torch – Death Dealer (punisher/enforcer), previous Widow Maker, grew up with Viking.
Chaos – Close with the NOMADS,
Ex NFL football player
Nightmare – Good friend to Viking and Exterminator,
club officer, previous NOMAD
Saint and Sinner – Hell Raisers, previous NOMADS
Smokey – Treasurer, previous Widow Maker
Odin – Vice President (VP), Vikings younger brother,
previous Widow Maker
Mercenary – Transfer from Chicago Charter
Scot – Deceased
Bronx - Deceased

NOMADS:
Exterminator
Ruger
Spider

Original Oath Keepers MC:
Ares - Prez
Cain – VP
2 Piece – Gun Runner - SAA
Twist – Unholy One
Spin – Treasurer
Snake – Previous President's son
Capone – Deceased
Smiles – Deceased
Shooter – Deceased
Scratch – Deceased

One

VIKING

Savage. That's what my mother called me growing up—a no good, filthy savage. I didn't know it at the time, but she was right.

If finding an ounce of pleasure by causing others pain makes me one, then so be it. I'll own that title because it's true. I fucking love pulling the skin away from others' flesh as they scream in agony.

I wish I could say that I haven't always been this way, but that would be a lie. Not that I'm above lying; if anything, I'll use it freely whenever it benefits me. For example, when I found this MC, I didn't come by it with any good intentions.

Arriving tired and irritated, I was sent by an MC called The Widow Makers. They wanted me to take out some rival Oath Keeper member whose road name was Exterminator. I was told that he had murdered some important members from another club—The Southern Outlaws.

The few SO Members that were left alive warned me multiple times during our meeting about how Exterminator's a ruthless killer, and I should watch him before making my move. Of course, I was planning on some recon; anyone who's been paid to kill before knows that shit. If anything, I was overconfident. Had it been me sent on the run to eliminate the Southern Outlaws, none of them would have been left alive.

After scouting Exterminator for a few days, I showed up at the bar he'd visited every night. I figured if I got there early, I'd have the one up on him.

My plan started to go to shit when I got into it with another club. The members had gotten me down on the ground, and I was struggling. I can handle three okay, but more than three I have to work at it.

Three of them had been taking turns at kicking out my right knee and then, in the end, striking me in the back with a metal stool to get me to fall. Once I hit the floor, five guys were on me like fucking leeches. They were determined to teach me a lesson but too big of pussies to do it one-on-one.

Exterminator and his boys stumbled into the middle of it all and bailed my ass out. Why? I'll most likely never know. They aren't the friendly type to most, but for some reason chose to have my back.

He saved my life that night. I didn't even know it was him until after it was too fucking late. Once a man saves your life, you don't take his cash—no matter what amount is offered.

The brothers helped me out, putting me up for as long as I needed. They were clueless, not knowing that I had my own means to make it. In time, they opened up some and showed me a brotherhood that I didn't know existed.

They aren't like the other clubs I'd been around. The Nomads from the Oath Keepers MC were all about themselves, but also each other. They never acted individually, but whole like a team.

With time, I was offered a spot to ride with them. It was hands down the best decision I've ever made.

I've never admitted my true reasons for going to the bar that night and my brothers have never pried. Eventually, though, I know my dirty deeds will catch up to me; they're always in the wind, riding my tail, waiting for me to fuck up and come barreling out.

The Nomads run differently than the rest of the clubs; we're freer. We don't belong to one Charter but float around to wherever we're needed or feel like going. The regular clubs' rules don't necessarily apply to our group. We have a structure amongst us, but not as strict as the Charters. A few of the brothers like Texas a lot, so we end up spending most of our time here when we stop for a bit. Otherwise, we keep on the move, rarely staying at one place for too long.

Scot and Exterminator pretty much call the shots when it comes down to things; otherwise, we work more as a unit. Ironic since we don't play well with others often. None of us own much; it makes it easier to travel.

Hybrid Collection

We aren't tied down by any women either. Scot had an Ol' Lady at one point, but when she passed on, he went Nomad. That was before I was around, though. Exterminator and Nightmare don't talk much about if they had an Ol' Lady in the past or not.

I'm fairly young compared to them, so I'm all about playing the field when presented with getting my cock sucked. Pussy's another thing entirely; it's gotta be worth it for me to get in it.

Ex and Night are pretty tight with each other; they handle a lot of shit together. It's not quite as excessive as Saint and Sinner; sometimes I wonder if they wipe each other's asses with how close those two are. They seem to share everything—room, food, women; they don't have any boundaries when it comes to the other.

Spider's pretty quiet most of the time, and Ruger just likes to shoot the shit. All in all, we make up our small group and we're each just fucked up enough to compliment the other.

Occasionally, we'll get a full-time member who transfers over to us, but they never last. Men all bitch that they want freedom, but then many can't handle the level of freedom that we have. We don't follow your everyday lifestyle; we say fuck the bullshit and do what we want.

We have our unspoken set of rules amongst the group that we follow. The main ones being: We don't rape women, we don't kill anyone innocent, we always have each other's backs, we never interrupt a fight unless someone feels we might die, and well, that's pretty much it.

Nancy, the bartender, sets a tall draft in front of me as my ass hits the seat. Immediately taking a large swig, I down half of the refreshing beverage, parched from the Texas heat. Saving the rest for the next drink, my glass hits the top with a thud.

My brothers quickly follow and place their empty cups back on the counter. Feeling a little more relaxed as we all settle into our favorite shitty roadside bar. We always stop in when we're visiting central Texas.

We just got back here; we were off on a run to California. The brothers and I were helping out the local Chapter here. They were having an issue with a notorious club known as the Iron Fists.

It all turned out to be a success, as we sat by and watched those fuckers burn to death. I enjoyed every minute of torching that ratty clubhouse with them locked inside. That's what they get for fucking with the wrong crew. The Oath

Keepers are well known for their loyalties when it comes to family, so this other club should have taken note. That's their fuck up, though, and in the end, they paid the ultimate price with their lives.

No sweat off my back, though. I couldn't give a fuck when it comes to killing scum. People around me thought I was a heartless bastard, and they're probably right about that. I don't have the guilty conscience eating me up inside like others get; I've seen too much and done too many things.

Taking a life is simple—almost poetic watching the life drain from their eyes. Why should I feel bad for removing them from a fucked up world anyhow? No one ever saved me, so in a way, I'm doing them a favor.

"Ye good, laddie?" Scot gestures to my neck, and I nod with an irritated grunt.

Ares, the VP of the local Chapter, and I got into it the other day. The fight wasn't anything serious, but he put his hands around my throat and left a mark. He was making Ex look bad in Church, and I wasn't having it; no one needs to make my brothers or myself look incapable. If anything, we're more than capable when it comes to handling things, and we should get more credit when it's due.

"Yep, I'm straight. Don't get it why they didn't just let us settle it, though. Now shit's unfinished, and I wanna have a turn to prove my point."

"I'm guessin' they put a stop to it, as it was their Church time. As for Ares, ye should just stick to yer own. No good will come from messing with the VP."

"Oh, I can handle my own, trust."

"Aye, I'm sure, but we're the friendly type with 'em. Let it be."

Nodding, I drop it and take a drink of the crisp, cool liquid. I'll be respectful to Scot, but damn sure believe I'll have my turn with Ares again. He's lucky I didn't take my hatchet to him like I do the others. I kept it clean, only fighting with my fists; the club should've stayed out of it.

No wonder they needed our help on that California problem if that's how they handle a little scrapping. *Bunch of pussies!*

Speaking of pussy, I could use some tonight and not the gash that was hanging around the clubhouse. Those bitches around there are a little too prim and proper for me. I need a naughty bitch, one who isn't scared of getting dirty as I fill her up.

Saint and Sinner take the seats on the other side of me, sitting back and relaxing.

"Where're you two coming from?" We all arrived here at the same time, but those two fuckers disappeared quickly.

Saint turns toward me, his light gray eyes meeting my gaze, with his full-on pretty boy looks. The man could be a fucking buff cover model for Abercrombie or some shit. Sinner looks similar, just the dark version, with his jet black hair and charcoal colored irises. I swear to God those fuckers are real brothers and don't know it.

"We wanted our cocks sucked." He shrugs and Sinner grins alongside him.

"Well fuck! I want my cock sucked too." Grumbling, I scan the room, instantly stopping on some sexy blonde bitch talking up one of the skinny Prospects from the Oath Keepers.

She's exactly what I need with those sultry lips, plump enough to wrap tightly around my dick and suck until her cheeks flush. I'd spray my load all over that flawless skin gracing her face.

Finishing the last of my drink, I stand and adjust myself; baby already has me getting full for her. Taking a deep eager breath, I swagger over toward the couple. Immediately turning toward the pissant Prospect, I snarl, "Thanks, newbie, but I'll take her from here."

Since when do Prospects chat up chicks? When I was prospecting, you shut the fuck up and were the last man on the totem pole to get any female attention.

His eyes grow wide, knowing he better back up, even though his forehead wrinkles in irritation. At least the cat's smart enough to keep his damn mouth shut.

I turn to the blonde, ready to show her I'm the better choice, only to find she's gone. Vanished like a goddamn ghost or some shit. Figures, she's the first one in a while that I want to stick my cock in, and she disappears.

"Where'd she go, Prospect?" I growl, and he shrugs.

"I don't know; I'd never seen her before. She was only in here a minute before you scared her off."

"The fuck you trying to say?"

"Nothin' man." He puts his hands up and takes a step closer to his Prospect buddy.

He's never going to get a full patch if he can't show some balls. The Oath Keepers would not let a weakling in full-time.

"You see her again, you send her to me. Got it?"

"Yep." He nods, and I take my seat again.

"No luck, brother?" Saint smirks.

Rolling my eyes, I ignore him and gesture so Nancy will bring me another drink. A small hand runs up my arms and a pair of big tits press up against my back. Hot breath hits my ear the same time as Saint and Sinner both break out in grins.

"You want your cock sucked, baby? Your friends sure liked it."

Glancing at my brothers, they nod, easily agreeing with her, so I stand and adjust my dick. My pants are still tight from the blonde so that I could use some relief. Twisting around, I find a mousy redhead with tits probably bigger than double Ds and a decent mouth.

"Let's go," I mutter as I catch her wrist and yank her toward the door. *Finally, time to get serviced.*

PRINCESS

I inhale another drag off the cigarette. My father would shit if he saw me smoking. I'm an adult, but my father's always treated me like I'm fifteen years old. So naturally that eggs me on even more to do shit that would piss him off. I know, real mature, but fuck him.

He made his choice long ago when he chose his club over his loved ones. I guess his real family wasn't good enough for him and his life, so he went and made his own. It wouldn't have been so bad if he'd included us in everything, but he kept my brother and me far away from it.

Then when I was younger, he was in jail for years because of his friends running drugs with him. What a loser. Being away from him for so long has been a blessing as far as I'm concerned.

Now, he suddenly wants to pull a stunt and show up at my mom's house all the time, like he fucking cares about her? Fuck that! He broke her so badly before. I'm older this time around, and I'm not letting him get away with it.

Hence the Prospect from the Oath Keepers I was just talking to—Scratch. I still can't believe he'd let people call him that, and frankly, I'm scared to find out how he got it.

At least I have a plan. Well, my best friend, Bethany, came up with it at first, but it's brilliant. I'm going to go from daddy's little good girl to his naughty biker slut, and I'm making sure it's personal for him. As soon as B mentioned it, I was sold.

Hybrid Collection

Paybacks will come swift and easy for me by fucking a few of his club brothers. Surely they would love a young blonde with a perky rack and tight cunt. I could probably walk right through that club door and get picked up by a few of them.

Once I'm done sleeping with some of them and I can rub it in my father's face, I'll embarrass him in front of everyone. I'll figure out when he'll be around his oh so precious fucking club and announce it. I may even point out which of his men dipped into the honey jar. Once he's mortified and disrespected, I'll be out of there. It'll teach the bastard to fuck with my loved ones once and for all.

In the past, I'd have never had the guts or would've thought about this plan, but now he has my older brother, Brently, joining that stupid gang too. I refuse to let my mom lose Brently as well. She sacrificed her husband already, and it's not fair to take her son also.

My brother met me to have lunch last week; it was quick but better than nothing. *Nothing* has been the norm for him lately. He's been pulling no-shows and not returning any of our calls or texts. Then, I couldn't believe it at the diner when he showed up proudly wearing a cut that was just like my father's. The only big differences were that Brent's said 'Prospect' and 'Snake' for his name.

Seriously? Because the experience from the psychos who carved him up and attacked him wasn't bad enough already? The club members went ahead and chose a name off of it for him?

It sounds more like a slap in the face if you ask me. They're calling him that shit after what the attackers did to torment him and the love of his life. I don't get it how Brent can stand to be around them after that.

My brother felt like me for so long, never wanting anything to do with the club or our father. We both graduated with good grades and went to college. I was on the drill team in high school, and he stayed busy playing sports. We both made our mom so proud; she supported everything when it came to us.

I went to a junior college since my father wouldn't pay for a larger school, and I had to go where financial aid would allow. It was extra shitty because I remember him getting a new Harley that year. At least, in the end, it meant that I still had my mom and Bethany around me.

Brently, on the other hand, got to go away to a decent college. He was awarded a sports scholarship that paid most of his way. Not like any of it matters anymore, with his chosen career path. He's turned into a giant asshole just like my dad.

After all the lying and cheating my father put my mom through, I just can't forgive him. Now Brently's going on that list too. He should be helping me, not making it harder. *Traitor!*

I haven't spoken to my mom in almost four weeks. I kept seeing my dad's new bike parked out front of her house, so I didn't want to stop by. Then, he's answered her phone every time I've called, so I gave up ringing her.

When it comes down to it, I don't have anything to say to him right now. I'd rather keep driving or hang up, than waste more breath on being angry at him. Obviously, my words in the past never did anything to change his ways, so hopefully this drastic plan of mine will.

In the beginning, when he'd pull his shit with Mom, I'd been able to speak to her about it. She was always saying that she needed him, which I know was a load of bull. I've been the one around her—all the time—even when I was in college in Austin. She's always been such a strong woman; she never sees it, though. He breaks her over and over, yet she rebuilds herself.

Sure, there've been nights when I'd hear her crying or when he'd call lit off his ass begging to talk to her, but he never showed up every day like he's been doing. We'd go for little spurts of him being around for like three days, and then he'd vanish again. Each time he'd show up with the same sob story of 'he couldn't take it anymore, and he loved her.'

I never understood back then or now, how she could easily forgive him. Her favorite justification, when confronted about it, was always 'love's blind and forgiving.' Well, I'll embarrass him so badly this time that he'll stay away from my mom for good. She won't have to make excuses for him any longer. I never want my dad to hurt her ever again; she deserves real love and happiness.

He's done all that and yet the guys he has with him call him the Prez. What kind of shitty man like that deserves to be called the President of any organization?

Ugh. Maybe getting my payback will end up opening my brother's eyes again.

When I showed up at that crappy bar tonight, it was pure blind luck on my part. I stopped in to see if they knew where I could find some of the Oath Keepers guys. The bar's located near the clubhouse, so I figured I'd give it a shot. I struck freaking gold when—pretty much right away—I ran into one of their Prospects. He was cute and seemed kinda sweet, definitely looking to get laid until the big guy showed up to interrupt us.

Hybrid Collection

The other man was insanely good-looking, but he was no Prospect. As soon as the wild group of bikers came barreling into the bar, my body went on guard. Their cuts said Nomad and my mother's warned me about those types of guys, as well as club members from back in her time with my father.

With the lifestyle they live, I seriously doubt I could handle one of them. But, I may try it out in the future, especially if it's with the guy I saw tonight. Sweet fucking baby Jesus that man was so delicious looking. He seemed rough and sexy all over, and to top it off; his name patch said 'Viking.'

It was the last thing I saw before I was headed out the door, needing to regroup and come up with a better game plan. Because fuck me, how on earth do you get called something like Viking? You know it can't just be because he's massive. It has to be more. I'm betting he's a very dangerous man, and the scary thing is, that sounds fucking hot.

Next week I'm damn sure dragging Bethany back in there with me to help. It was her idea originally, so she better be up on acting as my wingman. She'll probably flip out and offer to fuck them all. She's a total slut, but I still love her. I'm not the only one with daddy issues, but hers are far more fucked up than mine. The poor woman was beaten and molested by the man who helped create her. I don't know how she did it; I most likely would have stabbed him when he slept if it were me.

Also, some much-needed recon is due for the Prospect; any information on him at all would help me out. Oh and Viking too. But how? My mother wouldn't know either of them, not that I would get to speak to her anyhow. My dad's probably over at the house, and God knows I don't want to talk with him.

Not far from the bar, I pull into the parking lot of my quaint apartment. Climbing out of my car, I slam the door, relieved to be home.

It's nothing special, but it's become home to me and occasionally Bethany when she decides to stay over. I don't make a lot of money, but it's enough to get me by, thankfully. I've never been one for many material things, even with a name like Princess hung over me.

Tossing my clothes in my hamper, I sluggishly make my way to my awesome fluffy bed and face-plant. I'm buzzed and exhausted. It's the perfect way to end my day, with a good night's sleep.

Two

PRINCESS

The next night...

As I'm getting dressed, my phone goes off, flashing Bethany's name across the screen,

"What's up, chick?" I mutter into the phone as soon as I hit *accept*, propping it on my shoulder and pull on a sock.

"You have to get over here," she shouts loudly over the blaring music in the background.

"Where are you exactly?" A party or a bar, that's for sure.

"I'm at a Coop's place. You remember Cooper from eleventh grade?"

"Cooper Williams?" I guess, squinting my eyes as I picture him and Polo shirts from years back. He was somewhat popular back when we were in high school. Nice guy, but nothing special to me.

"Yeah! He's back and having a party, but that's not why I called you."

"Okaaay." I bite my lip waiting; she doesn't sound bombed yet, but she's on that route.

"There's a guy here! And, he's wearing a Prospect cut from your dad's gang. His name is Stitch or Scratch, or, umm...I don't know, something like that. Anyhow, get over here!"

"That's the same guy I met last night at the bar." *Scratch*. Thinking of him instantly has my mind flashing to Viking.

Hybrid Collection

"I saw the text you sent me this morning about meeting a Prospect; that's why as soon as I saw the guy's name, I called you. Is he the one?"

"Thanks, and yeah, I believe it is. I have to do my makeup and can be there in like an hour."

"What if he leaves? You need to come here now, this your chance."

"Okay, I'll try to hurry. Does Cooper still live in the same house as high school?"

"Yeah, same place."

"Okay cool, see you soon."

"Bye, bitch!" she shouts, laughing, and I hang up.

Lucky for me, Cooper had a ton of get-togethers in high school, so everyone from this area knows where he lives. I'm not looking forward to seeing that crowd; I'm sure it'll be littered with floozies, but oh well. This is about my plan, not partying.

Instead of taking my time getting ready as I would prefer, I lose the comfy socks and shimmy into my favorite pair of daisy dukes. I quickly slide on my new summer sandals, because they pair up perfectly. I look cute but casual. To top my outfit off and make it pop a little, I line my eyes with black kohl and brush on some bright pink lipstick. Men say they hate lipstick, but they love that shit, especially if it's smeared a little by them.

Thank God my hair's already dry, or it'd set me back another twenty minutes. The blonde locks damn near brush my waist, just like my mom's always have.

I stuff my ID and some cash in my back pocket, grab my phone and keys and then I'm on my way. The drive takes about fifteen minutes, and as soon as I park, I'm jumping out of my car. I can tell myself all I want that I'm in a rush to see if my dad's Prospect is still here, but even I know that's bullshit. Viking's who I want to catch a glimpse of.

Bethany's easy for me to spot as I find her playing beer pong—her usual—so I make my way over. Pinching her butt, I step to the side, messing with her a little, and she turns—surprised—until she realizes it's me. I get instantly embraced in an exaggerated hug and giggle, so she's been drinking awhile.

"Damn, that was fast." She smiles.

"I hurried. I want a beer and to see this guy again."

"Okay, come on, there's still liquor left too if you want a few shots." She pokes her beer pong partner's arm until he gives her some attention. "Play my turn; I'll be right back."

"You promise?" He slurs like the typical weak frat boy out of his neighborhood, causing me to roll my eyes. Another loser seems like, already pretty plastered and guaranteed to puke at some point.

"Be right back." She nods to him and yanks my wrist, so I follow her toward the kitchen.

"Who's the dude?" I gesture back to Mr. Beer Pong.

"I don't know," she laughs, "but he's kinda' cute."

"You could do better; he has *puker* written all over him," I argue.

"I'm not picky." She shrugs and I keep my mouth shut, grabbing a beer from a bald guy manning the keg.

"Thanks," I say, tipping my cup toward him slightly since he didn't fill it to the top and have it spill everywhere. The guy obviously knows how to pour a beer.

"Anytime," he smirks looking me up and down like I'm his next conquest.

Ugh, go polish your forehead, douche.

Bethany leads me back to the beer pong table so she can keep playing and the beat kicks up to one of my favorite songs by The Hills. The volume gets cranked even louder after a second in what should be the living room. The new song pouring through the oversized speakers draws my attention to the people dancing, and I spot the Prospect. He's leaning against the living room wall, just watching them all.

Scratch's giving me such an easy in right now, and he doesn't even know it. Swaying my hips like I want to dance, I make my way over into his direct line of sight. My gaze hits his briefly, just enough to draw him to me, as I grind my hips seductively to the beat.

Like bees to honey, he's on me in no time at all. Just like that, he's already hooked; I know it. He pulls my waist into him, gripping my hips securely. Following my rhythm, he moves along with me at first, eventually taking over the lead.

My red solo cup gets crunched, and beer starts to spill over, so I take a few big gulps and attempt to concentrate on not spilling it down my chin as well, while we continue to dance. I'd appreciate it if I could get some sort of buzz established; it'd give me a boost of courage to do what I need to later.

I wasn't the type who went out and fucked around in high school. I wouldn't be labeled as a good girl per se, but I wasn't a whore by any extent. College was different; I explored some and had a good time, but most of all, I learned what I liked. This situation, though, is slightly nerve racking. I'm planning to seduce Scratch when I don't want him. Like at all.

As soon as the red cup leaves my lips, he reaches around and takes it from me. Before I can get turned around to protest, he finishes the liquid off and tosses the plastic cup toward an overfull trash can.

"I wanted more," I state loudly and cock my eyebrow. I *needed* it.

Grinning playfully, Scratch tugs my front into him, until our faces are so close that our noses are almost brushing together. He takes the lead again as our bodies gyrate against each other, and his leg pushes between mine. His firm palms cup my ass, applying enough pressure so that each time he moves, my pussy rubs against his thigh and gets a little wetter. We're close enough that I can easily feel his cock hardening with each thrust.

"We can get more later," he says watching my eyes and mouth each time he presses me against his thigh. Giving him the reaction he craves, I imagine riding the big biker's thigh from the other night and part my lips letting a small, breathy moan escape, building up his ego.

Scratch's fairly good-looking with his fuller lips, hazel eyes, and shaved short hair. By the dancing, he doesn't appear to be in bad shape either. He's slightly more on the thinner side than what I normally would be attracted to, but this isn't about me finding a man and my preferences. It's strictly based on my mission to fuck with my dad and his club.

Running my hands over his back, I pierce my nails into his shoulders coercing Scratch to me so he thinks that I can't possibly get enough of him. He complies, feathering his lips over my neck, pressing wet kisses as he goes.

I need to clear my mind and get into it; I have to make this happen. I want to get it over with as soon as possible, so I'm going to make this nice and simple for him.

"Do you want to go somewhere with some privacy?" I suggest breathily next to his ear.

"Yeah, sugar, I'm cool with whatever."

Bingo.

Thank God he has no idea who I am, because if so, he'd also know that my father would strangle him for kissing all over me like he is. Not having a good relationship with my dad doesn't mean he wouldn't teach his Prospect a lesson. It'd take a certain kind of man for the Prez not to scare the shit out of them.

Thinking about it, makes me giddy inside. It's so fucked up, but I can't stop feeling this way, knowing I'll be one step closer to sleeping with a few of them. Then I'll get to break it to my father that his club has benefitted me as well. I'll finally get that small piece of satisfaction knowing I've hurt and disappointed my dad like he's done to my poor mom for so long. In the end, she'll be happier with him gone, and that's all I want.

Payback's a bitch, motherfucker.

"Great, let's see if we can find a room or something."

"Even better." He nods, following me down Cooper's narrow hallway until we find an empty bedroom. I should have brought a leash; it's been that easy so far.

Once I'm over the threshold and pulling Scratch inside the room with me, I kick the door closed. Ready to make this real for him and get my head in the game, I begin kissing him passionately. Closing my eyes, I search for my happy place. I'll be pushing it all to the back of my mind as soon as possible anyhow. I need to make this memorable for him. I want him to brag as much as possible, especially around the clubhouse. Then once it comes out to my dad, everyone will know about it already.

Scratch instantly reciprocates, his hands eagerly wandering all over my body. He rushes the entire process like he's going to burst in his pants. I was expecting his hands to be callused since he's a wannabe biker and all, but they're soft.

Why does that seem so wrong to me? Have I ever noticed callused hands before? Maybe it's because I would assume him being rough and tough, but I'm not even naked yet, and he's not meeting my expectations.

Shit! Fuck! What expectations? Erase them, bury that crap, and stick to your plan.

He pulls away breathing heavier, pushing his groin into me a few times. Scratch's so wound up; he starts kissing over my throat again as he pants, "Let me get you off first in case I don't last. You're one fine piece of ass, sugar; you ever been with a biker before?"

"No, and I don't want to talk about it either." God, no talking or his breath may kill me. Hot beer scent isn't something that excites my pussy. "I think the cut is hot, though." I throw in for extra measure like he's going to be some prize for me, hopefully building up his ego. "Please, I want you so badly, I can't help myself. I can't believe I saw you here; it must have been meant to be."

It all sounds so rehearsed and fake. *Because it is.*

Hybrid Collection

If I don't work on this better and end up getting an experienced club guy, he'll be able to see right through me. My entire plan could be blown to shit, everything going downhill if that happens. Or else next time I need to make sure I've had a few shots or something, and then I'd be able to blur it all and relax.

"Well I wouldn't go that far, but us havin' fun was meant to be, for sure," he mumbles on his way to my chest.

I get tired of him slobbering on me so I push him off, his eyes meeting mine, confused. The first dirty thought stumbles out to get him back on track. "I can think of better places for that tongue."

"Fuck yeah, that's what I'm talking about."

"Okay, over here."

"Perfect," Scratch says and catches my arms, pulling me to him. He guides me, walking backward as we're pressed up against each other. His body is warming me with each step until the pits of my knees hit the mattress. The bed's made up with a hunter green duvet and appears to still be clean. Thankfully, I don't think anyone's found their way in here yet. Regardless, I'm not touching the sheets, so I'll just lie on top.

He pushes my shorts down my legs, his hand shooting between my thighs excitedly. I use the alcohol and my determination to get my body turned on, wetting his overzealous hand.

I feel like a fucking whore right now. Tons of women would be stoked to be here with him; he's decent, just not for me. Time to fucking suck it up and do this to hurt my father. I'll wound him any way possible to pay him back for the heartache and distress he's caused our family, even if I have to play the bad guy for a little while. I want him to feel such disappointment and embarrassment, just as I have my entire life growing up. I want his fucking heart to hurt. Empty inside from the father that was never there.

"I thought I was getting your mouth?" I don't want to fuck him, so if I can get away with oral that would surely count toward my goal. No doubt he'll be back at the clubhouse bragging about how he had some blonde chick on her knees the night prior.

"You can have whatever you want with that tight little puss you got down there. I can't wait to taste you, sugar" he mumbles and squats.

His fingers leave my wetness and tangle in the strings of my underwear as he carelessly pulls on them, yanking the elastic toward him. I don't know if he thought he could rip them or what, but it doesn't work so he shoves them down to my ankles. He leaves them resting at my feet and pushes his face between my legs.

Scratch's nose bumps my clit instantly, causing my center to clench up in a jolt of pleasure. No way am I going to be able to do this standing up; it'll feel way too good if he has any clue whatsoever as to what he's doing. He seems rushed, but he zeroed in on my sensitive spot with the first shot, so this could end up not being so bad.

Sitting, I scoot back toward the pillows, making sure to leave enough room for him to climb on the bed also. As he follows my body to the mattress, he pushes my legs wide open. His soft hands run along my thighs, parting them as far as possible, giving him a full view of my pink center.

Scratch leans in, giving my pussy long powerful strokes with his tongue. Each enticing lick's being accompanied by skilled fingers relentlessly plunging in and out of my tight entrance. It seems like no time passes as my head's thrown back, moaning out my pleasure, riding the wave as it starts to hit me and make the entire world disappear.

Holy shit! Maybe I should fuck him after all.

I'm beyond surprised with his persistence as my hips thrust into his face, twisting and jerking as I work my way up to my release. My fingers rake through his short hair as I pull his mouth into me as much as I can to ride his tongue through my orgasm.

Once I'm depleted, I'm left panting and wide-eyed. Not often can a man eat pussy like that, and fuck if he isn't one of the best I've had in a long time. Maybe this mission of mine won't be such a bad thing after all. God, if the Prospect's that good, I can only imagine how Viking would be. I'd probably fucking die.

"Fuck, you got a greedy pussy."

I can't think of a reply; he's completely right. I let loose a low giggle, and he shoots me a goofy smile.

"What's your name, sugar?"

So now he's curious? Typical man, waiting until the panties are off for formalities. "Princess."

He thinks about it a minute, before repeating me. "Princess? That's your actual name? Kinda fits after I've tasted ya."

"Yep, my daddy said he knew that he'd be Prez one day, so they went ahead and named me Princess."

His eyes widen, and he swallows down a cough that's suddenly bubbled up. His face becomes sour as he thinks hard, his forehead wrinkling with tension.

Continuing on, it all comes out almost like a taunt. "You know, of the Oath Keepers? You're wearing the cut, so surely you'd know that you had your fingers and tongue all up inside his daughter." I feel like such a bitch giving him a snotty answer, but fuck it; I have to be one to drive my point in.

"Fuck…I'm dead! They'll fucking kill me for this!"

"No. Lucky for you, he doesn't care about his family, so you have nothing to worry about. If anything, now you have bragging rights to the brothers. You are, after all, the very first one who's touched me out of them."

"Oh, God, I'm really fuckin' dead now. I gotta go." Standing suddenly, he straightens out his clothes, wiping the sweat off that's suddenly on his brow with the back of his hand.

"But I thought you wanted to fuck? Or you wanted me to return the favor with my mouth?" Licking my lips, I smile devilishly, and I swear he whimpers.

Taking a step closer toward the door, he chuckles weakly. "God, you're gorgeous, but I'm trying to stay alive. If I fuck you, then I'd be signing my death certificate. Ares, our VP would chop me into little pieces. We all know if he wouldn't have claimed his Ol' Lady, then the Prez would want his VP with his daughter. It's like some unspoken rule in biker clubs. I have to go before the wrong person notices that I'm with you." Shaking his head apologetically, he's out the door in a flash. I don't even have time to get any argument out.

In his wake, I hit the mattress as I fall backward, bouncing and then slamming my fists onto the bed, irritated.

Damn it. He's so freaked out; I don't think he'll open his mouth about it. *Ugh.* What should I do? I don't think there's much I can do, besides put his name on my list and move onto another.

Surely there has to be one of them that will gloat about it and not be too scared. Hell, Scratch is a man; he'll have to open his mouth to someone. Men always brag about their conquests.

If anything, one day I may have to head over to the clubhouse when I'm certain that my father's not around. Ares knows what I look like, but most of them haven't seen me since I was a little girl. I'd be able to scope out the brothers and see if Scratch brags when the guys say something about me because they will. I'll make sure to wear something that easily gets their attention.

Sitting up, I pat my hair, smoothing the frazzled mess and collect myself for a moment. Scooting to the edge of the bed, I find my panties and tug them back on, and then stand to adjust my shorts. Inhaling a deep breath, I nod, satisfied with my orgasm and plan I've decided on. It'll work; I have to stay persistent.

Oath Keepers members were crawling all over that little bar I went to. I'll find another. Until then, my ass is going home to shower, sleep, and regroup some more. Scratch was a nice guy, but not my forever type. I want to get home to scrub the memories off as soon as possible.

Three

VIKING

Four days later…

Sitting at the small round table in front of the crappy hotel window, I watch across the street as Saint and Sinner leave with yet another new woman from that shitty little bar we've been going to. I don't know where these bitches come from; it seems like they multiply each night that we're there.

I'm not complaining; having my cock sucked regularly has been pretty fucking nice. It'd be even better if I found someone worth fuckin' though. The women available have been run through time and again. They serve their purpose when it comes to pleasing ya, but I'm not trying to stick my dick in one and have a bitch fall in love or some dumb shit.

The truth is, I've shown up every single night hoping to catch that sexy ass blonde chick I saw the first time my brothers, and I stopped in. We had come straight over after we handled some business for the MC. It was Saturday night, and she hasn't been back since; even the bartender confirmed that she hadn't seen her either.

I'm wondering if maybe 'cause it was the weekend? Regardless, I can't shake that mouth and those tits from my mind. I go to sleep thinking about them and wake up hard as fuck. I can only imagine what she'd feel like wrapped around me, hot and wet, her little cunt throbbing as I make her come.

She could be a college chick, maybe looking to play with some bad boys to get her kicks or some shit. Wouldn't surprise me, it's happened before. I have no problem whatsoever showing her just what a real fuckin' bad boy is.

I'd fuck her twenty ways to Sunday. She'd be begging me to stop 'cause she wouldn't be able to stand up anymore. That's what a real man would do with a piece of ass like hers.

Turned on again, I unclasp the button on my jeans and reach inside to start pumping my thick cock. Giving it an extra tight squeeze, I picture her tightness clasping down, grinding, while I made her scream.

Fuck! I groan, full of need. Pumping a few times, my thoughts switch to her tits bouncing while she rides me. My sac keeps tightening more and more, my balls ready to explode.

Pulling my eyes away from my throbbing length, a near silent gasp escapes my mouth as I watch a platinum blonde's ass in a short black skirt. She sashays across the gravel parking lot; her arm looped through another chick's, and the sight of her hips swinging has warm jets of my seed splashing onto my shirt.

The sun's setting so I can just make out everything perfectly, and I'd bet fifty bucks it's the bitch I was just dreaming of. Like a freshman excited for his first fuck, I jump from my chair. Pulling my jeans closed, I stuff my wallet in my back pocket.

Most of the guys are already over there, so I'll join them until I'm able to make certain it's her. Better get over there quick before someone else attempts to get in her pants like that fucking Prospect from last weekend. I wanted to beat his ass so badly after she disappeared but held myself back. My brothers seem to like this bar for some reason, so I'm trying to keep the peace.

Saint and Sinner have been in their room mere minutes when I head outside and can already hear the chick they had with them moaning loudly. Her long wails remind me of a cat in heat, maybe the rest of us will get lucky too, and they'll gag the bitch. It's not often they go off with someone alone. One would think they'd get tired of sharing all the time, I damn sure couldn't handle that shit.

The highway's never busy, so I amble on across and make my way through the pebbled gravel parking lot. Headed toward the entry, my gaze settles on a shiny group of bikes parked out front. My curiosity's peaked because none of them belong to the Nomads or the other regulars that've been here all week.

They'll be straight as long as they stay the fuck out of my way.

Hybrid Collection

The music from the jukebox pours outside as I head through the entrance and spot my brothers. Tucked back in the corner, they all sit facing the majority of the room. One thing about these guys, even if they've been drinking all day, they'll keep their guards up. The Nomads stay ready in case shit goes south. Never knew a group like that before and had come to appreciate them. It makes a hell of a difference knowing someone else has your six.

Scot nods hello as I make my way over to them. As I return it, Spider's fist pops out in front of me so I can bump knuckles with him. "'Sup, Vike?"

"Spidey."

Damn sure could use a drink; I sound like I just woke up.

"Brother." Nightmare nods in acknowledgment as I sit near him at the high top.

"Figured it was time for a cold one." I'm here to check out a female. Not that I plan on alerting them or the fucking media to it, though. Keeping her to me will be tricky, but I'll figure it out. None of these fuckers need a sample; that's for damn sure.

Stacy, a part-time bar girl, sets a glass bottle down in front of me. It's chilled enough that the amber colored glass is foggy, letting me know that she listened to me and grabbed it from the bottom of the beer cooler.

Taking the first sip, the alcohol hits my tongue like a burst of refreshing, icy bliss. *God, I love it when bitches listen to me, and a good, cold beer.*

"Would you like anything else to drink, Viking?" She cuts straight to it. Stacy doesn't try the bullshit flirting or anything like that. Setting her straight on day one, I let her know that I'm not some ass clown in here she can fool. Since then, we've been cool, and I tip her better. Like tonight, this beer just got her a kick-ass tip.

"Nope, I'm good. How's your night so far?"

"Same as always." She smiles, and I nod. "If you decide to change it up, let me know."

Handing her a five, she attempts to give me my change, but I ignore it. She smiles and then takes off back toward the bar.

Once Stacy's out of my line of sight, my eyes search *her* out. My gaze meets *hers,* and it hits me that she was already staring at me. I'm betting that she watched me from the moment I walked through the door.

Is she just checking me out? Or could she be jealous that Stacy was over here smiling? Nah, she's way too happy right now to be the bitter type. She and the little friend she's here with are playing a game of pool, giggling and drinking what looks like their second beer already.

Glancing around, I find that damn near every other motherfucker in the place is watching them as well. I haven't even sampled her yet, and she already has my adrenaline spiking. I can't remember a time when a chick has had my body humming like this, and especially it being from someone peeping on her.

A few scrawny bastards whistle as hot chick bends over to make her shot and my insides stir something fierce. My hands tingle, feeling like I could break a fool's fingers one by one for touching her.

I don't know if it's 'cause I haven't fucked in a whole minute or what, but she's got my dick wanting to stand loud and proud under this damn table. That's the last thing I want my brothers popping off, giving me shit for right now. I'm going to let her have some fun with her friend for a little while before making a move. She'll get a couple more drinks in her and probably loosen up some so she won't bolt again when I speak to her.

Sipping my beers, the night drags on with me sitting quietly, attempting to learn everything about her from afar. My brothers start to notice my unusual drinking activity and eventually realize I'm not paying them any attention, but instead, giving it all to her. I can't stop either.

The way her calves flex when she walks around the pool table in her sky-high shoes, makes me want to grab her wrists one handed, behind her back and bend her over. Then her long silky hair brushes the top of her ass every time she moves. It's fucking taunting me, waiting for me to wrap it around my fist and pull it. Sweetheart has no idea the type of hell I'd put her through, to bring her pleasure.

Taking another swallow of beer, I imagine yet another way I'd have her. This time, she'd be on her knees, cheeks flushed and begging me to let her swallow my cum. Letting loose a growl at the image, my brothers turn to me, eyebrows cocked.

Nightmare hikes his lip up slightly, almost in a grin, but not completely. He doesn't ever really smirk or smile. "Talk to her."

Scot chuckles. "Aye laddie, the lass would probably love a good ride." I shoot him a glare just as the hot chick shouts to her friend that she's going to go out for a quick smoke. She glances at me briefly as she's declaring it, almost like an invitation.

Hybrid Collection

She saunters closer to our table and as she does, her lashes lower, and her lip slightly pouts. I already wanted that luscious mouth the first time I saw her. With that bottom lip out a bit, it's doing fucking insane things to the rock hard cock in my jeans.

She checks me out from head to toe the entire time that she passes us. Swinging those hips a little too much, knowing damn well that she has every brother's attention at our table. It's so goddamn seductive and obvious; it hits me that it's no innocent invitation. It's a fucking dare. She doesn't think I'll actually go out there. *Challenge accepted.*

Like a dumbass, she strolls down the hallway toward the bathrooms. No doubt that she's going out the back door to have a smoke all alone. Doesn't she have any means of self-preservation? She can't announce that shit and then amble on out alone.

Some guy posted up against the wall near the same hall, follows her, easily catching up. I watch as the idiot smiles all friendly-like and holds the door for her. It's probably a good time to have my own smoke. I hadn't seen him out in the bar, so I have no clue who the fuck he is.

"I'mma smoke." Grumbling, I stand and think of squirrels in pink tutus to get my dick to go soft. The brothers nod, continuing with their conversation that I wasn't paying any mind to.

Stopping along the way, the alcohol's set in so I take a piss. Then head outside as well.

The door closes, engulfing the classic rock, leaving me in the quiet, humid night. Leaning against the building, I fish my cigarettes out of my front jeans pocket, shaking them so one pops out enough that I can put it straight to my lips. Shoving the packet back into my pocket, I dig my fingers around until they find my Zippo, and it comes out next.

Flipping the top open, I flick it, so the bright orange and blue flame comes to life as I cup my other hand around it, lighting my cigarette. Closing the lid, I stuff the non-descript metal Zippo back in my pocket and inhale a long, relieving drag, just as I hear the first low whimper.

Holding my breath and remaining still, my gaze starts to scan over everything around me. Nothing pops out, but I know what I heard. There's a small brick building about twelve paces away, most likely for the bar storage. A dim light hangs from behind the poorly built structure, not doing much to illuminate the area.

A pained cry comes next, louder, echoed by another; this one tainted with anger. Off to the side of the storage, it's shadowed, but I'm able to make out what looks to be a struggle happening.

Launching off the small porch, I bring the cigarette to my lips and inhale another deep drag before tossing it off into the gravel. With large, quick strides, I make my way over to the shadowed area. Remaining as quiet as possible, I creep the last few paces to get a good look at what's going on. It could be a wild fuck for all I know, or it could be someone getting attacked.

The shady looking guy from the hallway has the blonde shoved up against the brick, ripping at her clothes. She's not giving it freely, but fighting for her fucking life, pounding her petite fists into him over and over. He slams her into the building, frustrated, going for her lacey bra next and she emits a wounded whimper from impact, the sound stabbing into my soul.

Consumed by his dick, shady fuck hisses, "I've watched those bikers show up and take all the women around here, well not you. I'm fucking you, no matter if I have to kill you first or not."

Her hands fly toward his face, attempting to shove him away. "Get off of me you piece of shit!" she cries.

The rage inside grows, overtaking and overwhelming any bit of self-control that I once possessed. My body vibrates as I'm unable to hold myself back any longer, nor do I want to. Blood rushes through my body, my veins pumping full as the adrenaline hits me full force, wanting to explode. Deep red, the color of blood, begins to cloud my vision from witnessing someone physically hurt her like this, to hear the fear and helplessness in her sweet voice.

"She said no, motherfucker," I rasp, angrily. It takes so much to utter those simple words and not just rip him from her, but I don't want to frighten her more by slaughtering him in front of her.

He turns toward me with a snarl painted on his lips, but I give him no time to react. Eagerly wrapping my hand around his throat, I lift him completely off the ground. Thrusting him forward, I beat his skull into the wall. His head emits a loud smack sound each time it crashes against the rough brick, totaling three times.

It dazes shady fuck enough for me to glance toward the shaken woman. Her red lipstick's all over her mouth and chin, her mascara smeared down her cheeks from her tears, dirtying her up a bit. I've never seen a woman more beautiful before.

Hybrid Collection

Her gratitude-filled blue eyes meet mine like I'm some sort of fucking hero or a saint. As the wetness continues to trail over her cheeks, it ignites an entirely different creature. The urge to breed—to *fuck* her into submission—grows rampant. The animal wanting to claw it's way free and take over what this shady fuck was about to do.

I never said I was a decent man. Upstanding citizen hasn't ever fit in my description. There are these thoughts I have; it doesn't mean I've acted on them before. But fuck if it isn't the strongest right now, wanting to take this bitch and ride her hard.

The asshole starts to squirm, my grip slipping slightly and stealing me out of the spell. "Go," I grunt and tighten my hold.

"O-okay." She swallows, pulling her shirt front together attempting to hide her bra, from where the douche ripped it completely open.

Her tall heels are forgotten as she takes off in a sprint toward the front of the building. Fumbling along the way, she calls someone, continuing to run. Probably her friend, to let her know what happened.

Shady fuck moves again, and I release my grip. He falls, stumbling to catch his balance as I plant a powerful punch to his gut, causing him to gasp for air.

"Who the fuck are you?" Stomping my heavy boot into his foot, I grind my heel down, planting him in place.

"Fuck you Oath Keeper!" he replies stubbornly.

I've always been an impatient man, hitting first and asking questions later. This idiot got a courtesy and didn't even realize it. My curiosity wanted answers, but my need for punishment wins out.

Pulling the small hatchet from my belt, I let loose a dark chuckle at what I'm about to do. I wanted to laugh when I was hitting him against the wall, but I would've terrified the beauty. Without another thought, I flash a grin and impale the blade of my ax into the top of his skull. It's not an easy feat, but I've had many times to practice throughout the years, and not to mention my size.

The brother's call me Viking for a reason, with my thighs resembling small tree trunks and my arms massive enough to make grown men cringe. My height easily dwarfs the average man; hell, I even tend to make the bigger ones look feeble when standing near me—if they have the guts to get that close in the first place. Usually, if the size doesn't scare them, then it's the Nordic Viking tattoos all over my body and the hatchet I keep on me.

There's a large gasp on impact, and my gaze flies to his expression. His eyes widen in shock, his mouth gaping in a horrific, tortured scream as I use both hands to wiggle the conveniently sized ax back out. It's wedged snuggly into the hard shell of his skull and takes some plying to remove. My favorite part's when they scream like this. Their eyes always widen with terror and disbelief that I'm going to kill them, and it's going to be painful.

Once the blade's free, he becomes motionless, staring like he's in a trance and I bring the hatchet down again. This time, the sharp object reaches far enough into the brain to do the damage I was craving. The man's once evil gaze glosses over as he falls to the ground, his life finished.

My dick hardens further as the rush of adrenaline sets in with the fact that I just killed for her. *She's mine.* My body hums in triumph.

With that one thought, I know I'd do it again. I'd kill for her as many times needed, no matter the reason. There's something about her that speaks to my darkness. It's fucking with my mind; I know absolutely nothing about her.

Hearing the bar door, I turn from the shady fucker and notice the chick's black heels she'd left behind in her haste. The light hits the shoes just enough to pick up the glossy texture and make them shine. They stand out like that stupid fairytale the girls in grade school used to talk about. Only I'm no Prince Charming, more like the big, bad wolf ready for dinner.

"Vike?" Spider rounds the corner, flicking a glance at the dead guy on the ground then to me. He watches as I place my hatchet into its holster on my leather belt. "You need some help dumping the body?"

"Appreciate it, brother," I reply, and he fist-bumps me.

This is a prime example of why I'm a part of this crew; they always have your back no matter the situation. There's not a bunch of bullshit questions or accusations, and the best part of all, they're all pretty fucked up in the head just like me.

"You wanna bury or burn it?"

There's a river not too far away, so I have a different idea that may not gain us attention or make us get all tired and filthy from digging. The only way I'd get dirty tonight would be if a sexy Cinderella were involved.

"Do you still have that container of liquid acid in your saddlebag?"

"Yeah. Fuck, you're gonna melt him?"

Hybrid Collection

"I'm thinking we could pour some over his face and head where I hit him, and then dump the body in that river back there." I gesture into the darkness toward the sounds of rushing water.

Texas got so much rain this past week that it's been causing major flooding. The river here is up seven feet so far and still rising; authorities and weathermen are calling for everyone to stay away for fear of injuries and drownings. They've even closed some of the lakes as well. I'm betting it's the perfect scenario to dump a body easily. I could probably dump a dozen before anyone noticed.

"Good idea. I'll get it real quick." He takes off in a rush toward the front parking lot where his bike's located.

I'm drawn back to the shoes. Bending, I pick them up and inspect them closer. *Her calves in these were utterly fucking sinful.*

They look tiny in my hands and Cinderella's no small woman. I'd guess her to be around five foot eight or a little taller, but her shoes still look petite. There's nothing significant about the heels or on them to help me figure out who she could be.

Bringing them to my nose, I inhale, wanting some hint of her scent. I'm pleasantly surprised to find that they smell flowery. I'm guessing she must've put lotion on her feet before wearing them tonight.

I take another deep sniff like some psycho stalker, but I couldn't be fucked about that. She smells good—edible. This is the scent I would most likely incur as I ran my tongue up her calves, biting into the muscle tenderly while reveling in her smooth skin. You know it has to be soft; bitches like that always feel like they're an entirely different breed than the rest of us.

Spider hurries back; his chains secured to his wallet jingling with each step as he carefully carries the container. He peers over at the shoes I'm clutching for a moment, confused, but keeps his questions about them to himself.

"You want me to grab one of his legs so we can drag him?" His gesture doesn't go unnoticed. I know he only offered so I wouldn't have to put down the woman's heels and I won't forget it the next time he needs a brother to back him on something. Little shit like that goes a long way with me.

"Appreciate it, brother." I nod, carefully holding the pumps to my body and grab the right leg of the dead man.

Spider lifts the left ankle, holding the acid with his other hand as we set about dragging him in the dark toward the sounds of the river. He's fairly easy to move, save for him occasionally getting hung up on small bushes and what not. We both take careful strides; you never know where a snake hole or a dip may be, and I'm not trying to carry Spider's ass back 'cause he rolled his ankle not paying attention.

The aroma of rich topsoil grows stronger as we near the river's edge. The odor eventually becomes murkier—like muddy rainwater as we arrive at the bank.

We each drop the dead weight. Spider cautiously opens the acid, handing the container to me.

"Wait," he grumbles, pulling his cell phone out. The screen illuminates as he taps on it a few times. Eventually, a bright light shines out of it. "Flashlight app." He grins, pleased with himself.

"Nice."

Stepping toward the dude's head, but not too close, I tip the acid all over his face and the top of his skull where I had chopped a nice sized hole in it with my ax.

"Is it working?"

"I don't know. You sure do talk a lot when we're attempting to quietly dispose of a body, though."

"We're usually riding or drinking. Can't do much talking when there's a loud engine or music blaring."

"It's weird."

"I don't like the quiet."

Shrugging, I hand him the acid and the shoes.

I'm not checking if the guy's face is melted off; it's an image I can live without. I've gotten used to the blood and broken bones over the years, but I've never seen anyone melted before. The toxic smell floating in the air is enough to tell me not to look.

Not wanting to get any of that shit on me in case it really does burn your skin off, I turn the shady fuck over on his side and lift him, so his back is facing me. Inhaling a deep breath of burnt skin and damp earth, I powerfully toss his body out in front of me, biting my lip until I hear the splash of him hitting the water.

Spider shines his phone light over the water in front of us, and then along the banks. Either it's too dark, and we aren't seeing him, or the body landed in a good spot and is busy floating away.

"I need a beer," he mumbles after a beat.

Hybrid Collection

"Fuck beer; I want whiskey." I need a sexy-ass blonde who wears super high black heels also, but I leave that part out.

Taking the shoes from him, we make the short trek back to the bar.

Four

PRINCESS

"**I have to go** back tomorrow," I declare, glancing over at Bethany.

Her mouth gapes and she shakes her head. "Are you crazy, Prissy? No way! You were just attacked!"

She's called me Prissy for years. It only comes out when she's worried about something, though.

"Look, I know I was upset…"

"That's one hell of an understatement; seriously, think about what you're saying."

"I told you, that guy saved me. He didn't try anything either, just stopped that creep from hurting me further."

"How do you know the jerkoff who hurt you won't be there when you go back?"

"I just do."

"You're so full of shit."

"I saw the big guy hit him, and then when I was running away, there was a loud wail. I don't think the biker made it easy on him."

In fact, I know he didn't. Once I was far enough away, I had glanced back and seen him hit my attacker with something that wasn't his fist. The outline from the weak lighting made it look like a scene out of a horror movie.

The fucked up part about it all is that I'm not frightened. If anything, I'm curious. I want to go and see what he did to the bastard, see if he killed him.

Hybrid Collection

I've never had anyone convey that type of violence for me before. Being so terrified and then witnessing that same feeling wash over my attacker was exhilarating. My savior didn't scare me one bit; he empowered me.

I'll never be some biker bitch or approve of my father's ways, but deep down, I know his blood runs through my veins. Pair it along with my mother's and it's no wonder I'm suddenly craving an outlaw. *I need to see him.*

He'd watched me all night. I could feel his blistering gaze on my back; it had taken every ounce of self-control I possessed not to look back and meet him head on. I don't think he's used to aggressive women and at first, I was on a mission to add him to my list. Now though...well, I have no idea what to do, but like a moth to a flame, all I can think about is getting back to him as quickly as possible.

"I still don't like it. I think you should stay away from that bar; your father's MC has a ton of other guys you can go for. Look, I get it; you're used to being a badass around normal people, but Princess, these guys aren't everyday people. You're a little woman compared to them, and if you go in there alone, they could kidnap you or something crazy and I'm betting no one would bat an eye."

Huffing, I count to five, so I keep my calm. *Wait, why am I getting upset over her talking down about those bikers anyhow? I hate them just as much, if not more.*

"You forget, Bethany, that my father's in charge of them. Besides, I won't be alone. You're coming with me."

"It's been two hours since I had to drive my best friend home because she was attacked and too upset to drive, and now she's sitting here, planning to drag me back to the place where it all went down? No way, cuz."

"Yes, that's right, I am your best friend, and I need a wingman. And for the record, stop with the cuz and cousin shit; people are going to think we're related, and I don't kiss my cousins!"

"Fine, but I'm not fucking one of them," she replies, her nose going up in the air like she's calling all the shots.

Yeah, okay, I won't hold my breath on that one. Those guys have her name written all over them. My snort pops out before I can hold it back.

She shoots me a heated glare, irritated.

I shrug, not saying anything and after a few moments her frown changes into an evil grin.

"Shut-up, I'm not going to sleep with them," she mumbles, and I outright laugh.

"Want to put some money on it?"

"No."

"'Cause you know I'm right."

"Whatever. I'm sleeping in your bed tonight, and since you're dragging me back tomorrow, I'm borrowing your clothes too."

"You're only in my bed if you're naked," I flirt and kiss her cheek.

"Won't be the first time." She smiles and lifts her shirt over her head, exposing her pale breasts.

Nope, definitely not the first; we've had plenty of fun together, and I love her for it. She's always had my back, and when I was feeling low and unattractive, she let me know just how beautiful she found me, turning me on to something I would never have guessed would be mind-blowing.

Don't get me wrong, we both love men, but occasionally it's fun to have a woman too.

VIKING
The next day...

Shedding my shirt, I use it to wipe the sweat from my brow. The sleeves are ripped off, but it's no match for this Texas heat. Beads of perspiration run down my chest, and I quickly swipe over them too. South Carolina's hot, too, but it's a dfferent kind of heat, more humid than Texas. Here, I feel like my nuts are going to melt off.

"What the fuck could it be?" Nightmare hisses angrily, staring at his ride.

He has his bike partially taken apart; random pieces are strewn about in the motel's parking lot. I saw him get pissed and kick the old wooden picnic table outside, so figured he could use some help. We've been out here for a while and have gotten everything back together where it's supposed to be, but he's still irritated. I would be too if my shit weren't running right.

Letting out a deep breath, I pat the back of my neck with my shirt and then tuck a piece of the material into my jeans pocket, thinking about what the issue could be. "We've been over everything. The only issue I can think of at this point is if the gas had something in it. You filled up at that ghetto petrol station a ways out, and we all skipped it to eat. I'd clean out your tank with some fresh gas and hope that does it."

"If that weasel's selling fucked up gas and screwed my bike up, I'm going back and torching that fucking station."

Ruger steps out of his room, wiping down his piece with a cloth, right in the open. "'Sup." He chin lifts, and we return the gesture.

"Brother," Nightmare acknowledges.

"Talkin' about torching another place?" he asks, and I chuckle, remembering how much fun we had blowing up the last building.

Night shrugs. "If the fuck down the road sold me shoddy gas, I'm burning that shit hole to the ground."

"I'm down," Ruger replies.

"Yep, me too." I nod. If the owner has insurance on the place, we'd most likely be doing him a favor anyhow. It'd be good if Nightmare had a few of us watching his back as well.

"Has Scot mentioned a new job yet?" Ruger asks, and I turn toward Nightmare, curious as well.

I'm a bit surprised we've been stationary for this long considering we didn't get paid for helping out the Oath Keepers with their California problem. I'm not hurting for money; I don't use much out on the road, but some of these guys blow through it like they have an endless supply.

"Nope, he hasn't said anything."

"Surely one of the Chapters needs more weapons; we haven't taken shit up to Montana in almost six months," he mumbles, but brings up a good point.

"He has a point." I cock my eyebrow at Nightmare, and he shrugs.

"I think Scot has a thing for the bartender," he confesses after we stare at him for a moment.

"You fuckin' with me? That bitch has been ran through so many times; she probably couldn't keep a dick in her twat if she tried to."

They both laugh as a car passes by on the old highway that runs between the motel and bar, gaining our attention.

"Goddamn!" Ruger gushes as the driver and passenger drive by slow enough for me to realize it's Cinderella.

Once it registers, I let loose a loud wolf whistle, trying to get them to stop.

Nightmare's lip raises a touch in his 'I don't ever fucking smile' sort of way, 'but this is the look you'll get when I'm amused.'

Ruger grins. "I could stick around for some chicks like that."

Sapphire Knight

My temper ignites almost immediately, wanting me to teach his mouth how to stay shut when it comes to her, but I fight myself inside to hold back. Taking a few deep breaths, I begin to feel like my normal self again when a car turns into the gravel drive of the motel. It's not just any car, though; it's *her* car.

Ruger puts on a cheesy smile, strolling toward the passenger side that's closest to us. The girls have the windows rolled down and music blaring, but it gets quieter as they come to a stop directly in front of us.

Cinderella's gaze is trained on my naked torso while her friend is busy looking at Nightmare like she wants to eat him alive. I don't think she even really notices Ruger in front of her. She should, though, because Nightmare would easily break her.

Taking quick strides, I round the car to the driver side before Ruger notices that Cinderella's a twenty when her friend's barely a nine. He even thinks of touching her; I'll wire his mouth shut after I break it. Brother or not, I feel almost feral when it comes to her. I have no fucking clue why, but I'm damn sure going to find out.

She licks her lips, and my pants grow tighter at the sight of her tongue. She doesn't look like last night. She looks even better now—hair windblown, crystal blue eyes sparkling, wearing a little bikini top with short-shorts and flip-flops.

The savage inside me pounds his chest once I get a chance to take her in. I want to pull her out the car window, throw her over my shoulder and carry her straight to my room. I know that's not logical thinking, but fuck if I can't stop imagining it.

Her arms are scraped up a little on the backs; most likely from Shady fuck pushing her against the brick. She'll never have to deal with him again; I made sure of it.

I can hear her friend babbling on to Ruger about them being on their way to go swimming. I don't pay much attention, though, just gaze at Cinderella, cataloging each possible detail of her to memory. She's like an enigma that I can't figure out. What's so fucking special about her?

"Hi." She breaks the silence, and I'm forced to think of something to say. I have no idea what, so I just nod.

She chews on her bottom lip for a few seconds before swallowing and trying again. "So…umm, thanks for last night." She meets my stare, and I nod again like an idiot.

Hybrid Collection

I hear Ruger ask if he can go swimming with them and her friend happily agreeing, inviting Nightmare along as well. Of course, Night doesn't say anything. He eventually looks over at the chick in the passenger seat, his nostrils flaring when she smiles at him.

She says please to him directly, and I think we're all surprised when he huffs, throws his wrench to the ground and strides to his hotel room, slamming the door in his wake. I don't know what the fuck that was about, but I'm leaving it alone.

Cinderella looks up at me again. "Would you like to come with us?"

Would I ever, but I won't. I know that if I see her in a bikini, I'm gonna fuck her whether she wants it or not, and I can't have her hating me before I even know why she calls to me so damn strongly.

"No."

She taps her fingers on her steering wheel, her gaze leaving mine to stare straight ahead like she's frustrated.

Ruger gets in the backseat, and I learn her friend's name is Bethany when she shouts it as soon as the back door closes.

"Let's go woman; I want a good tan before we go out tonight."

Cinderella shifts the car in drive. "Me too."

"Wait!" Spills from my mouth and her irises jump back over to me.

Her shoes.

I walk-jog to my room, grabbing the black heels off my table and bring them out to her.

"Oh my god, thank you!" She smiles, and my mouth goes dry. She takes the shoes, handing them over to Bethany, who's wearing a pleased grin.

Leaning over, I look through the window that's behind her seat, straight at Ruger. He glances at me, puzzled, and then rolls the window down. "'Sup?"

"Eyes off Cinderella," I quietly order, but it comes out more like an angry growl.

Ruger's eyebrows practically hit his hairline; he glances toward the driver's seat, and it hits him what I'm saying. "Got ya, brother."

Nodding, I walk behind the car back to my room. On my way, I hear her repeat 'Cinderella?' dreamily and Ruger says, "Yep, that'd be you darlin'."

I waited around for hours, checking out the window whenever I'd hear a vehicle and every damn time I'd huff when it wasn't them returning. Finally, I gave up, took a shower, put some clean clothes on and walked across the street to the bar.

Taking a seat next to Saint and Sinner, I'm pleased when a beer's set down in front of me almost immediately. I'm surprised they're here and not corrupting some woman with both of their cocks.

"Angel," I nod toward Sinner. He's not so bad, but he's always around to egg Saint on. He's the type to plant a seed in someone's head, then sit back and watch them self-destruct on their own. You won't catch him fighting much, but he sure loves to fuck with people's minds.

"Devil," I fist-bump Saint, and they both chuckle at me giving them shit.

They know those names are more fitting, though. Chicks eat up Saint's 'sweet boy' charade he plays to get in their pants. However, I see him away from the women. Trust me when I say the only type of angel he'd ever be is a fallen one, and nowhere close to a Saint.

I'm about half way through my beer when Ruger finally waltzes through the door. I wait with bated breath for Bethany and Cinderella to enter behind him, but they never do.

Ruger plops down in the seat across from me, looking tanner than he did earlier. He may have gone for Bethany, but I still want to pop his legs off and beat him with them for the simple fact that he got to hang out with Cinderella today and I didn't. I sat at the hotel pouting like a giant pansy ass.

"Where're the chicks?" I ask immediately. He better not have fucked it up with them.

Saint and Sinner's gazes both land on me as soon as the words leave my mouth.

"They went to go change; they'll be here."

"You found some new bitches for us, Ruger?" Saint pipes up.

"Naw, just me and Vike. They were in here last night playing pool."

Sinner's eyebrows shoot up as he does a low whistle. "Damn, it's like that, huh? I would've chatted them up last night to get some pussy, but I got the impression they were skittish."

"What happened at the lake?" I interrupt, my jealousy nagging at me, wanting to know every single detail.

"Not much. Cinderella painted her toenails when we first got there. Then she floated around the lake on a small air mattress and on the way back asked if your name was really Viking."

Hybrid Collection

Saint leans forward. "No fucking way. Her name's Cinderella? The blonde one? I bet she's a goddamn fairy tale in bed," he finishes, eyeing Sinner.

Letting loose a deep growl, I slam my fist down on the table, hard enough to make the drinks bounce and everyone jump to catch them. I swear if he speaks about fucking her again I'm going to lose my shit. I'm not nearly buzzed enough to deal with bullshit comments about the woman I recently killed for.

"Damn, Vike, my bad." He holds his hands up in surrender. He's seen me get pissed, and no way in hell would Sinner be able to save his ass from my wrath.

Grunting in response, I turn back to Ruger. "You get some ass from her friend?"

I only ask because it was written all over her at the motel that she wanted Nightmare, not another brother.

"No, she's a fucking cock tease, bro. We hooked up a little, but she wouldn't let me get my dick wet, wouldn't even give me head. We had a few shots of tequila, but I'm hoping tonight she'll get blitzed and let me hit it."

Saint laughs and fist bumps Ruger, clearly approving of his less than stellar tactics to get laid. Can't say shit about it, though; we've all done it at some point.

Downing another beer, the night gets a little later before the girls finally show up. I'm fairly surprised to see her back so soon after the shit that went down. Most women would be locked inside their houses right now, too shaken up to leave. Is she just stubborn or could she feel safe coming back? Is it because she knows Ruger's here and that I will also be? Nightmare and Spidey-boy have joined us as well, leaving Exterminator to sit with Scot up at the bar flirting with the bartender he's got a hard-on for.

Cinderella walks her fine ass through the door wearing a fitted black leather miniskirt that barely comes to the bottom of her ass cheeks, paired with a red corset top and the shoes I gave her earlier. There aren't words strong enough to do her justice. Bitch makes my heart beat faster; that's the biggest compliment any woman could ever receive from me.

Surprisingly, Bethany holds her own. She fits perfectly alongside Cinderella, wearing daisy dukes, dusty cowboy boots, and a cut-up shirt coming to the bottom of her tits.

I swear to God, everyone at the table probably came in their pants a little at the sight of them. They're not just hotter than sin; they look like a biker's fucking wet dream, dressed like some badass bitches that belong on the back of our bikes.

"If you two don't want those chicks, I'll sacrifice myself to take one for the team," Spider offers and a few brothers chuckle.

Nightmare and I both mumble "shut-up," at the same time.

I catch it, but with the music on in the background, I don't think the brothers realize it was both of us who said it.

Five

VIKING

Cinderella came over to say hello when she first got here, but I ignored her. Up close her tits were nicely displayed, taunting me with each breath she took as they moved slightly. I couldn't peel my eyes away from them. I'm sure if I had, my brothers would have been glued to her chest as well. My dick was so damn hard under the table; I couldn't think, let alone speak. She needs to cover the hell up if she's expecting some sort of a conversation to come out of me.

It's been sweet fucking torture to watch her each time, bending over the pool table to line up her shot. After each ball either one of them sinks in a pocket, the other takes a shot of liquor. I've been paying attention because I'm not letting them drive home if they're both plastered. Right now Cinderella's on her fourth and Bethany's on her sixth.

She glances at me briefly, walking around the pool table until she stops directly in front of our table. Spreading her feet apart, she bends over, her muscular legs on full display as she adjusts her pool stick until she has it where she wants it. She inhales a deep breath then pushes her ass out more while she takes her shot. With that motion, her skirt lifts the few inches I need it to so I can catch a glimpse of her bare pussy lips.

My fist hits the table top again, loudly, causing her to jump up. She spins around, her hand on her chest and eyes wide. My nostrils flare as I breathe heavily, wanting to rip the skirt completely off her.

"Are you okay?" She asks breathily and Saint groans beside me, no doubt witnessing what I was just privy too. I could go for punching him right about now.

"Pull your skirt down," I demand, glaring at her for making me lose control so easily.

"Fine," she huffs back. Wiggling slightly, she shimmies the tiny piece of material hugging her hips down. It moves all of an inch at the most, and I grit my teeth from her titties jiggling.

She faces Bethany, her long platinum hair falling to the top of her ass. "I need you and a smoke."

Bethany gets a wicked grin on her face and downs a shot before eagerly following Cinderella through the bar. Either she's happy about having a smoke or they're up to something. Whatever it is, those girls are fucking trouble. People think bikers are bad, but that bitch is the type to make a brother lose it over her, and that's gonna end up being me if I don't keep my distance.

Slamming the double shot of whiskey I had resting in front of me, I'm stuck listening to my brothers talk about how they all hope that the chicks have friends that look as good as they do.

"You going out there?" Nightmare asks quietly, so the others don't hear him over their conversation.

"Nope."

"Why the fuck not?"

Shrugging, I take a gulp of my beer.

"You know with the cunt shot she just sent you, she wants to fuck. If you don't jump on it, any other man in this shit hole would be happy to, Saint included." My eyes fly toward the other brother busy carrying on, drinking and having a good time, paying Nightmare and myself no attention. Nightmare raps his knuckles on the table. "Somehow I don't think you'd let anyone touch her, though."

"What do you know about it?"

He copies me, shrugging and sits back in his seat, taking a long pull from his bottle.

Goddamn it. Fine. I hate the fact that he's right. I would go fucking apeshit on someone if they touched her. She has me so wound up; I'm liable to flip out on anyone at this point.

"I'mma smoke," I declare suddenly, so everyone at the table hears me.

Night and Spider nod, while Saint, Sinner, and Ruger keep on reminiscing over our last trip to Florida. They turned into some regular beach boys, going surfing and shit. We gave them all types of hell for it, but they ended up loving it regardless of our opinions.

Hybrid Collection

Trekking through the bar, I take a deep breath once I arrive at the door leading me outside where Cinderella is. I have no idea what the fuck to say to her or them both if they're standing there smoking and attempt to talk to me. I ought to make her put on my shirt while we're out back. It's the least she could do so I don't end up killing someone else for her tonight. At this rate, it'll end up being one of my fucking brothers.

I head outside, making sure the door closes behind me and that no one's followed me. I hope she was at least cautious enough to do that much as well. Standing beside it, I lean my tired body against the brick wall and dig a cigarette out of my front pocket, then my zippo.

It takes a few tries to get my smoke lit in the breeze, but it works eventually, allowing me a couple of drags before I hear the first soft moan. My eyes fly to the left of me where the building protrudes out in an 'L' shape.

In the full moon's bright glow mixed with the porch light, I can clearly make out Cinderella propped up against the building. They have the short leather skirt pushed up to her waist exposing her nakedness that I caught a glimpse of back at the pool table.

The real shocker is that Bethany's on her knees right in front of her, with her shorts pushed down to the ground. She has one hand between her legs, pumping away while her face is between Cinderella's thighs, licking furiously at her cunt.

Groaning, my hand immediately goes to my dick, squeezing it through my pants, attempting to ease some of the huge ache it's suddenly feeling from not getting the attention it wants. This is the last thing I was ever expecting when I got up from my seat. Cinderella's eyes meet mine as she moans again and I squeeze my cock harder. Fuck, I want in her so badly. This is no doubt the sexiest fucking thing I've ever seen.

Bethany starts sucking on Cinderella's pussy as her hand moves faster under her shorts; she squirms for a second before pushing her away. Bethany stays directly in front of her, using both of her hands to chase her orgasm.

Cinderella locks her gaze with mine again and inserts two of her fingers as deep as they'll go; my palm rubs my cock over my jeans, consumed by the sight in front of me.

Bethany calls out in bliss, finding her release as she watches Cinderella pleasure herself.

She pumps her fingers in and out, each time grinding her palm against her clit and moaning all while watching me. Cinderella's eyes suddenly fly closed, a loud moan escaping her as she rides the waves of her orgasm. The vulnerable look of surrender as she gives in and accepts the pleasure overcoming her body is fucking breathtaking.

She finishes and Bethany climbs to her feet, both of them wearing pleased smiles. Pulling my hand away from my dick, I take a drag off my forgotten cigarette as they fix their clothes, approaching me.

Bethany beams a bright smile as she passes by, heading back inside.

I'm panting like I just ran a fucking marathon when Cinderella gets to me. I'm expecting her to do the same as Bethany, but she pauses. Her blue irises take in my flushed face as her tongue glides over her lips, making my heart rate spike even higher from the simple gesture, and then she does something I'll never forget for the rest of my fucking life.

The bitch reaches her hand up, taking her two fingers she just came all over and brushed them against my mouth, leaving her wetness behind on my lips. It's more than I can handle; her scent on my mouth is my fucking undoing.

She flashes a sexy smile and disappears through the door. She's gone before I even realize it and I'm not sure if I'm in shock that she just did that or because she left me like this after such a brazen invitation. At least for her sake I hope that's what it was, or she's going to be highly pissed when I call her on it.

Licking my lips breaks me, and I go storming through the door, on a mission to have her. She thinks she can do that without any repercussions? I don't fucking think so. That bitch is so fucking mine; she doesn't know it yet, but she will real quick.

Once I make it through the hallway and into the bar, she's yet again bent over the pool table, just like she never left.

Perfect.

With a few powerful strides, I'm behind her; Bethany's eye's growing wide when she notices how furious I am. Cinderella gets a 'what' out to Bethany before I slam the top part of her body down onto the pool table. She attempts to move, but I hold her down with my hand in the middle of her back. She's no match for my strength no matter how hard she tries.

With my other hand, I release the button on my jeans, my zipper lowering immediately from my dick trying to burst out and lift her skirt up, uncovering half of her ass cheeks. She starts to scream in protest while everyone watches me claim her in front of the entire bar. After this, no one will ever touch her again around here.

Hybrid Collection

"You offered your pussy up, Cinderella; now I'm fucking taking it," I declare and she quits jerking around as I slam my dick inside, seating it in her fully. Once she hears my voice, I can feel the muscles in her back relax some; the fight left in her is purely because I've decided to collect in front of everyone.

Gripping her hip tightly, I take her hard and rough, our skin making loud smacking sounds each time our bodies meet a certain way. Her pussy's tight, so fucking good, squeezing my cock like an angry fist.

Within a few pumps, I have her moaning, pushing her ass back into me for more. I give it to her, driving in deep until she whimpers, making my dick throb. The brothers all watch eagerly, no doubt enjoying the free show I'm giving them.

Nightmare's over at Cinderella's table. I'm guessing he was holding Bethany back from trying to stop me, but now she's sitting on his lap with a worried stare directed at her friend. His arms are wrapped around her front, holding her to him. She has no need to stress anyhow; I can feel her friend's cunt squeezing and pulsing inside, wanting to come.

"My bitch," I state loudly as I thrust into her, so everyone understands exactly what this means.

"Fuck you!" She yells, muffled from the pool table.

"I am, baby." Releasing her hip, I reach around giving her tittie a strong squeeze as I push my cock in as far as it'll go. She feels so fucking good; I have to hold my breath, so I don't go off to soon.

I hear, "Oh, Viking," followed by that same moan from outside; then her pussy is squeezing me over and over, soaking my cock with her juices as her body gives in to me. Grinding into her, she rides my dick until her orgasm finishes.

"That's it Cinderella, soak my cock; I want every last drop," I growl just before pumping her full of my cum.

After a few beats, I step back, moving my hand that was holding her down. She stays in place, though, so I go about pulling her skirt down first. Once she's covered up, I tuck my cock back in my pants.

Some of the patrons in the bar have stopped paying attention, while others are still staring. The music seems louder than before since the majority of the people are quiet now.

She takes a few breaths, carefully pushing herself up from the table. Once she has her footing again, she faces me, her blue gaze blazing with fury. I've never seen her pissed before; I think it makes her even more beautiful.

"My name's Princess, not Cinderella," she hisses angrily and follows it with a powerful slap. The crack from her palm connecting with my cheek is so loud that I wouldn't be surprised if it fucking echoed. The bitch hit me hard enough that my face feels like it's on fire, even with the protection from my beard. She's got some balls; that's for damn sure.

My hand shoots out, wrapping around her throat. Her eyes grow wide, and I pull her body flush with mine. I lower my face to hers, close enough that we trade breaths. "It fits," I mumble as she watches my mouth.

"Huh?" she whispers, meeting my eyes.

"Your name. You reminded me of a fairy tale, but Princess is better," I answer quietly.

Her hands flutter up to her throat, following my fingers down to my wrist and then further until she has a hold of my forearm. She clutches on, using it for balance as she gets to her tippy toes, making her a bit taller. It gives her just enough height to bring her mouth to mine.

She sucks my bottom lip between both of hers and immediately my grip on her neck relaxes, releasing her throat so I can kiss her. Her lips part eagerly when I take over, our tongues meeting and mating in their own form.

She jumps up, wrapping her legs around my waist, and our kiss changes from exploratory to downright erotic. Her body already wants more. I've heard stories from other brothers that once a cunt is claimed and filled with your cum that it goes crazy, wanting to fuck for days. They said it has something to do with breeding and finding your mate or some shit like that. I thought it was a myth, but maybe it's not after all.

My hands fly under her ass to hold her to me securely as I break our kiss, so I'm able to see as I walk. If this is happening, then I'm taking her to my room. I glance toward the brothers, getting a thumbs-up from Saint. I don't respond, just concentrate on walking toward the door.

Princess runs her tongue over my neck, sucking hard enough that tomorrow I'm most likely going to look like I was fucking attacked. I don't mind it one bit. I'll wear that shit proudly.

I can't believe that I claimed her in a bar, in front of everyone. Where the fuck did that even come from? I'll think about it later. There's no way I can give a shit right now with her body pressed up against mine and her mouth on me.

PRINCESS

Just kissing him alone, it's like drowning. No matter how much I tell myself to struggle and fight against him, I succumb to the raging need he fills me up with inside. I want him, unlike anything I've ever experienced before.

There's never been a man in my life that was brave enough to fuck me like Viking did tonight. Any other women would be crying somewhere in a corner, acting as if they were violated from being manhandled, but I'm not most women. No, definitely not, 'cause I fucking loved it.

He was that hell-bent on showing everyone in the bar that he's the only one allowed to have me, well now I want more. That sample he gave me was only the beginning.

My tongue trails over the salty skin of his neck, nipping at the juncture meeting his shoulder. His cock is huge, pleasantly reminding me of its length and girth with each step he takes when it rubs against the bottom of my ass. "I want more," I declare, biting his shoulder between each word.

Groaning, he blows out a breath as his dick rubs against my ass again. We're nearly to his room already. He carries me as if I weigh nothing, taking large strides in a hurry.

His taste has left me in some sort of frenzy, wanting him any way I can have him. This isn't supposed to be part of the plan, sleeping with him multiple times. I feel lost, not wanting him to stop but at the same time my head chanting that it's not supposed to be like this. I never included in my mission the possibility of me actually wanting any of the bikers I planned on fucking.

We arrive at Viking's room, the key making a scratching sound as he attempts to stab it in the lock while juggling my wandering hands and me. He becomes impatient, slamming me up against the door. His closeness floods me in his scent of earth and leather. He's all man, everywhere, even his smell. Fuck, he makes my hormones race with all the possibilities.

Taking full advantage of his brief stillness, I hold onto his shoulders, pulling myself up a little way. He pauses, watching me lick my lips, and then I drop down slowly, grinding against his hardness trying to break free from his jeans.

Viking's cheeks flush, his eyes lighting with passion. "You don't hold the fuck still, I'm going to tie you up. Then I'll make you suck my cock while you beg for me to touch your pussy."

His words make me clench and ache with want. Luckily the door flies open as he finally gets it unlocked and we stumble through the opening. Viking starts to balance us, but I lose my grip, and we tumble to the carpet. He braces himself over me in the push-up position, so he doesn't land on me.

"Not what I imagined, but this position will work too," I chortle, and his lips part enough to give me a glimpse of his bright white teeth, clenched together.

Oh. He's not in the mood to play. I must have teased him a little too much.

"So, you like grinding huh?" he rasps with his face bent close enough I can feel the warmth from his breath flutter over my lips, taste the remaining whiskey left in his mouth from the pool table. He had thrown back a double shot right before he spurted his come deep inside my body, owning me in front of the entire bar.

I'd never been claimed before, and it's something I'll never be able to forget. The primal rage I felt radiating through his muscles as he powerfully drove into me over and over, then declaring I belonged to him in front of everyone. It wasn't only a declaration, but a dare. If anyone is remotely brave enough to approach me after tonight, then they become fair game for him. After what I witnessed him do to the last creep that threatened me, I know he wouldn't make false statements.

My heart doesn't stutter in fear thinking that there's a chance he could kill for me; no, it skips a beat, knowing for a fact that he really will kill for me.

His arms lower until he's resting on his elbows, his strong body blissfully pushed against my softer one. I've never felt small before with men, more on their level, but with him, he takes over every inch. Viking consumes me like no other, commanding me to submit and demanding control of everything. Shockingly, my body reacts as if it's being strummed like a melody, eager to please the one playing it.

Spreading my legs wide, my bare pussy lips become pressed against his jean clad cock, sending sweet torture through my body at the contact. "Yep," I eventually get out, starting to pant. He's so warm, his body heat blanketing me like a hot summer's day.

"Funny, when your tits are in my face, you always want to talk, but now that I have your pussy spread and wound up, you don't have much to say?" His hips press into me, delicious waves of pleasure slowly building me up higher

I manage a low moan, but nothing that makes any sense.

"My cock got you distracted, baby?" He pushes his jeans down enough, so his cock is freed, standing at attention, grazing the bottom of his belly button.

Hybrid Collection

"My God you're big."

His mouth hikes up as he rotates his hips in a circle, his cock pressing into my clit perfectly.

"That's right, Princess, I'm gonna fuck your tight cunt until no other man ever measures up."

"Trust me; I can already confirm that they don't," I ramble, as his fingers reach between us, rubbing my entrance, collecting my wetness. Each time he touches me or grinds into me, I feel my juices flooding, dribbling down toward my ass.

"You save your voice 'cause you're gonna be using it a lot tonight. I'm going to fuck you so hard that tomorrow your legs will shake when you try to stand. Each time you sit, you'll burn, but be reminded that I was there all night long. I'm going to have this pussy as much as I want, then I'll take your mouth." His hand moves lower, stopping at the entrance of my ass, the one place that hasn't ever been touched by anyone. "And when you think you can't possibly come again, I'm going to make you cry, baby." He shoves two fingers deep into my back entrance, a gasp escaping me at the new sensations, and he continues, "Yeah, you're gonna cry and beg me to stop, but I'm gonna fuck your ass, and after you're cleaned up and done crying, I'm going to spray my thick cum all over those pretty titties you like to flaunt in front of me. You may hate me by morning, but you'll fucking be mine." He ends on a growl, plunging his cock into my core while continuing to play with my ass.

He's right, I scream.

I scream in absolute fucking wonder at the amazing feeling of being taken by a real man. I should've saved my voice because it was only the beginning.

Six

PRINCESS

I'm awoken by a revving car or truck engine coming from outside. My body aches in new places, spots that I've never felt sore before, reminding me of last night. Viking had taken my body like a man possessed, never getting his fill, and I'm definitely feeling it all over. The sheets smell like us, leather and flowers. I would never have guessed that it would be a good mix.

The mattress beside me moves, and I crack my eyes open to witness his firm, naked ass as he stands, pulling on nothing but the jeans he was wearing the night before. I love the Nordic tattoos he has scattered over his arms, including one the size of my entire hand on his thigh. His entire back is covered in one massive tattoo as well. The details are breathtaking, making the Oath Keepers patch appear more sinister and threatening. The flag being held by the skeleton looks like it's being ripped from his flesh to wave proudly. It must have taken hours and several sessions to get something that would probably win an award if it were ever put on display. That would never happen; my father wouldn't approve of such exposure to his club or the surrounding Charters.

My father.

I wonder if what happened last night in the bar has gotten back to him yet. Surely someone must have said something about the dramatic public claiming performed by a notorious Nomad. Hell, it should be the talk of the town and surrounding area with how much people like to gossip.

Fuck my life. I can't believe I let that happen.

Hybrid Collection

I'm probably going to end up having to move away when this is all said and done. I won't put my mother through added stress; I do, however, have to complete my mission. The things Viking did to me, made me feel...I'm such a fool to believe I could get through this without any damage to myself.

He would never truly make me an Ol' Lady, and God knows I couldn't handle everything that comes with that title in the first place. I'm too much like my mother, an old soul. I want monogamy; I want a husband who comes home to me after work, and I get to cook him dinner every night. I couldn't deal with having a man that came home when he wished, fucked whomever he wanted and ended up in prison.

I'm not that strong, neither was my mother and she's taught me plenty. Last night should be enough, and I can keep my distance from Viking in the future. Between him and the Prospect, I don't think I could do anything else with another member. I know I said before that I would be with a dozen if that's what it took, but something's changed.

Viking's different for me; he's a game changer. I don't feel disappointed when I look at him, but the opposite and that scares the fuck out of me. I can't afford to let myself fall for a biker. I won't let him break me like my father broke my mother.

The motel door closes quietly on Viking's way out. I guess he knows who that engine belongs too.

Their voices are loud enough to carry through the poorly built motel and over the rumbling from the exhaust. It's hard to tell if it's a friendly visit with the heavy metal music playing amongst everything else. Despite my stomach telling me to stay in bed, that Viking can handle whatever's outside, my feet hit the matted carpet.

I scoop up the thin sheet, wrapping it around me and make a beeline for the door.

Opening it enough to fit my body through, I lean against the doorjamb, curiosity spurring me on to be brave or stupid. Immediately I notice two of my father's men, each standing next to a mean looking black beast of a car. The doors are wide open with the windows down, allowing the thumping from the rock music to escape into the parking lot.

Breezing over their cuts, I learn that the driver is my dad's Enforcer, Cain, and the passenger with the bright Mohawk is the club's Treasurer, Spin. They notice me immediately. Mohawk guy's face lighting up as he runs his eyes over my sheet. The other guy stares, his forehead wrinkling slightly like he's trying to place me from somewhere. He won't be able to, though, my father's never introduced me to these guys before.

The driver keeps talking through his curious gaze. "So 'bout that barbecue, my Ol' Lady's cooking and she doesn't mess around when it comes to food."

Viking and a few of his brothers stand next to the bike Nightmare was working on yesterday afternoon, listening to my father's men.

"Aye then, laddie, we're always up for some good cooking." A robust, red-haired man beside Viking answers in a Scottish accent. I've never seen him before, but he wears the same cut that Viking has, so he must be one of his Nomad brothers as well.

The Enforcer grins, a set of dimples coming out to play that make my stomach flutter a little. Fuck, he's hot. He doesn't have the same effect on me as Viking but damn is he nice to look at.

"Bring your Ol' Ladies too. I know the girls would wanna meet them." His friendly gaze meets mine causing Viking to glance between the other men and me.

The Treasurer stares openly at me as well, clearly enjoying what he sees and then like an afternoon storm coming out of nowhere, Viking's irises blaze.

Facing me, his nostrils flare as he breathes deeply, taking in my bedroom attire. He looks upon me with such heat; I can't stop myself from licking my lips nervously, remembering his taste. He had that same intense fire blazing last night while he took me relentlessly. He'd kissed me until I swore my face would be rubbed raw from his beard.

My fingertips lightly trace over my chin, finding a tender spot at the memory.

Spreading his legs out a little more, he crosses his arms over his chest, his shoulders becoming even wider by the new stance. His magnificent body's completely imposing, overtaking more space than what should be allowed; it seems like he grows even larger as he commands everyone's attention and points toward his room. With a deep grumble, coming out more like a growl he demands, "Get in the room."

Huffing in irritation, my temper flares to life, ready to spit nails if necessary. I open my mouth to protest, and he dutifully cuts me off.

"Now, Cinderella."

Glancing over to the men, I wait for someone to tell him he's ridiculous, but I notice they're all staring at me, not him. They've got on amused smiles and smirks, entertained at this biker bossing me around. My gaze settles on Viking again.

His eyebrow lifts, almost in challenge. It's like he's warning me that he'll put me in my place if I argue. This man clearly hasn't seen every side of me; I don't do well with taking orders. Well, orders that aren't sexual anyhow.

He'll learn—the hard way.

Keeping my mouth shut, I spin around and give them my back as my temper takes over. Being one that doesn't easily relent, I slam the door behind me. Making sure the impact is strong enough that it echoes through the nearly empty room, sounding like a clap of thunder, making the fake art on the walls shake.

The guys outside chuckle loudly at my outburst and the thin walls of the motel allow the sounds to float inside, taunting me, angering me further. Gritting through my sore muscles and my ass that feels like it could be on fire today, I slide on my leather skirt.

Glancing around for my corset, I land on a new package of wife beater tank tops. Those will be much more comfortable than attempting to squish my tits back into my top from last night.

I hated wearing it. Damn thing squished me like crazy, but it was all about the look. Ruger had told me that Viking would for sure be at the bar last night, and I wanted any advantage I could think of to get his attention. I would never have returned to that place had I not known Viking was there along with Bethany, just in case I needed help again. I hate to ever feel dependent on someone like that, but I learned my lesson the first time, going outside alone, barely two nights ago. My arms and back still have the stupid scrapes to remind me of my bad judgment call.

Throwing a tank on, I practically drown in it, so I tie it up at my mid-back, leaving a sliver of skin on my belly visible. I'm probably looking like a hot mess, but I couldn't care less. I'm making a point to this bossy biker, that he doesn't give me orders outside the bedroom.

Shit fuck. I like him being such a demanding ass. It's sexy to meet someone who's so damn Alpha; at times I worry my panties will catch fire being around him. Oh wait, I'm not wearing panties. Regardless, he doesn't need to speak to me like that in front of so many men.

Viking had been sweet enough to retrieve my purse from my trunk last night about halfway through our activities, so I snatch that up. Quickly, I shove my corset top inside the oversized bag that should most likely be classified as luggage rather than a purse. Tossing my shoes in also, which Viking admitted he's a bit obsessed with, I shoulder the wide strap and head back outside, ready to leave.

Bethany's standing next to Nightmare, this time, clad in his T-shirt and boxers with hair shooting every which way like she just climbed out of bed as well. I wonder if she got to hook up with him after all. When we went home to change she confessed that she was interested in him.

What's it with these grouchy fucking bikers that pull you to them? Nightmare seems broody and miserable, but she's still fascinated with him. Who am I to talk though? Viking could be classified as a quiet asshole, yet he has me twisted all over the place for him.

Nose and chin up, I use a dose of fake confidence strutting past the men and call back, "Come on, Bethany, we're out of here." Since I'm not in my high shoes and the gravel doesn't bother my bare feet too badly, I put a little extra swing in my hips making a few of the guys' mouths pop open.

Viking lets loose a frustrated growl, and it takes everything in me not to shoot him a smug smile in defiance. "Where do you think you're going?" he demands, but I ignore him.

"I'm coming! Let me grab my stuff," Bethany answers and runs back into Nightmare's room.

"*Princess*!" he shouts. His voice is strong and lethal with a warning ingrained in my name, just by his tone.

Turning to him and propping my hand on my hip, I give him 'the look,' "What?"

"Where do you think you're going?"

"I'm leaving."

"I'm not done with you."

Shrugging, I don't get a chance to respond as Bethany comes running out, yelling that she's ready.

"Fine. I'll call you." He plays it off.

"Sure you will," I retort, knowing damn well that he doesn't have my number. He didn't get it last night and I damn sure didn't leave it for him.

Bethany and I trek toward the two-lane highway, the guys loud enough I can still easily overhear their conversation.

"Her name's Princess? Or you call her that?" Cain questions Viking.

"It's her fucking name. I call her Cinderella. What's it to you?"

I try to do a sly glance back, but catch Cain openly staring at me, as if he saw a ghost. I don't think twice about it, though; there's no way he knows who I am.

"Definitely, bring your Ol' Ladies with you to the barbecue," I catch him saying right before we're too far away to hear anything else.

VIKING

Cain repeats himself, and I almost pop off that she isn't my Ol' Lady, but I did claim her last night. Whatever the fuck that means now, I have no idea. I was planning on hashing it all out with her later today, but that plan's gone to shit with her temper tantrum.

It's none of his business right now anyhow. I can't stand Ares, but the rest of the Charter here doesn't bother me much. Cain, for example, is good people.

At the same time, I don't want to say she's not my Ol' Lady 'cause if another brother goes after her, I'm liable to scalp them. The bitch was already under my skin, but after last night—getting a real taste—it's even worse. She makes me feel as if I've had my first hit of heroin and I want more.

Fuck! She came outside in a goddamn sheet, and she wants to give me attitude for it? I know these brothers and what goes through their heads. The moment they saw her dressed like that, there's no doubt that they were picturing the fucking fabric falling.

That's my fucking property; I own that body and the only time I want her seen in so little is right beside me. At this rate, she'll end up on the back of my bike permanently, and I'm not so sure that description fits with being a Nomad.

The chicks speed off, Bethany waving and smiling as they pass by. Princess stares straight ahead like we're not over here, still pissy I reckon. Good thing I remembered to use her phone to send myself a text message with her number once she had passed out. I doubt she'd have given it to me today.

"All right bro, we're smashing. Don't forget—three p.m. next Saturday." Cain fist bumps each of us, Spin doing the same before climbing back into the midnight black Hellcat. I'm not much for cars, but that's one badass vehicle.

The car creeps through the parking lot, and we all admire the impressive machine, throwing up a few fingers in a friendly wave.

Spin leans forward, cranking the music up as the car hits the highway and Cain romps on the gas. The powerful horsepower of the Hellcat sends Spin flying back into his seat, and we all chuckle. You know Cain did that shit on purpose since the brother touched his radio. I'd probably do the same.

"Fuck, I wanna drive that car!" Ruger wistfully declares, watching it speed away.

Saint claps him on the back, nodding, "Bet it's one hell of a pussy magnet." He turns toward Sinner. "We need one, man. Both of us in it, I bet bitches would be throwing themselves on the hood."

Sinner chuckles, shaking his head.

Nightmare snorts and rolls his eyes. "Whatever, I'm going back to bed."

The brothers agree and head back to their rooms. I won't sleep, though. I hardly got any rest last night, and I can't stop wondering what Princess is up to today.

Sitting on the picnic table, I light a cigarette and pull out my phone, turning on the screen. She's my new background, sleeping peacefully—fully naked—and absolutely fucking beautiful.

Spider takes a seat next to me, getting a peek at my device.

"Hmm?" Grumbling, I flash an annoyed glance his way for not minding his own business.

"She sure stormed off quickly."

"No shit."

"Do you wanna talk about it?"

"Of course not, why would I?"

"Look, man, you're the one clearly pissed about it and thinking of her; I'm just lending an ear if you need it. What's so fascinating about this one anyhow?"

"Fuck," escapes with a sigh. This guy likes to chatter all of a sudden. He's been so quiet up until recently, and we've gotten along just fine. "Hell if I know."

"You're too picky."

"Excuse me?" My eyebrows wrinkle as I take a pull off my smoke.

"We all see you sift through which bitches you allow to suck your cock and the few you fuck. This latest one, you took her in a bar and then all night, I'd guess by the whimpers and moans I heard through the wall. You can't shake her because you don't just fuck anyone. I wouldn't even call that just fuckin' either. I heard you being all sweet and shit when she got upset. You care about her, enough to console her."

"You've all seen me fuck in public," I defend.

Hybrid Collection

"Yep, we've seen you fuck on the side of a building and in a field at a party, but brother you claimed her in front of a room full of people. You mounted her in front of the brothers and everyone else in the middle of a bar, just so another man wouldn't touch her." He breathes deeply and mutters, "You're royally fucked, bro."

Shrugging, I glance up, watching the clouds filter over the sun. "Doesn't matter. She was pissed and left. I'll probably never see her again." Leaning back on the table with my elbows, they prop me up enough so I can stretch my legs out in front of me.

"Do you wanna?"

His question catches me off guard. Do I want to?

Squeezing my eyes closed tightly, I admit the truth, muttering, "Fuckin' A."

"Let me see your phone."

My eyes fly back open as I face him. "Why?"

I don't want him staring at Princess' picture; it's all mine.

"Because I'd bet five hundred bucks she gave you her number or you took it."

"You're not calling her." I take one last puff and throw the rest in the rusted coffee tin. *I need to quit that shit; the road hides most of the smell, but I still know it's there.*

He grins, his face appearing younger with the lightness. "No, but do you want to know how to find her?"

"You can do that?" I reply, sitting back up, my interest suddenly peaked.

"Seriously, think about who you're talking to right now." He places his palm in front of me, waiting for me to hand over the phone.

"Let me change something."

"I already saw the picture; I won't yank my dick to it, I swear."

I shoot him a brief glare, then give in, nodding and hand over my phone. My eyes never leave the device as he illuminates the screen. He quickly flips to the apps section and pulls up some tech shit about the phone. Spider loses me from that point on. I have no idea how he can know so much shit about technology, but if it finds her, I'll be grateful.

He chants, "Come on, come on, come on," quietly to himself, tapping his thumb against his jeans as he waits for something to happen on the screen. After a beat, he lets out a cocky chuckle full of triumph.

"How do you find her?" I'm assuming it must've worked by the grin he's back to wearing.

"I installed a program that works like Key Logger."

My expression mirrors my thoughts, becoming more puzzled.

He tilts his head and tries to explain again. "It's like the Key Logger program you install to monitor someone's computer activity."

I remain quiet, not having a clue what the fuck he's talking about. We didn't have money like that, for useless shit such as computers when I was growing up. It was hard enough to eat when I was fucking hungry.

Huffing, he simplifies, "It's an app that's going to track where she goes."

"She'll blow the fuck up knowing I'm tracking her."

"It's a ghost program; she won't be able to tell you're tracking her. Even a decent phone tech wouldn't know about it. You'd have to be a programmer or app builder to know where to begin looking."

Cocking my eyebrow in disbelief, he rolls his eyes.

"Look, man, I give you my word. Princess won't find this shit. Besides, your phone is an unlocked burner; she'd have no idea who it belonged to unless she knows your number. Does she?"

"No. I haven't contacted her."

"Yet." He mumbles, causing me to scowl. "Okay, it's finished." He holds the phone so I can see everything also. "Click apps. The box with a crown as the photo is her, click it."

Multiple options appear such as find, log, points of interest, home, listen, disable, and the last—delete program.

He hands me my phone. "The question mark next to each word will tell you what the option does, otherwise, just click on the words, follow the prompts, and it'll take you where you want."

Nodding, I mutter, "Appreciate it," while my eyes stay trained on the words, curious what they'll each do.

"I'm your brother, Vike. I'll always have your back."

My gaze meets Spider's as he stands and I fist-bump him, giving him the respect he deserves. It's easy to forget that these men are my allies, and they support me. I was surrounded by snakes for so long, that it's been hard to let go of the shit I dealt with in the past. Never again—these men are different, respectful, and loyal.

We tap knuckles, and he heads toward the office while I pull the app up again.

I start off by clicking the question mark next to the word 'find.' It's labeled in red, so I guess that one's the most important. A small white cloud pops up with a paragraph inside explaining that you use that option to find the person that's connected to the tracker.

Let's see if this shit works or not.

Holding my breath, I press the red lettered option. Google Maps opens up and hones in on a street view, showing me the last recorded image of the area. Below the picture, an address appears in white.

Let's see just how accurate this thing is.

Nodding to myself, I stride over to my bike and dig out my Bluetooth piece from my saddlebag so I can hear the directions my phone gives me. Once it's securely in my ear and I've clicked 'go' on the phone, I toss the cell into my saddlebag.

Mounting my ride, I quickly tie a bandana around my head and place my half shell helmet on securely. With a loud rumbling engine, I steer my way through the gravel lot, hitting the highway, a man on a mission.

Seven

PRINCESS

I dropped Bethany off and then came straight home to jump in the shower. I'm still sore from Viking, and I'm in serious need of a nap. That man has the stamina and strength of three men put together. When he got going, it was impossible to think about anything but him.

Once I'm not a zombie, I'm soaking in an Epsom salt bath and drinking water. I'm sure I need to rehydrate. Digging through my dresser, I find one of the large men's white T-shirts that I prefer to wear to sleep in when I'm here alone.

Pulling it over my head as I shuffle toward my bed in a sleepy haze, I hit the cool sheets, sliding between them and my big fluffy white feather down. My comforter's like a giant pillow, and it's pure heaven to sleep under. I close my eyes and my stupid cell rings.

Are you kidding me right now? Don't answer it.

It finishes its three-ring cycle then almost immediately picks up ringing again.

"Oh for fuck's sake." Complaining, I sit up, the covers falling to my waist as I reach for the irritating device.

Bethany glows on the screen. She'll just keep calling back, so I swipe my finger across the screen to answer.

"Hmmm," I mumble into the phone and crawl back under the covers, making myself comfortable.

"You're sleeping right now?"

"Ummhmm."

A loud cackle comes through the speaker causing my eyes to fly open in irritation. "What?"

"I just find it amusing that you finally met someone who can outpace you."

"Shut up."

She laughs loudly again. "Oh hell no. You drug me back there last night on a mission, which means I'm owed details and have the right to give you shit if I want to."

"You looked pretty cozy this morning coming out of Nightmare's room. I doubt it was a hardship for you."

"You're not turning this around on my night. You were irritated in the car, so I left it alone. I didn't pressure you, knowing Viking's dick was probably in your mouth most of last night, and I didn't want to experience that on your breath. You've had time to shower and mouthwash, so spill it."

"I can't believe you just said that."

"It's the truth, though, isn't it?"

"Why are you so nosey?"

"Yep, I knew it. You weren't angry at him bossing you this morning; you were heated because you liked it. In fact, I'm betting the entire time you spent in the shower; you remembered all the things he did to you."

"I can't talk about this right now. You know why I had to be with him. It's done. Now I need to find another."

"Another? Honey, are you crazy?" I know by her tone that her eyebrows are raised so high, they're probably closer to her hairline than her eyes.

"I may as well be. I can't believe I thought Viking was going to be an easy target."

"Look, I tried to warn you, but you saw it as a challenge instead, and now you're deep. What you pulled last night with me outside, basically egging him on to watch us and then giving him your orgasm? You opened him up to a whole new playing field. I don't know what you said or did to that man when I went inside, but even I know that after a biker claims you the way he did in that bar, you won't be having another."

"I hardly doubt he was sincere. You saw his brothers; there were no women with them that were more than a one-night stand."

"Hey! How do you know I was just a one-night stand?" she responds with a bit of hurt coming through her voice.

Hmm, I wonder what that's all about, why she'd be upset. Bethany's never minded before, always stating that she knows what it's all about and wants to have a good time.

"I knew it; you did fuck him!"

"We'll talk about me another time; right now, it's about you and Viking."

"There is no me and Viking to discuss. Did I sleep with him last night? Yes. Do I want to again? Yes. Am I going to? No way."

"You have it so bad."

"I'm taking my nap now."

"Princess, you need to call your mom." She sighs and my heart pings at the thought of my mom. I miss her.

"Why, so Prez can answer? No thanks. I'll call tomorrow morning when he hopefully won't be around, and if he's still there, then at least I know he'll be sleeping until noon like he used too."

"Okay, just...just don't push her away. Some of us aren't lucky enough to have a mother in our lives that love us so much."

"I know. I'm sorry if you think I'm a spoiled bitch about this whole thing; I've just seen her so hurt each time he leaves. She shouldn't have to cry for days—sometimes weeks—barely eating and moping around because some piece of shit doesn't realize how wonderful she is."

"You know I don't feel like that. I understand why you're this way. If I had someone like your mom in my life, I'd do everything I could to protect her and get her some payback for her pain. I'm on your side, and I'll always be, even if I don't think you're doing the right thing."

"I know. I love you," I respond, and my body relaxes with her reassurance.

"I love you too," she replies, and I hit the end button, turning my screen off.

Setting the phone next to my head, I roll over on my side, tuck my hands between my thighs and close my eyes. If it's cold enough, then this is my favorite way to sleep. I can still smell him, the leather and spice that seems ingrained into his skin. It smells amazing. And mint, from his mouthwash, it was all deliciously overwhelming to my senses.

I must doze off for a few minutes because I swear I can hear myself snoring, but that's not what startles me, it's the pounding on my front door. Someone's knocking so loudly, you'd swear the place was on fire or something.

Keeping my eyes closed, I pull the covers off my face and sniff the air a few times. *No fire.* Taking a few deep inhales, I attempt to get my mind back to nothing when the door lashing begins again.

Jumping up in a furious rush, I storm toward the front door. "Whoever the fuck this is, better be dying if they're hitting my door like that!" I huff to myself and the random houseplant placed next to my couch. I'm not a morning person, in general, and this lack of sleep is liable to make me scratch someone's eyes out.

Wrenching the door open in a flourish, I shout in a tired fit of rage, "What?"

On the other side, my eyes meet with a muscular chest covered in black leather.

My gaze flutters over the different patches decorating the front, one, in particular, drawing a swift gasp as I read over each letter. **-Viking-**

Fuck, shit fuck, fuckity, fuck! How many times has Brently warned me to check the peephole before opening the door? I've no doubt learned my lesson; you better believe I'll be using it from now on. How did he find me? What's he even doing here?

He stands so stagnant; he could be a statue. Clenching my fists, I meet Viking's intense stare.

I expect to find heat or the cocky confidence from last night, but instead, it's turmoil swirling in the colorful depths. He's confused like he's questioning something, maybe wondering if he should've come here.

Lacing my voice with venom, I ask the million-dollar question, "What're you doing here?"

His nostrils flare like an irate bull, ready to charge. "You left," he rasps, making it sound more like an accusation rather than a declaration.

"We fucked, it was obviously done." Shrugging my shoulders slightly, I continue, ready to drive it home and piss him off enough to leave. Anger and words have always been my defense I go to when someone can hurt me. "Besides, I always want a shower right away after a one-night stand. Don't you?"

A deep rumble shakes his chest as anger consumes his handsome face; suddenly his hands fly forward, each one grabbing my upper arms tightly enough to leave finger marks. Viking prowls forward, lifting me off the floor, and driving me backward into my living room. He kicks out behind him, effectively slamming my front door so hard there's a good possibility it could be broken.

A whimper bubbles up, leaving me, shocked at the sudden movement and the ferocity overcoming Viking's entire being. I've never been manhandled before; no one that I know would've dared to touch me like this. There wasn't a man that I dated brave enough to stand up to me or fight with me. If they had, my brother would've beaten him to a pulp if I hadn't already.

My back meets the wall next to the hall leading to my bedroom, and my head hits the solid surface with a small thump, momentarily dazing me. My stomach twists with a rush of adrenaline as the flight or fight reflex starts to kick in, commanding my body to survive. I want to struggle against his hold, to fight him, but my heart pleads for me to just stop this nonsense and apologize to him.

He releases one of my arms, bringing his hand between my legs. On reflex, I slam them closed around his palm.

"Open your legs, Princess," he demands sternly.

"Fuck. You."

"God, you're one mouthy bitch; of course, you'd be the one I'd find."

It takes everything inside to hold back from dropping my father's name. I refuse to let him win this battle for me. I can stand up for myself. I have to.

Viking releases my other arm to peel my thighs apart. I'm in pretty decent shape, but in no way am I strong enough to fight off the mountain of a man in front of me. Slapping my hands over his pecs, I drive my fingernails in as harshly as possible.

I'll make him feel something.

I'm expecting him to cry out in pain or surprise—anything. His gaze, simmering with rage, meets mine, and he smiles. The motherfucker grins like it feels good, exactly the opposite of what I wanted.

Two of his thick fingers drive inside me, stretching my tender flesh, going as far as my body will allow them. Every piece of me is wracked in confusion. I gave myself freely to him last night. Why is he here, why's he doing this?

A cry escapes me at the intrusion, while my pussy excitedly milks his fingers. The trader bitch has already been broken by him and is ready to do what he commands.

"Why?" I whisper brokenly, as a tear falls, cascading over my cheek until it drops from my jaw.

He stares into my eyes intently; breathing deeply as if he's just running a race and pumps his fingers into me a few times. "Because I made you mine," he murmurs.

Another tear drops as I attempt to speak, "I-I..."

"Who's in bed with you Princess?" His question catches me completely off guard, as if him finger fucking my pussy wasn't enough of a distraction that I can't come up with a response quick enough. "I *said*, who's been in *my* cunt today?"

Clearing my throat, my eyes hold steady with his. "What are you talking about Viking? No one's here, I came home alone."

Hybrid Collection

"You're naked under this shirt; your hair's a fuckin' mess, and your face had the just fucked look on it when you answered the door. Your friend here eating pussy again?"

Swallowing, my tears slow as I'm starting to understand why he just flipped out. A little, but now I can see how he would come to this conclusion.

"No, I haven't been with anyone, just you last night."

"I'll be able to tell," he retorts, his gaze dropping to my pebbled nipples.

"What? How?"

Viking slips his fingers free, showing them to me, covered in my wetness. "Like this." He sticks the fingers in his mouth, sucking the juices off them completely. As he tastes each digit, his cock grows rock hard between us, digging into my belly.

The site of him so turned on from a small taste is insanely hot. My breaths quicken as his cheeks flush, tattling that he wants me very badly. After his fingers are clean, he drops his hands, lightly grasping my hips and I relax my cat claws that've probably drawn blood under his shirt.

"You swear she wasn't licking on you?" he asks—his voice softer, normal—vulnerable. "I'm able to tell by your flavor; no man's had you but me. I can't tell, however, if she had her tongue on you."

I damn near stutter, rushing to respond. "I promise, no one, not even Bethany. I was asleep when you knocked; that's why I looked like that, and I always wear this to bed."

A deep breath leaves him as his shoulders finally relax. I can smell myself on him, and it's making me want to jump him.

"No one fingers, licks, or fucks this cunt but me now. You're *my* bitch."

"Umm, no. I'm not anyone's bitch."

His eyebrow rises, staying perked up for a few moments as he holds me hostage, waiting for his argument.

"I claimed you last night in front of everyone. Like it or not, you're my Ol' Lady now. You belong to me." He takes a step back as I desperately attempt to fabricate a response to justify why I'm not his Ol' Lady, nor could I ever be. Opening my mouth, he interrupts, "I'll give you space, but get your ass to the bar Thursday night. I'm going to have a few drinks, and then I'm eating that pussy for dessert."

And I'm speechless.

Eight
PRINCESS

"**Wait a minute...you're** telling me he did all of that and then just left you there? He didn't make you come first, say I'm sorry or anything?" Bethany's mouth hangs open in shock.

We're sitting on a small patio having lunch at a deli we like to eat at. I was filling her in on the whole Viking situation from yesterday when he overtook my apartment and then left me hanging.

Shaking my head, I take a sip of my bottled water.

"It happened exactly like I told you."

"Jesus Christ," she replies and takes a bite of her sandwich.

"I know. I pretty much froze up like an idiot."

"I still can't get over the fact he got you to shut up." She snorts and I shoot her a glare. "What! It's the truth, Prissy, and you know it. You have to be the most argumentative, loud-mouthed person I know. And I say that in a good way, take it as a compliment. You stand up for yourself and your beliefs."

Rolling my eyes, I dip my sandwich in my loaded potato soup and take a huge bite.

"Good thing you have a big mouth; I bet Viking's dick is huge."

My hand flies up to cover my lips as I damn near choke at her words. She says some random crazy shit. Chewing my mouthful carefully, my eyes water as I swallow the food down and clear my throat.

"I almost just died right then. Don't talk about his cock anymore."

"You're very much alive honey, and if you choke like that with his dick in your mouth, there's no doubt he'll shoot off like the Fourth of July."

"Shush, tell me how it went with Nightmare."

Her smile drops, and she briefly glances away. "Another time, we need to go, or we'll be late for our movie."

What the fuck happened and why isn't she dying to talk to me about it?

"You win this time, but you're telling me eventually."

She nods quietly and collects her trash, then escapes anymore conversation by going and throwing everything away.

I swear he better not have hurt her already.

VIKING
Three days later...

Thursday rolls around before I know it and fuck if I don't want to admit it, but I'm looking forward to seeing Princess. If I'm real about it, I've been thinking about her non-stop since I left her place. It's taken everything in me these past four days to leave her alone and not show up unannounced again.

I haven't completely left her alone, though. This app that Spider hooked me up with is like my secret weapon. Tracking her has been a fucking dream come true. Every place she drives to and stops, it logs on my phone with the complete addresses. Then there's the listening feature; I've been able to turn it on at random times and catch her voice. She can't hear me, which is perfect.

Fuck, I can't wait to listen to her moan when I'm inside her later.

With four days apart now, I assumed my attraction for her would dim and I'd be able to cut her off, now having had a taste. I'm a fucking fool. Staying away has driven me mad. I'm irritated about everything, grouchier than usual, and when I manage to fall asleep, I dream of her every damn time. Probably doesn't help that my bed smells like her flowery scent.

It's constant, utter fucking torture knowing what she looks like sleeping next to me and wishing she were in my bed, or how silky her skin feels when it's up against mine, and how hot her tight cunt feels squeezing the cum right out of me. That bitch fucking owns me. I know it already, and soon my brothers will also. If anything, that's pissing me off even more.

Being a Nomad is my life. I love being an outlaw and doing whatever the fuck I want, never being judged for scalping a motherfucker who crosses me. Right now Princess stares at me like I'm a god or some shit, but I know eventually that light will fade away, and she'll look at me with blackness, finally seeing the type of poison I really am.

When I was growing up, I dealt with that look from my mother, but my father couldn't give two fucks. He's even darker than I am. But Princess is my exception. I would hang myself or slit my goddamn throat if I ever saw the poison shadowing in her gaze.

With those thoughts, I angrily storm across the street to the bar. I'm early; I know she won't be here for a while, but I need whiskey and a lot of it. It won't solve my issues, but it'll help drown out any guilty feelings I'm having. I've turned off my conscience; I've had to, in order to become the ruthless bastard that I am today.

Princess, though, she lights a fucking fire inside my chest and with the many chances of me damaging her eventually, I need to start drowning it out now. When it comes down to it, I know that no matter how much I tell myself that I'm no good for her, I don't fucking care. I want her, and I'll have her.

"Whiskey. Double. Neat," I demand as my ass hits the stool and Stacy's eyes grow wide.

"No problem, would you like a beer too?"

"No. Keep them coming or give me the fucking bottle."

She nods, rushing to pour me half a small glass. Placing it dutifully in front of me, she stares up at me a little frightened. I almost feel like I should pat her on her head and tell her good job, so she doesn't piss her pants. I don't, however; instead, I grunt and swallow back the entire beverage, placing the glass down louder than necessary.

"Another one?" she asks before reaching for the tumbler.

"Did I stutter?"

"Okay then. You've had a shit day, and I know you're not driving, so how about I just keep pouring them until you've had enough?"

"Good girl." I nod, and she pours a hefty amount of the spicy, amber liquid.

Saint plops down next to me, sending Stacy a dazzling smile. Her face brightens at his light ash colored irises and good ol' boy charade he has her fooled with.

"Rough day brother?" He questions, gesturing to my liquor as Stacy places his Captain and Coke down. "Thanks, sweetheart." Saint winks and she flutters away in a daze.

"It is what it is, man."

"That's the fucking truth." He sighs and takes a hefty gulp.

"You got Sinner hiding in your ass somewhere or what?"

"Fuck you. He'll be over later." He chuckles and shakes his head. "You're not ready to hit the road yet? Usually, you're restless by now."

Shrugging, I finish my drink, catching part of two guys' conversation. Saint starts to talk again, but I'm trying to concentrate on what the other guy's saying. Holding up a finger between us, Saint notices and instantly quiets to pay attention also.

After a few beats, I'm able to locate the source. It's the stupid Prospect I ran into when I first saw Princess. Their voices grow louder as he gets wound up, making it easier for me to overhear everything.

"She was the sweetest I've ever tasted man, swear to fuckin' God! Blonde everywhere too; fuck, it was good."

"Damn, blonde pussy hair too?"

"Yep. When she told me her name was Princess I thought the bitch was joking, but I could see it with her looks an' all. Then she told me her father's the President of the fucking Oath Keepers! Was the dumb bimbo tryin' to get me smoked? Her old man would fall the fuck out if he found out."

"Scratch, you're good as dead even if Prez doesn't find out and one of the brothers hear about it. You know they'd string you up, messing with a family member like that."

"That's what I said too. I got the fuck outta there like my ass was on fire and shit. Don't get me wrong; I'm not saying I'd never hit it again. I'd probably have her come over for a midnight booty call then send her packin' out the back door, but that's about it, so my ass doesn't get shot."

This motherfucker needs to shut up. I've pretty much heard all that I can handle. It's a miracle I haven't broken something already, but I was concentrating on what was being said.

Saint's ashy irises—now dark and stormy—meet mine, having heard it all for himself. "That your little Miss Happily Ever After they're talking about over there?" He nods toward my next kill.

A furious growl resonates through my chest, unable to answer him as my fury builds inside like a Phoenix, destined to rise from the smoke and seek out retribution.

A malicious grin appears on his too pretty face as the real Saint decides to show himself. "Oh, let's have some fun, shall we?" He lets loose a loud chuckle, getting to his feet. "Been far too long since Sinner's let me play with someone, always keeping the peace." His eyes widen in glee. "What do you wanna do to him, Vike?"

"Get him out back; the bathroom will be too messy. It's about time I pay a visit to the club and let them know where the fuck I stand." He nods turning away.

Saint cackles as he saunters toward the two Prospects, excited to finally stir up some trouble. Snatching up his drink, I finish it in two swigs, watching as he claps the loud mouth Prospect on the back, filling him full of lies about wanting his opinion on a bike outside that he may buy.

Scratch, being green, follows Saint willingly out the back door as the other Prospect sits at their table, happily chugging a cheap draft beer. I wish I could come up with some sort of plan, but I'm honestly raging so much inside that the image of ripping him apart, piece by bloody piece runs through my mind like my own personal horror movie.

Standing, I move throughout the bar in a daze, not focusing on anything but the bristling need to get outside before I burst. If I'm confined for much longer, I'm liable to kill someone in here or at least break a bunch of shit that would end up getting the cops called on me. Laughter and voices are nothing but a blur, everything mixing as I make it to the back door.

Slamming through it, the Prospect's head whips toward me at the loud noise, fear and trepidation quickly consuming his features as he discovers it's me. He shuffles a step back behind Saint, gullible and stupid to think that my brother would ever save him. He's a nobody, and Saint owes him no loyalty.

Saint turns to Scratch wearing one hell of a scary looking smile and grabs his arms forcefully.

"Hey, what the hell?" Scratch yelps in surprise.

Striding toward them, I grumble, "Most of you candy-ass motherfuckers like to run when I approach them."

"What's this about? I'm cool, remember?" he pacifies, causing Saint to laugh.

Saint loves when they beg and plead. He'll torture a fucker for days just to see how long they'd cry for their life. That's where Sinner comes in, cleaning up the mess and putting the miserable to rest. He's always alongside Saint, ready to help keep a sense of balance.

"I heard you talking about my Ol' Lady."

"No way; I was talkin' about a chick I met at a party. I wouldn't be talking about your Ol' Lady."

Hybrid Collection

At my glower, Saint snickers, squeezing the Prospect's arms until he yelps and faces him.

"Fuck! What's your problem now?" he asks angrily.

Saint smiles brightly, confusing Scratch, then drives his forehead into the man's nose when he's least expecting it. Blood showers them both as Scratch cries out in pain, feeding into exactly what Saint wants.

"You don't speak unless spoken too, Prospect," Saint orders and I take a few steps closer, ready to take what's owed, unsnapping my large blade as I approach.

"No one speaks about Princess like that. You think her cunt tastes good? It'll be the last one you ever taste, so savor that shit. I won't walk around knowing some motherfucker has touched my bitch and fuckin' lived," I growl, leaning down close to his face, showing him who the real alpha is.

Sweat draws on his brow as he swallows, thinking of something to placate me, "Sh-she wasn't yours. I wouldn't do that."

"No," I respond quietly with a brief chuckle, "that's where you're wrong, Prospect. She's always been mine." I finish and watch the shock hit his face as I drive my hunting blade deep into his kidney. The fucker was too stupid to pay attention and try to get away. Not that he could've, but it would've been more entertaining for us anyhow.

Saint tosses the wounded man onto the ground, watching as he falls on his back, crying out in discomfort. Once he starts apologizing and trying to bargain with us, Saint lowers to his knees above Scratches head.

Giving him the nod, I unstrap my hatchet and sheath my blade. Saint's hands fly to Scratch's skull, securing it so he can't squirm away and cause me to miss. Planting my heavy, size fourteen boot on Scratch's chest, I brace him to the ground with my weight.

"Ready?" I ask Saint, and he cackles maniacally, excited at what's about to happen. We've gotten into some shit together a few times and each one he's been the same way. Torture and killing bring me satisfaction if anything, but it fills my brother with energy and happiness. I can only imagine what kind of life he had to shape him as he is. Mine was fucked up, but I have a feeling his was like nothing I'd ever imagine.

"Do it, Vike!"

Bending my left knee as much as I can behind me, I position myself as low as possible in the perfect spot over the Prospect and grip my ax with both hands.

It's much harder than one would expect, driving the blade through flesh and tendons, and fuck, there's so much blood. Not to mention my height making it harder to decapitate someone when they're flat on the ground as well.

Glancing at the man's terrified eyes one last time as they fill with tears, I say my piece, "I've already killed for her once motherfucker; you're just another one under my belt. I'll be goddamned if anyone disrespects my woman like that and lives. I may not have been her first, but best fucking believe, I'll be her last."

At that, I swing the ax aiming directly for his throat. The first hit makes a decent implant, but not completely sufficient. It's with the second swing that his blood splatters enough to hit my boot resting on his chest.

Saint laughs with each chop, getting covered in blood and loving every minute of it. Eventually, I have to get on my knees to get close enough so I can finish sawing through the last remaining fleshy pieces. The small stuff is always the hardest to get severed.

"Saint, you need to get cleaned up, you're a mess. Call Spidey to help you dump the body."

His gaze meets mine, his brow furrowed. "Why aren't you dumping it?"

"I need to pay someone a visit."

"Okay then," he answers, pulling his phone from his pocket as I grab the short hair on the Prospect's skull. He has just enough for me to grip it; hopefully, I don't drop it.

Saint climbs to his feet, swiping his tongue against a few drops of blood on his wrist and follows me around the side of the bar. He watches as I mount my bike, still holding the bloody head in one hand. I've ridden having to hold onto shit before, so it's not that difficult being that I'm a seasoned rider.

The engine comes to life, loudly announcing our presence and within seconds, I head toward the Oath Keepers MC Compound. I have something that belongs to them, and it's time they know that I'm not fucking around.

Neither the kill nor the quick ride to the clubhouse does anything to cool down my temper. Normally a long ride will do me wonders, giving me enough time to clear my head out and come down from when I rage. If I were smart, I'd hit the road straightaway after my pit stop, but I know I won't. I've had one thing on my mind nonstop, and I plan to have her as soon as possible.

The Prospect that's posted at the gate sits up suddenly when I come into sights. He takes one look at my extended arm, still tightly gripping onto the head and stays clear, so I can ride through without any issues. Smart move on his part. I wouldn't kill him if he tried to stop me, but he'd damn sure learn.

Having worked with this club in the past, I know the kid's calling up the Prez or VP right now to announce my arrival. It's exactly what I want him to do, get either of them to come outside. I plan to throw this motherfucker's head at the pussy-ass VP's feet then let the Prez know his daughter belongs to me. I did this club a favor, taking out their biggest threat not even weeks ago, and it's time they show me that they're grateful.

Easing off the gas, I slow down some more, eventually rolling to a stop not far from the main entrance. The Compound consists of a fairly large building that houses members, their chapel, kitchen, and a bar. Off to the side is their shop where they fix bikes and the occasional vehicle. The land it all sits on is surrounded by a tall electric fence and who knows what else.

It takes merely moments before the lot of them shuffle out. Ares, their VP, comes to a stop directly in my path as several of his brothers flank his sides. Cain, his Enforcer, takes the right, then Spin, the treasurer, and finally, their newly patched member, Shooter. To his left stands 2 Piece, the Road Captain and gun trader, then Twist, the unholy one covered in tattoos. He's the fucking crazy brother I've heard of. I thought he was going to join the Nomads for a while, but he backed out eventually. Lastly, the President's son himself, Snake.

I could probably kill half these motherfuckers before they got me down. Scot says we're friendly with them, and Cain's not bad in my book, so I offer a warning instead of bullets. I may be an Oath Keeper, but when it boils down to it, this Charter is not mine. I would support them when needed, but I ride with the Nomads. We make our own fucking laws.

Staring coldly at the VP in front of me, I release his Prospect's head—the heavy skull more resembling a bowling ball than the lump of mush it is at this point. As it rolls across the asphalt, heated by the scorching Texas sun, it eventually stops, sticking to a particular hot spot on the pavement.

He doesn't flinch, so my gaze expands, taking in the other members beside him. "Tell your club to stay the fuck away from my bitch. I won't say it twice."

Ares' eyebrows shoot up, his nostrils flailing as he breathes heavy, attempting to reign in his temper. I've heard about him too. He used to be the Enforcer for the club, known as the Butcher for sawing bodies up.

That's cute. I like to hack my kill up too. Only I drive my hatchet into their body repeatedly or sometimes scalp them, using my favorite blade to pull their skin away, exposing the angry red flesh underneath. I'll happily teach him how to be a real fucking butcher if he'd like.

"The fuck you do to my Prospect?" he eventually grumbles, angrily peering at the decapitated head.

"He thought he could touch my Ol' Lady then talk about it. I didn't agree."

Cain's hand flies to his forehead, massaging his temples as he mumbles a disgruntled, "Fuck."

Ares glances over at him, "Brother?"

Cain drops his arm flashing a look at Ares, then meets my stare. "The blonde from the motel when we were there? Princess?"

Snake's head snaps over to me at Princess' name, and I nod.

"You sick fuck!" Snake shouts, charging at me only to be held back by a few of the men.

Ignoring him, I speak loudly. "You've all been warned what will happen if you touch her. Don't even fucking look at her." Pointing at the head stuck to the pavement to drive my point across. "Now...get me the Prez."

Ares chuckles, shaking his head. "You're a ballsy fucker; I'll give you that. What do you expect's gonna happen when you tell the Prez you've claimed his little girl as your Ol' Lady and you never even asked him?"

"I don't give two shits what's going to happen or if he'd have given me his permission. There's nothing to discuss; she's a grown-ass woman. I fucked her in front of an entire bar full of people and let every goddamn one of them know that I own her. Just like I don't give a fuck what any of you think about it."

Snake makes a sound reminding me of a roar as the guys hold him back from charging at me again. The dramatics are interrupted when the heavy metal door leading into the clubhouse slams closed, announcing the Prez' presence.

Snake shoots his mouth off before the older man even makes it off the four steps leading to the parking lot. "He has Princess! This dick thinks he can claim her. Tell them to let me go so I can slit his throat."

Prez sighs deeply, striding toward us with purpose. "Brently, stick a sock in it, son. You have any idea who you're threatening right now? You're a Prospect, son of mine or not; you shouldn't be speaking right now."

Snake breaks the guys' hold, storming off toward the shop. Probably angry his father just called him out in front of the other members.

Prez comes to a halt next to Ares. He claps him on the shoulder affectionately. "Thanks for handling this son, but let me have a talk with him."

Hybrid Collection

Ares' brow furrows, his irises growing lighter as he relaxes and allows the Prez to take over. I can see why he was the Enforcer for so long; he's definitely the protector who loves his club. I can't stand him, but I do respect that bit of him. "You need me, I'm here," he mumbles, taking a few steps away and lighting a smoke.

Watching him, Prez huffs, "Your Ol' Lady's gonna have your ass if she catches you out here smoking again. You want babies and don't I remember that you agreed to stop if she'd get knocked up?" He glances at the others standing around. "Someone give him some gum before Avery chews him a new one on his health and he takes it out on the brothers."

Rolling his eyes, Ares stomps on the cigarette, then folds his arms over his chest. If the situation weren't so serious, I'd laugh. I guess his Ol' Lady's a stubborn one like my Cinderella.

The older man's kind gaze meets mine again. "Last I checked, your cut said Oath Keeper on it. You're welcome here, so how about you get off that bike and take a walk with me?"

"I'm not the strolling type, how about you just get out what you have to say."

"What did he do?" Prez gestures to the Prospect's head, so I fill him in on everything, including the part where his daughter's now my Ol' Lady. It takes a while to explain everything and eventually, I'm off my bike, walking with him along the fence line as I talk.

Shocked is probably the most accurate word to describe him at my news. At first, he didn't believe me, but when I described her looks, her car, where she lived, etc., he started to realize I was telling the truth.

"Out of everyone, she ends up with a biker and a Nomad at that." He shakes his head in disbelief.

His boots suddenly become interesting as he stares down at them and thinks it all over, the Prospect no longer on his mind now that his daughter's involved. I don't know if the man's happy or about to come unglued. One thing I've noticed is that he's hard to read about how he feels about anything. He could probably win a grip of money if he ever decided to try his hand at playing poker.

"I would never have pictured her with someone like you," he finally continues. "Prissy tell you that she was a good girl growing up? Went to college, stayed out of trouble. She hates me with a passion, but that's all right; it kept her safe overall."

"We haven't talked about her past; it's all happened pretty quick."

His eyes find mine again as he smiles slightly. "It always does. It was that way for her momma, and I fuckin' fell hard for her, and best believe she had a temper like no other." The happiness falls from his face, his gaze growing firm. "Just don't fuck it up. Her and I, we've grown so distant, I no longer have the privilege to make demands with her anymore. I lost the right to tell her who to love and be with when she gave up on me being her father. In many ways, I'd love to put a bullet through your skull, but in the end, I have to be grateful that she ended up with a member and a strong one at that."

We walk back to the parking lot, continuing our discussion.

"She knows I'm a hard man." It's the best answer I can give. I know I'll screw up sometimes, what matters is if I can fix it.

"I fucked it up with her mother—worst mistake of my life. When I tried to go back and fix it all, club threats against Princess and Brently started pouring in from my rivals. I had to let them go. It was the hardest thing I've done, leaving my family and letting them hate me. Tell me, you have kids, can you walk away from them and your Ol' Lady, then not look back to keep them safe?"

Adjusting on my bike, I sit back a little and reply truthfully, "No."

"So you're the selfish type."

"Hell, yes, I'm selfish. She belongs to me—they would belong to me. Best believe I would hunt down every last motherfucker with the balls to threaten my family. I'd feed them their fucking nuts as my entertainment and then take their lives as my payment."

"I thought I could too, tried for years, out on the road looking for any of them." He sighs. "It drove my children away from me, caused my Ol' Lady years of heartache. At some point, you have to figure out your limit. You ever reach that, you come find me so I can help you sort things."

No matter how sad his sob story sounds, I can't find it in myself to feel any type of sympathy for him. I grew up with a fucked-up family. I know firsthand what that's like, and I'd never put someone through that experience.

"That's the difference between you and me, Prez. Princess is my limit. She's the type of woman I'd happily kill a hundred men for. I'm not saying it'll be an easy life for her; in fact, she'll fucking hate me at times, but I'll do my best every day of my life not to break her. And I'll damn sure protect her."

"Good. I still receive threats against my family, had one awhile back from the Twisted Snakes. Fucked my boy up pretty good and threatened my daughter next. We snuffed the fuckers out, but the danger's always out there. The main thing is that she never knew about any of it."

"I'll keep her out of my business, but I won't lie to her."

"She knows you were comin' here?"

"Yeah, she helped me chop his head off," I retort, deadpan.

Chuckling, he approaches me. "Let's keep this between us then."

He reaches his hand out, and I shake it in return. I'm not making any promises, but it won't be a conversation I bring up to her first thing.

"You won't have issues from any of my brothers or my son for that matter. I hope you're able to bring her around with you; I'd love to finally see my daughter. This club's her family, too, whenever she's ready for it."

"I'll see you around, Prez." Replying, I crank the engine over, the loud rumble overshadowing anything else he'd been planning to say.

He throws up a two finger salute as I walk the bike backward a few paces, his men all standing around Ares, no doubt waiting to be filled in after I'm gone. Had this whole situation not been about his daughter, though, I can't help but think that I'd have a bullet through my skull right now for chopping off his Prospect's.

Nine
PRINCESS

Staring at the beat-up building, I let loose a long sigh. After questioning myself fifty hundred times today about whether or not I should show up to meet Viking, I decided to say fuck it and drove my ass to the bar. Debate about it all I want to, if I'm not here, then I know he'll be knocking on my door again. I can either face him in a room full of people when he's had a drink or when we're alone, and he's irritated again.

Bethany's supposed to meet me up here once she's showered and changed from work. I still haven't gotten her to confess what's up with Nightmare. I'm quite stunned at her persistence; any other time I've been able to crack her into confessing. Her silence is making a huge statement, and I'm hoping that with her showing up tonight I'm not setting her up for failure being around Nightmare. It's been four days since she stayed with him, maybe they've had time to cool off.

Crossing the threshold of the noisy bar, the music, and rowdy patrons' conversations envelop me as I start to scan the room for Viking. Halfway through my perusal, one of his brothers approaches me. He's a lot smaller than Vike, but still pleasant to look at with his dark features.

Stopping right in my path, he shadows me by a few inches. I'd guess him at five foot eleven or so. His sharp jaw is overtaken by at least two days of dark stubble from forgetting to shave, or not caring enough to.

A friendly smirk plays on his lips until my gaze meets his amused charcoal colored irises. "'Sup Princess." He flashes me a bright smile that's slightly bashful. "Sinner," he states, his hand grabbing mine lightly to lead me farther into the bar.

Confused as to why he's touching me, I follow a few steps before he continues, "My brother had a few things to take care of, but he'll be back in a bit."

Requesting any details, even something simple like what time he'll come back, would be a waste of time, so I keep quiet. I know how bikers and their business work, thanks to my mom's constant rambling about my father and his MC rules. It's been drilled in that you keep your nose out of their club stuff, not only for your safety but also because it'll cause pointless arguments.

The bartender notices Sinner approach and rushes over, ignoring the other customers waiting for their drinks.

"Refill?" the older lady questions and he shakes his head.

"Nah. Vike's Ol' Lady needs one of those red girly things you make." Her mouth turns up in a friendly coffee-stained smile, and then she's off busily mixing liquor and juices for me.

I wish I got service like that when me and Bethany order. Instead, it's usually a dose of attitude and a shitty made drink.

Cutting straight to the chase, I lift my palm up, covered securely with his. "Umm, why are you still touching me?"

"Just being friendly to my brother's Ol' Lady."

"Thanks, but please stop calling me that and I'm able to walk myself." Using my other hand, I point at my shoes. Dutifully he looks down. "See, I have two feet just like you do."

He flashes me a hurt glance about to say something, but the bartender approaches stealing his attention. Once he's thanked her and has my fruity drink in hand, he starts to tug me along toward the back tables.

"Where are we going?"

"You can come sit with the brothers while you wait. No one will bother you back here."

"Oh. They won't mind?" I'll admit it's nice of him to offer. Getting attacked by the creep was traumatic enough that sitting at the bar alone is slightly intimidating even if I am inside and surrounded by people.

"Nah, they're cool."

"And Viking?" I only ask because I've seen how he acts when another male's within two feet of me.

"Trust me; he'll appreciate you being at our table when he gets here." He plays it off as a random idea, but I figure it's so he can keep an eye on me for his brother; either way, though it's a win-win for me. I get to relax with a few free drinks and at the same time know I won't be harassed again.

Two sex and the beaches later, along with an abundance of information on the guy's latest conquests, and I can understand why Viking rides with them. Sure they're scary looking and at times crude, but overall there's a strong bond forged. Their easygoing nature and friendship with each other are enough to make any outsider want to be included.

With the vodka and sweet juice mixture working its magic over my self-preservation, I interrupt their banter by blurting out the thought that's been running through my head all day. "I need to break it off with Viking. It was only supposed to be a one-night stand, yet I've seen him a few times in the past couple of weeks and then there's tonight."

Collectively, the entire table of men quiet. Each one is staring me down, looking as if I have the plague, and they don't know what to do with me exactly.

"I tried to after what happened the other night, but then he showed up where I live, and I'm sure you know he's persuasive when he wants to be."

Spider cracks a smile, thawing the frigid awkwardness I'm suddenly surrounded with.

Taking a large gulp, I stammer on, "The man's beyond bossy. He's temperamental and demanding and….and each time I stand up to him, I swear he grows an extra five feet tall." Flailing my hand dramatically, a few of the guys' expressions lighten, amused at my description of their brother.

Scot, the older red-haired biker laughs to himself and Spider speaks up. "So, you're saying that you stand up to him?" His irises sparkle as he glances briefly at his brothers like he's conveying a silent message that I'm not privy to.

"Of course, I do. Don't you?"

The table erupts in loud chuckles and Spider nods, laughing with them. "No wonder he can't leave you alone."

"Aye, 'tis a good thing," Scot agrees, winking like he's proud of me.

They move on, picking their previous conversations back up without skipping a beat, and I grow quiet with my thoughts. Staring out the dingy pane of glass in the window beside me, my original plan that Bethany came up with plays through my mind again. Only now I feel incredibly guilty when I think of it instead of excited. Not guilt for my father, but for planning on using Viking. I should be happy right now, being one step closer to making my father miserable, but I know to do that, I'd have to give up Viking.

Hybrid Collection

What do I want more? Viking? Or revenge?

It's been no time at all; how can this even be an issue already? Sure, I've seen him a few times over the past few weeks, but think of those times. One was me escaping and being too chickenshit to speak to him. The second time, I was taunting him and got freaking attacked, which he saved me from, thank God. The third time, I teased him to no end with Bethany, turning him into some kind of amazing sex god who fucked me in front of a room full of people. The last time I saw him, he mauled me, thinking I was sleeping with someone, and then stormed off.

Yep, that's the extent of our relationship. It's been the most thrilling, life-changing experience of my life so far. What in the hell is he going to do to me if we stay together for six months? I'd be completely ruined for anyone else. Like he wanted to happen when we slept together, it'd happen with my heart as well. My vagina's already given up; she was waving the white flag the first time she saw him.

My heartbeat starts pounding stronger in my chest as I watch Viking pull into the gravel parking lot, rolling to a stop under the bright street lamp.

Minutes pass with him remaining on his bike, not moving to dismount. I can't make myself turn away nor do I want to, as I watch him eagerly. His ominous figure practically glows from the lamp overhead and the pitch blackness fanning out behind him, makes him appear incredibly powerful. Something must be on his mind to just sit there, lonely, not hurrying in for a drink. He knows I'm here.

I can't wait any longer. I talk a good front in my mind and to him, but every time I see him, my insides melt. He's like gravity, keeping me to him, even if I try to jump.

Leaving my seat without another thought, I weave around people trying to play pool and dance. My legs dutifully carry me through the bar and outside until I'm left standing in front of Viking, feeling more feminine than ever next to the powerful rumble of the huge machine between his legs and his needy gaze.

My mouth parts, drawing in a swift breath as I'm close enough now to notice the blood splatter that's covering his jeans and arms. Suddenly my mind's plagued with memories of the first time I met him. The image of Viking gripping the man by the throat, and then staring at my exposed chest is almost too much to think of. He may have saved me, but I could read it in his intense glare that he wanted to take me just as badly as my captor had.

"Get on." He breaks the silence, and I swallow.

"I don't ride."

Viking's nostrils flare as he revs the engine louder. "Didn't ask. Now climb on."

The liquor in my system does the trick, providing me with enough courage to place my palm on his solid bicep. Holding on securely, I swing my leg over the back. I've seen my dad and brother mount their bikes countless times, so I have a general idea. There's not much of a seat for me, just a small piece of padding wrapped tightly in black leather.

His other hand reaches back, landing on my exposed thigh, warming it instantly with his touch. Gripping my leg firmly, he slides my body forward until my breasts are molded against his back, and then he wraps my arms securely around his muscular torso.

Viking's so solid; holding him to my body like this makes me feel the safest I've ever been. I know I'm with a man who's able and willing to protect me; he's in control, and he's already made me his. He's also everything that I've never wanted but is turning out to be everything that I've always needed. I can feel myself healing. In just a short time, he's helping my anger fade away, replacing it with his heat.

Viking's movements are so quick and efficient it takes me by surprise, and the next thing I know, we're entering the highway with me holding on for dear life.

Too scared to look around at first, I take in the broad stretch of the endless dark sky above us. The stars twinkle proudly as he takes his time, steadily increasing our speed and making the ride pleasant. I've never ridden a bike before and with Viking being a seasoned rider; I'm guessing he can tell. Most people would never believe me if I was to admit I'd never been on a bike before, being the daughter of an MC President.

After about ten minutes of the quiet highway, my muscles and grip on him start to relax as I grow more comfortable being behind him. Laying my temple against him, I close my eyes and just breathe, taking in the peacefulness of the whole experience. Once we started going faster, the stuffy Texas air swiftly morphed into what I'd imagine a thousand butterflies kissing my skin would be like.

Time passes all too soon it seems, and I feel him start to slow down. Parting my lids, my senses become overwhelmed. The leather on his cut hits my nostrils, along with an undertone of exhaust, the humming vibrations growing stronger each time he downshifts sending delicious pulses to my core.

Hybrid Collection

My pussy grows wetter with each passing mile, a sinful torment as I do my best not to squirm and chase my pleasure. The last thing I want is to cause a wreck when he's showing me this other side to him. He'd probably never forgive me for ruining his motorcycle and this beautiful night. Judging by the blood decorating his clothes, it wasn't so pleasant for someone else.

At a bump in the road, Viking's bike shifts, the movement causing a powerful enough tremor to hit my clit. He must hear my whimper escape because he slows down, pulling off at the first abandoned dirt road he finds.

The bike comes to a complete stop and my heart pounds so erratically he has to be able to feel it against his back. My breath comes in silent pants; I'm so damn turned on after the sweet torture my pussy was just put through.

"Get off," He barks, causing me to jump.

"Ex-excuse me?"

"You heard me; get off the fucking bike, Cinderella."

At his words, I suddenly feel like there's a frog in my throat. I don't know whether to laugh at his nerve for ditching me way the fuck out here or cry. I'll most likely scream and throw what I can at him but then I'll get so angry that I'll end up crying. Who can blame me, though, we're out in bum fuck Egypt, surrounded by fields. It'd be pitch black if it weren't for the million stars and nearly full moon. With my luck, I'll be hoofing it home and get so nervous; I'll have a full-on anxiety attack and pass out on the side of the road.

Carefully I dismount, watching, so I don't graze any of the pipes or engine with my legs. That would be a miserable reminder of tonight. I learned about them getting hot when Brently was a kid and burnt his hand on my dad's pipes. That ER visit took forever as my mom kept having to explain that she didn't burn or abuse her kids.

Standing beside his massive thigh, I prop my hands on my hips and hit him with a glare that's so cold you'd think he'd turn to ice. "You have a lot of nerve."

"That so?" His gaze flicks to mine, eventually dropping to run over my body.

"Hell yes. I can't believe you're actually kicking me off your bike here," I retort angrily, gesturing to the emptiness around us.

"Well, maybe you shouldn't have been rubbing your tits all over my goddamn back. Your nipples are so fucking hard; I can feel them through my fucking cut!" he shouts back fiercely.

"My nipples? You have got to be joking right now. If you weren't too busy driving like some kind of maniac maybe, the wind would be warmer!"

"So it's my fault?"

"Of course. You're the one who brought me out here. I told you back there that I. Don't. Ride."

Viking peers down at me with his mouth drawn in a stern line, making me feel like I've been naughty and now I'm in trouble and about to be punished. It almost makes me want to lash out at him some more to see what happens.

Those thoughts flourish as his massive hand shoots out, snatching my bicep with rough precision. He yanks me toward him like I'm some rag doll, weighing nothing at all. Unable to catch myself quickly, my stomach collides with his thigh. The impact is forceful enough that it damn near steals the breath from my lungs.

I should be furious with him for manhandling me each time a situation escalates, but being so close to him has pure carnal desire running rampant through my veins. Beating my fists on his solid pecs, I halfheartedly shove against Viking and prepare to let loose an outraged scream. Pretending to fight and struggle like this, will only spur him on further until he satiates the ache building between my thighs the bike ride initiated.

On our first night, he had to hold me still as he took my virgin ass. I'll never forget how thick Viking's cock grew when I'd whimpered and attempted to move away. He'd stopped at first to try and ease the ache by coating the rim, inside and around my tiny puckered entrance. It felt sinful and erotic having him use the warm cum he'd filled my pussy with moments prior.

I'd begged, offering my mouth and pussy again while he'd worked his way in slowly. Then my tears came, and he fucked my virgin hole like a man obsessed. Fuck, it hurt but eventually his skilled fingers played with my clit until he had me calling out in ecstasy.

My cheeks blush, thinking about that once-untouched area, now fully being his. Someday he may want it again. I know it'll hurt for a while until I'm used to it, but I don't care, it's worth it.

As if Viking can read my thoughts, his mouth slams down on mine, ravishing my lips like he's famished and can't get enough. His dark scruffy jaw prickles my sensitive skin and turns me on more, knowing he's one hundred percent man. I love it when he's this way. There's nothing soft when he gets like this. His muscles are like rocks, his kisses relentless, his movements harsh, and his cock stiff.

One hand tangles in my long hair, gripping it tightly against my skull as his tongue takes mine hostage, demanding it to surrender to him.

Hybrid Collection

Meeting his hunger, my tongue twists with his, hoping to entice him even further. My body's brimming with so much need that if he brushes against my pussy, I'm going to come.

He frees my arm to grab the front of my shirt roughly where they cover my breasts, twisting the material tighter against my skin. Viking's mouth overtakes my every thought as he kisses me crazily, sucking my bottom lip between his and then pulling away to nip at my top one playfully. Not ready for the erotic moment to end, I draw his tongue into my mouth, sucking and rimming it like I would his cock, greedily taking whatever I can.

Within seconds, he's breaking off our lip-lock, panting and flushed. The crimson coloring his cheeks, more pronounced from the pale moon, reveals that he wants it just as badly as I do.

My mouth's left tingling in his absence, the rough whiskers bestowing a bittersweet memory as the night air tickles my skin. His soft lips leave mine behind, swollen and eager for more. I refuse to beg no matter how badly my body wants me to.

Viking's dark gaze drops to my chest, enraptured as my breasts rise and fall from my excitement. "You're not wearing a bra," he murmurs absently, and I shake my head out of habit, not needing to respond. The evidence is clear with my peaks stiffly pleading for his attention. He loves my breasts; I left my bra at home purposefully for him.

He clears his throat, his voice gruffer than normal as he demands, "I've got what you need, climb on." He leans back some more, sliding closer to where I was sitting on the way here.

Viking turns my body and then lifts until I climb back on the bike. This time, I'm facing the handlebars like I'm the one driving us. Staring out at the openness in front of me, I begin to panic. "I can't drive." Plus, his bike's massive, literally the biggest I think I've ever seen.

A deep chuckle comes from behind me as I feel his large, warm palm rest between my shoulder blades. "Baby, you'll never drive my bike. You belong on the back. And before you lash out with some smartass retort, I mean that in the best fuckin' way, just trust me."

He puts pressure on my back, having me lie forward until my breasts rest against the still warm tank of his bike. I'm curious what he plans to do. He probably should've taken my shorts off prior to me climbing on if he's going to have me from behind.

"What are you doing?" I mumble, laying my cheek on top of my fingers in case there's grease or something on the tank.

"I'm taking care of you like I should've done the moment I saw you." His hands grip my hips, lifting them up until each of my thighs rest on top of his, and my ass is slightly elevated. "Hold still until I say otherwise."

"Why, what are you doing?"

"Just hold still or it'll hurt."

Well, that's reassuring.

Drawing in a deep breath, I hold it in, waiting for whatever he's about to put me through. There's no telling, but when it comes down to it, I trust him. Something cold and metal touches the inside of my thigh, kind of like a cool pen tip. He moves it more forcefully, a ripping sound happening along with air finding places it previously couldn't get to. It takes an abundant amount of control for me to hold still and not freak the hell out as I finally come to the conclusion that he's using his large hunting knife between my thighs, sawing away at a pair of my favorite shorts.

"I could have taken them off," I whisper.

"Shhh, Cinderella. This way I get to that dripping wet cunt, and I also get to play with my favorite knife." Once he slices through my shorts completely, he pushes the material up, leaving my ass cheeks on display in the moonlight.

Viking jostles around some, his belt clinking as he unbuttons the buckle and pushes down his pants zipper. After a few moments, he adjusts my body more, having me scoot farther up his bike. Gripping my hips, he moves me until my lace covered pussy is pressed deliciously against the small part of the tank.

Two of his fingers trace the scrap of material barely covering my core, eventually pushing it off to the side. The brief rubbing he rewards me with is enough to have me squirming and forgetting all about his blade previously being there. One moment Viking's pressing his palm against my needy center tantalizing me further and the next he's entering me without a warning. His cock so full and thick, stretching me to the ideal point, right on the edge of pain.

"Ohhh!" A whimper quickly transforms into a moan of pleasure as I close my eyes, reminiscing in the sensations.

He palms my ass cheek with his giant paw, squeezing it roughly and thrusting again, deeper this time. He's long enough that his dick hits all the right places inside, making you wish it'd never stop. Viking's not the kind of man who hesitates; he dives right in. It may hurt some in the beginning, but then it'll morph into a crazy intense orgasm.

"Tell me," he gruffly commands.

"About what?"

"I want to hear how it was riding on the back of my bike."

"Scary at first." Gasping, I hold on tighter to the cool handle bars while he drives in, the action causing my nipples to graze the hard surface deliciously. "But when you changed gears, it felt so good."

"Yeah? That why your cunt's so wet?"

"Yes."

"Good. You know what I'm going to make you do?"

"Huh?"

"I'm going to pump your pink pussy full of my cum, 'cause my Ol' Lady needs to have my seed in her every fucking day, marking her as mine."

"Uh huh," I manage breathily as he pulls my hips into him, seating himself to the hilt.

"Tonight, I'm taking away that little string you got on that you call panties, along with all your other clothes. The only way you're riding back is with that cunt pressed against my seat, wearing nothing but my T-shirt. I want your pussy juice spread all over it by the time we get back. Got it?"

"But what if there isn't enough?"

"I'll make you cream plenty," Viking grunts, leaning forward for smaller thrusts.

Too consumed by his demands, I'm busy imagining how it'll feel on the back of his bike with nothing filtering the pulses that'll be directly hitting my core. This time, I'll be wearing nothing but his shirt.

I don't notice him grab the handle bars. With a flick of his wrist, a strong vibration assaults my clit as he starts the motorcycle. The wondrous purr makes me scream in ecstasy. With each loud rev his bike makes, he plunges into my core, causing my greedy pussy to convulse. It feels beyond erotic, the sensations out of this world, taking Viking mere seconds to break my body down into a withering mess of multiple orgasms, milking his cock for whatever it'll give. One after another he commands my body to yield, spanking my bare flesh like a harsh kiss in the moonlight.

Viking bites and sucks, turning my skin tender by marking me anywhere he can get to in our position. The bar may have been a public claiming, but this is by far a private one with him bending my stubborn will into submission. With this sample of what he'll do to me, next time I'll cut to the chase and gladly beg.

After my third orgasm hits, stealing more of my energy, his movements begin to slow. Eventually, he stops and has me turn my body to face him. He spreads my thighs over him so I can sit comfortably and still be impaled with his cock.

Peeling my thin tank top off, I free my breasts, putting them on display. Viking is a full-on tit man and after giving me so many orgasms, he deserves to be rewarded. He takes my shirt from me, tossing it away from the bike and plants his palm on the back of my neck, gripping it with just enough force to warn me that he can take back control anytime he wants it.

His other arm gets braced across the top of my butt so I can hold on to one of his biceps. In smooth, fluid movements, Viking rocks me, slowly, back and forth, entranced, as he watches me. My eyes roll heavenward as my clit grinds into him each time my hips fall forward, making me clench my pussy muscles inside, eagerly anticipating a possible fourth orgasm.

This started out with him wanting to teach me a lesson for teasing him with my tits, which I'd say he's definitely accomplished. I'll be rubbing my body against his, anywhere we go, if it means he'll make me ride him and the bike at the same time again. I'm also curious now what make-up sex would be like if we were to really piss each other off somehow.

The claiming at the bar and then again later that night in the hotel was strictly Viking taking what he wanted. I get it, not that I understand it completely, but it did teach me right away not to expect anything average when it comes to this man. Bethany was right about one thing; I set the standard to a whole 'nother level with him. However, I wasn't expecting him to meet it and then raise mine as well. In the end, when the night was over, I had loved almost everything he'd done to me.

When I had time away and was able to start processing it all, I came to the conclusion that deep down, I believe he would have had me sooner or later whether I gave it up to him freely or not. It's terrifying when I think of someone obsessed and violent toward me like that. On the flip side, it's unbelievably empowering, knowing that he wants me badly enough to claim my mind, body, and freedom. To know that he's mine so completely, that he'd kill for me.

Having Viking like this tonight covered in someone else's blood—enraptured by me and my body—is different. At some point during everything, I surrendered myself and became his. He didn't take me for a test drive; he signed the fucking contract and demanded I give him everything.

Right now, this very moment, he's allowing me to ride his cock, on his motorcycle, while he wears his colors proudly. This is Viking surrendering to *me*. Tonight he's showing me that not only am I his Ol' Lady, but he's my Ol' Man.

And, for once, that doesn't seem so fucking bad.

Ten

VIKING

Three days later...

"**When will you be** back?" I mutter, watching as my Cinderella walks around the hotel room, collecting her things.

Tossing her lip gloss and brush in her purse, she shrugs. "I don't know. I can't keep calling into work, though; eventually, they'll fire me."

Doubtful. If they have any clue who her father is, she'll still have a job waiting. I'm not going to complain, though; I've had her at the motel with me for three nights in a row. She met me at the bar on Thursday and hadn't left since. It's Sunday now, so we've finally gotten some good time together.

"I got invited to a barbecue next Saturday. I want you with me."

Princess sets her bag on the bed, coming to stand in front of me. "Is this the same one those guys in the black car were talking about?"

"Yeah." *Does she realize Cain and Spin belong to her father's Charter? I should say something, but she's the one who shoulda' fessed up that Prez was her pops the same night we fucked.*

"I may have to work," she mumbles, glancing off to the side.

I know she's lying through her teeth and fuck if it doesn't make me want to hurt her for it. I hate feeling that way toward her, but I've cut men's tongues out for the same shit in the past.

"Ol 'Ladies are going to be there; you need to be on the back of my bike if I decide to roll up with my brothers."

Hybrid Collection

Princess takes another step closer, her hands finding my hips as she presses her chest up against mine. "I'll see what I can do, okay?"

"Make it work." Grumbling, I graze my lips across hers in a peck. "Wanna have lunch before you take off?"

"Not today. I have to call my mom and Bethany as soon as I get home. We can during the week if you're not busy?"

"I said the barbecue is Saturday, not that I wasn't seeing you until then. I'll give you a night or two."

A beaming smile overtakes her mouth as she lets out a soft laugh. "You're going to show up and break my door down again?"

"Maybe, if I feel like it." My voice comes out raspy, as my lips brush against hers with each word.

"You're such a tease."

"Nah, I'm the real deal, sweetheart." Winking, I back away so she can get out the door without me taking her to bed for the second time this morning.

"So I should expect you Monday-ish?"

"Just expect me to be around anytime."

"You're really not going to give me twenty-four hours, are you?"

"You sayin' that like it's a bad thing. I thought bitches liked it when their man's up their shit twenty-four-seven?"

"I didn't mean it like that. Of course, I want to see you. I'm kinda sore though and was thinking about the downtime."

Letting loose a cocky chuckle, I'm beyond happy that I made her sore enough that her pussy needs a break.

"Just keeping my woman satisfied; can't have that juicy cunt needy."

She leans up, pecking my lips again, and then grabs her bag. "I'm going, thanks for the 'satisfying' experience," she cheekily replies, as she walks away, opening the door.

"I'll show you satisfying," I warn, striding toward her as she takes off outside in a rush. I easily catch up to her, popping her on her ass strong enough to make her let out a shriek of laughter.

Chuckling, I spin her around and push her against the car. Her face is completely lit up, a smile so wide it makes my lifeless heart skip a beat.

My mouth meets hers in a scorching kiss, the kind that has her wrapping her hands in my shirt, pulling me as close as possible, and about to climb my body by the time I'm finished with it.

"Holy shit, why do you have to kiss me like that when it's time for me to leave?" she asks breathlessly.

"Just owning that shit real quick so you remember it later."

"Consider it noted."

She pecks my lips again and hops in her car, rolling down the window and blaring her music.

"Bye guys!" she shouts, waving behind me as she backs out of the parking spot.

Turning back toward the motel, I'm met with Spider, Ruger, and Nightmare.

"Don't say shit." Grumbling, I shoot a glare at each of them, causing Spider and Ruger to grin.

Fuckers.

Heading back into the room, I grab up my wallet and slip on my boots. I'm starving, and since Cinderella had to bail, I'm going to find a big-ass burger. Making sure I've got everything, I head back to my bike, tying my black bandana on as I walk.

I barely mount my bike when Exterminator approaches. The other guys are suddenly nowhere to be found. I'm betting they heard us fooling around and came out just to be noisy.

"Ex." Nodding, I wait to put my helmet on to hear what he wants.

He stops next to me, resting his hands on his hips, appearing peeved about something. "We need to talk."

"All right; what's up?"

"A few brothers down the road need some shit."

So he wants me to run guns or narcotics most likely. It's not uncommon; we usually break off into smaller details. We're less likely to get picked apart by the cops if it's a few bikers versus a big group. If we're setting up a new business deal or handling blowback, then we take care of it as a pack.

"So what's the issue?" I don't like pussyfooting around; I prefer the facts, especially when it comes to the club's dealings. If he's pissed about a certain variable that has to do with our ride, he needs to tell me asap.

"Nothing, just ready for some new scenery. Scot wants to stay, so I'm heading up the run this time."

"We're all headed out, or just the two of us?"

"Everyone needs to be on this. I want to take off in thirty, so be ready to split."

Hybrid Collection

"You want to fill me in first on why it's taking all of us if we're only visiting a few brothers?"

Exterminator clenches his jaw, his mouth growing tight, not liking the fact that I'm questioning him. I don't give a fuck about his feelings when it comes down to it. I need to find out how long we'll be gone to give Princess a heads-up.

The MC's top priority, but after laying claim, she's my first thought over club business. I don't want her thinking I'm taking off and not coming back. Her ass is already stubborn about being my Ol' Lady, and I can tell I'm finally wearing her down about it.

After a few seconds, he finally answers, "We're headed to Juarez."

"Mexico! What the hell do we have goin' on? I didn't think we had anyone down that way."

"We're making a quick exchange and getting the fuck outta there. Take extra ammo. You'll probably need it. I have to get the others." He finishes and walks toward Spider's room, cutting off any other possible questions I may have.

Fuck. Extra ammo? But yet it's a simple pick and drop? Doubtful. What the fuck am I gonna say to Princess, 'cause shit's about to get real.

Either Scot is getting serious about the bartender and wanting to settle in with the Chapter here, or this run is a shit storm, and Exterminator doesn't want us thinking about it with the ride ahead. Either way, I can't help but think that I should have fucked my girl again before she left, 'cause you never know in this type of life if today will be your last. We don't have time to waste when you deal with scummy fucks on the regular; that's one reason why we're quick to claim a bitch and hope like fuck she's the one.

Is Cinderella the one for me? Just the fact that I'm even thinking about this shit and asking questions should be enough of a clue to let me know that she's got my dick on lockdown. She better get real comfy being my Ol' Lady, 'cause that bitch won't be getting another man until I'm rotting six feet under.

She handled the claiming, but can she handle the lifestyle that comes with it? I'm a fucking Nomad; she needs to come to terms that we work off my schedule, not one that some pussy-ass manager sets for her. One thing's for certain, when I return we're having a serious come to fuckin' Jesus moment when I lay it all out and clue her in. I'll set up roots and tie her ass up in a basement if I have to. I'm just fucking warped enough to do it too.

Digging my cell out, I pull up the finder app I have for Princess. Her mini crown blinks at her home address, showing me she hasn't gone anywhere else since she left here. *Good. I like when she stays home; then I know no assholes are hitting on her.* Closing it out, I bring up her number in the text.

ME: Hey, Cinderella, shit came up. I'll be with my brothers for a few days, maybe the whole week idk.

Closing the message out after I hit send, Sinner pulls up beside me. A large Taco Shop bag strapped under the convenient elastic net thing he made for his bike. Pretty fucking genius actually and the first time I'd ever seen it before. He took a car-sized trunk net you find that holds groceries and what not, customized it down to fit his bike and replaced the clasps with softer plastic hooks so it wouldn't damage the paint.

His engine quiets and he begins to climb off.

"You got any extra food in that bag?" I nod, as the delicious, spicy smell floats over, causing my stomach to growl.

"Yep. Exterminator hit me up a little while ago about the run. Made me crave tacos and figured half of you assholes would be hungry."

"That's what's up. Thanks, brother."

"No worries, I got you." He reaches in the bag, coming back with five wrapped tacos for me.

"Fuck, I'm starving," I mumble as he hands them over and I immediately unwrap a hard-shelled taco, shoving half of it in my mouth in one bite.

Sinner chuckles and shakes his head at me throwing a munch then strides over to Ruger's room. He beats on the door for a second, and when it finally opens, he's greeted with, "Hell yeah."

Guess I'm not the only one who was busy eating pussy for breakfast.

Later that day…

What should be a simple run down south, has morphed into a miserably long ride. The closer we get to the Texas/New Mexico border, the dryer the hot air becomes and even on a bike with the wind hitting full force, it does little to cool you down. I'm used to the humidity and have a rough enough time in central Texas with its smaller amounts of moisture. Down here the air is stale, making my skin feel dried out and filthy.

The sun's burned down on us the entire trip, thanks to Ex wanting to take off at a fucked up time. *Bastard.* This shit better be worth it. I don't bitch on runs. I love the road, but I would go fucking nuts it if I had to ride in this shit all year long.

Slowing, Exterminator signals and takes the off-ramp, leaving the highway that runs through El Paso. Right off the ramp, we're met with the entrance to the Mexican border. All the *You're now leaving the United States* signs they have posted does absolutely nothing to make me feel better. If anything, they make me want to tell Ex to fuck off about this run, but that's not how MC life works.

He picks a certain lane to go through, and we all follow suit, getting in line as a group. This could go down real fuckin' bad if they decide to search us. I'm packing like a motherfucker, and I'd put money on it that my brothers are loaded up to their ears with weapons and ammo as well. Princess will end up with a dose of reality if I have to call her ass from jail to bail me out or find me a decent lawyer.

The bikes rumble as we scoot forward slowly; it feels like it takes them forever to check through vehicles. The road and exhaust are making me stinky and sweaty. Nothing like being around a group of hot, tired, pissed off bikers. I'm thinking if we get flagged shit'll go down, border patrol agents or some ass-clown will get popped, and we'll all be shuffled to the pen on murder, accessory, and weapons charges.

Motherfucker.

Spider glances back at me, looking like he's going to upchuck. *Easy, Spidey, just stay cool and calm; hopefully, they'll let us pass.*

We can drop the majority of our ammo before heading back, so that's not the issue unless we're hauling something with us. Regardless, I'm not about to enter Mexico without packing some serious heat. I know a few brothers who've come to do a pickup and have wound up in a ditch, never seeing their home soil.

The cartel doesn't appreciate bikers on their turf who don't belong in their pockets. I've struggled too long to finally break away from pieces of shits like them, to be forced back under someone's thumb. Any of their minions or twisted pigs come at me, I'm shooting or scalping their asses, fuck the dumb shit.

Then yesterday we ate at the picnic table with Spider and Scot. Both guys were polite and funny the entire time. I enjoyed myself to where I was hoping we'd see them again. It was the total opposite of how I'd always thought bikers acted and treated people.

Was my mom lying? No, I can't go there. Dad seriously hurt her. I remember the days she'd lie in bed all day, face puffy from crying because he hadn't been home to see her, or he suddenly cut off contact. She never even went on a date with anyone else; I don't get it how she didn't eventually move on. The crazy thing is she's feistier than I am and she lets him treat her like this.

I remember one time we had to go up to my dad's old club. I think I was like eight years old. Anyhow, some woman kissed my dad in front of my mom. He pushed the lady away, but it didn't stop my mom. I remember my brother flying out of the car toward them and when I looked over my mom was straddling the woman just wailing on her. Once they were able to pull her off the lady, she slapped my dad in front of his brothers and then cried hysterically the entire drive home.

That time she stayed in her room for four days, only coming out to feed us until she felt better. No, she's not lying; I remember too much shit that happened. He's still the fuck up who screwed our family away.

I should call Brently this week. He needs to get the hell out of there and remember why we stayed away from Dad in the first place. I wonder if he's been to see Mom. That could be why she wants to talk and for me to visit. Dad probably left again, and she's going through her motions, alone.

"Yoo-hoo?" Bethany calls and I glance up, not paying attention to whatever she'd been saying. "Was the text that bad?"

A tear falls, my fingers swiping it away quickly. "Oh no, not at all. It's my mom; she wants me to come over."

"Are you going to?"

"Probably, let me call her really quickly. Do you mind?"

"Of course not; you know I love your mom."

Backing out of her message, Viking's name is next.

"Shit," I mutter with my gaze trained on his message.

"What happened? You haven't even dialed."

"No, yeah, I know. I was shitting because Viking had to leave town but doesn't know when he'll be back. He thinks a few days."

"Did he say where he was going?"

"Nope, bikers don't tell you that stuff."

"What the hell? He could have a wife and kids shacked up somewhere, and you'd never know."

"No, he doesn't," I defend automatically.

"How would you know? Think about it Princess."

"I have and well…When he was sleeping, I went through his phone and wallet." When I don't turn my back to her quick enough, I see her mouth drop open at my confession.

"You're so sneaky. Does he know? Do you think he'd actually have evidence on him?"

Grabbing an apple from the bowl using up a large portion of the counter, I take a hefty bite, starving with all the extracurricular activities I've been doing lately and face her again. "Fuck no, he doesn't know. He'd probably spank me until I couldn't sit down or something if he did; besides, this isn't CSI detective work or anything."

Her eyes light up at me implying he spanks, and I continue, "And yes, he would have something. I googled his home address. It was some little town in South Carolina. When I google mapped that shit and did a street view, it was an empty lot. It was literally grass and a mailbox."

"Geez, no wonder your phone died."

"Well yeah, plus I did reverse lookup on every phone number he had listed, which wasn't many, like fifteen."

"The next boyfriend I get, I'm calling you. How did I not know about this sneaky side of you? The one time we tried going out of your mom's house at night, you were so freaking noisy, she met us out back with a damn shotgun."

At that memory, I burst out laughing. Bethany eventually copies me, both of us giggling until my stomach starts to hurt.

"Oh God, I forgot about that! You were so scared I thought you were going to pee!"

"Yeah, pretty sure I did pee a little."

Laughter overtakes again, remembering her face and shriek when my mom scared the shit out of us, just waiting. It was like she'd already known it was going to happen and wanted to make sure we were so terrified, we'd never try it again. It definitely worked. We didn't attempt to sneak out from my house again—ever.

Once I'm able to catch my breath again, Bethany excuses herself to go to the bathroom, which ensures a few more chuckles, and then I bite the bullet and dial my mom.

I swear it feels like it rings for five minutes until the line's finally picked up. "Yeah?"

Fuck. It's my dad.

VIKING

Exterminator handed over a nice chunk of cheddar at the border and was able to get us through without an inspection. I'm thankful, but where the hell did he come up with that cash? We haven't been paid in a while unless someone else gave him some paper up front for this run that's magically appeared out of thin air.

We ride for a while longer, eventually stopping in a small town called Calle De Norte. I haven't a clue what it means; I'm not Mexican. I'm gonna guess it's something North since we're fairly close to the United States, though.

Ex checks us in, coming out of the office with four room keys. "Bunk together." He grumbles, handing them out.

Ruger always eager for a job, speaks up, "Are we riding more tomorrow?"

"You saw that Compound we passed resting up on that hill about ten miles back?"

We all nod, paying attention.

"Well get some rest, 'cause behind that wall is men loaded with heat, not excited to see us."

He ends his explanation, unlocking his hotel room door. He opens it wide then comes back to roll his bike inside the room with him.

Nightmare shakes his head in Ex's wake, disappointed most likely because Exterminator's been cutting him out lately. They're usually boys and all that, as much as two fuckers who never speak can be anyhow. Now Night's left out in the cold with us other fuckers when it comes to information it looks like.

A worn out sigh leaves Sinner as he glances at Saint. "Want to lock the bikes up and head down to that bar we passed? We might find us a feisty senorita to share."

"I want some Mexican snatch and some tequila, but it'll have to wait 'til tomorrow. I'm goin' to rub my cock in the shower and pass out."

Sinner nods, fist bumping us as him and Saint trek to their room. Realistically they'll probably end up jacking each other's cocks off, but whatever floats their fucking boat I suppose.

Spider grins, "Not knocking on the old man, but I'm so glad I don't have to bunk with Scot tonight. He snores so damn loud and sleeps with his hairy ass hanging out."

Ruger and I both chuckle used to sharing a room.

"I need something to drink," Ruger announces, and Spider agrees.

"You two share then, I'm headed in now."

"Cool." Ruger nods and I pound Spider's knuckles, wheeling my bike into my room.

Nice. No sharing tonight. I don't mind bunking up, but privacy is even better.

Taking a quick, hot shower, I worry about getting the initial layer of road grime off and decide I'll do a better scrub in the morning. The main thing I'm wanting is sleep. My body is sore, and my ass is chapped from sweating all fucking day long, thanks to Ex's asshole move making us ride during the hottest part of the day. This run better be worth it with the vague answers and bullshit we're going through for it.

Lying down on top of the hard, cheap mattress I'm betting is full of shredded cardboard, I power my phone back on. I've learned being a Nomad and always on the road to keep it turned off when we're on a ride. Saves my battery, since I never know when I'll be able to plug it in.

The first thing that pops up is a message from my Cinderella, sent about four hours ago.

254-200-8699: No worries. I'll pick up some extra shifts to stay busy. Ride safe, and see you in a week or so. XO –P

Good girl. I can't help but think as I read it.

She may be Ol' Lady material after all.

Twelve

VIKING

The next morning...

"**I got some grub.**" Spider walks in as I'm pulling my boots on.

"From where?"

"The front desk told me about a little trailer down the way where you walk up to the window, just like a food truck." He chuckles, sitting on the opposite, still made-up bed.

"It's probably ground up cat," I remark, staring at the brown bag skeptically.

"You guys are so fucked up. First with Saint and Sinner talking about feisty senoritas and tequila and now with you saying these people are cooking cats."

"Nope, we're all just telling it like it is. Mexico has good, cheap tequila; of course, they want that shit. I may even take a bottle or two back with me, depending on the haul. They want Mexican snatch because they always want pussy wherever the fuck we go. As far as the food goes, did you see any fucking cats or dogs when we rolled through town?"

He thinks about it and remains quiet, proving my point.

"Exactly, now get your dick out of your ass and chill. You act like we're trying to fuck your mom or something. We're bikers, harden the fuck up."

He's the newest one to our group. I don't mind his company, but sometimes you can tell he's not like the rest of us.

"On the plus side, the food's only scrambled eggs in a tortilla. I watched them make it all."

"Thank fuck; I'm starving. How much did you get me?"

Digging through the bag he comes back with four wrapped burritos, they're thin, so I won't get full, but it'll work until later.

"Appreciate it."

"How's that app working?" he asks, ignoring my gratitude, like we all do to each other.

"It's on point. I've been tracking her every day she's not with me."

"I got an alert from your phone in the middle of the night, Saturday. She was clicking on each of your phone numbers and then I got a notification of her searching the numbers on her own phone's internet."

"It's freaky how you know all that shit. Did you block the internet searches?"

"I redirected them to random places you'd use, like a bike shop, a few Oath Keepers main club house numbers—that sort of thing."

"Good. I don't need her finding out my mom's info, thinking she'll be Suzy Homemaker and give her a call or something." I especially don't want her calling any of my old contacts. They're drug dealers and killers, not the type of people I want to know her name, even if they are friendlies.

"Nothing to worry about, you know I have your back."

Nightmare enters the room, not knocking as well. We're used to being in each other's space. "Ex is ready."

"Ex? You want to fill us in?" I ask and Nightmare sighs.

"No clue. I know as much shit as you. He's shut me out. Whatever this is, it's important to him."

"That's all I needed to know."

Spider wads up his trash, tossing it in the miniature bin and makes his way outside.

Nightmare turns to me, "He good?"

"Yeah, he's fine, starting to adjust."

"Bet. He's too smart with numbers and computers not to have him with us." His voice grows quiet as he finishes, "I figured out that's how Ex got money to pass through the border; he had Spider transfer rich fucks cash into a fake account."

"Serious?"

"As a fuckin' heart attack, brother. I don't know where the fuck his head's at, but we'll find out soon enough."

Nodding, I stand and roll my bike back outside, next to my brothers. We wait on Ex for a few minutes; eventually, he walks out as well pushing his bike and coming to stand with us.

"Here's the deal." He gazes over each of us. "This isn't a regular run. We're not here on drugs. Well, we are, but only if we find some, do we bring it back."

Sinner cocks his head to the side. "Then why we wasting our time?"

"We're not." Exterminator meets his stare. "We were hired by an undercover cop—a very rich cop—who's tied to the Russian Mafia. He's been searching for one woman in particular over the past months and got wind she was in that Compound we passed yesterday. He's paying us a fuck ton of money to obtain her."

Nightmare interrupts, "So you didn't have Spider steal money from a bank? Why didn't you tell us about this sooner?"

Spider coughs when he hears Night's conclusion and Ex growls angrily, "Fuck no, how well do you know me?"

Night cocks his eyebrow, and if either one's temper raises a notch, we're liable to be pulling them apart, or one would be setting the other on fire. They both have a fire and dumpster fetish.

"I didn't say anything sooner because the cop swears these people hear everything. He thinks that once he gets close to finding her, that whoever is keeping her moves her again."

"So we could be heading into a shit storm and not even come out with this bitch?" I mumble.

"Yeah, but we get paid either way."

And everything's right in the world for me again, knowing this is a paid job. Just wish he would have given us a heads-up sooner, especially communicating with a fucking cop. He better be careful. If one of the brothers thinks he's turned snitch, he'll never keep his spot in the club. He'll probably be strung up somewhere with a cord wrapped around his throat. We don't expend our skills on snitches; we just snuff them out as soon as possible to get them removed from the equation.

"We'll leave here and enter from the southeast corner. Satellite shows the least amount of guards and people in that area at all times. I have a general description of the female, but no one's seen her since she was a girl I guess. She's supposed to be a tall Russian woman, thin and she used to be blonde. They don't know if her hair will be changed, what language she'll speak, nothing. She'll most likely be one of the servants or maids. Let me know if you see one that looks Russian."

We all nod and mount our bikes as he does. Before we start them up, he shouts, "As soon as we have her, bail the fuck outta there, shoot whoever you need to and we ride toward the border as fast as possible. This is the Cartel, brothers; they won't fuck around."

We should've brought more men. Fuck!

With a sound like thunder, we crank over our engines, placing weapons wherever we need them for easy access and as one unit we hit the road, ready to piss off the fucking Mexican Cartel. We may as well be headed into a bee's nest because that's exactly how crazy shit's about to get.

PRINCESS

I still haven't spoken to my mom; I hung up when my dad answered. I don't know why he'd be answering her cell phone anyhow. Bethany comes out of my room, hair pointing in every possible direction and mascara all underneath her eyes. She stayed the night since I knew Viking wouldn't be stopping over at any given time. Knowing him if he shows up sometime with Bethany here, he'll demand to smell my pussy again. That man can be so flipping pushy.

"Morning, Sleeping Beauty."

"Ugh. That biker's already rubbing off on you."

"Huh?"

"With the nickname, I seriously doubt I resemble a Disney princess right now. I feel more like road kill."

"Well, you do kinda resemble a dead bird." Shrugging, I blow her a kiss.

"Shut up, some of us need sleep. Why are you up so early anyhow?" She passes me by, going straight to the fridge to get a glass of her favorite orange juice. I keep it around specifically for Bethany unless my brother stops over, then he'll drink it all just to screw with her. They've known each other far too long that they like to torture each other in small ways.

"Dude, it's noon."

Her eyes shoot to the clock, verifying the time. "Shit! I was out of it. I didn't pay attention to the clock in your room, with it dim in there; I figured it was pretty early."

"Nope, it's just cloudy out."

"That would explain why I'm starving then. Did you eat?"

"I had a banana, but I'm getting hungry now. Do you want to go somewhere or make something here?"

Finishing her juice, she rinses the cup and places it in the dishwasher. Stepping away from the counter, Bethany twists back suddenly, launching her face into the sink bowl. Fisting her messy hair in one hand, she braces with the other, wrenching up all the liquid she previously consumed.

"Holy shit!" Rushing over to check on her, I snatch a hand towel on my way. "Are you okay?"

"Ohhhh." She moans, expelling the water she had drunk before bed.

Flipping the faucet on beside her, I grab the sprayer, rinsing it down the garbage disposal, so she's not stuck looking at and smelling it.

After a few minutes of hovering over the basin, she wordlessly leans back, bracing both hands on the counter, staring at the drain.

"Bethany? Honey, you okay?" Cocking my head, I try to meet her eyes and push the kitchen towel in front of her. Her brow's dotted with perspiration but her skin's very pale.

She stays quiet washing her palms with soap, then takes the towel from my hand, never glancing up.

"How do you feel?"

Tears build up, running over her lids, flooding her cheeks with wetness, truly worrying me. I hate to see my best friend upset, so I lean in, wrapping my arms around her and place my forehead on the side of her head.

"Oh babe, don't worry. You can stay here and just lay in bed until you feel better. I'll make sure you have everything you need."

She breaks her silence as a sob bubbles up, and she finally faces me. "I need diapers," she cries, looking heartbroken.

"Okay, in any other circumstance, I'd give you *shit*," I giggle at the pun. "For the rest of your life, but I know you're actually sick. We'll just toss your undies out, and you can borrow a pair of boxers to wear."

Instead of laughing or chuckling, hell, even calling me a twat face like I'm expecting her to do, she busts out in a pathetic wail. I've known Bethany nearly my whole life, and I've never seen her like this—including bad breakups or drunken moments we've shared.

Hybrid Collection

Bethany hiccups, her tearstained face swollen from crying, as I hug her to me tightly. Maybe we should go to the hospital if she's feeling this terrible. Shit, I hope whatever she has isn't contagious.

She takes a few deep breaths, her crying finally slowing down as she whispers, "I'm not sick; not technically, anyway. There's something wrong with me, though."

"What do you mean? Why haven't you told me sooner?"

"Because…I wasn't sure."

"You better not be fucking dying or something and just now telling me. I won't let it happen."

"I'm pregnant."

Shocked, I don't know if I should hug and congratulate her or cry, because in all honestly, there's a good chance she won't know who the father is. Her mom and stepdad will most likely kick her out even though she's an adult. They're dicks like that. She needs to find a better job so she can get her own place.

With my eyes wide, I mutter, "Wow."

"I know." She swipes her hand over her face, then fills a glass of water, chugging it down and refilling it.

"So that's what the puking was about and why you're suddenly drinking more water."

"Yep."

"Wow.

"You said that already."

"Who's the father?"

Grabbing the 409 from the opposite counter and a few paper towels, I spray the counter next to where Bethany puked. Once I'm done wiping it, she steps away so I can do the top of the sink. Coating the inside of the basin, I rinse it out and step back, still waiting for her to answer.

"B, do you know who the baby's dad is?"

"It doesn't matter, he doesn't want it, and I won't be letting him decide my child's fate. He's not the one carrying the kid around or who's going to be taking care of it, so it's not his decision to make."

"Holy shit, he doesn't want it?"

She shakes her head.

"What a dickhead; he should be castrated. Who is it?"

"I told you, I just want to forget about it. I have to figure out my life and how to support myself and a kid."

"Wait, is this the real reason why you called me so much and freaked out with Viking?"

Shrugging, she places her other cup in the dishwasher and runs her hands through her hair. "That's what started it, but then I did begin to worry about you when I didn't hear back."

"That makes sense. I'm sorry you've been going through these changes by yourself."

"Hey, at least I have you now. Plus, it's still too soon."

"What do you mean?"

"Well two days after I had sex, I was massively ill and went to the hospital; they couldn't find anything wrong with me, and then a nurse suggested that I could be pregnant. I thought she was crazy, but she said in certain cases a woman can be sick within days. She told me that my body may have registered the change immediately, where in others it takes longer to show pregnancy symptoms."

"That's crazy, so did they run a test?"

"Actually, I've had a fifteen-minute quick check with a nurse at my doctor's office daily since then. Yesterday before coming here, they ran a blood test, and it came back positive. My doctor was thrilled. I guess she's never had a pregnancy case like mine before."

"Why is that?"

"Well, because my test came back positive yesterday morning, making it eight days since I would have gotten knocked up. Today makes day nine. According to her, none of her patients have ever found out that quickly before. I have to go back in a few weeks for another test, but I'm convinced now after being sick every single day and then fine later in the day."

"I'm so sorry you've been sick. Is it that douche you were playing beer pong with, the night of the house party?"

"God, no!"

"But I haven't seen you go home with anyone else, except..."

Her head tilts as she nods sadly, "Nightmare."

"Ho-ly fuckballs."

Thirteen

VIKING

Monday and Tuesday drag by with no luck on breaching the Cartel's Compound. Princess hasn't contacted me again, and I don't know whether to be upset or impressed. She knows I'm with my brothers, and she's either keeping busy or letting me handle my shit.

I'm getting real sick of being here, though. I'm ready to slide deep inside my woman and eat a fucking burger. I thought the hotel mattress in Texas was shit, but it's a goddamn pillow top compared to the springy box I've been sleeping on here. It's going to be straight hell on us riding back, sore and grouchy, most likely with some runaway bitch while dodging bullets.

Now here we are, Wednesday morning and attempting to sneak in once again. We figured that if the place is usually loaded down with cartel thugs, then a quiet, early approach is probably best. The brothers are just as antsy as I am, ready to get the fuck away from here.

Ruger catches up to Spider, talking quietly, "Look, all I'm saying is, it's strange there isn't anyone in this part of the Compound. Where the fuck did they all go?" He gestures around us at the huge abandoned space as we continue our trek.

The back corner where we're located is littered with trees, a small brick building that we're assuming is storage, and random, massive-sized rocks, nearly the same height as me. It's weird, but who the fuck cares if it provides us some cover.

Shrugging, Spider glances around. "I showed you the satellite images. There were only a few heat signatures indicated with the program on the thermal mode. Unless they've decided to patrol, none of them are near this area."

Exterminator halts suddenly, whirling toward them. "Quiet the fuck down. This isn't school or some shit where you two can fuckin' gossip. If they hear us, they'll shoot. Now shut the fuck up," he orders.

They keep quiet, and we continue on our path toward a specific building Ex was told to search first.

Over the past two days, we've learned that the cop told Ex that he'd been watching the area closely and thought that this bitch he's looking for is being held in a certain spot. There are regular rotations that monitor it made by three guards at all times, which will be no biggie for us to overpower.

Spider had to wait until we penetrated the wall and were physically inside the cartel's perimeter to log into their camera feeds with his cell. Supposedly, whoever has this chick is insanely cautious and at any little glitch, he takes off with her and disappears. By waiting until we were on their land, the system they use wouldn't register it as an intruding device, just as one of their men trying to use the Wi-Fi. Fucking crazy shit that I'd never know about or even have a guess to think of; Spider's one smart little fucker.

Trailing along, I think of random shit, such as I'm grateful to have Spider with us and not against us. He's a good asset to have and will be even more valuable as he gets in more time on the road with us. I should have him set up some type of security over at Princess' apartment. I hadn't seen a keypad by the door when I'd left her place last week.

Sinner gasps, "You've gotta be fuckin' with me." He clears his throat as his steps falter. "Brothers, stop." He gazes around out in the field.

I don't know if he found an IED or a mine or what the fuck, so I stop straightaway. My gaze scans over the ground around us. With it being the Cartel, it could be absolutely anything. If it's not some explosive or drug, it's most likely a pile of dead bodies stacked up somewhere.

Next, Saint whispers, "*No.*" And we're all silent enough to hear it loud and clear. "Holy fuck."

"What?" Ex grumbles and Sinner nods to the open space off to the left side.

Everyone's eyes immediately shoot in that direction, concentrating to peer closely enough and pick out whatever Saint and Sinner have discovered. Personally, I'm looking for snipers. I wouldn't be surprised if they position a few out here to pick off intruders. It would explain the lack of heat signatures the guys were talking about earlier.

Hybrid Collection

The choking sound that leaves Spider as he finally sees them doesn't surprise me one bit. I'd probably choke also…if I could speak or even move my mouth.

Nightmare grumbles, "What the hell we supposed to do?"

"Anything to the right?" Ex whispers.

"When I looked at the map I saw a small cluster of buildings. I don't know what they house, though, could be guard quarters."

"Do we run?" Saint asks.

"If it's a nest for the sentries they'll shoot us on site."

Finally, able to conjure up words, I hiss, "Better than getting eaten by two fucking lions!"

Glaring at Spider and Ruger, I point at them heatedly, "Remind me to fucking skin your asses when this is over with."

Spider's eyebrows shoot up. "I swear we had no idea."

My fingers find the snap securing the large hunting knife to my belt. Pulling the button free, I grab my knife and clutch it in my left hand. My digits go to the clasp holding my hatchet, drawing it free as well; I grasp it tightly in my right hand. I'm as ready as can be if those scary motherfuckers come at me.

I'll most likely die, but I'll be taking some of their blood with me.

The brothers all follow my example, preparing. Saint reaches around to dig in his backpack, arming himself with a machete. He passes another to Sinner. The others remove various weapons they're skilled with, watching the lions closely.

They may be lying out there, looking harmless now, but they can easily outrun any of us if they're hungry enough.

Exterminator murmurs, "Back up slowly, one step at a time, stay as quiet as possible. Think of them as bears. Ruger, keep an eye on where we came from. Night, watch the path that we were goin'. Saint and Sinner, you got behind us. Viking, want your eyes on those cats. You're probably the most skilled motherfucker out here with those weapons, who has a chance in hell at killing a goddamn lion. I'll be monitoring them as well. If any one of us is gonna die, it'll be me, not my brothers."

I've held a sense of respect toward Exterminator since the day he saved my life. He earned that, but today I respect him for an entirely different reason. The fact he'll put his life in front of ours speaks of true loyalty and brotherhood. This is why we look to him as one of our leaders; he's willing to ransom himself before us and take responsibility. I won't argue with him, but if it comes to it, I'll be the one forfeiting my life so he may live. I owe him that, and I will pay my debt if needed.

We slowly begin stepping backward, steadily peering over at the enormous beasts, and it hits me that I should confess my initial intentions. That way they'll all hate me and not interfere when I need to sacrifice myself. The brothers in the Nomads have become my family over the past few years; I won't allow this to be their parting fate.

"That day, you showed up early and saved my life," I begin.

He cuts me off mid-sentence. "Why do you think I was early to the bar?"

"Because I'd been tracking you. I was there, waiting for you."

"Go on."

"I was sent to kill you from another MC, but you stepped in and stopped that rival club for me."

He grunts.

"You were the first brother to have my back, and you weren't even in the same club."

"You fuckin' proposing or some shit right now?"

"Just thanking you for offering me a new life."

I think it's the most serious conversation I've ever had with any of them. We don't do chats unless it's full of ribbing each other, planning club business, or discussing the best way to torture someone.

"You think we'd let you ride with us without knowing who the fuck you were?"

His statement surprises me, and I glance at him. He points straight ahead, ordering, "Eyes on the cats."

One of the lions decides that it's a good time to stretch, putting us more on edge as we keep shuffling backward.

"I know who the fuck you are or were. I chose that time to wait for you, knowing someone was tracking me. I found a young kid who had a shitty fuckin' deal handed to him and was following orders in place of the mercenary I was expecting. You've proved yourself to this club many times over; you fit with us. If this is your confession, I don't give a fuck about what it *was*. You're my brother, end of story. Now shut the fuck up, 'cause if those cats scratch me from you flapping your jaw, I'mma stab you in the same spot."

I would grin but watching the other lion stand as well, has my heart rate speeding up.

Hybrid Collection

"Move brothers!" Ex growls and our steps speed up.

Sinner speaks up, "There's a chain link fence."

We all glance in that direction, finding that it's not any ordinary fence. I'd guess it to be at least twenty feet tall of heavy twelve inch wired squares.

Nightmare voices exactly what I was worrying about. "You better pray to whatever god you believe in, 'cause there's a good chance that fence is electric."

Both lions' heads snap to us, licking their chops and begin to stroll leisurely toward us.

"Oh fuck!" Spider says shakily, losing his shit and taking off, sprinting toward the fence.

The lions perk up at him running, crouching lower as they prepare for their next kill.

Ex catches on, realizing we've suddenly become more interesting to the felines, quickly becoming their next prey. "Beat feet for the fucking fence, now!"

Our steps thunder against the dirt, running full force toward the only salvation in site. If we get electrocuted, we may as well give up, 'cause we'd be well and truly fucked. I won't let that happen, though; I'll defend my brothers till my last breath.

Making it to the fence, everyone jumps, scaling our wire savior as quickly as possible. I know the lions run and chase us; I can feel the sturdy metal bounce and sway as they jump after each one of us.

As soon as I reach the top, I leap. Not giving a shit if it's fifty feet below me or twenty, it's better than getting a limb chewed off from trying to climb down the other side. Landing roughly on my hands and knees, I say a silent thank you in my mind. My fall could have been much worse, and I was fortunate this time.

Nightmare calls out, his voice laced with shock and pain. Snatching my weapons off the dirt near me, I immediately look for Night, ready to help him if needed. I find him lying on the ground at the base of the fence a ways down from me, clutching his calf.

Striding over to him, the lion roars next to us, busily pawing at the holes trying to reach us. The other one jumps again, scaling the fence a few squares up before it falls. It angrily roars at my brothers, pissed off that its dinner just escaped.

"What happened?

"Landed up against the fence and he got my leg before I could scoot away."

The cat growls at us.

Nightmare meets its primal stare. "Fuck you," he grits out, flipping the lion off. "Can you walk?"

"Yeah, I need to wrap it, though. I can feel the blood runnin' down my leg, and the last thing I want is to attract more fuckin' animals." He shakes his head. "Of course, the Cartel would have wild fucking lions on their Compound. Makes perfect sense. I hope I see the motherfucker in charge, 'cause he's paying for this bullshit."

Chuckling, I cut the bottom of his pant leg. It's torn most of the length of his calf, but the very bottom is still sewn together. Parting the material, I discover a gaping hole. The lion didn't just scratch him; he tore a fucking chunk out of his leg.

"How's it look?" he mumbles, scanning our surroundings as I try to figure out how to fix him.

"You'll live brother, but you're right, we should tie it tight, in case there are dogs running around."

"Just fucking wonderful, thanks for that."

Taking my fresh bandana from my back pocket, I close the gash up as much as I can. Nightmare groans but holds steady as I snugly wrap the folded over material around his leg.

"Little tight, brother," he grumbles, wincing.

"Yeah, it'll fall off if not."

Liar. He seriously needs to be sewn up and who knows if the cut's deep enough to do permanent damage, but it'll bleed a shit ton if that wrap doesn't help out. I need to let Ex know.

We both stand him lightly on his injured leg.

"Someone should go with you back to the bikes."

"What? No. I'm no pussy-ass crybaby."

Shrugging, I drop it.

Sinner grumbles at Spider, "Thanks for that, dick. If you didn't take off, we could have had more time."

"That lion wasn't staring you down; he had me in his sights the entire time," Spidey defends.

Ex holds his hand up, telling them to stop. "Brothers, we need to find this bitch so we can split."

The guys nod, silently following Ex, hopefully in the right direction this time.

Fourteen

PRINCESS

Bethany glances over at me as we pull onto the side road that leads to my mom's. "We're going to your old house?"

"Yeah. Every time I call my mom, Prez answers."

"So?"

"I want to talk to her!"

"He doesn't let you speak to her?"

"I always hang up."

"You're such an asshole. He's your dad, Prissy. You need to just accept it, that this is how their relationship is and move on."

"I get that and to an extent I agree with you, but what happens if she gets so fucked up sometime down the road from him leaving her again that she pops some pills or something and kills herself?"

Bethany doesn't answer, staring out the windshield as we near my mom's house.

"I refuse to feel like I stood by and did nothing. I don't have to go through with our plan by slamming the Prez in front of everyone, especially because it would now affect Viking as well. But at the same time, it doesn't mean that I have to like him or talk to him. Father or not, he left my life a long time ago."

"Look, I love Mona, I do; but that's not your responsibility. Your mom can decide to stop letting him around. Her actions aren't yours to own and neither should the consequences be."

"They may not be, but you tell me all the time, I have one mother and she loves me. I'm not going to stand by and not do something."

Pulling behind Mom's Impala, I shift my car into park. "Are you staying? Or do you want to come with me?"

"Isn't that Prez' bike?" She nods off to the side of my mom's car at the navy and black Harley Davidson Softail. Cost my brother almost twenty-four thousand dollars to take that bike home.

"No, the Softail is Brently's. I forgot you hadn't seen it yet." Gesturing to the side of the detached garage, I point out. "That's Prez's."

My dad's very picky about his bikes. He keeps them for years at a time, but when he gets a new one, it's completely different than the last every single time. This one's a Harley Davidson, Ape Hanger Custom, low-Softail Deluxe.

I have no clue how much he spent on it, but I'd guess a ton with its glossy black paint and silver pin striping. He'd never tell my mom anyhow. The one time he told her how much he had spent on a Harley, she flipped her shit. I remember hearing her say that they could put a kid through college, but he had bought a motorcycle instead.

"Crap, do you need me to come in? If you do, then I will; otherwise, I was going to wait here."

"No, it's fine, the pickup's gone, so they must've come and traded vehicles."

"Okay, will you leave the car on so I can listen to music?"

"Yeah, of course. I'll be right back."

Slamming my door, I follow along the narrow, worn grass path and hop up the steps to the porch. Stopping at the front door, I take in the aged dark gray paint. It's fading enough to make out the wood underneath, and it sort of makes me sad. We painted this door right before my dad finally left us. Now, like the paint, we're all worn down, a little vulnerable and exposed when it comes to outside elements.

Taking a deep breath, I twist the door handle; only it doesn't budge. *Okay then.* Pressing the door chime and folding my arms over my chest, I wait for her to answer. It feels as if five minutes pass with nothing, so I try knocking loudly.

She still doesn't answer, which is odd because my dad never takes her anywhere with him and her car's parked out front. *Maybe I should call.*

Jogging back to my car, Bethany turns to me as I slide into my seat.

"Everything go good?"

"She didn't answer; I'm going to try her cell."

Bethany nods and sits back as I dial.

It rings and rings, but she doesn't pick up. Her voicemail clicks on, which I never use, but decide to in this case. "Hey Mom, it's me. Umm, I stopped over, but no one answered, so I guess you're somewhere. I was hoping to talk to you about the guy I'm seeing. It's becoming serious, so…well, I was thinking of bringing him by sometime. He's…different. Anyhow, let me know what you think. Love you more," I finish and hang up.

"That sounded a little strained."

"It's just weird because we've been talking over random messages, nothing consistent like it used to be. I sort of feel like I have this new life, and she's not in it anymore. Ugh, I feel so shitty admitting that out loud."

"It'll all work out; just bring the big guy over with you sometime. She's totally going to freak. You know that, right? He's pretty much everything you've fought against. Your dad's an alpha, in charge of all those guys, but Viking makes him look like a sweet old man. Not only that, but you're in love, and she's going to be so excited for you."

"I'm not in love." I turn the engine over, backing out. *It's too soon.*

"Please Ol' Lady; your ass is so in love." She rolls her eyes and no matter how much I don't want to, I laugh.

We head back to my apartment, and I swear to myself that I'm going to bring my Viking to meet her. She deserves to be included in my happiness, and I want my mom back.

VIKING

Another pint-sized thug charges at me, and I drive my blade into his chest, following up by swinging my hatchet into his kidney. It's messy, but it works. At this point of the trip, I'm done fucking around.

I don't know what the hell they're feeding these assholes down here, but they're goddamn runts compared to the brothers and me. It's not that I'm complaining, there's like twenty of them on us at a time. Not to mention they're loaded down with weapons and walkie-talkies to call for more backup. At least I figure that's what they're radioing for; I have no idea. Watch it be a tank or some shit. After the run-in with the lions, couldn't say it'd surprise me.

Shorty drops to the ground, gurgling in agony as he bleeds out. One of his buddies runs at me, and then falls flat on his ass when I extend my leg, getting him with a strong kick to the ribs. He gasps, attempting to catch his breath as I stride over to him and finish him off with a few swift kicks to his skull. Size fourteen, steel toed boots will do some serious damage when properly executed.

"Stupid fucker." Grumbling, I shake my head at the two dead idiots at my feet. "Drink a damn protein shake next time."

Saint steps beside me, covered in blood.

"Looks like you were playing with your food again."

He smiles widely, and then let's loose a loud, wicked laugh. "Hell yes, you know I like them bloody! Oh and Ex wants us to keep moving; he said to hit up the shed on the left. They're checking the right, and then we need to meet back behind our building in case we need some cover."

Nodding, I take the lead toward the small shack.

This place is trippy; it's littered with these random square structures built out of cinder blocks. Reminds me of something you'd see when building a basement. Each has a steel door with a padlock holding it closed and one window covered in bars. I don't know if they were making temporary cells to sort drugs or what.

Part of me's a little hesitant to open them, knowing they've kidnapped people and shit. I swear if I open one and find a kid that's been fucked up, I'm liable to go Rambo on every motherfucker here, taking them all out.

Saint digs through his rucksack again, coming back with some sturdy metal cutters. It takes him seconds to get the cheap lock off and step to the side. Putting everything away, he replaces it with his fully-automatic Glock Eighteen with a silencer. Once he's ready, he nods.

Heaving the thick metal open, Saint points his weapon, ready to shoot any potential threats.

"Fuck," I mutter out with a sigh.

"Holy shit, that's all heroin?"

"Looks like it. Ex said we could bring some shit back with us if we had time, but I'm not running no fuckin' H."

"I have lighter fluid; we could try torching the place after we find the Russian."

"Sounds good to me."

Closing the door behind us, we silently creep around the back and wait for everyone else to meet up so we can go over the rest of the plan.

Leaning against the building, Saint glances over at me. "You talk to your Ol' Lady?"

"Not today. What's it to you?"

"Nothin' brother, but bitches like it when you call them every day and text them pictures."

"Thanks for that life changing advice you just shared with me; I'm fucking touched."

He chuckles, "Just trying to give you a one up on keeping her locked down and all."

"Cinderella knows better than to pull any drama bullshit with me, making demands and what the fuck ever else chicks try to do. She's not going anywhere."

He shakes his head. "You think she's submissive and always gonna do what you want, but you're wrong. She's fucking smart, bro; she's an observer, like Sinner. He met her at the door the other night when she came to the bar. Didn't say two words to a soul all night; anyone else would've thought she wasn't paying attention, but I watched her the entire time. She has that same mask her father does; you can't read her. She only lets you see what she wants you to. At the very end of the night, she mutters out a few words about you, brutally fucking honest. I think a few brothers damn near choked when they heard her speak and not to give a fuck whether we agreed or not. She's got strength. She might let you think she's pliable, but I'm warnin' you, stay on your fuckin' toes, 'cause better believe she's gonna keep you on them."

After his big spiel, I'm stunned. How the hell did he get all that about her, but I haven't and I've spent the most time with her over anyone else? I know Cinderella's smart; it's one of the many things I find hot as fuck about her. *But* I also thought she was just naturally more of a quiet person like me.

I can see her being observant. He's also right that I do believe she's submissive. She could be a natural sexual submissive but not in another part of life. It would explain a lot. Not that I give her much of a choice, anyhow; I'm dominant. I've known it since the first female I fucked. Hell, even the first one I kissed, ended with me controlling it.

"I'll give it some thought. I'm fucking surprised you got all that."

He shrugs. "I have a lot of experience with chicks."

Pulling my phone out, I check to see if there's anything from her, but my screen's blank. I start to put it away but think of his advice.

Me: I may make it back by dinner. Fingers crossed. Be ready.

That sounds good and to the point, so I hit send and start to stuff it in my pocket when it vibrates. Immediately I draw in a breath, excited she replied so fast. Clicking the message icon, it's some shit telling me that the message wasn't sent.

I start to retype it when Sinner rounds the corner. Saint and I jump from leaning against the building, having relaxed our backs against the cool blocks in the shade. Holding the power button, the cell turns back off, and I stuff it in my pocket.

Sinner rests his hand on the shoulder of a dark haired woman, walking her forward.

"Who the fuck's this?" I mumble, scanning her over.

"She was one of them cleaning. Ex said if we found any of the maids that they may be able to give us intel."

"Where's everyone else?"

"They're still in the main house searching."

Saint gapes. "We were supposed to check the small buildings, not the main house. You should've waited for me."

"I'm straight; they had my six," Sinner replies, pushing the lady's back against the wall, so she's facing us all. "Should we question her now, or wait for the brothers to get done?"

"Ex has the most info, so let's just wait for him."

They both agree, and we grow silent, all staring at the maid, curiously. She must be used to strange men watching her because she stands still, not cowering into herself. Most women put on display to three huge guys would be scared out of their minds. This one's calm, like it's a normal occurrence.

Male shouts followed by multiple guns firing ring out, putting us on alarm. Saint peeks around the corner to see what's happening.

"Shit," he mutters, glancing back at us. "The brothers are running toward us."

Suddenly they go flying by, Nightmare shouting, "Get the fuck outta here! Come on!"

"You want her?" I ask Sinner.

"Hell yes, she could be our only hope."

Snatching her away from the wall, I toss her over my shoulder in a fireman's carry and take off after the guys. Saint and Sinner flank me on each side, shooting while I concentrate on not losing the maid as she bounces along.

Arriving at the outer property wall, we're trapped inside if we don't go over the fence and into the lion's den again.

Hybrid Collection

"The fuck we gonna do now?" Ruger huffs, staring down the solid barrier that's keeping us from our freedom.

"Follow my lead, keep your gun on you and shoot anything that moves too close."

I don't see any lions chilling anywhere, so I start climbing as quickly as possible. Eventually getting high enough to reach the top of the wall, I move my body until I'm lying on the ledge looking down on the other side.

Spider shouts for the other brothers to hurry up and climb faster because the cartel guys are catching up.

"This is gonna hurt," I mutter to the maid and push her off me.

She flies through the air, quickly meeting the hard ground with a yelp. Launching myself off afterward, I try to position how to land somewhat decently since I already know what to expect from earlier. The maid's obviously scared now as she silently cries, not looking at me but it's no love lost on my part. She's lucky I didn't drop her ass in with the lions on accident.

The brothers start jumping from the wall and as they land we help each other up, waiting until the last one's over, and then make a run for our bikes. We're about halfway to our freedom when we hear a surprisingly loud roar. Casting a glance back, while keeping my pace, I watch as a lion rips into one of the Cartel guys who'd just hit the ground. Two men sprint, taking off toward the front of the Compound and the other lion gives chase, eventually jumping on them and brutally attacking as they scream in agony.

"The wall!" I gasp as we reach our rides.

We'd blown a huge fucking hole into the barrier where we'd broken in. At the time, though, we had no idea it led inside a makeshift den. It looks like we unknowingly granted their freedom as well.

Nightmare cocks an eyebrow. "I think those fuckers trying to kill us, unintentionally saved our lives."

Ex barks, "Sinner, have the bitch ride back with you." Then he starts his engine with us following suit.

It's clear by Sinner's pissed off expression that he's not happy getting tasked with babysitter duties, but he's the one who found her after all. I never get a chance to text Princess as we race off in the early morning air. It's barely seven a.m., and we've already been through enough hell for the day.

At least I get to see my woman tonight. She'll make the eleven-hour ride completely worth it.

Fifteen

PRINCESS

It's been a few days since I received the text from Viking letting me know that he was going out of town, so imagine my surprise when my phone rings and of all people, it's Scot calling me.

Immediately, I spaz out, jumping to conclusions that Viking was dead, and Scot, being the one semi in charge, was calling to tell me about it. Talk about overreacting. Bethany's baby news has had me on pins and needles, automatically jumping to wild conclusions on everything, even the small stuff.

The poor man barely got three words in before I was peppering him with questions about why and how it happened. Chuckling loudly, he'd ignored my craziness and told me that it would be a cold day in hell when someone was able to kill that rotten bastard.

I'm not one hundred percent sure what Scot meant by that exactly, but it did indicate that Viking was okay. Bethany's words sunk in a smidge more, suggesting that I do love him. It's the first time as his Ol' Lady I guess you'd say, that he's on a run, so I can't help the nervousness bubbling up inside.

Scot was nice enough to let me know that they'd all be returning from their trip this evening, and he was hoping Bethany and I would go to the bar early and help the bartender prepare. Of course, I agreed, eager at the chance of possibly seeing Viking early. Plus, I'd get to do something nice for him and his brothers. They've been kind to me each time we've seen one another, so hopefully, the culinary skills I've learned from my mom will further win them over.

It's much easier for me to keep Viking at some distance if people are around versus being with him alone. I want to be with him a little too much, and that feeling scares me. I refuse to be left home all the time just because I'm an Ol' Lady. I won't let him treat me like my dad did with my mother and with how strongly I feel about him already, he could end up doing that if he wanted.

Per Scot's request, the majority of my day was spent preparing my mom's potato salad recipe and chocolate cupcakes with chocolate frosting. I tried to bribe Bethany to come with me, but she had to work and wouldn't call in sick. I can't blame her. I'm proud of her for turning me down; she has a kid to think about now.

After the food was finished and I'd taken a shower, I found a cute outfit consisting of a thin tank and jean shorts, then I loaded my car up and headed straight to the bar.

1 Hour later...

Dutifully, I've been getting everything set up and ready with the bartender ever since I crossed the threshold. This woman is a workhorse; I'd never guess she could pull this much off with so little notice. I'd think she'd be exhausted from closing the bar down each night and would sleep all day long too. At least that's what I would do.

That's probably why she's been quiet. I hate not knowing her name, but she didn't mention it earlier, and I don't want to guess and fuck it up. She hasn't been rude or anything, but besides asking me to set stuff in certain places or help her move the long table, she hasn't really spoken to me. I'm too used to having Bethany chatting my ears off when we're together that being around quiet females gives me too much time to think.

Hopefully, these bikers are starving; otherwise, I don't know who's going to eat all this food. So far we've got a buffet style table set up full of fried chicken, corn on the cob, potato salad, cupcakes, rolls, grilled chicken and pineapple kabob's, chips, dip, and banana bread. She had some serious help cooking, or else I need to step up my game when it comes to the kitchen.

"Will you hand me that bucket? I need to fill the ice bins back here." She points to a gray bucket beside the table. She used it to fill a few large bowls with ice to set under the salads so they'd stay cool.

"Sure." I place the plastic forks down and grab the bucket.

Handing it over the bar, she smiles friendly and uses both hands to take it from me. "Thanks."

"No problem," I respond just as the bar door swings open, letting in a burst of late afternoon sunlight. Normally the place would've opened hours ago and been busy with the regulars, but she posted a sign earlier saying the bar's closed for a private party. The guys have no idea about it either. Scot's supposed to be calling them later on, once we're all ready and let them know to come on over. I hope it's a surprise they'll be happy about with tons of food and alcohol.

My gaze is instantly glued to the entrance, waiting for *him* to cross the threshold because I know when I see him again I won't be able to breathe. That's what Viking does to me; he steals my breath away easily with his crazy demands and no-holds-barred way of living. He orders me around like he's lost his fucking mind and doesn't think twice about me standing up to him. He doesn't care about anyone else's opinions; he does whatever he wants, and it's fucking liberating.

A rough group of bikers enters the empty bar, and my stomach instantly tenses. I've never seen them around here before. My mother made sure I was pretty familiar with the clubs in the Austin area. She wanted to be certain I knew which ones were friendly with the Oath Keepers if there ever came a time that I needed someone else's help.

Pretty sure that time is now.

The intruders' cuts advertise one percenter patches, and when the last burly man turns around to shut the door, I make out 'South Carolina' on his bottom rocker. He swings back before I get a chance to see exactly which club they're from. The fronts of their cuts have each of their road names, the percenter patch and various other warnings sewn on, but no club name.

Damn. I need one of them to turn again; their name could mean so much.

My mother had also taught me about the types of patches that they sew on their cuts and what all they imply. I can tell you right now, these guys are at least into guns and drugs, possibly prostitution as well. It looks like they've all killed before, every one of them. A few have knife patches, and others have stripes marking their kills.

The two cuts with the tally mark patches most likely mean that those men are the club's Enforcers. Paired up with everything else they have on display, they're probably very mean bikers, taking care of the unwanted stuff thrown at their club. One approaches me, hardened features, glaring coldly like he wants to stab my eyes out.

His expression has me throwing on my resting bitch face. I'm pretty good at coming off to guys that I'm not interested or that I don't care about anything they may say. My gaze shoots to his title, reading 'Death Dealer.' *Definitely a damn Enforcer. Shit, fuck.* Whatever the reason is that they're here, it probably isn't good news.

With a road name like Torch, I'd hate to be on the receiving end of his anger. Thankfully, he keeps walking, heading toward the bathrooms.

The oldest guy with them spots me right away, and his eyes sparkle in triumph as he saunters toward me, wearing a malicious smile.

Just great. My stomach churns, knowing inside that this isn't going to end well. *Why can't these assholes just read the sign on the door and leave?*

"Well, well, well, looky here, Widows!" he announces as he comes to stand in front of me.

I'm not going to lie; I kind of want to shit my pants right now. This man is damn near as big as Viking; only he's scary as fuck. When I look at Vike, I see a man that worships me. This guy seems more like he wants to peel my skin off and wear it. Most men I come across are overly sweet, trying to get into my pants; but clearly, these guys don't use those tactics.

A skinny cracked out looking guy with greasy black hair snickers as he swaggers closer. "Nice. Her tits are bigger than the picture."

Any other time, I'd flip him off and tell him to lick shit off a toilet, but one thing stands out in my mind. He said 'the picture' as if he's seen me before and already knows who I am. It's like setting off a shrill siren or lighting a blazing fire directly in front of me—the warning written in his words.

My gut was right to feel uneasy; it was cautioning me that these men will hurt me.

Swallowing down my fear, my thoughts race to find a way out of this situation. I could try to make it out the side door, but most likely they won't let me back there alone, and if they did, then it most likely means that they have someone waiting outside.

Shit fuck. Could this be my father's fault? Did his damn club get mixed up in something bad enough that people would come for me? It's not a farfetched thought; it wouldn't be the first time.

Back when I was seventeen, I was leaving the movie theater and was left alone out front. My friend's boyfriend gave her a ride home, and she had taken off before my brother showed up. A rival club member of my dad's happened to be there, taking his Ol' Lady to a movie as well. They saw me waiting to leave and tried stuffing me into their old beat-up pickup truck.

Thank God my brother showed up just in time with a few of his college buddies or who knows what could have happened to me. My mom flipped out, scared for me to go anywhere alone and ripped my dad a new one. Come to find out, the other club had been threatening my dad for some time because one of his old members kept stealing the other club's drugs. The member got kicked out of the club and my dad made as much peace with the rivals as fifty thousand dollars would buy.

Then the Twisted Snakes came after Brently awhile back and nearly killed him, so why should I think that I'm exempt from such repercussions?

There's no way I can ask my mom for help with this. I have to figure out a way to call Viking. I don't want him to get hurt, but I think the Nomads are most likely the only ones who would be able to get me out of this situation right now.

If I don't do something fairly quick, I'll probably end up raped multiple times and then killed when they're all finished with me.

Viking's on my speed dial, but if I reach into my back pocket right away, I think the monstrous guy hovering over me will know exactly what I'm doing and take my cell from me. That's the last thing I want right now if I have any hope of making it out of this with minimal damage.

Clicking his tongue, the man looks me up and down. "Snatch got your tongue, baby?" He chuckles, and I clench my teeth together. I'm going to barf all over this jack off if he keeps talking to me like that.

Remaining silent, I mentally start slowly counting to ten, so that I don't come back with a retort that I'll end up regretting.

It takes no time at all for his weathered features to contort in anger at my silent defiance. His hand shoots out toward my face, his fingers digging into my cheeks as he pulls me in closer. Coppery flavor consumes my taste buds as my teeth sink into the soft flesh, carving out painful cuts inside my mouth.

Momentarily, I forget to breathe, in shock and in pain.

At his commanding voice, I draw in a few gulps of air, doing my best to concentrate on his words. "I asked you a motherfuckin' question. You don't open that cum guzzler real fast; I'll beat you 'til you feel chatty. You get me?"

Blinking a few times, I nod quickly, causing my teeth to slice in deeper where his fingers continue to hold my skin captive.

He sighs, and the anger melts away, almost like he just took off a mask and is a completely different person suddenly. His hand releases its fierce grip and falls away as a small grin appears. "Good, glad we understand one another."

Hybrid Collection

Another man strides over, coming to stand beside my tormentor. He resembles the older man slightly. This new guy's thinner but still muscular and young. I'd guess he's eighteen, if that. I wonder what could've been horrible enough in his life to make him want to be around someone so mean and just plain evil?

My gaze flutters over the man's cut in front of me; he wears the President patch on one side and his road name on the other. Jekyll. Taking in each material decorating his cut, one, in particular, scares me the most. It's actually more than one; there's an entire row of tiny red flowers sewn under his arm, all in a line.

Rape.

Those patches show me how many 'flowers' he's taken. I'm guessing he raped every single one of those virgins, as it looks like he's collected quite a few.

"You like those flowers?" he murmurs nastily, adjusting a little so I can get a better look.

Twenty-nine.

I'm able to get to number twenty-nine before he returns to his original position. That wasn't all of them either; that was just how fast I was able to count them. Shrugging, I pretend to be oblivious. Fake it till you make it, right? "I don't care for them."

Stepping closer, he places his finger in the 'v' where my thighs meet. "You sure?" He rubs my pussy through my shorts. "I could show you what they mean; then you could have your own. "He points to the last spot under the crimson line. "Right here."

"I'm not really a red person, more like pink."

He pushes against me hard enough to send an entirely new zing of sickness to my stomach. "I'll bet you are. Did my son get a flower patch from you?"

"Huh?" I'm confused. I have no clue who the hell this guy's son is unless he thinks I've met him before.

"Take off your shorts," he orders, causing me to panic. If I take them off, I lose access to my phone. *Fucking shit.*

"Not happening. I'm not some bar slut that you may be used to."

He snaps his fingers and instantly greasy hair guy along with another guy grab my arms, spreading them out. I can twist and turn, but they're strong enough, making it so that I can't go anywhere even if I do try to fight them.

Jekyll pulls the same long knife from his belt that Viking owns, wearing a cruel smile as he grabs my shirt, slicing up the thin tank top material. Once he has most of it cut away, he pulls the scraps off, tossing it to the floor.

I'm left in my bra, panting, my anxiety making me feel as if I'm about to have a heart attack. "You seriously need to stop; you don't know what you're doing!"

"That's where you're wrong. I'll do whatever the fuck I want, whenever the fuck I want to. You see this patch here." He points to the one percenter sign, and I nod, well aware of what it is. "Means, I make my own rules, and some snatch isn't gonna tell me what the fuck to do." He grabs my bra between my breasts; I try to wrench away, but they're too strong. I don't get back far enough, and when he slides the blade underneath to cut the bra, he draws my blood.

The sting to my sensitive skin is enough to have me spewing threats. "Do you have any clue who the hell my father is, you fuckwad?" I scream furiously. "He'll kill you! You're all fucking dead!"

Jekyll bursts out in a deep belly laugh, only pausing to send a quick punch to my stomach for my outburst. He hits me hard enough to make the air escape me, but not to break a rib. Watching me, he continues to chuckle for a moment while I gasp in discomfort.

The younger guy remains solemn, standing beside him and looking miserable like he's being forced to watch this.

"Blaze, come shut this mouthy whore up," Jekyll hollers at a stocky guy that has flames tattooed all over his arms.

Before he reaches me, I shout, "My father's the President of the Oath Keepers MC you fool! Let me go!" That's all that I can get out before Blaze is standing behind me with his huge hand, covering my mouth and muffling my shrieks of outrage.

"You think I don't know who the fuck you are, *Princess*?" He says it snidely, running the tip of the blade ever so lightly against the flesh of my exposed chest. I can't answer, just stand here helplessly and listen while my cheeks burn with anger and my gaze bristles with my newfound hatred for him.

"You're wrong. I know everything about you, where you live, your job, how long you've been sucking my son's cock, oh, and my favorite—the pictures from him fucking you right in this room on that pool table." He gestures to the old wooden billiards table with faded green felt.

He has no right to cheapen what happened on that table between Viking and me. He didn't just fuck me that night; Viking made me his. It wasn't some shitty show put on for the patrons like Jekyll's making it sound, what happened was carnal and raw. It was us.

Being a biker himself, Jekyll should know exactly what that entails. By the biker code, it means that if my Ol' Man shows up and witnesses what they're doing to me right now, he has every right to slaughter them without any repercussions coming to bite him in the ass. At this point, Viking could request the entire club to help him snuff out each one of the Widow Makers members in this room. Prez may be a shitty father, but he's always been one hell of a biker, and he'd be ballistic right now beside my man over this.

A shotgun loads in the background somewhere and then the bartender starts shouting, "Let her go and get the hell out, dickhead!"

Jekyll's head flies up with murder coating his irises toward her. He remains eerily silent, even as a shot rings out, followed by her pained scream.

Tearing up, I attempt to suppress the wetness from falling, but it's no use. I'm too irate at this point to not start crying. I'd use my anger by punching and screaming, fighting them, but they've stripped it away from me along with my modesty.

That woman was only trying to help me, and they shot her for it. These sick fucks are absolutely crazy. The only piece of comfort I find, out of everything, is that I can hear her crying. I can't stand it that she was injured because of me, but at least with her upset, I know she's not dead.

I'd give anything to be free right now and holding that knife in Jekyll's hand.

"Your father means nothing to me, same as you. I'll still fuck you and kill you when I'm finished, because let's face it, my son can't have an Oath Keepers dirty slut as his Ol' Lady."

My mind soaks up every word he speaks like a sponge, but my heart pleads with me not to listen. I don't want to believe anything Jekyll says, but he knows too much. I would be stupid to think he was lying and that there isn't a bit of truth to everything.

But how could Viking betray me like this? I was falling in love with him and now...Shit, fuck. Who am I kidding? I am so fucking in love with him, but there's no way I can be with him if he's going to be a part of this hateful club. The Oath Keepers will probably kill him for this anyhow.

Jekyll uses his free hand to twist my nipples painfully and sadly all I can do is whimper. I want to cry out, cursing him to hell, but I can't. At the strangled noise leaving me, he smirks, running his digits down my chest and stomach, pausing at the button on my shorts.

He leans in beside my ear, close enough that I can feel his short hot pants and pushes his fingers inside my bottoms, far enough to go under the elastic of my panties. "Let me fill you in, as I'm sure he didn't share the news with you," Jekyll mumbles quietly, "He's due to be patched as the President of the Widow Makers MC soon, and there's no way I'm letting you fuck it up. I'm ready to pass the gavel down and watch my oldest take my place."

No. Please be lying. I don't want him taken from my life. He's mine; he belongs to me. We haven't had enough time yet.

His calloused fingers rub back and forth over the smooth skin above my pubic hair, continuing, "He can have the gavel, and I'll have your snatch as my parting gift. You're one lucky little girl; in our club we share. Think of the fun you'll have being passed around until we dispose of your body."

Sickness whirls through me, my gaze blurring as my head becomes fuzzy and makes me want to wretch at the bitter flavor that's abruptly overtaken my taste buds. I'm confident and strongheaded, not letting people get me down in everyday life, but I've also been diagnosed with panic attacks. It was a wake-up call and also my doctor's way of telling me that I was trying to be too perfect for my father when I was younger. I wanted him to stay, so I tried everything I could think of, then he'd leave, and my mom would be a mess. I couldn't help but panic, and over the years, I've learned how to keep the attacks at bay by staying mad inside.

My anger's faded with Jekyll's torments, morphing into a sense of loss, fear, and sadness. His latest taunt has me conjuring up images filled with the room of filthy men sexually assaulting me and then killing me. Even with the air conditioner blasting cold air throughout the bar, beads of sweat trail down my back, catching on Blaze's shirt.

At the feeling of Blaze thickening and resting his cock against my back, shakes start to set in, racking my body with nervousness and fear. I can't stop the thoughts running through my mind that Blaze could easily rip my shorts down and force his hardness inside. *Viking won't want me.* More tears fall, and I gag into his palm, ready to empty the contents of my stomach.

Blaze's hand flies from my mouth like it's on fire, then sharp pricks of pain explode from my scalp as he grasps onto the back of my hair. Yanking the platinum strands harshly, he wrenches my head back in outrage. "You better not throw up on me, you dumb bitch." Growling, he shoves my head forward with such force, my neck pops, protesting the movement as he releases my hair.

Jekyll chuckles, amused at the display and steps back. "You can still have your turn whether she pukes or not." He's loving the fact that he's tormenting me enough to make me physically ill and that it's grossing Blaze out.

Blaze scoffs, "I'm not touching that twat if she's gonna fucking wretch. Maybe we should dope her up first. Besides, she looks like she's gonna pass the fuck out anyhow." He nods at me, and all the guys start to really stare at me.

"Well, I'll be damned, looks like Viking chose a weak-ass bitch," Jekyll chortles and the men all laugh in agreement. "Just throw the whore down, she can sit up against the bar. I don't want this one drugged up at first; I want to see if she'll try fighting me." They all chuckle again, and it takes everything in me not to toss my stomach contents.

The two bikers holding onto my arms drag me backward a few paces then propel me to the stained concrete floor.

My ass smarts as I land harshly on the solid ground, a smell yelp of "Shit!" escaping. Thankfully, no one pays me any mind because my cell phone digs into my butt cheek, reminding me of its presence.

A speck of hope rises, feeling the small square still in my possession.

Greasy guy crouches down, stopping about four inches in front of my face. Even with him this close to my nakedness, I can't help but pray silently that my screen isn't cracked, and I can get ahold of someone.

Smirking, he glances at my chest. "I'm fuckin' those titties when it's my turn." Flicking my nipple, he stands, staring at my breasts while adjusting what looks to be a tiny dick pressing against his dark wash jeans and turns around to face Jekyll.

Bastard.

He can think whatever he likes. As soon as I know that they're all distracted enough, and I get a chance, I'm calling for help. It's times like this that I'm my father's daughter, because when the anger comes, so does my clarity and I'm hoping that I get the opportunity to shoot this nasty monkey in his dick.

Sixteen

VIKING

We arrive back at the hotel after a long-ass ride and get settled in. We didn't speak two words climbing off our bikes, and I'm pretty sure the maid we brought along won't be able to walk for a week after a trip like that. I prefer the northern runs the most during this time of year, not this bullshit sweating until your nuts chafe, and you get a rash up your ass crack. It took me two showers to scrub the road grime off, and my balls are fucking tender enough that I'm not gonna be able to fuck my woman like I'd planned. It'll be slow and steady with her on top.

I'll give her a call shortly and head across the street for a beer to wait on her. I'm sure Exterminator hit up Scot and let him know we were headed back. I wonder if the old man knows what's up at the bar. There were about ten bikes parked out front when we rolled in. It's not unusual for the regulars to be drinking already; however, I didn't see any of theirs parked out front.

Nightmare had a hell of a time riding back. I'm thinking the heat and blood loss was making him weak after his adrenaline finally started to dissipate. At one point he was swerving so much, I thought he was going to pass the fuck out. I've never been worried about him like that. He's a tough dude, but I almost suggested he stop off at a hospital. I'm glad we were able to make it back first, that way no authorities will be flagged by him getting medical attention.

Heading outside, I check for him, but find his bike still gone. He decided to stop over at the Charter to see if they had a private doctor that'd look him over. Hopefully, Night gets that shit squared away; it would fucking blow if something serious happened to his leg because he was too stubborn to get it taken care of.

Hybrid Collection

Digging a cigarette out, I get it lit and the first drag filling my lungs as Spider leaves his room. He starts my way, glancing up, surprised when he notices me already out here.

"Can I bum one?"

My eyebrow rises as I stare down at him. "It tastes like shit. Why you want to smoke?"

"Because I guess with how everything went down south, the Nomads are going to pummel my ass. Might as well pick up a bad habit on the way."

Chuckling, I shake my head, "Nope."

"No?"

"You a parrot now?"

"My bad, I'll ask the desk clerk," he says sincerely and begins to walk off.

"Spidey, get your ass back here."

Halting, he turns back looking like someone kicked his fucking cat.

"Look, brother; shit always goes down on runs. You're just too new to know that. Brush it the fuck off and if anyone gives you shit, just tell 'em to fuck off. Don't show yourself to everyone or they'll end up running your life. And don't start smoking, for the love of Christ; we've all been trying to stop since we started. Chew a piece of gum."

He nods, silently thinking it over.

"You still have your Smith and Wesson?" On our first run together we were transporting weapons, and Spider pretty much jizzed his pants when he saw a small, flat black gun we had in one of the containers. That was one business deal that went through flawlessly.

"Yeah, I've been getting familiar with it. The different design is sick, but I've also been looking into other models."

Exterminator rushes out of his room, beelining for mine. What the hell is going on with people today and coming to me?

"Ex?"

"We gotta talk—now!" He slams against my door, shoving it open swiftly. "You too, Spider," he orders and we shuffle in quickly. "You speak to your Ol' Lady?"

Meeting his stressed-out gaze, I shrug. "Not yet, my phone was off for the run, why?"

"Fuck, fuck, fuck," he mutters, his fingertips squeezing his forehead.

Grabbing my phone off the table, I power it on immediately.

"It's not good, Vike. You're gonna lose it, brother. You need to stay calm so we can figure out what the hell to do," he finishes as six missed calls from Princess pop up.

One voice message.

Clicking the message icon, I hear whispering at first, and then sobbing. My eyes fly to Ex's, just as she starts sobbing and pleading, "Please no, don't take it, nooo." Then the screaming sets in, "Viking help me! Please, they're gonna rap--" And then it cuts off.

I'm going to filet whoever did this.

Exterminator positions himself in front of the door with his palms out. "Calm down, brother. I just spoke to Scot. He heard from the Prez over here. Nancy, the bartender, called him asking for help too."

"Get the fuck outta my way!" Roaring, I charge toward him.

"Vike! Wait, man, we'll get her!"

Halting directly in front of him, I send him a dark glare. "Move." His eyes shine with sympathy which has me almost ballistic. "You wanna fuckin' die? Get the fuck out of my way, or so help me, I'll take your motherfuckin' life, Oath Keeper."

"It's the Widows."

The little bit of spit in my mouth damn near chokes me at that name. That's no regular MC; that's my *father's* club.

"We'll figure this out, what would they want with your woman?"

"He doesn't want Princess. It was my birthday yesterday; he's come for me."

"This isn't the way to get you a fuckin' cake." He shakes his head, trying to figure out what to say.

"Jekyll doesn't want to celebrate; he wants to give me the gavel. I'll get her back; if not, they'll kill her. She'll fucking hate me for what I'm going to have to do, but at least I'll know she's still breathing."

Spider interrupts, "What the hell, this isn't old England; you're not born into shit, you vote, especially on patches."

"True, but in the Widow Makers, you have to be a son to be the President, and if you live long enough for your first born to reach a certain age, then you inherit the gavel and the previous gets to hang his leathers, just ride free the rest of his days."

"So fucked up," he mutters.

"Yep. Now I gotta go save my bitch, 'cause I have a good idea of what they're doing to her and I have a plan."

"What is it?" Exterminator questions.

"I'm going to kill my father, and then I'll kill any other dumb motherfucker who steps in my way of saving my woman."

He steps aside, and I storm out the door, striding purposefully toward the bar.

"We're coming!" he calls from behind me.

"Give me twenty first and keep a look out for her," I yell back as I see the first Widow posted up by the front door.

A young member slouching against the building jumps to his feet quickly as I near. He must be a recent patch since I'm not familiar with him. I know all the lifers and members dating five years back. Most could be dead by now, but I doubt it—shady fuckers.

The punk steps to the top of the stairs, crossing his arms like he's king ding-a-ling. "Who are you?"

My steps don't miss a beat as I hop up the few steps and shoulder check his ass, causing him to fly back a few feet, landing harshly against the old wooden porch.

"I'm your new fucking President." Muttering, I pass him by and head inside the bar.

The sight I'm met with is sickening. My girl's on the floor against the bar, hair in every direction, halfway undressed sobbing as my father and cousin, Blaze, taunt her. She's got blood smeared over her tits and Butters' greasy ass is smashing her phone under his boot.

My father's in the middle of telling her how he's about to tie her to the bar and fuck her in front of everyone when the men quiet with me storming inside like a freight train.

"Son!" Jekyll shouts jovially.

Such a fucked-up man.

My entire life was lived on the edge, because when you have a father like Jekyll, you never know what's going to happen. One minute he's laughing and the next he's driving a knife into your stomach. Psycho is too tame of a word to fit him. He got his road name after Dr. Jekyll and Mr. Hyde. His father was proud of the fact he had a son that was off his fucking rocker.

I never use guns—ever. I'm strong enough of a man to kill with my two hands, but when I see Smokey's Glock out on the table, I don't hesitate and pick it up immediately, shooting my father in the head. Brain matter sprays behind him, and he falls like the dead weight he is.

One thing I'm learning about my woman is that I can't handle shit when it comes to her. My normal way of thinking goes out the window, and I become obsessed with her.

Obsessed with being inside her. Obsessed with keeping her safe. Obsessed with making her mine. Just fucking obsessed.

"Cinderella!" I demand, loudly.

Her tearstained face finds mine, and she lights up. *I love her. I will forever.*

"Get the fuck outta here. We don't have space for filthy fuckin' sluts." Nodding toward the door, I turn away to give her my back.

My younger brother stares at me in shock while my cousin Blaze comes toward me angrily. "You shot the Prez!" he accuses, and I cock my eyebrow at him, my nostrils flaring.

"Last I checked, yesterday was the fourth. That means this club belongs to me now."

Glancing around, the brother's nod, keeping their mouths shut. This is how it works. I'm in charge now, and they know that. I could have let my father live out a peaceful old life, but he would never have changed and seeing a drop of blood on my girl, he's lucky his death was swift.

Her grief-stricken voice rings out, causing me to spin back. "You bastard!" she practically wails, heartbroken.

Her palm stings as she slaps me with everything she's got. I don't get an odd punch from her somewhere; I get her 'in your face' disappointment launched at me, and I'll have to live with that moment for the rest of my life. If she only knew it was done because I want her to be happy and alive. I'll make these men believe I want her gone if it means it'll keep her safe.

A few of the brothers stride toward her, and I throw my hand up, halting them.

"Get the fuck out." Growling down at her, I point toward the door.

Her eyes refill with tears; sorrow swimming in them so deep that I feel like my heart's being cut out. In some ways I wish it were, I know it would hurt less than this moment. As she turns away, a noise close to thunder gets closer, and immediately I think of Widow Maker's reinforcers showing up.

"Princess, get back behind the bar," I demand, and she actually listens right away.

"Who's that?" Butters, the dirty motherfucker, asks.

"You scared? Shut the fuck up."

Hybrid Collection

"Maybe your poppa should've stayed longer," he utters, and I shoot him next.

"Shit, man!" Blaze yells as Butters hit the floor.

"I never liked him. Anyone else in here wishing Jekyll was still around?"

The room stays silent as the powerful rumble comes to a stop outside.

"Good."

"You've grown hard," Blaze notes.

"No. I've always been hard," I respond and point to my dead father on the floor. "He's gone. This club runs my way now. Anyone have a problem with that; there's the fuckin' door, and best believe shit's fucking changing."

My gaze lands on Odin, sitting quietly at a table. "Why'd he bring you?"

"Why do you think?" he questions back, standing and coming near. It's like looking in a mirror; only I had more bruises back then.

He's a big kid now. When I left, he was about to turn eleven. Now he's riding around with a group of outlaws at the age of fifteen. I can only imagine what kind of man he'll turn into if I'm unable to get him away from the bad.

"'Cause he was going to use you to get me home."

He nods.

"What'd he do to you?"

"Not me. He promised to hurt a friend of mine."

"Jesus fucking Christ."

Ex and my Nomad brothers storm in, guns drawn, ready to fuck some shit up. The resident Oath Keepers, including Princess' father, pours in behind them, and the Widows get to their feet, prepared for a fight.

"Stand down," I order. "These are my brothers, the Nomads, and this is the local Chapter of the Oath Keepers. They have my six and being your President, I'm telling you, we're cool with them."

Charlie stands up, his nine out in front as he grumbles, "Fuck this, we ain't friendly with nobody." He raises the weapon toward me, but my old best friend, Torch, steps out of the hall and shoots Charlie dead.

I didn't even know Torch was here.

"He brought you too?"

"Yep." He puts his gun back in his holster.

"What'd he do to you?"

"Threatened to rape my ex-wife and sister."

"Meggie?" I name his sister who's the probably the sweetest woman alive.

"Yep."

"That shit's fuckin' done. You won't be living like that anymore. We'll figure this shit out later, but your friends and families are safe, you have my word."

Odin scoffs, "Like that means anything."

"The fuck you just say?"

"You promised to protect me too. Next thing I know, you're leaving me in your exhaust. Whatever, I'm over it."

"We'll talk; that's not how it went down."

Prez comes over with Ares and Exterminator. "Everything okay, son?"

"We'll get it figured out. We need to have a meeting though to discuss the clubs."

"You're family; my door's always open for you," Prez answers, and we shake. I'm going to need his help with turning this club around, and he's one hell of a President when it comes to running a semi-clean MC.

The bartender and Princess stand slowly, looking around to make sure it's clear. My woman has a bar towel covering her naked chest, and being the overprotective fucker that I am; I want to gouge everyone's eyes out. Shedding my shirt, I swiftly help her into it and place my cut back on.

She doesn't look at me, but I can feel her physically move her body closer to mine.

Glancing around at everyone, I declare sternly, "This is my Ol' Lady. None of you better have touched her or ever touch her in the future. If I find out otherwise, my boy Saint will gladly hold you down so I can chop your fucking head off."

Blaze stares at the ground guiltily.

"Blaze?"

"I was keeping her quiet," he replies honestly.

Glancing at Princess, I ask her loud and clear, so everyone can hear me and know exactly where I stand. "He's my cousin, but I will kill him for putting his hands on my woman. You want him dead, Cinderella?"

She looks over at him, her backbone a little straighter with me beside her.

"I swear I will protect you with my life." Blaze meets her gaze, pledging his loyalty.

She glances up to me. "No, as long as he doesn't touch me, we'll be okay."

Smokey grumbles, "So bitches are choosing our fates now? You told her to get the fuck out earlier."

"Yeah, I sure the fuck did. I didn't know who the hell was here or if anyone had hurt her. I wanted her to get out so I'd know she was safe, with my brothers." I nod to the Nomads standing closer to the door.

"As for being a fate-maker, best believe you decide your own. You touch my property; I take your fucking head. Don't test me when it comes to her. You need to realize right here, that this is your President's Ol' Lady. You call her Princess or Cinderella. Anything else, derogatory or sweet, will get you fucked up."

Prez speaks up, "We'll be gettin' outta the way now that you have it under control and I know they're safe."

"Appreciate it," I nod, genuinely. I'm humbled by the support and respect he's shown me, knowing that I'm his daughter's Ol' Man.

He steps over to the bartender, and I feel Princess' body grow stiff, the anger still radiating off of her as I try to eavesdrop.

Seventeen

PRINCESS

My father glances over at the bartender. "Thanks for the heads-up, Nancy."

She smiles through her discomfort, peering up at him with respect, "Anytime, Prez." She has a towel wrapped around her arm where the bullet grazed her. She's lucky she fell to the floor crying when she was hit; it probably saved her life and also gave her the chance to call my dad.

A gasp escapes me as the knowledge comes to light that she knew who I am and called my dad to tell him I was here. He turns toward me, his eyes soft as he takes me in and begins to speak, but I cut him off.

"How long has she known who I am? Was she calling you every time I was in here?" I fume, with the thought of being watched the entire time. She saw Viking claiming me for heaven's sake. What I do is none of my father's business; he gave up that right many years ago.

"Princess," he starts and I interrupt what I know is about to be some sugarcoated bullshit answer. They always are.

"No. Tell me the truth, damn it. I have a right to know; it's my life."

"I mean, what do you think? You're right down the road from the club, sugar. You're my daughter, and I'm the President of the Oath Keepers. Every bar in the county has had a picture of you and known who you are since you were seventeen years old."

"So...What? You've had people there to spy on me? And what would you have done if I messed up anyhow? You've always been too busy to be a father, so why even care to let them know? Does my privacy mean absolutely nothing to you?"

Hybrid Collection

His eyes become a little glossy as his expression falls flat. "You want the truth, fine. I told them to memorize your face, if you ever showed up, to make sure no one messed with you and if you had any problems ever, to call the club. I paid them well for the favor, but I also threatened to rip their fuckin' guts out if they didn't comply. Like it or not, Princess, you're my kid, and I protect my family."

His words hit my heart like an arrow finding its target. I want to scream and cry, lash out at him with 'why' questions: Why wasn't he there? Why didn't he want us? Why did he hurt everyone? Why weren't we good enough? Why didn't he ever come for us, or actually fucking stay and love us?

I've wondered those things my entire life, but he doesn't deserve my questions, and he hasn't earned my respect to listen to his answers. So, I revert to the only thing that's ever guarded my heart against being completely shattered by him—my words.

Standing a little straighter, I stare down the man standing in front of me. In so many ways we resemble each other. If he had a female version of himself, it would be me; only I don't abandon people that I love.

Many men in this area fear him, never being able to figure out what digs deep, they call him the 'rational' President. He's supposedly the one who thinks everything through and never lets a thing get to him. Well, newsflash, I've had years to perfect just what to say, so it hits home for him. He doesn't get off scot-free ripping our family apart with no repercussions.

I guess I really am like him in one way; I'm the strong one. But I've had to be.

Mimicking him, I shutter any trace of emotion from my face, and then I let the words fly. "I'm with Viking; he's the one who actually protects me. I don't need you; in fact, I've never needed you. My mother stuck around and did everything so you could be a piece of shit sperm donor and go off with your buddies, so please, don't stop now. And while you're gone, do us all a favor and stop breathing."

Brently steps beside us, placing his hand on my arm. "Princess, stop it. You don't know everything."

My father glances sadly at my brother and shakes his head. "No son, don't. Just let it go."

Brently huffs, sending me an irritated glance before letting his hand fall off my arm and moving toward the door.

Glaring spitefully at my father, I practically spit, "I see you've turned him into a good little puppet; nice job, Daddy." I can't help myself; my brother's not the man he used to be, and my father does nothing to steer him from the path he's on. He's going to get Brently fucking killed.

Brently spins suddenly, striding toward me in a rush, bellowing, "Will you just shut the fuck up for once?"

Viking jumps in front of him, stopping Brently mid-stride in his pursuit of me, "Snake, not trying to disrespect you or get involved in your family business and all, but that's my Ol' Lady you're talking crazy to. I won't allow it."

My brother turns toward my father like a good little soldier, waiting for his orders.

"He's right son; she belongs to him. He deals with her, not you."

"She's my fucking sister," Brently argues, and my dad raises his eyebrows. Irritated, my brother meets my hurt gaze. "Fine, you know what? Fuck it. Princess, you wanna act like a spoiled fucking brat? Well, stay the hell away from me."

Viking growls, ready to lay into Brently in my defense, but my brother raises his hands and backs up a few steps, then spins around, storming outside.

Stay away from him? But we've always been there for each other. He was just as screwed up inside as I was growing up. How did I suddenly become the bad guy in all of this? His words slash me inside like razors carving up my flesh. It takes every ounce of pride to stand tall and not start bawling like I want to. Nothing I said was meant to upset my brother.

My father clears his throat, his gaze peering down at my feet as he mumbles, "Sug', when you're ready, we'll talk." He takes a deep breath and turns away.

Passing Viking, my dad pauses long enough to rest his hand on Vike's bicep. I watch intently as he thanks him, expecting my dad to give Viking shit for what just went down, but he doesn't. They shake hands; a mutual respect exchanged and then my father's swiftly out the same door as my brother.

He's gone again. The same as every other time I've seen him in my life. He always takes off, never staying and fighting with me like I wish he would.

"Princess." A raspy grumble comes from the other side of me as Ares angrily follows suit, leaving now that my father's obviously ready and waiting.

I keep quiet as Viking watches the exchange like a hawk.

After a few moments the bar's finally empty, minus the nosey bartender who's stuck cleaning up the huge mess that we've made. Viking strides toward me, pulling me into his embrace. His warmth cocoons me, and I break.

I fucking crumble.

Hybrid Collection

The tears come at me with such a powerful force that my legs give out. I could fall to the floor, and at this moment, I don't care. Everything that just happened with Viking's dad, all the new information and secrets he was hiding from me, from his brothers. After that huge revelation, there was so much hate and violence; I've never seen so much blood before.

The argument with my brother and my father...Brently's words—I can't believe he told me to stay away. I love him; I was protecting us. How can he not see that I'm angry to keep my family from hurting?

Sucking in a sob, my heart and body ache so badly, the only comfort I feel is the heat from this man holding me so desperately, his strength promising me that he'll never let me go. With one arm across my back, keeping me up and against him, he bends a little, tucking his free arm under my butt so he can lift me fully into his embrace.

Complying, I run my hands over his solid chest, wrapping them around his neck and tuck my face against his throat. I'm able to find a sense of peace, being pressed against his heated skin, feeling the pulse beat strongly, reassuring me that he's safe and not leaving me as well.

"Shhh, Cinderella; I've got you, baby," he rumbles quietly, and I feel him start to walk, carrying me to his hotel room.

I try to quiet and slow the tears, but no matter what I think of, my body does what it wants. Viking doesn't complain, though; he just holds me tighter to him.

Once we get inside the room, he carefully lays me in the middle of his bed and then takes his boots off. I turn over to my side, giving him my back and tuck my fists under the pillow I'm lying on. My tears still fall freely; they're just silent now.

The bed dips behind me, and I start to protest that I can't possibly turn it off enough to have sex right now. Viking distracts me so much, but at this moment, my body needs time to process and heal. Before I'm able to form the right words, so I don't hurt him by turning him down, he pulls my back into his body.

His heat engulfs me like a blanket, and I'm shocked to realize that I was so cold and alone when he had laid me down. I felt his warmth on the way over here in his arms, but once I was away from him, I felt nothing.

How can someone break through enough that even when your body is in shock, it still recognizes them?

It feels like we're in bed for hours with daylight fading to dusk. I lie completely silent and still against Viking as my tears escape. He doesn't move once, holding me snuggly against him with his right arm. His head is resting on his left bicep as he softly plays with my hair, gently pulling it off my face as he soundlessly watches me cry. He doesn't have to speak to fix me; he holds me, offering his support and comfort.

For a woman like me, that's all I'll ever need.

The brightness outside slowly disappears until it resembles dimmed lights flooding throughout the room as the sun finally sets and my emotions come to a crashing halt. I've found balance again, but my body's exhausted, feeling as if I haven't slept in days.

The tears stop completely, my tender cheeks starting to dry as my eyes get droopy, and it hits me that for the first time besides my mom, I feel cherished by someone. My heart doesn't weep from being devastated anymore because of my father's actions. Sure it still hurts me a great deal, but I can almost picture it mending back together—piece by jagged piece—as someone else fills up all the little voids with glue, making me whole again. Teaching me to open my heart and love again, not to push them away, but pull them near.

With that blissful thought, my eyes close and I whisper the words that have the power to crush me if they wanted to. They could dismantle me in the end, pull me apart by the seams if used against me. But even with that scary vulnerability exposed, he deserves to hear them, because even if he's my undoing, my heart belongs to him.

"I love you, Vike."

The whisper's soft as it leaves my lips, but with the weight of what those three little words mean to me, it may as well have been a shout as I finally admit it to him out loud.

He doesn't skip a beat, continuing to play with my hair. It's okay, though; I didn't expect him to answer me back. I like to believe inside that he truly cares for me, and right now, that's enough.

Snuggling into the pillow as wonderful sleep starts to overtake my senses, Viking breaks the silence with his deep rasp.

"I know, Cinderella."

Holding my breath, not letting myself succumb yet, I wait for him to tell me it's over, that he can't be tied down, even if I am supposed to be his Ol' Lady.

A few beats pass before he continues, "I've loved you since I found you behind that bar and you looked at me like I was your savior instead of a monster."

Hybrid Collection

He grows quiet, and one last tear slips free as my heart sings with his declaration. Moving my hand to his at my waist, he threads our fingers together and pulls me a little tighter. His lips meet the back of my neck sweetly as I fall into the best sleep of my existence.

Eighteen

VIKING

The next morning...

A door slams closed, the noise echoing throughout the small room and disturbing my sleep. Parting my lids, the overly bright sunlight shines in, mocking my splitting headache. Yesterday was a fucking train wreck, to put it mildly.

At some point, Cinderella will hear about me showing up and talking to her father if we end up hanging around the Charter for the barbecue and other get-togethers. Not looking forward to that shit storm.

The bathroom door swings open, my girl coming out with her belongings loaded up in her arms. She heads straight for her purse, dropping everything inside the oversized bag.

"Hey, baby." It comes out sounding extra gruff, my voice a little raw from all the shouting yesterday.

Her fiery gaze meets mine, an eyebrow lifting as I scoot back to sit against the headboard. She ties my wife beater tank at her mid back, so it doesn't swim on her small frame and messily twists her hair up, securing it with a pen from her purse. You'd think with how big the bag is that she'd carry a hair thing in it. Remaining silent, she picks up her cut off shorts from the floor, sliding them on and heads for her flip-flops.

"What're you doing?" I rasp, feeling my forehead wrinkle as my head pounds.

She slips the other shoe on. "Exactly what it looks like. Leaving."

Hybrid Collection

Turning quickly, my feet hit the floor next to my pants. I pull my jeans on, leaving the button unclasped and head over to her so she can't get outside without telling me what's going on.

"You wanna be a little more specific?"

Last night everything seemed to be okay once she calmed down and fell asleep. I know my father scared her, but she's a tough bitch. Besides that, I killed the fucker; she doesn't have to worry about him coming back, ever again. I know my brother will leave her alone, so I don't get why she's upset.

Unless she's pissed at her pops all over again? She's clearly mad about something, as I tower over her, and she glares, probably wishing she could light my ass on fire.

"Nope, sure don't."

"All right, cut the bullshit, Cinderella. The fuck's going on?"

"How should I know? My Ol' Man." She makes quotation marks in the air as she says Ol' Man. "Doesn't tell me anything. I'm just a good little woman, fucking him like I'm supposed to. Guess it makes me the stupid one for thinking we actually had something real."

Pointing my finger close to her face, I warn, "First off, don't you disrespect that title. You'll get a lot of fucking respect you deserve to have from my name being the one attached to it. Second, I don't have any idea what the hell you're talking about. Last night I thought we were straight when you fell asleep. Unless something went down while I was passed out, then shit's still real."

Her gaze lands on the door, and she huffs, "I need to leave," trying to shut me out.

"You can go once we settle this."

"Oh, can I? That's so kind of you. Biker or whoever, you're not my boss and if I want to climb in my car and drive away, then I will." Her stubborn eyes meet mine as she crosses her arms over her chest defiantly.

She's so damn cute, wound up like this.

Smirking, I let out a cocky chuckle, "Baby, if I want you to stay somewhere, you will. You try getting in that car before I say it's okay, and I'll slit your fucking tires."

"You're infuriating. I'll walk if I have to."

"No, you won't. I'll be damned if my woman's walking down that highway. I'll tie you to the bed and eat that pussy until you beg me to let you stay."

"You are pretty talented with that tongue; good to know you don't only use it for lying."

Her retort confuses me. Why would I lie? And about what?

It takes a few seconds until I realize why she's so angry.

"You're pissy 'cause I didn't tell you about my father."

"You're not just some Nomad for the Oath Keepers; you have your own freaking club!"

"You're wrong. That's not my fucking club. I haven't been a Widow Maker in years, and I'll never be again."

Her hands fly up, drastically as she rolls her eyes, "And that name! A widow maker? Yeah, I'd definitely have that on my cut; it sure is something to brag about. I can't believe you haven't told me. Look at the danger you put me in. You kept your past from me, and it almost got me killed. You could have at least told me so I would've been on the lookout."

"You were in the wrong situation, and I'm real sorry about that Princess, but you were never in any danger."

"Look at my arms!" she exclaims, thrusting them out, showing off the ugly bruises my father gave her. "You haven't even seen the cut between my boobs yet. Thank God it wasn't deep!"

My hand goes to her heart, a little rougher than intended and her wide eyes meet mine. "You fuckin' feel that?" Growling angrily, I put pressure on the top of her breast, driving her backward until she hits the wall. "That's your goddamn heartbeat, thumping away. I came for you; I got there as fast as fucking possible, and I killed as many motherfuckers as I had to, to get to you. Don't you tell me that you're hurt unless you're sure you absolutely fucking mean it." And she's wrong; I did see that cut.

Her chest heaves as she gets worked up. "You did save me," she admits quietly, "but you rescued me from your own family that I should have known about."

Sighing deeply, my other hand rakes through my hair, pulling at it in frustration. "I know I fucked up, but you kept your shit from me too." My palm slides over the shirt, stopping at the base of her throat.

"I-I couldn't talk about him to you," she finishes on a whisper, her eyes cresting with tears.

"Yeah, babe, you could. Believe it or not, I do listen to you. I know what it's like to have hate consuming your heart because of fucked-up circumstances."

Hybrid Collection

"He respects you, I could tell. You're angry that I didn't confess, but you already knew who he was to me, didn't you?"

Nodding, I watch as a tear falls down her cheek, then a second, and another, until I can't take them anymore and use my thumbs to wipe her cheeks, wanting her tears to dry. "Shhhh, calm down, everything's all right."

"But it's not." Her lip wiggles as her tears come full force, and I drag her into my arms, holding her tightly to my chest.

"What's going on in that head of yours?"

"You'll hate me," she replies, her voice muffled by my shirt.

"Cinderella, I don't know how you haven't noticed by now, but I'm fucking batshit crazy in love with you. I can't see myself hating you anytime soon, babe."

Her words make me uneasy, but I won't give that away to her. Staring ahead at the beige painted wall, I attempt to swiftly prepare myself mentally for whatever she's going to say.

"I slept with you on purpose."

That's not what I was expecting to leave her mouth, and it almost makes me laugh. "I sorta got that when you rubbed your cum on my lips and flashed me your cunt while you were playing pool."

"God, I'm such a slut."

"Nah, I fucking loved every minute seeing you like that."

"I hooked up with another biker before you."

My hackles rise at the mention of another member. I don't give a shit who the biker is; she belongs to me now.

Princess leans back to look at me, her face red and splotchy from crying, "Me and Bethany had a plan so I could get back at my father."

"Go on."

"I met one of my dad's Prospects before you came along. I used him to upset my father, and I was planning to do the same with you, but you wouldn't let me. Once I was with you, I couldn't even think of anyone else."

"You fuck any of the brothers?" The Prospect was nothing, and I took care of him right away anyhow. No sweat off my back but she better fess up if there was one I don't know about.

"No. You're the only biker I've slept with."

"Good answer."

"It's the truth," she responds, and I close the distance between us.

My palm slides up her shirt, squeezing her full tit as my lips find hers. My other hand eagerly unclasps her shorts button, as my tongue swipes against hers passionately. Within seconds I'm inside her jean shorts, my fingers moving in circles against her clit.

Her dainty hands fly to my jeans, shoving them off my hips as she becomes immersed in sexual need. Her tight fist wraps around my cock eagerly, pumping away with purpose. Tearing my lips from hers, I order hoarsely, "Get on your knees." It's been too long since I've had her. I need to be inside of her now, especially after she gets all mouthy and emotional. She's so fucking beautiful all tearstained and vulnerable, eager to love and please me.

"My knees?" she repeats in a daze.

"Now, Princess."

For once she does exactly what she's told, holding onto my thighs as she drops to the floor directly in front of my cock. Without hesitation, she takes me in as far as she can. It feels incredible, and I'm probably not going to last long like this.

"Deeper, I want to hear you choke on it."

She complies, taking me in several times until she starts to gag. Her reflex and throat massages the sensitive tip making my precum trickle out excitedly.

"Holy fuck, you're gonna make me come so hard like that." Groaning, my mouth hangs open slightly as I watch the fucking goddess in front of me.

Sweat builds on my brow as my nuts begin to tighten in anticipation, yet she continues the pleasurable torture, barely hesitating to catch her breath. Wetness coats her cherry colored swollen lips and chin, making Princess the sexiest bitch I've ever seen before.

She goes even farther on her next pass, causing one of my hands to fly to the wall, steadying my body, so I don't fall over from my knees becoming weak. *She's so damn good.*

"Fuck baby, you wanna swallow my cum, or you want me to fill you up somewhere else?"

She pulls back briefly, staring up at me with desire filling her eyes, continuing to work my cock over with her fist. "I want to please you, Viking. Where do you want it?"

Fuuuuuck. I could shoot all over the place right now with that look and those words.

"I want my cum all over you, especially that pretty face and pink pussy."

Hybrid Collection

Licking her lips, she nods, then bends forward to suck my cock some more. Each pass, she copies my fingers from earlier, swirling her tongue around the head of my cock and sending me one step closer to bliss. My dick begins to throb, and she sits back on her heels, busily pumping me.

The next time I glance down, she's eagerly watching me, her face tilted upwards with her mouth wide open and waiting.

"God, I love that look. I'm going to fuck you so good and hard, everyone will be able to tell I've been beating that pussy up."

A loud growl escapes as cum bursts from my cock, the hot liquid spraying her flushed cheeks and mouth. Halfway through my climax, I spread my seed over her puffy lips and then shove my dick inside. The last of my offering is welcomed by her tongue, as she savors it in her mouth, waiting for me to give her permission to swallow.

"Damn, Cinderella, you make one hell of an Ol' Lady." Muttering, I pull her to her feet and shed my shirt to clean her face for her. "Swallow it."

She nods, softly moaning to herself afterward.

Once she's all taken care of, I walk her over to the bed, having her lie down. My hand shoots between her thighs ready for my turn to play. "Spread those sexy thighs for me, baby."

"I thought you'd need a few minutes?" She gasps as I find her clit again.

"Fuck that, now open up so I can watch as I finger fuck that sugary cunt."

With each pump of my fingers her core clenches, trying to pull them in further, her pussy creaming around my knuckles.

"I swear if I can eat you out every day of my life, I'll die a happy man."

"The stuff you say to me, it's crazy. I'm not used to anyone talking to me like that, and it makes me want you constantly."

Pulling my fingers free, I use the wetness to insert them in her ass while my tongue hungrily swipes up any leftover juice in her slit. Her honey hits my taste buds, and my cock instantly stiffens, ready for more.

"Ahhh!" she calls out, her body tightening up on me.

Keeping up my assault, I run my tongue from her pink folds, spreading her wetness down her taint, eventually pushing cream and saliva into her back entrance. She goes wild, her body squirming and as soon as it's lubed enough, my digits go right back in, working her over as my lips slurp her slit and suck on her clit.

I don't stop until she screams, coming all over my chin and lips. Like the greedy bastard that I am, I lick up every last drop my tongue can find then flip her onto her stomach.

"Oh my god!" she mumbles into the bedspread.

Grabbing her hips, I prop her ass in the air, rubbing my tip all over her cunt until she starts gyrating, attempting to get my dick to slip in farther. After a few moments of teasing her, I line myself up with her asshole. She stills just like I figured she would, sliding my hand around her hip and between her thighs, I find her core. Shoving three fingers in deep, I plant my cock in her ass at the same time.

"Please not like the first night," she whispers, but even low, I can still hear the tears in her voice.

I loved the first night.

Stilling, I take it down a notch and start kissing up her back, pausing next to her ear to murmur, "I don't think you realize how much control you really have, Cinderella. I loved the first night, but I love you so much more. Tell me what you want, baby; tonight is all yours."

Nineteen

VIKING

Saturday...

"**All right, take a** seat."

Nancy, the bartender, was nice enough to let us borrow the bar for an hour before she has to come in and do her daily setup. Scot offered to take her to lunch on my dime, and she excitedly obliged. I had no clue that she's the one who owns the place. I've gained a lot of respect for that lady since I've been here.

"Stacy, the chick that helps out at night here, dropped off some muffins and shit that she baked. Help yourselves, just remember it next time you leave her a tip."

Everyone eagerly grabs three or four different muffins, munching away, content. I'm glad they have something to help smooth over what I'm about to discuss with them. "Odin, grab a few pitchers of water and some plastic cups."

"Seriously?" He cocks his eyebrow at me like I'm fucking nuts.

"You want a real shot at being in the MC? You want to go to the barbecue later?"

"You're really going to boss me around and shit now, huh?" He so much like me, it's unreal. Princess told me last night that she's going to go bald in a few years having two of us broody assholes around. I just laughed and asked if she'd bake us a cherry pie.

Breathing deeply, I attempt to tune in the patience that Princess has been helping me with the past few days. "We talked about this yesterday. I'm not fucking Jekyll, and things will be changing, for you, me, for all of us." I glance around at the brothers surrounding our makeshift church table. We pushed a few small square tables together, and I'm at the head. Blaze and Torch are at my sides.

Eventually, Odin will take his spot beside me. He's my brother, and once I'm able to teach him about true brotherhood like I've learned with the Nomads, he'll become my Vice President. Right now, though, he's not allowed at the table. My father treated him like a regular member, so he was pissed to hear he'd been essentially demoted. What he doesn't understand is that he should have been treated like a kid and never even saw the table in the first place.

Smokey's at the end along with Bronx, he's the new kid I had gut checked outside the bar. I think with Ares and Exterminator getting hits in after me, the kid was traumatized enough to welcome some change. Butters and Charlie would be down there as well, but they're dead. Can't say that I care either. If anything, I'm glad because they were fucking scum, just like Jekyll.

Rapping my knuckles on the table, everyone's gazes fall to me.

"First off, let's make one thing clear, I'm not Jekyll," I repeat myself from earlier, but this time to the brothers. "Got it?"

I'm met with 'ayes' all around, and surprisingly they seem excited about that aspect. It shouldn't be a surprise I suppose with the miserable tyrant my father was. Odin comes back setting everything in the middle of us, then sits back at the bar as I instructed him to when we first arrived. Glad he's paying attention.

"What's the deal with the clubhouse?" We used to have a rundown building in the middle of nowhere that the MC drank and discussed business. It wasn't anything compared to the Compounds I've grown used to in the past few years.

Torch speaks up, "We use it as a chop shop now when we're home."

"Fuck. You'll get popped and do years in the pen."

Blaze huffs, his eye still a deep purple from my fist finding out that he touched my woman's hair. "A few of us tried to say that, but you know when Jekyll got an idea, it was no stopping him."

"Who ran it?"

"That was O's contribution."

I swear to Christ my eyes bug the fuck out of my head. "My brother?"

Everyone nods, not meeting my eyes.

One, two, three, fifty, a hundred, think of Princess, don't break anyone's face, and just breathe.

"No more. It ends now. Blaze, find someone you can hire to gut it out and fucking burn everything."

He chuckles. "And how do we pay for this?"

"Who usually handles the books?"

"Charlie, but there wasn't much of anything to be counted. The money we're using now to be here was from our recent drug sale on the way over here."

"Fuck. Okay, was it a decent pay out?"

"We each got a five hundred dollar cut."

"You fuckin' with me right now?" How can you do a drug run and only cut your men five bills for serious possible jail time? That doesn't build loyalty; it builds rats and sellouts when they're presented with more paper.

"Odin, call my woman and ask her to stop by with five g's."

Everyone stares at me, shocked and silent.

"That's bad business and bad dealing. I'll give you each a grand. Don't go screw it off on blow. Save a few hundred for shit you need to take care of. From now on, we'll be voting on club business. Temporarily, I'd like for Blaze to sit as my VP until Odin is ready. It could be two years or ten, who knows. Torch deserves the Death Dealer patch. Smokey if you're still decent with numbers, you can start up the books and trade your patch for Treasurer? We need a decent cash counter, and I'll be paying close attention to all of it. Bronx, we'll give it a little time and see if you get something other than member. Everyone agree to that?"

They all reply 'aye' except Blaze.

"I'll lose my Death Dealer patch? But what happens when Odin is ready to take over as VP?"

"You can have your Death Dealer patch back, or we can vote on a different one if that's what you want."

"Okay, I vote 'aye.'"

"We'll be recruiting, but not many. I want us to get our feet on the ground and adapt before growing too much. There were at least nine more when I was at home. Where is everyone?"

Blaze takes a drink of water and replies since everyone else stays quiet. "Dead."

"Fuck." I shake my head, nine dead, plus the two from the other day, eleven members. That's horrible. "I'm meeting with the Prez from the Oath Keepers

Charter here later. I want to see if he'll offer us a patch over and a few potential business partners."

"What the fuck? South Carolina already has an OK Chapter," Smokey declares. Being an older member of the MC, I'm expecting a lot of fight from him.

"I know, which will give you three options. One, if this patch over happens, you will be given the option to leave. Two, you will have a place in the South Carolina Charter or pretty much any other location. I actually know the Prez down there, and he's a good man. Three, I will step up and run my family's club, but my Ol' Lady's life is here. As it turns out, my life is going to be here with her, so my chapter will be built in this area, and you will be offered a place in it. I won't have the Compound in this exact place, but close. There's many clubs in Austin, and they have a good relationship with the Oath Keepers."

Torch sighs, "Well fuck, some of us can't afford to just pick up and move our shit; I have a little girl to think about."

"Actually, since there's only a few of you, yes, you can. I'll make sure you get here."

"And where will we sleep, what will we eat? I wasn't really getting by, and that's with anything from the club and a part-time job."

"I'll look into purchasing land and start a build on a basic clubhouse. Singles can have a room there, but you'll have to keep it clean. Anyone with a family or kids, we'll get it figured out."

Bronx interrupts, "I'm in; I don't need to go back at all."

Smokey takes a drag of his cigarette, rasping, "And where will this money come from exactly?"

"For the past five years, I've bought a new bike, food and stayed in occasional cheap-ass motels. I don't have a lot, but I have enough to put a chunk down to get started. I'm gonna ask my Ol' Lady's father for input and help. The Oath Keepers are different from the Widows; they make some pretty damn good cheddar. It'll be tough at first; I'm not going to lie, but I believe in a few years, shit will be really good."

Blaze sits up. "I'm in."

Smokey releases the toxic smoke from his lungs as he talks, "Why would you do this for us? You took off when Jekyll fucked you up and sent you on a stripe, never coming back."

"Because that stripe saved my life, they took me in and showed me what brotherhood is. After experiencing it, I know everyone deserves it."

He nods.

"That's another thing, the Nomads. You saw them the other day, except for one. If this works, I'm inviting them to join the Chapter and just saying this up front; they'll be full members and offered officer patches."

A few grumble and it takes everything inside to tamper down my temper.

"That's fine, you feel that way, but one saved my ass the other morning from a fucking lion. How many of you know of a brother that has your six like that? I've never met a more loyal, fearless group of men before. Do not underestimate any of them, ever."

Bronx rolls his eyes, but he'll learn when Ex beats the hell out of him for that shit.

"We're all invited to their barbecue later, and I think it would be in our best interest to go and make friends. The Prez offered to let you stay in their guest rooms if needed. I know a few of the members from handling a job with them and stopping through on runs. You can relax around them and have a beer; they won't try to kill you in your sleep. You'll get a good look at the Oath Keeper life." They stay silent, so I figure it's time to call it to an end. "Anyone have anything to add?"

Torch nods. "We're in."

Smokey follows. "Yup, me too. Been wanting to get outta SC for years, just wasn't able to."

"Welcome to Texas, brothers."

Rapping my knuckles against the table to note the end of the first church I've conducted, I'm wearing a smile when it's over.

PRINCESS

Having Odin ask me for five grand in cash, had me a little skeptical, but being Viking's brother, I figure I should give him a chance. I went to drop it off, and he climbed in the car asking if he could come back to the apartment with me instead of staying with his older brother. I ended up taking him with me grocery shopping to get a few things for the barbecue tonight, and we left with two hundred dollars' worth of food.

To see him so excited over having that much food, kind of broke my heart a little. He shared with me that he never really went grocery shopping like that before. I guess he only visited the store for basic things that he could stretch out to last him a long time, like peanut butter and bread. Once I heard that I encouraged him to throw whatever he wanted into the cart. Viking had stuffed five hundred dollars in my purse a few days prior, making up for all the food I was cooking them, but I didn't want to use it. If it's for his brother, though, then I don't mind.

Never in a million years would I have thought that he's only fifteen. I knew he was young, but he's weathered for his age, and that makes me so sad for him. My father sucked, but Odin grew up without love, like my Viking. And shit can he eat; my God, he clears his plate and eats anything else I load it with.

Viking had brought his stuff over to my apartment so Odin would be able to sleep on the couch and not be left alone. He's worried that Odin may get pissed about something and just leave without letting us know. I was a little nervous about them being in my space twenty-four hours a day, but I love it. I didn't realize before that I was so lonely all the time when Bethany wasn't around.

I've loved having Viking talk to me a lot over the past few days and ask my opinions on everything. We've been trying to come up with a plan that would make us both happy. He's so distraught about the fact that he has to leave the Nomads. They're his family, people who get him and don't judge. Now he's being thrown into something he never wanted in the first place.

When he told me that he was going to stay here and be home a lot, I almost did cartwheels I was so excited about it. He wants to find a small two-bedroom house for us to rent, so he can give Odin some stability here, and I can't blame him. After meeting Jekyll, Odin's going to need every ounce of help and structure he can get. I'm young and know jack about teenagers, but I swore to Vike that I'd do my best and support him as much as I can.

My father and I haven't spoken since our blowup, but I've been thinking a ton about what all he and my brother were saying. I was so upset that I didn't pay much attention at the time it was all happening. Now, though, I'm growing curious.

We stopped by my mom's yesterday, but again, she wasn't home. I wanted her to get to meet Viking. It was the same way as before with my dad and brother's Softails parked there and the truck missing. I'm starting to freak out; it's been two months since I've physically seen her and about a month that we've spoken to each other and not just in random messages.

Viking told me that he was meeting with Prez today but that he wasn't going to the barbecue. I'm relieved I won't have to worry about a confrontation, but I was kind of hoping to at least ask if he's seen her. I just want to make sure she's okay. In her last message she sounded like she was desperate to see me, but now it's almost as if she's avoiding me.

There's nothing I can do, besides keep trying and ask my dad or Brently if I see them.

Once my mom's famous Italian pasta salad is complete, I paint on some light makeup and dig through my closet. I need to find something that's fit for a biker bitch to wear but also says I'm the Ol' Lady to a President of an outlaw MC. One benefit of having my mom as the Prez' Ol' Lady, she knew how to dress.

Settling on some thigh-high black leather boots with four-inch heels, I pair them with a cherry red leather miniskirt and my black Harley tank top. Finishing the look, I use a blood red lipstick that's smudge proof and tie my hair in a high ponytail. We'll be riding his bike, and I'm not showing up with my hair looking like a hot mess.

His stack of bandanas that I washed sits folded perfectly on the counter spurring my idea further. I pick out the nicest looking black one, fold it a few times and wrap it over my hair. It reminds me of those workout headbands you use to hold your bangs back; only this one is much more badass.

"Odin, do you drive? I can't carry the pasta salad on Viking's bike; the bowl's too large." He doesn't respond, so I turn around to make sure I'm not waking him up or something.

I'm met with large eyes and his mouth slightly hanging open.

"Odin?"

"You're wearing that?"

"Umm, yes. Is it not good?"

"Do you want my brother to kill someone tonight? 'Cause if you wear that outfit, that's what will end up happening."

"Whatever, it'll be fine." I laugh and roll my eyes. "Do you drive?"

"I can."

"Perfect, I need you to follow us with the pasta salad."

"Cool."

"Thanks."

He nods and the front door opens; Viking's finally back.

"Hey! How'd it go?"

Viking takes his boots off next to the door like I previously asked him to and started peeling the few chunky rings he wears and such off, not glancing up yet.

"Fucking perfect. We did a little tweaking and shit, but overall it's going to work out. We're going to settle about twenty miles out at an old pig farm. Best fuckin' part is, your dad's gonna work with me on making him payments so I can start the build on the club right away."

"That's amazing news!"

"Yeah, I'm so fucking stoked." He glances up and goes silent, just standing and staring.

"Vike?" I raise my eyebrow.

"I'm going to kill someone tonight," he finally answers, and Odin pops in.

"Told you."

"Should I change?" I don't want to and wouldn't any other time, but this is the first time he's riding with his club to meet another MC. I want it to be his night.

"Fuck no; you're the sexiest woman I've ever seen."

"Hell, yeah," Odin comments and Viking growls.

"Shut up." His eyes glaze over looking at me again. "I need to shower, or we'll never fucking leave." He storms off, and I do a little dance inside, knowing that I've made him proud.

Twenty
PRINCESS

The ride over isn't bad at all; if anything, I'm really starting to enjoy Viking sharing this with me. I know he loves the wind and road when he's on his Harley, and that means something special to me because I love him. Pulling into the Compound is a little nerve racking. I was made to stay away basically my entire life and now to be invited, is just surreal.

The night passes in a blur; Viking's introduced me to so many people. Blaze and Torch actually smiled at me; I thought their faces were going to crack or something. I think my favorites are still the Nomads. I got used to their banter and rough exteriors. Plus, I know they truly have Viking's back, and that's important to me.

God, I wanted so badly to rip Nightmare a new one, but know that I can't. He's Bethany's baby's dad, and she needs to fight that battle when she's ready. I'll always support her decisions even if I don't agree with them.

However, I was a little taken back though when he was talking to me like nothing was different. Nightmare has to know I'd be pissed at him on my best friend's behalf. Once he said hello and started telling me that Viking had to patch him up on their run, I just walked off in the middle of him talking. He's Vike's brother, not mine.

I met the Oath Keepers Ol' Ladies, which was interesting. They all have big personalities, and you can tell they love their own type of sisterhood that they've formed. I was nervous, but Ares and 2 Piece's Ol' Lady, Avery, walked right up to me and started talking like she'd known me for years. I couldn't believe it when she told me she had two Ol' Men; I wasn't sure if I should feel bad for the woman or congratulate her.

There was also a rumor floating around that my dad may pass the gavel to his VP, who happens to be Ares. I was freaking shocked, and now I do want to speak to him. The only part of the night I'd take back if I could, would be catching Odin with an Oath Keeper's little sister bent over the trunk of my damn car.

Pretty sure that it was Spin's little sister too, but I'm pretending like I didn't see a thing. Maybe Oath Keeper women will end up falling for Widow Maker men, who knows. I did warn Vike, though, and he had a 'talk' with Odin. The kid was mortified, but it was hilarious and the least he deserved. I don't think he understands what kind of hell he can stir up for himself messing with a biker's little sister.

After this brief time, I'm starting to see why my mom loved this life in so many ways; I can understand why it made her so happy with my father. Bikers don't just love you; they obsess over you. With that fierce love, comes a protection like no other, willing to kill for their women at a drop of a hat. Getting together didn't make me feel uncomfortable or out of place like I imagined it would. I felt like I was finally home and surrounded by family. I was hugged and welcomed, complimented on my food and asked to come back.

If this is club life, no wonder my father loves it, because I do too.

VIKING
The following day…

Yesterday I met with Prez and my Nomad brothers. I wanted everyone's opinion on my ideas to merge the club over. They were a little hesitant at first, but once I explained all of it out in detail, they were much more open then I'd expected.

There was a vote, and I was named the new President of a hybrid Charter. Prez said he'd contact the other Charters to inform them of us and the decision. After being a part of the Oath Keepers, I know what types of men are in the MC, and I'm pretty honored to be a President affiliated with them.

Ares was in that meeting and surprisingly he approved of the plans.

I also found out about the run to Mexico we pulled since Exterminator was there. He said that he let the cop know about the maid and then hours later some mafia guys in suits showed up and took her. According to Ex, the Russians are on a massive manhunt for one of their sisters that were taken. The cop asked to use us in the future, and Ex agreed as long as there are no exotic animals involved.

I'm hoping with the time it'll take to build our Compound and get everything set up that my Nomad brothers will trade their wanderer patch for one that says Texas. I can't think of any better men to have in my club.

Nightmare showed up to the meeting. He thought Ex was bullshitting him about everything that was going down and he needed proof. It was pretty fuckin' hard to watch him walk in using a cane. He claimed that once it's healed, he won't need it, but I was the one who saw the gash first, and I'd be surprised if he ever walked without it again. He was at the party but stayed sitting, so I had missed it.

Scot came too. He asked the brothers to approve his request to hand in his Nomad patch. He's not planning on leaving Nancy anytime soon and asked to be a part of my hybrid crew. I was honored.

Being surrounded by my brothers made me realize just how lucky Odin is going to be. He not only has Princess fawning all over him, feeding him too much, but he's going to learn the true meaning of brotherhood and loyalty.

Before I left yesterday, Prez pulled me to the side and requested I bring my woman to her mom's house. I tried to let him know I wasn't getting in the middle of their relationship shit, but he reassured me it's because her mom needs to see her and that he wouldn't cause trouble.

We're headed to her house now, and I'm a tad bit nervous how she'll take the news of Princess and me. Of course, I won't care if she's not welcoming, but I want this part of our relationship to be somewhat easy on my woman. She's already dealt with way too much when it comes to me and our family drama.

"You straight, Cinderella?" I check as we dismount off my bike.

I've been asking her randomly ever since I found out how bad her anxiety can get. I never want to see my Ol' Lady shut down like she did when my father had her. She admitted that it happened the first night we saw each other also with the attack. I guess she felt strong with me there beside her, but that once she was away from me her tears and shakes set in for a few hours.

"I'll be fine; I'm just happy we're finally getting a chance to visit, and you're meeting her."

"Me too, baby." I place a swift peck on her lips and follow her up the pathway.

We climb the stairs to the porch, and she stops mid-stride. "The door's painted," she mutters softly.

"Yeah?"

Clearing her throat after a moment, she knocks on the front door. Pulling her hand to her chest, she rubs her knuckles with her fingertips. I don't know what's up with the sudden weirdness, but somethings gotten to her.

Her brother opens the door, stepping out of the way for us to enter. "P." He greets her, then turns to me, "Viking." He nods and I return it.

Prez comes into the dainty living room looking exhausted; he has dark bags under his eyes, and he's dressed in plain clothes. You'd never guess that he's the President of an MC, seeing him like this.

The couch has sheets, and a pillow pushed carelessly to the side and a half eaten grilled cheese sits on the coffee table in front of it. Princess notices and becomes annoyed, "Geez Brent, you need to clean up your crap. You're too old to be making Mom do it. Did you move back in?"

He huffs, "No, of course not. That's Dad's, not mine."

Prez approaches us, "Heya, sug', thanks for coming," he says to Princess then turns to me shaking my hand, "Brother."

"Brother," I respond, paying him the same respect.

"Mom?" Princess calls but gets no answer.

Prez cuts straight in, "We need to talk about your momma."

"What's wrong with her? What did you do this time?"

PRINCESS

Furious at the mess my dad's left my mother to deal with, I question him, ready for him to admit that he's staying here to have her wait on him like he sometimes does. He'll walk through the door after being gone months, and you'd swear he was a long lost king or something with how my mom treats him.

His hand tangles in his overly long sandy hair as his head drops, his eyes on the floor instead of meeting my irate gaze. He opens his mouth to say something, but then a huge crash comes from my mom's bedroom.

"I've got it, Dad," Brently jumps, but my dad rushes in front of him.

"No son! Not unless it's absolutely necessary."

"It is, talk to Princess so that she can stop this bullshit."

"Excuse me?" I gape at him. Who the fuck does he think he is, suddenly being a dick to me all the time. I've barely walked in the freaking house.

Hybrid Collection

A moan comes next from my mom's room, and I quickly skirt around the table, beelining for the bedroom door.

"Wait!" My father shouts, but I ignore him, throwing the door open.

"Mom?" It takes a second to see a table knocked over with stuff spilled everywhere. I find her on the floor, crumpled in a small, frail ball, a small amount of throw up beside her.

"Shit! Mom! Are you okay?" Rushing over to her side, I start to help turn her over when I'm stopped by a firm hand. My head shoots up, finding my father's stern gaze.

"Don't move her like that," he orders and I yank my shoulder out of his grip.

"Get off me; I'll take care of her. I always make sure she's okay."

"I know," my dad croaks as tears start to fall down his cheeks. I've only seen him cry one time in my life, and I thought I had hallucinated it all. "I know you do sweetheart, and I'll owe you for the rest of my life for taking such good care of the woman I love."

"What are you talking about?" I'm so fucking confused. What is going on?

His shoulders shake as sobs begin to take over. Brently comes in to help Mom to bed, and Dad just bawls, so much to the point that I start crying. It's so fucking scary to see the man that you've always known to be unreadable and hard, crack before your eyes.

"Dad, talk to me please, what the hell's happening?" I glance at my mom, clearly on a ton of medication looking the weakest I've ever seen her. Brently fixes her pillow and softly wipes off her cheek with a baby wipe.

That's when I notice it...I see a big piece of her hair's missing, and I know exactly why she's been so absent. She's been hiding it from me. With a hoarse cry I turn to my father, my watery eyes overfilling and blurry to where I can only make out his shape. "God no! Please, no, please, please, please tell me she's okay. I have to be wrong; this can't be happening."

"I'm so sorry, sugar."

"No!" A guttural bark leaves my mouth, shaking my head.

"I'm sorry," he repeats, and I get so irate inside.

"Fuck. You! Get out of my mom's house, you piece of shit! Get the fuck out, all of you; she was fine when I was here with her!"

Viking forcibly wraps his huge arms around my body, pulling me up off the floor and carrying me out into the living room while I scream at everyone, blaming them for this tragedy. It's not an easy feat for him as I kick and scream, weeping that my mother is in that bed dying, and he's taking me away from her.

"Shhh, Cinderella," he repeats softly into my hair, tightly cocooning me in his warmth until I'm too sad and worn out to fight any longer. The one person that's been there for me my whole life, my constant, is lying in that bed, struggling for her life. And no one told me before it was so late.

Once I'm silently crying, he sits on the small sofa with me in his lap, sweetly playing with my hair like he did the night he saw me freak out. The thought of my mother looking so frail is terrifying. She's always been so stubborn and strong, her only weakness being my father, and now this.

My dad and brother eventually come out of her room and sit on the couch, both with their own tears coating their scruffy faces.

Viking, ever my strength, starts talking. "I can understand why this wasn't said over the phone, but Princess should have been notified sooner. How can she have time to make peace?" he directs at my father.

"None of us have. My wife's been sick for a long time, but she's kept it from her family. She's always been like that, though when something's been wrong with her. I came over one night and found her passed out on the kitchen floor. The doctor said by her body and tests that she had probably been there for longer than twenty-four hours. We don't know if she was out the whole time or not, but he said her body shut down to throw it in protection mode and that if it would have been longer, then she would have most likely passed. That was about two months ago."

"When you started answering her phone?" I ask quietly.

His defeated gaze meets mine. "Yeah. Then it progressed so rapidly. She told me she could beat it, and she didn't want either of you to know unless it looked like she wouldn't make it. The minute she had an ounce of energy, I'd call you and have her leave you messages. This last week's been the worse; she was in the hospital for most of it. I was hoping she would bounce back, but at this point, there's no telling. It's up to her body and the medicine to work together and fight back."

"She can't have surgery or something to get it removed?"

"Not until she makes it through this round of medicine. Believe me, honey, I'm on them, calling her doctors daily, leaving messages about her having surgery. I even tried to bribe the doctors with the money I have set aside for you guys. Ares went as far as threatening to kill one surgeon. I had to talk him down and pay the man off. He wasn't even the right kind of doctor had he gotten the guy to agree eventually. It's been one giant clusterfuck."

"So what do we do then?" Sitting up, Viking's big hands wipe away my tears, always taking care of me.

"We wait and see, but in the meantime, you tell her you love her as much as you can."

"I can do that." I nod. "Does she have a nurse that helps out?"

"Yeah, but she doesn't like anyone seein' her like that. You know how beautiful your momma's always been and stubborn. She doesn't like help when she's sick."

"So what happened in there earlier?"

"If she wakes and is going to be sick, she tries to make it on her own instead of saving her energy like we beg her to do."

"I don't even know what to say."

"You don't have to say anything, sug'."

"I'm surprised you're here so much. Is that why there's rumors about Ares being President?"

He nods. "Yeah, I uh, I told him that I've had to stay away from her long enough, I'm not wasting anymore time."

"You could have been here the entire time; you made her fall apart every time you left. I was the one behind with her, helping her pull it back together. You didn't just do it once either; you did it over and over, and she'd be a mess for days, weeks; hell, sometimes for a full month. But now that she's sick, you want to play hero?" I can't stop the words tumbling out as my emotions spiral.

"I know. I tried to stay away, but I loved her too much. I'd stay gone for as long as I could handle, but I always came home eventually."

"Ha. That sounds pathetic; really you had to stay away? Really? We were your family, your wife, and children. We wanted you!"

"I know it, but I couldn't fucking help it!" His voice increases as his eyes start to dry. "I had to stay away. It wasn't my choice; it was for your safety after I received threat-amongst threat against you all. I had to keep you safe. I knew if you hated me, you'd stay away from me and no one could get to you. I get it; I fucked up your life. I know that, and I live with it every fucking day. You don't think I wanted my life?" He points toward my mom's room, "That woman has owned me since I first laid eyes on her!"

"So what's different now that you can come right back into everything?"

"My son is grown and has brothers that will help him if needed. My beautiful daughter is the Ol' Lady of the President of an MC club, who'd blow up half the fucking country to find her. You're both safe, *finally*. If they come for me, well they can have my life. I only care about my wife being alive and healthy and my children."

"Look, Dad, I want to believe you, I really do. I promise to try, okay?" My mother's sick, she wouldn't want her family fighting like this. If I have to bite the bullet and back off, I will.

This whole time, I was trying to protect her, and I'd even go to extreme lengths to do it, just like my father did. I only wish that I'd known that I was protecting her against the wrong thing. I was too busy hating my father when I should have been loving my mother.

Thank God, I've found a love so strong with Viking because I'm going to need the extra backbone and support when I help my mom kick cancer's ass. She's a stubborn Ol' Lady who leads the pack; in my heart, I know she'll win, and she'll finally get her man.

Epilogue

PRINCESS

One year later...

"Get more plates!" I yell toward the main room at Odin.

"Yes, ma'am," he calls back, using his sweet manners he's developed over the past year. Viking's been ruthless about Odin growing into a decent man and not like Jekyll. When we finally have kids of our own, they're going to be little angels or risk getting 'the talk' from Viking all the time. I love his voice, but he can drone on to teenagers, and they hate that shit.

Odin comes in carrying a stack, stopping at the end of the table, "Where do you need them?"

"That's fine; you can stack them there and then when everyone comes in they can fix their plates and either sit with us or wherever. I don't want any pressure since they've been good at letting me take over the clubhouse for the past few days."

"They should be in here helping; you did cook enough food for an army."

Shrugging, I smile kindly at him, "No big deal, it's Thanksgiving, and this is how it should be for everyone."

Nancy passes in the hallway, waving when she notices me. She wanted to help out, and I gladly obliged. She's made all the desserts for tonight, and they look so delicious. I can't wait to try out her key lime pie.

"Are we still stopping by Mom's later?" Odin started calling my mother "Mom" about six months ago. I couldn't be any happier about it either.

"Yep, you're still coming right?"

"Of course."

"Okay, just checking, I didn't know if you had plans with Mercy or not."

He's been dating Spin's younger sister off and on for a while now. The only way Spin agreed not to kill him was because Viking promised to take care of it himself if Odin got her pregnant. Mercy's about to turn sixteen and full of mischief. But she's close to Odin's age, which I love because he spends too much time around adults.

"Nope, I'll be there," he replies as Viking carries food in from the kitchen.

"Damn, Cinderella; this shit smells so fuckin' good."

"I know, I'm starving. Is my dad here yet?"

"Yeah, he's drinking a whiskey."

"Shit, again?"

He nods.

"Try to keep him distracted or pour some water in it, something. I don't want him blurring today out. We need to be happy and eat some good food."

"I got it, baby, don't worry. Ares is here, too. You know that's practically his father too. He'll keep him talking."

"All right, God, I really don't know what I'd do without you. I love you so much, Vike. More every day."

"You want some D, huh?"

Laughing, I shake my head "I say love, and you automatically think of your cock?"

"Hey, I'm pretty sure that's why you fell for me," he says aloud, then mouths out 'cunt crazy.' He's been teasing me about it more here lately with Avery popping up pregnant. He's lost it if he thinks it's happening with me anytime soon. I'm too selfish, I want him all alone, at least for a few more years. I don't think I'll ever get my fill of him.

As we gather around the massive tables we rented for this dinner; I can't help but think about how lucky I am. I'm surrounded by friends and family I adore and sitting next to the man of my dreams that I never even knew I wanted.

Oh, and then there's the billiards table Viking brought home on our anniversary. That alone is enough reason to love him forever.

VIKING

"Hey, Prez?"

"What?" Ares and I answer at the same time, then chuckle. We've grown used to it now since we're together a lot.

It's one of his guys; Shooter comes closer to speak to Ares about a shipment of weapons, and I turn away.

"Brother, you can stay," Ares mumbles.

"Nah, I'm good, I need to go be sociable." Chuckling, I head through the club, just taking it all in.

Every day, I walk through with a cup of coffee, first thing and check everything over. It's surreal knowing that I built this club. We've grown a lot too. It's still Smokey, Blaze, Torch, and Bronx, but now we also have Scot, Nightmare, Saint, Sinner. And our newest brother, Chaos.

When the club was built, I asked all the Nomads to join us, but they weren't ready to trade in their patch yet, which is fine. They stop in from time to time and catch up. I've made it very clear that they'll always have a place here waiting for them.

Growing up, I thought I'd never have anything, and now I feel like I've got it all. I have strong, loyal brothers at my table, and Odin is thriving. He actually walks around smiling sometimes. My club is running successfully, finally making some decent money and I've got the best fuckin' bitch a biker could ever wish for.

ODIN

After we eat, I help Princess clear off the table. I've learned that if I help her out, then she'll let me use her car or take me with her when she grocery shops. I've gained twenty pounds since I came to live with her and my brother. At this rate, I'll be bigger than him in no time.

Making an excuse to be back, I grab my favorite club whore's wrist, tugging her along behind me. They don't realize I'm about to be seventeen, or they do and just don't care. We get to the bathroom, and I pull her into the largest stall, pushing lightly on her shoulders.

Sinking to her knees eagerly, she opens my pants enough to free my stiff cock. The food was good, but once the turkey settled, all I could think of was how damn horny I'd become.

Immediately, she takes my length in her warm, wet mouth as far as she can go, her eyes widening as I get closer to her throat. The club whores like to take turns with me to see if one can make me say anything. I don't moan or talk; I'm there to get off not hear my voice.

She starts in on my favorite move. I like to call it the 'Triple Whammy.' She's the only one who does it, gripping my cock tightly she twists her palm over the base, at the same time she uses her nails to scratch lightly over my sack and continue to suck on my cock. All at once.

Within minutes she has me exploding, pumping my cum down her throat in pure ecstasy.

Once we're cleaned up, I offer to find her later and finger fuck her if she wants. She's a club whore, so of course she agrees.

Mercy sends me a text, freaking out because I haven't messaged her all day, but I ignore it. Instead, I grab the flowers off my dresser that I bought earlier when I went to pick up ice for the club. Tossing them in the passenger seat of Princess' car, I head over to Mom's; thinking on the way about Mercy breaking up with me a few weeks ago. I haven't told anyone about it yet.

Last year when Mom got so sick, we were over there pretty much every day with Princess. When Mom was having a good day, I'd sit in her room with her, and she'd tell me a bunch of crazy stories about everything. Then when she'd had a bad day, I'd hold her hand and tell her how important she was to us all.

My brother thinks I've made changes because of him, but it was really for her. I didn't want mom to know my cold side, especially when she filled my heart with so much love.

Picking up the flowers, I remove the outer plastic wrap, throwing it on the floorboard. She was in luck at the store; I found her favorites, a big bundle of Gerbera daisies. I try not to slam the door as I climb out, but the wind catches it, making the noise echo around me.

Princess still meets me with a friendly wave regardless. She thinks she's like her father, which she is, but she's also filled to the brim with warmth from her mother.

My brother lets her go long enough for her to wrap me in a hug and smell the flowers. Tilting her head up, her eyes shiny with tears, she smiles softly and whispers, "She will love them, Odin. You make me so proud to have you in my life."

When she releases me, I bend; kneeling at Mom's grave to whisper how much I miss her, but also to thank her for leaving me with someone who loves me.

Hybrid Collection

Note:

This may not be the ending you were hoping for. It wasn't for me either. I cried the entire time I wrote it, even during the sexy times because I could feel where this story was taking me, and I was fighting it. I'm still crying as I write this. I feel like I'm betraying Prez by not giving him his happily ever after, but through life comes hardships. While this is fiction, I want to bring you pieces of realistic hardships people face as well.

I want you to smile at funny parts, get excited during a sex scene, anxious when there's suspense and most of all I want you to cry if a part makes you sad enough to. If any of that happens, then I did my job by making you *feel*. If you were able to experience even a fraction of what I felt when writing it, then thank you. That's the best compliment I can receive.

XOXO Sapphire

an
oath keepers mc
novel
DAYDREAM
INTERNATIONAL BESTSELLING AUTHOR
SAPPHIRE KNIGHT

Hybrid Collection

Daydream

Copyright © 2017 by Sapphire Knight

Cover Design by CT Cover Creations

Editing by Mitzi Carroll

This book is a work of fiction. The names, characters, places, and incidents are products of the writer's imagination or have been used fictitiously and are not to be construed as real. Any resemblance to persons, living or dead, actual events, locales or organizations is entirely coincidental.

All rights reserved. With the exception of quotes used in reviews, this book may not be reproduced or used in whole or in part by any means existing without written permission from the author.

The author acknowledges the trademarked status and trademark owners of various products referenced in this work of fiction, which have been used without permission. The publication/use of these trademarks is not authorized, associated with, or sponsored by the trademark owners.

DEDICATION

I don't even know who this one should be dedicated to honestly. I think I'm going to say this one is for me. I missed my bikers like crazy, and Daydream poured from my fingertips in a matter of weeks. That's never happened to me so quickly before, and I'm over the moon, completely grateful and proud of myself.

I reached a new personal goal that I didn't realize I had tucked away inside. After publishing so many books it's easy to lose focus of the little things; writing Daydream brought that focus back.

So whoever helped motivate and inspire me, thank you.

This one is for me, for you, for all of us.

PROLOGUE

NIGHTMARE

15 Years Old...

She's crying again. I hate it when they cry, makes me feel sick inside. My stomach churns as her hands cover her face and my father rolls his eyes at her. He hurt her; he hurts them all. They treat him like a king, and he breaks them. *Every. Single. One.*

"Come on, Dad, let's finish." I try to distract him.

"We are son. Had to teach the stupid bitch a lesson."

Her shoulders shake as her silent weeps rack her thin body. He's a bastard, and I hate him for it. He's the only person I have in my life, so in same aspect, I love him. He's my father—abusive drunk or not. This one makes wife number four. They're always young and beautiful and so, so dumb for believing his lies.

"I can't believe we're almost done." I splash some gasoline over the rebuilt carburetor so he can try and crank it over.

"This old beast will be good as new. Hell, even better—just you watch, boy. Nothing like a three-fifty small block in a Chevy like this. She'll blow any motherfucker away who tries to come up next to us." He cackles and climbs behind the wheel, taking a large sip of his beer as he slides onto the seat.

I push the piece of metal a few times that my dad pointed out last time. It pumps gasoline into the system without flooding it if you do it the right amount of times.

"Here goes!" he shouts out the open door. I poke my head around the hood and give him a thumbs-up.

The starter turns over, the fan whirring as the powerful, small block screams to life. The three-inch straight pipe running off the newly-installed headers makes the oversized piece of metal sound like one powerful beast of a machine just like my father said it would.

It roars loudly as my dad gives it a hefty pump of gas and my chest bursts with pride. *I helped do this.* My father and I actually did something together from start to finish.

He waves his hand out the window, gesturing me over. "I want you to drive it. You helped, so you earned it."

"No, Dad, you first."

"Chickenshit, boy?" He loves to give me a hard time, wants me to think I'm weak, but inside I'm not. I'm one person he can't break; my walls are too accustomed to his angry words when he's piss drunk.

"No, sir; I want to watch you and then take my turn."

"Well, load up, and we'll go fuck with old man Percy up there glaring down at us from his porch. Stupid bastard!" he hoots, pretty lit from the twelve pack he's already killed today.

No doubt he'll be taking the truck to town for more beer as well. I don't want to be along for that ride. It's not even four p.m., and he's downed twelve beers. I don't know how he can walk, let alone function like he does. It's normal though, he's this way a lot. When he's sober—which is rare—he's almost normal. It sucks, but this is life.

"I need to watch to make sure there's no smoke from anything."

Hybrid Collection

"Good thinking." He nods, buying my excuse.

I know not to argue with him; he can flip a switch from happy to angry in a flash. I don't know what makes me come up with the excuses this time, but something pushes them out of me, telling me not to ride along.

He casts a mischievous grin my way, turning up "Welcome to the Jungle" by Guns and Roses as he slams the door closed and throws the truck into gear. The music pours out the open windows as he guzzles the rest of his beer. The exhaust competes with the speakers, eventually winning out as he romps on it to spin the tires.

The now-empty can he had goes flying into the yard, and then he's off. Tearing up the street toward the neighbor's house.

Percy Dickson hates us; he's always hated us. My dad says it started back when he was in middle school, and Percy was in high school. My dad supposedly kicked Percy's ass in front of a group of people, but I don't know if it's true. Dad says he was being bullied and stood up for himself. I doubt that's really what happened though. My dad always likes to start trouble. He's been in the back of a cop car too many times to count.

It takes mere moments before my father's driving in Percy's front yard, steering the big blue Chevy truck in circles. He does donuts over and over, chewing up the neighbor's grass. The ground's still a bit soft from the rain we had yesterday, so dirt and bright green turf fly off the tires in every direction.

The angry neighbor stands on his porch, waving his hands, screaming something, and I shake my head at the scene. I know my dad's loving every minute of it. This isn't the first time he's done something like this either.

"You should go clean yourself up while he's busy," I suggest to wife number four and nod toward the small house. My dad built it with his own two hands. It's not much, but he never lets us forget that he created it and he can take it away.

Besides being a mechanic and a drunk, my dad's one hell of a builder. His skills in masonry are something men around here admire. If only he could stay sober long enough to be successful with it. No one admires his inability to finish products or stay professional.

I watch the woman curled up on the floor, as she wipes her tears away and tries to pull herself together enough to get in the house. If he comes back and sees her like this, he'll get even angrier, and no matter how badly I feel, I can't ever save them from him. He's too strong. I can only sit back and hope she smartens up soon to get away from him before he does some serious damage.

A shot rings out, echoing in the hills surrounding us. It's a normal sound with my dad letting bullets fly when he sees a stray cat on the property, or he goes hunting for turkeys with his brothers. The noise didn't come from the hills though; no, it came from down the road.

The roaring engine from the Chevy quiets to a rumble, idling as it comes to a stop. My gaze flies back to the porch where Percy stands, still pointing his shotgun toward the oversized blue truck and my breath catches.

There's blood splattered all over the back window, and I know deep down inside what's happened. You see, over the years there's been many threats from both sides, promising to shoot the other if the property lines were ever breached again. It never happened though; the threats were empty. At least I always thought they were.

The man glances to me next, his gun pointing to the ground. He sends me an irritated glare and stomps across his porch, slamming his front door as he passes through it and goes safely back inside.

He expects me to come get the truck from his front yard. The problem with that is I know my father's dead inside. He'd be yelling at the neighbor, shouting words full of revenge if he were still here with us.

I hate him, but he's all I've got. He's all I've had since I was six years old. Nine years of living this life—adapting and surviving—rolling with the punches dealt my way.

Hybrid Collection

The rest of my father's family has been no help to me—ever. They're just like my father only a bunch of drunken cowards, worrying only about themselves. My dad's always been a survivor like me, until now.

The crushing feeling in my chest grows heavier. It begins spreading throughout and weighing down my body as I realize I have no one or nothing anymore. All because of this neighbor and his almighty shotgun. They've claimed their vengeance. Only now, I'm the one who's paying.

My eyes linger a moment too long on the scuffed lighter resting on my dad's pack of Marlboro Reds. He teased me so many times for coughing whenever I'd try to show off to him and smoke. The bright red gas can topped full with fuel sits at my feet. The italicized lettering spelling *flammable* cultivates an entirely new idea. It's one full of clarity; I know what I need to do to right this wrong.

On autopilot, my fingers pick up the faded zippo, palming it in my left hand and then lifting the gas can with my right. My frame moves on its own accord, practically possessed as it carries me toward the neighbor's house. It should take me longer to get there, but my quick strides carry me at a swift, determined pace. In no time at all, I'm at the run-down wooden structure, known as Percy Dickson's home.

I wonder if he was man enough to build it with his own two hands as well.

My feet continue to lead me over the trail circling around the residence. The fuel spills from the open gas can as I go, eventually stopping at the front door. I remain stoic, staring at the piece of oak that will lead me to my father's killer—to my retribution.

Flipping open the top of the lighter, my thumb switches over the metal, igniting a flame full of revenge. Percy may have kept his promise, but I'll be damned if he gets away unscathed.

My grip releases, dropping the cool metal to the ground beside me. Flickers of fiery yellows and blues dance next to my feet once the flame makes contact with the igniter. The fire spreads on its own mission, following the path of gas I left surrounding the entire residence.

Minutes pass with me standing and staring—entranced at the door—and waiting. My legs and face grow warm as smoke envelops the air around me, the house catching the brunt of the flame as it climbs toward the source that can feed its scorching desire to burn. As it all burns away, piece by piece, it sets me free.

Loud thumps grow near as Percy stumbles in his heavy construction boots, coughing behind the very door, I'm standing in front of. Like a moth seeking the brightest light, the doors handle jiggles, and then it stops. After a beat, with a loud cry from the man trapped, the metal begins to turn. He's seeking his freedom, but I'm not granting it; not today, not ever.

I blink, coming out of my daze and grab the handle, holding it in place. The metal scalds my palm, but I won't release it no matter how bad it burns. The man pounds on the other side of the door, screaming for help as I stand still, the fire flickering full of life beside me. Everything smolders around me, but for some reason, the heat doesn't harm me. It melts the skin on my palm—a reminder, no doubt—but I embrace it.

The old man struggles to breathe with the smoke and begins to burn alive. For the first time in a long time, I smile. The harsh stench of burning flesh brings me peace.

Once he's dead, I dump the remaining gasoline over the blue memory holding my father and light it up next. Everything burns away, and, in that moment, I vow to never look back. It's nothing but a fucking *nightmare*, after all.

CHAPTER 1

You had me at a point where I would've left the entire world behind for you.
- iglovequotes.net

BETHANY

I can't go home alone again; I need someone to numb the empty feeling of loneliness I get night after night. I hate letting myself get down like this as if I don't have anyone and it's the end of the world.
My mind slips back to the one-night stand I had three years ago, nearly to the day. It is the reason I'm feeling this way after all...

Nightmare.

He called me his daydream, whatever the hell that meant. It was probably the sweetest compliment I'd ever gotten from a man. It was a compliment, right?

It had to be.

God, he'd freaking worshiped my body that night too. He didn't care that I was high on percs. He'd growled and then laughed, and it was like seeing light for the first time in my life. That man made me feel, and for once, I wasn't trying to block out the pain. I wanted to see him, to remember him.

That story didn't have a happy ending for me like I'd foolishly let myself believe it would. I guess in a sense, it did, though; it brought me Maverick. However, it didn't turn out like I would've thought when I'd first laid eyes on Nightmare.

He was everything I wanted—the forbidden fruit—or so I thought. Boy, was I wrong, and I took one hell of a big bite.

The first thing I noticed about Nightmare that day we pulled into the shitty beatdown hotel parking lot wasn't the long, dark, wavy hair shadowing part of his face. Not even the black tattoos painting his skin or the thick, corded muscles overtaking his massive body.

It was the jagged silver strip running through one of the deep brown depths of his eyes. It started at the far corner of his eyebrow and sliced straight over his eyelid, nearly touching his nose. It was tiny but must've been a significant enough wound to change the color of one of his irises.

It was creepy and enthralling how he could stare me down like he could see completely through me. He wasn't fooled one bit by my loud mouth or the too-bright-too-fake smile that I always wore. He saw me for me; the plain-Jane, broken Bethany.

My life wasn't butterflies and rainbows. It was rough, and my mask was the only thing I owned that I could hide behind. Well, besides my best friend Princess. I hid behind her beauty a lot. She's not like me. She's strong and never lets anyone push her around, and it made me gravitate toward her like a dog to a bone.

My phone goes off, the ringtone blaring Avenged Sevenfold loudly. Grabbing it quickly, I take off into the bathroom, so it doesn't wake up Maverick. He fell asleep in the car after I'd picked him up on my way home from the restaurant. As much as

Hybrid Collection

I want him to be up and alert so I can spend some time with him, you don't wake a toddler at bedtime; you just don't do it.

"Hello?" It's whispered in a rush as I close the thin bathroom door and swipe across the screen to answer.

"Hey! Are you having sex? Oh, my God, why in the hell did you answer the phone?"

Her excited rush has me breathing out a giggle. "No. dumbass, Mav is sleeping, I was running."

"Why were you running if he's asleep?"

"Because my ringtone would've woken him up." With my little boy being around me every moment that I'm not working, I've forgotten what it's like to live without having a kid. Princess has her man and his little brother, who's not so little. More like a six-foot-three, eighteen-year-old that eats her out of the house practically.

"Oh, well, I feel like an ass."

"Don't, you'll figure it out someday."

She huffs, and in my mind, I can picture her rolling her eyes. "Viking still says he needs more time with me, to himself."

"Trust me, don't rush it. Enjoy each other while it's you guys. Maverick is the best thing that's ever happened to me, but it's not easy, Prissy."

"I must sound so ungrateful to you, and you're the one always over-working yourself."

"I don't mind; he's worth it. Plus, I don't like you sending me money. It makes me feel guilty, and I don't like that hanging over our friendship."

"I've known you my whole life, and that kid is my family too. It's nothing. Besides, what would I do with it anyhow?"

"I don't know, go grocery shopping maybe?"

She laughs, and it brings a smile to my face. I miss her so much. I miss the many nights we were off screwing around, just having fun together.

"You're still coming, right? No excuses?"

"It's your wedding, I wouldn't miss it."

"You promise?"

"For the millionth time; yes. I promise I'll be there, with bells on and Maverick at my side."

"Okay...it's just...well, I told you that it's going to be at the compound."

"We'll be fine. No one will remember me and nobody knows anything about Mav. He's the only concern I have."

"Night and Vike have grown close since Nightmare gave up his Nomad patch." She admits softly.

"He's not a Nomad anymore?" I trail off, not being able to hold back from asking about him. His name has my mind racing with the few memories I have of him.

"No, he's not; I thought I told you?"

"You, ah, haven't mentioned anything." I would remember if she had; I remember everything she says about him, and it's been kept to a minimal, even over a three-year period.

"Right, sorry. I don't want to bring him up. I just don't want you to be blindsided either. You're finally coming home after three years, and I don't want anything at all to go wrong. I need you here, standing beside me when I tie the knot."

"I still can't believe he asked you to marry him."

"Me either. From Viking, it was the last thing I ever expected, but he's calmed down a bit, you'll see."

"Doubt it," I reply immediately, and she laughs again.

Hybrid Collection

"Okay, you're right. He's still a dick, but he's mine."

"He is. I'm so happy for you."

"And I'm so happy I'll see you guys. It's been six months since my last visit, and that's way too long."

"I know it is; I miss you." Tears crest and my throat begins to feel thick with emotion. I won't let her hear it though; I never do. "I have to work early, so I've got to get some sleep, but the promise is still good. In three days, I'll be heading your way."

"I love you."

"Love you, too."

"See you *soooon*!" she sings out happily, and I end the call with a smile.

I'm a bit leery because, in three days, I'll see the man who ruined me for anyone else. He's the man who broke my heart and also knows absolutely nothing about his three-year-old son. If he figures it out, he may also be the man who ends up killing me.

I switch my phone to silent and search out the box of cheap wine in my refrigerator. If I drink enough of it, it'll make me fall asleep without any dreams taking over my rest. The bad dreams are the worst. During the day, I can block everything out if I stay busy; but there's free reign on my mind when I'm sleeping.

That's one thing Maverick will never know—abuse as a child. I'll spend my last dying breath protecting him if I have to. I never cared about much before him; I would wash any memories I had away with alcohol and sex. If I was giving it up freely, then it could never be taken from me again.

Now, I have this little man depending on me, so I have to be extra careful. That includes not leaving at night unless it's an emergency or for work. Like tonight, for example, I got off late, but I had to. I make so much more money when I work the night shift, and I need it if I'm taking time away to visit Princess.

I hate not being home to put Maverick to bed, too. That's usually our special time together, and I want him to have some sense of normal. Not just thinking that his mom is gone all the time working.

It's an unfair balance you have to find it seems. If you work too much, you're a bad parent for never being home with your kid. If you work too little and don't make enough money, your kid suffers by not having what they need. How on earth is that fucking fair? It's bullshit.

I down another glass of the cheap wine and the alcohol's trance kicks in, making me drowsier from my busy day. It's enough that if I go to sleep now, I don't think the dreams of my father will come to haunt me. I can never be sure though.

Peeling off my work uniform, I climb into bed in my bra and panties. I can shower in the morning; right now my body needs rest. Nightmare's silver and bronze gaze is the last thing I think of as I fall into a blissfully drunken sleep.

I miss him.

CHAPTER 2

I broke my own heart loving you.
- Unknown

"Thanks, Barb."

She casts a friendly smile at me as she stands in the doorway and holds Maverick's hand in my direction. I reach my palm out to him, and he eagerly grabs it, a happy grin taking over his face, excited to be home. "You're welcome; you two have a safe trip and try to have some fun."

"We will. Enjoy your free time, too."

"Oh, I don't mind having Maverick around; he makes me feel young again." The older woman chuckles, waves, and heads toward her car.

Usually, I pick Mav up on my way home, but Barbara was out running errands and saved me the trip. It worked out perfectly, too; it gave me enough time to get my car loaded up with everything for our trip. My nerves were kind enough to show up as well. I was hoping to leave them behind, but, apparently, they didn't feel the same way. Hopefully, the drive will chill me out some.

It looks like we're going across the country or something when it's only four hours away. Anyone with kids knows that you have to pack everything but the kitchen sink practically, to keep almost-three-year-olds busy, especially at a wedding.

Bikers or not, I don't want to bring too much attention to us, or any attention at all.

"Hey, buddy." Pulling him in for a snuggle, I wrap my arms around. "I missed you today. Are you ready for our trip to see Aunt Prissy?"

"Yes! She has gummies?"

Six months since her trip here and he still talks about her spoiling him with gummy bears. He was in such a sugar rush during her visit; I thought I was going to strangle her. He doesn't need a grandma to feed him sugar on visits when he has Princess.

"Knowing her, probably. The car's all ready. Is there anything I'm forgetting?" I made him pick out some toys to fit in one backpack, no more. He tried to tell me we needed to bring his toy box, but it wasn't happening.

He taps his chin, looking around the living room.

He's so freaking adorable with his black locks he gets from both Nightmare and me, along with big brown eyes from his father that haunt my memories. Hopefully, no one looks close enough, or they'll be able to figure out whose blood runs through his body pretty easily.

"Ummm...snacks?" Surprise, surprise; snacks was one of the kid's first words.

"Got 'em."

"Ummm...Mr. Bwair?"

"Got Mr. Bear, too."

"Ummm..." He looks at me, his eyebrow raising and shrugs.

"That's what I was thinking. First trip this far away, I'm sure we'll figure it out soon enough."

Hybrid Collection

Yeah, so I ended up forgetting my cash, and two hours down the road had to turn around when I stopped to get gas and only found a twenty in my purse. A four-hour road trip turned into eight hours, and let's just say, Maverick was not amused in the slightest, at my mishap.

"I thought you'd never get here!" Princess squeezes me tightly, again. She's done it three times since she opened her front door.

"God, me too. Just be glad the kid passed out, or you'd be ready for us to leave already."

"No way, I love the little guy. I was hoping he'd be awake. I'm thinking once Viking gets around Maverick, he'll want to have some kids of our own."

"Trust me, he was super grouchy the hour before he finally gave in. His favorite word was 'NO.' I'm pretty sure he said it fifty times and threw so many damn action figures, they'll forever be lost in my car."

She laughs, finding enjoyment in my mini ride of torture. Payback—one day she'll be calling me, flipping out because her kids being a brat and then I'll laugh. It's what best friends do.

"Well, hopefully after some rest, he'll be in a better mood tomorrow. He can run after Odin and get some exercise too."

"That sounds good to me. Now, please tell me you have some wine?"

"I have vodka and OJ; will that do the trick?"

"Definitely, hook it up." I follow her into the kitchen and take a seat at the table. "Thank you for letting us stay with you, I hope we don't bother you though. Mav still gets up really early."

"Of course, I wouldn't want you anywhere else. And besides, I've stayed with you, and he's a lot quieter than I'd expect."

"Yeah, cartoons and a bowl of cereal and he's pretty calm. He needs time to wake up and get going."

"Just like his mom." She winks, and I smile. I love being here, even after a long trip and an hour of kid yelling to make it here.

"So what's the plan for tomorrow exactly?"

I'm nervous, but at the same time, I'm excited to see the guys. I don't expect them to remember me, but I could never forget the rough group of bikers. They're Princess' family now, and I'm so happy she's found her tribe. I always knew she belonged in the MC world. Her parents and brother were deep into it; she just needed the right piece to make her fit as well. That turned out to be Viking, and he's the President of the entire club. Go figure.

She sets the glass in front of me, taking the seat to my left and sips her own drink. "Pretty much just hang out. We're having a barbecue at the club to welcome some visiting members, mostly the Nomads coming in for the wedding, but both clubs will be there."

"The hybrids and the Oath Keepers?"

"Yes, but don't call them hybrids; the Widow Makers were patched over to the Oath Keepers. Oath Keepers essentially took over the Widow Maker name. They let a small charter keep the patch in South Carolina, but Viking's club here is Oath Keepers. You already know that much though. He works with Ares a lot; they're practically BFFs now."

"That's crazy, considering they hated each other with a passion in the beginning."

"I know, but they both love my father, and, thankfully, were able to bond over him and work through their shit. It makes things so much easier."

"Okay, so the same guys that were with your dad and Ares are under Ares, and the others belong to Viking's charter?"

"Right, that's why we moved a little ways out of town. This way they can each have separate clubs."

"Jesus, y'all must run Texas by now."

Hybrid Collection

"With the size of the clubs, we're definitely dominant in this state."

"Listen to you, no doubt a President's wife."

"Ol' lady." She winks. "And it has taken time to get there, believe me."

"You fit so well, though. Who'd have thought this is how your life would turn out?"

"I know, and the freaky part is, I've never been happier. I wish my mom was here to be a part of it all."

"She is, Princess. That woman wouldn't let you out of her sight when it comes to the club. I know she's looking down on you every day."

"I hope so." She wipes a stray tear away as the front door opens with Viking and Odin piling through.

"Well, there's trouble." Viking acknowledges me, walking to his woman and giving her a blistering kiss.

"Hey." I smile, and Odin bends over, giving me a half hug.

I've met him before; Viking makes him come with Princess on each visit. He says it's to keep Odin busy, but we all know it's to protect Princess if she ever needed it. He may only be eighteen, but he's a tank—a lethal one at that—and Princess is the closest thing he has in his life now to a mom, older sister, female friend, etc.

"'Sup Bethany, how was the drive?" Odin nods, heading to the fridge.

"Long; glad to finally be here."

"Bet." He nods again, pulling out a pack of lunch meat and some mayo, heading to the counter to make a sandwich.

Viking detaches from Princess after a moment, "Where's this mini version my ol' lady won't stop talking to me about?"

"He's asleep, but you'll meet him tomorrow." And Maverick will no doubt be curious with Viking. He already thinks Odin is the greatest thing since peanut butter and jelly because he spins him around a million times like he enjoys.

"Good. I'm hitting the shower," he grumbles, glancing at Princess. They have their own language it seems; they always have.

"Night, Viking." I smile politely, and he salutes me, heading toward their bedroom.

He's not a man of many words, but, from what I remember, none of the bikers talk much. Kind of weird for them to have a barbecue. Do they just stand around quiet, drinking beer? I will no doubt laugh if I see it happen tomorrow because it's so not what you'd expect to see with a bunch of bikers.

I'd met most of them a few times before I found out I was pregnant and moved away. They stuck together out in public, and when I was with Nightmare, no one bothered him. Some of Princess' dad's bikers had shown up the next morning, but they were all talking about a car when I made it out of the hotel room.

I wonder if Ruger will be there. He was friendly; I think he liked me, too. He went swimming with us once and was pretty funny. He'd attempted to get fresh, too, but I shot him down right away. I'd only ever had eyes for one brother.

"I should get some sleep, too. Maverick will be up early, and I'll need energy to keep up with him tomorrow around everyone."

"He'll have a few other kids to play with, too. London and Cain's kids will be there, and their youngest daughter is the same age, I think."

"Oh, good. It'll be nice to have a beer and some adult conversation that I actually want to have. I get so tired of the assholes hitting on me at the restaurant."

"I can imagine, but don't be surprised if the guys hit on you tomorrow, too."

"But, I'll have my son with me."

She snorts, "*Pahleese*, a little boy won't scare any of them off. They'll take one look at those hips and won't care about anything else."

"That's what I'm afraid of," I mumble, and her grin falls.

"You'll have fun, I promise."

"I know, don't worry about me. I'm here for you, remember?"

"You don't know how much it means to me that you are."

"No worries, woman. Now go attend to your fiancé. I'm pretty sure he was sending you silent messages with the looks he gave you on the way to y'all's room."

"He's insatiable." She laughs, and Odin makes a gagging sound.

"Don't wanna hear that shit," he says around a mouthful of sandwich, and Princess picks up an ink pen that was on a notebook in the middle of the table. He looks at us, and she throws the pen at his forehead.

He ducks, cursing, and we both laugh. She knows how to keep him on his toes, I'm sure of it. If Prissy and Viking do ever have kids of their own, the kids are in for a ride no doubt.

"Goodnight, you guys, see you tomorrow." I climb to my feet, and Princess follows.

"Yep, I'll be the pretty one."

"Oh my God, he's made your head get bigger since I left," I retort.

"Shut up! Love you."

"Love you." I squeeze her one last time and close the door to the guest room they're letting us stay in. It's perfect for us, too; we have a small, private bathroom and a king-sized bed to share.

I take a quick, super-hot shower to scrub the road grime off and then hit the sack, grateful to be snuggled next to my son in my best friend's house. I missed being around her so much; it even feels good to be back to the place I grew up, even if my life wasn't the greatest.

CHAPTER 3

Yeah, I'm hurting but on goes the mascara and lip gloss.
That's right, I'll be the prettiest fucking wreck you've ever seen.
- Unknown

"Hey, Bethany," Viking grumbles while sitting on the couch watching cartoons with my son. "Why's Maverick look so much like my homeboy?"

My chest tightens at his words.

He means Nightmare, his brother. I knew I never should've come here; at least, not with my son. Princess has kept my secret for which I'm beyond grateful. Honestly, I never expected her to be able to keep it from her ol' man and for this amount of time too.

Deep down I've been waiting for the angry pounding on my front door, but it hasn't come. My big secret could really stir some shit up between them if Viking were to find out who Maverick belongs to. With their wedding in the works, that's the last thing I want to do. I would never want to hurt or cause trouble between them.

The thing is, Princess doesn't know just how much has been kept in the dark. I've misled my best friend, and I hate myself for it. At the time, it was all I had. I was hurt by Nightmare's words, and I didn't want anything to do with him after.

Hybrid Collection

That's a lie. I've thought of him countless times over the years. I have wanted him, every fucking piece of him, but he wouldn't want my son—our son.

I still remember his words like they were said yesterday.

"I'm sterile and clean," he rasps against my neck. "I told you this already, the other night when we fucked."

I've been sick each morning since that first night, too. I can't get ahold of Princess because Viking has her trapped in his room, and her mom never answered her door when I went over. I have no one to talk to about this.

My own mother would just tell me that I'm a whore and kick me out. She doesn't have time for me; she only cares about her husband. She's made it abundantly clear many times.

Naturally, I ran back to Nightmare. I'm scared. The doctor says I could be pregnant, but how do I say the words out loud to an outlaw? He's a Nomad for Christ's sake. I seriously doubt he's the type to win a father of the year award; even I know that much.

"You're sure?" I mutter, my breath catching, waiting for his deep voice to offer some kind of reassurance. But he doesn't. He breaks my heart instead because I know the truth, I just have to hear him say it.

He plunges inside me deeply from behind as he grumbles, "Of course. The fuck I'm gonna do with a kid? I'm not father material, none of us are. I wouldn't be fuckin' you bareback like this if I was gonna knock you up. Clearly, I like my freedom."

My eyes crest with tears because, just like I knew his words were going to sting, I also know inside that the doctor is right. I have a little life growing inside me. It was created by this man—the one taking my body right now—and he wants nothing to do with any of it.

He wants to take his pleasure and leave me with the consequences.

"Right, I'm just being paranoid or something." I swallow as he pumps into me again. No matter how good he feels filling me, I won't get off. He basically told me that if I were pregnant, he wouldn't want the baby. He wouldn't want a piece of me.

No one does. My father abused me in ways I would never wish for anyone to experience. My mother hates me; I'm a burden that she's counting the days to be rid of. And now the father of my own child doesn't want the one thing I'm able to offer him- life.

"Or sumthin'," he agrees, continuing with his pursuit of pleasure.

Silent tears trail over my heated cheeks, but I don't utter a word. He won't know my pain, no one will. I'll be the very thing I've needed my entire life. I'll be strong.

Princess thinks I told Nightmare that I was pregnant, and he pushed me away. It's why she hates him. She's never said it out loud; she won't since it's Viking's brother and club business. It's not her place to tear him down for his choices, even if I am her best friend. She respects her ol' man, and I respect her for it. Not only that, but it's a lie. She came to that conclusion on her own, and I let her run with it.

Nightmare doesn't have any idea that he has a kid out there. At least not with me, anyhow. Who knows if there are others out in the world. I was so damn naïve to believe him the first time we were together, and he told me he couldn't have kids. More like he was in denial and I proved him wrong.

They can all hate me for my decisions, and that's fine. I've made my choices, and I've lived with them every damn day of Maverick's life. Would I go back and do it differently if I could?

Maybe, but I doubt it.

I had my reasons for keeping him a secret, and, at the time, I felt like I was doing what I had to. Time only built my confidence stronger in my decision. Nightmare never looked for me. For all I know, he never even asked about me. I was nothing, probably not even a memory.

I don't want that in my kid's life, someone who won't remember him. Maverick is everything. He won't have a life like I had. He'll be surrounded by people who love him, and will protect him.

I'm surprised to hear Night isn't a Nomad any longer considering his freedom was so important to him after all. Things change, I suppose. I'm guessing that having Viking as the President of his own Charter most likely has a lot to do with it.

I hate lying to Viking. He's never done anything to me personally, and he takes care of my best friend. However, the safety of my child is everything, and if Nightmare wanted me dead for keeping this from him, the club wouldn't even bat an eyelash, and Mav would be left without a mother.

I shrug, glancing to the side, and deflect, "I think he looks like his mom. Lucky kid, since I'm hot."

Vike snorts, turning back to the show.

My reply worked…for now. But if Viking can pick him out first thing in the morning, then I may have a harder time when Mav is around people that see his father every day and have a chance to really get a good look at him.

If Princess wasn't so damn important to me, I never would've come here. There's no reason to after all. My mother doesn't know about Maverick; she wouldn't care, and that's fine with me. She's not a good person and doesn't deserve to know my son. And wherever my father ended up, I hope it's six feet under, and he suffered.

The only one I would've gone out of my way to have in his life would've been Mona—Princess' mom. I loved her so much; she was a great mom. She died of cancer a few years ago, so having her in Mav's life isn't an option.

I was too broke and struggling to make ends meet with Maverick; I wasn't able to attend her funeral. I hated it, but I know she would've understood. She was just like that—always caring for and worrying about others.

She'd have been pissed at me if I'd tried to travel and then something had happened to me or the baby on the road. I said my piece to her at the time, and I still talk to her randomly. She may not really be there, but I talk to her like I believe she is.

"You're wearing that?" My mouth falls open as Princess comes out of her room.

"Yeah, it's hot."

"Exactly, you'll bake in black leather."

"They're shorts, I'll be fine. Besides, the halter top doesn't have a back to it." She spins around, and my mouth drops open again. She's straight up doin' the hootchie momma thing.

"Viking!" I mutter and tilt my head toward my friend. He'll let her out the door like this?

He glances at her, a pleased smirk taking over his lips. He's as bad as she is.

"How do you go anywhere? Won't he chop off guys' heads?" Her ol' man is nutso when it comes to jealousy, and that's the last thing I want myself or my kid to see at a barbecue.

"They know better," he declares, his voice confident and stern. I wouldn't fuck with him.

She shrugs, waving it off. "They either stare at my face or look at the ground. I could be naked, and no one would comment."

I hear a growl come from Viking's direction.

"Jesus." I shake my head. It's a wonder he has any club brothers left at this rate.

"Is that what you're wearing?" She points toward my boobs, flicking her gaze over my dress a few times and basically cringes.

"Yes."

Hybrid Collection

"Since when do you wear maxi dresses?"

"It's one of the halfway decent things I can get away with. Regular dresses? Maverick thinks it's hilarious to grab the skirt part and take off running. This is long enough and stretchy."

"You look like a hobo. It's definitely the wrong size for you."

"Gee, thank you, assface."

She giggles. "Come on, I have something you can borrow."

"Uh no. I have hips, remember? Having a baby changed some things."

She rolls her eyes and grabs my hand to drag me to her room. "In your case, it finally gave you an ass."

I end up coming out in a different dress, surprise, surprise. This one's a sun dress though with stretchy material. Fingers crossed my kid doesn't flash my new ass to anyone today. I expect to see someone's boobs at some point, it being a biker compound, but none of those body parts need to belong to myself.

After letting her screw with my hair and makeup which I bitch about the entire time, but secretly love, we're finally ready. It helps having other people around to distract Maverick. I don't usually have time to do anything special to my hair before work besides a quick ponytail. Mom duties overshadow hairstyles when it's just the two of us.

I smear a healthy coat of sunscreen all over my son and grab his backpack full of Matchbox trucks and action figures. All he needs is some snacks and a little dirt to play in, and he'll be one happy little boy.

"Ready?" Smiling, I fix his black tank top I have paired with army green camo shorts and chucks. He looks freaking adorable as usual. It pays to have a cool mom on your side.

"Ummm…yep."

The 'ummm' thing drove me a little nuts at first, but the pediatrician said it's normal for kids to pick a favorite word. Right now, Maverick's favorite happens to be 'Um.' Guess it's better than 'mine.'

"He'll fit in just fine with the other biker kids." Princess shoots me a look. She knows I'm tripping out inside over seeing Nightmare after so long. Even being separated for a while, she can still read me like an open book.

I nod, we're good. At least that's what I keep telling myself. Fake it til you make it has been my life motto thus far. Why stop now?

"Follow behind Odin, and Viking will let the brother at the gate know you're with us, okay?"

"All right. Just give me a sec to strap him in his seat, and we'll be right behind you." I look to Odin, and he gives me thumbs-up. For being raised by a badass, he doesn't usually reflect it.

"Later kid." He holds his fist out, and Maverick fist bumps him.

Only one morning being here and Odin's already teaching my son to fist bump. Viking does the same, letting Mav fist bump him, too, before heading out the door, and then we're off.

I've never been to Viking's compound before. It was built after I left, and, well, I'm amazed. I was expecting it to be a crappy little building in the middle of nowhere to hold a bunch of rowdy bikers, but it's not. Not even a little bit.

Princess' house is on the back side of the property, so it's really close to the actual building, but you have to drive in a sort of circle around a bunch of trees to get there. Viking did it on purpose. He wanted her close to him, but not too close, so if any shit ever went down, she wouldn't be harmed. He can cut through the trees on foot to get to her, but vehicles and motorcycles have to drive around. It's perfect actually.

Hybrid Collection

They stop for a second to talk to the member standing at the gate, and then we all roll through, the biker nodding to each of us as we pass. He's young, probably closer to Odin's age. I've never seen him before. As we pass by slowly, I catch his name patch, *Bronx*. Definitely never met him; I'd remember the name.

I watch Maverick in my rearview mirror waving at the guy. Instead of acting cool and ignoring him, Bronx breaks out in a grin and waves back. I won't lie; it brings a cheesy smile to my face. Maybe today won't be so bad after all. Lord knows we're about to find out.

CHAPTER 4

Until you cross the bridge of your insecurities, you can't begin to explore your possibilities.
- Tim Fargo

"I haven't seen him yet." I glance around again making sure Nightmare hasn't suddenly appeared. The place is littered with men in leather cuts visiting with each other, but none resemble the man I remember.

"He was on a run this week; he'll be rolling in soon with Chaos."

"Who's Chaos?"

"Another member." Princess winks, being a smartass.

She failed to mention yesterday that he wasn't even in town; it would've saved me a lot of immediate worrying. What if I'm spazzing out for nothing? He could show up and completely ignore me. It never crossed my mind before, but what if he shows up with another woman?

Holy shit, how could I not think of that? I'm not with anyone, so I automatically picture him with no one as well. I'm a freaking idiot. It's been years; he could have his own wife!

No. He likes his freedom; he flat out told me that. He won't be married—he *can't* be.

Fuck.

"It's not what you're thinking, it was a gig."

She knows what I'm thinking? I hope she can't tell. "A what?"

"You know, a job. He still plays. One thing he didn't give up over the time you've been away is his sticks."

What the hell is she talking about? Sticks?

"What's he play, exactly?"

"Wait, you don't know?" Her eyebrows raise, and I shake my head. "He's a drummer. All this time, I thought you knew that about him."

"Nope, I had no clue. We don't exactly talk about him, you know."

"I'm sorry; I try not to bring him up to you. I don't want to hurt you after the way he treated you and all."

I nod. Not sure what else to say right now. I thought he was just a biker, but now that I'm here, I find out he's not even a Nomad anymore. He's a drummer, and I had no idea. I feel like I don't know him at all. We fucked, and I fell. I didn't need to know anything to want him and then let my heart get broken in the same breath.

"Are you okay?" My friend's worried gaze meets mine.

"Yeah, I'm fine." Lies.

Brush it off, B.

"Maybe you should have a beer. I'm here. I'll help keep an eye on Maverick; besides, he's completely fine with London's daughter. She won't let anything happen to either one of them."

"It's kind of early; I was going to wait until later when we eat. I only have one beer if I have to drive somewhere."

"Listen to you, all responsible. I'm so fucking proud of you, Bethany."

"I have to be and thank you."

"Well, if you want to drink, go ahead. We can always walk home if we need to or one of the Prospects can drive us. You're safe here, try to relax and let yourself have a little bit of fun."

"You're sure?"

"Yes. I know you can't be the crazy girl you used to be, which is completely fine- I understand and admire you. But you can cut loose here; you know I'll never let anything happen to you or Maverick."

"Thank you." I let a pent-up breath free.

I can have a beer now and then another later when we eat. I'll be able to be momma and still function, but the alcohol will help calm my nerves a bit. No hard stuff, it's been forever since I drank tequila and the last thing I want to do is pray to the porcelain god in the morning. That would be a train wreck, no doubt.

The sound of motorcycles arriving catches my attention as multiple loud exhausts rumble into the parking lot. Three bikes come to a stop, and I know who it is before he has a chance to climb off.

Exterminator swings his leg over, his back patch still reading Nomad. At least there's one thing that hasn't changed. Another man, a bit older comes to stand beside him, and I'm guessing that must be Chaos. He's gorgeous, distinguished, I'd say mid-fifties and fit. Built like a football player with a look of pure trouble.

Then comes my demise; I can feel him, and he's nowhere near me. My gaze finds powerful thighs, still the size of small tree trunks like I remember. Surprising, too, after the attack Princess had told me about. I figured they'd be skinny from the damage, hidden away by jeans, but that's clearly not the case.

Hybrid Collection

He turns around to grab something off his bike and the deep brown, shoulder length waves I loved running my fingers through are gone. In their place are long dreads, unruly but neat in a sense. And sure enough, a pair of drummer sticks stuck in one of his back pockets. How did I never notice them before?

His shirt sleeves are cut. Big gaping holes show off his arms that've only gotten larger with time. He's a beast, and I missed that body something fierce. The only man I didn't faze out when he took my body. I was present with him, I felt everything, I wanted everything.

"Shit," Princess whispers beside me. "I wasn't expecting them until a little later."

I blow out another breath. "How about that beer now?" I ask, watching Night light up a cigarette. That hasn't changed either. I can still smell him—leather, smoke, and spice with a touch of exhaust and wind mixed in. The guys chuckle beside him and his lips tip at the corners, always a broody bastard. Being that hot shouldn't be allowed on an asshole.

"Good idea."

One thing that didn't escape my perusal is that he was alone on his bike. Just as I was hoping, too, whether I want to admit it or not.

"Come on." She takes off toward a few large tubs filled with ice and various beverages. "We have some really good moonshine that we get from Alabama, wanna do a shot?"

"No, it'll put me on my ass. Maybe later after I've eaten and absolutely no tequila." She laughs, knowing tequila turns me into a hellion.

I check on Maverick as we walk, but he's content surrounded by toys, a juice box, and a couple small kids. I'm glad he's busy; it'll wear him out for a nap later. At this rate, I'll most likely need one, too; my nerves are fried already.

She cracks open a Smirnoff for herself and hands me a Bud Light. It's cold and refreshing. I don't miss drinking itself, just hanging out with friends and not caring about anything.

"We can set up the food. I'm sure everyone's getting hungry by now."

"Is this what you always do?"

"What? Set up the tables?"

"Yeah, just take care of everyone and help take care of the club?"

"Yeah, this is what an ol' lady does, especially since Vike is the President. It puts more on me."

"You like it?"

"I love it. I understand now why my mom was so lost when my dad started keeping her away from the club. They become your family, and this," she waves around her, "becomes your whole life."

"I know you're involved with stuff, from the calls and your visits, but I didn't know it was like this. It reminds me more of a reunion than a rowdy barbecue."

"They have their moments, trust me. Today is a family event. They know it's to celebrate me and Viking, so they'll tone it down for me and the families visiting."

I catch her wrist, so she pauses and meets my gaze. "I want you to know, I truly am happy for you. I always wanted you to find your place and be happy."

Her grin's a little shaky as she pulls me in for a hug, "Thanks, B. Hopefully, someday you have it too."

"I hope so." It leaves me on a whisper, but it's true. It never hit me so hard as it has in this moment.

I want this.

Maybe not being a Prez's ol' lady, but the sense of family, of belonging, of purpose. I love being a mom, but I want Maverick to grow up surrounded by people who love him, not just a few, but many. I want him to have a family, people who love him that I never had.

Hybrid Collection

A few bikers stand around in the kitchen, no doubt quietly speaking about business of some sort. They glance at us briefly as we unintentionally interrupt them.

"Hey, Torch, will you carry that potato salad for me?" Princess requests as she opens the fridge door and gestures to the top shelf.

"You got it, boss." He grabs the massive plastic bowl that most likely weighs fifty pounds knowing Princess.

He's new to me. She's told me about the guys, but I haven't seen a lot of them before. Her description of him was right. He reminds me of the Terminator—menacing, but hot. Torch is supposed to be one of Viking's oldest friends, and a biker around here called Blaze is supposed to be his cousin. I haven't seen him yet, though.

"Thanks. Bethany, will you get the paper plates and forks?"

"Yes, ma'am." I grin, and she rolls her eyes.

They head out of the room, while I load up a plastic bag with a bunch of plates and utensils. She said forks, but may as well get everything; I know she'll ask for it next. The other bikers in here ignore me, going back to their chat and I do my best to not overhear anything. The last thing I want is to be putting my nose in other people's business.

Once the bag's full, I make my way to the hall that leads out the club's back door. I hate not having Maverick in my sight, but Princess says I can trust London. She'd never let either of us get hurt, so I believe her.

My heads in la-la land as I walk the long hall, not paying attention to the shadow in a passing doorway. The shadow sees me, however.

My wrist is snatched in a tight grip, my gaze flying to the source of strength.

"Bethany?" he utters deeply, and the air catches in my lungs. How could I not know he was standing there? *Fuck.* My pussy clenches from his voice alone.

He gazes at me, confused and a little surprised to see me. I'm guessing that I'm the last person he was expecting to be walking around their clubhouse.

"Ummm." I begin to stutter, the word instantly making me think of Maverick. I know where he gets it from now. Shit.

"You're here?" His voice swallows me whole, coating my body in tingles as his other hand finds my cheek. His palm's rough and big, easily covering part of my face and jaw with warmth.

How does he expect me to speak when he's touching me like this? I could barely say anything before when I didn't hate him. And lack of words has never been an issue for me; if anything, it was always the opposite.

His touch is everything—caring and controlling—just the way I liked it before. The heat from his palm ignites my body in sensory overload. I want him to feel me everywhere, rub me all over.

"Yes?" I nod, a little unsure of what he even said. I know he spoke and I need to give him a response; to what, who knows? I can't think, I only feel him and take in his features.

He's aged a touch, but nothing too noticeable. The few lines from his ever-present glare and his time out on the road have gotten slightly more pronounced, but that's about all. His hair's throwing me a bit. It's so much longer, and I've never cared for dreads, but I like them on him. He wears the look well, reminding me of one of the guys you see in a heavy metal video—forbidden and wild.

"Where have you been?" He's angry; I can hear it in his voice. He's pissed over something. Over me leaving? No way; he has no reason to be. I was the one who left hurt and upset, not the other way around.

"B?" Princess comes into the hall, a concerned gaze at Nightmare's hand on me. Her wake never falters, coming to me immediately and grabbing onto my free hand, holding the plastic bag in a death grip. "Come on Bethany, I need you to help me." Her eyes snap to Nightmare's, full of her own warning. She can't say anything to him; it's not her place in the club, but she can tell her ol' man if something bothers her.

He drops his hands from me, releasing my cheek and wrist. Taking a step back, his gaze shutters, and without another word, he watches my best friend cart me toward the door. He never says anything, and part of me wishes he would stop us, while the other can't stop thinking of how it felt when he touched me.

How did I ever think I could come back here and he wouldn't affect me? I've never been that strong. I am for Maverick, but never for myself and never when it comes to Nightmare.

Maverick.

"Mav—" I begin, and Princess cuts me off.

"Is fine. I checked on him. I don't think Night has seen him yet."

"Thank you."

"Of course; I have your back."

"We should go."

"Already? Please stay. What if you go back to my house and take a breather?"

"Okay, I can do that. Maverick will probably be ready for a nap soon anyhow. I just need some space from him." I nod at the back door.

"I've been with Viking for a while now; I get it. They have a way of overtaking everything, nearly smothering you at times."

"Exactly." I set the bag down and toss the half-full beer in the metal trash bin. Smother is a good word to use whenever I'm near him; consumed would work as well.

Collecting my kid and his stuff, we get out of there as quickly and quietly as possible, not wanting to draw any attention.

It doesn't take long before Maverick's down for a nap, and I'm lying beside him, tears flooding my face. I was a fool to think I wouldn't be that messed up at seeing Night. It's been years—actual years since I saw his face and heard his voice—yet he has this control over me within minutes. Not only did he suck me right back in, but he twisted my heart all over again knowing that the innocent little boy playing right outside is unwanted by his own father.

Fuck you, Nightmare!

My own tiredness sets in, and I succumb to sleep. Unfortunately, there's not enough alcohol in my system to drown out memories that like to torment me in my dreams—my nightmares.

CHAPTER 5

*And the stars blinked as they watched her carefully,
jealous of the way she shone.*
- Atticus

NIGHTMARE

My leg aches as I stand on that side for too long causing me to shift and relieve some pressure.
Fuckin' Lion.

Of course, I'd be the motherfucker who was attacked out of the brothers. That's neither here nor there; it's been forever since that fucked-up day. I need to let that shit go already. I've gotten a lot of my strength and movement back with a shit ton of work, but my leg will never be the same as it used to be. Guess that's what happens when a Lion decides to use you as an appetizer. I damn sure can't run for shit; guess if I'm being chased I'll have to shoot instead of run.

Stupid fuckin' cartel. Those bastards always fuck shit up. I still think we should find every one of those sneaky bastards and light them up. It'd solve a lot of problems, but the brothers think I'm crazy.

'I'm angry, and they get it.' They don't get shit. They weren't attacked, their lives weren't completely changed. Thank fuck it didn't mess with me playing too. It screwed me out of riding for about a year. Hell, the doc said not to ever ride again.

Fuckin' idiot, like I wasn't gonna ride again. I told him to get the fuck outta here with that shit. I'm not a pussy; I'm not giving up my bike.

I lean against the wall a bit more, my sticks digging into my ass, reminding me that they're there. I usually stick them back there if I have a gig and then forget about them. I played last night with a local band. Chaos and Ex came out to show some support, then we got pretty fucked up on whiskey afterward. Damn sure beat this barbecue going on right now.

Don't get me wrong, Viking's my brother, and I have his back one hundred and fifty percent. I even think Princess is good for him. It's not them; it's Bethany. She was the last person I was expecting to see.

When Vike first announced he was getting hitched, of course, I instantly thought of B stopping through. Princess hasn't said a word about her since she split. One minute she was here in my bed and the next she'd left town. The bitch doesn't even visit her best friend. I thought maybe they stopped talking or something.

Then to top it off, she only says two words to me. The last time I saw her, I thought for sure she was into me. She would stare at me like I was a goddamn puppy or some shit. She's a prime example of why I don't let women in too close. The club is my family; they're all I need.

There's just one little detail that's driving me crazy. So much so, that I find myself making my way to Viking's office. He's not supposed to be working this week since he's getting married, but I saw him sneak into his office. He's either in there for some quiet or because he's a damn control freak and can't stand letting other people handle shit for him.

Opening the door, I slide in quickly and shut it, so no one knows we're in here.

"Brother?" He glances at me, eyebrow raised.

"Saw Bethany."

He nods, taking his seat behind the desk. I do the same, sitting in one of the broken-in leather seats opposite him. We're not big talkers the two of us. We both think a lot before opening our mouths, so our conversations are usually short and straight to the point. This is one time I don't know how to bring something up, though.

Very few members know how I feel about Bethany. Vike found out by pure luck when he was on the hunt for Princess. I slipped up a few times and my brother caught on. The others are like a group of gossiping broads and too wrapped up in themselves to pay attention to my shit.

Viking, not so much. We're broody fuckers who often growl at people more than we speak, so he pretty much knew by the second look I gave the chick that I was planning on fucking her.

"She's here for the wedding." He takes a healthy gulp of beer.

"Figured."

After a few moments of silence, he speaks again. "That all brother?"

"No."

He nods again, staring me down, but I don't know how to sugarcoat shit, so I stay quiet for a few more minutes, making shit awkward. Eventually, he goes back to working on whatever he was doing when I interrupted him, and I blurt out the thoughts bothering me.

"She had a kid with her." So what if I followed her when Princess took her. I wasn't about to let her escape that easily. Then she grabbed up a little boy. That had my step faltering and letting her go without me interfering. Now I can't stop thinking about it.

"Yeah, I met him this morning."

"First time?"

"Yep."

"She married too?"

He barks out a laugh. "This is B we're talkin' about. She doesn't have a fucking husband."

I let loose a relieved breath, and he grows serious again, seeing how much the thought was eating me up. I was racking my brain trying to think if I'd seen a ring on her hand, but fuck, I was too distracted. One look in those eyes of hers, and I couldn't give a fuck about anything else in the moment. I wanted to rip her clothes off and sink balls deep into her tight pussy right there in the hallway. I wanted to demand that she tell me why she left and why she hasn't come back sooner. Maybe make it hurt a little and punish her ass for keeping me waiting so long.

"She bring an ol' man with her, too?" Not that it matters; if anything, he'd get his feelings hurt by the way she still looks at me.

"No. Just her and the kid. Maybe you should talk to my Cinderella; she'd know the shit you're asking." Her name's Princess, and he calls her Cinderella. Fucker has a shoe fetish now, too, from what I hear. Not my business, but kinda ironic.

"She won't tell me anything. Your ol' lady's harder than some of the bikers I've met in my life." It's the truth too; the bitch is cold as ice toward me.

He cracks a tiny grin. "Fuck, yeah, she is." He finishes off his bottle and tosses it in the small wastebasket beside the desk. "Not sure I can give you the answers you're wanting, brother."

"Those were the main ones I had. How long's she staying? I'm guessing she'll beat feet back outta here pretty quick?"

"You have a week."

Huffing, I drum my fingers along my thigh. "They've stayed friends this whole time, then?"

"Yeah, they have, man. Cinderella visits her and shit."

"That's where her and Odin go then." It's not a question. Details are just starting to click into place, and I want him to confirm I'm correct.

Hybrid Collection

"That's right, brother."

"Appreciate it." Nodding my thanks, I leave him to his business.

He shakes my hand. "Good luck."

I have a feeling I need more than luck this time. One thing that running into Bethany has showed me, is that she wasn't happy to see me. She was surprised, but not pleased, and that's a problem.

I head back toward the other brothers, grabbing a beer on my way. Viking will give it to me straight if he thinks I'm stupid for asking about her. I can trust him. He didn't mention anything about me being a fool or that I should keep my space, so that's something.

Do I really want to get involved with her again, though, now that she has a kid? Baby daddy drama and all that shit in tow. I'd end up throwing the bastard in a dumpster and lighting it up if he gave her any kind of grief with me around. Not sure she wants that sorta shitshow in her life.

It could be my chance at having a brat, though, if it were to work out. One thing that's always ate away at me was not being able to have kids someday. I enjoy my freedom a lot; but hell, I want to have my own family eventually.

I usually fall back on it as a way to push people away. You're less likely to get hurt by anyone if they think you never want anything with them more than a quick fuck. I'll be real, for a while tapping pussy and riding was exactly what I wanted. I'm getting older now and am no longer a Nomad, and having a family isn't looking like a hindrance anymore. Quick fucks are great. I love that shit, but I want to have a son to carry on my name and my blood. I want to have the chance to be a good father, unlike my own old man.

Princess has everything set up all nice and organized so everyone can load up their plates. She stands on the opposite side, helping the younger kids pick out what they want to eat. She's always around the club, helping out and making sure everyone has what they need. Except for me, she usually pretty well ignores me. I don't know why. I've never wronged her in any way, and I'd like to think of myself as being close with her ol' man.

Grabbing a plate, I fall into line behind the kids. Sure, I could grab what I want and go around them, but I need to speak with her, so I not-so-patiently wait until she's free and it's my turn. Of course, she instantly busies herself stirring the foods in each of the bowls, so she won't have to acknowledge me.

"Where'd your friend take off to?"

Her irritated gaze meets mine. "Why do you care?" She's straight to the point, as always. One thing I admire about her. Nothing scares or intimidates her, and if it does, she hides it well like her father.

"Just curious, haven't seen her around in a whole minute. Wanted to catch up." And reacquaint myself with her body while I'm at it.

"You wanted to sleep with her again, you mean?" She damn well knows that isn't her business. My personal life is no concern of hers, but I let her get away with it since it's her best friend and all. I need to play nice if I want her to give me the information I'm looking for.

"Of course I do. Still, haven't forgotten that sweet pussy sitting between those thighs. But no, I wanted to actually find out what all she's been up to."

"Hmph," she snorts and rolls her eyes. She's lucky I'm a decent man. Back in the day; she'd get put in her place quick.

"Where is she?" I'm done with the pleasantries. I asked her a fucking question, and if I have to talk to her ol' man about her mouth, I will.

She's quiet a minute, being stubborn, but eventually, caves with a deep sigh. "She went to my house."

"Oh, yeah?"

"Yeah, but she wasn't feeling well. With the heat, the alcohol made her sick. She was going to rest up." She follows her confession quickly. Obviously, B wanted

Hybrid Collection

some space if Princess is going to lengths explaining, to make sure I don't head to her place searching out Bethany.

"That's shitty."

"She'll be around once she's feeling better."

"Hope so, hate to have to disturb her and all, just to get some time with her."

"No need. Let her rest, please. Once Bethany's back, I'll tell her you wanted to talk to her."

I watch her closely as I reply, so she knows I'm dead serious on seeing her again. "Bet, appreciate it, I'll keep my eyes open for her then."

She nods, and as soon as I leave her be, I watch her take her cell out of her pocket. She types a text quickly and then stuffs it in her back pocket, glancing at me. I meet her eyes straight on, making her turn away immediately.

She knows I saw her type that message, and I'd bet every penny in my wallet she was warning her friend right now that I was looking for her. I just can't figure out why she'd need to. I thought Bethany and I left things on good terms. One day she was in my room letting me fuck her like a madman and the next she was gone. If anyone's upset, it should be me. She left me high and dry, not so much as a 'fuck you, I'm moving.' Nothing.

Women are confusing to me; they always have been. Should I show up at Viking's house and surprise Bethany? As much as I want to, it's probably not a good idea to pop up unannounced and all. She has a kid now; I have to watch how I handle this. The caveman approach Viking used on Princess won't work for me, as much as I wish that were the case.

I can't believe she even has a kid. And that I'm still interested in her after all this time as well. Of course, I thought about her randomly over the years, but now that I've seen her, it's like I've missed her.

Did I really miss her? How is that even possible? We had a few fun times, nothing to get hung up on. I think it's the fact that she took off and then years later shows up, kid in tow and isn't instantly sprung on me like she was in the past. It's fucking with my head.

"You good?" Exterminator mutters as I post up next to him and survey the people spread out around the compound. All these people here and I'd bet Princess is nice to every damn one of 'em except me. Wonder if any of these fuckers hit on B?

"Fine."

"Princess?"

"Damn Ice Queen." I shrug, and he chuckles to himself.

They find it entertaining that she doesn't like me. I'm starting to wonder if her little friend has anything to do with that and what the hell Bethany would say to turn Princess against me.

I mean, I never called the bitch after we were together, not like I could anyhow. I didn't have her number. I could've asked Princess for it, but I don't like people in my shit, and I was attacked by a lion right after that for fuck's sake. I'm pretty sure lion attack pulls the trump card in anything.

Clearly, I had my own shit to deal with. Bethany would've ended up hating me if she would've stuck around here anyhow. I was so damn angry after my attack happened, I couldn't be near a woman anyhow. Not just because I was miserable, but I wouldn't have let her see me so fucking weak and hurt.

Nobody witnessed my struggle—not a single fucking person from this club. No one knew I went to specialists or spent hours upon hours in physical therapy, choking down orders from some dumb preppy fuck griping at me to 'keep going.' Christ, I wanted to kick his goddamn teeth in, but I didn't. Preppy fuck still has every gleaming white tooth, probably thanks to some rich parents.

It was all so I could get my leg to be in the best condition it could be and ride again. There was no way in hell I was giving up riding for the rest of my life like the doctors wanted. Fuck them and fuck that lion. I overcame the struggle just like I knew I would.

Hybrid Collection

I'm good now, I think. I've had years to heal and calm my anger. Now, it's time I find me a good woman to settle down with. Bethany just doesn't realize it yet, that it's gonna be her I choose. She'll figure it out soon enough, and just like riding, I'll get what I want.

I won't stop until I do.

CHAPTER 6

"I don't believe in magic." The young boy said.
The old man smiled. "You will, when you see her."
- Atticus

BETHANY

Glancing at my phone, I read the text again for the fifth time since I've woken up. My dreams sucked, but I survived as usual. Maybe one day I'll be able to push the memories so far down that they'll stop finding me each time I dare to close my eyes.

When you're abused by someone who you love and is supposed to love and care for you in return, well, it screws you up inside. I'll never be like everyone else—normal. Probably why Nightmare draws me in so easily; his darkness soothes my own in a sense.

Princess messaged me while Maverick and I were taking a nap. Her text said that Nightmare was asking about me, wondering if I'd be back to the barbecue. She said he's waiting.

Should I go back? Why does he even care? I can't stop thinking of how it felt when he touched me. His presence is so large, it's impossible not to feel him on absolutely every part of my body.

Hybrid Collection

The doorbell rings and I jump—startled a bit—secretly hoping it's Night, but dreading it in the same breath. If it's him, I'll most likely shit my pants, being alone with him and our son. *Shit, I've dug myself a deep hole.*

Checking the peephole, I find London on the other side and let loose the breath I'd been holding.

Opening it with a smile, I greet her with a "Hi," and gaze at her curiously.

"Hey, chica. I asked Princess where you ran off to, and when she said you weren't feeling well, I wanted to stop over to check on you."

"Oh, wow. That's nice of you, thanks."

"I know what it's like to have a little one and feel like ass. Can I get you anything or help out?"

I let her in and shut the door quickly, like Nightmare's hiding out in the bushes or something. I know he's not, but seeing him earlier has me semi-paranoid.

I don't really know what to say. Part of me wants to throw my arms around her and hug her. There've been many times, I've been sick and had to carry a trash bin around with me in case I randomly had to puke while trying to take care of a baby on my own. It was hard and every minute sucked, but I gritted and cried and puked my way through it. I never let anyone know it either, not even Princess. She would've been knocking down my door to help me, but I had to prove to myself that I could do it on my own. So far I have.

"No. I appreciate it more than you know. I think it was just the heat that got to me. I don't spend a lot of time outside anymore, and it wore me out quick."

"I know how that is. If it's not spring or fall, I don't attempt to be outside unless there's a pool nearby."

"Gotta love Texas."

"I do, just not the summer heat," she says seriously, and I grin.

"Me too," I agree and decide I really do like her.

She was nice at the compound, but one thing I admire about London is she's genuine. It's hard to find that in a lot of people, especially when you first meet them. I discovered earlier she's Cain's wife. Cain belongs to Ares' club, and he's pretty wild according to Princess. He was busy grilling when I was there earlier, so I didn't get a chance to speak to him.

"So, are you feeling better now, then?"

"Yeah, I am. I knocked out with Mav and got to recharge a bit."

"Awesome. You heading back to the festivities?"

"I should. I'm supposed to be here supporting Princess. So far, I haven't done a great job of it, either."

"Want to walk back with me then?"

"You walked?"

"Hell yeah, my mom's coming to get my kids later. I'm having some delicious drinks tonight, namely anything with tequila in it."

"Nice." Grabbing Maverick's bag, I shuffle through it to make sure we have everything already.

His toys and pack of cheese crackers are there, along with a twenty dollar bill. I doubt we'd need any money, but I stuck it in there earlier just in case. I've learned the hard way that being unprepared sucks, big time.

"Let me go check on him and see if he's fully awake."

"Okay." She nods, and I make my way to the guest room.

Maverick was awake earlier, but he was still in sleepy mode, plucking at his stuffed giraffe's hair. It's his routine until he fully wakes up and goes from zero to fifty with energy.

"Hey buddy, are you awake yet?"

"Hmmm?" he grumbles, turning toward me. He's definitely Nightmare's son; he can be so grouchy if you don't let him have 'his time.' Same as in the mornings, too, when he needs cereal, cartoons, and quiet. Just like I need coffee to function and get myself going.

Shit, maybe it's me he's like and not Nightmare.

"Do you want to go back to Prissy's barbecue and play with the other kids?" His pediatrician told me to speak to him in full sentences as much as possible. It's supposed to help with his vocabulary development.

"Ummm…yep." He sits up, already more awake than two seconds ago. I'm glad he'll have someone to play with again because he's about to be bouncing off the walls.

"Okay, I got our stuff ready. You go to the bathroom and then we'll go back. Make sure you wash your hands."

"'Tay', Momma," he replies and I go out to wait with London.

"He's coming, just having him use the restroom."

"I get it; I'm a boy's mom too. Mine's just a bit older now. He's off doing man shit and fishing with my brother. I've learned that girls are fun but dramatic."

I'm laughing when my own little man makes his way into the living room, and we take off for the compound again.

I'm about to crack open a new beer when a large hand takes it from me, opens the top, and hands the cold beverage back.

"Thank you, I could've opened it though."

He shrugs. "What kind of man would I be if I let you open it?"

"Let me?" I mock, and Ruger grins devilishly, his eyes skimming over me from top to bottom.

"You've gotten hotter."

"Well thanks, I think." Laughing, I take a good-sized gulp of the beer. I need it after earlier. "I honestly didn't think you'd remember me."

"Of course, I do, and I'm not the only one either." His eyebrows go up, and he flicks his gaze to the side.

Mine follow along and meet an irritated Nightmare's dark glare. *Well, shit.* "He's still charming, I see."

He snorts, smiling widely. "Brother or not, that's not the word I'd use for him."

"Come on, Ruger, you know you follow his lead." I giggle, and he laughs with me.

"You're gonna get me in trouble smiling like that, B, with him watching us. You know he still hasn't forgiven me for going swimming with you guys. I've gotta stay hands off when it comes to you."

"What? That was years ago!"

"I know." He shakes his head. "Still, he had his eye on you, and I should've known better. Just like Viking with Princess."

"We're nowhere near that level and never were. And I'm single, by the way, so he has no right whatsoever to be pissed at you for making me smile or being over here talking with me."

He snorts again. "Yeah, that's what you think, sweetie. I just wanted to say what's up, but I better go find someone to hit on before my brother decides he wants to beat my ass to show off in front of you. I happen to like this nose much better when it's not broken."

"You're just a flirt, no harm done. It was good seeing you, Ruger."

Hybrid Collection

"You too." He winks, flashes a quick look at Night again, and takes off toward another chick like his ass is on fire.

That was weird, but I brush it off. Nightmare rarely said two words to me in front of his brothers back then. I don't know what Ruger's talking about, but I'm not going to argue with him. If he says Nightmare was territorial, then I'll take his word for it. Clearly, I never received that memo.

The sun's beginning to set, so I shuffle Maverick closer. I don't want to lose sight of him in the dark. I'd freak out. There's so much land around here, and God forbid he finds the pigs by himself. He'd try to touch them and end up hurt. I'd never forgive myself for it.

Princess told me earlier that we could take Mav to go feed them, but I don't want him out there at nighttime. Maybe I'll surprise him, and we'll walk over there tomorrow. My son seems to be infatuated with monster trucks and farm animals. I don't know if it's an age thing or what, but those two things garner his attention if he notices them.

Princess comes over to my spot with two plates of strawberry pie. My guess is she made them yesterday before we arrived. Her mom had an amazing recipe she'd use when we were teenagers. "Hey, would you keep an eye on little man for a few so I can visit the ladies room?"

"Of course, take your time." She smiles, and I know she's going to let him eat his weight in pie while I'm gone.

"Save me some." I point accusingly.

"I make no promises."

Shaking my head, I go inside to take care of business and should've guessed that Nightmare would be there for me once I finished. P said he was waiting; I should've taken her seriously. I figured he was just speaking to her, being nosey.

A strong arm wraps around me from behind, pulling me into a hard body. His warm breath hits my neck as his nose lightly brushes over my ear. He smells just like he used to—enrapturing.

"You need to let me go." *And right this minute*. Not only does he feel good, but it's more difficult for me to protest with him touching me.

"Why should I?" His deep voice grumbles, coating my skin in heat and my stomach flutters like I'm on a roller coaster. He's always done this to me whenever he was near, made me feel as if I were falling.

"I have to get back outside."

"You should just relax and come spend some time with me."

"I don't need to be anywhere near you, and you have to stop touching me, Nightmare."

"Mmm, I love it when you say my name. Now let me make you scream it."

My breath catches, every nerve in my body waiting, practically salivating at feeling him. "Not happening."

"You never objected before." His teeth bite into the soft spot where my neck and shoulder meet. Goose bumps flood my body. I want to grind my ass against him and make him pant, but I don't. "I can make you tremble with need, make you crumble to pieces in my hands. Fuck, I missed your taste."

I never should've worn this dress.

"I'm protesting now."

"Naw, you just need a little coaxing. I can work it out." His other hand finds my thigh, smoothing up my skirt toward my center. "Remember the last time I touched you like this?"

"How could I forget?"

"Exactly. I had my fingers inside you in front of an entire bar and damn did you come hard. I can make it happen again. I can sink them knuckle deep right now."

"So generous of you."

"I missed that smart little mouth of yours, too. Close your eyes and remember how I made you shake, dollface."

The heat from his palm has my eyes slamming closed. Briefly, but it's enough to stir up the memories from the first night he ever touched me.

Three years ago...

I'm standing on the opposite side of the pool table, downing tequila and waiting for Princess to take her shot. The bar's a total shit hole, but fuck, it has some sexy-ass bikers. The huge biker she'd been tormenting outside, comes storming toward her.

He looks pissed, so I attempt to warn her, "Princess!" I call, but the music and patrons are too noisy for her to hear me, and my voice drowns out amongst the chaos.

In seconds, he's slamming her face down on the pool table and ripping her skirt up. I can't believe what I'm freaking seeing.

Oh shit, oh shit, oh shit. This isn't happening.

I stand still, shocked at first. Nobody does shit to help, so I take off for them. I have to help her!

I'm halfway around the pool table when an arm wraps around my middle. It's strong like a vice and pulls me into a body that's harder than any other I've ever been against. He even smells strong and manly, like smoke and whiskey. It's the type of smell from someone you're sure you don't want to fuck with.

"Shhh, little daydream, leave them be." It's rasped into my hair, but loud enough for me to hear him clearly. I begin to stir and pull away from the mountain of a man, but he's way too strong, easily subduing me.

He tugs me backward with him until I'm planted directly on his lap beside one of the small round bar tables. His boots part my feet, his knees and thick thighs, easily opening my legs wide for him. I can feel his hardness against my ass, and any other time I'd want to rub all over him, but I'm too distracted right now. My best friend needs me.

"I need to help her." I attempt to squirm from his hold again, but it's no use. His other hand lands on my thigh, the size making me feel dainty with him wrapped around me like this, practically consuming me.

The arm around my stomach brushes the underside of my breasts causing the peaks to stiffen almost immediately. I was an idiot thinking I'd show off and not wear a bra with a shirt cut right underneath my tits. Young and dumb comes to mind, in a biker bar no less.

"No, you need to let them handle it. You can't go startin' shit. He's claiming her, that's gonna be his ol' lady."

"His ol' lady?"

"Yeah, watch them. He's fucking her, and she's loving it."

She really is. I know my best friend, and she's enjoying every second of it. If I'm honest, it's so damn hot too. She's absolutely gorgeous with her cheeks flushed and her hair wild.

His hand trails up my thigh until it reaches my cutoff jeans. The shorts are so tiny, there's practically no barrier to keep him from touching me. "Fuck, dollface, this pussy's just waiting for me?" he growls against my throat.

I swallow and nod, becoming more and more turned on as I relax and listen to his voice. He adjusts, his cock thick and hard—ready. I know he wants me, and it spurs me on to wiggle on him just enough to make him groan.

His mouth lands on my neck, sucking and biting just as his fingers find my swollen lips. The tequila and Percocet I took earlier is thrumming through my body, heightening my pleasure. There are people everywhere, but they're all watching

Hybrid Collection

Princess and Viking go at it in the middle of the bar. No one's paying any attention to Nightmare and me.

"Jesus, you're wet," he mutters against my skin, and my nipples tingle, aching for his attention as well. He's the sexiest man I've ever seen—swear to God. Mix his voice with the narcotics, and it's a potent aphrodisiac on my body.

His fingers part me, rubbing my wetness before pushing inside my core. I'm still wet from making myself come moments ago outside when we went to go smoke. His movements are making me drip down the side of my thigh. Probably getting all over his jeans, too, but I don't care. I want to leave a reminder behind; I want him to remember how I felt sitting on his lap tonight.

"Ride my fingers, baby; let me feel that sweet pussy." He pumps them in me over and over while we watch Princess and Viking fuck like animals. His arm holding me tightly t him has my body going crazy at being controlled so effortlessly on his part, and in minutes, I'm coming again, all over his knuckles.

"That's it. I feel your little cunt gripping my fingers; take what you need, baby. Let me make you feel good."

Moans escape me; it's so loud around us that I don't hold back at all. I'm sure some people have noticed what we're up to, but no one will dare say a word to the enormous biker bracing me to him. After the tremors subside and my body relaxes, his grip loosens.

I have to see him. I want him to notice my own flushed face. I want my wetness all over his lap. I've craved this man since the first time I saw him, and he's going to know it. He's that quiet bad boy you notice across the room and then dream about nearly every night for the rest of your boring life.

Twisting around, I climb over him to straddle his lap. My center rests on his hardness, and I reward him by grinding my hips in a circular motion. He made me come; now it's his turn.

"Fuck, that's good," he groans, one hand holding my ass so my pussy remains pushed up against his cock. The other lifts my shirt just enough for him to see my bare tits. His head falls forward, drawing a nipple in his mouth and grazing his scruffy beard between them. It feels absolutely fucking divine and has me picturing that beard between my thighs next.

"So good," he grumbles and sucks the wetness from his fingers, still nuzzling.

My mouth meets his right after, my tongue swirling with his, copying the motions my hips make on his lap. The kiss is short, but sinful and sweet all mixed as one.

"Pussy taste sweet?" I ask as I pull back and whisper it against his lips.

"Hell yeah." He's so close I can taste his breath mixing with my own.

"Now you know how both our pussy's taste." His gaze is confused until I tilt my head toward Princess.

"Her?" He stops, his mouth staying open as his mind races. His gaze is blistering as he stares me down, waiting to tell him that I'm kidding. I'm not.

"I was licking hers outside."

"Jesus fucking Christ." His eyes flair as he immediately stands. He grabs my arm tightly and yanks me along with him outside. "She's not the only one getting fucked tonight, dollface," he growls.

I blink, coming back to the present.

"That was such a good night, baby," he whispers, his tongue finding my neck as his palm rubs my core over my panties. He knows I love being kissed there; at least he did when we were together those nights.

Not only was it a good night, it was the night I got pregnant.

That thought has me pushing away from him. I'm panting and turned on, but thinking about my pregnancy is like a bucket of cold water when it comes to Nightmare.

Hybrid Collection

"I have to go," I utter, my mind fighting against my body and take off back down the hallway. I'm almost outside when I hear him call after me. His voice has my steps faltering to listen.

It's deadly serious as he grits, "You can run, Bethany, but make no mistake, I'm a hunter. I always catch my prey. When I catch that pussy again, I'll lick it, eat it, and fuck it. Hell, I may even keep it. Be ready, baby."

I push through the screen door, and it slamming behind me loudly as I nearly run back to my best friend and son. The son he doesn't have a clue exists.

CHAPTER 7

Nyctophilia- (n.)
Love of darkness or night, finding relaxation
or comfort in the darkness.

NIGHTMARE

I didn't see Bethany at all yesterday. One full day of being away from her, and I haven't stopped thinking of her. It's like she crawled inside my mind, planted her ass down, and hasn't gone anywhere since. It's fucking with me.
I'm beginning to think she took my threat serious from the barbecue the other night. That's good; I wanted her, too, because it was the truth. The chase only makes me want to have her again even more. Christ, that bitch looked so fucking beautiful when I touched her, too. Jesus, took my breath away.

She's foolish if she believes I'll let her hide out the entire week she's visiting, though. I'll show up at Viking's house if I have too; I'm not above finding her. I'm trying not to be too pushy since she has a kid and all, but I won't stand completely to the side either.

"You good, brother?" Viking questions me as he stares from across the table. I sorta just zoned out in front of everyone during church. We all do it, so I shrug it off.

"I'm straight. A little distracted or whatever, but it's all good."

Hybrid Collection

"He needs some pussy; his mind's too busy." Ruger snickers, and I glare in return.

I saw his dumb ass flirting with B the other night. I should make him taste his teeth for that shit. He knows we fucked before. He should also know she's off limits. He wanted her back then, and I told him to take a damn hike. Besides, he's still a Nomad, so ride off into the sunset, motherfucker.

I don't care about much, especially when it comes to the club. They do their thing, and I'm there with my support. The brothers rarely see me showing interest in any of the females around. If I like a bitch, they should back the fuck up and find another.

"It's not too busy to know you need to mind your own."

"Oh, I am brother; I assure you. I have no curiosity in her this time around. You made yourself clear the last time."

The brothers sitting around the table all watch us curiously. This isn't typical club business, but Ruger's decided to air my laundry in front of everyone apparently. *Stupid ass.*

"Good." I shut him out, not about to let everyone see me worked up. I'm glad the fucker learned quickly, though. No more going swimming and trying to hit it. That shit won't fly this time. No one's touching that pussy but me; I'll make sure of it.

Odin clears his throat. "You know she's leaving in a few days, right?"

Jesus fucking Christ. I can't believe we're discussing this shit in the middle of church right now. They all need to mind their own damn business instead of being knee deep in my shit.

"Thanks for that, Sherlock. Now can everyone mind their fuckin' business or should we go about holding hands next? Maybe watch each other take a piss?"

Blaze grins and Scot chuckles. Viking just rolls his eyes and waits for us to be quiet so he can get back to his discussion. Odin shuts up immediately; he is after all the lowest on the totem pole besides the prospects. Sure, he'll be VP someday, but he's gotta earn that shit in his brother's eyes.

Torch is like me—quiet and sticks close to Viking. Hell, we all stay close to our Prez. Who knew the craziest fucker in our group would end up being an amazing leader.

"Now, back to the women we have working for us. Does the bar still have enough security? I don't want deputy douchebag showing up and catching them whoring out the back building."

"Aye," Scot confirms. "Makin' good bit of cash too."

"No issues at all? Blaze, you've been over there a lot. Anything?"

"Nope, the whores have been staying clean, and the johns have been leaving satisfied. They're getting repeat customers and no one's beating them up any more like when they were on their own. It's going smooth as silk, Prez."

"Good. Keep them safe and clean. If anyone wants to leave, make sure they have a way too. We get a decent cut, but overall, they work for themselves, and I want to keep it that way."

The brothers nod. We've never been the type to be running pussy, but it's worked out well for everyone involved so far. The crime in Austin against the whores was skyrocketing. Women were ending up dead or nearly beaten to death, some from overdose and not making it to the hospital in time.

Since they came to us asking for help, they've had no issues, and we've gotten a healthy profit from it. I'll admit, it's nice having another form of steady cash coming in rather than lump sums from random runs. When we have brothers visiting, they can have some company if they choose to.

I haven't touched any of them either. I won't—ever. A few of them are sweet and talk to me, try to catch my eye, but it never works. I don't care about them being around the club and fucking the guys or whatever, but I prefer not to shit where I eat. I can only imagine the drama when someone gets feelings or whatever. No thank you. No easy pussy is worth that trouble.

"How was the gig?" Vike turns to me again.

"No issues." I shrug.

Hybrid Collection

"Bet and Exterminator?"

"Ex and Chaos handled the drug swap while I played and kept watch."

"That's what's up. Good looking out." He takes a swig of whiskey and turns to Chaos. "Did the Mexican offer anything besides weed again?"

We've been attempting to heal the rift we have with the Mexican cartel, even though I fucking hate the thought. It's all in hopes to flush out the leader and start taking out bits of the organization. If any type of mob's around, we want it to be the Russians. We've worked well with them for years now.

"Nope, we made ourselves clear we don't want anything besides moving some green."

"No coke?"

"No, Prez. We told him we'd light his ass on fire if he brought it to us again."

"Good. Twist from the other crew handles that shit, and I don't want us dipping into their shit cause some Mexican's gettin' greedy."

"We won't cause any shit with Ares' club; you know this," I grumble, and Viking nods, sighing.

He's stressed. I'm guessing over the wedding. He's supposed to leave for a few days, too, and he's not used to taking time off. If he leaves, it's 'cause we have a run or some other reason. This time he's supposed to take a few days and do absolutely nothing with his ol' lady. My money's on them staying here. They'll post up in the house going at it nonstop, but he won't stray far from his club.

"Anything else?" He glances around, and we shake our heads. He slams the gavel, and we shuffle out the decent-sized chapel room he had built specifically for church.

"You need to get her alone with a few drinks in her system. Have the old Bethany come out and play," Ruger suggests, walking behind me. *Nosey bastard.*

"How am I supposed to do that?" I mutter. She has a kid now; I can't get her toasted with a little one to take care of. I'm a dick, but not that sort of a dick.

"I can help with that." Odin comes up beside me. I swear it seems like Viking's younger brother grows half an inch each week.

"How?"

"I'll offer to babysit so she can come to the party with Princess tonight. She was planning to stay at the house and watch movies, but if I offer to babysit, she'll come."

"Why would she let you?" I stare at him skeptically. It's a longshot, but it could work if we get Princess on board to talk Bethany into it.

"Bethany trusts me. I've seen her over the past few years. You haven't, and Maverick likes me anyhow."

"Maverick?" I ask. Cool-ass name for a kid. I shouldn't expect anything less from B, though.

"Yeah, that's her son's name. He's almost three."

"Right." I nod, but I really have no fucking clue. Why does finding this out, make me feel like an ass for not already knowing? Maybe because she's here alone, without a man and I know if it were my kid, I'd be posted up beside them nonstop. "You're sure you don't mind?"

"Yep."

"Why would you do this for me?" I'm blunt, but Odin owes me nothing, and he's young. I remember being his age, babysitting was the furthest thing from my mind.

"Because you're my brother. I have your back, and one day, I'll need you to have mine."

Ah, the fucker's smart. He knows that one day we'll all be voting on him being Vice President. He's already chalking up favors from us. He's no doubt Viking's blood. He'll make one hell of a leader someday like his brother.

Hybrid Collection

"All right, Odin. You do me a solid, and I'll owe you one."

"I'm counting on it." He smirks, heading for the parking lot.

"Spider?" I turn to the shorter, dark-haired brother.

"Yeah?"

"Can you figure out where it is exactly that she lives? I need to know how far this commute is gonna be if I'm getting serious an' all."

"Of course. I can get her plate number from the security tape and run it through the DMV system. As long as her registration's up to date, her address should be current in their program. But why are you going to this trouble? It's been years since you were with her."

"I know that. Maybe it took a few years for me to realize what's important in life."

"And what about her son?"

"He fits in those plans."

Especially since I can't have my own kids.

"Okay then, give me about an hour to search the feed and get her license plate number. I'll get you an address and phone number."

"Appreciate it," I reply, and Spider's off toward his room. It's like a tech center in there with five computer monitors and a few laptops. He's got all kinds of shit going on all the time. He helps watch the club security footage when he's not out riding with Ex and them. He does pretty much anything else we need him to tech wise as well. I'd describe him as an outlaw nerd. He won't blink to bury a body and can hack into pretty much anything.

It's convenient having him around when he's here, but I try not to ever bother him for any of that stuff. Makes times like now come in handy because he doesn't even blink, offering to help out.

With Odin watching her kid, there's no reason for her not to come out to the clubhouse tonight. Her one excuse is taken care of, and Princess will want her best friend there celebrating with her.

Now I just have to figure out how to get her to talk to me. I've done a shit job of it so far. She's been avoiding me as if I have the fucking plague or some shit. Why do chicks have to be so complicated?

"You think me goin' after Bethany is pointless?" I ask my brother once he finally walks out.

"Not if you want her. Just keep in mind, it's not only B anymore. I don't want my ol' lady up my ass cause her best friend's hurt by my brother. Shit won't be fun for me or you."

"I got you; I won't mix my pussy in the club's business. Shit goes south, I'll make sure it's not her caught in the cross fire."

"Don't know how you'll manage that one, but glad you're at least considering it could happen."

"I need her to come tonight to the party. She's gotta chill the fuck out at some point so I can get her to talk to me."

"I can't believe we're having this fuckin' conversation. Last time the bitch was all over you like she was in heat or something. You just glared at her, and she couldn't get enough. What's the issue this time around?"

"Fuck if I know. Maybe because I'm not ignoring her this time? It's fucking with my head though. It's like she had my cock before and doesn't want it again. Trust me, she loved my shit, ain't no way she can deny it."

He chuckles. Viking flashing his teeth tells me that he's thoroughly amused with me tripping out over this. Fucker never does it unless we're lit off some whiskey and weed so he must be loving this a little too much.

"You sayin' I'm gonna have to drag her ass here tonight so you can have a shot? Just show up at the house and make her come with you."

Hybrid Collection

"I can't do that in front of the kid. It may traumatize him or something."

He snorts, glancing heavenward. "You're turnin' into a pussy. That's why she's not after you, she can probably sense it. Chicks are smart, she thinks you're a pussy, she won't want your dick man."

"I am the fuck not. Just trying to think of not messing her kid up is all. Trying to be considerate; females love that shit."

"How would you know that? Since when do you make it a habit to notice women's feelings?"

"I read it somewhere, and I am now; that's all that matters."

"If you say so, brother. You want my advice? You see her tonight, pick her ass up and carry her to your room. Show her you're still a man. Tie the bitch up; fuck her until she can't walk, then be all sweet and shit. My ol' lady loves it like that."

"Princess gets her here tonight, and I'll take care of it."

"Just lock it down, brother. A good dickin' and she'll be all over you like white on rice. Hell, you may not want it after you hit it again anyhow. Could be you forgot what it was the last time."

"It was good, trust me."

"Then lock it the fuck down."

I nod, tossing back the shot of whiskey sitting on the bar waiting for me. I'm going to need about ten of them to make her feelings become invalid to me enough that if she fights me, I won't give two shits. Viking's right; I need to take care of business and remind her who's in control here. She came back, and I want her. She was mine back then, and she'll be mine again—this time for good. Once she comes to her senses, I'll move them back down here, and we can get settled together.

I can't believe after all the years out soul-searching, I'm ready to put down some roots. She's a good woman, though, just wild enough to keep me on my toes. At least she used to be. I have a feeling if she gets a taste of that again, she'll want more.

Now I'm around more and not into as much dangerous shit. Before we had our hands in dirty business, and it was a liability to care about anyone, a weakness. I wouldn't want a woman tortured or killed so enemies could get to me. They did it to Princess and Viking was a goddamn wreck. He never let anyone know it, but the man was about to completely lose it. Not sure I'd be as strong in his situation. I'd be liable to go in, guns blazing, and murder the whole lot of them if they ever threatened my ol' lady.

CHAPTER 8

Carpe Omnia
- Seize Everything

BETHANY

"I hope they'll be okay," I repeat myself for the tenth time.
Of course, I've left Maverick with a babysitter before, but this isn't the same. Odin doesn't babysit regularly, and I'm just slightly worried he'll do something out of the norm.

There's a decent-sized chance we'll come back later, and my son will be covered head to toe in fake tattoos. Generally, it wouldn't concern me, but in two days when Princess says, "I do," I don't want my kid looking like a hellion in any of her photos. Although he'd fit in with the men around him, and maybe he'll blend in more that way.

"They're right over the field at the house if they need anything. I'm sure they won't, though. This is good practice for Odin anyhow. The club sluts follow him around like lost puppies. He needs to see what happens if you're not careful."

"Thanks." I wince.

I wasn't careful; I was too trusting and ended up a single mom because of it.

"I didn't mean it like that. You were older—in your twenties—when you got pregnant. He's only eighteen and thinks he's untouchable by anything. I don't want a surprise to land him on his ass, at least not until he's older. You had a chance to be free and crazy, he's just getting to that point."

"I know what you meant. Really, it's fine. I was older but still living with my mom working a crap job. Things could've been easier. I hope Odin gets a chance to live his life some before facing the challenges I did."

"Me too, B. I won't let him be some shitty father, bailing on the back of his bike, either. I promise you that whichever woman he ends up with, he'll do right by them."

My smile's a bit shaky as I ponder over her words. She's turning into her mom, and she's so lucky for that. So are the rest of the guys; Mona was good to everyone.

It's also shaky because she still believes that Nightmare left me out to dry. I mean, he did in a way, telling me he didn't want kids and couldn't have them. He said it himself. *What kind of father would he be and why would he want that anyhow.*

Every time I begin to feel guilty or question my decisions, I have to remind myself of his words. He didn't want me; he didn't want Maverick. Nightmare didn't want us. I would've given him everything I had, too. It wasn't much, but I would've worshiped him with every beat of my heart. Too bad I wasn't enough for him.

"Enough seriousness. You have a free pass tonight. You know what that means, right?" She pulls me to her in a side hug, grin full of mischief.

"Free pass? Hardly. I still have to function tomorrow." Grinning, she rolls her eyes.

"Tonight, we have fun, Bethany. Suck it up and hold on sweet pea, it's goin' down."

"Oh, God. Why do I feel like we'll regret this tomorrow?"

"Let's not think of that now. You're trying that apple pie moonshine I told you about. That stuff is freaking amazing."

"All right, bartender, pour me one ... but only one. No puking tonight."

Hybrid Collection

She laughs and leads the way into the clubhouse, straight toward the bar. She's full of trouble, and everyone always thought I was the bad one growing up. She was just as guilty as I was at getting us into something we weren't supposed to be in.

First time we drank? *Her fault.* Yep, she opened her mom's brandy cabinet and made us vodka and orange juice. It was disgusting, and we spilled it everywhere. Her mom had to know half the bottle of vodka was really water. She never said a word about it, but she didn't need too. Princess and I were so paranoid that Mona knew, we didn't enjoy it one bit. I think we walked around with our eyes wide and hands shaking for an entire month, waiting for her mom to lynch our asses.

Part of me wonders how we even survived as teens, being linked to a notorious biker club and her brother being Mr. Super Popular in school. Girls hated us for being close to him, and weird men watched us all the time. I know it was because of her father. Whether they were friend or foe, I still haven't the slightest clue.

However it happened, we made it, and now she's still trying to kill me—with moonshine. I love apple pie and doubt the liquor tastes anything like it, but if it does, I'm in trouble. You can't have too much apple pie, especially if they have whipped cream behind the bar, too. Geesh.

"Hey, Blaze? Can we each have a shot of apple pie, please?" She leans over the bar, smiling at a guy our age. His arms are covered in tattoos that look like they're on fire. So, this dude must be the cousin she's told me about. He's decent looking, but not on Nightmare's level though.

Princess filled me in how he was a total dick to her the first time they met. She said he's cool now, but for the longest, I wanted to castrate him for treating her so badly. I'm surprised Viking didn't kill him when he found out. She said he offered to and that gave him some more brownie points in my book.

He carefully pours us a few shots from a jar and sets them in front of us, then he takes a big swig straight from the jar for himself.

"I told you only one!" I protest over the loud music filling the small room.

Blaze grins at Princess, then at me. "No way, darlin'. You'll want another, trust me." He winks, and I understand how he's charmed her. Manners and a cute dimple with some southern twang will no doubt make your heart flutter. Mix in some moonshine, and women don't have a chance.

"Ugh." I groan, knowing I've already lost. She's got the freaking bartender on her side, so no doubt he'll feed us drinks all night as long as she bats her eyelashes at him.

"Blaze, whiskey and coke, brother." It's grumbled from behind me.

"Brother." Blaze nods and turns to make the drink.

My backside feels like it's on fire and being able to make out his grumble, I know Nightmare is close. If I guess correctly, I'd say way too close knowing him. The man has been persistent for sure and doesn't hesitate to overtake my personal space.

"You gonna say 'hi' at least, little daydream?" he mutters making my nipples harden in response. *Traitors.* The man's voice has a straight shot to my core it seems. One hand lands on my hip, and my body falters for a moment, wanting nothing more than to lean into him and rest against his strength. I want to touch him everywhere, for him to do the same to me. God, he's so good at it, like he knows all the perfect spots to hit.

"Princess," he acknowledges, playing nice.

"Nightmare," she replies, not impressed and the tension grows thicker around us. I wouldn't be surprised if P clawed his eyes out if she was given the chance to. It's my damn fault entirely, and I hate that I've created a rift between them.

"Try the shot dollface, you'll love it." His breath hits my neck, caressing the sensitive flesh, my eyelashes fluttering as it does. Thank God, he can't see my face, or he'd know I'm halfway there to giving in to him.

His drink lands on the counter in front of me as Blaze's gaze flickers over me. He's curious no doubt, why his broody brother is hovering behind me, like an overprotective bear—like I belong to him.

Hybrid Collection

Prissy shoots him an annoyed look and passes me one of the rock's glasses with two fingers full of clear alcohol. "Come on, B; a toast to good friends and good times."

I tap my glass to hers, lightly bumping the bottom to the counter and then bringing it to my lips. It doesn't even smell harsh like moonshine normally does. The taste splashes over my tongue, and it's like biting into a fresh slice of cinnamon apple pie, just like she said.

I'm fucked because I instantly love it and know I'll want to drink it until I'm sick which is not good. I don't get out much—like at all—and have no alcohol tolerance anymore, so I there's no way I can hang with my bestie drinking anymore. I've turned into more of a chug-wine-before-bed or sip-a-beer-until-it's-room-temperature type.

"Damn, that's good." I sigh, setting the empty glass in front of Blaze. Nightmare's grip tightens on my hip briefly until I wiggle away. He and alcohol don't mix—I'd end up pregnant again, and that's not happening.

"Told you." She winks, and I giggle.

I actually giggle, because I'm so happy to be here right in this moment getting to drink and relax with her. If I knew how everything was going to turn out, I would've cherished the time we had before, much more. I hate living away from her, but I didn't have a choice. I had to get away and start over. I had to go somewhere where a decent apartment was cheap to rent and where we could survive on a waitress's salary.

"Too bad Maverick's father wasn't in the picture to help you with him, or else we could do this more." She glares at Night behind me, and I choke, coughing.

"Princess!" I gasp and yank her away from the bar, away from him. "You can't say that stuff, please," I plead, the music drowning our conversation away. I can't believe she just said that next to him.

"Why not? I'm your best friend; of course, you're going to tell me what happened. Does he think he can just stand right there, touching you like he owns you, without me opening my mouth? He can't have his cake and eat it too, doesn't work that way. He wants you, he wants Maverick. There is not one without the other."

My eyes become watery. She has no idea what she's talking about. I should admit everything to her, the entire story. He doesn't know Maverick's his, and even if he did, I don't think anything would change. I seriously doubt he'd care, but I'm not wanting to feel that heartache in my soul as well.

Being shot down once from him is enough for me to remember for the rest of my life. I wish he wanted us both, but I'm not going to fool myself into believing that fairy tale can be mine. He doesn't want to be a father; I won't force him into that position.

"Please. I just want to relax and have some fun."

"What's going on?" Viking's inquisitive gaze flashes over us both as he pulls Princess to his chest. Always in protection mode when it comes to his woman. She's lucky.

"Nothing, your ol' lady's making me drink moonshine."

"Ah." He grins. "It's good."

"It's amazing!"

"Then let's have some," he finishes, pulling Princess with him to the bar. She, in return, tugs me along with her.

We each pick up the other full shots we'd left behind, and Blaze pours Viking a tumbler that's three-quarters full. The man's the size of a mammoth, so naturally, his shots are supersized too.

"Come on, brother, join us in celebrating." He includes Nightmare, and, of course, Night readily agrees, saddling up next to me as he's poured his own super-sized shot as well. At this rate, I'll be trashed within the hour.

"What we toasting too?" Night asks while staring down at me, his eyes saying so much but I'm unable to read him.

Hybrid Collection

"To women we can't forget," Viking mutters, while tinking his tumbler to Princess' shot. "To women worth being better for."

She finishes, "And to men who're nothing but trouble." He sends her a curious glance but doesn't protest. Instead, downing the alcohol in two gulps and finishing by pressing his lips to hers in a scorching kiss.

I'm happy she's found the love of her life. I'm even slightly jealous of it. Not in a bad way; I just want that love for myself.

Nightmare's knuckles find my chin, tipping my head up to his, but I don't give him the chance. Turning back to Blaze, I put on a large smile. "Hey, Blaze, can I get a Sprite, please?" I need something to cool me off.

"Just a Sprite? Want me to add some vodka and cherry or anything?" I hate vodka, and even that sounds delicious. No wonder he's the bartender.

"No thanks, just the Sprite for me, please. I need something other than alcohol in my stomach or I won't be able to hang with this one for very long." I tilt my head over toward my friend who's still making out with her man. Years later and they act like two horny teenagers, never getting enough of each other.

"Hmmm, that's not what I've heard. According to the boss lady, you were quite the partier back in the day."

"Yep, I was, but I've calmed down since then. It's not fun being hungover the next day I've learned."

"Truth," he agrees, handing me the large, fizzy soda. He threw a cherry on top for me, so that was sweet.

"We had fun, and I don't remember you being so bad off that we couldn't roll around the next day." Nightmare pulls my face back toward him, and I lick my lips. My hand falls to his chest, attempting to keep some mandatory space between us. Any closer and I'll melt right here in front of him.

He leans down, brushing his nose against mine as his deep voice continues to mutter, "In fact, I remember we had a great time—fucked up, posted against the side of a bar. Remember that, dollface? You had marks all over your back from the brick." Princess' eyes grow wide as they meet mine, and the memories flash through my mind of the night he's talking about.

He'd pulled me outside the bar. Rushed and hot after I'd divulged my secret of having tasted Princess mere moments before he'd sucked my taste off his fingers. I wanted him so badly at that point I thought my body would explode if he held out.

It'd been like he was teasing me in the days before. Each time I'd seen him, he'd throw me a brief, irritated glance and nothing more. I knew he wanted to fuck me. I could feel it in the air, in the way his pissed-off gaze practically singed me each time it landed on me.

"So, I'm getting fucked too, hmmm?" I giggle, following behind as he rounds the corner of the building. I'm practically thrown up against the brick, his body coming to mine in a hurry as if he can't feel me fast enough.

"Bet your sweet ass, you are. I'm gonna fuck you so hard, you won't be feeling anyone else there but me—ever. I'll be your goddamn Nightmare all night tonight, baby, and you'll be my daydream."

Those words coming from his mouth as he pulls my shorts free are like ice on a hot day. Just what I need to hear for my core to crave him sinking blissfully deep into me. Most men are pansies, overworking to get me to spread my legs for them. Nightmare, however, gets right to it.

"Then fuck me, Nightmare," I whisper, relenting and his eyes alight with a fiery storm. He's big and strong and hung like a goddamn horse. His cock stirring between his legs is the biggest dick I've ever seen in my life. Long and thick and needy, exactly what I want from him. He's right about me never feeling anyone else. How could I with a man like him?

"Oh my God." Gasping in delight, I take his length in my hand—my fingers not being able to touch each other, his girth is so dense.

Hybrid Collection

"That's right, dollface, you won't be walking tomorrow." He winks, a roguish grin painted on his lips.

You know how many guys say that shit and then it never holds true? All of them. In this case, Nightmare is one hundred percent telling the truth, and for the first time in my life, I'm scared of a cock.

Pulling my hand free, he takes both my wrists in one of his much bigger hands. Nightmare posts them above my head, against the rough brick behind me. He wraps his other arm with muscles the size of my thighs around my waist, lifting me clear off the ground. The man clearly knows what he wants and fuck if it isn't unbelievably sexy.

A small moan escapes my lips at his movements. The control and no hesitation on his part has me panting to have him inside me. His cock bobs, straight up, seeking out my center. It's so fucking big, he doesn't even need his hands. He simply lowers me down on him, my pussy swallowing him up like the greedy, overly excited bitch she is.

One powerful bounce of his hips and I'm sliding down farther, his length ripping through me in the most delicious ways that I've experienced.

"Sweet baby Jesus," I groan, and he chuckles darkly. *"You are one big boy."*

"I didn't descend from above beautiful; I ascended from hell. Nothing good and pure could have a cock like this. And I'm all man, no boy around here," he growls and drives into me hard.

I scream loudly and love every second of the pain, of the perfection. There was a reason he was holding out on me, but no more. I may not be able to walk tomorrow, but I'll make sure he's so satisfied that he never wants another.

He may believe he's from hell, an outlaw biker who's mean and dangerous. But I don't agree with him. Nothing this perfect could come from below.

He fucks me with purpose, the rough edges of the brick scraping my back with each harsh drive. I don't know if he's proving his point to me or trying to make me praise

God about him some more. His arm must be torn to shit as well from bracing me and taking the brunt of his motions.

"You gonna cry, baby?" *he mutters, watching me with delight. He must be used to weak women. I may not be too strong, but one thing I'm not is weak. And if I were, I'd never let a man like this see it. He needs a mate that can match him, and I'm determined to be that one for him.*

"No, I want it harder."

His eyes widen as his eyebrows raise, surprised at my admission. "Harder?" *He must not be used to hearing that request.*

"Yes, harder, Nightmare. Make me feel you."

"Oh, you'll feel it all right." *It's muttered darkly as his body slams into mine, the breath nearly leaving my lungs as he sinks into me fully. There's hasn't been a man like him before, and it has me spinning. He's purely sinful, everything I crave and desire, yet everything I shouldn't have, everything that's bad for me.*

Nightmare calls to my dark side, I want to drink a little more, take another pill, and fuck even harder. He could be my destruction, yet it's the first time he's been this close to me—the first time I've felt him.

He bounces his hips again, thighs with thick muscles, built like some sort of Greek god. His cock drives through my core, taking its pleasure and giving me mine in return. He's so deep that his dick hits the perfect spot. One more caress and his cock has me grinding into him, seeking more.

"More, please, right there!" *I call, my eyes clamping shut as the sensations begin to make me see bright colors behind my eyelids.* "Ohmygod more, just fuck me, already!"

The words flip a switch; he drops my wrists, his free hand coming to my throat. One harsh squeeze, cutting off my breath has me coming, a scream fighting to break free as he pounds into me. It must be the tipping point for him too, as he stares at me full of fury, pumping into me over and over, so quickly that my head hits the brick. It hurts, but each sample of pain only heightens my pleasure he so easily supplies me with.

Gasping, my mouth falls open as dizziness starts to cloud my vision. His forehead is against mine, his mouth taking my own with a vengeance as his cock bursts inside my core. His cum is hot and thick, each splash warming my center in a blissful assault, and all I can think of is how I want more.

I want all of it, everything he'll give me. I want him.

"Fuck, you're sexy when your cheeks redden like that," Nightmare mutters, and it brings me out of the memory, of the first time he had me. The first time I had a piece of him. It was the night he possessed my body and my soul. I knew he owned me.

"Ummm," I reply, blinking quickly, trying to clear the thoughts away.

"You okay, Bethany?" Princess interrupts, garnering my attention.

"Yeah, just a little…dizzy." Sighing, I gulp some of the Sprite down.

This is why I can't drink around Nightmare. He doesn't even have to touch me; the memories alone could make me self-destruct.

CHAPTER 9

I'm a daydreamer and a night thinker.

NIGHTMARE

My knuckles brush her flushed cheek, and her breath catches. She's so fucking beautiful. I was stupid to let her slip through my fingers the last time we were together. Each time I'm around her, I see more and more what I've been missing out on.
Had I never been attacked, I'd like to think things would've turned out differently. She was so fuckin' crazy back then, too. Just plain wild; I would've loved taming her. I doubt there would've been any dull moments between the two of us.

"Please?" she mumbles as her head turns to the side away from my touch. Almost as if it hurts her each time I do it. I don't know why she's being like this, so stubborn. I'll break through her barrier; I just need a little more time with her relaxed like this.

"Dollface?" I stare down at her, wanting to place her cheeks in my palms and own her lips.

"Just stop touching her already!" Princess interrupts, about to take a step forward when Viking catches her arm, holding her in place.

Hybrid Collection

Flashing an irritated glare in his direction, one he's easily able to read, I remain quiet. He needs to keep his bitch in check. I'm getting real tired of her attitude toward me when I've done nothing but be respectful toward her since day one. She has no reason to treat me the way she does, and I've kept my mouth shut, but enough is enough.

I don't want to disrespect my Prez or his ol' lady, but if she doesn't butt the fuck out, I will say something. It'll get ugly, but me and Vike have been cool for a long time. He'll at least hear me out before he tries to break my neck.

"Cinderella," he warns gruffly at my glower and pulls her closer to him. He whispers something into her hair behind her ear that we can't hear. Whatever it is, she doesn't like it, but her trap stays closed, and, for that, I'm grateful.

"Come here, B, do a shot with me." My hand grasps the tips of her fingers to tug her toward me a little more.

"I can't." Her head shakes, her eyes sad.

"Fuck this shit." Princess steps forward, furious, not heeding Viking's warning any longer. "Here's an idea, Nightmare. Don't fucking touch her anymore! Can't you get the message? You didn't want her when she was pregnant with your kid; why the fuck should you have her now? You're a real piece of shit, you know that? All this time I've kept my mouth shut out of respect for Viking and Bethany, but I'm done. You deserve to at least get one ass chewing from us. What kind of motherfucker deserts his own kid? You shouldn't even be anywhere near her, you piece of shit! You're lucky I didn't slit your throat myself," she spits out angrily, staring me down like I'm worse than the scum on the bottom of toilet.

Her words begin to register, and my stomach turns. I feel sick like I could puke. My first thought is that it can't be true. I can't have kids; the doc told me a long time ago that my guys were slow swimmers. I guess it doesn't mean I couldn't have kids for the rest of my life, but at the time, he told me not to be too concerned about getting anyone pregnant.

But with Bethany? How did this happen and I didn't know. My kid? With her?

My eyes flash to my brother, but his are wide with shock as well. He didn't know, and that brings me a little bit of peace, knowing he didn't betray me. But Princess no doubt knew, and she took all those visits to see Bethany and *my* kid. And then B, staying away for so many years and then showing up out of the blue, and what thinking we'd forget who she was or some shit?

My eyes snap back to the woman in question. Tears drip down her cheeks, and she looks so fucking guilty. She's kept this from me this whole time. She made my son into a big dirty fucking secret and kept that secret from me, his own father.

I've never wanted to knock someone's teeth in so fucking badly in my entire life. I've never felt such fury, such deception, either. My body becomes hot, shaking taking over my limbs as I attempt to stay rooted in place.

For this right here, I could kill her. In this moment, I'd love to wrap my hands around her throat and squeeze until she takes her last breath. She took something from me. She stole from me. She stole something I can never get back. *Time.*

A roar escapes, loud enough to be heard over everything in the bar. Rage overtakes my vision as I slam my hands to the bar, swiping my arm through the glasses. They fly in all directions, glass shattering as it lands everywhere.

"You fucking bitch!" I yell—beyond pissed. How could she do this to me? I've done nothing to deserve this treatment from her. My hands clench in fists, the shaking making me feel like my body's completely losing it.

My gaze clouded, I snatch her arm, yanking her to me, with such force her mouth pops open, and her eyes widen, terrified at my outburst. "You fucking stole from me, woman. I should take your motherfuckin' life for that shit. I got a kid—a *motherfuckin'* kid—you kept from me? That boy you got with you, he belong to me, Bethany?"

"Ummm..." She stutters, breathing heavy, shocked.

"You should be scared, bitch. You open that fucking trap right now and you tell me if that's my kid. Don't you dare lie either; I'll cut your goddamn tongue out if you try that shit. You fuckin' feel me?"

Hybrid Collection

Every eye in the bar is trained on us. I don't do this; I don't lose control—not ever and not in front of my brothers. I'm the calm one who's always pissed off but keeps to myself. They don't see me yell, and I'm usually only violent in front of Exterminator when we need to torture somebody.

And I never raise my voice at women. I saw my father do it too many times in the past that I promised myself to never be anything like him. But this woman has me angrier right now than I've ever been in my entire damn life. I've never wanted to beat the life out of someone like I do right now. I feel so hurt and betrayed it's consuming any feelings I had for her.

"Yes," she replies, her lip wobbling as tears rain down her face.

"You get the fuck back to that house and check on my son. And don't you dare think about running, 'cause I will hunt you down to the ends of the earth if I have to. Tomorrow we talk, but right now…right now you get the fuck outta my sight, so I don't do something I'll regret down the road." I release her roughly to where she stumbles back a few steps and Princess catches her.

Princess' empathetic gaze meets mine; she bites her lip and whispers, "I'm so sorry, Night; I thought you knew."

I glare at her for a moment then turn my back to her. Blaze immediately sets a glass down with a bottle of Jack beside it. Any man here knows I'm getting wasted. I have to drown out this demon trying to break free before he causes unfixable damage. If I let myself free and I end up hurting B for this, I will never forgive myself for it.

She thought I knew? How could I? And how could they believe I'd be a deadbeat father? No one has a clue about my life growing up; it's nobody's business, so they just assumed I'd be a shitty dad? Fuck that.

Yes, I'm dangerous. Yes, I'm violent. Yes, I'm an outlaw biker that was a Nomad for many years.

Not once in my lifetime have I ever hurt a woman, nor have I hurt a child or treated them wrongly. Sure I've been a dick, fucked then left, but they always knew the score. Bethany knew what it was all about from the start.

Her question that night comes back to me, the last time I saw her.

"We don't need a condom? What if I get pregnant?"

"I'm sterile and clean; I told you this the other night when we fucked."

"Right, I'm just being paranoid."

I kept kissing down her neck, sinking inside that tight cunt of hers, not thinking anything more.

Shaking my head, I take a large gulp of Jack. I'm a goddamn idiot, and she knew; she had to. After that conversation, it was like she was a ragdoll, not into it. I waved it off as her not feeling well. But she was fucking pregnant, with my kid inside her, and she never said another word about it.

Growling, I slosh more liquid in the tumbler and drain it. I hear Viking and Princess arguing behind me before he finally cuts her off.

"My brother needs me tonight. You go find her and deal with that shit," he says angrily, and the barstool beside me fills with his oversized body. No kiss or anything goodbye to his woman. Yep, he's pissed. It's shitty, but it makes me feel a touch better knowing that he was clueless and that he's angry too.

Sure, it didn't happen to him, but his ol' lady was keeping secrets again, and the last time that happened there was a huge blowout between them. I was in the room next door to them, and they like to yell when they argue. They're supposed to be getting married in two days, too, and this pops off.

Just fucking great. I hate being the source for the drama this time around. It wasn't voluntary that much is certain. I can't believe the Ice Queen knew and didn't say shit this entire time. She thought I knew? No wonder she treated me like dog shit all the time.

Hybrid Collection

He signals for a cup, and Blaze grabs another tumbler. Viking pours his nearly to the top and takes a healthy swig, sighing.

"Don't know what the fuck to say, brother. I'm just gonna sit here, so you aren't alone. We don't have to say shit if you don't wanna, just know, I'm here."

I nod. I'm not a talker, but I'm so damn mad inside, I should open my mouth. If I don't get it out somehow and drown it with the alcohol, I'm liable to throw a couple bodies in a dumpster and light that shit on fire.

"Truthfully…I want to kill someone right now."

"Bet. Want to head into Austin to one of the bars? We may at least find a fight."

Draining the rest of the Jack, I turn his way. "Let's fucking do it. I need to pound something, and a low-life piece of shit may help get some of it out."

"All right then." He lets out a sharp whistle, calling everyone's attention. "Bitches need to stay back, we're gonna take care of some shit."

The club sluts look disappointed, a few wives worried, but the guys? They're up for a good fight any day of the week. Most of us have demons inside we like to expunge when we have the chance to, and tonight's definitely one of them. I need to hurt someone, to get this blackness out that's trying to take over my heart.

We all load up on our bikes, the rumble of the club rolling out together sounding more of an angry roar. No doubt they'll hear us coming, wherever we end up. May God be on their side, 'cause they're damn sure gonna need His help tonight.

BETHANY

I slept terrible last night. I couldn't stop crying, and now my face is so puffy, I look like I ate a giant marshmallow. Princess was livid. It's been a long time since I've seen her that upset over something and it was directed at me.
She feels like she's helped me betray her ol' man by keeping my secret. I hate that she thinks that. It was entirely my fault; I take full responsibility for it.

Sure, I didn't tell Viking, and neither did she, but Princess believed that she was just keeping mine and Nightmare's business private. But it was only my business since Nightmare didn't even know about it.

I can't believe it went down like that last night; what a clusterfuck. I can't be angry at my best friend for saying something; I can only be upset at myself over this whole thing. I shouldn't have kept Maverick's existence from Nightmare; but, at the time, I believed I was doing the right thing. I felt like I was protecting my son, and I would most likely do the same thing if I were to go through it again.

Night was livid; I've never seen him like that. But was he angry because I kept Maverick secret from him, or was he angry that he has a child? Or that he has a kid and didn't know about it? Is he happy about it at all?

I know he was mad, but know nothing else. I wish he'd have told me his feelings last night. We're supposed to talk today, and part of me is terrified he's going to kill me.

"He's going to kill me," I whisper it out loud, a tear dropping free, and Princess shakes her head.

She glances at Maverick sitting on the couch, watching cartoons with his bowl of cereal. "He won't. If it weren't for you being Mav's mom, though, he probably would have last night."

"You're not helping."

"I'm just keeping it real with you. He won't hurt you; he knows Maverick needs his momma."

"Everyone in the club is going to hate me now, too." Sighing, I shake my head. I don't want them to hate me.

Hybrid Collection

"They won't hate you, but they probably won't say much to you either. What you did affects Nightmare, and that affects the club. They'll all wait to see how he treats you first because that's their brother."

"I should just go." My lip trembles, feeling absolutely horrible inside. I don't want to be here with everyone angry at me. My son doesn't need to see or feel that either. This trip was supposed to be fun, and I've managed to ruin it.

"No, that's the last thing you should do. Look, you ran and hid the last time, B, and that didn't work out so well for you in the end. I believe Nightmare when he says he'll hunt you down. It'll be much worse if he has to go looking for you versus you staying and facing the music."

"I can't let Maverick see him hurt me. I promised myself that my son will never experience abuse or hate. It doesn't matter if it's directed toward me; I don't want him to be around it at all."

"I told you, Nightmare won't hurt you, not like that. You should've thought about this shit when you first moved. I still don't get what you were thinking. Protecting your baby, yes; but keeping him from his father is no good, Bethany. You really dug a deep hole."

"I know, fuck." Swiping at the tears, I attempt to pull myself together. I don't want Mav seeing me like this. He'll freak out if he witnesses me crying and will probably start crying too.

"What should I do?"

"About which part?" She hands me another tissue.

"All of it."

"You pull your big girl panties on and deal with it, babe."

"I hate panties," I grumble, and she laughs. It's the first time since before all this blew up in my face. "You think he'll want to be a dad?"

"Only one way to find out, I suppose; but if how he reacted last night is any indication, my bet would be yes." She shrugs as the rumble of bikes grow louder. "Looks like you may be finding out sooner than later."

"Oh God."

CHAPTER 10

Carpe Diem
- Seize The Day

NIGHTMARE

I take her to IHOP because what the fuck else am I supposed to do? I'm no good at this talking thing, and we damn sure need to do a lot of it. And about everything, it appears.

"I'm surprised," she admits, sipping her coffee.

"You're surprised? Should probably be the opposite, dontcha think?"

"I mean with you bringing me here." She gestures to the restaurant. "I wasn't expecting us to go anywhere or you to let me ride on the back of your bike."

That wasn't the smartest of moves on my part. She kept her distance until I took a turn and then she was pressed up against me. I'm still too pissed at her for it to turn me on, but I still felt something tilt in my chest having her that close to me.

"I'm too angry to be alone with you. I don't trust myself yet, and the last thing I want to do is hurt you. Figured breakfast was a good place to start. We have a barrier between us." I point to the table. "As for my bike, only an important woman rides back there. You being the mother of my child, I'd say that makes you pretty fucking important."

She swallows, nodding, and I think her eyes tear up. Her gaze locks on her lap, so I can't get a good enough look to know for sure, though. I don't get why she'd be so upset if that's the case.

I'm not one to sugarcoat shit; I've made it clear in the past. Just because she wasn't honest with me, doesn't mean I'm going to stop being honest with her. I've kept it real with her since day one. I have no reason to pussyfoot around or keep shit from her besides club business. That will never be her business.

"The fuck you expect, B? You want me to just brush it off and forgive you? That's not how this is gonna work, baby. You may as well just bite the bullet and make peace with it now. Ain't happenin'."

She clears her throat, her gorgeous irises meeting mine for the first time today. "Maverick means everything to me. I thought I was doing what was best for him."

"What, having him grow up without a father? Having him believe that I'm some shitbag that doesn't want to be in his life? You're a goddamn fool if you think there's one ounce of justification or truth to either of those options."

"You told me you weren't cut out to be a father, Nightmare. You said it yourself, what would you do with a kid? What was I supposed to think? I was young, pregnant, and scared. My life was changing!"

"That's just it, you didn't fucking think. Or just maybe you would've discovered I wanted kids and still do. Maybe if you weren't so goddamn selfish, you'd have let me have a chance to explain. I'd have told you that my doc made it clear I didn't need to be too concerned with making babies. It wasn't something I thought was an option at all or I would've wrapped it up. Not saying I don't want my son, just that I would've protected you better."

"I did think, I just didn't think about you. I had to do what was best at that moment for *my* son. I'm sorry that I took the option away to be a father from you. I was under the impression you didn't want kids, period. I was just some random fuck to you, Nightmare. I wasn't stupid enough to believe you'd change your ways to be father of the year. For once in my life, I did think clearly; those thoughts just didn't include you."

Her words damn near cut me they're so sharp. At least she's finally being honest with me.

"Christ, you infuriate me. I've never wanted to snap someone's neck so fucking badly as I do yours. You get that, right? That I'm enraged by what you've done? He's my kid, B, *my kid*."

"I'm sorry, Nightmare. I really am. If I had even an inkling of belief you wanted Maverick, I wouldn't have ever left."

"That's another thing. You fucking took off and didn't come back for years. You basically snuck off and kept my son a secret. I don't even know what to say to you about that. I will say this, though; don't ever think you can pick up and leave like that again. I meant what I said, Bethany, I will find you. I don't care if I have to search until my last dying breath, you will never hide *my son* from me again."

A tear falls down her cheek, and I'm a bastard because I enjoy the sight of it. I'm hurt inside, and I want to make her hurt in return. She kept the one thing I've always searched for, away from me—family.

Why else would I join a damn biker club? I was a Nomad to be on my own, but I always had a few brothers with me, just as fucked up as me, it seemed. I thought that life was what I'd needed all along to be happy until I started seein' brothers getting serious and having kids. It opened my eyes to more that I was missing in my life. For years now, I could've had it too.

Fucking bitch.

"I won't, I promise."

"I have a place here. We'll get you moved in after the wedding."

She snorts, and my brows rise. "We're not moving. Maverick and I have our own apartment, and I have a job that I need to show up for next week."

"Don't give a shit about any of it."

"I mean it. You can meet Maverick, but we aren't moving."

"Oh, I can meet him? How fucking generous of you."

"Can we go now, please?"

"Huh?"

"We aren't getting anywhere, and this is pretty embarrassing having the people around us overhear this conversation."

"Oh, sorry, I'm embarrassing you? Guess you shouldn't have kept my fucking kid from me then, huh?"

"You're a bastard."

"Yeah, I am. Get used to it dollface, you're stuck with me for life."

Another tear falls, and I grin. I really am a fucking bastard. Time she learns who's in charge. She'll quit her job and move down here; I'll make certain of it.

She can think that she's stubborn, but I'll be up there riding her ass and seeing my kid every weekend until she gives in. I set up roots here; Bethany and Maverick are now a part of those roots, and I need to stay close to the club, to my brothers. Hope she enjoys club life, cause it's about to become hers if I don't kill her first.

"Grab your shit. We can take off, and you can introduce me to my son."

She sighs and climbs to her feet, grabbing her phone. We head out to my bike, and I secure my helmet to her head. I only have one, and at this point in time, her life is far more precious than mine is. She's the mother of my child, and that's pretty fuckin' important.

"So, you like animals, huh?" I watch as Maverick stands on one of the two-by-fours that encase the pigpen so he can see them better. He keeps oinking and snorting at them like they'll talk back. It's pretty entertaining.

"Ummm...yep."

Hybrid Collection

He waves to a pig as it walks in front of us. Maverick sounds just like his mom. I thought little kids weren't supposed to talk really well, but he does a good job. He rambles a little, and I lose track of what he's saying 'cause it's excited and fast, but everything else I've heard just fine.

He likes animals and trucks and my motorcycle. It's a trip seeing so much of myself in him, too. If I had kept my hair shorter, we'd probably look even more alike.

"I like playing the drums with my band," I admit randomly. Not too sure what to say to a kid really. I'm not around them much; well, not enough to have conversations and all. I could teach him how to play, though, if he wanted to learn. If the Flying Aces didn't only have gigs in bars, I'd have him come and watch too.

He stays quiet, so I try again. "Maverick, do you know what dads do?"

"Ummm…" He shrugs his brown gaze just like mine, flicking to me briefly before going back to the hogs.

"We teach you cool stuff like moms do; only man stuff. We're kind of like moms, but different," I try to explain but realize I suck when I hear Bethany giggle behind us. "What I mean is, I'll be here for you when you need something, like your mom."

"Momma?" Mav cocks an eyebrow, glancing at B and then back to me.

"Yep, just like her, only I'm bigger and stronger so I can protect you good."

"Snacks?"

"You're hungry?"

Bethany interrupts. "No, he wants to know if you'll get him snacks like I do."

"Oh." I blink and nod. "Yep, I'll get you snacks, too."

He grins at that, and it's like my whole world tilts with that small smile.

Snacks and animals, I can do that, no problem. First off, I need to get him a puppy, and then he'll never want to leave. Bethany has no idea what she's up against.

BETHANY

I have to keep chanting to myself not to cry. It's amazing seeing Nightmare and Maverick together like this, even if Nightmare has been anything but kind to me today. He's treated me like I'm nothing, and, sadly, I know that I deserve this from him. He should hate me, especially after seeing how happy he is with Maverick.

Now, I wish I could go back and do everything over. I'd tell him that very night I asked him about us using protection. I'd share with him that I was sick and the doctor believed I was pregnant. We'd argue that it wasn't true and then he'd learn it really was. He could see Maverick be born and hold him that very first day he came into the world. Things would be so different, life would be different, and he wouldn't detest me as he does now.

Nightmare doesn't have to hate me; I'll punish myself enough for what I've done. I thought I was protecting my son, but really I was only keeping him from someone who loves him already. These past few years could've been so much easier having Nightmare in our lives to help. Even just being there would've made an impact. I could've come to see Princess more, and the entire club could've known about Maverick this whole time.

I was so stupid. I'll never be able to forgive myself from keeping Maverick away from someone who loves him like Nightmare so easily does. One look at my son and he didn't even question it. It's easy to see looking at Mav's little face, who he belongs to. He's Nightmare's son, no doubt.

"Night?"

"Yeah?"

"Do you think you have any other kids out there that you don't know about?"

"I doubt it; I make it a habit of using protection."

"So, why was it different with me?"

Hybrid Collection

He shrugs, turning away and cutting me off again. Maybe someday I can get him to answer the question, but it definitely won't be today. And Maverick damn sure gets the shrugging from him, not me.

Princess' wedding passed in a blur filled with me apologizing a million times. Not only to Night but to the few of the club members who actually spoke to me. I was nervous prior to coming, but it was nothing compared to how I felt inside knowing that everyone around us knew what I'd done.

I felt like a giant asshole, and while I was excited for Princess to tie the knot, I'm extremely happy to be back home now. I get four days of peace to myself with Mav, then Nightmare will be here visiting. To say I'm shitting a brick knowing he'll be in my home is an understatement.

What are we supposed to do while he's here? It's going to be so freaking awkward now that he hates me so much. It was weird enough seeing him before he knew we had a child together.

At least now he'll stop trying to get me to sleep with him. Not that I didn't want to; it was just…he'd hurt me. Well, I thought he did anyhow. These past few years were wasted with my stupidity, all from a misunderstanding.

I'm still trying to figure out if it's a blessing or a curse now with Night. He could make the rest of my life hell if he wanted to. All we can do is wait and see what happens, and that's the scary part.

I hope he can move on enough to forgive me one day even though he swears he never will. To witness the hurt and betrayal in his eyes when he found out crushed me inside. I thought it was terrible him hurting me back then; it was nothing to how awful I felt knowing I'd caused him so much pain inside.

Me: We're home.

Nightmare: Good. Hug Maverick for me. See you guys Friday.

Me: Okay, I will. You got the address I sent you earlier?

Nightmare: Yes.

Me: Okay.

See, not awkward at all. *Ugh.* What am I going to do? I have to figure out a way to fix this. Not make it all better, I'm not that naïve to believe that could happen overnight, but there must be something I can do to help a little.

My gaze lands on Maverick's baby picture. It's one of my favorites with him in an old-fashioned tin as a bathtub with bubbles flying all around him. Princess took us to have his pictures done when he turned one, and they came out so adorable. I'd have never been able to afford it, and she gave me one of the best gifts ever.

Nightmare missed all of it, nearly three years' worth of firsts, and he saw none of it. I can start by sharing it all with him, so I use my phone to take a picture of the photo.

Me: Maverick turns one, my favorite picture of him.

I don't get a reply, but I didn't expect one. It could help or make him angry; I'm not sure which one. I'm going to do my best to share with him everything he missed, so each day for the rest of the week, that's what I do. I pick out a picture that means something.

Day two I sent him a picture of our son drooling, showing off his first tooth. Day three I sent him a photo when Mav decided it was time to walk. Day four I sent him a picture of Maverick grinning, giving me a thumbs-up. He'd just fed a giraffe at the Cameron Park Zoo in Waco and thought it was the coolest thing ever.

Day five Nightmare shows up on our front porch, so I skip the text, surprised to see he actually came. I don't know what had me doubting him, but I shouldn't have. The first thing I notice—his hair. The dreads are gone, and he looks like the old Nightmare—*my* Nightmare that I remember. Strong and imposing and just plain beautiful.

CHAPTER 11

Carpe Noctem
- Seize The Night

NIGHTMARE

"You're here," she squeaks. Bethany's eyes are wide as she pulls the front door to her apartment open.
"Told ya I would be." I wink and walk past her, coming inside without an invitation.
"Maverick?" I call loudly since he's not right there when I first enter.

"Dad? Momma, is my dad here?" he yells. It's an excited jumble, but I still figure it out easy enough. My chest swells, hearing him call me his dad. He knew it was me, just from hearing his name.

"Yes, he's here! Come say hi," she replies toward a narrow hallway off the side of the living room.

He comes out running, going full speed, jumping when he reaches me. My knees bend, and I catch him, lifting him until he nearly touches the ceiling. In one week, he's become my entire world.

"Yow're here, for weal."

"I am." Nodding, I grin. I can't stop the smile overtaking my mouth at getting to see him again. I'm overjoyed by hearing him talk and visiting with him. "When I promise you something, Maverick, it'll always happen, you can count on it. I don't break promises. Got it?"

He nods, and we fist bump as I easily balance him in my grip with one arm.

"Missed you, little dude."

"Missed yow." He smiles, and I set him back down, turning to find Bethany watching us wistfully.

Setting my backpack down, I glance around the small space. "Where am I staying?"

"Wif me," my son instantly answers, and I chuckle.

"Hey buddy, your bed's a little too small for Daddy. His feet would fall off." B laughs.

Maverick's finger goes to his temple and he taps it a few times, clearly thinking it over. "Ummm..." He shrugs, and she laughs again.

"You can sleep on the couch. We don't have a spare room."

"Him will fit in yowr bed, Momma."

She swallows roughly and shoots an uneasy smile at me. "We'll figure it out, Mav; don't worry." Her gaze meets mine. "Have you eaten?"

"Nope."

"Well then, guess we can start there," she replies, and I'm not sure it's for me or her. I think she's reassuring herself.

"You don't have a gig this weekend?"

"Nope, bar's got another band visiting."

"I'll get some food started."

The day flies by hanging out with the kid, and it's not until the next night that I'm really drawn to Bethany.

Hybrid Collection

Turning over on the uncomfortable couch, I steady my breathing to listen.

"No!" B grounds out, and the sound carries out my way from her room. The living room is in the middle, separating hers and Maverick's rooms. I doubt he can hear his mom, but I definitely can.

On alert, I grab the blade from my pants that I'd discarded beside the couch earlier and quietly creep toward her hall. Her door's cracked open, in case our son needs her in the middle of the night. I use it to my advantage, following the wall so I can be hidden by the partially-closed door.

"No, please?" she groans, sorrow and fear coating her voice.

She sounds as if she's being tortured, and no amount of anger I had from her secrets can keep me from wanting to protect her, to save her from whoever's hurting her in there. It's in this moment that I realize that no matter how much her deceit hurt me, I'd die for her if I had to. She's my son's mother, and he needs her more than anyone else on this planet.

Leaning toward her door, the floor creaks, and I instantly flatten myself against the wall, holding my breath. I want to have the drop on whoever's in there, not the other way around.

There's silence for a few moments and then a soft cry. It's the last straw. I jump through the opening, in a fighter stance, ready to stab to death whomever I need to, so I can save Bethany.

The room's empty; her window's even closed and locked securely. It's just her, tossing and turning while grumbling. She's dreaming, but whatever it is, it's making her scared or hurt.

I could walk away right now, go back to sleep on the couch and pretend like this never even happened. I don't need to worry myself over her comfort, and I shouldn't want to after what she pulled. But I do.

Her being upset makes it hard for me to breathe for some reason. It's confusing and infuriating. I'm a criminal, an outlaw; I don't care about shit if it doesn't concern me or my club.

Yet, she concerns me. She digs at my heart that I once believed didn't exist, and that's answer enough. I need to comfort her. I don't have to fuck her or have a relationship with her, but, in this moment, I can at least make sure she's okay. There were so many dreams and so many times I'd wished someone would've done the same for me.

Standing beside her bed, I watch her a few moments more until she calls out loudly, scrunching her face up. In pain or in sadness, I wonder? Who knows, but something is definitely not right in her head tonight.

I can't help but think it's me in there, terrorizing her. She's acted pretty scared and nervous since I've arrived, but, honestly, I've relished it. I've taken each little terrified look she's sent at some of my remarks and have added them inside, collecting bits and pieces, letting them offer me what small comfort they can.

Revenge...I love getting payback when it's due to me, but how do you take out your hurt and anger on the mother of your child? I kill her for the shit she pulled, and, then suddenly, I'm the bad guy in the equation. I refuse to be the villain in my son's eyes. I may not be some real hero out there, but to him, I will do everything in my power to look like I should be one.

I could shake her, rouse her enough to pull her free, but I don't. I'm stupid, I want to feel her against me, and this is offering me the perfect excuse to do just that. Pulling the puffy comforter away from the pillows, I climb into the bed next to her.

One hand on her shoulder, I place my other palm to her face. She whimpers and the sound's beautiful. I'd love to have her whimpering underneath me, but in pain and pleasure combined.

"Bethany." It comes out in a bit of a grumble. I'm still tired and watching her half-naked has me flexing and hard.

She doesn't wake, so I stroke over the side of her face, calling her again. "Little Daydream...wake up, baby."

"Night?" Her eyes crack open, dazed and confused. I'm sure she's wondering what I'm doing in her bed and touching her as well.

Hybrid Collection

"I'm here, you're safe."

Tears well up, her pouty lip trembling, and then she's in my arms. Her own wrapped around my neck, head against my chest as sobs wrack her body.

"Shh, shh, you're okay. I got you, baby, don't worry."

"Oh God," she whispers, still crying.

"Was it really that bad? What happened?"

"I-I don't want to talk about it. If I talk about it, it becomes worse, because then it's real."

"Fine. Just tell me...was it me making you like this?"

"You? No-no-no...it was...it was my father," she admits, her warm breath fanning over my pecs. A few shuddering breaths and her tears begin to dry up.

I lie back, pulling her on me until I can wrap my arms around her securely. We l like that, chest to chest for what feels like hours. Truth is, I have no idea how much time passes; eventually, we both drift off to sleep.

It's in the early morning when she's sleeping soundly that I crawl free from her touch, wrapping the blankets around her cozily. That was close enough for now. I have to keep reminding myself that I hate her for what she did, that we could never be.

I would never be able to trust her to even give her a chance.

However, I can't help but wonder why it was her that got pregnant with my child. I'd lied to her about being careful. I wasn't; in fact, I was careless. No woman ever got pregnant no matter how many times I fucked them...and then there was her.

BETHANY

I wake to a cold bed and groggy thoughts of Nightmare holding me all night long. Part of me believes that last night never happened, but I know it did. My bed still smells like him.

Rolling over in his spot, I deeply breathe in his scent. It's been a very long time since a man was in my bed in any form, and smelling him has my body wound tight, senses in overdrive.

My hand crawls over my stomach, fingers almost going into my panties when I get a wake-up call.

"Momma?"

"Hmmm," I groan, rolling over to my back.

"Cereal's wready"

Shit. That means there's a mess from hell in my kitchen and probably no milk left. I thought we talked about him fixing his own breakfast; it never works out for either one of us.

"'Kay, I'll be right there."

Clumsily, I head for the bathroom, taking care of business and washing my face with cold water, so I'm awake enough to mop up the milk that I know is coating my kitchen floor. At least it wasn't eggs this time; cleaning those up suck.

When I round the corner, I'm met with essentially two Nightmares—one big version and one mini version. They're sitting at the kitchen table, both staring into the living room at cartoons while they eat cereal. Surprisingly, there's no mess either.

"Hey," I mumble, heading for the coffee machine. It's a fresh pot. Neither of them glance in my direction, zoned out on *Transformers*. I pour myself a cup, adding in a splash of cream and two scoopfuls of sugar.

Throwing away the empty sugar container, I come across what looks like an entire roll of wet paper towels in the trash as well. My gaze lands on Nightmare.

Hybrid Collection

"Did Maverick make breakfast?" I ask, curiously, and Nightmare finally glances over at me and nods.

"Yep. I woke up when he yelled, 'Oh shit.' Turns out the milk was a little heavy for him."

And being a typical man, he used every paper towel in sight to clean it up versus just grabbing the mop. But one thing stands out; he got up, helped Mav, and then cleaned up the mess. He actually cleaned it up and let me sleep.

Checking the clock, it reads nine a.m., and it makes me giggle.

"You all right?" His eyebrow tips up, concerned with my weird behavior. He doesn't understand the only time I ever get to sleep in is when Princess visits every few months, and I rarely do it then too. I could jump up and down and cheer right now.

"Fine." Grinning, I bring my cup of coffee with me and sit in the chair between them. I have cartoons to watch with my son and my baby daddy. Never in a million years, did I imagine I'd ever be able to say that.

CHAPTER 12

> She dreams more often than she sleeps.
> - Jonny OX

"When wiw he be back?"

"We've been over this Mav; he had to go home to where he lives so he could work." He, meaning Nightmare. We've been over this daily since Nightmare left.

"But when wiw he be back?"

"Soon."

"Soon," he grumbles, copying me as his gaze turns out the window to watch the scenery as we drive. It's weird, but I miss him, too. Sure, there were many nights I thought of him over the years, but this past weekend went well—really well.

He was a dick to me Friday when he first arrived, but then I cooked him dinner. The next night he held me when he didn't have to. It was nice and different. It felt like we were a family, and that's the scary thing, because I loved it, and I know I can't have it. He may have offered me comfort, but he still hates me.

We get back to the apartment, and I give Princess a call. She's another one pissed at me. She has every right to be; it still sucks, though.

Hybrid Collection

"Hey."

"Hey, you still mad at me?"

"I told you, I'm not mad. I'm disappointed; it's different. I wish you would've told me from the beginning. It almost feels like you didn't trust me enough to have your back."

"Of course, I trust you. You have to look at it from my point of view, too, though. I had just found out I was pregnant. I was tripping, freaking out over my life changing, and Nightmare's words hurt me. Of course, I took him at face value; I didn't know him well enough not to."

"And you do now?"

"Hell no. I wish I could change how I went about things, but if I'm honest with myself, I would probably do the exact same thing again. I didn't have options when Maverick's existence surfaced. I had to bite the bullet, grow the fuck up and take care of the both of us, so that's exactly what I did."

She sighs. "I know. It's just…now Viking thinks I kept this from him and is questioning me on what else I've kept from him. You need to start coming down here and being around the club."

"Why would I do that? Those guys despise me for keeping Maverick away from Nightmare. I'm the bad guy, remember?"

"They only see it from his side of view; they don't know you or your story like I do. Start coming around so they can see for themselves you're not trying to keep him away any longer. Trust me, you'll want them on your side. It may suck for a little while, because, I'll be real with you, they most likely will be jerks. Not to Mav, but to you. Once you choke through it, they'll have your back. Most of all, they'll have Maverick's, and I know how important family is to you, B."

"I don't care if they support me in any way, but you're right about one thing. I do want my son around family, and I know the club is loyal to their own. I don't necessarily want Maverick growing up to be a biker, but I do want him surrounded by people who'll have his best interest at heart."

"That's us."

"I know, Prissy; I know. Nightmare was coming back up here this weekend, but maybe I'll see if I can take it off and go there instead. He saved me a lot of money being here last weekend to hang out with Mav while I worked."

"See, Nightmare being in your life could be good in multiple ways."

"I know, I keep reminding myself of the benefits. It's still hard to be around him, and even more so, now that he hates me."

"He doesn't hate you, Bethany."

"Oh no, believe me, he does. He sat right across from me at a table and told me he'd like to peel my skin from my flesh. Pretty sure that equals hate."

She chuckles, and I huff.

"He has it so bad for you."

"Yeah, like the man may kill me in my sleep one night."

"No as in he was all over you to get in your pants again, and now he's threatening you with bodily harm. He knows you're the mother of his child. He fucking wants you."

"Yeah, well, I'm not going to make any bets or hold my breath on it."

"Oh yeah, what was that bet you made me when this whole thing started? Oh no, it wasn't a bet…but I remember your words." She laughs, then in a snooty tone, pretends to mock me. "'Fine, but I'm not fucking any of them'." She bursts out laughing like a hyena. "So busted. We have DNA proof you're full of shit."

"You're such a bitch, Prissy."

She laughs again, at my expense, and I laugh, too. I'm just happy the guilt trip for not telling her about Night is letting up.

"I am, but you still love me."

Hybrid Collection

"Ugh, God knows why, but I do."

"Good. I love you, too. Now let me know if you can come this weekend. I'm sure Nightmare will have you staying at his house; but if not, you can stay at mine."

"There's no way I'm staying with him. I want to keep my skin, thank you."

"You'll have to fight with *him* about that, but anyway, let me know."

"I will."

"Okay, byeeeeee."

"Bye." I hang up, rolling my eyes. I am happy that we ended the call on a good note, though. It's hard when your best friend is upset with you.

It's also time I start planning Maverick's birthday party. Usually Princess would come to visit, and I'd make a cake for him, but I have a feeling Nightmare will want to be involved this time around.

Each day that passes, I continue with the daily texts. I always send a new picture of Maverick and let Nightmare know of anything significant. Usually, it's just a small message from Mav. Today's was: Maverick wants to know if you like meatballs and with sauce or no sauce?

Random, I know, but I'm hoping it makes Nightmare feel a little closer to his son. Maverick thinks it's neat, too, and has started helping me pick out which picture to send. Nightmare could think it's stupid for all I know, but, as a parent, pictures mean something.

At least they do to me. It's like little perfect moments frozen in time that you can look back on and remember. I could be having a rough day and look at Mav surrounded in bubbles, and no matter how blue I am, it makes me smile. I'm crossing my fingers that they do the same when I send Nightmare his daily text from us.

My phone beeps.

Nightmare: Yes and yes. Tell him I'll see him tomorrow and I'm teaching him to play my drum set. Be safe driving.

Me: I will.

He argued with me about us staying with Princess. I knew he would, but I still had to try. It's awkward enough, but at least staying with Princess would provide some sort of barrier.

I'm going to pick up groceries before we leave so I can cook dinner tomorrow night. I think it'll be a good way to break the ice. I think when it boils down to it, it's the small things that really matter. Dinner may seem like nothing to some, but Nightmare and Maverick haven't gotten the chance to sit down at dinner together. Last weekend was the first time, and while I can't make up for everything Night has missed, this is one small thing I can give them both.

All of this is new, and I'm lost. I'm not used to worrying about sharing my son with anyone. The thought was always in the back of my mind that one day it could happen. That's not true; the actual thought was that there was a chance of Nightmare showing up and taking my son from me completely if he were to find out the truth.

So, this visiting or whatever it is we're doing, I'll gladly do my part, because, in my heart, I know it could be so much worse. He could want nothing to do with our son ever, or he could take him away from me completely. Nightmare has the means to just disappear if he wanted too. He's an outlaw, and those types of men do what they want and know how to do it without getting caught.

With a sigh, I down the large glass of wine and pray that I'm able to sleep tonight. I'll definitely need my wits about me tomorrow. Who knows what kind of mood my baby daddy will be in. Not only that, but I have to face his brothers, and some of them are as ruthless as he's known to be. Fingers crossed I make it home in one piece.

Hybrid Collection

NIGHTMARE

Having them in my space is strange; not bad, just different. Not like I'm here much anyhow. I'm usually at the club or gone doing something—a run, a gig, whatever. Maverick's discovered my drums and thinks they're pretty bitchin'. Those are my words, not his. His were more along the lines of "Ummm…wow." Bitchin' sounds better in my mind. His mom would have my ass if I taught him that word, though, so we'll save it for when he's older.

I'm not going to lie to myself either. Having Bethany floating around in the kitchen, cooking dinner, is pretty fucking nice. I haven't brought anyone here except for a few brothers. Club whores are meant to be kept at the club, not brought home.

I don't touch any of them anyhow. I haven't been abstinent by any means, but I hit it out of town. Bethany or my son will never have to worry about running into past pussy.

I like it that way; less bullshit for everyone involved. The gigs and runs help make that possible. I don't know what the hell to do now, though.

Nearly two weeks ago I had getting in Bethany's pants, and possibly keeping her, on my mind. Last week after the news of my son being kept from me came out in the open, I hated all women. This weekend, I just have no idea where I sit with anything.

Part of me still hates Bethany. I think I'll always have resentment toward her for that. However, other thoughts have been creeping in as well. Like how I'm unbelievably grateful to have a kid and a son at that. Also, that she's the mother of my child, and so far, appears to be a damn good mother to my kid.

What more can a man ask for, but a woman that takes care of your kid well. I could go into little details like decent whiskey, tight pussy, etc. but that's all irrelevant when you get down to the shit that really matters in life.

Do I still want to fuck Bethany? Of course, I do; I'm a red-blooded male in his prime. I've thought of fucking her to make her mine. Then I thought about hate fucking her, then fucking her and killing her, then more hate fucking. Now I'm almost to the point of make-up fucking.

I'm pretty sure if she would suck my cock dry for the next few years, I could find it in my heart to forgive her. It's shallow, but I'm not a fake motherfucker. Every man out there with a dick who loves women would feel the same way. They're just pussies and won't admit it; I'm not.

So, here I sit, at the club having a drink and thinking while B and my kid are at my house—hopefully, sound asleep. She thought she could fight me on where they're staying. Not a chance. She owes me, and she knows it.

It's gonna be my way on a lot of shit for the foreseeable future, so she needs to come to terms with it. I should be at home with them, but I need time to clear my head after spending a quiet evening with them both.

"Another?" Blaze gestures to my empty bottle.

Shrugging, I nod. "Sure, fuck it."

"How you holdin' up, lad?" Scot stares at me curiously. He's the oldest member here at the clubhouse, and I've ridden with him for many years. He was sort of in charge when we were Nomads; but here, he's my brother—another officer in the club.

"I haven't strangled her yet."

"Aye." He chuckles. "Have ye fucked 'er again?"

That's the question of the night it seems. Every brother I've come across has asked the same damn thing. Fuckers, all thinking with their cocks.

Hybrid Collection

"Nope, sure haven't."

"Stronger man than I." He laughs again, finishing his draft. "Time I go check on my ol' lady."

"Be safe, brother."

"Aye, you too, lad." He shakes my hand and heads out.

His ol' lady runs the local bar about twenty minutes down the road, and Scot always shows up when it's near closing time. After Viking's father shot her, Scot's been stuck up her ass and with good reason. I'd be even worse if it were my ol' lady, I suppose.

Blaze sets the fresh, cold beer in front of me, and I gulp down a large swig.

"So she came back, huh?"

I grunt, not saying anything really. Everyone knows my business and that shit drives me crazy. I don't do drama, especially when it comes to the club.

"Look, I know I haven't been around you as long as Scot or say Viking, but I'm your brother nonetheless. I just want you to be happy, and I'm glad she's giving you the chance to be in your kid's life."

I've never had an issue with Blaze. He's Viking's cousin and very loyal. But his admission makes my respect for him rise. Stupid, how just a few words can make you respect a man, but it's true.

"Appreciate that."

He nods. "But what are you doin' here, brother? Your son and a woman, who you no doubt care for, is right down the street at your house."

"I know; fuck, I know. We had a good night, I just needed to breathe."

"Ah, yeah, that's a big change. We're here for you man, any one of us has your back if you need something."

"Even a shovel to bury a body?"

"As long as it's not the kids, then fuckin' right."

"If it's the kids, I'd be slicing and dicing whoever is responsible."

"And I'd help you in a heartbeat."

Ex better watch out. Blaze seems to want to fill his spot as my closest friend. Not that it would happen, but Blaze has opened my eyes to him a little more tonight.

CHAPTER 13

It will cost you nothing to dream, and everything not to.
-GeniusQuotes.net

Church, four days later...

"We have a run coming up this weekend. Nightmare and Chaos, are you both still good for it?"

We both nod. It sucks because I'll have to miss my visit with my son, but I'm not going to shoot down business. It's my responsibility as an officer in the club. I'll have to make a trip up during the week or something to see Maverick it looks like.

"Prez." Blaze interrupts.

"Yeah?" Everyone's gaze shoots to Blaze.

"How about I head out with Chaos this weekend?"

"There a problem?" Viking grumbles.

"Nah, but Nightmare's just gettin' to know his son. He needs off weekends more right now than the rest of us."

My mouth drops open at his admission. I'm stunned, but I guess I shouldn't be; we're a family and try to step up when someone else needs it. I didn't realize it was me that needed it though. I try not to ask anything of my brothers besides their loyalty.

"You good with that, Night?" Prez asks, and I nod, confirming. Hell yeah, I am.

I'm so damn grateful. I didn't even have to say a word, and a brother stepped up for me. It's another reason why the club means so much, and I've dedicated a large portion of my life to it.

"I appreciate it."

No one says anything, blowing it off. It's what we all do when someone says thank you like it doesn't even need to be mentioned. It's true, though. I am thankful, and now I get to visit my family—my other family, that is.

I guess that's what Bethany and Maverick are, after all—my family. It's been a long time since I've had someone actually blood-related to me. Ever since my father was killed, family has become whoever I chose, whoever has earned the title in my eyes.

"It's settled, then." My thoughts are interrupted. "Chaos and Blaze will do this weekend's run. We have a club run coming up in two months. We all need to be on board, as it's to welcome in a new Prez to an Oath Keepers charter."

"Taking over the motherfuckin' world." Bronx snickers and we either chuckle or roll our eyes.

He's young but has come a long way since we first came across him. Bronx was a part of the giant shit show when everything went down with Scot's ol' lady and Princess got held up at the bar. Viking overtook the old club. The Widow Makers MC and Bronx was one that patched over, along with Blaze, Torch, Smokey, and Odin.

"Night, you planning to get B to move down here with you?"

"Yep, working on it," I answer Viking, everyone's attention on me, yet again. I hate that shit.

Hybrid Collection

"Bet. Let us know so we can make sure we're available to help move her shit if you need it."

"I will."

"Now, back to the pussy. Anymore issues?"

Torch speaks up, "Everything was smooth this last week, and the girls turned good profit as did we."

"Thank Christ; last thing I want to deal with is pussy problems."

"Aye, yer ol' lady holdin' out on ye then?" Scot riles and Viking growls causing the rest of us to snicker to ourselves.

We're quiet because Viking has a temper like no other. While he wouldn't put a bullet in our skulls, the fucker would damn sure throw a punch, and he's no small man to tangle with. The first time I met him, he was fighting off five or six guys at once. He wasn't winning, but that was beside the point.

"Don't be worryin' about my shit, and I won't worry about your wrinkly ass," he replies, and Scot laughs loudly. "All right then, everyone good?"

We all reply with yes and aye. Viking slams the gavel down and we head out. Another successful church meeting for the books, and now it's time to have a drink with the brothers. It's one of the best parts about having church; we take a moment afterward to visit.

I plant my ass on the barstool as my phone chimes with a text from Bethany. Opening the message, it's a new picture. This one is different than her usual daily text. The photo isn't of just Maverick; it's of them both and fuck if it isn't my favorite yet.

B: 2nd Birthday, he took a bite of cake and then smeared it all over my face. Speaking of, Maverick has a Birthday coming up!

I stare at the photo, grinning like a goddamn fool and decide to make it the screen saver on my phone. They're both covered in blue frosting, and it's hilarious.

Maverick looks so proud of himself while Bethany's mouth is gaping open in shock. Whoever snapped the picture, timed it perfectly. *Probably Princess.*

For the first time in two and a half weeks, I look at her and don't become angry when doing so. Has to mean something, right? She's a natural beauty, stealing my breath away in a ponytail with frosting smeared across her cheeks.

"Hey, Scot, can I borrow your truck and trailer this weekend?"

"Aye, ye need some help?"

"Nah, I'm good. I'm going to load it up with Bethany's furniture while she's at work. Figure she can't argue with me if she's not there."

He chuckles and removes a key off his keyring. "Take it anytime, lad. Can't wait to see thee lass spit fire over this one."

"Not sure it'll be fire, but no doubt she'll be pissed I'm moving her shit without telling her. I'm counting on her anger, looking forward to it actually."

"You're going to turn her into one of those psycho bitches that chop your dick off in the middle of the night," Bronx interrupts.

"I'm counting on that, too. Only I'll keep my cock and enjoy driving her crazy at the same time." I smirk and motion to Blaze for a whiskey.

"Want me to come with you?" he asks, and I shake my head.

"No, I can handle her, and she doesn't have a lot of stuff. Mav is easy; I'm going to tell him he can have a puppy."

The guys around me all laugh, knowing I'm playing dirty by swaying my son with a dog. I'm not above getting down and dirty, though; I'll do what I need to. I didn't become an outlaw by participating in a fucking hotdog eating contest. I became this way because I'm a bastard. I'm not above doing what I have to, for what I want. Hell, I'll get my son a damn piglet if it's needed; I'm not opposed to bribery.

"Nightmare," Viking grumbles, coming to stand behind me.

Hybrid Collection

"Brother?"

"I just got a call. Prospect says one of the girls was roughed up pretty bad last night. He just found her and had to take her to see the doc. I want you and Saint to go pay a visit to the dumb fuck that was stupid enough to take it too far."

"I'll go with Night," Blaze suggests, eavesdropping on me and his cousin.

"No, you stay here. This will take a certain kind of finesse. I want an example made," Viking grits, evil dancing in his eyes, and I know he wants us to make the guy hurt really bad.

"No problem, but Saint and I...you know, we each do shit differently." I clench my hand, feeling the thick scar on my palm. The mark from holding the door closed as a teen has never gone away. It's a constant reminder of how I became the man I am today, of what my methods are. I like to watch them burn, to smell the stench and hear their cries of agony.

"I know, brother. Let Saint play for a while, then do it your way to get rid of the evidence."

In other words, let Saint get bloody, and then I can light the fucker on fire. The hard part will be controlling Saint though. He goes a little psycho when he sees blood; the brother practically bathes in it when given the chance. I tend to stay cleaner. I save getting dirty for when I'm working on bikes or sweaty when I'm hitting the drums for a set.

"And Sinner?" He's usually attached to Saint's side to keep him in check. They balance each other out or some shit. The point is, you don't see Saint out and about much without him. I'm not about to have to leash his ass. I'm not Saint's keeper.

"Sinner's preoccupied. Like I said, let Saint have some fun, and he'll be fine. It's when you hold him back, he loses it. You know how he is."

I nod. Looks like it's time to get bloody and teach someone a lesson.

It didn't take much to find the fucker who messed up one of the whores. It never does, though. We have a nose for sniffing out filthy fuckers. This guy was a repeat, so the prospect recognized him immediately.

Punching the weasel is cathartic. I love taking care of issues with my fists or with fire. He flies to the floor, and Saint's eyes go a little crazy, and he cackles, "Can I?" He stares at the man who's gasping for breath at my feet.

I hit pretty damn hard, and he's only experienced a small taste of my anger. I could tear his body apart with my hands, break bone after bone if I wanted. Instead of crushing his skull with my boot, I decide to heed Viking's suggestion about holding my brother back.

"Go for it."

At my go ahead, Saint kneels beside the guy and removes his blade and begins to stab the piece of shit woman beater to death. He plunges the sharp knife into the man a good fifteen times through protests, cries, and gurgles until finally, Saint drops the weapon to his side. His hands go to the weasel's throat, squeezing until the guy stops making noises.

Next, they trail to his chest, smearing the blood everywhere before collecting what he can in his hands and wiping it over his own arms. It reminds me of some crazed Indian ritual or something. The brother has some serious loose screws.

Saint's fucking crazy. Did I mention that before? It's completely opposite to his preppy, pretty boy model appearance too. One look at him, and you'd think he was a rock star or something, not a serial killer on a leash.

He laughs again. "Want me to peel his skin off next?"

This is why he and Viking get along so well. Viking is off his rocker when it comes to people pissing him off too.

"No man, he's already gone. It's a shame, too. Really would've liked to burn him alive; it wouldn't have ended so quickly."

His smile drops, and his gaze grew serious as he stared at the lifeless body before him. "Viking said he wanted him to bleed."

"You killed it, literally," I snort and grab a can of old gasoline I'd found in the garage when we first arrived.

Saint grins, grabbing his favorite hunting knife and backs away as I begin to soak the mutilated body in the petrol. We leave a trail from the body to the front door, where I use my trusty zippo to start the fire that will erase any implication we were ever in the house. The body will be too far gone by the time anyone gets here that the authorities will never be able to tell it was us.

"You good?" I ask, a little concerned with his appearance.

We climb on our bikes, and I wait for Saint to get situated. He looks somewhere between a horror movie and a car-crash victim. The blood's already beginning to dry on his arms, turning a reddish-brown, and he reeks of the metallic scent that blood gives off.

A shower may not help. He needs a deep cleaning to scrub that shit off. I feel like I should take him to the carwash and hose him down, but Viking and Sinner wouldn't find that as amusing as I would.

I'm sure Sinner will be all over my ass when we get back, for letting Saint's "crazy" out to play. The man's like a demented angel of some sort—pretty-boy looks with blond hair and light gray eyes. I'm sure if you peeled that layer away you'd find a soul as black as can be. How Sinner cares for him so much, I'll never understand.

"Yep, I am. You ready to take off?"

I nod, and the rumble from our bikes drown out the nearby chirping birds as we take off for the clubhouse. Business is done—for now.

"Hey." My eyes rake over B from top to bottom. She's dressed for work but still looks sexy as fuck.

"Hi. Perfect timing." She steps back so I can come into her apartment.

"I liked the pictures this week." Muttering, I follow her into the kitchen.

She smiles, her eyes lighting up. "Oh yeah? He's pretty great, huh?"

"Yeah," I agree as my son comes tearing down the hallway at my voice. He flies into my arms, and my body feels warm all over because of his tiny embrace. You never know what you've been missing until you finally have it.

"I missed yow." He squeezes me tighter, and I chuckle.

Around him, I don't have to be so serious. He doesn't know the dark side of me, and I love that fact. I want him to know me as dad, not Nightmare.

"Missed you, too, kid." I squeeze him back, and he acts like I squish him, sticking his tongue out and rolling his eyes back.

Bethany's smile grows. "Thanks for being here. I should be off around six thirty when the last girl clocks on for the dinner shift."

"No rush. We're going to hang out and maybe eat some ice cream. I brought the Monster Truck movie Maverick asked for. Besides, you should just quit."

She laughs, rolling her eyes. "Yeah, right. Maybe someday in a far-off land when fairies pay my bills, then I'll quit and eat ice cream with y'all." She winks, and I smirk. Little does she know, but her ass will be quitting whether she likes it or not. She'll find out when she gets home, and all her shit's packed and loaded on the trailer outside.

"I'll be back later; you two have fun, and Night, call if you need anything."

"I will."

"Ummm…we wiw. Love you, Momma"

Hybrid Collection

"Love you, buddy." She blows him a kiss and grabs her purse.

She's off to work, and it's just me and little man left at the kitchen table. I may as well not waste any time. Turning to him, I grin. "So...you like puppies, Maverick?"

CHAPTER 14

You can't rush something you want to last forever.
- Love Quotes

BETHANY

I pull up to the apartment, noticing a truck parked across a few spots with a trailer attached. The bed and the trailer are packed full of what looks to be my couch amongst other belongings. Weird cause I could've sworn our building was full, and it's even stranger that it looks like my furniture secured under the bungee cords and rope.

If Nightmare replaced my furniture, I'm going to be pissed. That takes a lot of nerve coming to someone's house and getting rid of their things.

Getting out of my car, I approach the vehicle on my way to my front door, paying closer attention. Yep, there's my ugly yellow lamp that's normally on the table beside my bed. But what in the hell is it doing out here, packed up? Did something happen? Oh, God, was there a water leak or something?

Fuck! My heart begins to beat quicker as I jog to the front door. It's locked, so I find the right key and burst in, drawing Maverick and Nightmare's gaze and a...puppy?

"Hey, what's going on?" I ask in a rush, closing the door. The dog runs at me, tail wagging like crazy. "Whose dog?" Bending down, I scratch behind his little floppy ears, because, duh, it's a puppy, and they're adorable.

Hybrid Collection

"It's Maverick's," Night replies and Maverick nods his head crazily, a huge smile overtaking his face.

"But we can't have dogs here."

"Not my problem." The broody bastard shrugs, and I bite my tongue from calling him a dick.

I'm going to be the horrible mommy by taking the damn puppy away from my child. Not like I wouldn't give my son a dog or cat, but they'll kick us out of here, and a place to live is far more important. Not to mention dog food and vet bills—a luxury I can't fathom right now.

"We need to talk," I huff and glance around, noticing my furniture is indeed not here. "Did something happen? Why is everything outside?"

"We packed, Momma!" Mav yells and jumps up, coming to bother the puppy.

"I see that, but why. What happened?" I grin. It's completely fake and forced. I know none of this was my son's idea, and I won't take it out on *him*. Nightmare is in an entirely different boat though.

"You're moving." Nightmare shrugs, like I should already know this.

"Ummm…no, we're not." My eyebrows rise.

"Pretty sure I told you before; you're coming to my place."

"And we get a puppy!" Maverick cheers, making me cringe.

"Shit, shit, shit. This isn't happening. I told you no. I distinctly remember saying the actual word 'no'."

"And like I said, *not my problem*."

"It is if you don't unload that truck and put everything back where I had it all."

"Nah, it's only an issue if you don't come to terms. Me, Maverick and that dog," he points to my feet at the little puppy wiggling around, "along with the truck full of shit are leaving tomorrow morning. The real question here is, are you coming with us?"

I'm so angry at him right now for putting me in this position, I can't speak. I storm for the bathroom as tears fill my eyes. I just want to scream and punch him, but I won't let my child witness me behaving like that. This man is infuriating! What gives him the right to walk in and suddenly think he can change my life however he sees fit?

He's insane, packing up my apartment while I'm at work. And he bought Maverick a puppy...a fucking puppy! Who does that shit?

Nightmare does, obviously.

This is how my life is going to be, too, for the remainder of time until Maverick turns eighteen and moves out. Fifteen more years of this overbearing alpha taking control of everything. I'm going to go batshit crazy at this rate.

Pulling my phone out, I turn it on and hit the speed dial number for Princess. She's probably the only person who will understand what's happening right now, and she'll let me vent without freaking out over whatever I say.

"What?" It's Viking. *Shit.* Not who I was expecting.

Clearing my throat, I huff out, "Is Princess there?"

"Yeah, but she's busy."

Dickhead. I'm surrounded by them as of late, it seems. Is it something in the water all of a sudden? Christ!

"Well, will she be un-busy soon-ish?"

"Is it important?" He's just like speaking to Night, I swear.

"Well, I'm trying not to stab your brother in front of my child at the moment, so I'd say yeah."

He chuckles. The badass over-the-top Viking, just laughs at my frustration.

Hybrid Collection

"Lemme' give you some advice, B. Whatever my brother's doing, just suck it up and go with it."

"Even if that includes giving up my apartment, my job, and basically what little bit of a life I have?" It leaves me in a dramatic huff, pissed to my core.

"Yep," he responds, and I hang up the phone. He's just as nutty as ol' boy in my living room. Fucking control freaks.

The bathroom door opens, and the small space grows tiny with Nightmare's overly large presence. He comes in and closes the door behind him, making the fit even tighter.

"You calm the fuck down yet?"

He stares at me like I'm the one being irrational. Thankfully the tears went away speaking to Viking, but the anger not so much. It's still there. "Calm down? You seriously have some freaking nerve."

His hand flies up, pointing at my chest. "Oh, I have nerve? How about you look in the mirror, dollface. Pot calling the kettle black, dontcha think?"

"You're going to hold this over my head for the rest of my life, aren't you?" I ask outright. Fuck beating around the bush at this point.

He steps closer, my back hitting the counter as his thigh comes between my own. The position is unbelievably intimate, and if I drop from my tippy-toes to standing normally, I'd be pressed against his leg. I can't handle him touching my clit right now in any form; it's hard enough with him in the same room.

I draw in a deep breath at his scent surrounding me. It's the type of manliness that envelops you and makes you forget about anything else. Did I mention before that he has a beard, too? That detail alone makes my insides twirl.

Leaning closer, he brushes his nose up the side of my cheek causing my stomach to tighten up in anticipation. Eventually, his dark gaze comes to mine; the silver line standing out in stark contrast as our noses nearly touch. He grumbles low enough it comes out as a threat, even with grape soda on his breath. He's serious. "If I have to. I'll use it for however long I need to."

Tears form again as I swallow and my throat grows dry. He fights dirty, and he doesn't care who it affects. I should've known him finding out about our son would be a losing battle. In a sense, I did, but I hoped it wouldn't come to this—him taking control over me and my life.

Swallowing, I whisper as a tear falls. "If you make us leave with you, I'll never be happy there."

He backs up, an evil grin coming over his stern features. "Baby, that's where you think I care about your feelings. I don't." He shakes his head as another tear tumbles over my cheek. "You'll grab your purse, suck it the fuck up, and move your shit. You know why, Bethany? I'll tell you why. You fuckin' owe me. That's why."

His fingers go to my chin, and he tips my head up so I meet his gaze and he drives it home. "You kept my kid from me for three fucking years, and I'm playing nice. Oh, baby, I'm being *so* fucking nice to you, you have no clue the hell I could rain down over you."

His hand drops, and he blinks, glancing away. "Fix your face; it won't work on me. Be ready at six a.m. Set your phone alarm if you have too. I don't give a fuck, but Maverick, that dog, and I will be loaded up no later than six fifteen."

Swallowing again, I nod shortly, my eyes falling to the floor. I can't look at him right now because, in this moment, I hate him all over again.

He hasn't changed; he's still as heartless as he was when I first met him. The beast I thought I'd tame, the broken man, meant for me. I was so fucking wrong.

He leaves the bathroom, and I pull my phone out to set my alarm. I damn sure won't be letting him go anywhere with my son without me. While I'm at it, I send a text to the day manager, Brenda.

Me: I'm sorry to do this to you on short notice, but I won't be back to work again. Thank you for everything you've done for me, giving me a job, working with my schedule and sick days.

Hybrid Collection

Brenda: Oh no, Bethany! I'm sorry to see you go, I hope you're all right.

Me: I am, my life is just changing and I can't stop it.

Brenda: Life happens honey, I understand. You and little guy will be in my prayers.

Me: Thank you.

Thank God someone's praying for me; Lord knows I'm going to need it where I'm going.

I wake up at five a.m. and get the groceries packed and clean the apartment as much as I can. It's not great, but I'm hopeful the landlord won't charge too much. He's been nice, letting me make payments for the deposit and what not in the past, so hopefully, he'll do the same with whatever bill I have left.

I can't believe Nightmare's making me break my lease. This will only add more to my already full load of trying to support Maverick and me. I need to see about getting another job this week. Something where I won't have to leave Maverick too much but will give me some money to pay the bills I'll have haunting me with this impromptu move.

Maverick and the puppy ride with Nightmare in whoever's truck he's borrowing, and I follow behind in my car, alone. It's terrible, but secretly, I'm hoping Mav goes on one of his 'no' sprees for like an hour straight. I need to get some sort of payback, and while that's nothing major, it's enough to bring me a bit of satisfaction. Nightmare is nuts if he thinks it's going to be all rainbows and sunshine having us in his space.

He's never dealt with a sick kid who pukes and cries for three days straight or a toddler who decides to make breakfast once a week and destroys the kitchen in the process. He'll learn, and while he's figuring it all out, I'll be saving any money I can. That way when he gets sick of playing daddy, I'm one step ahead and ready. I hope for Maverick's sake that he never realizes just how much of an asshole his father really is.

CHAPTER 15

Love is not an emotion, it is your very existence.
-Rumi

"So, how's it going?" Prissy sets her soda down, staring at me intently.

I sip from my cherry vodka Sprite and roll my eyes. "It's been a week and the best way I'd describe it is, awkward."

"Still? I figured with some time it would get better or easier."

"He's a good dad, so I'm thankful for that. He's fine with me for the most part, too, but he's still pissed. I know it."

"You did keep his kid from him."

"Fuck, I know, okay. Jesus, I get it. I fucked up majorly, and now I'm paying for it by letting a biker control my life."

"It could be a lot worse; at least Night wants you guys in his life."

"Whose side are you on? You're my best friend, but it's sounding more and more like you're taking his side."

"I'm Switzerland, okay. I think you both screwed up, and you're both having to learn how to fix it now. Look, I don't agree with how he got you here. But, I am grateful that you are. I missed you. I feel like he's brought my best friend back to me, and he does sorta earn points from me for doing it."

"So, you are on his side."

She huffs, pushing the soda away and drinks from her beer. "I'm always on your side first."

"Mmmhmm." I lean against the bar, watching the brothers around the room, chatting, laughing, and drinking. London asked if Maverick could have a happy meal and a playdate with her daughter. Of course, I agreed, so here I am, having my own playdate.

Some twat walks by Nightmare, running her hand over his chest, saying something in his ear. He shakes his head and moves her hand off.

I smirk, my gaze shooting to Prissy. "Who's the hood rat?" I nod and she groans.

"Ugh, it's Honey. She's a club slut. She's been after Nightmare and Viking since she first showed up. I already put her in her place with Vike. Looks like you need to do the same."

"Why should I care? If he wants that, maybe he'll forget about me."

"Well, because that's Nightmare, Bethany. Wake up, sweet cheeks. You may be pissed at him, but that's your baby daddy. You don't want some club whore sniffing around him, even if he does brush her off."

"Seriously, he's a big boy; he can tell her no. He's never needed me to stand up for him, and he doesn't now."

"B, I'm telling you, don't let it fester. It'll drive you crazy to see her hit on him every single time you're here at the same time he is. You guys have a fresh start; she's just a dirty vagina trying to screw that chance up."

I snort at her description and a few brothers glance at us. Blaze winks, and I grin. Finishing off my drink, I ponder over what Princess says. I know she'd never lead me astray; she always has my best interests at heart, so I take her words seriously.

Hybrid Collection

"Ready then?" I smile mischievously, and her concern turns to a smirk full of trouble. She knows me too well.

"Always."

Heading straight for Nightmare, I garner the brother's attention as I pass by. Everyone's curious to see what I'm going to tell Nightmare. I think they're all wanting to witness some drama, and I'm about to give it to them.

Nightmare remains seated as I approach, tilting his head up to me. Bending before he can react, I place my hands on each of his cheeks and press my lips to his. He's a moody fucker, so I know the women around here don't have the balls to take control when it comes to him.

His palm warms my thigh as it pulls me closer, and the kiss turns from me showing off to something full of lust. Breaking free after a moment, I pant against his lips, wet from my own mouth sucking on them. "Wow," I whisper and blink, remembering my initial purpose. Backing away, I nearly misstep from the kiss that put me in a daze, quickly righting myself.

Honey glares, and I can't help but smirk. At Honey's huff, I pull my arm back and punch her right in her eye. She stumbles backward, clutching her face as a scream of pain breaks free.

"Mine." I declare sternly, turning on my heel and making my way back to my spot next to a giggling Princess. Viking appears impressed, and Nightmare, completely shocked. The other guy's chuckle, amused at my antics, and Odin helps the whore to the bathroom.

"Better?" I mutter and finish off my mixed drink.

"Hell yeah, glad to see you're still the crazy woman I love."

"Shit, baby girl, you just opened up a whole new can of complicated." Blaze shakes his head, in his usual place behind the bar.

"Damn, I thought that's how bikers communicated? Don't you beat on your chests and punch people?"

He snickers. "You're trouble, you know that?"

"I may have been called that a few times in the past."

Princess leans over "Uh, no, she's crazy, Blaze; don't get it twisted. She always has been, and that right there proves she's still the same wild woman I grew up with."

"Hey, I've toned it down a lot, thank you very much."

"Maybe around your kid, but not when it's you and me. No way sister, I see you trying to break free. The good news, B, is that these guys here are even crazier. You fit in here like a lost puzzle piece, just you wait and see."

"If you say so," I sigh.

I haven't really fit in anywhere, ever. I became the crazy party girl prior to getting pregnant, so I could drown out my lack of everything and not care about anything else. That's why Princess and I became so close; she was different like me, her family belonging to a biker club and all.

"Another one?" Blaze grabs my empty glass, and I nod.

Why not? Maverick does have two parents now. I think I've earned that extra drink.

NIGHTMARE

"Fuck was that?" Viking grumbles after Bethany walks off. He's attempting to act serious when I know he's most likely busting up inside over this.
Personally, I'm still shaken from her pulling that shit. "No idea, brother."

"Chick's a goddamn fruit loop." He downs his whiskey. "Can't believe she just claimed your ass in the middle of the clubhouse, too."

Saint laughs beside me, and I growl, thinking about punching him next. No way was she layin' claim. "That was a fuckin' tantrum, that's it. Bitch was showing off for

Princess. Anybody claims anyone; it'll be me fucking her until she can't run that damn mouth of hers."

"Trouble in paradise?" he asks, and I glare. He's the only fucker in this place, besides Ex, who has enough guts to give me shit, especially about Bethany.

"She's driving me crazy," I finally admit.

"Crazy is how I'd describe her." He nods, and I grunt.

"She stares at me all innocent and shit at the house. Just wanna bend her over and spank her ass."

"Maybe you should. It'd bypass this bullshit y'all are going through right now. I had to just say fuck it with Princess and make her mine so she'd quit fuckin' around."

And none of us will ever forget it, either. One of the hottest things I've ever seen; not to mention, I had B on my cock right after that went down. Shrugging, I tip my longneck back and finish off the beer.

I'm not sure what I'm going to do about her yet. I'm still pissed inside and want her ass walking on eggshells a while longer, but I'm not sure how much more I can take. This last week she's slept right down the hall from me, and I've held her twice. Her and those fucking dreams, they screw her up in the middle of the night, bad.

Crazy thing is, once I hold her, she sleeps like the dead. I can move around, shower, get dressed, whatever, and nothing wakes her. When she's by herself, she tosses and turns, cries out, you name it. I know because I like to watch her sleep. I witness it every night.

I can't believe she just came over here and pulled that on Honey and me. I have to give Bethany some credit; she completely surprised everyone with that one.

"Your band have a gig this weekend?" Chaos pipes up. He's pretty quiet; one of the reasons why I don't mind him.

"Yeah, out at Shorty's."

"Bet, I'll head over with you. Friday or Saturday?"

"Both."

He nods. "You should get some pussy, take your mind off her." He gestures in Bethany's direction. While that would've sounded good before, it does nothing for me now. The only pussy I want riding my dick belongs to that hotheaded chick that just laid one hell of a kiss on my mouth.

"She smells another bitch on you, you may not wake up in the morning." Viking chuckles, and I grin. It's probably true though. Good thing I won't have to worry about that.

"Fucked up." I shake my head.

"How 'bout I tell Odin to babysit. Me and Princess could ride up, you could show B?"

"Not sure she'd like that sort of thing."

Chaos sighs. "Bullshit. Chicks are all over your cock once they see you play."

He has a point; it could win her over a little. I can keep fucking with her here and there and then really hook her. This time when she falls for me, I plan to make sure she never goes anywhere.

"Why you single, Chaos?"

He shrugs. "I had a woman when I first started playing football. She gave me my daughter then split. That was enough for me."

That's right. His daughter visits on her college breaks sometimes. "You haven't been on a run to Alabama in a whole minute. Your kid okay?" That's also how he met our moonshine contact. The stuff here at the club is the real deal—homemade and everything.

"She moved up north with her boyfriend."

"No shit?"

He nods. "He went to play for the Patriots."

"Holy fuck, brother; that's awesome."

"As long as she finishes her degree, I won't kill him," he admits, and we all chuckle. Makes me glad I have a son. Not sure I could handle having a daughter.

I get home after Bethany does, and there's dinner already made and waiting for me. I'd never admit it to my brothers, but I love every bit of having her here. I don't know why I want to torment her so badly. My guess is, I'm still hurt. I hate that bullshit. Makes me feel weak, like a chick worried about feelings and shit.

It's true, though. Finding out I had a kid and knew nothing about it, fucked me up inside. I was already screwed up, but this is different. It makes me think that she believes I'm not good enough to be Maverick's father.

However, I will be a good dad to him; I'll make sure of it. I may not be a good person or even a decent man, but I won't let myself fail at being his father. I had enough of that growing up; I won't torment my own kid with that kind of life.

Trekking down the hall, I peek in and check on Mav. He's knocked out, with his feet up on his pillows. Kid sleeps like a wild animal in every direction besides the normal one. It's all good; his mom and I both march to the beat of our own drum, too. Fuck the standards.

Next, I check on Bethany. Cracking her door open a little more, I peek in. Her sleepy eyes meet mine, a tired smile on her lips.

"Thanks for dinner."

"Of course." She yawns, snuggling into her covers more.

"I have a gig this weekend. I'd like you there."

"Okay."

"Viking and Princess are coming."

"Oh cool."

"Night," I grumble.

"Good night." She sighs, her eyes closing. I can't help but pause and stare for a few seconds before leaving her doorway.

Peeling my clothes off, I leave them on my bedroom floor in my wake. I lie flat on my own bed; it's a California King since I'm six feet four. Regular beds don't work too well for me.

My eyes close and I see Bethany's smirk as she punches Honey. I didn't say it outright, but it was hot as fuck. If she had really been claiming me, I'd have her in my bed right now, rewarding her with my face between those thighs.

When she kissed me, I had to touch them. Every time she puts on a pair of shorts, I want to run my hands up the backs and give them a good smack, leaving a pink handprint behind. Fuck, the things I'd do to her body.

Groaning, my hand finds my semihard cock and I give a few rough pumps. It hardens quickly, precum spilling from the top as I pretend it's her doing it.

"Ummm…Night?" Her voice breaks my thoughts, and my eyes pop open, landing on her flushed cheeks.

"Yeah?" It's gruff, but fuck, five more minutes and I would've been spilling all over myself.

"Can I lay with you?" It's so soft and innocent, I could break down a door with how hard it makes my dick.

"Yeah, come 'ere dollface," I reply and let her scoot under the covers, coming to lie on my chest.

It's going to be one hell of a long night for me. I should just fuck her right here, right now. But I won't. I'm going to let her fall for me before I claim her and finally make her mine.

CHAPTER 16

Live your life by a compass not a clock.
-Stephan Covey

BETHANY

Watching him play the other night at the bar was insane. I had no idea Nightmare was that talented. Makes me wonder why he ever became a biker in the first place and not a professional drummer. He's at that level, and it's not often you come across someone who is.

"What are you doing?" I ask, pausing in the doorway to the bathroom. He's got a few drops of oil he's rubbing between his palms.

"I'm putting beard oil in my beard." His gaze meets mine while staring into the mirror above the sink. His eyebrow rises like I'm off my rocker.

"Beard oil?"

"Yeah, you know, to make it softer?" His gaze flicks back to the dark hair as he runs his hands over it.

"Hmm," I reply and watch as he smooths it over the long scruff.

Knowing he uses products like that, I have to admit is pretty damn stimulating. Men like him, you think are naturally good-looking, but he works to take care of himself, and that is so attractive in a man.

I caught him in the garage the other morning lifting weights shirtless, and I swear the guy gave me hot flashes. He busted me gawking at him them, too, but I didn't care. Any woman in their right mind would watch muscles like his flex with each lift.

A biker who wears beard oil, lifts weights, plays the drums, and can kiss like the devil himself. Why is it I'm protesting living with him again? Oh right, because he packed my shit up and moved us here without having a real choice in the matter. Doing things like that makes me stabby, no matter how fuckable he may appear.

And let's not mention that he also holds me at night when the dreams haunt me full force. The asshole's not making my life any easier being sweet like that.

"You coming by the club later?" He stands in front of me in the living room on his way out.

"I wasn't planning on it, why?"

"Just checking."

"I need to find a job."

He shrugs. "Not really, but I'm done arguing with you over it."

There's no way in hell I'm letting him pay for my stuff. I won't depend on him any more than he's already caused me too.

"It's not an argument if I want to work."

"Whatever. You could come to the club."

"And do what? Watch one of the whores rub all over you again? That's not my idea of fun."

"She didn't rub on me; she asked if I wanted my cock sucked. I turned her down and then you punched her. Pretty sure the message was clear, and that was a week ago. You're still thinkin' about it?"

"Of course. Women don't let that sort of thing drop."

"You're being a bitch right now, you know that?"

He did not just say that shit to my face. "You better leave before I take a knife to that pretty bike you have parked out front."

He huffs, stuffing his wallet in his pocket.

"And Nightmare?"

"Yeah, B?"

"Next time you call me a bitch or say I'm acting like one?"

He remains stoic, glaring at me.

"You won't be the only one known as Nightmare," I finish and walk toward my bedroom. I'm getting dressed and finding a fucking job if it's the last thing I do today.

Why would he want to know if I'm coming to the club anyhow? It doesn't matter; Princess said she'd watch Mav while I go job hunting, so that's what the plan for the day is.

NIGHTMARE

So moody and for no damn reason, I think as I take my spot at church. Everyone else is already here; I'm running late thanks to Bethany being pissed over old shit. "Everyone straight?" Viking peers at each of us, waiting for somebody to speak up.

Chaos grumbles, drawing our attention. "Spoke to Cain, he said the charter over there is having a shit time with another club again."

"Iron Fists are back?"

The name rings a bell. Pretty sure that was the club we went on a run to Cali for and torched. We burnt every dirty fucker alive inside too. The club shouldn't be having any issues with the Fists; they should all be dead.

Chaos shrugs. "I don't know if they're back, but they have video of two wearing their colors vandalizing a building next to the compound. They can't pin down a location on them."

"Fuck," Viking mutters. "Ares hasn't called yet, so we'll leave it for now. But…keep your eyes open for them. We killed a lot of those fuckers the last time we chased them down. Doesn't mean we got 'em all, though, and they could be coming for retaliation."

"It's been what, three years?" Sinner blurts.

"Yeah; however, if you think about it in terms of revenge, it's plenty of time for us to be forgetting about them. It's smart. We're not lookin' for them, and they can snuff us out before we get our feet on the ground."

"True. So we just sit back and wait? Not our usual style, brother." I give my two cents.

"I know. I don't like it either, but if we keep watch and wait on 'em, we'll catch them. Hopefully for good this time. I'm sick of these stupid fucks. If we don't have any other business, I'm going to head over to the other club. See if we can get a church session with the other brothers and come up with a more concrete plan. I'm sure Ares is already plotting."

"I'll head over with you."

It's probably not a good idea to be out riding alone if there's someone on the hunt for us. The other brothers agree with me and decide to come along as well, strength in numbers and all. Viking gives Ares a call to see if we can do church with them now versus waiting.

"Appreciate you sitting down with us and having us at your table," Viking grumbles once Ares calls attention to everyone piled into their small room they use for church. It's smaller than ours, but since we wanted to talk, we came to them.

"You're welcome here anytime, brother," Ares replies and glances at each of us. I'm sitting across from Twist, crazy blond fucker covered in more tattoos than myself. Most of the brothers stand, lining the room, as only ten of us can fit around the table. "Now, what's going on?"

"Chaos brought it up that the Iron Fists may have returned."

Collective growls and murmurs scatter amongst the members.

"You heard right. Wasn't gonna drag your members into it unless shit got heavy."

"I'm thinking the bastards may be jonesin' for some retaliation with my crew. Figured it best we hit you up."

Cain sits forward. "You're probably right. We need to fuck 'em up before they hurt anyone like the last time they came through." He glances at Ares as several of the brothers agree with an 'aye.'

My gaze hits Twist briefly, stopping on the scar running along the top of his forehead. He got some of the blow back from the Fists the last time they were in town. Brother had to be transported to the hospital after shrapnel made him flip his bike. That feels like a lifetime ago though.

"We're not here to overstep, Ares. Let us know your plan, and we've got your back." Viking ignores Cain's suggestion, concentrating on the other Prez.

None of us have any issues with Cain, especially myself as his kid plays with mine. Cain and his ol' lady are good people, but this is a discussion held by the Presidents to then be voted on by all of us.

"Your friendship is valuable to this club, we won't forget that or how you've helped in the past," the Prez says to the other, and they clasp hands.

Once enemies, they're now brothers, friends, and each other's full supporter. At one point, I as well as most of the club thought we'd catch hell because we were sure Viking was going to end up killing Ares. They surprised us all by bonding over Princess. There's so much history between us all; we've grown to respect each other a great deal.

"Now," Ares clears his throat, "we've discussed this. We're watching the feeds around the compound and have taken some funds to send the families on vacation, minus a few of us. Avery will stay here along with London to help keep the clubhouse running. London's mom and brother have taken her and Cain's kids out of town, so they're safe."

Of course, those two would be left behind. The Prez's ol' lady along with Cain's. Cain won't let London out of his sight from what I hear, along with those two women being kamikazes. They're almost as bad as Princess and Bethany. The four of them together could seriously cause a shit storm if they wanted to.

"With them gone, we're tryin' to figure out where these jackoffs are stayin'. Once we find out, we're blowing them sky high. Fuck the dumb shit; I'm done with them existin'."

"That sounds all good, except, what if this isn't all of them?" Blaze grumbles, sitting next to Viking. "We've all heard how this club has chapters in Texas and Cali and that some of the compounds can't be found."

"We torched their south Texas or Mexican border club years back," 2 Piece answers. Not only is he a club officer; he's Ares' property. Yes, you heard that correctly. Ares has an ol' lady and an ol' man. "Then the Nomads torched the Cali club," he finishes, and I nod, confirming his explanation. 2 Piece actually rode with us on that hit. He's cool in my book, true to his position and loyal to the club.

Hybrid Collection

Viking sips some whiskey from his flask, his eyes shooting to Spider. "Spidey, can you do some tech shit and find out if these fuckers have been popping up anywhere else?" He rode back in last night and couldn't have timed it any better.

"Yeah, I can, uh, run the club's video against a facial recognition program I have that's linked into the justice monitoring system via stateside."

"Whatever the fuck you just said, do it." Viking nods, and a few of us chuckle. We have no idea what the hell Spider is talking about half the time, but it sounds good. He's one smart fucker, probably bordering on genius. No idea what someone with his head is doing riding with a bunch of outlaws.

Pulling a smoke free, Ares watches as I light it up, swallowing and staring longingly. We've all heard the stories how Avery has his nuts in a vice when it comes to him smoking.

"Pass me a smoke, lad." Scot holds his hand out, and I dig my pack back out, handing it over and gesturing for him to pass it around. None of these idiots thought to bring their own, just their drinks. Everybody started staring at me like a fucking kicked puppy when I flicked open my zippo. May as well share, so they stop their silent whining.

Once everyone's had some nicotine hit their system, the talk continues, and a plan formulates. My girl and kid will be fine, as no one knows about them. Princess lives with Viking and Odin, so she'll be straight as well. Bronx will be posted up at the bar with Scot's ol' lady to offer her some protection in case the Fists stop through at the bar. I'll keep Bethany and Maverick safe, and if shit hits the fan, I can move them to my room in the club for the time being.

Extending my legs, I roll my ankle around as much as I can in my heavy riding boots. My leg is achy today. Not sure why, but I may need to adjust the leg weights or something. I want it strong but not reinjured. Bad enough it'll never look the same, but it hurts a lot of the time, too. Nothing a decent double shot of Jack can't fix, though.

Church comes to an end, and we head back to our clubhouse after sharing a drink with the original Oath Keepers.

CHAPTER 17

I hope to arrive to my death, late, in love, and a little drunk.
-Atticus

BETHANY

After job hunting, I decide to say screw it and stop by the compound. Nightmare obviously wanted me here for some reason. I don't know why, but whatever, guess we'll find out.
Heading into the clubhouse, I see him instantly. How can I not? Anytime he's in the vicinity, I'm immediately drawn to him. He calls to me on a deeper level, as if his soul is an old friend of mine.

Honey has her hand wrapped around his bicep, and it's all I can take. Princess was right about it sparking jealousy inside me. I'm not a jealous person either, but Nightmare is my hard limit. No one needs to touch him like she's doing.

Stopping, I decide it's best to just leave, rather than hit her again. I don't know if he enjoys her attention and pretends otherwise, but fuck that. I don't have time for bullshit, especially when I already have enough grief from him.

I'm a grown-ass woman, and while I like to tangle, I won't put up with club crap. I'm not an ol' lady; I don't have dibs on him, even if it feels as if I should. In reality, he's not mine. He never was, and he probably never will be.

Hybrid Collection

I barely poked my head in, and, thankfully, no one noticed me. I make my way back to the parking lot full of bikes and my car. It stands out like a neon sign amongst the beautifully painted motorcycles. Especially Nightmare's. I've always loved the glossy black finish. It's humongous up close, definitely a bike fit for a big man. The best word to describe Night would be imposing, and his bike, no doubt, fits that description as well.

My fingertips trail over his seat, the same place I sat on when he took me with him to see him play at Shorty's. God, I loved watching him beat on those drums. It was practically sinful, his hair going in every direction, his biceps flexing as sweat beaded on his forehead. *Yum.*

My anger ignites again as I glance at the carefully airbrushed sandman on the tank. It's creepy as fuck and fits his name perfectly. He's the shit that nightmares are made of if you piss him off in the wrong way.

I made a promise that he wouldn't be the only one around here known as a Nightmare if he crossed me. My actual words were him calling me or insinuating that I was being a bitch, but I'd say this instance counts. It's the perfect time to teach the man a lesson.

I giggle to myself. It's probably more like a cackle, a crazy one, but who's paying attention at this point. My mind's made up. It's time to play with my food, my meal being Nightmare.

Pulling my keys free from my purse, I open the small pocket knife I keep on my keyring and bend toward his back tire where no one can see me. Finding the softest spot on the back tire, I press the blade into the thick rubber. It's no easy feat, but I get it with some pressure. It won't go flat immediately with the clean slice, but it'll do the trick with a little time.

Wearing an evil grin, I let out a deep breath. That felt freaking great! Not one to let my handy work go unnoticed, I head for the beautiful white airbrush design and scrape a large *B*right in the middle of the sandman.

Fucking piss me off bastard biker, and I'll show you what crazy is. I could never be his ol' lady because of shit like this. I'd end up slitting a hoe's throat for touching him; I'm not patient like Princess is. She gets club life; she belongs here. Me, well, he'd probably strangle me by the time Maverick turned ten years old.

I found a job. It's nothing special, but it'll do. Obviously, with my little tantrum here, I'll need it, too. He'll want me to pay to have his shit fixed no doubt, but it won't happen. At least this way he should be pissed enough to make me move out, which is the end goal after all.

Sucks he's so damn good-looking and enticing, makes it harder to be evil toward him. I would've loved it if we could work things out, but he hates me for keeping our son from him. I can't blame him for feeling that way, but I refuse to be around him twenty-four hours a day, in his arms if he can't forgive me.

I can hear the air slowly escaping the tire. The sound's barely there, and if he leaves soon, he won't notice it right away more than likely. I'd think he'd see the gash in his tank first off and then the tire would be the little kicker following up my handiwork.

Ugh, I hope he doesn't try riding it like this though. While I want to piss him off and screw with him, I don't want him to wreck and seriously injure himself. He's been a decent dad to Mav so far...No, he's been a great father to our son. I'm a bitch, but he already knows that. He mentioned it earlier. Perhaps I should carve *bitch* on the other side.

Nah, that may be pushing it. I want him furious, not feeling lethal.

One last glance at my special surprise, and I make the trek back to my car, grinning the entire way.

Welcome to crazy town motherfucker. Next time you'll remember why I punched the slut in the first place.

For you.

NIGHTMARE

We head out to the parking lot; half of the brothers are planning to hit up Scot's ol' ladies bar. I'm done, ready to go have dinner with my family, especially after brushing Honey off all damn afternoon. It seems as if she's more persistent now that Bethany's come around and let her presence be known.

It's getting old fast. I haven't given her any reason to believe I'd be interested. It's fucking annoying. I don't fuck club pussy—never have, never will. They all know this, but a new bitch shows up, and it's like everyone forgets to leave me the hell alone in the process. Maybe my glare isn't as menacing now that I'm getting older. Back in the day, one nasty look would send a chick running scared.

My rear tire looks a bit low. I may need to pull it over to the garage and top it off with the compressor before hitting the highway. A low tire and some gravel can screw up anyone, even seasoned riders. We need to be extra careful and prepared with the talk of the Iron Fists being in town as well. Last thing we want is to be caught unprepared by some dickwads with an axe to grind.

"Daaaaaamn." Saint laughs and points at my tank, clearly amused by something.

"The fuck?" I grit, pulling a smoke free and lighting it. Fucker's losing it, I know it. Sinner needs to reel his homeboy's shit in.

"You pissed someone off, brother." Sinner chuckles, shaking his head, and I finally come to stand beside them.

Sure as hell my tank is scratched up—deeply. This was no accidental brush up or dip from someone. This was intentional and caused some serious damage. Taking a deep breath, I run my hand over the deep indentions. My scarred palm sits on the warm metal, and it hits me.

It's a motherfuckin' B.

"Motherfuckin' woman, Jesus Christ. I'm gonna strangle her ass for this."

"You need help taking care of whoever did this?" Saint offers, and I shake my head. I'll smack her ass cherry red for pulling something this ballsy.

"Nah. I know exactly who did this. I can handle her on my own."

Sinner's eyes widen. "Shit, no way, it was Bethany? You pissed her off pretty bad for that one, huh?" His charcoal irises glance to Saint, an amused grin painted amongst the dark scruff overtaking his jaw.

"I didn't do shit to her. Bitch is fucking crazy in the head. She's gonna put me on my death bed with her antics if she keeps it up."

There's nothing I can do besides order a new tire to be delivered because I'd bet my left nut that's her doing as well. I'm sure there's a hole somewhere if I look close enough; hell, maybe one in the front, too. Glad we came out pretty early; would've been bad if it was at night and I didn't notice right away.

How she came up with this in the first place is beyond me. You'd think I made her life hell with the torture she put my bike through.

If it were anyone other than her, I'd be hunting them down for retribution. You don't mess with a man's bike. It's like rule number one in this lifestyle. I need to call Spin at the other club, too, and see if he and Twist can repaint and then airbrush my tank this week. This blows and not in a good way.

Looks like I'm borrowing Scot's truck again. I hope for B's sake she's not home, 'cause this is going to take more than the drive home for me to calm my shit. She has some serious explaining to do, and she's either sorting it out to be fixed, or she's paying me in pussy. Whatever it is, she better get on board, because she crossed a fucking line. *Again*.

I end up stopping for gas for Scot's truck and then driving around for an hour trying to think and cool off. Cooling down is not my usual behavior. Normally, I'd find the person and make them pay in however I saw fit, but, this time, it's different.

I don't want to do something that she won't be able to forgive me for. Why I care, I don't know. Do I have feelings for her? Of course, I do. I had a soft spot from the moment I pulled her onto my lap in that stupid bar.

Hybrid Collection

She was lit up on alcohol and painkillers, but that's not what I saw when I looked at her. I saw someone who was damaged like me, yet she was beautiful. Somehow, she'd survived and was put in my path. Then I lost her and thought maybe I was being an idiot.

Clearly, I wasn't since she's the mother of my child. I don't care what anyone says, what anyone tries to make you believe, but when a woman has your child, she automatically carves out a piece of you. I could hate her with every breath I have, but, in the end, she carried and gave birth to my son. For that alone, I'll owe her forever.

I should despise her for what she's done, but after seeing how good she is to Maverick, I can't. I ought to, I know it, but I don't. Truth is, I want her, and as each day passes us, my anger from her deceit dissipates, and my hunger to have her grows.

I've never wanted a woman so badly in my life like I do her, and especially after pulling something crazy like she did today. It makes me want to fuck her until she begs for my forgiveness. I want her to plead with me to make her mine, so I don't look like the weak one in this. When it boils down to it, I am. I'd probably do anything she asked, and that's so goddamn scary, to let someone own you like that.

Pulling up to my house, it all looks the same. Well, the same since she and Mav have arrived. The front porch light shines brightly, as does the one over the garage. The blinds are closed, but I can see Bethany left the kitchen light on over the sink, and I'd bet there's a plate full of whatever she cooked waiting for me in the microwave, too.

It's something I never had growing up or throughout my life—consistency and care. My father's wives never did it; that's for sure. Hell, they never had a chance to. Life was probably terrifying living with a man whose moods were constantly swinging from one side to the other. It was rough for me being his son, can't imagine having to be married to the bastard.

I don't want to be that way with Bethany. I know I'm a bit moody and quiet, but that's just who I am. I never want her to fear for her safety when it comes to me. Her sanity maybe, since she drives me just as crazy it seems.

I bypass the kitchen, going straight for the room she's taken over since moving in. She belongs in my bedroom with me, but we haven't hit that level yet. She wants her space, and I'm attempting to give it to her.

Maverick ought to be knocked out by now, so he shouldn't hear shouting if there turns out to be any. While arguing may be a natural part of a relationship, I don't want my kid witnessing his mom and me going at each other. Her actions today tell me she wants a fight.

Pushing the door open, Bethany's gaze meets mine, and instantly her eyes widen. She knows she fucked up. I probably look like an angry bear storming in while she's in her normal nighttime attire. The first time I saw her wearing only her cami shirt with no bra and a pair of panties, I thought my dick was going to pop out of my pants on its own accord.

She's already beautiful—the kind of classic beauty that she thinks makes her look plain. She's nowhere near ordinary, she's perfect. Pair that with barely any clothes and it's enough to tongue-tie me, making me think of other things I want to do with her. Not right now, though. I need to get my point across.

"You fucked up," I growl, grabbing her by her biceps and slamming her onto her back against the bed.

Grabbing at my hands, she sputters, "Please, I'm sorry, I know, okay?"

Taking her wrists into one of my palms, I grip them above her head. Then wrap my other around her neck just tight enough to make her nervous, and I bring my nose to hers. "You don't touch a man's bike. That kind of crazy ain't cute dollface," I growl. It's hard to be pissed when my body's laying over hers on top of a bed. I can feel her curves in all the right places.

"Night, I can't breathe." She sucks in a breath through her lips.

Hybrid Collection

"Bullshit." I flex my fingers tighter, and she sputters again. "See, you got breathing room." My lips nearly touch hers as I peer into her shocked irises. "You owe me, Bethany. How you gonna repay me for this little tantrum of yours?"

"I, uh…"

My mouth whispers over her lips, "You finally gonna give up that pussy, baby?"

"You want it?" she replies breathily, making my heart stutter.

"Fuck yes."

"Good, keep wanting it. You won't be touching it anytime soon."

"Fucking bitch." My nostrils flare, and she leans up, quick enough to bite my bottom lip savagely. "Shit!" I pull back as the coppery taste of blood overtakes my tongue. "I should bruise your ass for that one."

"You won't, not until I give in, and right now, it's not happening. And don't call me bitch, bastard."

Grumbling, I push off the bed, releasing her as I stand and adjust myself. The woman's going to be the goddamn death of me. "You have to give me something. You fucked my shit up."

"Fine." She stands, coming chest to chest with me. "You want something?"

I watch her. She could be baiting me. This is Bethany we're talking about. She's not like other women; she likes to keep me on my toes. I'm always guessing when it comes to her.

B licks her lips and drops to her knees. Seeing her below me like that has me awestruck. She's breathtaking.

Quickly she unbuckles my belt and unsnaps my jeans, letting the zipper down. My cock is throbbing with need, wanting her to touch and feel me everywhere. It's been too long since I've been with a woman. Having her here, like this has me damn near jittery with excitement.

"Still a boxer brief man, I see," she states, pushing my pants and underwear down my thighs.

I mutter a reply, but it comes out more as jibber-jabber. She probably didn't understand me; hell, *I* don't even know what I said. All that matters right now is her hand gripping on to my cock like she's about to downshift into second gear or some shit. It's tight and feels magnificent.

"Fuck," I gasp, with her tongue coming to lick my tip like a lollipop.

"Oh, Nightmare, you still taste good, too." Bethany winks up at me, and my stomach tightens with lust. I want to taste her, too, feel her against me.

"Let me bury my cock in you."

"Mmm, no." The tip of my dick sinks between her plump lips before she pulls back and finishes. "I won't be that easy for you, again," she promises and then sucks my cock all the way to the back of her throat.

I'd probably offer her a ring at a moment like this if I knew it would sway her, but it won't. Bethany's never been the marrying type. She'll be loyal for life, I can tell, but she doesn't need a man's last name to do so. She reminds me of myself in so many ways. Maybe that's why I've wanted her so badly from the start.

Her head bobs and she swirls her tongue as she draws backward. I'm damn near to the point I should probably say a prayer thanking whatever being is responsible for creating her. That mouth of hers is torture in the best and worst of ways when it comes to me.

"You weren't easy. I never gave you a choice; I was having you and we had fun." Groaning, my hands tangle in her brunette locks. "Fuck, you're good at that, baby."

"Say my name."

"Huh?"

Her eyes look up, stopping on my own. "I said, 'say my name,' Nightmare. Who am I? Who's sucking your cock right now?"

Hybrid Collection

"Bethany." It leaves my mouth in a whoosh as her lips sink back over my length. I have to hand it to her; the bossy shit turns me on like no other. "Suck my cock, Bethany," I demand, and her teeth graze over my sensitive skin, causing my nuts to tingle, building anticipation.

She pauses, licking the tip in short, quick strokes and prickly sensations overtake the arches of my feet as amazing sensations shoot in every direction throughout my body. One powerful twist around my cock from both of her hands at the same time while she draws me inside her warm, wet mouth and I'm gone. My feet flex inside my motorcycle boots, my leg achy from balancing. Next, my hands that're already gripping her hair, close into fists, pulling and groaning as my mind fades into pure bliss and my cum shoots down her welcoming throat.

Pump after pump she swallows what I give her, and for the first time since she's arrived, it's like I can think clearly again. The fog she's had me in finally begins to thin, and everything's not angry or fuzzy. I'm here, in this moment, with her.

"Are you still mad?" she mutters, climbing to her feet. She wipes over her lips and I swallow thickly at the sight. I don't think I could ever get enough when it comes to her.

Shaking my head, I fix my pants. "Nah, but what knife did you use to cut my tire?"

"It's ummm…the one on my keyring." She gestures to the dresser and then goes and gets her keys. Holding her palm out in front of me, I lift them up, finding the small pocket knife. It's the definition of cute to a chick. To me, it looks like something I would've had when I was six.

"Dollface, let me get you a knife, yeah?" I remove her *knife* which would be considered a nail cleaner to me and hand her the keys. B nods, her stare curious.

She follows me to my room, where I go to my closet to retrieve an actual knife. It's the type she should be carrying for safety or whatever it is she uses it for. Holding out the dark purple handle, she takes it from me.

"Wow, a switchblade?" She palms it in one hand, looking it over, then switches to the other hand, weighing it.

"Yeah, baby, you need something better than that scrap of metal you had on your key ring. You're lucky it didn't break in my tire and cut your damn hand. I'd have been more pissed havin' to call up the doc because you needed stitched up," I mutter, and she rewards me with a bright smile. "What?" She's not going to fight me on it?

"Nothing, just…thank you for this." She presses the lever with her finger—with a bright blue polished nail—and the blade shoots out. My breath falters a bit like some sort of candy-ass.

"Now, be careful with that shit."

"I will." She grins, sheathing the blade again. She twists around, heading for her room.

"Where are you going?"

"To bed! Dinner's in the microwave," the troublemaker calls behind her like I should already know.

I can't believe she didn't fight me on the knife. The downfall to that is if she gets pissed again, she can really screw up some shit with it. Hopefully, it's not my bike that takes the heat again…or me, for that matter.

CHAPTER 18

Shit's gettin' real. Saddle up and hold on.

A week has passed in pretty much a blur. Bethany started a new job that I wasn't happy about, but on the plus side, it's close to the house. She only works during the day, too, so that's an advantage.

I like what consists of family time that we get together even if I piss her off half of the time. She picks up Maverick from Princess and heads home, and then I show up sometime later. We've began our first routine it seems.

It's crazy how much things change when you have a woman and a kid in your life. I no longer want to sit at the club, drinking and bullshitting with my brothers. I'd rather be home with them. Sure, I enjoy my time at the club, but I also enjoy my time with her and Maverick, too.

Before, if I wasn't working out or fixing up a bike, I would go a little stir-crazy at home alone. I've always been sort of a loner, but after being around my brothers for so long, I've grown used to them and their company. Having B and Mav at the house has taken away the quiet. They're always doing something, too, whether it's watching TV, listening to music, or Maverick's busy building some sort of fort in the living room.

Pulling my bike up beside her car, I park the freshly-painted beauty and make my way up the small walkway. That's another thing she's done; she's planted flowers. Never gave two shits about that sort of thing before, but I like them, too.

The small touches make the place seem homier rather than just a crash pad. It's got me thinking about painting the trim and front door as well. The chick is domesticating my ass just by bringing plants around. Ruger would love to find that out and give me some shit over it, I'd bet.

Heading up the walkway, I immediately catch sight that the main door isn't shut all the way, which has me curious. I wonder if Maverick was screwing with it. B asked me to install a chain lock up high, and I haven't done it yet.

Seeing the door cracked, though, I'll make sure and get to it this weekend. The last thing I want is our kid outside when no one is watching him. He's smart, but he's no angel, I've come to discover.

Entering quietly, I hear her. It sounds almost like she's pleading with someone not to hurt her son. *Our son.* I don't have any clue what the fuck's going down, so I draw my blade free from my pants. Flicking the large, heavy blade open, I creep stealthily through the entryway. They're in the living room which throws me in the middle of the scene immediately.

Some fucker in an Iron Fists cut is in my living room, holding a gun at Bethany, who's standing in front of my son protectively. He notices me immediately, switching tactics. He pulls her in front of his body and aims his weapon toward me.

"Get over to where I can see you, Oath Keeper," he hisses, and his teeth are black, from a bad Meth habit if I had to guess.

Doing as he says, I hold my palms out to my sides. I keep a solid grip on my blade with my thumb, but act as if I don't want any trouble. My gaze is surprised like he has one up on me.

I watch in utter amazement as Bethany holds her keys tightly in her palm, keeping it together. She must've been coming home from her new job when this asshole saw her and followed her and Maverick home. I have to give her major props for staying strong and protecting our child while I wasn't here.

"Momma?" My son steps forward and Bethany sputters.

"No, no, no buddy." She holds her free hand out in a stop motion. "You stay over there and hold onto that puppy for Mommy. I don't want you coming over here or I could get hurt."

"Ummm…hurt?" His little worried gaze takes in the scene before him as he holds the sleeping puppy.

"Yes, I don't want any owies, so sit with the puppy; he needs you to cuddle him while he sleeps."

He sighs and slowly sits with the dog, watching everything unfold. I don't think he buys it completely, but he's smart so he stays where he is.

"Who the fuck are *you*? Why are you in my house?" I grumble toward the man I'll be killing shortly. He'll be lucky if I don't string him up and torture him for pulling this little stunt with my family.

"I'm Shadow. And your fucking club killed my older brother."

"Who was your brother?"

At this rate, it could be anyone. We've had our fair share of killing shitbags throughout the club. I'm guessing it was an Iron Fist we torched, as his cut advertises he's affiliated with the same club. None of it matters anyhow; I'm only concerned with keeping him talking.

"Ghost was my brother. Someone from your club killed him," he repeats.

I know exactly who it was, too—Twist and Ares. I remember the exact day, as a matter of fact. They'd called us over for a beer to fill us in on what went down that afternoon. I was still a Nomad at the time.

"I'm coming to kill each one of you." As soon as he finishes, he aims and fires his Glock at me, gripping the back of Bethany's neck tightly with his free hand. Her cringe, has me wanting to extract what teeth he has one by one, so he can feel my wrath for laying his filthy hands on her.

The kick causes the shot to go wide and the bullet hits me in the shoulder. It stings, but that's not what hurts. It's the screams leaving my girl and my son that wind me. He just signed his death certificate. *Bye-bye motherfucker*.

Shaking it off, I spread my feet and grit through the burning sensation. I've been attacked by a motherfuckin' lion; a bullet won't drop me. Not today, at least. I have to protect my family, and I'll do it with everything in me.

"Again, why are you doing this to me and my family?" I need to distract him enough to get his hand away from Bethany's throat, so I can get to him without her getting hurt badly.

Thank God Maverick is a good kid and listens to his mom telling him to stay away from her. He clutches the puppy to his chest as tears roll down his cheeks, confused and scared by what's happening in his own home. I want to kill this asshole for touching Bethany already, but the fact he's making my kid cry, it makes me want to filet him—slowly. I swear if I don't get to finish him outright, I'll burn plastic until it melts into scalding hot liquid then I'll coat his flesh in it and peel him like a goddamn orange. This motherfucker won't know what pain is until I get a turn at him.

B's eyes flick to Mav again, full of concern, I know she's torn on what to do. He sits only a few feet away from the hell happening in our living room. Hell, I want to grab him and take him someplace safe, but I know I can save them both.

This dipshit, Shadow, didn't come prepared. He was expecting to have access to Bethany without any interference and came alone. It was a dumb mistake on his part.

I told dollface before that you never mess with a man's bike. The other two rules that go along with that are: You never fuck with a man's club, and by all means, you never touch a man's property, so you better be prepared if you do. What comes after screwing with those three things is retaliation, revenge, and murder. I cannot wait to get my hands on him, 'cause I will end him.

Hybrid Collection

She takes a deep breath, and I read her before it even happens. She releases the switchblade, nervously glancing at me, and I nod. *Do it baby. I got you.*

It feels as if it happens in slow motion. Her hand jerks upward, taking assface off guard as she drives the blade into his thigh with everything she's got. He yells, releasing her in shock, and she dives for Maverick. I've never been so proud of her.

In the same breath, I jump for Shadow, bringing my own blade to his throat and ripping it across. Bethany holds our son and the puppy to her chest, covering Maverick's eyes as she watches. Blood showers out from the wound, coating my clothes and the floor beneath my feet.

Flicking my head to the side, Bethany hops around the mess heading for the other room. She doesn't need to see all of this; I wish she hadn't witnessed any of it. Watching the man bleed out below me, I wait until I know he's completely gone before I check on my family.

"You okay?" I mutter, pausing in the doorway.

"We will be." She holds Maverick to her still, sitting on the edge of his bed as the puppy noses a few of my son's toys lying around his room.

"You can come out now."

"I can't let him see that out there. And you need to change."

Glancing down, I see I'm coated in blood spray. "I'll be right back."

I stuff the ruined clothes in a trash bag, put a fresh set on and scrub some of the blood from my hands and arms so I don't freak them out. Then check on Shadow again; he's still dead, so I make my way back to the bedroom.

"Better?"

"Yes, thanks and thank you for what you did in there."

"Of course. I'll always protect you in any way that I can. It didn't freak you out though?"

"Well, yes it did, but you had to do it. That man was going to kill us, and you saved us."

"It was you, Bethany. You did the right thing with that knife; I couldn't have planned it better myself."

"The scariest part of all," she whispers, meeting my gaze, "is that I liked it. I enjoyed every second of watching you slice that guy's throat."

I flick my eyes to my son, and bring them back to hers. "It's because you knew you were safe by me doing it, that's all. Don't worry about nothing, babe."

She nods, taking a deep breath. "I need to pack."

"What? Why?"

"Because, we can't stay here with *him* laying out there in the living room. It's bad enough that Maverick saw as much as he did. I can't keep our son here with the house like this."

"Oh, yeah, I get it. I have a room at the club we can stay at for a few nights until this is all cleaned up."

"Okay, I can get us a couple days' worth of clothes."

"The carpet's no good though. It'll have to come out, most likely the whole room. How about wood floors? Unless you have something specific you'd like."

"You are seriously talking to me about flooring right now?"

"I mean, it'll have to go. It sucks. I liked that carpet too, but—"

"Oh my God! You're going over flooring options with me right now!"

"Well, it's your house, too; I want you to have what you like," I reason, and she bursts into a fit of giggles. It's a beautiful sound and makes me grin, even though I don't know why she's laughing right now.

"Jesus. Okay, Night. How about we go with a dark walnut color?"

Hybrid Collection

"Walnut? Like a tree or nut you buy from the store?"

"Yes, if you go to a floor or hardware store they should have it, and it'll look nice with the furniture."

"Sounds good. You'll need to drive to the clubhouse."

"Without you?"

"I'll be behind you in case anyone else is waiting or tries to follow."

"Okay, just be careful, please. I don't know how you can ride like that." She gestures to my shoulder.

"You gettin' soft on me, Daydream?"

"Maybe just a little," she admits and my thumb grazes her cheek. She's so goddamn stunning, even after all the bullshit she went through today. She shouldn't have to deal with any club blowback, but she got caught up in it regardless.

"I need to text Vike, and then we need to head out," I grumble, pulling my phone out. My adrenaline's pumping too thick right now that the pain in my shoulder hasn't hit me full force yet. I'm not looking forward to when it does, either.

Me: My crib was infested when I got here.

Viking: Bet. I'll get my ol' lady, you should come back.

Me: On our way.

Viking: Be safe

Taking a deep breath, I pull up Chaos next, texting everyone in code.

Me: I need your help with a remodel. Grab Spider and head to my place.

Chaos: Will do.

Me: I'll meet you there shortly.

Chaos: No problem.

"Come on baby, grab Maverick. I'll get the dog and your bags. Chaos and Spider are on their way."

"Will they be okay with..." She points to the other room, and I chuckle. If she only knew just how okay any of the brothers would be, she may lose her shit.

"Yeah, they'll be straight. They'll help me clean up and put the new floor in."

"Okay, make sure you order pizza or something for them."

I chuckle again, shaking my head. There's a dead body in the other room and she's worried about feeding company. And it's not normal company either; these are my brothers who are coming over to help me dispose of a body.

She's definitely a keeper.

We load up, and in no time we're on our way to the club. I can't stop thinking that one of the best decisions I ever made was giving my woman a knife.

CHAPTER 19

*I love the 3 am version of people.
Vulnerable. Honest. Real.*

BETHANY

"Wait, how did he get into the house? Was he waiting behind you or something?" Princess gapes, asking me a zillion questions about what just went down with Shadow.

"Not exactly. When I first got home, my hands were full, and I was too busy worrying about putting the puppy outside that I didn't lock the door behind me. We let the dog out, came back inside, and Shadow was there waiting for us."

"Fucking creepy." She shudders.

"I know, Prissy, trust me. I wanted to freak out so badly, but was trying to keep it together in front of Maverick."

"You were so lucky Nightmare came home earlier than expected. Who knows what could've happened to you guys if he'd been running late."

"I know, I was thinking the same thing. Luckily, he had to pick up his bike from Spin and was close to the house so decided to come home. To think, if I'd never slashed his motorcycle up, there's a chance we could be dead right now."

"Well, your temper definitely paid off this time. I'm so glad you all are all right."

"God, me too, lady. I hope this isn't something Maverick will remember as he gets older. Nightmare literally slashed the guy's throat in the middle of the living room. With the blood everywhere and Shadow shooting Night in the shoulder, it was gruesome and scary. I can only imagine how he must be feeling right now."

"I know what you mean, babe; the stuff that went down with me in the bar a few years back was pretty crazy, too. We're lucky to have strong men in our lives."

I nod. It's true. If it'd been some "Joe Schmo" down the road, he'd have pissed his pants in fear—not killed the guy. I always believed Nightmare was sort of a badass, but he's really one bad mamma jamma. I witnessed him kick ass with my own two eyes.

"I'm sure Maverick will replace those images of his dad. He's so small now; hopefully, he'll believe it was a dream or something."

"Fingers crossed," I mumble, thinking about how young I was when my dad began hurting me. I have my own demons and know just how daunting dreams can be inflicted by true events.

"Viking flipped his shit when he got Night's text. He had Odin and Torch come get me from the house in case anyone was lurking around the property. When something like this goes down, it usually happens in more than one place, sort of like a distraction. The club is livid. They'll find these guys."

"Good. Is it bad that I hope they seriously hurt them or even kill them? I feel so guilty saying that, but after meeting Shadow...well, I have to think of my own family."

"No, I agree with you. And to be honest, they won't be turning up again after the club finds them. A threat to family is like a cardinal rule when it comes to these guys. Took me being the Prez's ol' lady to realize that and how important we were to my own father growing up. I really had no clue just how much the club protects its own."

"But we don't belong to the club. I'm not Nightmare's ol' lady."

"No, maybe not, but you are his family. Maverick is his son and you mean something to him. That means a lot to the brothers."

"Do I, though?"

"Yes, B; everyone knows it," she reassures me, her statement full of finality making me believe her.

"So, what now?"

"Now, we settle in, maybe get some dinner going because the guys will get hungry. They'll take care of everything else."

"Just like that? You sit back and let them?"

"Yes. This is their club. While we're a part of it, they run things in this lifestyle. We show them support and love them fiercely. In return, they do the same for us."

Taking a deep breath, I nod and send her a smile. "Then lead me to the kitchen. I need something to do, preferably with chocolate involved."

She returns my smile. "Follow me, this kitchen setup is perfect for cooking a ton of food."

NIGHTMARE

"Spidey and Chaos should be there already," Viking mutters, busily texting someone. "Your shirt's soaked. 2 Piece is already here waiting in case any of you need medical care. Now that I see you were shot, I'm glad I'd called him after all."
"I'm fine. It was just a shoulder graze. Nothing I can't handle."

"Look, I don't give a fuck if you're fine. You have a kid and a woman now, suck it the fuck up and get stitched up," he glowers and I roll my eyes like a petulant child. Last thing I feel like doing is having 2 poking around my shoulder with a damn needle.

"Fine, fuck it. 2 Piece?" I gesture, and he brings his glass and a small tote with him.

"Where did it hit you?" he questions, eyes raking over me quickly.

"My shoulder." I yank my shirt over my head. It's pretty bloody, and I just changed before we left. Good thing my shirt's black. It sucks ass trying to get blood out of clothes.

"Damn." He cringes and pulls a few bottles and other supplies from his bag. "It went straight through, luckily. You'll be tender here for some time, though, and the shoulder's an easy spot to rip stiches out for us. Careful riding, fighting, lifting, fucking, that sort of stuff."

"So, basically, everything then." Grumbling, I get situated. Fucker should've gone to medical school, not joined a biker club. "Appreciate you fixing me up," I acknowledge and he waves me off, getting to work. Bad enough he had to ride over here with shit hitting the fan.

I turn back to Viking, ignoring the pain from 2 Piece cleaning and digging into my flesh while he sews my wound up. "I told Bethany that Chaos and Spider needed to come by to help me redo the floors."

"Good. You having them use that deep pit out back of your place to burn the body?"

"Yeah. I figured they'd look him over for any more information as well. Spider can snap a pic for the photo search he's been doing this week too. May help us find some more answers."

"Bet. I'm sorry this happened to your family, brother, but it may end up being a blessing in disguise."

"I thought the same thing, actually. We need to find these motherfuckers and snuff them all out. Put an end to whatever future plans they may be up to."

"Agreed. I'm talkin' to Ares right now, working on keepin' him up to speed."

Hybrid Collection

"'Kay. If you're straight here, then I'm heading back to my place to help them clean up."

2 Piece grabs the bloody gauze and other supplies, heading for the bathroom and I pull my shirt back on. The shoulder area's a bit stiff from the blood drying, but it'll do for now. I can grab another back at the house and burn all my bloody clothes with Shadow's body. No body, no blood, no evidence, no murder is the way I see it. That motto hasn't let me down yet.

"We've got it handled. If I find out anything, I'll hit you up. You three keep a lookout for any more joiners coming to the party late, and hit me back if you see any Iron Fists period. I'll see about getting the other club here by the time y'all are back for church."

I nod and bump his knuckles. I know he'll make sure Bethany and Maverick are safe here while I go take care of business. I hate leaving them at all after what they just went through. At least B has Princess here to help her process it all. Probably no one better for that job anyhow.

Shadow coming around shakes everything up. It went from us looking out for the other club to a direct threat against us as well. The other club, they aren't as … how do I put it? Not as savage as we are. I think that's the best way to explain them.

They're hard, sure, but we were Nomads before turning over our patch to a home charter. We dealt with the worst of the worst and prospered. That Nomad brand of crazy still pumps through our veins, and this is giving us a prime excuse to cash in on it.

Before I leave, I search Bethany out. She needs to realize that not only was Shadow a game changer for the club, he was for me as well. I'm done fooling with her. I flat out want her. Yes, she fucked up, and, yes, it will forever be in my mind, but I'm moving past it. I'm putting what matters most in perspective—her and my son. Nothing is more important to me than the two of them.

"I'm taking off." I find her and Princess in the midst of a huge mess in the kitchen. I can't help but grin, thinking about how this'll piss the club sluts off something fierce having to do cleanup duty. I know Princess, though, and she'll give zero fucks. My girl need P right now to show her how to cope; I'm glad she has her.

"You have to go?" Her gaze flicks to the floor, and I can tell she's biting the inside of her cheek. She's still shook up. Can't say I blame her.

Grabbing her forearm lightly, I tug her in my direction. "Gotta go and make sure no more idiots are lurking around. You know how I am about you having bad dreams about shit. Figure I'll squash them now and you'll sleep like a baby." Winking, I bring her against my chest.

It's true. Her nightmares drive me up the fucking wall. If I hear her having one, I've started to automatically carry her to my bed so they stop and she sleeps. I don't want this giving her more shit at night as well.

"I know. I really don't want you caught riding alone though."

"One of them couldn't handle me with you in the middle of it. Trust me, B; they damn sure can't handle me alone."

She sighs, still worried, and I pull her closer until her chest is flush against mine and my arms are around her securely. "I'll be fine, Daydream," I utter as I bend down until her lips are to mine.

My hand tangles in her long, dark, chocolate-colored hair and my tongue glides over hers tenderly. The kiss is full of so many feelings I've been holding back, hiding away inside. If I could tell her with merely a kiss just how I feel about her, I would. I'm not sure she'll get it, but I do my damndest anyhow.

Her palm lands on my chest, bunching my T-shirt fabric in her hands as she gives it back just as well as she takes it. I wish the lip lock was under different circumstances and I wasn't about to leave. If anything, the kiss is good motivation to take care of business quickly and get back to her.

"Behave," I murmur, as I pull away. My toes tingle as I remember what her mouth's capable of doing.

Hybrid Collection

She grins as I bump my nose against hers gently, and then I'm out the door, in pissed-off biker mode, ready to fuck up some Fists, if needed.

Thankfully, cleanup went quick, and we made it back to the club in one piece. Having to lift shit with my shoulder sucked, but I got through it. There's nothing more relaxing than lighting a body on fire—other than sex. To me anyhow. I relish in that shit. It can't just be anyone, either. It has to be a piece of shit whose flesh gets melted off by my hands for it to do the trick.

"This crazy goin' on better not be giving you ideas to go Nomad again."

Grinning at Viking, I shake my head. "Nah, you'd miss me too much."

"Not to sound like a bitch, but yeah, I would actually. When we were Nomad, you and Ex were the two brothers I trusted the most. You didn't run your mouths and you owned your shit. I want to be surrounded by that in my own club. I have Princess now; I can't have a Nomad charter."

"I get it, and you don't have to worry about me either. I have Bethany and Mav now. No way I'm leaving them. Truthfully, though, if they weren't around, I'd love to go back to being a Nomad, but my fucking leg can't handle the amount of riding it takes."

"Your leg?" He stares at me, confused. "But I thought it was fine?"

I shake my head. "No. The doc told me to stop riding forever when it happened, but I refused. I did what I could to make it stronger. Well, at least strong enough so I could ride with you guys locally."

"Fuck, why didn't you tell me any of this before? I've sent you on so many runs. I never would've had I known."

"And that's why. I didn't want you to see me any differently. Hell, besides that, I know you would've blamed yourself, and I couldn't have that on my conscience.

You finally found Princess and your calling being the Prez. I wasn't about to piss all over it."

He holds his hand out and I place mine in his, as his other palm comes down on my uninjured shoulder. "You're my brother, Night. Anything you need...any fuckin' thing...it's yours. You just let me know, man."

"Appreciate it."

"And you won't ever hear a word out of me about it again."

"Thank you." I don't mention those words often, but what he's saying, means a lot to me.

"Now, let's get on with church. I'm sure everyone's wondering what the hell's going on. We need to bring them all up to speed."

CHAPTER 20

*Everything has changed and yet,
I am more me than I've ever been.
-Iain Thomas*

BETHANY

"What do you think's happening in there?"

"I don't know, but that Lamborghini that just pulled into the parking lot?" She gestures out the window and I glance to where she points. Sure enough, there's a black sports car parked outside right next to mine and all the guys' motorcycles.

"Yeah?"

"It belongs to the Boss of the Russian Mafia."

"No fucking way." My eyes grow wide, waiting for her to explain.

"Yep."

"Why would the Mafia be here?"

"Well, you know London and Avery from the other club?"

"Yep."

"Their duo is really a trio. The third best friend, Emily, is married to the head of the Russian Mafia. Hence, the connection with the guys."

"Holy shit."

"Uh-huh. The brothers did some work with them awhile back, but I can't get into any details."

"That's still crazy he's here right now."

"I know. I'd guess that things are a little more serious than we'd anticipated. If Mafia and the other club is involved, it's a bigger threat than our guys are letting on."

"Who's that, then?" I point out the same window as a gray Phantom pulls in next.

"Holy fucking shit," she says, copying me from a minute ago, and I laugh. She turns to me and whispers, "That's Thaddaeus Morelli." The way she says it, makes him seem to be some magic creature.

"Okaaaay…Who is that, exactly?"

"Uh, that's Chicago m. o. b.!" She spells out mob, and it nearly makes me laugh. I don't, though, because this is serious according to her shocked gaze.

"So, is this bad, then?"

"Supposedly Cain did some work for him, but I've never seen him in person. I only know who he is because Viking showed me a picture in case I did ever see him."

"Wow, I wonder why they're all here at the same time. It kind of scares me being here with a ton more criminals than I'm used to."

"For once, B, it scares me too, because it means my man is knee deep in something."

"I take it he hasn't mentioned to you about whatever he's up to?"

"That would be a big fat no, but you better believe I'll be asking him tonight."

Hybrid Collection

"I should ask Nightmare to tell me."

"You can, but don't be surprised if he doesn't say anything."

"Why would he keep it from me?"

"Because, it's club business. He may not tell you to keep you safe."

I hope that's not the case. I may go crazy if he doesn't share what's going on. Prissy has me a little wigged-out with all these people suddenly showing up.

"Come on," she calls and takes off out of the kitchen toward the main entry. I follow along, because I need to find out what's happening one way or another.

The heavy door opens with Cain coming through on a mission and Thaddaeus hot on his heels.

"Princess." Cain nods in acknowledgment. Of course he'd stop to greet her; she's the Prez's 'ol lady. "Bethany," he says to me next, and I nod, remaining quiet, stomach twirling with nerves.

The breath leaves me in the next moment as my hand's engulfed by a large, strong completely male hand. "Pet." His gaze meets mine, and I think my heart skips a beat when they do. "I'm Thaddaeus Morelli." His other hand falls on top of mine as he introduces himself. His deep voice invokes hot flashes. The man is the definition of GQ power and beauty. *Holy fuck.*

"Ummm…hi," I reply quietly, and Princess steps in to save me. I'm grateful for the interruption as I have no idea what to say to a man like that.

"Mr. Morelli, Cain…I'll take you to see Viking." She turns and leads the way, leaving no room for argument.

My hand is set free from his warmth, but Morelli's eyes linger on me for a moment longer and then he's gone.

My feet remain planted in the same spot as my nerves cool down. I'm going to go ahead and call that "The Thaddaeus Effect." Holy shit, if I wasn't so far gone for Nightmare, I'd probably follow that man around like a devoted groupie.

NIGHTMARE

Taking my place, I glance around at the brothers. Every one of them from ours and Ares' chapters is here, including Tate, the Boss off the Russkaya Mafiya, and Morelli, from the Chicago mob. It's like a goddamn convention for criminals taking place. Rarely do you see this many of us in one spot at the same time and usually there's either a big deal going down or cops involved if so.

"My woman was attacked today. This needs taken care of immediately," I growl, and everyone's stern gaze looks to me. I'm sure the majority of them have heard through the grapevine what went down, or, at least, the short and sweet version, but it needs to be brought up in front of everyone.

"Bethany, the woman I just met?" Morelli's cold stare lands on me, and I send one straight back. He shouldn't be speaking. He's a guest here. Clearly no one told him to shut up before he entered our clubhouse.

"Yep, she belongs to me."

"Noted." He nods with a smirk on his face.

The fucking *Joker*, huh. I'll wipe that look clean off his mouth if he gives me a reason to, and I'll do it fucking smiling the entire time too. Show him how bikers handle business.

"We'll find them all, brother," Ares growls, angry that pain has touched our club once again. He, of all people, knows how I feel. His ol' lady, Avery, has been targeted in the past. So has Twists ol' lady, Sadie, and Princess. It seems to be a favorite spot for our enemies to hit us—our women, our hearts. You'd think they'd steer clear, knowing that's a line you don't cross, but apparently, they're fucking idiots.

"All of 'em dead this time," Twist mutters, his fingers tapping in some random rhythm.

Hybrid Collection

I've heard he plays guitar, and he's damn good, too. I find myself tapping out beats all the time as well. It must be a musician thing. I could use some music therapy right about now. Beating on some drums would help me get some of this energy out, that's for sure. Or a good fight. I'd take either.

"Why are you here, Thaddaeus?" Ares brings up the question we're all sitting around wondering as well. "Cain said you had business to discuss?"

"It can wait until after this other matter."

"No, go ahead," Ares orders.

"As you know, my uncle is in charge of Chicago; he runs everything with the Italians."

The majority of us are well aware of who he and his family is, so we nod and he continues.

"I want you to clean house for me. In return, I'll take over his territory and offer you the area you've been wanting."

"Shit," Ares mutters and takes a large gulp from his water bottle.

"Fuck." Viking sighs. "So you expect us to go in and do your dirty work and you'll give us a Chicago charter in return? How does this benefit us? We'll lose half our club cleaning out the mobsters up there."

"Right. In return you get your colors in my state."

"Who's to say you wouldn't turn on us, sell us out, and have your mob buddies come after us after we 'clean house' as you put it. As you can see, we're already dealin' with our own shit."

"I'm not a rat, and I'm loyal. I'm doing this because the man wronged me; otherwise. I'd never cross him. It's time I take back what was mine to begin with."

"Why would we encroach on mob territory like that? We run weapons, we deal. You guys already have your system up there."

"Right. I run all the shipping and such, meaning I could offer you a partnership in that aspect. Like I said, some things have come to light, and it's time he was dealt with."

"Break it down a little blunter for us Southern folk," 2 Piece interrupts.

"You run weapons for the mob like you do the Russians." His gaze flicks to Tate's and we all hold our breath briefly, waiting to see if we're about to have a mob war on our hands next.

After a tense moment, Tate shrugs. "We are eastern-southeastern. I don't see any conflict of interest with the Midwest, as long as you remain good on our deals we have in place. There are more of you now; I'd be an idiot to expect you to not work with others."

Viking rubs his temples, then nods at Morelli. "We'll discuss it and then vote. It's club business so everyone has to agree. We'll be in touch with what we decide."

"Good. I look forward to speaking with you soon." He stands, as does Ares and Viking. He shows them respect by shaking each of their hands and then Cain shows him back out. Cain being so close to Ares is the only reason Thaddaeus Morelli was allowed in here and heard out in the first place.

"Now, how about you, Tate?" Viking's gaze hits the Russian. It is his clubhouse, so while Ares is a President, he respects Viking's status in his own club. It's the same as when we were at church in their club last week.

"It started out as just a trip so Emily could visit with her friends. Then I caught wind that something was going on, so I left her with the girls at the other club to see if y'all needed my help. Well, the Mafiya's, specifically. Whatever's going down, do you have enough weapons or enough men to keep everyone safe? Especially after what Nightmare brought up in the beginning?"

2 Piece claps him on the shoulder, grateful. They're friends, along with Cain, because of their wives and have grown to do a lot of business together over the years. We've done some work for Tate's cousin, Beau, as well. That's actually why I got attacked by that damn lion. We were down in Mexico searching for a woman

the Russians were hell bent on finding. We came away with nothing, but that's beside the point.

"We're good as far as members go, but we can always use more weapons. Did you bring anything with you?"

"I didn't, but one of my soldiers will be here tomorrow with a few cases. I figure what you don't use, you may want to sell?"

"Sounds good," Ares agrees instantly. "Brother?"

"Yeah, we're in," Viking confirms.

Tate stands next. "All right, I'll let you handle your business in private then. If I can help out, let me know." He shakes Viking and Ares' hands on his way out.

What a busy damn day. I swear it seems nice and quiet around here and then everything comes at the club all at once. Shit can never just trickle in to be dealt with one at a time.

"Fuck, now back to what we're going to do to catch these assholes." Vike takes another swig of his drink and continues. "Spidey, run that photo of Shadow you took today through your face program."

"Will do, Boss. I'll let you know what I find."

"I've called the other Nomads, Exterminator and Ruger. They're on their way into town to provide some backup, but let's hope we don't need any. The rest of the crew is on a run up north so they won't be heading down with them. The mess at Nightmare's crib is cleaned up. I say we go on full lock-down until we figure out what the fuck to do next. They got a little too close to home today, and I don't want to see it happen to anyone else, especially when we haven't even found their location."

"I agree. We need to vote. All in favor of the plan?" Ares finishes, and we go around the table agreeing.

With church coming to an end, the brothers and I pile out into the bar area while Spider runs the photos he got of Shadow through everything he can think of. I've barely thrown back half a beer, and, in no time, he's calling us to his room to see what all he's found.

Blaze, Viking, Ares, Cain, and I all pile in and take a look while he explains everything he was able to uncover. He found it in mere minutes with the right information to search for. Fucking crazy how you can be hunted down through random cameras positioned throughout the world.

"So, the facial recognition was able to pick up Shadow all over the place. One in particular was his mugshot which came paired with his legal name. It also found him at several gas stations that have been under surveillance after being robbed. Lucky for us, he had several buddies with him during these times. I was able to feed those camera shots into the system and figure out where a cluster of them have been gathering."

"A cluster?" Blaze's eyes row wide, glancing at Viking.

"Yep, not a small one, either. It looks like they've been holed up in a little town four hours north of here. My guess is they did it on purpose, waiting to make their move. It's way too damn convenient they're that close and they weren't planning something."

Ares grumbles, "I don't get it. How could everyone miss them? We have allies everywhere. It doesn't add up, none of it."

"Actually, it does. The spot where they're hiding out is technically Oklahoma, which puts them out of our main territory. And it's also right off a busy highway so they can be on and off in no time, with hardly anyone seeing them. In this case, random gas stations were the only thing that pulled them up. If Shadow hadn't got caught by Nightmare, there's a chance we never would've caught on. They're smart, and I hate admitting that about enemies."

"Makes sense." Cain shrugs. "Random Casinos run by the Indians, pussy, drugs, all right there, and not closely monitored 'cause it's Indian Territory."

Viking huffs, cursing. "Where are the fucking Indian bikers in all this? We couldn't go through Oklahoma on a run without them being up our asses for a payout to pass through."

Blaze tsks. "I'm sure they're getting a payout somehow. You know the Iron Fists roll around in heroin and meth. Bet they're cooking some shit up for the Indians to keep quiet. The entire thing smells bad to me."

"Goddamn, motherfucker," Ares mumbles, rubbing his temples. "The fuck we gonna do then? We can't go guns blazin' on the goddamn Indian reservation; Uncle Sam would be breathing down our throats in a heartbeat. We've gotten around with mild heat for many years, not trying to get in trouble with them now."

"Actually," Spider interrupts. Smart little fucker has an answer for everything. "Where they are, it's not technically the reservation. It's closer to the Texas line, so if I give you a location you should be fine. You have to light it up and get the fuck outta there though. No sticking around to see the outcome. It would be hit it and quit it."

"Good work, Spidey." Viking claps his shoulder. "Get us a location, and we'll plan a visit."

"We need to discuss this ASAP," I mutter as we pile into the hallway.

"We'll have a drink and wait for Spider to finish. When he's done, we'll go back into church. I think everyone's still here." Viking glances at us and Ares nods.

"Sounds good, brother. It's been a while since I've had some fun. I'm ready to take care of business."

"Brothers, we have news," Viking begins as we're all crammed back into church, Spider with printouts spread on the table in front of him. "We have a location and an estimate in numbers."

"'Bout time, let's finish this," Twist grits, and I couldn't agree with him more.

"Ares and I discussed a plan we'd like to run over with everyone. We're wanting to pay them another visit like before. Think Cali all over again. We torch the place and get the fuck out of there. Come home and batten down for potential blowback. We can knock a bunch of them out with one big hit. Let them scamper away like roaches, same as they did the last time."

"We all going?" Torch questions, ready to get down and dirty. He used to be a Widow Maker in South Carolina before they were patched over, along with Blaze and Bronx. He's a pretty mean fucker; I have respect for him always keeping his word.

"We'll have Exterminator and Ruger; I know they'll want to be in. From our charter: Chaos, Torch, Nightmare, and I will go." His irises flick to mine. "If you're up for it?" Everyone else's gaze falls on me as well. He's never asked before, but I know he wants to make sure I can handle the ride with my leg. I'm touched and irritated all in the same breath.

"Of course," I mutter, glowering so I don't come off as a weak spot in front of anyone.

"Scot, Bronx, Blaze, and Spidey will stay here to hold down the club."

"I'm going, too," Twist interrupts and Ares growls.

"Yeah, Twist, Cain, Snake, and I will ride up. The rest of my charter will stay at the club."

"Everyone good with it?"

"Aye," we each respond pegging our gaze on Viking and Ares.

Enough fucking around. I'm ready to leave right the fuck now and handle this shit. I'm sure the others are antsy as well.

"Everyone watch your backs until then. We'll see what Tate's men bring up and then plan to hit the road the following day. Expect to ride out Friday. Those assclowns will get fucked up Friday, and we'll be able to surprise their asses when they least expect it." Ares and Viking rise, done with business for the time being.

The only thing on my mind is finding Bethany and kissing her again. Her lips were perfect earlier.

CHAPTER 21

His love roared louder than her demons.
- |writtenbyhim.

BETHANY

I'm half asleep by the time Nightmare crawls into bed behind me. Maverick's passed out right next to me on a cot Princess found in the storage room. It's a tight fit in here, but we'll make-do for a few days. It's not so bad either, since I've gotten used to sleeping next to Night most of the time, and we have to share a bed here.
"Mmm, you smell so fuckin' good," he whispers in my ear, and I can make out whiskey laced with mint on his breath. He must've been drinking with his brothers a bit before and then swished with mouthwash before coming to bed.

"And you smell like whiskey and mouthwash." I grin and he chuckles.

"Sounds like a damn good combination to me." He wraps his strong arm around my waist, pulling me into his warmth. It's like being covered with a fluffy blanket, and I love the feeling.

"It is."

"You finally gonna let me in your pants, baby?"

Hybrid Collection

"And there's the whiskey talking."

"Dollface…" It's nearly a whine which makes me laugh.

"Oh no, you don't crawl in bed half-lit and expect me to spread 'em for you, the first time in years, at that. Maybe eventually, but not tonight, handsome."

"You think I'm handsome?" he asks in an unsure mumble.

"Of course, you're handsome. You're freaking hot. I'm not afraid to admit that much. Besides, you know it anyhow, all those chicks going crazy over you when you play the drums."

"That's just the rocker vibe. But *you* think that, even with the scar and fucked up colored eye?"

Can he really be unsure about it? I would never peg him being insecure about anything, or caring for that matter. He's nuts if he doesn't realize women love mismatched eyes and scars like that. He's not only gorgeous, but he's got the bad-boy-kind-of-scary-but-damn-I-could-fuck-you kind of look going—always.

"I think your eyes are beautiful, and the scar is sexy."

"Hmm…You're beautiful."

"And you're horny."

"I am," he admits and I grind my ass against him just to tease him a bit.

"You're bad, Bethany, and bad one's get spanked. You better watch it or I'll pull those panties down, then you'll be begging to be fucked."

"Jesus Christ, why do you have to say shit like that? Our son is right next to us. I can't go at it; you know I could never be quiet when you were in full-on pound town mode."

He chuckles, and it sends tingles all over me. He sounds absolutely delicious. "Fine, but I'm having some fun," he declares as the palm resting on my stomach flattens and skims under the elastic of my panties.

"Ummm…whoa, buddy," I sputter as his palm rests over my clit and he applies some pressure.

"Enough being patient," he grumbles, his soft lips coming to my neck where he nips and sucks the tender area.

Holding my breath so I don't squirm and intensify the erotic tingles, I go with it, closing my eyes in the moment. It takes everything in me not to be loud with him. I don't know what it is, why he gets me so flustered like he does, but it's like his hands are magic.

I have to be quiet, but it doesn't mean I can't enjoy his touch, the feeling of him holding me so closely to him. I've wanted Nightmare since the first day I set my eyes on him. He's absolutely crazy if he doesn't realize how gorgeous he is or how women gawk when they see him. Fucking sinful is more accurate.

His middle finger dips between my folds making me gasp. It's been too long since I've felt him. Everything is right on the edge, wanting to explode and waiting for his next move.

He leans over a bit and I turn my face to him, letting him take my mouth with his. As his tongue strokes mine, his finger sinks into my depth. He catches the moan that attempts to escape from my lips, keeping all of me for himself.

Pulling my bottom lip between his, he bites it, just rough enough to make my eyes pop back open. He's wearing a wicked smile. The fucker knows he turns me to putty with his touch.

"Feel good, dollface?"

"Yes, fantastic."

"Oh yeah, that good, huh? How about when I do this?" He dips another finger in, moving them in long strokes. His thumb circles my clit at the same time, and it's a miracle I can breathe or think through the sensations.

"Fucking shit," leaves me on a breathy gasp. So unladylike but I could care less. He knows exactly what it means.

Hybrid Collection

"Yeah?" he growls, his teeth biting at my bottom lip again. My eyes roll back, submitting to his blissful torture. Smelling him, feeling him, hearing him—all have my body waving the white flag to whatever he wants to do with it.

His fingers plunging in deep has my mouth popping open. He uses the opportunity to kiss me again. It's the feelings that the best types of dreams are made of. The twists and flutters spiraling all around as you're enraptured in the sweetest bit of euphoria between a man and a woman.

"I want you seeing motherfuckin' stars when you look at me, baby," he admits. If he only knew. He's been making me see stars for far too long already.

"I do, oh God, I do."

"Fireworks, Bethany."

His growl has me wanting to climb over him and ride him like a fucking cowgirl. I'm not one, never have been, but pretty sure I could give him one hell of a ride to convince him differently.

"I do."

"Swear to me."

"I swear." I'll tell him anything he wants to hear. The only thing clouding my mind is the building orgasm and the fact that it's Nightmare giving it to me.

"It's what I saw when you had my cock in your mouth—stars. Fucking bright-ass stars and your beautiful face. Had me shooting my load off like no other." His finger presses against my nub harder, and the breath catches in my throat.

"Now, dollface, give me more fucking stars," he orders, pressing his fingers in me, stroking quicker, and I explode.

My pussy quivers with delight, attempting to pull him in deeper as my body rides the wave of pleasure. The wave that only Nightmare makes me feel whenever I'm with him—no one else. No other man can play my body so easily and make it do whatever he wants it to; they never even come close.

"Night." Groaning, my hand clutches his forearm to me, not letting him move away immediately. The aftershocks flutter through, and he waits patiently while dropping kisses all along my neck. I could lie here and let him pepper kisses all night long and be a happy woman.

"I saw stars."

"Promise?" he whispers against my throat.

I nod and the only dreams that come that night are ones filled with a broody man, there to protect and love me. They're the best types of dreams to have.

NIGHTMARE

"You have to leave?" Bethany peers up at me, worried.
"I do."

"Please be careful."

"I will."

I stuff the saddlebags with my belongings. She stands at the back of my bike, holding Maverick's hand as they watch me. Everyone's loading up, a few of us having to say good-bye to our other halves. We haven't made anything official or said it out loud, but that's what she is to me. Maverick is just icing on the cake when it comes to our family. I'd do anything for that kid.

"I feel like we've barely had time to reconnect," she admits, biting her bottom lip.

Nodding, I stand and pull her into my arms, Maverick's hand wrapping around my thigh. "It'll be all right. Once I get back, we'll have more time," I mumble in her hair.

Hybrid Collection

"Princess told me what happened with this group before; just watch your back. You have a kid waiting for you."

"Just a kid?" I pull her in my arms, holding her tighter.

"You have me, too."

I nod again, taking in the flowery scent from her shampoo. "Go inside. I probably won't call you or text 'cause I'll be riding most the time."

"If you aren't coming back right away for some reason, you need to at least text."

"I will, I promise." Pulling back, I press my lips to hers gently. I want to own her mouth, kiss her roughly to take as much as possible, but I don't. I'm gentle, giving her my sweet side, relishing in her taste so I can easily remember it later.

"Later alligator." Putting my fist out, Mav bumps it with his, giving me a happy grin.

"Bye, Daddy."

In no time we're loaded up, our engines shaking the ground as the nine of us take off on a mission of revenge. It's time to head to Oklahoma and fuck some shit up.

CHAPTER 22

There is my heart, and then there is you, and I'm not sure there is a difference.
-A.R. Asher

"What is it?" Viking growls as we pull off at a gas station out of turn. We'd already filled up and were set for another two hours at least before breaking.

"Fuck, I don't know, but my phone has been going off nonstop, continuous for the past hour."

"Just Bluetooth that shit, we're wasting too much time."

"I would, but I can't hear good with that thing in my ear. Besides, who the fuck you know would be callin' me like that? Someone who's lost their motherfuckin' mind," I grit in return, and pull my device out to see what the hell is going on.

It says Bethany: 240 missed calls.

"What the ever loving fuck?" Holding it up to Vike, his gaze widens, and he gestures for me to call. I was going too anyhow.

"The fuck's goin' on, Bethany, Christ?" I damn near yell when she answers.

She's sobbing, and I can't understand a damn thing she's saying. "Baby, calm your tits, the fuck happen?"

Hybrid Collection

She's crying something fierce, mumbling words that make no sense whatsoever. She's hysterical to the point I would be thinking of sedating her if I were there, and it's crushing me inside. "I cannot understand you at all. Is Princess there? Put her on so she can talk."

"Nightmare?" Princess comes on the line; no doubt she's been crying, too. I hear Viking swear in the background, once he powers his cell on and discovers his missed calls too. Her voice has me on edge; this is the Ice Queen I'm talking to. She doesn't show weakness like this, especially to me or to anyone besides her ol' man.

"Yeah, the fuck's goin' on over there?"

"Y-you guys need to come back, right now."

"Why? Talk to me, damn it!" I shout, and all the guys stare at me, with 'what the fuck' expressions.

"They have him. They took Maverick. You guys left and so many showed up. They killed Bronx; ripped a knife up his stomach and pulled his guts out in the middle of the parking lot. Scot…he's gone. Th-they cut his fucking throat! Blaze is barely breathing; I have the doc coming right now." She lets out a shuddering breath, her voice choking up as she fights to get words out. "But Mav, h-h-h-he-he's gone, Nightmare. We fought them; I swear to God, we fought. But there were just too many. They threw us to the side like flies. Puppet, their leader said they were leaving me and Bethany alive to warn you. They s-said the Fists always collect their debts owed."

I growl into the line, my mind beginning to spiral out of control with the many ways I'll kill them all, and she continues.

"We took a son from them, so they're taking a son from us. Oh God, Night, I don't know what to do. Bethany is losing it; she's going to kill herself at this rate. You guys have to get here now. There's blood everywhere, and her son's gone. I-I don't know what to do."

"Keep her safe. Call 2 Piece and tell him to get over there now."

"I've been calling everyone; I think the Fists are hitting them too. It didn't seem like they were finished when they left."

"Call your father. Tie B up if you have to; I don't give a fuck. Just watch her. We will be there as quickly as possible," I order calmly, even though I feel nothing of the sort. Every nerve in my skin is jumping, and I'm so angry I could peel someone's skin off their body with my bare hands and feed it into a fire piece by bloody piece at this moment.

I hang up, stuffing the phone in my pocket. Everyone stares at me in anticipation. I'm so fucked up inside, yet I have to tell them what has happened. I have to find the strength.

Climbing off my bike, I stumble a few steps away and then puke. I wretch up every last thing in my stomach, eventually dry heaving, with the strong taste of stomach acid left behind in my throat. It takes an empty stomach before I'm able to pull it together enough to speak.

I turn to my brothers with tears in my eyes. Swallowing, I take in each of their faces and then relay everything Princess just told me on the phone.

Viking is on his bike and out of the parking lot before I even finish. We all follow quickly, and it's amazing I can even concentrate enough to ride. All I know is that my son is gone, my girl is an absolute wreck, and I have to get the fuck back home.

I have to fix this; I will fix this, if not for me and my club, for Bethany.

The ride home is the longest I've ever been on. I shook the entire way, not just my hands, but the inside of my stomach quaked with worry and anger. I have no idea what to even do. Should I just hold Bethany while she cries, or should I immediately hunt down the bastards that have my son?

I decide on both. As soon as I see her, I wrap my arms around her battered body and just breathe as she sobs into my chest. Tears fall down my cheeks hearing her so beyond broken. How do you get through something like this? What on earth do you say to someone who just had her child literally ripped from her hands, in a place where she should've been safe?

They came into our home, killed members, and stole our son. There's nothing I can say to bring her peace in this moment. I'm barely standing upright on my own two feet.

I can't remember the last time I shed even a tear for anything at all, but my cheeks are wet as her body shakes against mine. I have to be strong for her, for him, but I feel anything but. My physical being feels weak and beat down all over, I'm not even the one who took any of the physical blows either.

Two brothers are dead and gone forever. If anyone could've been somewhat of a father figure to me, it would've been Scot. The man never passed any judgment and welcomed me immediately when he recognized I was young and lost. He led us for a time with the Nomads, and I'm honored to have had the chance to ride with him for so many years.

Bronx was just a fuckin' kid. I'd only known him since he patched over from the Widow Makers. He'd barely cleared his Prospect patch and been patched a full member with us. He was a punk the first time I'd come across him, and I'd gotten the pleasure to watch him evolve into a young man. He'd grown into someone honest and loyal over the past few years, someone worthy of wearing the Oath Keeper patch.

I can't help but have the festering rage building inside me toward Twist. I know I shouldn't blame a brother for what has happened, but his woman brought the Iron Fists to their front door initially. They'd had run ins and issues with the club trying to claim our territory, but it was her that brought the brunt. It's because of them that my son isn't here with his family right now.

We never should've ridden off and torched that clubhouse for them in Cali. The Nomads should've told them to take care of their own shit. But we were the hard ones, the true death dealers of the club. When shit hit the fan, they called us, and we were there to answer. Now it's us who needs the help, my woman and me. Every motherfucker better step up to help out, too.

Saying a silent prayer to a God I'd long stopped believing in, I can only hope I was wrong. Hope that He's up there, listening to my heartfelt plea for assistance and helps me find my son and some peace in this life. Why is it we have to hit a new level of low to seek comfort and redemption from up above? It took a three year old to bring me to my knees and want to change my ways. I want to become a better man in life not for me, but for him and for Bethany.

She shutters and I keep holding her, trying to give her some ounce of warmth to keep her with me. Bethany's so fucked up, I'm afraid she's mentally checked the fuck out. She weeps and stares into space. She won't speak to me. She mumbles his name and sobs some more. She's broken, and I can't fix her, but I'm hoping to get our son back because I know he can fix her.

"I have you baby. I will do everything to make this better, I promise you with everything I am. I'm so fuckin' sorry. I will get our son back if it's the last thing I ever do," I murmur in her hair, my voice laced with heartbreak, rocking her in my grip.

She doesn't answer, just cries more and I feel like each tear that falls from her eyes rips more of my soul from my chest. I'll be completely black inside by the time this is over. My heart will match the bruises on her face.

"I have Spider searching any cameras in the area. We'll find them," Viking declares, but part of me doesn't want to hear him. A piece of me is locking up and pulling away from everyone. If I don't get Maverick back, I know I will never be able to forgive my brothers or this club. Whether it's their fault this has happened or not, I will hold them responsible for my pain.

One thing is for certain: I will never stop looking for him.

"I'm so sorry, Daydream," I repeat, not able to convey my true feelings. I wish I knew how, but I don't. All I know is the person I love is hurt, sad, and broken, and the other person I love is missing.

The doc finds us after fixing up Princess to check over B. Once she completes her exam, she asks if I want a sedative. I don't take one, but have her inject Bethany with a mild tranquilizer.

Hybrid Collection

She's too fucked up right now. She may hurt herself, and I can't let that happen. I'm here and I have to protect her, even if that's from herself.

She'll probably end up hating me for all of this, and I can't blame her for that. One thing I've come to discover, though, is that I love her a great deal more than I'd begun to realize these past weeks. She's it for me—the one—my everything, and that includes Maverick. So she can hate me. I'll take it, own it, and wear that badge every day of my life. But, I'm going to do whatever I have to, to make her love me like I do her, with every single beat of my cold, once-dead heart.

CHAPTER 23

I love how you take care of me. How you keep working to be a better man. Even on days I fail to be a better woman.
-IntentionalToday.com

BETHANY

The days come and go, passing me in what feels like a drug-induced haze. I let Nightmare be my strength.
I've been strong for the past few years. I took care of Mav when he was sick, up all night crying through fevers and puking. I took him to the hospital when he stepped on that rusty nail and held his hand and promised him the entire world to get him through his pain. I've been brave for him each time he's gotten scared, but this time I just can't do it. I need someone to be strong and brave for me, and that's Nightmare.

He takes it in stride, letting me cry when I feel that I need to. He accepts my hits each time I blame him, and he stands still when I pound on his chest in anger. Most of all, through everything, he keeps trying and he shows me love.

He loves me so much, that if my little boy wasn't missing, my heart would be so full, it would overflow. Through the anger consuming me over my son being taken by a rival club, I love Nightmare in return. I hold on to him for dear life and let him take the reins, knowing inside that he won't let me drown. He can't, because I won't survive on my own anymore.

NIGHTMARE

My cell rings, and it's a number I've never seen before. "Yeah?" I answer, not in the mood to deal with spam calls. I may rip their throats out if presented with the opportunity.
"This Nightmare?" A gravelly voice replies.

"Yep, who the fuck is this?"

"I'm the one keeping your son alive."

"Motherfucker! You better not hurt him, or I'll—"

"You'll do what?" he interrupts, chuckling. "You forget, I'm the one in control."

"Fine." My voice is dark, coated in fury, wanting to rip him to shreds as I do my best not to plead. "What the fuck do you want so I can have my kid back?"

"Oh, I'm afraid that's not going to happen. It's quite simple, you see. You took something from me, now I take it back."

"What did I ever take from you?"

"Well for starters, your other club took my son."

"I'm not responsible for that!"

"I know that, but you took something from me as well."

"I don't even know who the fuck you are!" I can't stop the shouting. I'm so pissed, I feel like my head is going to explode.

"Shadow was my son, and you killed him."

"He was at my house, threatening my woman."

"He wouldn't have hurt her. He was only there for the child. Like I told the women, you take a son from me, I'll take one from you."

"Why? Why my son? There are so many other members that have club brats."

"I know that, we've been watching. However, *your* charter was the one to torch my clubhouse in Cali. So when that sexy bitch Bethany showed up with your kid in tow, it was the perfect opportunity to get my payback."

"So you've been watching the entire time and planning to take him since she showed up?"

"I have…and now he's mine."

"The fuck he is. I will find you, and I will get my son back."

"No, you won't, but I have a deal for you. You'll get him back, eventually. He's going to be raised by me, and when he's a grown man, I'll let him go back to you. If he wishes."

"Not fucking happening," I grit and the line goes dead, making me shout.

Throwing my phone against the wall, it smashes and I begin to hyperventilate. His words crawled right under my skin and have begun to fester already. I think he's crazy enough to believe what he's doing is in his right. He can't take my son and keep him.

That's medieval shit, sending your kid to live off with the enemy or another king. In our case a rival club and I'm assuming Puppet is the President over them all. We didn't snuff out the Iron Fists; we poked the fucking nest and now they've come back to swarm.

I'd heard they were a hard club—hell, we all had. That was why we were sent in the first place. We were warned that they don't fuck around. Neither did we. At least I thought we didn't. Clearly we had no fucking clue what the hell we were doing.

Hybrid Collection

There's so much more here, so much under the surface. I can't just kill the Fists I find like I'd want to; this is going to take planning. How the fuck can I possibly pull this off? There has to be a way.

To think the Iron Fists have just been sitting back and waiting, biding their time for retaliation. We were stupid enough to believe we'd outdone them. The opportunity arose, and they took it, leading us straight into a goddamn trap. I'd bet their clubhouse isn't even in Oklahoma. It was all a ruse to make the club weak enough for them to easily take what they intended.

"Talk to me," Ex grumbles.

They haven't left yet; he and Ruger have been by my side waiting to help me—everyone has. We buried Scot and Bronx yesterday, but I wasn't present. I loved my brothers, but I have my own shit to deal with. I know if they were here they would understand and want me to keep looking for Maverick.

"What's going on?" Viking asks immediately, noticing me flipping my shit. I puke again. I've lost weight this week from being sick so much, but it's the only way my body is coping with the stress and pressure I'm under.

"Breathe, brother; tell us what just happened." Chaos rests his hand on my shoulder, another good friend of mine, having my back. Regardless, without Mav I will blame them, no matter how much I tell myself not to.

"It was him," I get out between heaves.

I feel like my chest is seizing up, and I'm having a fucking panic attack or some shit. I can't breathe. It feels like my ribs are squeezing me in a vice grip. Like my heart's going to burst straight through my chest. It's not like running too much. It's like sticking your head under water and being forced to suck in nothing but water. It fills your lungs, weighing your body down, choking you the fuck out.

My vision goes blurry for a moment, and I puke again, but this time nothing comes out. I have nothing left to expel. Acidic aftermath fills my mouth and I gag a few times. The blurred vision is new and not something I want sticking around.

Eventually it passes and I'm able to explain what just happened. I tell them about Puppet and everything that was said. I feel like I'm losing my mind, like this is all a sick joke or a goddamn nightmare and I need to wake up.

Letting it hit me all over, I shut down and go on a rampage, punching and throwing everything I can find. I down a bottle of Jager and then upchuck it all back up, damn near immediately. It gets so bad that I'm pricked with something in my back, and then everything goes black.

BETHANY

Princess shakes me awake, upset.
"What's happening?" It leaves me in a groggy mumble as I meet her concerned gaze.

"It's time for you to snap out of it, B."

"I can't deal with this, Prissy. There's nothing I can do." Brushing her off, I fall back against the pillows. My body aches from lying around and sleeping so much. I have to, though; I can't handle being awake and not being able to do anything. No one here will let me leave to go find my son. No one has answers. I can't cope like this.

"The fuck you can't," she replies angrily and suddenly she's straddling my waist. She rears back and unleashes a harsh slap. Copper overtakes my mouth as my lip splits on the inside, and, for the first time in a week, I'm seeing her face clearly. "Shit is happening!" she screams, her bruised face scrunching up in sadness and anger. "No more, Bethany. You've fucking slept and moped for a week."

"Well excuse the fuck out of me, Mrs. Fucking Perfect, but my son was stolen from your husband's club!" I shout back and the bitch rears back, hitting me again.

It's enough to infuriate me to the point of throwing her off my waist and jumping out of bed. "Bitch!" I yell, my hand coming to my face as I get some distance from her.

"Do I have your attention now?"

"Yes. What. The. Fuck."

"Time to pull yourself together and stop being selfish. Your man lost his shit today, and he needs you. He's doing what he can to hold it together for the both of you, but girlfriend he's fucking falling. He got a call last night about Maverick that rocked him. He went off the deep end, and your ass needs to pull him the fuck back so he can get your son!"

"What do you mean? What call? Tell me what the fuck you're talking about, Princess."

"Nice to finally have your damn attention. We need coffee and I'll explain everything to you."

Hours pass as he sleeps, and I pace the clubhouse like a caged animal. Princess was right. I needed coffee, and then I needed her to hold me while I broke again after hearing what Puppet told Night. And then I became angry. It's what's keeping me going right now waiting for Nightmare to wake up. He freaked his brothers out so badly, they fed him a mild horse tranquilizer. Thank God the man's the size of a mountain or they could've killed him.

"Ermmm," he mumbles, waking from his own fog. He's been asleep since last night.

"I should fucking punch you for letting them knock you out. Really, Nightmare, a whole bottle of Jager?"

"Huh?" His sleepy gaze meets mine, bloodshot to hell. "You're up?"

"Well one of us had to be since they put you out."

"They put me out?"

"Yes, sleeping beauty. Now wake the fuck up and find our son, it's been long enough."

"What happened to your face?"

"The new shit? Princess."

"Jesus, I don't even want to know."

"It was my wake-up call, now here is yours. Get up, get your shit together or I'll be the one stabbing you in the throat." I hold my hand out, coffee cup near the brim. He's going to need it just like I did.

"I can't believe you're out here." He sits up from one of the couches in the bar.

"In the flesh." I hand him the coffee and take a seat beside him. "We need a plan, Night. This self-destruction shit we're doing to ourselves is getting us nowhere. We'll be stronger together and our son needs us to save him. No one else will."

"All right then, what did you have in mind?"

CHAPTER 24

You put your arms around me and I'm home.
-Love Quotes

"You think your plan will work?" Prissy asks, sitting across from me in the kitchen.

I haven't eaten in days, and I'm trying to choke down some soup to get some strength back. We're failing Maverick, and he doesn't deserve this. He needs to have two parents he can count on who will go into battle for him. We have to fight for him; I'll never forgive myself if we don't.

I can only imagine how scared he must be, away from everyone and everything he knows. And I have no idea if Puppet is being nice to him or even feeding him. I have to have faith with what we know.

Puppet said that he wanted to keep Maverick until he was grown, so I have to think that he's feeding him. I need to keep telling myself that he's okay so I don't lose it again and go off the deep end.

"It has too. We don't have any options, and I refuse to let this shitbag keep my kid. I don't care if Nightmare killed his son or not. Shadow was a grown-ass man and knew what he was doing. Maverick is a three year old little boy; he has no part in any of this. I can't believe we missed his birthday. That piece of shit not only stole Mav from me, but his third birthday. The first one Nightmare was going to get to celebrate, too, and it was stolen away."

"I know it, B; I wish we could freaking gut Puppet for this. I don't normally want such evil to touch someone, but I hope this guy slowly rots for what he's done. If the brothers have any say in how Puppet goes, we can have faith that they'll make it very painful."

"I want to do it myself, Prissy. I told Nightmare that they need to catch him alive because I want to be the one to end him. He says we have to wait, though, and that as much as he wants him gone, the Fists are more than what they originally thought. Nightmare believes our revenge will take time to get."

She remains quiet, picking at her sandwich. I've never had hate for someone like I do for Puppet. I want to take his life like he so easily has taken mine.

That evening we crawl into bed; this time, together. It's the first time since Maverick has been missing. After seeing Night so messed up over everything, I know he needs me. I have to show him that he's loved and that I believe in him. Without him on his game, none of this will work the way we need it to.

"I spoke to Spider; he's going to hack into the phone company to get me the number that called before I broke my phone."

"So we'll get to call tomorrow then?"

"Yeah. Spider said he'll have it for us first thing along with a new untraceable phone."

"Good. I really hope this works."

"It will. Puppet was livid over losing his own flesh. He'll be all over this new information."

I nod, trying to stay positive. This will work. It has to. If not, I have no idea what to do.

Hybrid Collection

Night kisses my shoulder softly and I pull him to me, feathering kisses all over his face. It's like worry lines have appeared out of nowhere. My beautiful man is falling apart. I don't know if it's because he's exhausting his body or if the stress of it all is making them suddenly appear deeper. I hate seeing him like this; he's normally so strong.

My kiss lands on his lips next and he takes it up a notch, adding his skillful tongue to the mix. Within seconds his hand's under my shirt, squeezing my breasts and tweaking my nipples. It feels divine to have my mind distracted for the first time in what feels like forever. I'm mentally drained, and his touch is a blissful reprieve.

"I want you," I whisper, my nails dig into his forearm, begging for more.

"Yeah?" His husky breath trails over my shoulder as he presses more kisses to a spot I never realized could be so erotic. "I always want you, Daydream," he states as his hand pushes my yoga pants down, freeing my lower half to him to do with as he pleases.

His warm palm disappears momentarily to push his boxer briefs down and then he's pushing his length inside me from behind. His cock stretches my center, the burn a welcome feeling.

"Ah," groaning lowly as he sinks in deeper.

"You okay?"

"Mmmhmm."

One more push as he grips my hip tightly with his fingers and he's seated in me fully. It's been years since I've felt him down there, and it was never like this. It was never soft and gentle like he's showing me right now.

His lips work their way to my back, kissing and biting me sweetly, enough to cause my hips to jump eagerly.

"I missed you." It takes a lot inside for me to admit feelings I've kept locked away, hidden from the world. But my words are true; I did miss him. Everything about him, especially the way he feels when he fills me so fully.

At my admission, his teeth sink into my shoulder as he thrusts just a touch rougher.

"Keep saying shit like that dollface. I love hearing you talk."

"Even here, like this?'

"Especially like this. You mean everything to me, B. Wish you'd see that."

My throat grows tight and I swallow through the impending tears wanting to appear. Now's not the time for them, but he just said something I've wanted to hear leave his mouth for years. Growing up, I didn't think there was a man out there for me; I'm too much of a mess. Turns out I needed someone just as messy to get me and need me, to love me and keep me, like I want them to.

"I hope so, Night, 'cause I don't know if I can continue to go through life without you."

"You don't have to, I'm here," he rasps as his mouth makes a blissful assault to my neck. His thrusts grow rhythmic, playing my body in its own sweet melody he's slowly creating.

He needs me to show him love right now, but I didn't realize that I needed him to show me love too. When you're a mom you learn to put your desires on hold. But Nightmare's breaking through that, slowly filling up holes I didn't know existed. He's making me complete, and the crazy thing is, it's all happening in the opposite order.

Usually relationships begin, and you get time to build on to them, to be happy and in love before you face obstacles. For us, it's been completely different. One thing after another we've been fighting through. At first, we fought against each other. Now, we fight against them together and it's an entirely new feeling to have.

"Don't leave me again," he mutters in my ear, pushing inside deep.

"I won't." I reach back, my hand weaving into his hair, keeping his mouth to me.

"Promise me, baby."

"I promise, Night, I promise." Moaning, my legs clamp together tighter, making him feel even bigger as he glides in from behind.

"I want stars, Bethany," he orders, and I nod, concentrating on the amazing feeling, letting my orgasm build. He's so damn bossy, but I love it.

"Please." The moan leaves me on a breath, but I have no idea what I'm asking for.

He does though, as his grip on my hip tightens and his drive increases. He pumps into me over and over, pushing me over the edge. "Stars," I gasp and he growls, finding his own release as I spiral through mine as well.

"You fuckin' blow me away, B." He pulls free after a moment, moving to lie on his back.

"That's not the only thing I blow." I turn to him winking, and for the first time this week, he grins.

Day made.

NIGHTMARE

Spider hands me the new phone with the number already programmed in. I'm shaky. I want to call, but then I don't. The last conversation I had with this motherfucker made me lose my shit. I don't want B seeing me like that or my brothers for that matter.
My gaze meets hers. She looks hopeful, and it gives me some strength. Taking a deep breath, I hit dial.

"What the fuck do you want?" is said when he answers.

Obviously, this crooked dick already knows who the hell's calling. Bethany told me they'd stolen her phone before they took off. Spider tried searching for it, but they must've just used it to get my number and then turned it back off.

"You know what I want, motherfucker."

"Ain't happenin', cunt, done told ya' that."

"That was before. But you don't know what I know."

"Cute, doubt it'll help ya sort it out."

"You'd be surprised."

"Hurry up then."

"You said a son for a son, but what if I told you that you had a grandson? A grandson with your own blood running through his veins?"

"Oh, you're good. Stop trying to fuck with me."

"Swear to God, this kid was Ghost's."

"Ghost?" His voice comes out a bit unsure all of a sudden.

"Yep, and I happen to know who was pregnant with his baby when he was killed."

"If you're lying, you'll never see your son again. This, I promise you."

"It's no lie. I want my kid back, and I'll throw any motherfucker under the bus to achieve my goal."

"Noted. You expect me to give little Maverick up just for some information? If so, you're mistaken."

"What if I could arrange for you to meet this kid? He looks just like your piece-of-shit son. He's close to my son's age, so plenty of time to become a part of his life."

"A part of his life? Ha, if what you say is true, that kid should be here. He'd be treated like the club prince he is."

"Well, you'd have to go through my brother, Twist. He killed your son and is raising your grandson as his own kid. He'd drill you full of holes before he let you anywhere near him. But, I could arrange it."

"And, in return, you want your kid back?"

Hybrid Collection

"I wouldn't help you otherwise."

"Who says I need your fucking help? You couldn't keep your own kid safe."

"Listen fuck face, I didn't know he was in any sort of danger or you would've never been able to breathe the same fuckin' air as him. You want to meet your grandson, you go through me, and I get my kid back. That's the only way this works. Your grandson is so well hidden, you'd never get to him."

"Fine. But I don't give Maverick up until I get a DNA confirmation. If he's really my blood, then send me a lock of his hair, and it will match with mine. If not, your son is toast after this scheme."

At his words, I choke out, "Done." I want to retch, thinking of him harming Mav.

"Have it tomorrow. Go to the market and give it to a cashier named Sonya. I'll call you when I get the results."

"Let me talk to my son."

"Fine." He speaks to a few people, and then my heart shatters in a million pieces as the small voice comes over the line.

"Ummm…Daddy?"

"Mav!" I shout. "Shit, are you okay? We love you, Mav, we'll get you home. I promise you, son." I ramble until Puppet's demented laughter comes over the line.

"I'll be in touch." He hangs up.

Handing the phone to Bethany, I turn away from her. She has tears coating her cheeks, and it's more than I can take. I puke up my toast from earlier in the nearest trash can. My body won't stop shaking either; it's to the point where it looks like that shaking disease folks get sometimes.

Dainty arms wrap around me from behind, her face pressed into my back, just holding me. She's giving me her strength and I need every bit I can get. I couldn't let her be the one to speak to Puppet, to allow him to taunt her like that.

"It's okay, Nightmare. He bought it, and that was the first step."

"Twist will never forgive me. I'm trading one son for another," I reply, shaking my head, sick with myself.

"No, we're doing what we have to, to get our son back. They brought this on us, we never asked for this. Now we do what we have to in order to protect Maverick, even if that means giving up a club secret."

"You realize my brothers can kill me for this?" I turn, finally facing her so she can see the sorrow in my eyes. I may get Maverick back, but there's a good chance I'll be taken from both of them.

"Listen to me, if that happens, we'll run."

"No, we won't. I ran one time in my life when my father was killed. Never again."

"Then we'll face them together. They won't kill you, and, if they do, I swear, Night, I will make it my life's mission to put every one of them in the ground."

Not gonna lie, my girl's a goddamn badass. She's so sexy when she turns into this overprotective alpha female.

"I love you, Bethany. You know that, right?"

She nods. "I know, Night, and I love you, too, with every breath in my body. I love you and our son. I always have."

Pulling her to my chest, I place my lips on her forehead, pressing a kiss there and smelling her hair. It brings me comfort, enough so my shakes subside and my head clears a bit more. I have to do this; there's no other option. She's right, and if my brothers can't understand it, so be it. That's a cross I'll bear if I have to.

I'll do anything for my family, for my daydream.

CHAPTER 25

I broke my rules for you.
-Love Quotes

Surprisingly, Twist doesn't try to kill me, as I was expecting. Neither do my brothers. I had forgotten something very important about Twist, that his little girl and first wife were murdered. So he understands why I had to tell his secret. He's prepared to help. Sadie's terrified, but I think she knows Twist is way too psycho to let anything happen to her or their son, Cyle.

Everything goes down according to plan. I get a hair sample from Cyle with Twist's blessing. I drop it off at the store with Sonya like Puppet instructed and then we wait.

I don't know how Puppet pulls it off, but he has results within twenty-four hours. I shouldn't be surprised; the man has obviously been around awhile and wants to know if this boy is part of his family. I was ignorant to think the Iron Fists were stupid. You don't get a reputation like they have by being total dumbasses. It's the last time I underestimate anyone—ever.

The time comes for us to actually meet up. I'm a wreck inside. We've thought about the absolute best ways to go about everything. We've even argued with Puppet over where to meet. Eventually, we come to an agreement, and my woman is vibrating, she's so wound up. Can't say I blame her; I think we all are. Not only does this involve Mav, but there's a chance people will die today.

Bethany follows me in her car, Twist and Cyle ride behind in 2 Piece's truck, and a swarm of our brothers follow behind them. We've agreed that the brothers will stay back, along with Puppet's club. They are here to escort us to and from the meeting point and be ready to come in if it goes south and we need them.

The meeting point is at a scenic overlook on top of a mountain. There aren't many in this area of Texas, and we happen to know the State Troopers travel this route frequently if we need them. We got lucky with Ares' old Prez being in good with the Troopers. They weren't dirty-dirty, but they looked the other way a lot for our club. This is a time we may need to have some law on our side.

Yes we do some bad shit, but we also help make their job easier by cleaning up the filth around the city for them. In return, some things slide under the table, "unnoticed."

Pulling off the side of the road into the gravel, I park. Putting my kickstand down, I glance back to watch Bethany stop and then Twist pull in behind her. The brothers idle near us, waiting.

There's a decent chance this whole thing could go to shit. I hope not 'cause there's two little boys stuck right in the middle of it. I feel like a fucking failure dragging another kid in it, but shit happens. I have to grit through it and do what I have to.

A line of bikes appear from the opposite direction, a truck smack in the middle of the formation. I'm pretty sure we're all in shock. We were expecting their club to be some floaters, maybe some new recruits.

It's fucking huge; I'm talking a good twenty-five rolling up. With what we've discovered about them, too, I doubt this is barely a decent sized chunk of the club. I wouldn't be surprised if the club is a hundred deep or more after seeing them roll up like this. I fucking hate this. Why couldn't it just be a few hellions that I could easily take out. Instead it has to basically be a mob of men for me to work through to get to the middle.

Hybrid Collection

"Motherfucker," I mumble to myself. They could easily shoot us all down if they wanted to; our ten to their twenty-five, no good. I'm glad I told B to stay the fuck in her car or they could take her too.

Sonofabitch. I can't stand feeling as if I'm unprepared, and, in this, it's exactly how I feel. This jackoff has the upper hand besides our wild card being Twist's son.

The motorcycles pull off opposite us, staring us down as the truck pulls to a stop directly in front of me. I make out an older man driving, a little dark head in the middle, and another beefy guy about my size in the passenger seat. If they hurt one hair on Mav's head, you won't be able to peel me off them, I swear.

The older guy says something to the passenger, his gaze flicking over all of us. He gets out, slamming the truck door and I take in the man who's caused so much grief for me. I want to slit his throat so badly that my hands begin to shake. Toeing my kickstand in place, I throw my leg over and come to my full six foot four inches towering over him standing before me.

He doesn't show me any sign that I intimidate him in the slightest which says a lot about his balls right there. I make many men shit bricks, and this one doesn't even blink.

"My son?" I immediately demand, not about to fuck around.

"My grandson?" he counters, and I grit my back teeth together.

"So you believe me now?"

"I told you, I got the DNA results back. I still want to see his face and see if he looks like my boy."

"You bring my son over here, and I'll have Twist show you Cyle."

"I could just kill you and take them hostage you know. We have you out numbered times three."

"Yep, you could. Maybe you haven't heard 'bout Twist though? He'll kill your grandson before he lets you take him. You want any chance of knowing that kid—your blood—you follow through with our agreement."

"Ya know, I like to do whatever the fuck I want usually, but something tells me, you're not fuckin' with me."

I shake my head, glowering down at his five foot-eleven frame, thinking of ten different ways I could kill him right now with my two hands. I'd enjoy every crunch of breaking bone, too.

"Fine," Puppet huffs. "You fuck me over, and my brother," he nods across the street, and I glance, seeing a guy pointing a gun toward my woman's car, "shoots your ol' lady."

"I'm not fucking you over. If he shoots my girl, mark my words, I will slit every motherfucker's throat wearing the Fist's cut."

He grins, showing me a mouth of chipped teeth. He's definitely a hard fucker and has seen a lot. I wouldn't want to be in a club run by him; that, I'm certain of.

Puppet lets out a sharp whistle then meets my gaze as the passenger gets out. I'm able to breathe when I see the big guy grin at Mav and hold his arms out to him. Maverick jumps in his arms and smiles. This tells me that whoever this big fucker is, no matter how much I want to filet him, he was good to my kid.

"Daddy?" Maverick yells and starts waving.

"Hey buddy," I say and hear the car door behind me slam. Bethany comes running to my side.

"Maverick!" she yells, choked up at finally seeing him.

"Mommy!" Our son smiles widely and keeps waving.

The guy carrying him, comes near. I see his name patch says *Viper*.

"My grandson." Puppet holds his hand out, so Viper stalls.

Hybrid Collection

Twisting my head toward Twist, I give him the signal, and he gets out of the truck, Cyle walking beside him like a little badass. With Twist as a father, that kid will no doubt grow up fearless.

Twist stops beside me and flicks his gaze to Puppet. "You fuck with my kid, I slit your fuckin' throat. Got me, pops?"

Puppet flicks his tongue against his teeth and drops his hand. Viper gives Mav a high five and sets him down. Once his feet touch the gravel he's running for Bethany.

"Mommy!" he shouts happily, and my throat grows tight when I see him back in her arms where he belongs. She scoops him up and takes him to her car quickly, not skipping a beat. This is what we planned, and she's followed along perfectly so far.

Puppet asks a few questions, staring at Cyle in a near trance. I tune them out, though. My son is safe. I kept my promise I made to Bethany, and we got our boy back.

"One day, he'll join his family," Puppet states, and Twist rolls his eyes.

"Yeah, okay, old man. He may be your blood, but he's my kid. He carries my name, and I'll continue to raise him. Your blood is part Oath Keeper whether you like it or not. He's a club brat, an Oath Keeper brat."

Puppet hisses, but bites his tongue.

"Where's your President?" he asks me next, still gazing at Cyle.

I turn and gesture to Viking. He rides over, parking next to me.

"Brother." He nods to me.

"Brother," I reply, then gesture to the piece of shit in front of me. "This is Puppet, President of the Iron Fists."

Viking nods, glaring down at the shorter man. "Can I help you?"

"Before I'd have replied, yes, by killing yourself. But I see circumstances have changed."

"You've got guts speaking to me like that, Fist. I'm sure you know who the fuck I am," Viking growls and Puppet smirks.

"I've heard. That being said, I see my grandson is being raised and protected by the Oath Keepers."

Viking nods again.

"Instead of exterminating you, this is grounds for peace from my club."

"We will take the peace, but that does not mean you are welcome in our territory."

"Fine, same goes for your club."

Viking nods again, being his normal solemn self. I wonder what he's really thinking right now. I know we'll take the peace, but once everyone's safe and we're back on our feet, we'll be hunting again. I will kill this motherfucker if it's the last thing I do.

"Twist, you take good care of my grandson. And you ever find yourself in a bind and it has to do with my grandson, you have my help. Otherwise, you better pray you don't die, 'cause if you do, I'm coming for him."

"You fucking wish. I'm going to outlive every fucking cunt here," Twist grits out and spits. He needs to just nod and keep quiet; I'm trying to get us the fuck out of here without any bullets flying.

Viking holds his hand out, and Puppet shakes it. I think both sides let a breath out when they see it. "I'll be in touch," Puppet states, then gestures to Viper, both of them heading back to the truck.

"You okay, brother?" Viking asks out the side of his mouth, keeping his stare trained on the two retreating forms.

"I will be once we're back at the club, and I have them both in my arms."

Hybrid Collection

"You and B take off; we'll follow to make sure you're safe. You, too, Twist; your brothers are at our clubhouse waiting for you."

"Bet," he replies and I crank my engine, waving for Bethany to pull out. I cannot fucking wait to get home with my family.

CHAPTER 26

You know you're in love when you can't fall asleep because reality is finally better than your dreams.
-Dr. Seuss

I watch my daydream as she giggles with Princess and London. It's been a month since she and I got Maverick back home safely. None of us were expecting to reach peace that day. I believed that we would've ended up in a bloodbath, and I'd have been lucky if B and Mav made it out alive. I'd do anything for them—even pretend to be at peace with a rival club.

Thankfully, the bloodbath didn't happen. I don't know who was watching over us during the exchange, if *He* finally heard my plea when I'd hit rock bottom, but something saved us all. It hasn't made me religious in any stretch, but it's made me thankful. I've put things that actually matter in perspective, like my love for Bethany and Maverick along with their happiness.

Her laugh is loud, her smile big, and it makes me feel warm in my chest as the three of them gossip about something. Bethany's grown more beautiful to me the better I've gotten to know her. I haven't touched her like that night we made love though. It was the same night we came up with our plan, and I have to make sure she's one hundred percent ready to go there with me. I have to know she's in love with me as much as I am with her. I would give it all up for her, my club, my life, and my heart.

Hybrid Collection

It may be fucking with me a little bit, too, not touching her. I find myself staring at her all the damn time, to the point my brothers comment on it. She hasn't been back to work either. I barely let her out of my sight. I can't. I know a potential threat is out there, no matter what Puppet says. I won't let harm come to them again.

I need to make her mine. I know inside that she's already mine, but it has to be official. She needs to become my ol' lady in the eyes of the club so I know she has their protection as well. I'll be able to relax more knowing that if something happens to me that they'll look after her and Mav.

"I'm going to do it." I turn to Exterminator, and his eyebrow shoots up.

"No shit?"

Nodding, I repeat myself. "No shit, I'm going to do it." I don't want to wait longer, to hold myself back. I love her too much.

"Good for you, brother." He claps me on my shoulder as Chaos comes to stand next to us.

"'Sup?" he mumbles, tipping his longneck up.

"He's finally gonna do it," Ex grumbles.

"No shit?" Chaos murmurs, and I roll my eyes. These fuckers.

"Jesus, yes, I'm doin' it."

"When?" Viking asks from my left.

Meeting his gaze, there's a challenge shining in it. He doesn't think I'll buck up and actually do it. Taking a deep breath, I admit, "Tonight."

He whistles, and I huff, taking off toward Blaze for another beer. He's chilling, propped up against the counter, finally healed up enough to tend bar. He has to be careful and not move too fast, but he's here. That's what matters, too. We've lost enough brothers over the years. Thankfully, he fought through his injures and came out swinging in the end. If it wasn't for the doc and 2 Piece rushing over to get him to the hospital in time, he'd have died.

"They giving you shit?"

"Yeah, what's new though?"

"What about now?"

"I'm gonna do it." I nod toward Bethany, and Blaze's eyes widen.

"No shit?"

"Oh, for fuck's sake," I grumble throwing my hands up and head straight for her. She's standing at the other end of the bar. These fuckers are going to have me do it right now, just to prove that I'm serious. And I am; I'll do it.

Her gaze hits mine, amused. "Well, looks like someone needs a nap and possibly a spanking." She chortles and the women to her sides giggle. She's gotten ballsier as the days pass, too, and, if I'm honest with myself, I love every damn minute of it.

I've been known to be a bit grouchy around here, and she has me grinning or chuckling like a fool at times. I haven't forgotten what she's done as far as keeping my son from me for all that time, but I've learned to move past it. I'll never forget her actions, but I've forgiven her.

Life is too short and way too precious to fight over shit that's taken up the past. I have a chance to make her and Maverick my future, and I have every intention to do so.

"Aw, baby, someone take your popsicle?" She giggles next, her eyes joyful, knowing she's going to stir me up. Usually I'll just throw her over my shoulder and make her scream when she's in front of her friends like this, but she's in for a surprise today.

"That mouth, Bethany. I swear it'll have my cock in it."

"Oh, he's going to play today." She grins and winks at Princess and I growl. It's a good growl, though. She's making it hard for me to stay serious right now, but I have to.

This won't be real if I don't mean it.

Stepping in front of her, I tower over her as if she's my prey. B's mouth snaps shut when she figures out I'm not going to crack. My fingers go to her face, holding her chin tightly until she can't move away. I can see the heat in them. She can goof off all she wants to, but I know what she wants.

At my touch, she gasps, drawing in a silent breath and my thigh shoots between her legs, parting them for me to squeeze in close. Her back hits the bar and my cock rests against her center, her cheeks tinting at the delicious contact.

Blaze watches from behind the bar wearing a smirk, and I give him a nod. Reaching over, he grips each of her biceps in his palms, securing her in place. She's going nowhere with the hold he has.

Her chest moves quicker as her breaths pick up. My Daydream's getting nervous, thinking that mouth has finally gotten her in the trouble I keep promising. It has, and I couldn't be more excited over it.

I've waited too long for her. She's mine now, and Bethany's about to learn that firsthand right in the middle of the clubhouse bar.

"No more fucking around, you belong to me, Daydream," I promise, my mouth trailing over her neck, teeth grazing her smooth skin until goose bumps appear.

There's no question, no option given, it is what it is, and I'm declaring that shit, no argument permitted. She gets hot when I speak to her like this, and I have to admit it's no problem for me. She wants me to boss her ass and take control in times like these and it's my pleasure.

I slide her hair off to one side, clearing my path and bite into her flesh. I know she loves it. I remember everything she's enjoyed when we've been together. Later I'll have her ride me and I'll pull her hair back while I suck all over her neck, marking her. Everyone will know she's been claimed. They all know she's mine, but she's about to know it and really feel it.

"I do?" she mumbles and I breathe her in. She smells divine like sweet flowers, her usual scent. Everywhere I go, flowers will forever remind me of her, of this moment.

I push the thin material of her slutty red dress up that I know she wore specifically to tease me with. My fingers find her slit, finding her already excited. Bethany's teeth sink into her bottom lip and she's never looked sexier to me. Innocent but oh-so-completely bad. She's just the right mix of crazy to keep me and lock me down as hers forever.

"So fucking wet, too." I slide my digits up and down, readying her for me. "You want me to fuck you right here, right now. Admit it, dollface, you like being fucked where everyone can see us, don't you?" My woman loves filthy talk, gets her even more worked up. My fingers find her clit, rubbing circles, playing with the sensitive bud as she fights to keep quiet and not draw more attention to us.

A moan escapes her as two of my fingers push into her warmth. "Yes," she admits nodding, and I drive them in deeper, rewarding her. Moving them fast, her mouth parts making her pant as I add a third. They pump in and out, stretching her tightness, readying her for my length.

I hurt her our first time when she made me fuck her roughly outside the bar. I wanna be able to fuck her like that again. This time, however, I want her to enjoy every second with no pain from my size.

"No panties either, you bad, bad girl. You must've known I was gonna fuck this pussy tonight," I growl, using my free hand to unbutton my jeans and lower my zipper. This is happening right here, right now, in front of everyone.

Pulling my cock free, I pump the long length a few times, not being able to stop myself. I'm too wound up for her, so damn hard that my dick aches. I want to ram my cock in her and break her in half. Precum tops the head as I imagine bending her over and sinking into her savagely.

Hybrid Collection

The brothers begin wolf-whistling and a few cheer as they see what's going down, finally realizing that I'm one hundred percent serious about claiming her as my property.

"Shit," I hear Viking say from behind me. "Maybe we should make this a club tradition. You want to claim your bitch, you do it in front of all the brothers."

Not surprisingly they hoot and holler, agreeing. Next he's muttering about needing to lick and fuck Princess. I tune them all out as I concentrate on the striking woman in front of me. She's more than ready and more than I could have ever imagined.

Her pussy trembles around my fingers, growing wetter by the moment so I pull them free. "I want your cunt sucking on my cock like that," I groan and line myself up to her entrance. Pushing inside her wet heat, I reach around and press my soaked fingers into her ass at the same time, making her scream out in ecstasy. She never was able to be a quiet one. I guess everyone will know that now as well.

"Mmm," I growl against her throat. "So goddamn tight. This pussy's all mine, you hear? I catch any motherfucker sniffin' around what's mine, and I'll slit their motherfuckin' throat. You understand me, baby?"

"Oh my God," she moans loudly. "Yes, God yes!" she responds, pressing her chest out to brush against my own as I pound into her. Her back is going to be sore as fuck tomorrow, but this will be something that she never forgets; I'll make sure of it. Every time she glances at this bar top, she'll think of me and this moment.

Glancing around briefly, I state loudly, "Mine, you hear? This bitch is all *mine*. My property."

Her pussy drips around my cock, her juices running down my nut sack witnessing me practically beat on my damn chest like a caveman. It's one of the sexiest things coming from a woman that you adore, knowing you have her that turned on. And the fact that it's because I'm claiming her, makes me fall for her even more. I didn't think it's possible, but she easily consumes every single inch of my heart. She loves me with everything, and I love her even more. What else could I ever ask for from my mate?

Her legs clamp around my waist as I drive into her, my fingers matching the rhythm, pressing into her ass again and again. I've had that ass before, and I plan to be there plenty more times, probably starting later tonight. I'm going to sample it all, those plump tits, that ass, and this pussy all over again. I'm going to make her body feel like it's floating on a motherfuckin' cloud, worship her like I would've these past years we've missed.

Minutes pass us, my mind and body lost in complete bliss. "I'm going to fill you up with my cum, then I'm going to eat this pussy until your legs shake," I threaten, yanking her to me with force as my cock explodes inside her with my release. I'm no longer able to hold back, my control completely demolished. She feels too good; I'm too enraptured by her to suppress myself.

After every last drop is free from my now overly-satisfied cock, I lift her off me, her ass landing on the edge of the bar top. My cum dribbles out of her slit making me groan with pure lust. Bethany's like no other woman before. She sets the standard to an entirely new level. I want to lick her from head to toe, nip her skin from top to bottom, and love her like the queen she truly is.

"Give me stars, baby."

She leans back against Blaze's chest as I dive between her thighs, lapping every drop up. I lick and nibble and bite on her until her orgasms peaks and she breaks, coming in front of myself and my brothers with a loud moan.

She sounds beautiful. Knowing I've done that to her, made her feel completely lost and enraptured has me standing a foot taller it seems.

Bringing my forehead to hers, she whispers the sweetest words. "You give me stars, Nightmare. You give me good dreams and you give me love. You can have me. I'm yours, forever."

"Christ, woman."

"I love you, Night."

"I love you, Day," I mutter against her mouth, kissing her passionately with her delicious taste coating my tongue.

Hybrid Collection

It's true, I love her with everything I am, and she's truly the light to my dark, the day to my night, the dreams I've always wanted but have never had.

CHAPTER 27

She knew she loved him when 'home' went from being a place to being a person.
-E. Leventhal

BETHANY

"I know it's been a few months now and things have been quiet, but do you think we'll ever get to kill Puppet for what he did to Maverick?" I stare at Nightmare, curious.

Since making me his ol' lady last month, he's been pretty open with me when I ask him things about the club. Sure, some things he keeps to himself, but it's usually just the business stuff. I don't need to or want to know about any of that anyhow.

"Trust me, B; I will always have a target on that motherfucker's head. Twist is keeping him alive right now because of Cyle. He doesn't want to have any retaliation harm his family, which I get. But mark my words, dollface, if we ever have the chance, that fucker will be dead before he can blink."

I smile. It's a bit twisted I know, but I have a rage festering so crazy inside to kill the man who stole my son from me, it's insane. I'm not a hateful person, I've always been more peaceful, and the can't-everyone-get-along type.

Hybrid Collection

Something inside you changes when you're a mother and your flesh and blood gets stolen from you. I was beaten and Maverick was forcibly removed from my hands. I'll never forget that experience or the terror he had in his brown irises as they carried him away from me.

Nightmare rarely lets us out of his sight unless he has to go away on business. I know he'll do everything in his power to always keep us safe. He got me a new switchblade, too, and I always carry that sucker everywhere I go. He's taught me how to shoot a gun, and, with practice, I'm getting better.

It all sounds so violent and scary, but it's not. He's teaching me how to protect and defend my family; for that I will forever be grateful to him. I hope I never have to use any of the skills he's taught me, unless the day comes where I can teach Puppet a lesson.

"I hate knowing he's out there," I admit, and his eyes grow distant. He feels the same way. I can sense that in him—the feeling of unfinished business.

"I have a suspicion we'll be seeing more of the Iron Fists in the future. They're like roaches, coming up through the cracks. Besides, Spider won't stop looking for any information we can get on them. We ever lock down a confirmed location and have a way, we will kill them. This, I promise you, dollface."

Shuddering, I wrap my arms around his waist and lean my head against his chest. "I love you, Night. I don't think I ever said the words when we got Maverick, but thank you for getting our son back."

"Daydream, I'll fight until my last breath to keep you both safe—always

"I know. We're lucky to have you."

"Nah, baby, it's me who's the lucky one. I love you, too, Bethany."

"So, what's the plan now?"

"Well, the floors have been replaced. I even repainted the living room and hall at the house, so you guys can finally come home. I can't believe it's taken so long. I just had to make sure it was safe first."

"I know. So we'll be okay then?"

"Yeah, I also had Spider hook up some security features. We have some cameras and an automatic door lock. It locks as soon as the door closes on its own and you can only enter by using your thumbprint, so no jimmying the lock or getting a spare key to break in. I put the chain on the inside too, so no explorer Mav getting out."

"Wow, that sounds high tech."

"It is, but I have to know you're protected when I'm not at home."

"And here I thought you liked keeping us at the clubhouse."

"I do, but too much shit goes on around here, I don't want Maverick seeing it. Plus, I'm afraid one day Honey will piss you off enough that she'll go to sleep and never wake up again. I did get you that new switchblade, and I know a few brothers whose dicks would be sad if that happened."

"As long as none of those dicks belong to you, then I'll let her keep breathing." I wink and he chuckles.

"You're such a badass, babe." He grins and places a tender kiss to my forehead.

"Only for you guys. I'm just protecting what's mine," I mumble into his shirt and he squeezes me to him more.

"Exactly, I'm yours." He kisses me again, and I feel his breath in my hair. He's always smelling it and sighing. I've kept the same shampoo just for that reason. "Now, we ready for this late birthday party? There's a three year old who deserves to get spoiled by his family."

"Definitely, I can't wait to see him surprised."

"As long as he likes a motorcycle cake, then we're good."

"He will absolutely love it; he's just like his dad." I smile and kiss his cheek.

Hybrid Collection

If I could go back in time, would I do things different? I'd like to say no, but that'd be a lie. Nightmare deserved to be a father from the very beginning, and I took that away from him.

I plan to spend the rest of my life showing him just how much I love him and give him the chance to be a father. Who knows, maybe down the road we'll have another. Right now, though, I'm being selfish and only sharing him with Maverick.

Time's so easily lost; we need to learn to spend it with the ones we love, doing the things we love. In the end, the small things will be the big things. I'm just grateful to have learned that now before it was too late and more time was wasted.

I'll never get those years back, but I'll love Nightmare every single day for the rest of my life. He is, after all, the one who made me see stars.

EPILOGUE

*There are two gifts we should give our children;
one is roots, and the other is wings.
- Unknown*

MAVERICK

13 years later...

"Umm...what do you mean I can't have a motorcycle? I'm sixteen, Mom, and it's my birthday."
"Not happening, Mav. You have to wait until you're eighteen, you know this. We've already talked about it." She shakes her head and my dad's gaze hits his boots. He's in a huge pile of shit with her and he knows it. She doesn't though, not yet.

"Uh, Daydream?" he mutters, clearing his throat. It's pretty entertaining, we both dwarf my mom, but she's the boss in the end. She can bring a grown man to his knees. My dad with a simple kiss, anyone else and her switchblade will do the trick. "I, uh, sorta got the kid a bike." He coughs and I snort. He gives me so much shit when I choke up fessing something to my mom.

"You didn't."

"I did." He sighs and I grin at mom.

Hybrid Collection

Interrupting, I pull my leather jacket on. "Yeah, so you two sort this out. I'm taking off."

"And where in the hell do you think you're going exactly?" Her attention snaps to me, pinning me down with steel in her gaze.

My Aunt Princess has the same look when she's serious, too. Thankfully, she thinks I can do no wrong, so it's never turned on me. Mom. though, she'll shoot it at me every time I'm two minutes late coming in the door.

"I need to pick up Jessie."

"Jessie, as in Jessica? Cain and London's daughter?" Her eyes widen.

"Yes, ma'am."

"Oh, Jesus Christ." She stares down my dad next, "I'm so blaming you for this shit." She shakes her head, exasperated and walks off.

She's too concerned with Jessie's father getting pissed that she's not even thinking of the bike anymore. I've learned how to distract her like Dad does.

He turns to me with a devilish grin. "Go get her, son." We fist bump and I'm out the door.

It's on like Donkey Kong. Hope Jessie knows she's mine, cause if not, she's about to figure it out.

I am, after all, just like my dad, and life's nothing but a daydream.

Thank you for reading Daydream! I really hope you enjoyed Nightmare and Bethany's story. Many of you sent me messages asking me for more from them. I hope this satisfied that craving and has made you excited for the next.

Sapphire Knight

Yes, there will be more; you can never have too many bikers! I'm working on Saint and Sinner next and can't wait to unleash their brand of crazy on you all.

Once again, thank you. Your support means more than you know! If you enjoyed this book, please take a moment to leave a review. It can be short and sweet, every bit helps.

XOXO- Sapphire

Hybrid Collection

Baby

an *Oath Keepers MC* novel

INTERNATIONAL BESTSELLING AUTHOR
SAPPHIRE KNIGHT

Sapphire Knight

Baby

Copyright © 2018 by Sapphire Knight

Cover Design by Simply Defined Art

Editing by Mitzi Carroll

This book is a work of fiction. The names, characters, places, and incidents are products of the writer's imagination or have been used fictitiously and are not to be construed as real. Any resemblance to persons, living or dead, actual events, locales or organizations is entirely coincidental.

All rights reserved. With the exception of quotes used in reviews, this book may not be reproduced or used in whole or in part by any means existing without written permission from the author.

The author acknowledges the trademarked status and trademark owners of various products referenced in this work of fiction, which have been used without permission. The publication/use of these trademarks is not authorized, associated with, or sponsored by the trademark owners.

Hybrid Collection

DEDICATION

To those of you who think outside of the box. To the one's who walk to their own beat. To the dreamers.

Sapphire Knight

PROLOGUE

Tears shed for another person are not a sign of weakness. They are a sign of a pure heart.
-Unknown

The ominous double oak doors are massive, leading into the magnificent church. St. Mary's it's called, and I've passed it every day for the last six months. Each time, it's taunted me, beckoning me to take a step inside its walls.

I have to do it, you know—see if I'll really burn by coming in here. If it'd happen to anyone, I'd definitely be a viable candidate.

Inhaling, I'm met with a spicy scent. Oil perhaps? The building reminds me of a castle from the outside, and the inside doesn't disappoint in that aspect either. It's the type of place that when you enter, you feel small and insignificant; no doubt it was built this way on purpose.

My middle finger dips into the glass bowl encasing what these religious freaks refer to as holy water. What the fuck's so holy about it? Is it the fact that a priest has prayed over it? If that's how it's even made...I wouldn't know. I was never around one of these places growing up.

The cool water coats the tip of my finger as I skim the surface, and amazingly, nothing happens. I was expecting burning flames to encompass my flesh in mere seconds. I'm considered evil, after all; I've heard it before. Not from any voices in my mind, but from child services attempting to steal me away from my family.

The silence encompassing the room is interrupted by a deep, accusing voice. "Sinner!"

My gaze shoots to the front of the room convinced I was right after all; they'll burn me for coming here. That's how all the holy ones are; they like to peel you apart

Hybrid Collection

and make you crumble in an attempt to heal you. I've been warned the entire time I was growing up to steer clear of them.

I never needed their healing, only blood occasionally from a bad soul. My father was the same and taught me how to make sacrifices. He said our Native American heritage called for it. Our ancestors needed it to live on through us. It's our job to continue coating the earth with the black soul's blood to give back for everything they've used up.

My father was a true, proud Indian with long, straight, jet-black hair and black eyes to match. His skin was tanned and leathery due to his heritage and exposure to the elements. His time was spent outside when he was young, and he says it forever changed him like our ancestors. I never understood why I had to favor my mother. Her cloud-colored eyes, fair complexion, and light hair made her angelic in a sense, opposite of my father.

I've kept my promises to him, sacrificing when the madness inside my head gets out of control. He'd be proud; I know it was an important ritual to him. It's become sort of a cleansing for me as well, to show my devotion to the gods of the world. People may not understand my rituals, but the gods do.

On a podium set at the front of the room stands the man I heard dressed in thick robes. Behind him is a large, imposing marble table, covered with objects. I'm too far away to recognize what they are, however.

He's the priest—the holy one—who can burn me, according to the stories my father shared when I was a kid.

A young man cowers below him, completely bare. He's hunched over his naked front, his bloody back showcased for the man standing over him. Crisscrosses of bloody welts decorate his back, and I cringe. I've been whipped before. I know it hurts. The battered being draws me to him, wanting to see for myself if he's worth the sacrifice.

"Forgive me." The young, broken man pleads and the leather whip in the holy one's hand slaps against his flesh again. Blood splatters in its wake, leaving behind evidence of the punishment. The site of the garnet-colored liquid doesn't bother me; it's the purity of the man's voice begging to be set free. He doesn't sound guilty of anything worthy of his punishment.

"Sinner!" the priest declares again, and I begin to make my way around the room to get a better look.

I stick to the shadows to keep my presence unknown. That's essentially what I am anyhow, a shadow amongst everyone else in the world. Multiple colors cascade over the glossy pews in the middle of the room, almost making them appear inviting.

Almost, but I see through their motives.

Glancing up, I'm met with stained glass windows depicting the church's beloved saints. In the center of the raised ceiling is an ancient looking painted mural filled with fluffy clouds and golden angels. I wonder if that world ever existed. If it did, according to this, it must've been forever ago.

Smack!

My eyes snap back to the podium, drawn to the sound. The priest slashed another bloody welt into the young guy's flesh. Cringing, I can't turn away. It's like a car crash—you know it must be painful, yet you have to watch regardless.

"You must ask for forgiveness, Sinner."

"For-forgive me, father. I beg you."

No father should hit his son like this. He should teach him, rather than punish him. My own father taught me this. We worked together, never against each other.

"You've sinned, you must repent," he repeats, bringing the leather down again. This time the man on all fours gasps in pain, tears raining down his face, and stuttering something about hail Mary being full of grace.

This is his father? Surely, he feels the darkness in his soul as I do. The man with the evil soul deserves punishment, not the beaten one at his feet.

Hybrid Collection

Creeping slowly and quietly, I approach the man from behind. I'm good at being quiet; it's how I always get away when someone searches for me. It's how I sneak up on those I plan to offer as a sacrifice. The moon god always helps hide me.

"Priest," I hiss, sounding more snake than human. The older man spins around, his middle-aged face lined with surprise. "Repent," I hiss at him again with a scowl and drive my small blade into the center of his throat. It's not a fancy way to kill, but it stuns the opponent immediately. Being smaller than many of the men I kill, it's important to catch them off guard.

He stumbles back a step, as his eyes bulge, gurgling and choking on the sharp metal. Blood spurts, raining warm sangria droplets over my face. A genuine smile graces my lips as my hands rub the blood into my skin. I've killed a bad man, and there's no better feeling.

Sacrifice to bring this man peace. Use this blood to replenish all that was stolen from you by this soul. Sacrifice for my ancestors no longer here. I offer this token of evil to you. Sacrifice for life.

The older man drops to the ground, dead, and the boy at my feet turns to peer up at me. His face is drenched with tears, his back leaving behind droplets of his blood on the floor around him. He's paid his own sacrifice, offering his blood so easily without a fight.

He gasps, his mouth falling open in shock at the site of me.

He's frightened.

My hand opens, palm up, going toward him. He'll need help getting up, I'm sure of it. I don't want to worry him any more than he already appears to be.

"S-S-S-Saint Michael?" he proclaims, his eyes growing more fearful, "For-forgive me, for I have sinned."

"Sinner?" I test, holding my hand to him once more. Is that his name?

"I am not worthy. Forgive me for speaking your name." His gaze falls to the floor, and he bows before me.

He's absolutely perfect.

I will keep him and protect him—always.

"Come, my Sinner. I'll protect you now. No need to be frightened of me. You just call me Saint; no name, okay?"

His callused palm finds mine, and I tug him to his feet. "You will stand for me, Sinner, and you'll be strong."

He briefly glances to the priest, his eyes full of gratitude when they meet mine. No doubt he's grateful, but guilt will plague his heart for feeling that way after the shock subsides.

He's beautiful. Dark to my light, he could be my brother—my opposite. He's everything I once wished I could be, and together we'll be perfect.

"Okay, Saint," he agrees, and I lift the thick, white robe from the floor for him. We need to leave, and I have no idea when someone will show up. The last thing I need is another run-in with the local cops.

"We have to go."

He complies and allows me to help him place the robe over his battered flesh. He's close to my own age I notice. I hit fifteen six months ago; he's gotta be right around there as well. I hope his back only needs to be wrapped. I can mix up a paste for it, but I can't sew very well if he requires stitches.

"Is there a way out of here other than the front door?"

"Yes, I can show you."

"Sounds good little Sinner, lead the way..."

And just like that, I've met my obsession. My Sinner to my Saint, yet I know the truth. I'm the Sinner, and this beautiful, broken creature is my Saint.

He's mine. *Forever.*

CHAPTER 1

*I am not a saint, unless you think of a saint
as a sinner who keeps on trying.*
- Nelson Mandela

Sinner

"Sin, you have to reel Saint in, brother. He's losing his shit today," Viking, the Oath Keepers MC Prez grumbles. Like this is something new; this is Saint in a nutshell, but they all seem to forget that. The brother can't be cooped up.

I've been riding with Viking for years now, first as a NOMAD, and now in his own club. Saint and the other brothers of the Oath Keepers are the closest thing to family I have. The club means everything to me as it does to the brothers as well. We may be a bunch of misfits alone, but together, we get each other.

Saint...well, he's so much more than just a brother to me. We seem to balance each other out a bit. I don't know if I'd have survived this far if he hadn't stepped in and helped me stand that day, so long ago.

"You need to let him out, Vike. You know how he gets when you try to put a leash on him." They believe that if they keep him at the clubhouse, he won't hurt anyone. It does the opposite though. You'd think they'd have figured it out by now that cooping him up, drives him a little crazy inside.

"I can't have him out in town hacking up some motherfucker and then bathing in his blood. Find something to keep him busy."

No one understands him. They believe Saint is nuts—a pretty boy with the drive to kill and coat himself in his victims' blood. I wish Saint would just tell them he's Indian, that he does this for a reason. I thought he was crazy the first time I saw it as well; hell, I tried to take off and leave him behind. I didn't get very far and haven't been able to leave his side since then.

I think he enjoys the fear in the brothers' eyes when his skin's stained scarlet. Not to mention, he's the whitest Indian you'd ever come across. Shit, half the brothers probably wouldn't believe him even if he did tell them about his heritage. We practically grew up together through our teenage years and so on, so I've seen it all firsthand.

"We'll barbeque this weekend." I suggest the first thing that enters my mind.

It's not ideal, but it's the quickest rationalization I can come up with. "We can head over to the pigpen and get some hogs; it'll keep him busy, if he can chop them up." I leave out the part of him offering up some of the pigs' blood as a sacrifice to his ancestors and the various gods he chooses to worship.

He absently agrees, his distracted stare locked on his ol' lady, Princess. "Appreciate it, brother. I'll catch up later; I got shit to take care of."

"Bet," I mutter, but he's already striding toward the Ice Queen also known as Princess, his ol' lady. There's no telling what he has to deal with. Being the Prez, he's always taking care of business.

Drinking deeply from my vodka-cranberry-Sprite cocktail Blaze conjured up for me, I can't help but think of how I ended up here. I'd be nothing if it weren't for Saint. He saved me and has continued to do so ever since I was a teenager. If I have to defend his brand of crazy for the rest of my life to repay him, I will.

"Sinner?" Cherry, a pretty little redheaded club slut saddles up next to me.

She's nothing special—mousy nose, a spattering of freckles...the usual. Her looks do next to nothing to garner my attention, though other brothers around here seem to appreciate her attention toward them. As long as she sucks my dick well and doesn't talk much, then I don't mind her bothering me too much.

"Hmm?"

Hybrid Collection

"Do you two want to have some fun?" She squeezes into the spot between my body and the empty barstool next to me.

She's a wild one and loves fucking both of us. Can't say I don't approve of her type of fun. Saint usually has a decent time with her as well, and she's nowhere near his type. He likes the college girls, but I prefer the older women. Give me a woman ten years older than me, and I'll enjoy every moment of their experienced asses.

Shrugging, I let loose a sigh. "You wanna fuck both of us? Who's to say I'd even let you fuck us?" I would, but she doesn't need to know she has any type of allure over either of us.

"I was-I was...umm, I do want you both," she stammers, attempting to conjure up the answer she *thinks* I want to hear.

The truth is, no one has the slightest fucking clue what I actually wanna hear fall from their lips. The ones that give in easily lose my interest the quickest. Of course, I want to boss 'em around a bit, but when they're not too scared to give me a little lip in return, that's when my dick gets the hardest. It's usually the Mexican bitches that'll give me just enough spice to make me want to have them over and over.

"Ah, but you think you can handle it? Two cocks in you at once? Didn't you cry the last time we fucked you?" I have to screw with her; hell, I screw with pretty much everyone. I've learned along the ride if you fuck with people enough, most leave you the hell alone. After living through my own version of hell, I'm determined to never go back there. I'll be the biggest psycho dick around if it ends up protecting me. Saint was the one who taught me how to protect myself.

"I enjoyed it."

Scoffing, I roll my eyes at her unimpressive answer. She wants me, yet she's doing fuck all to get my cock hard. "Right. How bad do you want this cock? More than Saint's, or do you want him more?"

"I want you both."

She's playing it safe. It's typical for chicks that've been around Saint and me before. They want bad, but they're never too sure just how bad they actually want it. They either love our brand of crazy or it scares them.

My eyebrow hikes, my eyes skirting over her tits she has nearly on full display for anyone in the club to see. "Yeah, but surely you must think one of us fucks better than the other. I bet it's me. That's why you came to me, huh? You better not let my brother hear. He may carve your sweet little ass up if he does."

"Please, Sinner. I didn't mean to come off that way. Please, don't let him get angry." The rumors obviously hold up merit as she scrambles to backtrack, in fear. She has no reason to freak out though; Sinner only kills people he thinks are evil. Cherry's just a whore; she's not a wicked being.

Chuckling, my fingers brush her chin tenderly, enjoying the sound of her begging. "Relax, Cherry; I'm sure he won't hurt you...much. Let him fuck your ass, and he'll be nice. Me, well, you better wrap those fat lips around my cock if you want my attention. Think you can handle that?"

"Yes, I promise I can."

The chicks around here practically salivate at having the chance to sample us both at the same time. I'm used to it. We've been a team since shortly after he stepped in that shitty day so long ago. I still look up at him with wonder in my eyes sometimes; I can't help it. Where everyone else notices evil, I only see a saint.

"Careful what you promise, Cherry. What do we get if you break your word? Saint will want blood; no matter how sweet you bitches around here believe he is...he's not."

It's the truth, but so many of them are too fucking dumb to see through his pretty-boy charade. That's all it is—an act. He doesn't give a shit about any of them. Hell, neither do I. We're just interested in fucking. End of story.

"But yo-you're the nice one, right?"

I shoot her a sinister smirk, swirling the liquor in my glass while her mind races. Her stammering answers full of fear are pathetic. I love knowing I have people on edge, but if they don't buck up, eventually, I get bored. It's the same shit, different day in my eyes.

Shrugging after a moment, I swallow down the rest of my beverage without replying. Am I the nice one? Compared to Saint? Sure, I can be. I'd never outright let any of them know that though.

"I'll find you later *if* we wanna fuck."

"Okay," she responds with a slight grin. The bitch has won, and she knows it. One thing about my brother and me is we like to fuck—a lot.

Saint's palm lands on my forearm, wanting to pull me in closer, but I turn away. We're in front of the compound—not the right place for us to be close. I'd rather wait until we're in one of our rooms, and he knows it. "We're headed to the farm." Changing the subject, I take swift strides to the parking lot putting some distance between us.

"Someone fuck up?" Saint questions, following me to one of the brothers' trucks. It used to be Scot's, God rest his soul, but he was killed a while back. Now we use it as a communal truck. I know it's what he would've wanted if he'd had any say in the matter.

"No, we're going to barbeque this weekend, and we need some meat." *And I need to get you preoccupied.*

He grunts. "I thought you were headed out of town this weekend?"

I'd mentioned I might have plans, but, I'm surprised he remembered that. I told him when we were piss-ass drunk, in hopes he'd forget. Then, once I left this weekend, and he called me, pissed off, I'd have the excuse of already telling him but him forgetting about it.

It's kinda fucked up, I know. I don't have a choice though. One small lie to keep him happy and it's worth the guilt I feel in return.

"Yeah, I might. Nothing set in stone though." Total bullshit, I'm out of here as soon as I can be.

Fuck man, what else does he remember? I don't normally keep shit from him, but I do have one big secret I've managed to keep buried. He would most likely flip his shit if he found out too, especially since we don't make it a habit of keeping stuff from each other. He can't know, and I'll do whatever it takes to keep it in the dark.

On a run a while back, I made a horrible drunken mistake that I've been kicking myself in the ass for ever since. Of all the stupid things to do, I got married. And the real kicker is, I never told Saint about it. I knew if I did, he'd carve her up like a Thanksgiving turkey, and I can't have that on my conscious.

She may not be the best woman, but she's also a mom—albeit a horrible one. Call me a pansy ass or whatever, but I've stuck around for her kid. I couldn't just leave her high and dry when her mom's already done that. Two months into the sham of a marriage and she popped smoke, leaving her daughter behind without a backward glance. At least that's what Jude, her daughter, believes.

I've been able to mostly keep in touch with Jude by cell, but occasionally if I can make my way over there, then I do it. I like to check on her and see how she is with my own two eyes. She's not a baby or anything; hell, she turned eighteen right around the time I met her. Doesn't mean I don't worry about if she's still breathin' or if shit's not messed up around their trailer. The fact that she's insanely gorgeous doesn't make it a hard feat to visit either.

Her mom pretty much set her ass up for failure, living out in the middle of nowhere. The girl's smart; she has a part-time job at the library, and she takes classes online. That's not the issue; it's that her mother left her to pay the rent and everything else without giving her any money for it. They live in a tiny ass town with hardly any jobs, and if she works more hours, she won't have time for her college classes. She probably would anyhow, but the library's too poor to offer her more time even if she wanted it.

Hybrid Collection

I've stuck around these months to make sure she has what she needs, and partially from guilt. So far all she's needed has mostly been money. Thankfully, not sure I could handle much more. This feeling inside me when I attempt to cut free of her swarms my chest, and in a sense, I blame Saint in a way for being my savior. I don't owe this girl shit, but I find myself attempting to be my own version of a savior for her.

The first time I showed up after her mom's disappearance, she was completely out of food. Never felt so livid inside before—not even when it comes to Saint. Maybe because I know he can hold his own; Jude, on the other hand, not so much. The worst part of all was knowing that it was my fault. Her mom had disappeared because of me.

The girl was sweet and quiet in the beginning, unnoticeable in a sense. Then she got more comfortable with me, and the teasing started, and it was like I finally noticed her. She had the most perfect set of tits and plump lips that I didn't see anything else afterward.

The first time she had the guts to flirt, it began with her calling me 'daddy.' Boy, it drove me up the fuckin' wall. I wanted to be anything but her daddy at that moment.

That shit hasn't ever turned me on before, always more of the opposite. She thought she was something else, too, grinning full of mischief. It made me want to bend her over and smack her ass to show her just who that 'daddy' was she was mocking.

Another thing, I've never been too picky when it comes to pussy. If I'd had the option to choose in the past though, it'd always be an older, more experienced woman. I love it when a woman knows exactly what she wants, and this one is the complete opposite. I've wondered if even Saint would know what to do with this one. Not that I can seek his opinion on it with the shit hole I've dug for myself.

Jude's too innocent, untouched, and enticing like no one before, and those are the exact reasons why I shouldn't have her—why I can't have her. Not to mention how Saint would react if he found out I was going out of town and omitting the truth from him for this young woman. He'd be off his rocker with anger courtesy of my lies and the fact it was for a female.

"Where you headed?" He glances my way as we drive down the dirt road, approaching the other side of the hog farm owned by the Oath Keepers MC. The farm has become a staple to the club; we've created nightmares for many motherfuckers crossing the club. You never know just how loud a grown man can scream until he's eaten alive by a hungry hog.

The original Prez bought it awhile back, but since then has split it between Ares, Viking, and Princess—Viking's ol' lady. She and Ares are damn near siblings, and with both of them tied to each chapter, it works out for all of us. Vike built our clubhouse on the same plot of land, just farther down the road. We could've walked I suppose, but we need to load the meat in the back of the truck.

"Viking has me going on a run." It's an outright lie, but as long as it keeps Saint in check, Viking should cover for me if asked.

"Want some company?" There's longing in his voice, and it has me swallowing down the truth. He wants to be needed, it helps keep him calm. And I do need him, just not for this.

"Nah, you heard what Prez said in Church the other day. It's essential to keep the clubs full right now after all the shit that's gone down with Nightmare's kid getting stolen. He may be home now, but we still have to make sure there are enough brothers at the clubhouse just in case any motherfuckers show up."

"I'm not a babysitter. I didn't give up being a NOMAD to sit home all day and play with my cock. Either you find something for me to do, or I'll go on my own ride."

"I did. You're taking care of the hog now and then chopping him up for the barbeque."

"That's bullshit. I should be handlin' shit with you. Since when do you go on runs alone anyhow? I'll tell you since we turned in our NOMAD patches, that's when. I don't like it. I should be around to watch your back."

Hybrid Collection

"You are, and if I thought this was going to be dangerous, then you'd be riding with me."

"Right." He rolls his eyes like a petulant child, his stare trained out the passenger window watching the trees and brush as we pass.

I don't like that he's upset or that I have to keep lying to him. It's only for a little while longer, once I get everything squared away with ol' girl then it'll all be in my rearview, and Saint will be back to being my top priority.

"Ruger's been gone awhile," I bring up, attempting to change the subject, but he just shrugs, not in the mood to talk about the guys.

I try again. "Cherry came around lookin' earlier. Wants to fuck."

"Yeah?" he murmurs, not impressed.

"Said she was feeling lonely, wants us both to fuck her." I try on a grin for size, hoping it'll lighten him up. It does nothing.

"Another loose pussy." His irises flick over, skimming briefly before turning back to the window. "We ought to head back down to Mexico and try out some more Latina pussy."

"So, no to Cherry, then?"

"I mean, if she wants to fuck, and you'll be there, then I guess I will be too." His gaze sparkles as he meets mine and a little bit of his annoyance has faded. His signature charmer grin pops up, and it's hard not to smile back. He's full of mischief, one thing that's always drawn me to him.

"Stop," I weakly protest, putting the truck in park.

His hand grabs me before I can bail out. "Just sayin' we could fuck now and forget Cherry."

Releasing a groan, I nod, giving in. "You win, Saint. We fuck now, and then we have a hog to kill. Come on."

CHAPTER 2

Viridity
(N.) Naïve Innocence

Jude

Reaching forward, I stack another book in the correct place and breathe a sigh of relief. My days don't suck quite as much when I'm scheduled to work; it's when I'm home that I get to thinking. I try to watch TV sometimes to keep my mind occupied, but I just don't care for it much. My online courses tend to keep me busy a lot of the time, but it all boils down to being home alone.
My mother was never around much, but she was occasionally, and she always had her friends with her or her flavor of the week. I never looked forward to them though—most were total creeps. Well, except the latest. I learned not to expect much out of her, and in return, she was the same way with me. Not the perfect mother-daughter relationship, but it was ours.

The craziest part of this last guy that my mom brought home is his name is Sinner. I refuse to call him that though. The first time he told me what to do, a snarky comeback popped to the front of my mind, and it started the nickname Daddy. It drives him crazy—I know it does—but that's part of the fun of it.

And Lord help me, the man is sinful looking. His voice is a lazy rasp, his words drawn out like a true Southerner. I love listening to him speak or just watching him breathe. That sounds totally creepy, but it's true. He's gorgeous just living, not doing anything. Some mornings I'll even catch a peek of him putting his shirt on straight from the shower; my imagination loves to run wild with that.

Most of the men before him, I flat out ignored or tried to have minimal amount of interaction with as possible. Their attention wasn't the good kind, and I didn't want any of them to think they could cross the not-so-subtle line I'd drawn between us. I was lucky in that department, and they stayed away.

Hybrid Collection

There were lewd comments here and there as to be expected, but that was the extent of it. However, there were plenty of nights I didn't sleep—worried I'd have unwanted company. Thankfully, none ever crossed the threshold, or I'm sure I'd be a totally different person than I am today, and not in the good sense.

Besides all of that and the fact my mother was always messed up on something, I miss just knowing someone else is in the house. Sharing a pizza or hearing the radio play from her side of the trailer always gave me just enough comfort to not need much more from her. It gets quiet, and when it gets too quiet, I go a little crazy inside. Pretty ironic considering I do online classes and work in a library. You'd think I'd be the type that wouldn't want any interaction with other people, but that's not the case.

I speak to a few of the older ladies that stop by regularly to either check out books or to donate them and also to Carissa down at the corner Stop N Shop. The only other real human contact I have is when Sinner stops by to check in on me. I don't know why he took it upon himself to do it, but I'd be a bit more lost if he hadn't. His visits give me something to look forward to—if only there were more of them.

My mother's always come and gone as she's pleased, especially once I got older and could pretty much look after myself. The kicker was, I wasn't expecting her to decide to not come back home. Ever. She's been gone for months...part of me wonders if she's dead in a ditch somewhere having gone off with another bad man. I wouldn't know the first place to go searching for her either if I did want to attempt to hunt her down.

I honestly can't say it would surprise me if she was dead. Would I be sad? Who knows; I barely saw her before. I like to imagine I would be, but I'm also a realist. It sounds horrible, someone not mourning their mother, but she never much deserved that title.

"All set, Mrs. Muncey?" I enquire kindly and smile up at the seventy-year-old senior who has an addiction to smut books.

I enjoy when she stops by the library. I could talk about books all day—not to mention her outfits. She shows up wearing the most random things. Sometimes she looks as if she stepped straight out of an old-fashioned movie, all dressed up for tea time. There have been other days where she'll show up looking like a nineteen-fifties housewife, with a freshly baked pie and all.

"This'll do, Jude. Any update on that new release I was asking about? What was that name I told you to check for again?"

"No ma'am, no news. I put in an order request, but Mrs. Turpin likes most of our books to be donated since the budget's so small. I wrote it down though. I can look it up if you'd like."

She pats my hand. "No need, dear, I know you do your best. Maybe one day I'll stop over to make a donation so you can do a big order." She winks.

"That'd be great; the library would appreciate any kind of support," I reply with the same thing I say to her each week.

We have this conversation at least once, sometimes twice a week, and it's always the same. It reminds me of that movie *Groundhog Day*. I don't know if she does actually have some money stuffed away somewhere that she could donate, but I just take it for what it usually is—an empty promise. She's a nice old lady though, so I really don't mind repeating myself.

"You have a good afternoon, my dear, and keep your nose out of trouble." She squints and wags her finger in my direction making me smile.

"Yes ma'am, enjoy your book."

"Oh, I intend to." With a smirk, she takes her leave.

I can't help but laugh a little. I bet she was a spitfire when she was younger if her book choices have anything to say about her. I've read them all, and she has a taste for suspense and lots of sexiness. Not that I can blame her, I love those types of books as well. They give me wild dreams if I read them at night.

My so called "crazy" afternoon consists of a new yogurt flavor that I have a feeling could be life changing or traumatizing. I'm nervous and excited all at the same time to try it. Unlike me, Carissa's boss actually lets her order new products to try out at

Hybrid Collection

the store. As soon as I walked in yesterday, she was beaming, telling me about a new whipped Boston cream pie flavor they just got in.

Yes, the town really is that small. It's a blessing and a curse. I can walk to pretty much everywhere, which is convenient. The downfall is that there's a whole lot of nothing here. When I say nothing, I mean we don't even have sidewalks, and the only stoplight is on the main road to slow traffic down a bit. Our town's so little we don't have a Dairy Queen, and those places are all over Texas from what I've been told.

We have a diner though that specializes in fifty-cent burnt coffee, soggy grilled cheeses and the best apple pie I've ever had. But again, no sidewalk; they have a gravel parking lot. There's the Stop N Shop that doubles as a grocery store and a gas station. They have a deli in there to get a fresh sandwich, but it's a waste of money.

We have our library that's a single large room with bookshelves lining the perimeter, a desk in the center, and a smaller table to hold our one community computer. The selection is so poor as far as libraries are concerned; I'm surprised it's still in business. Mrs. Turpin put in a tiny bathroom last year, thankfully. Before that, I'd have to lock up and run to the store every time I needed to use the restroom.

The town has a hole-in-the-wall bar that's painted a hideous yellow color on the outside, so you don't miss it. I've only seen the inside once, and I wasn't impressed. Everyone younger than eighteen is bussed to the next town over for school. There's a thrift shop, and the neighbors have yard sales from time to time, so that's how most of us get a different clothing selection.

I think the only reason any of us is even employed is from the people passing through. We're in a part of Texas that doesn't have a major highway, so we get a lot of people traveling to get to the highway from small surrounding towns. Half the time they aren't even trying to be on this road, and they're lost. It keeps us locals entertained.

I don't know why anyone would want to live here and have a family, but I've never known any different. As far as I'm concerned, I've lived here in the trailer—a few blocks back—my entire life. It's been a boring life at that, and I suppose most would be grateful. I'm not; it's left me with nothing to do but age well beyond my young years.

If it wasn't for my birth certificate saying Dallas on it, I'd almost assume my mother had an at-home birth, and it was a miracle I didn't die. That didn't happen though. As far as that piece of paper states, I was born in a huge hospital in the city of Dallas. I even have a picture of my mom holding me in the delivery room as further proof.

When I was little, I'd dream that my nonexistent father was there waiting for me to return. I wish that were the case. I highly doubt my mother has a clue who the lucky man was, to begin with. And it's not like there have been any men popping up over the years claiming to be my father, so who knows.

If it wasn't for the computer and school, there'd be an entire world out there that I didn't know existed. My old high school teacher said it's borderline neglect keeping kids cooped up in these insignificant, good-for-nothing towns. I'm taking her advice and working on college courses to get out of here someday. She showed me how to get financial aid, and it's been a game changer for my future. I work my butt off to get good grades, so they never question whether I'm worth funding.

The change of scenery couldn't come soon enough, either. I want to travel the world and discover everything I've missed. Someday I'll leave this place and never return, just like my mother has.

I haven't left here yet, but I promise myself I will no matter how long it takes me. I don't have a car, but I save every extra penny I can. I'm hoping after I finish this degree that I'll find a job online to help with the costs of everything else. I'll literally move anywhere and give it a shot—just get me out of here. I figure if it comes down to it, I can get a college loan or something to get a cheap car and finally escape if I have to.

My stomach rumbles, and I'm drawn back to my lunch. I'm the only one in the library, so may as well pop open this little plastic container of mystery. Peeling the lid back, I take a sniff.

Hybrid Collection

It doesn't smell bad, so I grab my spoon and dip into the thick, whipped yogurt. *Please be delicious*, I silently chant on repeat. I really don't want to have to chuck it in the trash and be left hungry for the next few hours.

The coolness mixed with the creamy texture hits my tongue, and bam! The delightful sweet flavor of cream and a hint of chocolate hit me like a warm gust of wind. It's freaking amazing. Carissa is a genius. I can easily see why she's in charge of the ordering. Pair this with Muddy Buddy's peanut butter chocolate Chex snacks, and the two are basically life changing. I don't know how she finds this stuff, but I hope she continues.

The bell above the door jingles, and my sweet vacation with bliss is cut short by Herald coming to exchange the latest book he's borrowed. What I wouldn't give to have that crazy life Mrs. Muncey had mentioned as she left. Herald's not much entertainment for me around here.

"Hey, Herald."

He's in his usual khaki slacks, suspenders, and a short-sleeved flannel printed shirt. He tops the look off with a New York Yankees ball cap, and he's always dressed the same, alternating the colors of his shirts. "Hi, Jude. Good day so far?" he asks, pushing his wire-rimmed specs up higher on his nose.

"I can't complain much; the sun's shining outside."

"That it is," he agrees, hurrying over to his favorite bookcase.

The strong wooden case is painted a crisp white and consists of five shelves full of mysteries. He's read them all, probably a few times. He starts at the very top and reads book by book, stopping in every few days to exchange them for others he's already read.

I wonder what he'd do if one day he came in, and a new book was in the next book's place? I wish Mrs. Turpin wasn't such a tightwad. I'd be ordering new stuff to read left and right. This town would finally have a spark in their imagination if we got some new paperbacks around for them to devour.

"I scrolled through the order and wanted to let you know, they're all in the right place, Jude."

"Oh, thanks, Herald." Smiling pleasantly, I mark the notebook with his returns and the others he's checking out. Not that it really matters; he always returns them, nearly to the very hour each trip.

We had to adjust a few numbers because Herald freaked out awhile back saying they were in the wrong order. It doesn't matter much to us if a few are off, but we changed them, and it made him happy. Since then, he comes in each week and tells me if they're in the right order. I already know they are though since we never get anything new.

"Any plans today?" I question, changing up our usual exchange as I imagine being able to travel to some far-off place. I wonder if he's ever lived anywhere else or has an exciting story to share.

"Plans?" He stops his glancing around, his confused gaze locked on me.

"Yeah, anything fun to do later?"

"Nope, just getting an apple and then heading back home. I can't leave Felix home alone for long, you know."

"Oh, right. Well enjoy your new book and tell Felix hello."

"Thanks, Jude." He takes his recent selection, leaving me in silence again.

I don't want to end up like Herald, mid-forties and acts like he's sixty. Felix is his cat, and the furry ball of fluff probably wouldn't notice if he was gone twenty minutes or two hours. Maybe if he missed a meal, 'cause Lord knows that cat is fat. In a sense, I guess I already am like him. I do the exact same thing, every day, just like all these people I greet coming in here.

Maybe I should change it up and attempt going to the bar again now that I'm older. I did once when I was fifteen and was kicked out. I doubt they'd care much now that I'm considered an adult, although I don't want trouble and I'm sure that's what I'd find there. That or a bunch of old men with drinking problems and that's not my idea of a good time.

My cell phone beeps. It's the one that mom's soon-to-be- ex-husband, Sinner, left behind for me, signaling a new text message. His is the only number I have in here besides the Stop N Shop and the library. I had very few friends when I was in school, and I stopped talking to them once we graduated, so I don't have to worry about hearing from any of them. The girls got married right away, and most of the guys are busy helping their families with their farms. Those two options pretty much sum up the after-graduation life around here…so exciting.

Sinner: I'm stopping through. Do you have food at your place?

It's the same message he sends before each of his visits, and every time I do a silent happy squeal inside. The first time he came back, and Mom was gone, I didn't have any food in the house. I didn't have any money to buy it since my wonderful mother had stolen it. and he went a little ballistic when I told him exactly that. Since then, he's made it his mission to make sure I'm fed whenever he's around.

Me: I have yogurt and popcorn.

It's pretty much the best thing to snack on while doing homework. If I get really hungry, I can always buy a loaf of bread and some peanut butter or something. It's not the greatest of options, but it does the trick, and I'm able to save money. Any penny helps.

Sinner: I'm ordering you a pizza right now. You need more food than that. You home?

Me: No, I'm at work still.

Sinner: When are you off?

Me: 4:30

Sinner: I'm sending it at 4:45 then. You should get it after you're home and it'll be paid for. Don't tip them either, I will.

Me: Thank you.

I receive no reply, but that's normal. I've also learned not to argue with him over buying food or try to tell him I'll pay for it. That gets me absolutely nowhere except having to deal with a pissed-off biker. And angry motorcycle dudes are pretty scary when they want to be.

And hot! He's *so* freaking hot with irises the same shade as graphite, and hair as dark as iron. Not to mention way too old for me, but for some reason, that fact doesn't even register whenever he's near. All I can think of when I look at him is that his jawline is so sharp, covered in his dusky five o'clock shadow and how I want to lick it.

I've never licked a man before, but I want to lick him. Pretty much anywhere he'd let me. He won't though. I've tried throwing myself at him like in the books I've read, and it gets me nowhere. It's pretty embarrassing, too because you'd think a bad-boy biker would want to have sexy time as much as they can. I know I'd like to have it at least one time in my life.

At first, it was subtle hints I'd send his way, but that wasn't working. So, I went full-on hussy, and in return, he acted like I was a total weirdo. That sort of thing's not good for a woman's ego, especially one who's never had sex before. You'd think that would entice him even more, but he doesn't know. We've never gotten far enough for me to bring it up.

Yes, I get that it's a bit strange since he's technically married to my mom, but we both know she couldn't care less about him or me. In return, why should he care? At this rate, I'll die a virgin, and that can't happen. I refuse to be some shriveled up timeworn woman living in the middle of nowhere and not at least attempt to get the one hot guy who comes through to let me lick him.

I thought guys liked that sort of thing? Who knows, but apparently my books are wrong. The men my mom has brought home wanted to be all over her all the time, so I thought I was onto something, but I guess not. Lord knows none of it even fazes Sinner.

Hybrid Collection

Hopefully, it's not too awkward when Sinner comes for his visit this trip, given my poor flirting skills. Maybe I'm not _being_ patient enough, and persistence is the key? Regardless, I don't plan to give up on getting what I want any time soon.

It's pretty sad how excited I am about the fact he's sending pizza. However, it's the only time I ever get to eat it. The Stop N Shop sells the frozen ones, but they're nowhere near as good as the pizza he has delivered. Then there's the part where I could never afford it, so it's a treat.

Last time he even brought ice cream. He ate it straight from the carton, and each time his lips sucked that spoon, I got goosebumps. I couldn't stop imagining him doing something similar to me or him letting me eat the ice cream off him. My guess is it would've tasted even better that way. I nearly suggested we give it a try but didn't want to push my luck too far.

Clearly, I have some pent-up need if only he'd satisfy that like he does my hunger pains. I wonder if he has another woman. That could make sense, but I'd be surprised if she didn't get angry with him for coming to check on me. I'm glad he's divorcing my mom, but at the same time, I'll miss him not visiting me once that happens. I remember she'd fly off the handle if the guys she was seeing even mentioned another woman's name in front of her.

I'm not like that though. I don't see the point of jealousy if people are open with each other from the start. I figure you either want to be with someone or you don't. There's no middle ground in it, and one thing is for certain, I want Sinner. I'd never had the chance to keep him in my life for the long term so I'll settle for right now if he gives me a chance.

All I can do now is watch the clock and wait while the minutes pass by, and they always go by extra slow it seems. How ironic. I actually want to go home now and can't leave quite yet. With pizza and Sinner on the way though, I'd be a fool not to be excited about one thing if not the other. This trip could be the one where I get lucky and am finally able to run my tongue along that gorgeous jaw of his— amongst other things.

Maybe eat that slice of pizza off his body this time around...

CHAPTER 3

*Every saint has a past and
every sinner has a future.*
-Oscar Wilde

Sinner

Getting Saint distracted is fairly easy now that his cock's satisfied along with his need to offer blood up in sacrifice. He was pent up in more ways than one, so hopefully, he'll remain relaxed for a while. Our relationship may be out of the ordinary, but I couldn't imagine not having one with him. As for what we do sexually, well, we keep that between us and whoever we're sharing for the night. There've been many times I've wanted to show him affection but have held myself back. Maybe one day that'll change.

As for now, I have other things on my mind; namely, a young woman named Jude. I'm able to eventually sneak away while he's busy having a drink with Spider and Exterminator. The two are still NOMADS, so we don't see them much. They stopped through town when they heard we'd be having a hog roast.

Little do they know that hog roast will be compliments of the pigs we feed our enemies to. Can't say I'm sorry to miss it. I'm sure the bodies' remains are long gone, but it still gives me the heebie-jeebies just thinking about it. Saint could care less though, as he drinks blood from them with each sacrifice. I'm, however, not on that same level.

It sucks the two brothers didn't hang up their NOMAD patches to stay at the club with the rest of us, but I get it. The life of a wanderer calls to a biker's soul. There's nothing like being out on the road doing whatever you want, whenever you feel like it. I miss it somedays, and I'm sure Saint feels the same.

Hybrid Collection

Viking's aware of me going out of town again and wasn't thrilled with the idea, but I wanted to at least let the Prez know in case he needed me. Ever since Nightmare's son was kidnapped by the leader of the Iron Fists, the club hasn't been quite the same. We've been on edge, just waiting for something else to pop off even though we've all been promised that it won't.

I don't trust the Iron Fists for shit, so their word means nothing to me or to any of us. We're just sitting back, waiting for the right time to finish snuffing them out. Unfortunately, we have to find out where they are first before we can make any headway with retribution.

Saint wouldn't understand if I told him the truth that I'm going to go check in on Jude. He'd think I was nuts for buying her food and giving a shit. He'd also be beyond pissed to hear I'm married. Not only did I not tell him about it, but he's my best friend. You don't keep shit like that from each other, and I've broken that unspoken rule.

As soon as I can get it annulled, I'm going to put it in my past and do what I can to forget it ever happened. I still haven't figured out what to do about Jude afterward though. I have a feeling she won't survive if I leave her to depend on herself. I can't have her survival weighing on my conscience for the rest of my life, so I have to come up with some sort of plan.

I wonder if Princess has any ideas. She's young herself, but she may know what I should do. After this trip, I'm going to discuss it with the Prez and see if he thinks it's a good idea I involve his ol' lady in my mess. I have to do something though; I can't continue omitting shit from Saint. He means too much to me, and the worse the outcome will be if he finds out on his own.

The ride passes by quickly, anything under four hours always does it seems. Jude only lives about two hours east in bum fuck Egypt, so I hit town about nine.

Stopping off at the Stop N Shop gas station, I pick up a six pack of beer for me, some lemonade, and a few fruit parfaits for Jude.

She loves them but never pays the extra for the parfait, settling on the cheaper yogurts instead. You'd never think of granola and fruit as splurging, but in her case, it is. I've made it a habit of paying attention to what she eats. Otherwise, she won't tell me. The girl's got pride, and I can respect that.

Money's not much of an issue when it comes to me. I usually blow it on food or alcohol out and about with Saint; otherwise, I sleep at the clubhouse, so rent's free. I pay my dues each month but the runs we do make us plenty of money to live off of. Viking has done a good job at helping us fill our pockets.

We've recently gotten into overlooking the local hotel that deals in pussy. They needed security, and we could use the extra cash from it. We don't pimp them out or anything, that's not our style. We just sit back and keep an eye on them to make sure the john's don't mess with them in any way.

Drugs have never been much of my thing either with the trippy past I had, and then Saint doing his sacrifices. I have a feeling they'd give me a bad high if I were to use. Anyhow, I save a lot not throwing away my cash on any of it. Not that I judge my brothers who do enjoy the high, it's just not for me.

As I get closer to the shack of a trailer that she calls home, my abs constrict. I've been thinking about her a little too much since the last time I saw her. She practically threw herself at me, and it took everything I had inside not to rip her shirt and shorts off and fuck her against the wall. I wanted to, Jesus fucking Christ. I wanted to plow into her.

Self-control.

I chant inside my head multiple times and exhale, pulling to a stop. Shutting the engine off, I take in my surroundings and swing my leg over, climbing off my bike. It's so quiet out here besides the occasional car passing on the main road that I can hear crickets chirping. It's a touch surreal after listening to the steady roar of my engine for the past two hours.

Hybrid Collection

The warm yellow glow from the porch light shines brightly, reflecting over the chrome on my bike as I glance around. I warned Jude about that before—having the light off at night. She has fuck all out here to protect her. The least she can do is light her place up to help ward off any piece of shit creepers.

If I knew it'd help, I'd tell her to get a dog out here to make some noise as well. However, that'd end up being an argument about her not being able to afford it, and it's not like there's a vet anywhere near if she needed one. So, I haven't said anything, yet. That's not saying I may bring it up to her one day.

I stopped at the bar on the way out of town the last visit to let them know to hit me up if she has any sort of trouble. I wore my colors, too, so they'd know exactly who they'd be fucking with if they didn't take me seriously. Her safety is not something I want to be compromised. It's a miracle the young woman has survived this long without anyone to care for her like they should've.

Emptying my leather saddlebags, I head up the three rickety, wooden stairs. The two-by-sixes groan with each heavy step, the unpleasant creak gives me away; not that she didn't already hear the rumble from my pipes. I'm stunned the split weathered pine will even hold my weight; they're definitely on their last leg.

I'm not heavy by any means. I'd describe myself as "fit," I guess. I should probably fix the damn stairs for her. If I don't do it, then they'll end up breaking, and she'll hurt herself.

Being a biker, I have to stay in shape to accommodate my lifestyle. You never know when you may need to bury a body or get into a good ol' fashioned bar fight. Hell, we've even been chased down by lions. That was probably one of the scariest moments of my life, thinking I was gonna be a snack for an oversized, pissed-off cat. In this case, though, I can easily fix shit that's broken for her.

The door swings open before I have a chance to beat on the rickety metal, her beautiful form waiting just past the threshold. She's a site for sore eyes, that's for sure. "Hi," she greets, wearing a grin and fluttering her lashes. She's obviously been looking forward to seeing me, which isn't good, 'cause I wanted to see her too.

She's fucking gorgeous and completely untouchable when it comes to me. Back in the day, I'd have fucked her ten ways to Sunday without a second thought, but now, I'm married to her mother. Even if it is a fake ass marriage, it still counts, right? Boy, do I wish the circumstances were different; I'd break her body in with no questions asked.

"Hey." The greeting leaves me in a rasp, my groin already growing heavy with lust at the sight of her.

I swear she does this shit on purpose—a plain white fitted T-shirt with no bra underneath and a pair of tiny women's boxers. It sounds like nothing, but then imagine them being threadbare and a size too small. Fuck, it could be college-aged lingerie right out of a goddamn porno. She has an innocent look to match and throw in the fact she's a librarian...she's a man's wet dream waiting to happen.

"You brought me lemonade?" She beams, surprised, and jumps a little in excitement, clapping her hands together.

The movement's just enough to bounce her tits and the hardness of my cock has me needing to hit something for a touch of relief. She's so easy to please and a genuinely grateful person. It makes her like a goddamn angel. An angel that I can't touch. Ever.

"Of course." The reply comes out as a croak as I hand the bag over with the beverage and her parfaits. She could ask me to rob a bank for her right now, and I'd do it.

"And parfaits! Yummy! Thank you."

Grunting, I shove my way passed her to head for the couch. I need to slam a beer ASAP to get my mind preoccupied before I rip her shirt in two. Of course, in my haste, my arm brushes across her tits, and I grind my teeth to keep me from yanking her frame to mine.

She draws in a quick breath at the unintentional caress, and I'm tormented with the stiffness from her nipples. I want to palm each globe and draw the peaks into my mouth. I could probably make her come from touching her tits alone.

Hybrid Collection

Bless me, Father, for I have sinned.

The chant begins in my mind automatically at the prospect of defiling this perfect being. I want to dirty her up a bit but have to hold myself back.

The prayer hits me immediately, asking for forgiveness as I imagine my father whipping my back like he did when I was a child. It's the only thing I can think of to turn my thoughts away from deflowering this young woman's magnificent body. She may as well be a piece of chocolate cake sitting in front of me, telling me I can't eat it. In the end, I'm a man; I'm going to at least stick my finger in the frosting.

Man, I fucking love chocolate cake too. I'd eat the shit out of it, just like I would her pussy. Christ, I can't think like that about her. I have to stop this.

"There's pizza left if you're hungry," Jude offers, and her perfect mouth's enticing with each word.

"I already ate." Besides, I wouldn't be eating pizza with her. The only thing around here that I want to taste is between her legs.

"Oh, okay." She sounds bummed, but I don't give a shit. The last thing I need is to sit here and watch her putting things into her mouth. The one item I want to see there is my dick, and that can't happen. I won't let it.

Plopping down on the worn-in peanut butter suede couch, I grab the remote and flip on the TV. A black screen appears, but no picture. "What happened to the TV?" I ask, keying in random channels but still come back with nothing.

"It got shut off. They let you float the bill for three months then cut it off."

Shit! Because her mom never paid for it. I swear that bitch is something else. I should've asked if she needed me to pay anything besides the house note. Not having my own place has me forgetting about other bills she may have around here.

"It's all good, I have a Netflix account. I can just sign on, and you'll have stuff to watch whenever you want."

"I've seen it advertised online, but never watched it. Is it like regular TV?"

"Yeah, babe, it's pretty much the same thing—just cheaper and everything's on demand. I'll show you." Clicking through options, I find the app and use my sign in information. Then I go through, step by step, showing her how to browse and select shows.

"That's cool. I don't watch anything really, but at least you'll have something for when you're here. That first category, are those, uh, adult films?" Her voice becomes breathy, and it's an unintentional stroke to my cock.

Clearing my throat, I pretend not to hear her and reach for my beer. My throat's suddenly gone dry. I wonder why that is?

I wish she'd let me take her away from this place and have her...

Wait, where did that thought come from? I can't bring her with me, unless, well...maybe if Princess helps. But then again, Saint couldn't know, and I have a feeling Jude isn't the type to hide her friendship with someone. I can't imagine my brother taking kindly to her attachment with me either.

She's already told me that's exactly what we are—friends. Saint is my best friend. I have my MC brothers, and apparently, according to Jude, I have her friendship too. I don't know what to do with it if I'm honest about it. That's not really what I crave from her anyhow. I want to dip between her legs and make her scream my name.

Friends...the word's like poison when I connect it with her. Friendship isn't enough. I need to fuck her so badly, I can feel myself gritting my teeth right now just thinking about it. I don't imagine "friends" are supposed to fantasize about each other like that. But then again there's Saint, and our relationship definitely isn't the usual either. The brothers all believe he and I fuck, but what goes on behind closed doors is between me and Saint, no one else.

"You have any plans?" I mutter absently as I turn on the *Hatfield's and McCoy's*, quickly browsing past the more unsavory films Saint and I usually watch. I need some sort of action to keep my mind distracted from her and damn sure nothing with tits or ass in it.

"No, today was my last day of work. I'm off for the next three days. My boss can't afford to have me on any more hours than I'm already scheduled for. She said the other day that she may have to let me go."

"Right." Nodding, I slam the rest of my beer and crack open another, not paying much attention to her words. I can't. Her voice does things to my body it shouldn't be allowed to, as well as her mouth. I feel like a ticking time bomb. Maybe it was a bad idea coming here, after all.

It's going to be a long night being this close to her without being allowed to touch. Don't understand why I subject myself to this sort of torture with her. I shouldn't give a shit about any of it—her mom or fucking her—nothing. Instead, I find myself attempting to preserve her innocence like some sort of Good Samaritan. Such a joke. I'm far from a decent man, that's for sure.

"How was your week?" she probes, saddling up way too close for my comfort. She sits right next to me on the couch and leans back, her legs slightly spread. It seems all fine and dandy, but it's not. The bitch's pussy lips are outlined perfectly, taunting me to lean over and graze them with my fingertips.

Or cock. I could fit my cock right there perfectly. I'd finally be putting myself out of my misery too.

Ugh, how was my week? When was the last time someone even asked me that sort of thing?

My week was the usual, taking care of club business and trying to keep my brother from going crazy being stuck in the compound for too long. Fucked a few chicks with Saint, but they didn't mean anything. They never do, just someone to pass the time and make me feel good.

Being intimate with Saint, that's different. As much as I don't want to admit it, the sex does mean something to me, but I haven't exactly figured out what. We've been beside each other for so long that I can't imagine being away from him in the future. Is it enough to have an exclusive relationship though? I enjoy women too much to give them up for good.

Shrugging, I swallow, attempting to collect myself and rasp a typical guy answer. "Same shit. You need anything?"

I must not be paying her the attention she wants because she begins her teasing. "No daddy, but thanks for asking." She winks, wearing a playful smile. "Do you need anything, daddy?"

Shooting a glare in her direction, I grumble to myself, though there's nothing menacing behind it. She's got me by the nuts at this point. It's damn near impossible to be pissed with this bitch; she's too fucking cute to stay mad at. "Shut it," I order, and her smile grows, pleased.

I throw back my second beer cause if I don't I'll end up fucking that too perfect pouty mouth of hers. She's got those dick suckin' lips, and I'd bet money she doesn't even know what the hell that is. I could teach her though.

She's going to be one of those good girls that's a freak in the sheets, I just know it. Now if only I could be the first to tap that ass. Or school her in all things cock related...

Can't fucking happen, damn it!

I can't touch her. She deserves better. I'm a nobody compared to her. Not only am I damn near old enough to be her father, but I'm also not a good man—at all. I kill people. I hurt them and fuck with their minds without thinking twice about it. She needs one of those good ol' boys to come around and put a ring on her finger.

But why does the thought of another man sniffing around make me so angry inside?

"You can sleep in my bed tonight if you want? I know the couch is too small for you." Her shameless stare drops to my crotch, and I gulp, my throat parched all over again with her attention.

"Jesus, fucking Christ...seriously, Jude?"

Hybrid Collection

Her eyes widen. "What? I thought it'd be more comfortable? There are other ways I could help you relax, too, if you'd let me." Her tongue trails over her mouth, and I nearly lose my voice—my hands shaking with her implication.

"Shouldn't you be in bed or something? Pretty sure it's past your bedtime, little girl." I throw in the last part to be a dick and to remind myself that I'm not sleeping in her bed—with her—preferably naked. She'd help me relax? I'd have her climaxing so hard she'd think she was on another fucking planet when I finished with her.

She huffs. No doubt I've hurt her feelings. It's a normal occurrence, though; I have to keep some sort of boundary between us. So far, being an ass has been working. She's not used to men like me and doesn't know what to do or say when I give her shit about being young. Bet she'd clam up quick, too, if I was honest about what I want to do to her.

A club bitch, however, would strip and pretty much pounce on my cock, but Jude's no club slut, that's for sure. "Night-night little girl." I wave her off and open my third beer. I'm going to down this six-pack, then crash. It's the only thing I can do to stop myself from going in there and showing her just the sort of man I really am.

"Goodnight, Sinner," she whispers and makes her way to her room in a rush.

I'm pretty sure there were tears in her voice, and I hate it. I can't stand knowing that I put them there when she doesn't deserve them. She shouldn't be treated like shit by any man, but it's the only way I can protect her from myself.

The trailer's lit up from the sun when I peel my eyes open the next morning. Hearing voices, I drag my tired body off the too small couch and peek out the window toward my bike. There's a lime colored Lamborghini parked out front, and that fucking thing doesn't belong to me.

What the ever loving fuck is going on? I damn sure know it's not her mom...I took care of that problem already.

"Shhh, baby," I overhear a guy croon and instantly get pissed.

If Jude has a motherfucker over here, world war three's about to go down in this bitch. I'll teach that kid a lesson to show up over here when I'm around. And when I was asleep, to boot; that's some goddamn nerve.

It's not her that surprises me when I stick my head in her doorway though.

"Saint?" I utter his name in disbelief.

They're lying in her bed with him behind her. He's kissing all over her neck...his hands under the covers. My chest rumbles with a growl at that discovery.

"Brother." His stare is pinned on me and defiant. He's pleased that he's shocked me.

"What the hell are you doing here?"

He tsks, shaking his head, then licks up the side of Jude's neck, causing her to giggle. It's like nails on a chalkboard because I'm not the one making her do it. Nor did I give him my permission to come in here and touch her like he's doing. I've held myself back and not to leave the option open to my brother.

"And where in the fuck did the car come from? When did you even get here?"

"'Bout one a.m. or so. I've been talkin' to Baby all night about you. When I came in, you were passed the fuck out."

"How did you know where I was?"

"You didn't think you'd be goin' out of town without me knowing where you were, did you?" He rolls his eyes, the irises the same shade as a cloudy sky. He's clearly annoyed at the thought of me believing I could keep something from him. Little does he know, I have a whopper of a secret. Let's hope he hasn't figured that one out as well.

Hybrid Collection

"Who's car?" I repeat with more grit behind the words, knowing he damn well doesn't own the expensive luxury vehicle.

He shrugs. "Don't know, and I really don't fuckin' care either, brother. I saw it down the road at a hotel in town, keys in it. Figured they wanted it off their hands and I obliged."

"Jesus fucking Christ, Saint. The only motherfuckers leaving keys in cars is fucking mafia! How could you be so careless?" Yanking my phone out of my back pocket, I hit the speed dial to call the Prez.

He's going to be livid when he hears about this if he hasn't already. There's a decent chance someone's already told him. I'd like to think he'd have called me, though, if that were the case.

"Viking." He answers, even though his ID should show it's me on the other end.

"We have a problem. Saint's here where I am, and he's in a lime Lamborghini. Needless to say, we don't own it." Like he doesn't know that bit already, but I throw it in anyhow.

"Motherfucker. I thought you were going to tell me it was the Fists on your ride over, but this is pretty fucking bad too."

"Is it Chicago?" I guess aloud. It was the first thing I thought of when he said the car had the fob in it.

"Nah, Joker's Lambo is marmalade or some fancy orange shit, or his was a Phantom? I can't remember what that overpriced foreign piece of metal is that he drives. This is Masters' I'd bet. Beau's the only one I know with that color. It was a gift from his father, he said."

"Masters, as in Russian mafia Masterson? Are those the same?"

"Yeah, he's the one that sent us to Mexico looking for that chick."

"Holy shit. The cop?"

He grunts. "If Saint showed up in that car..." Viking leaves off, but I already know what he's thinking.

"I'll fix it. Later," I promise and hang up, glowering over at Saint. "You have any idea who that damn car belongs too?"

He ignores me, still kissing on Jude's neck and my fist flies into the wall beside me. The fake wood paneling erupts, a hole the size of my hand left behind as well as splits going in every direction. I'm too angry to feel the impact on my knuckles, immediately sharing the information Viking just enlightened me with.

"It's the motherfucking Russian Mafiya. You steal their shit, they'll know where that car is, and you know as well as I do what'll happen. They'll be here in no time, smoking you, me, and her. Get it back, now, Saint...before we can't fix this. Why in the fuck would you take it in the first place?"

"Because I wanted to," he responds nonchalantly. "Who's going to fuck with an Oath Keeper anyhow? Rich pussies don't have a nutsack large enough."

"The Mafiya, Saint! The motherfuckin' Mafiya, that's who."

He stands, the blanket falling away. He's clad in only a pair of jeans that hug his hips. I can make out the outline of Saint's cock, hard as stone beneath the material. It was only a matter of time before he fucked her and stole her innocence away.

"Come on, baby, you can ride with me," He offers, smirking as he jerks Jude to her feet as well.

"No, no, no. Jude, you're staying here," I demand and Saint cackles, sounding so evil it could be the devil himself.

"Fuck that, Sinner. The bitch is coming with me. I'm not finished having my fun."

He croons in her direction, "Isn't that right, baby? Come with daddy." He shoves past me, hauling her behind him. She's in the clothes from last night, what little material there is, thank God. At least he didn't have her naked yet.

"Jude, listen to me," I argue, attempting to stop a train wreck from happening.

Hybrid Collection

She follows him along, laughing like this is some big adventure. They're out the door in no time, with me following to the porch. "Don't get in that car with him!" I'm yelling at this point. Fuck the neighbors.

He'll kill her or get her killed and not think twice about it. "Saint! Stop! Don't take her; she's too fucking good."

"Fuck you, Sinner. You thought you could keep her to yourself? I'm not finished with her yet." He opens the passenger side, pushing her into the car. "Get in, baby; we're goin' for a ride." He laughs and slams the door.

Rounding the car, he gives me his middle finger the entire time. I've pissed in his Cheerios, and I haven't the faintest idea how to stop him from leaving without putting a bullet in either him or that too-fucking-expensive piece of metal he's stolen. I can't do either without repercussions. Fuck, it sucks being the rational one sometimes.

The moment he's in the driver's seat, the engine cranks, and he's flooring it to the point rocks spray across the side of the trailer, and I jump inside to grab my wallet. Shoving the leather fold into my back pocket, I run like my ass is on fire to my bike. I can't get out of here as fast as he can, but eventually, I make it out to the main road.

Shifting, my speed increases faster, the speedometer shooting higher. Eventually, I get to 140, and they're nowhere in sight. Saint probably has that car over 200 miles per hour. I'll be lucky if they don't wrap that death trap around a telephone pole before I can catch up.

Fuck, fuck, fuck, fuck! I should've known he'd figure out where I was this entire time. I believed I was sneaky; I was actually a damn fool, underestimating him.

Let's hope this Russian is as easy to work with as his cousins are. I've heard stories of how he was a ruthless undercover cop and then went rogue, joining the family business. His cousins are the Russian Mafiya, and Saint has just stolen his fucking car. Viking is going to be enraged if this doesn't blow over.

And he has Jude...

CHAPTER 4

Can you remember who you were,
before the world told you who you should be?

Jude

Saint has a grin nearly the entire time he's driving like a maniac. He'll randomly glance over, wearing a smirk full of trouble. I don't know where we're headed or what's going on. He stole the car apparently, and now we have to get it back right away, or someone from the mafia will be angry.

This is the most excitement I've had in my entire life, and I'm loving every minute of it. It's the adventure I wished for yesterday in the middle of my boring work shift; never in a million years did I think it would come true. These things don't happen to people like me; we go about living our lives like robots. Now I'm involved with not only one biker, but two. And who knows what's going to happen next.

Saint showed up out of the blue in the middle of the night looking for Sinner. When he saw him sleeping, he explained that he's Sinner's best friend and asked if we could talk. I wasn't going to turn him away. Sinner's done so much for me, that the least I could do is be friendly to his best friend.

I quickly learned that Saint is nothing like the man I've come to look forward to spending time with. Where Sinner's features are dark, Saint's are light. The contrast is striking and confusing because they're each beautiful.

He's funny and a bit wild and wasn't scared in the least bit to touch me. He treated me so sweetly at first, talking to me and complimenting me like I'm the prettiest thing he's ever seen before. Guys I meet are either creepy about it or fall flat, but he had just the right mix of charisma. I don't understand why Sinner didn't bring him around sooner.

Hybrid Collection

Saint's name matches his face too. He reminds me of someone you'd read about but never actually see in person. I liked him nearly instantly and even more so when he leaned over and kissed me on my bed. After that, I didn't want him to stop. I got his shirt off and let him touch me everywhere. I couldn't help myself; I pictured his hands were Sinner's sometimes too.

He caressed me in ways I'd been dreaming of Sinner doing, all the while telling me how special I am. He said I have to be different, for Sinner to take care of me like he has been. That has to mean something, right? I wish I knew how he felt; it would make everything so much easier.

"We're home, baby," he mutters randomly, gesturing toward the foliage out in front of us.

Peering at the scenery around us, I take in the quickly passing land. There are lots of trees and a dirt road that he drives over so fast, we could be flying. We drive through a giant open gate then hit a large paved parking area where an imposing building finally comes into sight.

Saint yanks up on the brake handle resting between us, causing the car to jerk and spin wildly. A scream breaks free as I grasp for something to hold on to and not get slung around. He must love it though because he hoots and howls, laughing as we spin, gunning the gas over and over.

A group of angry looking men come pouring outside, their hands shading their eyes to watch us as Saint slings random rocks around and smokes up the parking lot from burning tires.

I have to close my eyes after that because if I don't, I'm sure that I'll puke. "Pleeease stop, Saint."

"I told you, baby, you call me daddy, just like you do my boy, Sinner. He may not appreciate it, but I think it's sexy as fuck."

"Okay-okay, just, please. I'm going to puke." The nickname was a joke toward Sinner, meant to get under his skin, but Saint seems to enjoy the word falling from my mouth. He keeps reminding me that it turns him on. "For me, daddy, so I don't get sick."

He cackles at my begging, and the car comes to a stop, rocking as it finally halts in one spot.

It's as if I'm still moving, even though the engine's quieted to a near silent purr once again. Is this what a boat's like? "Oh God, I don't feel so well."

I open my eyes again just as a monster sized man looking like a Nordic god storms toward the vehicle and nearly rips the door from the hinges. Impossible you'd think since they open upward, but this man's so ripped, I'm sure he could tear it off if he wanted to. Yelping in surprise, the shock makes me freeze up, gawking as the scene unfolds right beside me.

"The fuck!" He roars and reaches in, grabbing Saint around the neck. He yanks him from the vehicle and slams his body across the hood like a rag doll. I'm about to scream again—this time for help—until I hear Saint laughing about it all.

"Damn, man! You need to drive this whip ASAP, Vike! Fucking a-mazing!"

My own door opens much less dramatically, and a grouchy guy wearing a frown nearly the same size as the one called "Vike" glowers down at me. He's got a crazy scar on his face, the silver slashing through one of his mocha colored irises and dark, wavy, shoulder-length hair.

"Hi?" The question escapes in a high pitch, nearly a squeak.

His hand comes toward me, and my eyes widen as my heart rate again quickens. He watches, breaking out in a surprised chuckle after a moment, then flips it over, giving me his palm. It takes everything in me to swallow my fear down and place my much smaller hand in his.

The man helps me climb out, steadying me as I stand, which is a good thing, considering I'm quite wobbly. "Oh, thank you," I acknowledge and hiccup, as I silently pray I don't upchuck in front of all these guys.

"You all right, darlin'?" he mumbles as a shorter guy comes to stand next to him.

Hybrid Collection

"Night, don't be calling her that. Your ol' lady hears that word leave your mouth, and you'll be peelin' her off this chick."

Night, or whatever his name is, shrugs. "Brother, my woman knows she's mine. This pint-sized woman looked like she was gonna be sick, and I don't want her puking or sitting in the Russian's car when he shows up. Unless you feel like cleaning up puke, Spidey?"

The other man shakes his head and offers me a kind smile.

Night grunts. "I'm Nightmare, this is Spider." He gestures to the less buff, amused guy to his right.

"Um...hi," I manage, with a brief wave that makes Spider snicker.

Can't say I'm too surprised hearing the big dude's name is Nightmare. And Spider for the other; that's kind of creepy. He doesn't strike me as strange right off the bat, though, so maybe he got it for another reason.

"Stop staring, Spidey," he gripes. "Saint or Sinner catches you. I'm guessing Saint will be carving you up. They don't go to the trouble for bitches, so this one must mean something or know something we don't."

Gee thanks. I don't know if I should be flattered or offended. "I'm not a bitch; I'm Jude."

Nightmare's eyebrow hikes. "Hey, Jude. Do you have shoes in there?" He nods toward the vehicle, disregarding my proclamation.

My gaze falls to my feet...my bare feet. "Oh, shit. No, Saint pulled me out of the house so fast, I didn't have a chance to stop and get any. I didn't bring anything, actually," I admit, wishing I'd at least have paused long enough to collect my purse and flip-flops.

Spider shoots a look I can't decipher at Nightmare and then glances toward Saint, still pinned on the hood. "This is going downhill fast. We need to get her inside while we handle club shit. We don't want certain people showing up with her out here."

"Prez, what should we do with her?" he calls across the car, and 'Vike' scowls over at me.

"Fuck," he grits, then nods toward the largest building. "Get the bitch inside."

Okay, enough with the name calling. No wonder Sinner's so freaking grouchy when he comes over, dealing with these guys. "My name is Jude! Use it!" I demand and nearly all their mouths drop open.

I may be young and polite and quiet, but that doesn't mean I don't know how to stand my ground. Did any of them not just hear me screaming in that car? Clearly, I have a voice, and I'm able to be just as loud as they are. Instead, they act like a group of barbarians, speaking as if I'm not right here beside them.

A deep rumble grows near, and if I'd have to guess, I'd say its Sinner's motorcycle. It's been long enough for him to catch up to us—I think so, anyhow. He was not pleased in the least when Saint loaded me into the sports car with him, but I wasn't about to pass up an adventure. Maybe I should've thought it through first.

"Viking?" Nightmare interrupts the sound of the bike, "You want her at the bar?"

Big guy waves me off. "Don't fucking care where you stick her, just get her the fuck out of here."

Jesus, is he a dick to everyone? That word seems to fit him; he's not nice at all. I'm being shoved through the building door, just as I see Sinner come speeding into the parking lot on his motorcycle. He looks amazing straddling that motorcycle and also completely furious with a scowl the size of Texas on his face.

Pushing against Spider's hold, I'm able to watch Sinner hop off his bike and practically run toward Saint, and then I'm inside with the freaking door blocked.

Saint

Hybrid Collection

Sinner's borderline manic as he strides toward me, fury written all over his striking features. The brothers leap between us, large bodies attempting to block us, with hands out to hold him back. He's on a mission to cause some pain, no doubt. Everyone knows as well as I do that he'll regret it after we've had a chance to cool down. You don't stick together like we have and not have a few fights thrown in over the years.

"All this...for her?" It escapes me in a roar, my jealousy pointed in his direction.

I can be just as cross at him over the shit he's pulled. I have every right. He's lied to me for a female and for who knows how long. We're supposed to be brothers. And he's supposed to love me, just like I love him. Yet he's been sneaking off for some pussy and then has the nerve to turn around and lie to my fucking face about it.

"Yes, for her, Saint. You don't know shit about what's goin' on." He peers around, eyeing the clubhouse. "Where is she?"

"I know you haven't fucked her, 'cause I had my fingers all up in that pussy last night, and it's tight." I spew the first hurtful thing that comes to mind. He's merely arrived and already searching her out like some lost puppy. "Can't wait to stick my cock in her. I bet the brothers will enjoy it too."

He snarls, "Motherfucker!" lunging in my direction.

Exterminator and Nightmare move to hold him off, but I'm not sure it'll work. Sinner's the calm one of the two of us and to see him this angry, has me questioning everything. Does she mean more to him than me? It's childish to think that way, but I do. He's mine.

"You keep wasting time, Sin. She likes me already. I'll take her, Sinner. I won't let you have her. You'll lose me and her both."

The Prez scowls down at me. "Back the fuck off, Saint." His forearm presses into my chest, holding me in place. "Sinner's going to put a goddamn bullet in you and he'll never forgive himself for that shit. Stop running your fucking mouth, brother. She's just pussy."

It takes all the self-restraint I have, and that's not a lot I'm afraid, but I do it. My mouth clamps shut on the hate it wants to emit, and I attempt to climb my way back from the chaos I so greatly crave. I may be pissed off at Sinner, but I don't want him to kill me. I don't want him to bear that burden.

"Fine, just cage me up like you always do."

"Can I let you go?" Viking probes, no longer applying as much pressure. He was holding me down with so much force, it felt as if he may crush my pecs under his massive arm. A few of us have caught his temper before, and the man doesn't fuck around.

My foggy gaze meets his. "Let him kill me."

"He's not going to fucking kill you, brother. Christ, relax."

"The hell I'm not!" Sinner interrupts, and the brothers break out in a varied chorus of 'shut ups.'

"You never should've taken her, Saint. She's not like me and you; she's a good girl, damn it."

"She wants to be really bad," I supply with a shrug and get back to my feet as Viking gives me some space. He remains a barrier between us but stops touching me.

"It's not your place to get her to be bad. Leave Jude alone," Sin warns, spurring me on to reply.

Spitting, blood mixed with my saliva lands next to my feet. I must've bitten my cheek when Prez slammed me on the damn hood. "Go to Hell, Sinner."

"We need to reel it the fuck in, right now, goddamn it," the Prez orders. "Spider, take that Green-Goblin-looking fucking thing back to Masters. He's at the fancy hotel down the road. I've already spoken to him over the phone, so he won't put a bullet in ya. Nightmare, follow in Scot's old truck and y'all get back here, quick."

Spider's face lights up, eager, as he rounds the car and hops in. He's no doubt satisfied that he's the one being tasked to take the chartreuse whip for a spin. Nightmare agrees and heads for the truck.

Prez's scrutiny falls back to us. "Now, you two fuckers hash this shit storm out, inside preferably, without knives or guns involved."

"No need for weapons, I can strangle him with my bare fucking hands," Sinner mutters with a huff.

His comment makes me hoot with laughter, and in response, he beams a glare full of menace in my direction. He doesn't realize that look does nothing but turn me on. Maybe we could go and fuck the anger out on Jude together. That is if he isn't too busy coddling her like a fucking newborn.

We get inside, and I head to the bar, needing something strong to help wash down my frustration. If I can't fuck or fight, then may as well drown the feelings a bit with some good ol' fashioned liquor.

"Where is she?" He levels his gaze on me before flicking it around the room. She's nowhere in sight though, and despite my irritation, it makes me want to laugh in his face again to be a dickhead.

Blaze places a tumbler with some Johnny Walker Black Label on the rocks in front of me and mixes a gin and juice for Sinner. "Spider brought a chick in a few minutes ago," he comments, taking a drink of his soda that'd been resting on the beer cooler.

"That's her," Sin affirms.

"I had her go to the kitchen and make a sandwich." The brother with tattooed flames up his arms gestures to the other room. "She said she hasn't eaten today and I didn't know if she was tweaking or whatever." He shrugs, his cerulean irises filled with curiosity. "Figured it helps sober her up if anything."

"She's not on drugs." Sinner's grimace turns to me. "Unless you fucking gave her something? Is that what happened?"

Scoffing, I roll my eyes again. "I didn't give the bitch shit, besides make her feel good. Something you obviously didn't offer up." His glass goes flying toward my head, and I duck. It makes me chuckle again.

"Fuck," Blaze comments, grabbing a towel and broom. "This is bullshit. You wanna throw shit, don't use my rocks glasses." He strides from behind the bar to collect the shattered crystal. He doesn't usually clean up our messes—we do that ourselves—but he obviously realizes Sinner's one breath away from throwing blows.

Taking a sip of my liquor, I attempt to reason. "Tell me, Sin, how the fuck does she have you tied up in knots like this? It's rare that I'm the calm one when shit pops off and you have me actually living up to my name right now."

He mocks, his voice carrying just an ounce of too much bite. "You're far from a saint."

"Exactly. It's good you fucking remember it too." I hate fighting with him, but I have a right to be pissed off too. He fucking lied to me. After everything we've been through, he lies to me over a woman. I think that's the part that has me the maddest.

Jude appears in the doorway, and Sinner hops up from his barstool, striding over to her. His hands cover her forearms, and the motion has me swallowing tightly.

Taking a large gulp to ease my thoughts, I stand as well, calling over to her. "Baby girl, tell our boy Sinner here, that I didn't hurt you."

Grinning widely, I approach them both wearing the look of innocence. It's the same smile I offer up to bitches to make them believe I'm their dream man. Then they learn what I am when I fuck them until they scream and beg or offer them up to the gods. I'm not that way with everyone, but Lord knows I'm far from virtuous in any way.

She shakes her head, lips in a perfect pout. "No, Sinner, he didn't hurt me. I promise."

Hybrid Collection

That's it, baby, tell him what he needs to hear. I didn't hurt her, but that's not saying I wasn't thinking about it in the beginning.

He runs a frustrated hand through his midnight locks, blowing out a heavy breath. "Let me take you home, sweetheart."

Her brow wrinkles. "But I don't want to go—not yet, anyway."

Wrapping my arm around her shoulders, I press a bit further. "See *daddy,* she wants to stay and have some fun." Smirking, I tug her into my chest and away from him. "Wanna share how you got that pet name?" With an amused chuckle, I plant a chaste kiss on her left temple.

If he pisses me off, I'll break her fucking neck right here in front of him. If he wants to play nice, then maybe I'll just fuck her and let him take her home without drawing any blood. The outcome of her fate's up to him. The best part of all, the brothers here won't even blink at my decision. In fact, they'll help me bury the body if needed.

Nibbling her lobe, I rasp, "I'm your daddy now; huh, baby?" *She wants someone to spank her ass rosy and tell her what to do, that's no problem for me. That's one thing I've always been good at, and Jude's just my type when it comes to women. She's hotter than sin—young, dumb, and gullible—my favorite type to play with.*

She gasps, and with wide eyes, she watches for Sinner's reaction. His own gaze shutters as he hits me with an obscure look, "Fine," he relents. "But if you're not going home right now, then you'll sleep in my bed tonight. No arguments, either."

Her cheeks turn a delightful shade of rouge, giving away her intimate thoughts. She bites down on her plump lip for a moment, thinking it over. It's no need though; we already know what she wants from the color gracing her flushed skin. "Deal," she nods, agreeing a little too eagerly.

Yeah, fucking right, I don't think so.

Sinner's in my bed on the regular with whomever we choose to join us, together. He's off his rocker if he thinks this bitch is going to be in his bed without me there to share it. I'm the one who brought her here after all.

We have an unspoken agreement; it's been there for years. We're together always. I watch his back, and he's got mine. Same goes for fuckin'. We do it together, and it's better that way. That's one account as to why I was completely caught off guard when I found out he was hiding Jude from me. Of course, it made me instantly interested and a touch covetous.

Who's this woman he'd lie for? And that he'd visit when he believed no one was paying him attention? Sinner's mistake was overlooking that I always have him in mind. When I came to terms he wasn't going to let me in on whatever he was up to, I had to go off and find out for myself. I can't stand secrets, and this one didn't bode well with me not knowing what it was.

I'd thought through everything trying to figure it out too. Was he running drugs by himself? Was he two-timing the MC and hitting up another club? Was he on drugs himself? None of it was adding up.

Never once did it remotely cross my mind that he'd be sneaking off for this woman. He doesn't even like young chicks; his preferences are the older women. So, imagine my surprise when I figured out he wasn't visiting the lady at the address his bike was parked at. She's pretty much a ghost, and the only other one living there was a young woman registered in college.

Then when Jude answered the door last night, I was left speechless. Clearly, she'd been asleep. I don't know how Sinner didn't hear me, but she did. When she'd told me he'd drank a six-pack and passed out, I knew it was the perfect chance to find out just who the hell she is. For not being my brother's usual type, she damn sure was right up my alley.

Her sleep tasseled hair and tired smile was a welcome sight to my groin. She greeted me with wide open arms practically. Her mistake. Getting close to her took no time at all. I could've snuffed her life out within minutes if I'd truly wished.

Her naiveté was so fucking adorable, and it was a turn on knowing she had two killers in her house, and she was clueless. I couldn't keep my hands to myself—didn't want to, and she welcomed me in no time at all. A few hours of innocent questions and flirting and it was like taking candy from a baby. She fell into the palm of my hand so easily it was almost boring—*almost*. There was still the fact it was all happening while Sinner was in the other room, keeping the bit of deception of my own exciting.

He thinks he can keep her all to himself, but he's mistaken. She already wants me. I made sure of it. He'll share, or I'll kill her, it's as easy as that. Sinner belongs to me; he always has. What's his is mine...

CHAPTER 5

*Counting other people's sins
does not make you a saint.
-Pinterest Meme*

Sinner

He's had his arms around her all damn day. Laughing and making her giggle while feeding her drinks. I doubt Jude's ever drank alcohol before now, and she's well on her way to full-on drunk. He's doing it on purpose; I've seen his game many times over. Hell, most of us have done it at least once in the past.

It's different this time. I don't want her broken. And he'll be the first to do it to her. He'll get her toasted and then use her up until he's had his fill. She'll be left with a shell of herself, wondering how a man could take so much and give nothing in return.

It's unfair of me to think of him like this; after all, he's been so good to me personally over time. However, I know him the best, and I've seen how he has no regard for a woman beyond scratching an itch. It's been great while I wanted the same thing, but my feelings are beginning to change. I have Jude to blame for that. All I do is attempt to stay away from her and keep her safe. But clearly, that's gone to shit with my brother stepping in.

She's fallen into a twisted web, and I'm the one at fault. I should've covered my tracks better. Jesus, I never should've stepped into Jude's life in the first place. If I'd just stayed away, Saint never would've gotten wind of her. But I couldn't force myself to keep away and not make sure she was okay.

And overall, how can I fight for her with a man I love? When it boils down to it, that's how I feel about him. I assumed with our lifestyle, we'd never have to cross a bridge where a woman would be placed in the middle of it.

Hybrid Collection

I can't possess Jude like I desire; I know that. However, I don't want Saint to hurt her, either. If he's angry enough, he'll bleed her dry in sacrifice, and a piece of me will hate him for it. I don't want to despise him in any way; he's been everything to me since I was a teen.

Slamming my fist on the table, I interrupt their laughing, "She's had enough." Standing from my stool, I shuffle the few steps around the table to collect her. I'm done watching him and her like this. I want her in my bed—with me.

Saint grins, not fazed. "We're having fun, brother."

"And you've had enough entertainment for tonight. She's drunk and fuck if I want to be holding her to the toilet all night while she pukes her guts out."

"So, don't." He waves me off. "Let's fuck the alcohol out of her. She'll sober up."

Jude giggles, tucking her face into his chest, not realizing what exactly that entails. The action makes me rage inside. I want to yank her away and yell at her that she's mine, not his. I found her first. He doesn't get to have her without me; he should know better. I can't believe I'm even dealing with this right now. I worked so hard not to fucking touch her before.

"No. She's sleeping it off."

"Fuck you, Sinner. You don't make decisions for her. She's not your bitch; she's community property right now."

I want to punch him as the words fall from his lips. Of course, it's no big deal to him; he hasn't been around her for the past few months and watched how beautiful she really is. Yes, she's beyond sexy, but sometime along that line, she became more than just fresh pussy when I look at her.

"The fuck she is." The argument rumbles my chest with a displeased growl. Tugging her off the seat, she falls easily. Jude's trashed and immediately seeks out my arms.

"Oh, hi, Sinner!" She giggles.

It's impossible for me to be annoyed with her when she's so adorable, even piss-ass drunk. I love hearing her laugh; I just wish it was under different circumstances.

"Come on, Jude. It's time to go to bed."

"Finally!" she declares loudly. "I've been waiting for you to touch me like Saint did, for forever it seems," she admits brazenly, compliments of the alcohol stupor overtaking her senses.

My nostrils flare as my glare meets his over the top of her head, my words grinding with their meaning. "No, you're going to sleep. Saint won't be touching you."

Ever, at this rate.

He rolls his eyes. "The hell I won't. If you don't satisfy her, I will. I'll teach her how to beg and suck cock too."

"Shut up." My arms scoop her up into a sturdy embrace since she can't walk for shit at this point and her nose finds my neck, giving me pleasant chills.

"Please take me to bed, Sinner," she slurs against my throat. "You smell so freaking good."

The brothers witness the entire thing, amused, but no one utters anything about it. They all know the same thing I do; this is a clusterfuck already, and it's going be one hell of a long night. *Again.*

Jude

Oh my God, my head hurts so badly. The pounding is unreal. What was in those fruity drinks Saint gave me yesterday? They tasted delicious—like punch and bad decisions. Blaze is definitely talented when it comes to mixing drinks—you don't know it's hit you until it's too late. Thankfully, there are curtains snuffing out the bright Texas sun, or I may not have survived opening my eyes today.

"Mmmm." Moaning as I turn over, my stomach swims and not in a pleasant way. Stupid juice. Jesus, it's like a sugar overload mixed with brain freeze or something.

A grunt comes from beside me, and I lift my head up a little too fast to see who it came from.

"Ouch." My fingers fly to my forehead and massage my temples, attempting to offer an ounce of relief. After a moment, I pry my eyes open again, finding a mop of neatly trimmed ebony hair on the pillow next to mine.

My perusal dips lower, discovering a naked muscular back, covered in scars. The sight of them makes me cringe, those had to be agonizing however he received them. They're various sizes, long and short, some wider than the others in various crisscrosses.

The poor man; I can only imagine what he's been through. Who or what would do such a thing? I know there has to be a significant story behind them, and I want to ask about it, but I'm not sure it would be a welcome topic.

I can't stop myself from being curious if the rest of him is naked as well. The covers have him hidden from the hip down, not that it does anything to stop my imagination from running wild with ideas. My fingers find the grossly disfigured indentions and lightly trace each one. I don't know what spurs me on, giving me the courage to do so. Maybe I feel safe because he's sleeping.

He's broken, but yet so perfect.

Seeing him dressed, you'd never guess what his clothing hides. The front of him is a thing of beauty, dips and plains showcasing his strong stomach. The muscles aren't overly pronounced, just enough to make your eyes linger a bit longer. Then there's his back, and it's like reading a completely different story. If he were a book, the front cover would mislead you entirely because he has two very different sides.

His physique stiffens as my fingertips follow along their unplanned path, lightly caressing the alabaster blemishes. "What do you think you're doing?" A gruff voice sleepily mumbles, startling me.

My touch falters for a moment as my heart rate increases before I go about my inspection as if undisturbed. "What happened?" I eventually choke out, not wanting to think of this man being tormented.

"I was whipped."

"Wow," I answer breathlessly, even though it was a scenario I'd already considered. Hearing it come from him, though, puts merit behind the brief thought. "I'm sorry that happened to you."

He shrugs the comment off, but it doesn't stop me from touching them. "Does me doing this bother you?"

Sinner shakes his head, holding perfectly still. "No," he rasps. "To be honest, I like it. Your hands are soft, dainty."

"You like the pain or me touching them?"

"Both."

His answer's confusing. How can anyone enjoy a pain such as this? And what did he ever do to deserve something so harsh? Sinner's a kind man; at least, he is to me. It's hard to fathom why someone would want to torture him in such a remarkably cruel way.

"Do the marks still hurt you?"

He shrugs again. "Depends. They can be a slightly sensitive sometimes, but nothing I can't handle."

"And what about your arms? They're completely covered in tattoos," I state the obvious. "Did those hurt worse?"

"Jesus, is there any part of you that isn't so virtuous, Jude? Have you really been sheltered this much your entire life?" His questions catch me off guard. I'm not used to him speaking much past grunts and mumbles and definitely not about personal things. Usually, he's grouchy with random short answers, almost like he's attempting to get me to shut up and stop bothering him, but not now.

"Umm, well, I've seen stuff on TV and the internet before. I've read plenty of books, but if you're asking if I speak to people about these sorts of things regularly, then the answer would be no. The only other people like you, stop at the bar on the way through town. I don't go there, so you're my first."

He groans, and I frown. What now? I didn't say anything bad; I was just being real with him.

"And the drinking last night—you ever drink alcohol before, sweetheart?"

"My mom's never cared, so I've tried some of her lemonade flavored malts."

"Fuck! You mean Mike's Hard Lemonade?"

"Yes, that's the one."

"So, you've never been drunk before—like last night, ever?"

"Nope."

"Why not?" He moves his back in an impatient squirm once I stop touching his scars, so I continue to rub over his skin casually.

"I don't know how to make drinks taste sweet and yummy. Plus, I've never been around anyone I felt safe with if I was like that."

"And you did with Saint, of all people?"

"I do with you," I admit softly, loving that he hasn't made me stop touching him yet. "I know you wouldn't let anyone hurt me, Sinner."

"Motherfucker."

Huffing, I shoot a glare toward the back of his head. "What? I don't understand why any of this is a big deal."

He flips over so quickly my mouth drops open. How anyone can move that fast after a night of drinking is beyond me. He pounces, flattening me back against the bed, his body hovering over mine. He makes me feel so small, being near him like this, his body heat radiating toward me.

All I can do is remind myself to breathe in this position. I've daydreamed of him like this before, and to have him just like this, is enough to make my body tingle with need. I want to touch him everywhere and let him do the same in return.

"You don't know shit, little girl," he declares gruffly. Lowering his lips to linger above mine, mimicking his frame, he confesses, "I would be the one to hurt you. I'd be the one to fuck you until you couldn't handle it...I almost did, many times. Especially last night when you were fucking adorable, like a needy kitten."

Sinner's lips close over mine in a powerful kiss. His tongue dips into my mouth, forceful and full of desire. The weight of his body warms me, as he lowers his body to mine. Gripping my hair in one of his hands, he gives it a powerful tug, causing me to reward him with a moan.

His sturdy hips grind into mine, the perfect amount of pressure creating delicious friction where I've been craving him so desperately. He's more than anything I'd ever imagined, and he's merely just begun to touch me. A simple taste and yet I'm spiraling, ready to beg for him to never stop.

He kisses me hard, skilled in tormenting his prey. I love it and can barely breathe—my mind and body so frantic having him touching me like this. It's everything all wrapped up in a few movements of his mouth on mine, the surrendering, the owning, the claiming.

If I wasn't his before, I am now. I could never not want a man like him. No matter how hard I could ever endeavor, fighting against it...it's no use. He calls to me like a beacon in the night. I'm meant to belong to him.

He wrenches back barely enough to watch my face as he jerks my hair again, my mouth open as I pant lustfully after his touch. "You yearn for me to touch you, Jude. Your body fucking melts when my tongue traces it, begging me for more. Yet you let Saint have you too. Why?"

Hybrid Collection

"He said you wouldn't care. He promised you'd like it if I let him." My gaze shoots to the side, feeling a bit guilty, before admitting the rest. "I-I melted for him too."

"You think I want another man's fingers inside your pussy when even I haven't been there yet?"

His words have me shuddering, just imagining the way he'd feel in my core. "Oh God." A moan escapes as he bears down against my center. "I want you there."

My mind races, picturing his fingers inside me over and over making my panties soaked. "I would let you touch me if you wanted to, Sinner…Any time, any place," I finish breathily.

"Babe, you couldn't stop me if I wanted to play with your pussy," he promises, but it's not needed because I would never stand in his way. He'd be allowing me to live out the fantasies I've been having of him for months now.

I'd let him have every piece of me if he wanted. His hand hastily skirts down my side, pausing to rub the juncture between my thighs over my shorts. Sinner's mouth meets mine again, and I wrap my legs around his waist, praying for him to quench my thirst and go further.

Our kiss is interrupted by loud banging, and then his doors flying open.

"The fuck?" Sinner yells, glancing behind him at the intrusion.

"Brother." Saint comes in, uninvited. His curious gaze flicking over us, amused. "I thought I heard moaning." A grin eventually overtakes his mouth as his eyes seek out Sinner's hand between my legs.

My body warms even more, embarrassed that others could hear me but still thoroughly turned on. Sinner had me so wrapped up in him kissing me and his hands finally headed to where I wanted them that I wasn't paying any attention to how loud I was being. I wonder if anyone else heard moaning.

"I told you already," Sinner gripes. "She's mine. You need to leave."

"The fuck I do." His amusement drops, irritation overtaking, "We share bitches, remember? And she's not only yours."

"Y-you share them?" I stammer with a gasp from hearing him admit it aloud. Good Lord, no wonder Saint told me that Sinner would approve of it if I let him kiss me. They're friends, but this is taking it to another level entirely.

He chuckles while Sinner's body tightens in response, beating him to reply. "Of course we do, baby girl. You either please both your daddies or you get the boot." He winks playfully, and I gulp.

"Don't call me that, damn it." Sinner replies with a growl.

Saint ignores him, closing the door while wearing a triumphant grin. "You ever sucked a cock before, baby? Or two?" he inquires, and I nearly choke, not knowing what to say.

"Saaaint." Sinner draws the other man's name out, a warning in his tone.

"What?" He raises his hands. "I'm just asking questions; no harm there, brother."

Somehow, he doesn't seem as innocent as he's attempting to imply. I'd bet that he knows exactly what he's doing and is enjoying it immensely. Saint is far from stupid; he's too smart for his own good.

Sinner stares down at me, and I realize he's waiting for my answer as well. He clearly wants to know too. Shaking my head, I swallow again, attempting to speak, "I, uh...no. The answer to that would be a no."

Sinner leans back, putting more distance between us. "We can't do this, Saint." He shakes his head, rubbing his hand through his sleep tasseled hair.

"The hell we can't." He disagrees immediately as he approaches the bed, keeping me in his sights. "Jesus, baby." He licks his lips, and his eyes dance with anticipation. "We're gonna fucking ruin you for all other men."

Saint's so confident in his statement, I don't know if I should be excited or scared. I'm a little of both I think, but mostly turned on so freaking much that I feel like my body may explode if it doesn't get some sort of attention from the two. If we'd had a few seconds more, Sinner would've had me satisfied with his tongue and dirty words alone. Add in Saint, and there's no telling what they'd do to me. Or the amount of pleasure I'd receive.

"We aren't doing shit to her right now, Saint. We need to give her a chance to think through all this and what it entails exactly."

He scoffs. "You have to be joking. What the fuck is wrong with you, Sin? She's ripe and fucking ready, brother. Let's break her in already."

Sinner sweetly lifts the covers over me some more, tucking them around my breasts before replying, "I told you." He stares into my eyes as he speaks. "She's innocent, and she's...different."

Pretty sure my heart flops over and surrenders to him with that proclamation. Different good, I hope.

"Fuck it, fine!" Saint declares, rolling his eyes. "But if she's not sucking my cock soon, then you will be."

Sinner nods, agreeing, and that surprises me even more.

"Now that's settled, let's get baby girl fed. You two stay in that bed any longer, and I'll be in it next, and I won't be kind enough to keep my clothes on."

CHAPTER 6

Sinner

The situation's not ideal, but it buys me some time, and it keeps Saint from killing her. I can't believe I agreed to us sharing her, but I don't have much of a choice in the matter. He was telling the truth about us always sharing the women before. Sure, we've had sex with chicks on our own, but it's never gotten down to this, where we're fighting over a damn woman.

We make sure Jude has plenty to eat before Viking calls us into Church. Saint takes the seat next to me, per our usual. I'm still pissed and confused about what the hell to do, but I keep my mouth shut, ready to handle club stuff.

"Brothers, Oath Keepers... Let's take care of business," Viking begins, and the gavel slams down, officially marking the start of Church. "First up, this Mafiya shit storm brought on by our thoughtful brother."

I can't help but sigh as he looks to Spider. This shit storm is Saint's fault, and that pretty much makes it mine as well for not having him on a tighter leash. "Spidey, what went down with Masters?"

Spider shrugs. "Honestly, he was fine. Unless he can put up a front like no other, I'd say he was more entertained than anything."

"He's going to let it go, just like that?" Prez's brow furrows.

"Yeah, pretty sure there will be no blowback. He said that he's familiar with the club's ties to his cousins and that he appreciates our previous business venture."

"Mexico," Viking supplies with a huff.

Hybrid Collection

"Yeah," Spider agrees. "My guess would be that it bought Saint a free pass." His scrutiny falls on my brother beside me. Saint chuckles in return, amused by it all, but refrains from commenting, thankfully. I'm sure his two cents would only spur on more drama.

Viking frowns. "Not too funny, brother. You could've fucked us, and that's the last thing we need after dealin' with the Fists. We still haven't found out where they're holding shop this time around either. We don't need a new beef with anyone."

Fucking Iron Fists—it seems like they're always around fucking with the Oath Keepers somehow. First, it was with the other charter of ours and them discovering the Fists kidnapping women. Then Twist's ol' lady having ties to their club and her ex, Ghost, showing up for retaliation and us torching their club in California to send a message.

Then there's the latest in that whole mess of them showing up to kidnap Nightmare's kid, and finally finding a shred of peace. It was all thanks to Twist's oldest son, Cyle, being the grandson of Puppet, the President of the Iron Fists. It's been a total shitshow that I'm grateful has chilled the hell out for a minute.

We've lost too many members going back and forth with them. Bronx was just a damn kid, and they slaughtered his ass, pulling the guts straight out of his dead corpse. They killed our other brother, Scot. That man was a father figure to a few in the club. Then there were others from our sister charter as well.

Our compound was left unprotected, with half of us on the run up north and the other half on their way to find the Fists' makeshift clubhouse. Blaze was pummeled within an inch of his life. We think the Fists believed him to be dead, and that's how he ended up surviving. Princess and Bethany were beaten to shit, left alive to deliver the Iron Fists' message to the club. And worst of all, we couldn't kill them to get a bit of justice when it all came to light.

The whole situation leaves a bad taste in my mouth. The last thing we need now is to start a new war with a longtime ally, the Russians. We can't afford to lose more club members, more family.

I especially don't want Jude around here if we're constantly watching our backs. It's one of the main reasons I never considered having a woman in my life for good. She's a liability, and with Saint, he's like me. I don't have to worry about him like I would with a female. If someone were to hurt her, I would go off the deep end. I know it.

Hell, Viking and Nightmare both lost their shit when their women were injured due to MC business. That's never been my thing, wanting someone to belong to me like they have with their ol' ladies. But Jude...she has me thinking about things I never thought possible.

"The keys were in it." Saint defends eventually, growing defensive, from everyone's mocking glares. "Half of you fuckers would've considered taking it to a chop shop. I only took it for a spin," he huffs with a shrug.

I can't help but grin. It's true; a few of us would've called an old buddy up for some easy cash. Saint does that shit pretty frequently. It gives him a rush, and he makes money from rich fuckers. It's not right, but we never said we were good men. There are plenty of other things out there that're much worse that we could be doing.

"No," Vike rumbles. "We aren't NOMADS anymore; we need to coexist with the people in town. If we mind our own business and leave shit alone, they'll leave us alone in return. We've been fortunate having the other club near; the civilians don't look twice at us. You start boosting cars and shit that close to home, we'll be in jail quicker than we'd like."

His gaze hits Torch for a second, but it's long enough for most of us to notice. There have been a few rumors about Torch doing some time floating around. How true they are, I'll never know. I'm not the type to delve into other people's business, even if I am curious.

"Fine." Saint sulks, irritated with the Prez's lack of enthusiasm. What can he expect, though? It's Viking's responsibility to keep things running smoothly. Saint's problem is he's not used to living by any rules. None of us really are.

Hybrid Collection

"Sinner." The boss turns his regard on me next. "Who's this bitch to you, and why were you flipping your shit in the parking lot over her?"

Saint snickers, coaxing a growl from me aimed in his direction.

"Her name's Jude." Swallowing, I admit the truth, "She's the one I've been going off to visit this entire time."

Saint's eyes grow wide, "Hold the fuck up," he interrupts, his scowl pointed toward the Prez. "You knew where Sin was going all along?"

Viking grimaces and nods at him. Looking back to me, he asks, "Now, she's here...why?"

I can hear Saint breathing heavy beside me. He sounds like a bull, thoroughly pissed off by the newest bit of information. I'm guessing he thought I was keeping it a secret from everyone, but it was only him. Not that the others knew about her either, but it wouldn't have been a big deal if they'd found out. None of them cares like he does.

"Not by my choice, Prez. I was planning on talkin' to you about Princess maybe helping her out to come up with some sort of plan. Her mom split and left her out in the cold. I've been making sure she's got shit to eat and a place to live. She's a real good girl, taking college classes online, trying to get her future figured out."

"She's young," Torch speaks up, unhelpfully and Smokey grunts in agreement.

"You think I can't see that?" I retorted, glaring at him.

"All I'm saying is, it's fucked up her mom popped smoke and all, but is she even old enough to be in the club? Not looking to go to jail for a minor, brother."

I have to respect that, but for a second, I thought Torch was implying that I'm fucking a minor. Maybe he really did take a visit to jail at some point and is trying to watch his ass instead of doing a repeat.

"She's eighteen," I confirm, and Exterminator, one of the NOMADs, lets out a low whistle.

"Damn near jailbait," he comments as if I don't already know that. Her age is one thing that's been holding me back from her for months. Had she been thirty, my cock would've already been buried in her pussy the first night I laid eyes on her.

"She knows you buried her momma?" Saint asks, wearing a smug sneer while divulging my big secret to the table.

"How the fuck do *you* know that?" My eyes shoot to his, anger rising in my chest. Jude can't find out. Her mom may have been shit, but she doesn't need to know she's dead.

"Goddamn it." Viking's palm slams on the table. The sound echoing throughout the room like a clap of thunder, "Is he telling the truth, Sinner? Did you kill the bitch?"

"Yes, I did. It was an accident." I lie. I did it on purpose, but denial is going to save me with this one. I'll deny it to my grave if Jude ever suspects too.

"How the fuck is killing a bitch an accident?" Everyone's scrutiny falls to me, waiting for me to answer our President. I guess he's not buying it.

Fuck, fuck, fuck.

This wasn't supposed to come out like this. I needed to hash it out with Viking privately. I get it. These are my brothers, and we don't keep fuck-all from each other, but I'm lost with this shit. I value his opinion and wanted it firsthand. He'd know what to do or at least help me figure it out.

"She was on something, tripping hard and came after me. This was after I'd met her kid and was trying to get her to agree to an annulment," I declare, the revelation slipping without thought and Saint stands, his chair crashing to the floor behind him.

"You married the fucking cunt?" he bellows, rage beating down on me from his gape.

"It's not like that, Saint," I backtrack, making an effort to placate him, "I was fucked up when she got me to agree to anything."

Hybrid Collection

"Excuses!" he shouts.

I can only gape, scrambling to come up with something to say.

"After everything...after everything I've done for you. I fucking loved you; you were mine," he finishes, fishing his favorite blade free from his side pocket. Thank God he's not near his beloved machete. With a twist of his wrist the blade gleams, the sharp metal exposed and ready to do its damage.

"Calm down, brother." Viking jumps to his feet, the others hurrying to follow suit.

"Don't tell me to calm the fuck down. Sinner belongs to me." Saint's voice warps, going dark; I've never seen him so irate before. "I'll show you what happens to those who betray me."

Everyone springs into action as he lunges for me. I'm in shock. Never in a million years did I expect him, of all people, to turn on me. My body remains rooted in place as his hand grows near, connecting before I can blink or process what he's doing.

He's never hurt me in anyway before, always playing the savior when I've been in trouble. He's killed many in our time together, but not an ounce of that menace was pointed in my direction. He's forever been my Saint—my lifeline in a sense.

It takes a moment for me to register what he's done, my heart breaking into a million shreds with the outcome. "You stabbed me," I utter brokenly, shaken to my very core that he'd ever harm me in any way.

"You made me do it," he proclaims as brothers wrench him away from me, separating us as much as the small room will allow.

"H-how is this my fault?" Gasping, my throat grows tight as the pain strikes me not where the gash is, but straight in my heart.

"You touched her, you married her, and you forgot who you belong to," Saint retorts, shaking his head. He's convinced that I fucking deserve this. In his mind, I'm guilty, and he's punishing me for it.

"No, Saint." My palm covers my side, growing slick with my own blood. Pausing, I try to collect my thoughts, everything a bit hazy.

Swallowing, I continue. "I never forgot. I killed her for you. She wouldn't agree… Sh-she tried to keep me, so I killed her…for you." Finishing, I grow weak.

Glancing at my rib area, there's so much blood. My hand's coated in the thick merlot liquid, my adrenaline draining away at the same time. It wouldn't mean much in any other situation, but it belongs to me.

My eye's close just as I hear our Prez. "Oh fuck, somebody catch him! Call 2 Piece now; we need him sewn up," he orders and a wounded scream like no other escapes Saint as he fights against our brothers. Everything grows silent as the compassion of passing out finally sets in against the blood loss and my broken heart.

Saint

Sinner's eyes close, and he tumbles out of his chair—unresponsive—and the reality of what I've done sets in. I didn't aim for an area that would kill him, but to see him drop like a sack of potatoes has my stomach dropping and my mind going wild with ideas. "Do something!" I shout as the brothers pin me up against a wall, keeping me away from him.

A fist flies into my stomach, but it does nothing to slow me down. I've got too much adrenaline coursing through my body. My head slams into Torch, busting his nose wide open and blood sprays over my face. This time a fist coming from him hits my temple with enough force that I'm out for the count, like a kid taking his first dose of Benadryl.

Hybrid Collection

CHAPTER 7

Softness is not weakness. It takes courage

to stay delicate in a world this cruel.

- Beau Taplin

Jude

I'm sitting at the picnic table out back soaking up some sunshine and sipping on lemonade when a gorgeous woman approaches me. She's nothing like the skanky looking females I've noticed scattered around the club who hang on a few of Saint and Sinner's brothers. Her hair's in a ponytail; it's blonde and reaches the top of her butt. She wears a perfect smile as she gets closer, and I take in her short, black leather shorts, white wife-beater tank top, and matching white Chucks.

"Hey," she greets and sits across from me. "You must be Jude."

"Yes, ma'am." I nod and smile in return. Me calling her ma'am brings out a giggle in return.

"Please, the last ma'am was my mom. I'm Princess."

"Your name is Princess, or do you get a nickname like everyone else?" Does she ride a motorcycle too? She looks like a different type of woman compared to the other females around here, and I wouldn't put it past her owning her own bike.

"No, my name is actually Princess. The only nickname anyone here has given me is the Ice Queen and Cinderella." She turns, throwing a thumb toward the back of her shirt, wanting me to read it.

"Viking's Property?" I read aloud, the words coming out as a question and she faces me again with a nod. She's pleased about it, obviously.

"Yep, that's my ol' man."

"Wait, the big, Nordic looking guy who slammed Saint on the hood yesterday?"

She snickers. "That sounds like him, so I'm going to go with yes. He's my husband and the President of the club."

"Oh wow, how does he not scare you? The guy is massive." My honesty pours from my lips, not used to censoring what I have to say around others.

She sighs, her eyes growing all dreamy. "I think it's hot. He goes all barbarian on me sometimes, and I love it."

I can understand, the bad boy vibe is definitely alluring. I have it myself for both Saint and Sinner, and I suppose they come off as frightening to some people as well.

"So, are you here with Saint, then, or Sinner? My ol' man wasn't sure which one when he gave me the CliffsNotes version of you."

"Well, Saint drove me here, but then Sinner made me sleep in his bed, so…" I shrug, not having a clue how to answer her the correct way. I probably sound like a whore admitting I'm kind of here for them both.

Her smile brightens again, flashing straight white teeth, "They've never brought anyone home before," she divulges. "I was curious about you." She scans over me from my hair down to my lemonade. "You're a bit young for them from what I've heard, but you're also blunt. I like that."

Shrugging, I take another drink. I've never been any other way. I'm glad to finally meet someone around here that seems to be friendly. The guys haven't spoken to me much, and the skanky chicks just frown my way.

"Oh!" She reaches around pulling something free from her back pocket. She holds up a pair of black flip flops. "These are for you. I almost forgot. Viking said you didn't have shoes with you."

"Thank you so much. I've been wearing a pair of socks, but it's felt kind of awkward. Maybe that's why the women around here have been so blatantly scowling each time I walk by."

"No, sweetie, those bitches are just jealous. That's why they're rude and give you dirty looks. You possess something they desire and can't get, so you have to put them in their place right away."

"What could I have? They're surrounded by guys! And besides, I'm just me." I point to myself and make a goofy face.

"Yeah. However, you just showed up with not one of the brothers, but two. Members are dropping like flies around here, coming home with ol' ladies. When that happens, the club sluts are less and less needed around here, and they become more possessive in return. I look forward to the day that the majority of the members have a steady woman in their lives."

"Club sluts?"

"Yep, the hoes trying to land on the back of a brother's bike, and in your case, the hateful stares you've been receiving."

"That's kind of harsh, don't you think?"

"No. In fact, you'll learn quickly that they don't give two shits about you at all. They want your man, and they'll do what they can to replace you. If I remember correctly there's one here that has had her eyes set on Saint and Sinner."

"Lovely."

She sighs and continues. "I try not to pay too much attention to which chicks they're sleeping around with and just concentrate on Viking. He keeps me plenty busy."

"She wants them both?" I don't know why, but that thought pisses me off. She's greedy, trying to have two men—the specific I'm here with. I'd have no idea either if it wasn't for Princess letting me know. The guys never would've mentioned it, I'm sure.

She nods. "Keep an eye out for Cherry. You're young, so she'll try to push her weight around with you. Just remember she's irrelevant to the guys, just a piece of easy ass. Honey's not much better, either."

What the hell is up with these names? Honey and Cherry? Is there a Blueberry and Syrup running around some place also? Geez, they make my name sound so plain in comparison. Jude, just boring old Jude...

"Wow. I appreciate the heads-up, Princess."

She grins. "No problem. I'm happy about them going. Less shit I have to deal with. Odin's bad enough. So, have the boys claimed you yet?"

"I'll be honest here; I don't know what you mean."

"Then it hasn't happened. Trust me; you'll know when it does." She winks and the back door slams open.

The bartender, Blaze, comes outside, huffing with blood spray on his shirt. "Oh, good. Viking was just asking about you." He pins his gaze on Princess.

"Me? Is he okay?" She's a lot calmer than I'd be. If someone came searching for me with blood on their shirt, I'd probably freak out.

"He's fine, it's..." He quiets, with a sidelong glance in my direction. I'm guessing he can't say with me sitting here. That's fine; I have no desire to know their business, especially with blood obviously involved in some way.

"I see. Do you need my help or? Are you the one bleeding, Blaze?"

"Everything's straight, 2 Piece should be here anytime. This is from Torch, but he's fine too. Maybe hang out and keep Jude company since we're busy?"

"Yeah, that's no problem. Are you going to be behind the bar?"

He shrugs, disappearing with a slam of the massive back door.

"That was weird," I mutter.

"Guess they're going to take longer than usual. Want to get a drink? If he's not in there, I can make us a mean margarita."

I have no idea what that is, but hopefully, it's good and doesn't make me sick in the morning again. "Okay."

"Bethany, my best friend should be here soon too. She's dropping her son off with the babysitter so some girl time will be fun."

"Should we be worried about that guy bleeding?" I gesture toward the closed door.

"Nah," She waves it off. "They'll take care of it; that's what 2 Piece is for. Plus, they don't like women getting involved with their club business. It's best if we just make a few pitchers and relax."

"A few pitchers?" My voice is weary at the amount that implies.

"Hell yeah, lady. I'm telling you, I make 'em good." She grins triumphantly and climbs to her feet.

Following suit, I grab my lemonade glass and silently pray that whatever she's planning on making isn't too sweet. I was nauseous until I ate with the guys earlier, and I'm not looking forward to that happening again. I hope Bethany's as friendly as Princess too. I could get used to being around them if they're both always like this.

"And then, I punched her!" Bethany hoots, nearly falling over on her barstool. She's funny and outspoken, not like the women I've been around at home. They're boring compared to these two.

I take another gulp of the sweet and tangy concoction as Princess giggles. "It was so great; the scream Honey let out, you'd think she was dying."

"You actually walked up to the woman and just hit her?" My mouth nearly falls open, and Bethany nods.

"Pretty much, but that was after I laid one hell of a kiss on my man."

Princess leans forward a bit over the round, counter-height table between us, "I told you, Jude, you have to stake your claim and let these hoes know that you mean business. Once you stand up to them, they wiggle their way back into the cracks they seeped out of."

"I'm not sure Sinner would be thrilled if I punched someone." I rationalize. "But Saint probably wouldn't care."

"Saint would probably jizz in his pants," Bethany snorts and then downs half her glass.

"I don't actually know how to hit someone though," I admit after a moment, staring down at the black painted table top.

"I can teach you," Princess offers with a wink and a smile full of mischief.

I don't know if I've stumbled upon trouble or two of the best types of friends I could've wished for.

"How long do you think it's been since the guys went to Church?" I glance around, noticing a few of them in the bar drinking as well. They weren't here when we first sat down, the place was empty. Princess and Bethany had to school me on the concept of biker church too. I still don't understand why they call it that, but whatever.

"They should be done soon." Bethany glances at Princess. "Right, P?"

"It's been a few hours, so they should be fine by now. I'm sure someone would've said something if that wasn't the case."

Hybrid Collection

"Jesus, the time has flown by," I mutter, as Saint finally comes walking toward me. "Oh, Saint! Are you guys all done?"

He flashes a sad smile. "Yeah, baby girl, I think so."

"So, isn't that a good thing?" I thought church was where they discussed the important club stuff, or at least that's what the ol' ladies told me.

"Not in this case." He grabs my glass and chugs the rest of my margarita then refills it. "You havin' a good time with these troublemakers?"

"Yeah, they're a lot nicer than the other women around here."

"Yeah. We need to talk."

"Okay…?"

He grips my arm with one hand and the glass with the other. "Ladies, we'll be back." He leans in closer. "Can you walk all right?"

"I feel fine." I wave him off, climbing down from my seat and attempt to stand.

My hand shoots to the table to steady myself. "Oh my God, those drinks did not seem that strong!"

The girls laugh at me, and Saint tucks me in closer, slipping his arm around my waist. "I got you; let's go to my room for a bit."

It takes longer than usual with my wobbly strides, but eventually, we make it. He lets me plop down on his bed, the fluffy mattress a welcome sight.

"Where's Sinner?"

"He…uh…he's resting."

"That sounds so nice right now; maybe we should go to his room instead. We could all take a nap."

"Not yet." He shakes his head and sits so close the entire side of my body presses against his. With the alcohol helping me relax, all I can think about is these two finally having their way with me.

"I feel good, Saint. We could get naked like you mentioned earlier."

A surprised chuckle falls from his lips, and he presses them to my forehead, leaving behind a soft, chaste kiss. "I like you drunk, baby; you're fun."

"Why do you call me that?" I mumble, lying back against his fluffy, sangria colored comforter. My shirt rides up, stopping just underneath my breasts and exposing my stomach as I rest my arms above my head.

"Fuck, you're one sexy bitch," he growls, crawling farther onto the bed, resting beside me. His fingertip draws a line from the top of my shorts, over my bellybutton and stops at the juncture between my breasts. I hold my breath the entire time, relishing in the sensation.

"Baby girl?" he asks, and I hum in response. "Because you're the youngest Sinner's ever had any interest in and hearing you call him daddy, kinda cemented it in place."

"I like it," I admit and yawn, the alcohol stupor overtaking my brain.

"Yeah?" His voice grows near as his lips find my neck, licking and nipping like he did before.

"Mmm, I like that too—more than the nickname."

He chuckles; the sound is raspy against my skin. "I was wondering why he found you interesting, but I think I get it now." His hand spreads, resting under my breast. It's enough to make me squirm, wanting him to touch me there. My nipples silently beg for his attention.

"Why?" My voice is breathless with the anticipation.

"Because, baby, you're perfect for us. You are for both of us."

Hybrid Collection

"Even you?" I can't help but repeat. I know he just said it, but my foggy mind needs to hear him say it again. It'll mean more if he repeats it.

I've barely met the man, but I've learned so much in a very little time. Sinner cares for him like no other, and he's special to me...so that means Saint is part of it too. These guys are a packaged deal if I want one. I need to want the other as well.

"Yeah sugar, even me. I was thinking about killin' ya when I found out about you."

I find myself sputtering and attempting to sit up with the alcohol causing my head to spin a bit with the quick movement. I don't get far though as his large hand pushes me backward, flat against the bed. His statement has me reeling, who says stuff like that?

"Calm yourself. I said I *was*. I don't want to anymore." He complains as if it should make me relax. The man was going to freaking murder me!

"B-but your name is Saint! How can you execute someone with that name?"

He snickers to himself over some private joke while pecking my forehead. "So fucking cute, baby."

Saint shakes his head, charmed with my outburst. "I do what I want. Sin gave me that name a long time ago, but that's a story for another time. He can tell it if he wants to."

"Can we go see him now?" Being around Sinner may make my nerves calm down a bit. I have a self-proclaimed assassin beside me right now; I need time to process everything.

He says he won't hurt me, but can I trust him? He's acted a bit senseless ever since I met him. I'd chalked it up to him having the bad boy allure. Clearly, my vision was skewed just a touch.

"Not yet."

"He won't mind if I wake him up, I promise."

"We have to let him get up on his own." He shoots me down.

"Why? I've never waited before." It's true too; every time he's visited, I've woken him up. Somedays on purpose, others on accident; regardless, he was never upset about it.

"Because he's been hurt. Now, how about you take a nap or let me get you naked?" His palm skims lower, dipping just under my waistband. It's distracting, even after his little truth telling session.

There's the attraction of him informing me that he wanted to kill me. It's sickening for me to be enticed by a man capable of such things, but for some ungodly reason, it makes me yearn for him even more. I guess I'm being tempted by the forbidden fruit in a sense. The edge and mystery of divulging further into the unknown has me nearly ready to beg him to touch me.

Even through those thoughts, there's still one thing at the front of my mind. "Saint, I want you, don't get me wrong," I admit. I meet his intense gaze and then stop his hand from traveling any lower. "But what happened to Sinner?"

He sulks. "I may have stabbed him." He comes clean finally with me asking him the direct question, and this time I do sit up in a flash, completely stunned.

My hands go wild slapping all over his chest. It does the opposite though. I want to hurt him, but instead, he chokes out a surprised laugh and catches my hands. He's stronger than he appears, his grip like a vice. I'm nowhere near a match for him physically.

"Holy shit!" I shriek, and he tackles me, laying over me to keep my body still. I've never had someone subdue me like this before.

"Hush up."

The adrenaline kicks in, sobering me up a bit and I warn him, "I'll scream, and I'll kick you in the nuts!"

"And I'll slit your fuckin' throat, now shut it," he promises, his breath skirting over my lips.

Hybrid Collection

I don't know if it's the fear or what, but my body vibrates in a way I never imagined possible. He's dangerous and controlling and nothing like any man I've met in the past. None of them had any balls compared to Saint; he truly is the real deal in terms of a bad boy. Clearly, the motorcycle and the I-don't-give-a-fuck façade is not a front.

Is this why my mother was always chasing after the guys she'd find? Was it the danger or the possibility of the unknown? Was she seeking an adventure like me? After this shaky, insane feeling that courses through your veins in the face of madness? It's addicting.

A frustrated, girly growl bubbles up, and I shoot forward, biting the shit out of his chin. He's provoked me to the point of losing control. This isn't me. I don't bite people, but Saint...he pushes me, tests my limits.

"Ah!" His eyes widen as the opaque irises darken to a shade resembling graphite. I don't know what it means, but somehow, I don't think it's a good thing. My heart rate spikes, even though you'd think it's not possible with everything happening so fast already.

He breaks free from my mouth and dips his face. Pain explodes in my shoulder as his teeth tear into my flesh. I let loose a piercing cry, gasping for breath afterward. The only defense I have is to drag my short nails down his biceps and scream.

He rasps a warning against my ear after he releases his bite. "Be careful what you wish for, baby. You give pain, you get pain in return."

Tears drip down my cheeks as I release my grip and whisper, begging, "Please?"

He draws back a bit, using his thumbs to wipe my cheeks. Saint's touch is back to being tender, and it confuses me. One thing is for certain; I'm sober now—that's for damn sure.

My scared gaze finds his as I plead, "Please don't hurt me." I sound so weak, but he easily overpowers me. I have no doubt he could really torment me if he desired to do so.

"Shh, precious," he murmurs, wiping my cheeks again. He bends, dropping a gentle kiss on my forehead. "I mean it; you play nice, I do to."

Swallowing, I nod and attempt to think. I don't know what to do. "So, umm, Sinner will be okay, then?" The faster he's better, the sooner I can let him know about this.

"Yeah, he's straight. 2 Piece came and sewed him up. I would never really hurt him; you need to believe that."

"Then why did you st-stab him?" I stammer, still a bit unsure what exactly to say. I want the truth from him directly, without him omitting anything important.

"Because I found out he married your momma. Sinner belongs to me; he always has. He betrayed me, marrying her."

"But it was fake. She wanted drugs and thought he'd get them for her. He told her he wanted an annulment. I remember listening to them fight about it."

He thinks it over, carefully rubbing around the spot he bit. "I know it was fake, baby. He told me that afterwards" He dips his head again, placing tiny kisses all around the mark he's left behind.

"And me? Am I a threat to you? Or do you realize I have no part in that?"

"I thought so when I found out aboutcha. Like I said, I was going to kill you. But he was right, you're innocent in this. I can't hold you responsible for his fuck up. Plus, I don't want to have to hurt you. It's not you who's done this to me, it's him."

I swallow, my throat feeling dry as a desert at his revelation. "That makes me sad that you'd ever want to take my life."

"You're safe now, from me and from anyone else. I won't let anything happen to you." The pad of his thumb trails over my nipple closest to the shoulder he just kissed.

The promise is less than reassuring. I fully believe him at this point about his threat to kill me if I don't chill out. The killing was not the metaphorical type I'm guessing.

Hybrid Collection

Now if I can trust him not to hurt me, that's an entirely different thing. He is no doubt a bit unstable.

Why Sinner loves him so much is the real question. Like I said before, I know to possess one, I have to want the other. Can I forgive Saint for scaring me like this enough to want him the same way I do Sinner? Can I forgive him for injuring the man I've already fallen for?

CHAPTER 8

Sinner

My side aches; shooting pain greets me as I come to. I must've passed out when shit hit the fan with Saint. Jesus, what a catastrophe. I hope no one killed him. Knowing Saint, I wasn't the only one injured in his outburst, either. It won't surprise me if there are two or three other brothers with stiches somewhere on their body as well.

Glancing around, I find myself in my own bed and alone. My side's bandaged up, nice and neat with a lump of white gauze secured with medical tape. 2 Piece must've stopped by and fixed me up; it looks like his work. Thank God that guy's close to us and on call whenever anyone needs him; we'd be fucked, if not.

My bed's comfortable, the room at the perfect temperature, yet all I can think of is what went down in Church. Also, where did Jude end up? I hope she didn't see me out of it and freak. Worrying about Saint losing it is bad enough—add another person to the mix, and it gets even more complicated.

Saint went flipping psycho earlier. I knew he'd be pissed if he ever found out, but not violent with me. I figured for sure he'd try killing my ex or Jude...but it was me he went after in the end. I can only imagine how it would've turned out if he'd have found out sooner and the brothers wouldn't have been around to stop him in his rage.

The sound of the cry he'd let out as I'd drifted off, was haunting. I think he finally realized what he'd done once he was pulled away and there was distance between us. And that fucking knife...when I'm feeling better, I'm torching that damn thing until it melts down to nothing. He'll never touch that blade again.

Hybrid Collection

And now, here I am left to wonder what the fuck happened afterward. If I move, I'll probably bust a stitch or two, but that's never stopped me before. I need to find out if Saint's dead first off, and then check on Jude. If she found out what happened, she's probably traumatized. And if my brother's dead, then I'll be dealing with whoever dealt the final blow.

This mess wasn't any of the club's business, but with Saint bringing Jude here, he made it theirs. It would've been much easier for me to break it to him slowly without Jude in the mix, but he somehow found out about her mom regardless. It probably doesn't make sense to some why I'd seek an annulment. But if I pretend I don't know where she is, then it won't look so suspicious if the cops were to overturn any evidence. Sounds fucked up, but it's the only way I can think to stay out of prison.

That's another reason why I've been fighting myself to stay away from Jude. I fucking killed her mother. And the worst of it all is that I didn't even care. The only worries I had was to not get locked up because of it.

I had to make sure Jude was taken care of too. Without her mother there to help her pay bills and what not, she needed me. I keep reminding myself that the chick could've starved had I not kept coming around. Saint should see that eventually...one can hope anyhow.

And yet I find myself hung up on her ass way more than I ought to be. Each time I'd go for a visit, I'd swear to myself it'd be my last time there. I had to get a plan together in order to cut ties. We can see how that worked out for me.

Obviously, it wasn't soon enough if Saint was able to see through my excuses. The other brothers never asked where I was going. Hell, they'd have been mind fucked if they had. I answer to no one except the Prez and occasionally Saint.

Slowly jostling my body, I move to sit myself up, getting met with more stabbing pain. It quickly reminds me of my wound and the importance to let it heal. I hate this shit. I don't do well having injuries, it reminds me too much of when I was younger.

Saint is nothing like my father though. He's never hurt me like this before. I wouldn't have stuck around in the past if he had.

Slowly standing to my feet, I grit my teeth as the skin on my stomach stretches out again.

Fucking shit. Thank God I was out when he sewed me up, that shit would've sucked if not.

Blowing a deep breath free, I curse a few times and take my time heading out my door. Saint's room is next to mine, so I don't have to go far to search for him. I find his door unlocked, so I enter without knocking, as we always do.

"The fuck?"

He has Jude in his bed, and he's lying on top of her. Thankfully they both have clothes on still. I'm injured, and he's working to get in her pants. Can't say I'm amused in the slightest. He has some nerve, that's for sure.

"Brother!" Saint gapes and leaps up, coming toward me, and I cringe holding my arm up between us.

His expression falls seeing me react to him as if I'm frightened. I'm not. I'm just sore and a little confused on how he's feeling and why Jude's in bed with him. Is he still furious from before, or has he calmed down enough to talk?

"You okay?" I ask, seeking her out, my gaze trailing over her swiftly.

Her eyes fill with tears, but she nods.

"You hurt her too?" I question Saint, watching him look like his usual self. Well, minus the bite mark on his chin and his swollen temple. That must've hurt. Can't say I mind him being a little fucked up, though, after what he did to me.

"Nah, the bitch bit me, so I bit her back." He motions in Jude's direction and a rumble of irritation takes over my chest.

"If she bit you, you should've left her the fuck alone."

Hybrid Collection

"I was tryin' to be straight with her, and she flipped out."

With a scoff, I tell Jude, "Come on, you're coming to my room."

She peers over at Saint, unsure of what to do, and it pisses me off. Jude was mine first. She was all for me before she even knew Saint existed. Now a few days with the brother and she's giving a fuck what he has to say?

"Now, Jude." I drop the order, no room for argument in my voice, and she hops up, doing as she's told.

She passes in front of Saint, and he snatches her arm, not letting her go. "Not so fast. We need to talk, Sin." His movements have the tension radiating from me. I'm not in the mood for any more of his shit today.

"Let her the fuck go."

"Not until we get some things straightened out. She won't go anywhere."

"I'm not discussing this in front of her, and she's sleeping in my bed tonight."

"It's fine, Sinner. I can wait." She stares at me longingly and fuck if I can't wait to get my hands on her.

Just touching her will make me feel better, I know it. I'm taking her to my room, and she can lie next to me, dragging her fingers all over my flesh like she did this morning before any of this went down. Maybe for a small amount of time, she can forget and just relax.

"See brother, she's all right. Now why in the fuck did you pull some shady shit like that?"

"I told you, Saint, I was trashed. Part of me is even considering that she could've fucking drugged me. I don't remember anything but waking up and seeing the damn marriage certificate. I didn't believe it was real until I spoke to the lawyer. Like I said, I wanted it reversed immediately."

"Hmm." He snorts, and Jude places her hand over his.

"I wouldn't doubt it, Saint. My mom is not a decent woman. She was with a lot of guys always trying to get what she could out of them. I can't say I'd be surprised if she ended up in a ditch somewhere because of it. Please don't take her plotting out on Sinner."

His grin warps into a wicked smile as he gazes down at her. "Oh yeah, dead? That so, baby?"

"Don't, Saint!" I order, and his silver irises fly back to me.

"Fine," he huffs. "You want me to stop, Sin? Then you better figure out a way for this whole thing to work." His finger moves in a circle, motioning to the three of us. Of all things for him to demand, I wasn't expecting him to even consider the three of us being anything together.

I'm flabbergasted he's seriously going to blackmail me right now. Over Jude, a woman he's barely met, yet he's willing to go this far for her after being angry at me for wanting her. "Seriously, Saint? Since when do you want to have just one chick in your bed?" I don't want to hurt her with this, but I can't stop the truth from breaking free.

He shrugs, placing a kiss on Jude's forehead and surprises the shit out of me. "Since you." He peers down at Jude, mumbling, "Since her."

He finally releases her arm, letting her come to me, his gaze humble. "I know it's the only way to have you forever. I'm not willing to give you up, Sinner, so I'll share you."

Jude wraps her arms around me, and I draw in a deep breath, the ping of pain not so welcome, even if her embrace is comforting. "Easy, my side is fucked." I heard him, but having her in my arms is enough to momentarily distract me from the seriousness of his proclamation.

"Oh no, I'm sorry." She wrenches back, worrying as she checks me over. "Are you sure you're all right?"

Hybrid Collection

"I am." Drawing her back, this time against my good side, I breathe in her clean smelling hair. I'm so much better with her here, like this. Running my nose down her temple, I whisper, "I want you to come lay with me."

"Okay."

"Saint...are you hurt?" I ask as he comes up to me as well. He stares at me with so much in his gaze, like he's trying to see straight into my soul. I'm still upset, but I want to make sure he's all right. He may have hurt me, but I'll always love him.

He shakes his head. "Nah, I'm fine. Deserved it after what I did to you," he admits, brushing his nose against mine softly—stealing my breath with the move. He's not always hard and temperamental; sometimes he's gentle. "Take it easy, Sin, I'm hitting the bar."

Swallowing, I rest my arm over Jude's shoulder, letting her take on some of my weight. I was stabbed, but yet I feel exhausted as if I ran a marathon. Not that I know what that would feel like, but I can guess. It's most likely from my adrenaline spiking then falling like it did. "I'll be in bed then."

He grunts, knowing it's an invitation for when he's had his fill of liquor. He rarely sleeps if he's left alone. I hate knowing he's in here awake by himself, thinking about a million things and driving himself crazy. It's comforting to have him beside me, sleeping peacefully. Plus, it helps chase away my own restlessness.

We make it back to my bed, and Jude lies down beside me. My body has a chance to relax again and in doing so realizes a woman is up against it. My cock begs to have some fun, but the chance to rest calls to me stronger. She snuggles deeper in to my side, and I sigh, content for the moment.

"Sinner?"

"Yeah?"

"Do you think Saint will kill me?"

"Not while I'm still breathing." My eyes snap back open at her question. Just what the fuck did he do to her while I wasn't around? "What did he say to you?" He was clearly on a roll today, Christ.

She leans up, half on my chest so she can meet my questioning gaze. "He said that he was going to kill me, but he's changed his mind now." Her shoulders lift, her gaze unsure. "I don't feel unsafe around him though. He'll get upset about something, but then when he calms down, he's really sweet to me."

A relieved breath leaves my lungs as I muster up a grin for her. "Then you'll be fine, sweetheart. That's how Saint is when he's comfortable with someone. Besides, what he was implying just a second ago wasn't that we kill you."

"What exactly was he implying?"

"That we keep you." I bring her hand to my mouth, placing a soft kiss on her knuckles. Her hands are so small, I love holding them in mine.

"Oh." Her wide eyes shine with something...maybe hope or excitement? Whatever it is, I hope she holds on, 'cause she's in for a wild ride. When Saint gets his mind made up on something, it's hard to break him away.

Saint

"Give me another." The request comes out in a grumble, and Blaze pours me some more Crown Royal, nearly filling the entire glass. I don't fuck around; I like my liquor. Not to the point where I drink until I drown every single feeling in my body regularly, but I enjoy relaxing with a few here and there.

He sets my glass down on the bar top, "You wanna tell me about earlier, brother?"

Not really, but I did stab another brother and then smash another's nose. Guess I sort of need to offer them more than just a quick, 'I'm calmed down.' Blaze's been around for a few years now, but I still don't look at him like I would Nightmare or

Hybrid Collection

Exterminator. I've been through some shit with those brothers, not so much with the old Widow Makers-patched Oath Keepers.

Not sure if I'll ever look at the hybrids as full members. I shouldn't think that way, but I do. I've ridden with the others for far too long to look at the hybrids all in the same sense.

"I didn't know he was married," I admit after a tense moment, not wanting to admit the truth. The words sting my tongue, a poison to my ears as I hear them aloud. They're bitter to the taste, knowing exactly what they imply.

Honestly, it was the last thing to cross my mind, and when he admitted it, I'd thought the world had come crashing down on me. You don't love someone as much as I love Sinner and just let shit like that fly by without some sort of repercussion. His admission cut my insides like a knife when the words fell from his lips. My actions in response were straight autopilot; my mind was gone in that moment. My soul had gone black, I didn't know how else to react.

"But you thought that was reason enough to slice him up?" He takes a hefty drink from his longneck of Corona, setting it down next to my glass.

"I was fucking pissed." My brow begins to sweat in irritation of having to think about it more. "So much so, that I didn't realize my blade was even in my hand until it'd already happened." My eyelids slam closed as I wince, remembering how stunned Sinner's face had become at that moment. I hate myself for hurting him.

"Viking was fucking livid. You got blood all over the rug and the wall."

I shrug and take a swig of the liquid gold. As if I give a fuck if they were briefly inconvenienced. My fucking life stopped, and they're worried about a scarlet stain. It'll add a new touch to the room and serve as a reminder to the others as to what happens when you betray me. As for the wall, well it'll add character. Last I checked we're a goddamn outlaw MC.

"You might wanna apologize to the Prez," he offers, and I roll my eyes, his suggestion going in one ear and out the other. I don't need his recommendations on how to run my club life or what to say to my brothers. He might be so far up

Viking and Princess's asses that he can't find the light, but I don't roll that way. I've always been a dick. They know that, and I won't be changing it anytime soon—if ever.

"Nah, Viking knows me. I've been through some shit with the brother." As for Princess, all she has to do is point, and I'll slice a motherfucker's throat for her.

"I get that, but..."

Cutting him off, I slam the glass down on the counter. "The *fuck* you do."

The muscles in my body grow taut, laying it out. "You're his cousin, Blaze, his other family. You have his back and good for you. But never forget that I have his back too. What happened with Sinner has nothing to do with you, brother. *Nothing*."

"Fine." Letting it go, he backs down with an exhale. "I'll drop it. You need to talk to someone, well then, I'm here," he finishes, finally permitting me to have a bit of peace from his inquisition. He may be acting VP for the time being, but he needs to remember I didn't vote him there.

"Appreciate it, but I won't need to."

I don't want to speak to anyone about shit. I never needed it and never will. The only person I give two fucks as to what they think is that man laying down the hall with a slice in his side. A wound that I was warped enough to put there.

Torch saddles up on the stool next to me, and I roll my eyes again, preparing for shit from him next. "Saint."

This is not my idea of a relaxing time at the bar. It reminds me of what a loveless marriage would be like with a hateful chick who bitches constantly. A prime example of why I'm a biker, so I don't have to listen to it.

"Torch." The bored response rolls off my tongue, not in the mood to hear his input either.

These two, both Viking's boys from his old crew, and neither are my favorites of the brothers around here. Guess they think their past gives them the right to come and try to speak to me about my business. If they only had a fucking clue, it takes a lot to get to that level with me. Hell, it was six years before I agreed with Sinner to hang up my patch for Viking. Before that, it was Ex, and fuck anyone else trying to come around.

He signals for a beer and Blaze sets his usual in front of him. "You feelin' all right?"

"Fine. Not that it's anyone business."

Taking a swig, he side-eyes me, "Look, man, I was just asking because I decked you pretty hard, and then you hit the ground. Just making sure there aren't hard feelings and shit. I'm not trying to have a beef with anyone in the club. I moved out here to get away from club drama."

Finally, someone not nosing into my life. "I deserved it, I know that. There's no negative shit coming from my way. I appreciate you stopping me before I fucked anybody else up. Sometimes my mind gets fuzzy, and I hurt people. Your nose busted?"

"Yeah, but no worries, it's my job." His shoulders lifted in a shrug, letting it go and just like that, the subject's dropped. He is one of the club's death dealers, essentially a club enforcer—just a step up. He'll kill you if he comes after you. "Shots then?"

"Fuckin' right." Grinning, we fist pump, and he calls Blaze back, ordering a double round of tequila.

The life in the MC, a shot or a punch can hash out some hard feelings, and you move on about your business. In Sinner's case, I owe him one hell of a blow job. There's no way a shot will make up for my earlier rage.

I don't know how many shots Torch, Blaze, and I end up doing, but it's enough to smooth the strain between everyone and make my body begin to feel numb. My head was tender after being punched, but the pain is a simple reminder of me hurting Sinner. I'll never forgive myself for that. I need to make it work with Jude for him too. I owe him that.

I can only hope that eventually, Sin will forgive me though because I meant it when I told him I want forever. I've known him most of my life, and there's no one I'd rather be with. If we get Jude in the mix, it's just a bonus as far as I'm concerned.

I enjoy a woman as much as he does. With our lifestyle, you never know when tomorrow may be your last, and I don't want him lying to me for another woman—ever. I may not let the next one live if he does.

In my drunken haze, I end up finding my way to his room, per my usual when I drink without him. I'm completely exhausted and ready to leave my resentment at the door. After today's events, I just want to be near him and move forward.

"Saint?" he mutters as I shuck my boots, followed by my clothes.

I sleep naked, we both do. No clothes mixed with alcohol was how we first had sex together without a woman involved. We've never stopped since.

"I'm here."

Swaying a little, I use the silvery blue glint from the moonlight shining through the window on the far side of the room to find my way to the empty side of the bed. Jude's tucked into Sinner's chest, lying in the middle. His wound's wrapped and away from her on the opposite side.

"You good?" He watches sleepily as I climb into bed on the other side and pulls some more blanket over for me to use.

"Thanks, fucked up off tequila," I admit with a yawn and fall back into the pillow.

He chuckles; it's a welcome sound after my stressful day. His sleepy rasp has my cock tingling, but nothing more. "Got whiskey dick," I confess, and he snickers quietly.

"Good. Go to sleep."

With his order, I close my eyes. "Mmm." Groaning, I pull Jude my way a bit, tucking her ass into my groin and I'm out like a light.

CHAPTER 9

I am definitely an angel, but careful,
my wings have fire.
-S.L.

We're woken up and ushered into church well before my body's ready to leave its peaceful slumber. Glancing around the table, I'm not the only one feeling that way, either. Every brother that was in the bar with me last night is looking a bit rough around the edges. I'm guessing this must be important if we're all here and no one's bitching about it.

"Long night?" Prez smirks, his regard beating down on the few of us that are a little worse for wear.

I keep quiet, reserving my energy. I may snap and bleed someone dry if I don't get a nap at some point today. I distinctly remember plenty of nights he drank like a fish and looked like hell the following day.

"Let's try this shit again," he grumbles. The dig's directed at me particularly. "I received a call the other day enlightening me that shit's not so kosher with the Chicago charter we got set up."

Can't say I'm surprised; we knew it would be tough to try and break in a new charter in a highly trafficked turf. The only reason we got an invite to set up shop in the first place was because the Chicago mob boss needed our help in taking out his uncle who was in power at the time. Blowback of some sort was almost guaranteed, but the money the charter would have a chance to bring in was too great not to give it a shot. Me, Sinner, Smokey, and a few others rode up to get it going.

The brothers up there are nuts in my opinion. It's too fuckin' cold. And who'd want to be that close to the damn mob anyhow? That's just askin' for trouble.

"A brother up there's having a tough time. Looks like he enjoys breaking skulls as much as we do," he continues. "The only problem with it is he broke a few of Joker's guys wide open. Joker wasn't pleased, to say the least. He was furious enough to pop off in Italian. I didn't understand the words but caught his meaning."

Oh, for fuck's sake.

"He's the one who called or the charter Prez?" Odin questions and my eyelids flick open, interested as well. Joker rules Chicago on an iron throne, ready to cut down anyone in his way. His middle name may as well be 'blood and business' when it comes to that territory.

Can't say I blame him either. Those Italians up that way tend to be a bit fucking crazy. I may slice you up, but they'll cut out your tongue if you snitch and stuff you in a goddamn meat freezer. Hell, they'll probably serve you up on a pile of pasta while they're at it. Around here, if you go running your mouth, we just tie a rope around your neck and let you go for a swing.

"Both." Viking glares, not fond of being interrupted, even by his younger blood brother. Odin's close to being voted as Vice President, so he's been speaking up more lately. "Chi town Prez says do whatever we can to help keep the peace. He doesn't want war with the mob, and neither do we."

Viking shakes his head with a sigh and continues. "Joker demands that Mercenary either disappears from the entire state or he'll make an example out of him."

Torch lets out a low whistle, mirroring most of our thoughts. The Italians don't fuck around, so whatever lesson they have up their sleeve, it won't be pretty. The brother wouldn't make it out alive, that's for damn sure.

Smokey lights up a cigarette and sits back. The brother's so quiet all the time you forget he's even here. When he does talk, he's one of those, "what if" types of people. Gets on my fucking nerves.

"Is there a plan then?" Spider questions with his pen and paper in front of him to take notes on what he needs to prepare. He's always the technical one, making sure we're ready for whatever's thrown our way. We would've been in some deep shit if it wasn't for him being organized all the time.

"We vote on it," he voices although we all know that's given, "If y'all approve Mercenary transferring here, then I'd hope the NOMADS would be up for a run to pick a brother up. If not, I'll hit Ares up to see what their club thinks. Their members are getting low anyhow."

He glances from Spider to Exterminator to Chaos and on to a few others. "I don't want to chance him trying to make it here on his own. I wouldn't be surprised if there was an unexpected accident. He'll need someone watching his back for any heat. You guys get him south, and Texas will have him covered from there."

I nod, with my finger raised, eager to get a word in.

"Saint?" The Prez's stare lands on me once more.

"I want to ride with the NOMADS on this." I need to do something around here other than just drinking liquor and arguing with everyone.

"No," he disagrees. "We need you and a few others at the border for the exchange."

My frustrated glare lands on Sinner to back me up. He knows I need a bit of crazy in my life to keep me from going batshit wild. And, if nothing else, I crave the wind in my hair, bringing me a sense of peace. A fourteen-hour ride sounds blissful after the yelling and arguing.

Sinner glances to Viking and then shakes his head, backing the Prez on his decision. "Iron Fists could be waiting to start some trouble. Motherfuckers may claim peace, but I need you beside me at the border if they decide to put up an ambush. We still haven't figured out where their compound is; they're being careful."

Of course, I'll give into his request. He's the one I need to protect the most out of anyone. I'll always defend my other brothers, but I'd never forgive myself if something happened to Sin and I wasn't there to help. Every piece of me wants to argue that he could come with me and the NOMADS but instead bite my tongue to keep the thoughts to myself.

Hell, we could just say fuck it and vote to go NOMAD again altogether. We'd be free of these small-time orders and get to travel all over again. That's the whole point of being a biker—to do whatever the fuck you want to. But now he's brought Jude in our lives, so I doubt he'd go for it.

Odin sits a bit taller, drawing attention from his brother, waiting for permission to speak. Viking gestures him to continue, and O speaks up again. "We need a vote; all in favor of approving Mercenary's transfer say aye."

We should be voting for the young man becoming VP already. The kid has paid his dues. Maybe I'll bring it up at the next church session, see if we can get him a new patch. He's no doubt earned it, always taking care of the grunt work even though his brother's the boss around here.

The Prez nods, mumbling "aye" first, shadowed by the rest of us agreeing as well. We'd be happy to increase our body count. It makes it less of a threat coming up against another club if our numbers are high.

Vike follows up his brother's remaining vote with everyone's orders. "It's settled then. I'll head to Ares' charter afterward and let him know we have a new brother in the area. Don't want any of the other brothers to fuck Mercenary up for thinking he's representing our colors without permission. Odin, you and my ol' lady, make sure there's a room ready for our new brother."

"Will do, Vike," he replies.

"Ex, Spidey, and Chaos, prepare to roll out first thing tomorrow. Joker wanted Mercenary gone as of yesterday. We just had too much shit goin' on to make it happen that fast."

They nod, and Spider scribbles on the paper a bit more. He's probably making a travel list as well as planning out the easiest route already.

"Saint, Sinner, Nightmare, you three set up a rendezvous point with Spider along the border and get whatever you need to meet up with them. Make sure you're packin' plenty of heat; I don't want you caught unprepared. If anyone fucks with you, shoot first, and we'll ask questions later. We've lost too may brothers not to send a message at this point."

"All right," I mutter, and the other two agree as well.

I'd have preferred us being with Ex and Spider, but the Prez has the final say, and I have to roll with it or else be voted out to go NOMAD again. At least Viking isn't a pussy when it comes to handling business. I couldn't imagine belonging to a club who had one for a Prez.

"Blaze, let the club sluts know we have fresh meat on the way, and they need to give him a warm welcome. I'm sure the brother is stressed; the club would be coming down hard on him for this. And do inventory; it may be time for Chaos to pick up another batch of moonshine."

"Bet."

"Torch, get with my ol' lady so she and the others can set up a welcome party for our new brother. I want Ares' charter included in it as well, so get with Cain. His ol' lady will want to help, I'm sure. Also, take Smokey with you to check on the whores. We need to keep that steady money coming in from the johns."

"No problem, Prez."

"Good. Like I said, he could be tense. Keep it in mind if he comes off hostile at first. Anything else?"

We glimpse around but all remain silent, ready to carry out our orders.

"It's settled. Get shit done," he commands and slams the gavel down, officially ending this session of church.

†

"Chicago, Saint?" Sinner mutters coming up beside me as we tread down the hall.

The walls have various club photos lining the way, leading straight to the kitchen. We left Jude in there, and I'm betting she's either still in the same spot or sitting outside.

My boots feel heavy hitting the stained concrete, the alcohol stupor still not completely lifted. It doesn't stop my brother from talking though. "It's cold as fuck up there. We ride at night, and our dicks will freeze off. We got it easy, sticking to Texas."

"Don't care, just tired of being cooped up."

He chews the inside of his cheek and says, "Why don't we take Jude somewhere for the night? We can drop her back off tomorrow and then take care of club business. We have enough time."

"She's staying? You asked her already?"

We hadn't actually gotten to speak the words aloud, but he knows what I meant by telling him to figure shit out. She has to stay here for good if my idea works and he needs to get on the ball about it. If she commits, then I'll have her and Sinner for good, which is exactly what I want. If he thinks taking her out of town for the night will help steer her in our favor, then I'm all for it.

"Well, no," he admits, appearing a bit sheepish. "But she hasn't asked to leave yet."

"So, you're finally giving in? She told me the first night about how she'd flirt with you and shit, but you'd shoot her down each time. You're stronger than me; I'd have been all up in her pussy before she could even blink."

"I figured you'd gut her if you did find out and sleeping with her would've made it harder to leave her behind when it was time. I already struggled when I couldn't go check on her when I felt like it. I didn't think this would be the outcome, to be honest."

"Thought about it," I admit, shrugging it off. "I needed to be around her to see why you even gave a fuck in the first place. It's different; you caring about her like this. I wouldn't just randomly kill someone you care for in spite. I have my reasons for doing the shit I do."

"I know that. At first, it was the guilt for killing her mother, eating at me. Then I started looking forward to seeing her whenever I could. I guess it grew from there without me even realizing it. One day she was cute but annoying, the next I couldn't get her out of my head."

"You should've spoken to me sooner. After everything we've been through, I don't get that part. That's what bothered me the most, not finding out from you telling me directly and from the very beginning."

"I'm aware of that now, but you've been kind of stir-crazy lately. I'm not making this your fault, don't get me wrong. I'm being real about it all. Whenever I'd think of telling you about her, I'd picture you in a rage, sacrificing her or scaring her. She's not like us; she's never been through the shit we have been. You and me, we're not exactly normal."

I reply, cocking a blond eyebrow up in his direction, a bit wounded by his preconception. "You of all people know I only do that to bad souls. I would've killed her mother from what I've heard of her. Then maybe just fucked baby and left her alone after. Hard to say. She's more my type then yours, anyhow."

He gives in after a few beats. "I was judging you like everyone else."

Sighing, I nod, because I'd already figured that much out. Hiding her like I'd torture the bitch or something. Nineteen years by my side and yet he forgets one of the most important things about my heritage.

The sacrifice of bad souls is to pay tribute and give respect to my ancestors that've long passed. Do I enjoy the kill when it happens? Of course, I do.

It doesn't mean I go on a rampage slaughtering innocents for shits and giggles. I'm not a fucking psychopath. If I was, I wouldn't love him so damn much, that's for sure. And, I wouldn't give two shits about keeping Jude with us.

"Forgive me," he finally whispers, saying the words I needed to hear.

Grabbing his forearms, I stare into his pebble-shaded irises, the one's I've come to seek in comfort. "You don't have to ask, Sin; you've already been forgiven."

He swallows roughly, watching me with so much sadness in his eyes. I can see the boy that I saved that day inside him still. He fights those demons his father planted down deep to this day. I'll never let them hurt him again. As long as I breathe, I will be his savior.

Leaning in, I gently graze his nose with mine. A breath escapes me, being so close to him. I want to take his mouth desperately, but he doesn't like it unless we're behind locked doors. I have to respect that; our relationship is a step out of the ordinary when it comes to club life.

Moving to the side, I caress his earlobe with my nose next and rasp the same promise I've made to him over and over, "I will always fight for you." With my entire being, the statement is true.

His knuckles push into my stomach briefly as he releases a deep breath, and then his fingertips are up, gripping my chin. He draws my face to his, brushing a hard kiss against my mouth. It takes everything in me not to slam him against the hallway wall and rip his clothes off.

I settle for a moment of my tongue twisting with his. The need built up inside me pours from the very depths of my soul into him. His teeth graze over my lips as he pulls away, leaving behind goosebumps in his wake. It's everything I've come to look forward to when we touch like this; it's what my body's learned to crave more and more.

The pad of his thumb trails over my lower lip wet from his mouth, his shadowy gaze trained to the spot full of heat. A noise in the other room breaks the spell, and with a blink, he's backing up, putting space between us. "I couldn't stop myself," he confesses, shaking his head and spins to walk away.

Catching his arm, I stall him briefly, not ready to put an end to what we've just shared. "I didn't want you to."

Hybrid Collection

With that, I release him, and we finish our search for Jude. He claims I have him, but there's a twisting in my stomach telling me that I need to own her heart to have him forever. I'll let him fall for her too, as long as she falls for us both. One thing is for certain, he'll never completely be hers, not while my heart's still beating.

Jude

Saint and Sinner's handsome, scruffy faces finally appear after about an hour. I've had time to wake up and even miss them. It seems silly and too soon, but it's true. I've begun to enjoy every moment that I'm around them now that Saint isn't angry anymore.

What time frame is normal to know how you feel about someone? My mind and body are all for Sinner and Saint. However, I don't know if it's foolish to listen and go with my feelings or to hold back. Sinner says that I'm naïve, but is that a bad thing when it comes to love? It took merely one day with each of them to know my life would never be the same.

It has to mean something, right? Every hour that passes, I find myself enraptured with them even more. It's my own type of madness, being torn between two men at the same time. Do I absolutely have to choose only one? Because as of right now, I want them both, and I don't see that changing anytime soon.

"Hi," I greet, sipping some of the strong black coffee I'd made earlier. This stuff is awesome.

"That smells good," Saint comments, his tired gaze looking as if he could use some extra sleep or a giant cup of coffee.

"It's strong and very yummy. There's more if you want some."

"It's chocolate chicory coffee baby girl. Gotta have that sort of shit with a compound full of men." He winks, planting his body in the spot beside me. He twists until I'm positioned between his legs and presses a kiss to my temple.

It's become sort of a habit of his to leave behind sweet kisses on my face. It makes me feel kind of cherished, especially after he bit me, and I freaked. I think I'm figuring Saint out though. He loves strongly and in return his anger is an even more powerful force to reckon with. As long as I know that much about him, I can relax. He won't hurt me because I won't hurt him.

Sinner sits on the other side of me and winces as he does, his inky eyebrows downturned with the frown on his lips. I can't help myself and show my worry. "How's your cut?" I wish I could do something to help.

"Hurts, but I'll survive." He sends me a sweet grin. It's so unlike the grouch I've grown used to visiting me out at my mom's trailer. If I think I have it bad for him now, a little more of this side of him, and I'll be done for before I take my next breath.

"Do we need to change the bandage or anything?"

He lifts his shirt up enough for me to see the clean dressing, "I did after I took a shower this morning. Not much I can do with it; the stiches have to do their job." He fixes his shirt, and I'm disappointed to watch the sexy strip of his stomach disappear. "We want to take you for a ride, but I'm not so sure that Saint's boxers and T-shirts would be good to ride in. Let alone the flip-flops."

"I guess it's too hot to just stick me in a leather jacket, huh?"

His inquisitive gaze scans over me, and I dip my head, looking over my makeshift outfit of borrowed clothes. I'm dressed like a total bum, but it's comfortable. And besides that, the only people I have to impress are sitting right next to me.

"Not to mention if she doesn't get a bra soon, I'm gonna lose my shit—having to watch her titties bounce each time she fucking moves," Saint gripes as his hands fist tightly, glancing at my chest. They relax after a moment, and my lips turn up

Hybrid Collection

into an amused smile. He's never one to hold back on what he's thinking. Some may find it intimidating; I think it's charming.

I'm glad I'm not the only one feeling ready to burst. My eyebrow shoots up, teasing him. "Like you've never seen a naked woman before."

"Oh, I've seen plenty, baby girl; make no mistake about that. None of them quite measure up to you, however." He flashes his perfect, white teeth with his flirtatious grin. I don't know how it could be possible, but that look makes him even more freaking gorgeous.

It seems like the more sinister they are, the sexier they are as well. He reminds me of the big bad wolf, and I'm Little Red Riding Hood, just waiting to be devoured. Only, in this case, I'm between two wolves. If only Red had known what she was missing with only one chasing her.

My cheeks warm, loving his compliment. Men don't ever talk to me like he does, and it makes me hold my breath, just waiting to hear what he has to say. It's either some sort of whispered threat or sexual innuendo it seems, and I've found that I'm growing used to it the more I'm around him. I wonder what his reaction would be if I were so brazen in return? Could I make him suck in a breath at my thoughts as well?

"We need to get you some clothes." Sinner finishes his earlier observation, ignoring Saint. "I'm going to check if any of the girls around here have something that'll fit you. What size pants and shirt do you wear?" He's always attempting to think of everything.

Saint interrupts before I have a chance to open my mouth. "You're not supposed to ask women that shit. I read about it somewhere, I remember. Same goes for their age and weight. Don't do it, man."

A snort leaves Sinner. "Fine. I'll figure it out, then." His finger tucks my hair behind my ear, and the movement makes my heart flutter. His touch is electric. "When's your birthday, sweetheart?"

It's the last thing I was expecting him to say and the pet name has me racking my brain like I don't know my own birthday or something. "It's in two months." Not sure the exact date at the moment because the only thing I care about is staring at his perfect mouth whenever he speaks. He could be speaking Chinese, and it wouldn't faze me, just as long as I could sit here and stare.

"You'll be nineteen?" He tucks my hair back on the other side as well, and my legs damn near fall open, wanting his attention between them too. I'll welcome his touch anywhere.

Nodding, my stomach seizes, preparing for the spiel about how I'm too young for either of them and so on...

"Good." He breathes out a sigh of relief. "You're not as young as I thought. I thought you'd barely hit eighteen."

"Nope." I smile, relieved as well he didn't go into a lecture about the age gap, and his finger caresses my jaw before falling away. I almost let the daddy retort slip, to egg him on further, but hold myself back. It makes him uncomfortable even though Saint seems to enjoy it.

"Saint will keep you company." He waves to the man who's most likely going to get me in trouble at some point—in the most devious ways, I'm sure. "I'm going to check around for clothes and boots."

"I wear a size seven and a half for shoes." I'd tell him my other sizes as well, but I don't want to prove Saint's article wrong. Some women really don't care about telling people their size, weight, and age.

"Noted. I'll be back." He stands, and Saint runs his palm up and down my spine, the rhythm warm and relaxing. I could probably fall asleep if he were to do this while lying down.

"So where are we going?" My attention gravitates to the striking man left beside me. His chin's still red from my teeth, but I kind of like it. He's wearing my mark, and that makes my stomach spin in satisfaction.

"It's a surprise." He chortles, sharing another glimpse of his bright white teeth.

Hybrid Collection

Gah, it's so sexy, having men who take care of their bodies, such as Saint and Sinner. I mentioned wanting to lick Sinner before; well, I definitely want to lick Saint as well. And preferably every square inch of him if he'll let me.

"Sounds like fun."

"How, if I haven't told you anything about it, yet? We could be stealing you away to never let you go again."

"Considering I've never been anywhere else besides my hometown and here, it sounds pretty awesome. Besides, you two are anything but boring, so I know I'll most likely love it. Steal me away."

"Jesus, baby." His head shakes and his eyes the colors of raindrops, lose a bit of their teasing glint. "We'll take you places; I promise." He utters it with so much sincerity that I can't help but wish it comes true. "You'll have a good time; we'll make sure of it."

"Saint?" I briefly pause, conjuring up the nerve to say what I'm thinking as easily as he does. "Can I ask you something?"

He grunts but continues to rub circles on my back so I guess that's not necessarily a no, per se.

"Why are you letting me stay here with you and Sinner?"

"'Cause, you may not realize it now, but Sin wants you."

"But you don't?" I meet his gaze, inquisitive. I'm attempting to understand where exactly I fit into this dynamic. I don't want them to get tired of me and leave me in their rearview mirrors.

"Of course, I do. Maybe not in the same capacity as Sinner, but you serve a purpose for both of us. I'm sure with a little more time, I'll want you the same amount, if not more than my brother." His answer's brutally honest, and I have a lot of respect for it. I appreciate that he's not one to sugarcoat things for me but be open about them when I need him to be.

"What's my purpose?" Not that I'm too excited to hear it if I'm only here for sex, but I have to find out. I need to know where I stand and what to expect being intertwined with the two of them.

"It's too soon to get into all this. For now, I want you to learn to relax and enjoy the ride. Don't worry yourself sick about our feelings. We want you with us, so you're here."

"I don't want to go back home," I admit, barely loud enough for him to overhear. There's nothing left there for me. I didn't want to say the words out loud, but they're the truth.

"Then I guess that's gonna work out just fine for us, baby girl. 'Cause, trust me, we're not ready to take you back yet."

Remembering home has me thinking of everything else too, such as my puny job manning the library desk. "I have to work the day after tomorrow." Not that I want to. I love working, but this trip is far more entertaining than being stuck there.

"So, quit." He shrugs as if it's no big deal which, to him, I suppose it isn't. I doubt he's ever even worked a normal job. He strikes me as the type to get bored and tell everyone to go to Hell.

I could easily quit; it's not like I have many hours, but what would I do when he and Sinner get sick of me and take me back home? I don't want to go back to no job and no way to survive. I have to be responsible because I've learned that no one else will be for me and I have goals I want to reach.

"I can't." Shaking my head, I plant my elbows on the table and my chin in my hands with a sigh.

"What are you so scared of, baby?" His lips trail over my neck, placing a few random chaste kisses along my throat. His lips and short, blond scruff against my skin are distracting in a wonderful way.

"Well...I guess that I won't have anything to go back to when it's time for me to return to reality."

"Why would you even have to go back? To work at your shit job, or hang out in your trailer all alone?"

It's like he echoes my thoughts exactly.

He backs away just a touch, his penetrating gaze serious as he continues, "Or maybe you wanna go back because me and Sin aren't what you thought we'd be? Baby, we don't take any shit, neither of us. We won't let anything happen to you either if that's what you're worried about."

I wished for those very words last night while I was lying in bed next to Sinner and then again this morning when I woke up snuggled between two warm bodies. But now that I have them the rational side of my brain is pumping the brakes on my newfound adventure. I crave the fun of course, but I need some sort of assurance on things as well. I don't want to get hurt by Saint, Sinner, or both. There's no doubt in my mind that they're more than capable of demolishing my heart if they chose to.

It's like he can feel my mind fighting me on what to do, jerking in multiple directions at once and turns my face toward his. Saint leans in until our lips are nearly touching, his breath just a touch away from me to taste. He murmurs, "Not everything has to be complicated, baby girl. Sometimes what you see is exactly what you get," he finishes, and his lips meet mine.

He's kept his distance since our whatever you want to call it happened in his room. I screamed and bit him, and he bit me in return. I cried, he got even angrier, then we both had a chance to calm down and come back to our senses. I'd never been so unsure in my life if I wanted to punch a man or take my clothes off for him. Neither happened, but that was probably for the best at the time.

I guess when it boils down to it, Saint does have his own effect on me like Sinner after all. Only his influence makes me feel completely different. While Sinner causes my heart to flutter whenever he's near, Saint makes my soul burn.

His dirty thoughts and heated threats leave me panting to the point I think there could be something wrong with me. Hot flashes being brought on by a gruff growl can't be normal. Like I could be part cuckoo wanting not one man, but two, and neither of them are completely sane themselves.

His mouth easily takes control of mine, parting my lips so his tongue can slip inside—a sweet torment making me feel as if I may wither away if he ever stops. His strong hands explore, fingers weaving through my hair, anchoring me to him. If I doubted his motives before, those thoughts are slowly being forgotten. He kisses me like Sinner, powerful and consuming—filling me with painful anticipation.

His tongue teases mine, coaxing it to play his little game until I'm panting, attempting to catch my breath. His kiss is enrapturing, making me forget that anything outside of this—me, him, and Sinner ever once existed. My body moves on its own accord, craving his touch, squirming to be closer, but he holds me still. My fingers climb their way up his muscles, the tips raking against his flesh, silently begging him for more. I want him to tear my clothes free and fuck me right here on top of the table.

After a moment that's far too short of ravishing my mouth, he pulls back enough to chuckle and kiss my chin. His lips, teeth, and tongue trail down along my throat, making me no longer want to move in fear of him stopping. His scruff leaves behind the most delicious tingles in his wake.

He mouth on mine is everything—full of promises, hope, and so much raw passion.

"You wet yet, baby?" he rasps against my skin, clearly feeling the kiss as much as I did. His warm breath amiably torments me in its own way, inflicting the desired affect he's seeking.

Am I wet? More like so damn hot my clothes may catch on fire from the burn his touch elicits.

"You could find out," I coyly retort, and he growls, drawing me over his sturdy jean clad thighs to straddle his lap.

He's pulling my hips to him, his tongue and mouth against my throat when Sinner comes through the door with a pile of clothes in his arms. These two are always interrupting the other, it seems, and at the worst times. Maybe he'll join us, and I can feel them both, right here, right now.

Sinner's eyebrow hikes at the site of us, an amused grin overtaking his mouth, "Enough fun for now. Go change, Jude, so we can split." He nods over his shoulder, toward the hall.

"Okay, daddy," leaves me breathily, poking the bear, and his grin's accompanied by a fake glare in response.

Saint stops and pulls away, a chuckle escaping as he plants a chaste kiss to my lips before helping me stand. It's the most connected to him I've felt since I arrived, and it has my head spinning. I never pegged him to be the one to have a serious chat with; I always expected it to be Sinner if it were to happen. However, I'm grateful it did; we needed to connect after the fight we'd had.

He stands beside me, towering over me, and Sinner tucks me under his arm, warming me all over again as he walks with me to his room. If they can do this to me with their touch and kiss alone, I can only imagine what a full night would be like with the two of them. I'm beginning to think Saint's earlier statement is completely true—they're definitely going to ruin me for anyone else. It looks like I'm going to find out firsthand tonight too. I'll finally get my fantasy I've been dreaming of...one of them, anyhow.

"You ever ride before, Jude?" Sinner inquires, and suddenly I'm thrilled for an entirely new reason.

He hands over the various clothes, and I gratefully take them. I do miss the small wardrobe I've left behind, but not doing laundry is also pretty cool.

"Nope, but I can't wait!" I'm scared and excited all at the same time. The best part is that I get time alone spent with both of them. No distractions and hopefully no clothes either, if I have anything to say about it. I may be a virgin, but I've waited far too long, and I'm ready to find out what I've been missing.

Best adventure ever.

CHAPTER 10

Sinner

Dallas is pretty close to the club, so Saint and I decide to head there with Jude for the night. We take her to Sea World, buy her ice cream, and watch her smile the entire too warm Texas day. I never in a million years would've thought spoiling a woman a little would give me so much happiness inside. It makes me want to do this with her every chance I can.

She's never been anywhere interesting, and her sweet innocence is intoxicating, even for two grouchy, seasoned bikers. Saint and I explored all these places when we were younger and could sneak in. I'd forgotten what a little old-fashioned fun was like.

Of course, we were stared at all day by anyone around us. It was hot and sunny, so Saint refused to wear anything besides his jeans, boots and cut. Most of those women about fell over seeing his tight stomach and blond hair tied up in a man bun. I'm used to it, so it's easy for me to forget just how good-looking he really is. That's Saint though, always the pretty boy of the group.

We've given him so much shit about it over the years, and he's learned to roll with it. Even the Prez likes to poke around, telling him that Abercrombie called, and they want their model back. Saint looks nowhere near his age either, fooling anyone who attempts to guess. Women are quick to fall for him without realizing he comes with a backpack full of baggage as well. And me...he comes with me, and most women can't handle two men at once.

While he and I were panted after by every damn woman in the vicinity, it seemed, Jude wasn't privy to the same welcome. Chicks can be beyond hateful toward one another without knowing shit about each other. After we noticed the jealous

Hybrid Collection

bitches glaring in her direction and another was rude while she asked for ice cream, Saint and I took over. We had to or else our trip wouldn't have turned out so good 'cause I would've lost my shit.

If she noticed anything throughout the day that she even briefly thought was worth considering; I went over and ordered it before she had the chance. If a bitch shot a glare her way, Saint was kissing her and pulling her in another direction. Between the two of us, she didn't deal with anymore haters and ended up having a great time. Seeing her so free, exploring, and having fun, made us happy.

Not only that, but we got to show her another side to us. She was able to discover the part where we like to take care of each other and laugh. We're not always so serious or fighting; in fact, Saint and I rarely fight. Jude, however, came at a time where she got to witness everything firsthand, the bad and now, hopefully, the good as well. I wished she'd met Saint sooner; maybe we could've avoided this back-and-forth had the circumstances been different.

We made a brief detour and stopped off at a store on the way to the hotel to purchase her some new panties and a bra. Thank God we did, too because the moment she found out there was a hot tub, she was stripping. The little woman was on a damn mission, having never been in one before. I tried getting her to pick out clothes as well, but she wouldn't have it. Usually, she knows better than to argue with me over such things, but she refused, after our spending money on her throughout the day.

Witnessing her make her way into the steaming, bubbly water, and her excitement over it gives me peace knowing I killed the bitch that gave birth to her. She didn't deserve Jude. She damn sure didn't cherish and care for her; I can do a better job than she ever did.

I don't understand how someone can do that to their own kid, not give a shit about them. I couldn't imagine, even with my own warped childhood. Yes, I was whipped and was raised up in the church, but I never went hungry or worried if the electric was going to be shut off. I guess demons come in all forms; we each have our own, no matter how different.

Of course, when Jude peers up at me like I've hung the moon, the guilt sets in as well. The ominous feelings overtake the place of the peace I shortly experienced. I took the one person she's had in her life away from her.

And the worst part of all is that if she finds out, she'll hate me forever for what I've done. I'm in too deep to let her ever hate me. She has me too wrapped up to let the truth seep out and ruin it all. At this point, I plan to keep her, especially after Saint made it clear about what he wants as well.

"This is awesome." Her face lights up as her skin flushes, a light rose blush dotting her cheeks from the hot water. "Are you coming in?" She beckons with her pointer finger, and I nearly follow.

Witnessing the tops of her breasts float above the water, teasing me, has my cock hardening, coming up with its own plans. The sheer lilac material of the bra doesn't nearly cover enough. Fuck, do I want to be in there with her right now. She's so damn sexy.

"I need to stay out with this." Gesturing to the bandage covering my side, her smile falls.

"Crap, I'll get out. It's not fair for you to sit there and wait while I'm in here." If she only knew. Not fair? Shit, I get to stare at her, soaked from head to toe. I doubt she realizes her bra and panties have become see-through and oh-so-enticing.

"I don't mind." At all.

Jesus, I'm a fucking pervert, but I couldn't care less right now. She's insanely gorgeous. I get to watch her fine ass float around in the overly warm water, her pink skin giving me a glimpse of what it'd look like after I've had my way with her.

Saint remained in the room once we checked in to take a cool shower, and I can't blame him. A rinse sounds like bliss after the semi-humid day walking around. If he'd seen her like this though, he'd say fuck the shower, and you wouldn't be able to peel him away from nearly-nude Jude.

"Are you sure you're okay? Were you supposed to be running around all day after me or riding your motorcycle?"

Hybrid Collection

She rode up on the back of my bike with the agreement in place she'd ride back home with Saint. I won't lie; it hurt my side, but I won't freely admit that to her. I've had much worse so I can get through this. Her tits molded against my back the entire trip was plenty of motivation and comfort for me.

Chuckling, I snag her dainty wrists and tug her toward me. She stands all the way up, water dripping down, so our faces can be close.

"If you haven't noticed yet, let me fill you in. I don't follow rules, sweetheart. I do whatever the fuck I want, whenever the fuck I feel like it."

A rumble shakes my chest, witnessing the beads of hot water continue to trail over her soft skin. They fall down her breasts tempting me further. "It's one of the benefits of being me." I end the statement pressing a chaste kiss to her perfect lips but craving so much more from her. It's probably a good thing I have to stay out of the water, cause if I was in there with her, she'd come out having felt me everywhere.

"You're just an everyday badass then?" She giggles, her eyes glittering playfully.

"Watch your mouth," leaves my throat, the sound coming out gruff with the tightening of my pants. The bossy side easily shows itself around her, wanting to take control of that delicious body of hers. "Saint should be done by now. Let's join him before I end up fucking you in that hot tub and get us all kicked out."

"Oh…I thought you said you didn't mind waiting? I had no idea you were so impatient." She fake-sulks, and I can think of a cock that'd like to be pressed between those pouty lips.

"Well, staring at your tits and pretty mouth has me changing my mind. I could stick my cock between those lips and let you stay longer if you'd like?"

Her eyes grow wide at my bluntness, not used to hearing that sort from me.

A chuckle escapes, as I tug her out of the hot tub, pulling her behind me, so any guests aren't privy to witness her looking so damn sexy. She may not be accustomed to me speaking to her like Saint does, but that's only because I've held myself back. I won't be doing that any longer though. "Cat got your tongue?"

"Something does," she mumbles, flicking her gaze toward my groin several times as we make our way to our shared room. My cock's hard and definitely not hiding its eagerness any longer.

"You getting scared of me?"

I won't make her do anything she doesn't want to. I hope she realizes that. I think she's freaking out inside now that we're alone in a hotel together and we've both made it clear that we don't intend to hold back from taking her body any longer. Glancing at my groin, it's clear as day, I want to fuck her until she can't stand up.

"No, but..." She trails off, and eventually, I glance her way. She continues, "Do you think I'm a ho?"

Anger claws its way up my back with her question. Did someone call her one? Where did she get that shit from? Nobody, and I mean not a motherfucking soul, better have called her a ho. I'll have Saint wearing their skin like a goddamn cape in retribution.

"No. Who the fuck said that?" The words are harsh to my own ears as they leave my mouth. I can only imagine how she'll take it, but hearing her even question it, has me furious. Jude's one of the purest individuals I've ever come across.

"Uh...no one, but I know people will think it's wrong."

"Think what's wrong? Baby, spell the shit out for me. I'm a man, remember?"

"That it's wrong for me to want you both, at the same time."

"Well, too fucking bad. You know why, Jude?" I ask, and she shakes her head, looking to me for guidance.

"Because I said so, that's why. Besides, ain't nobody looking in that mirror each day besides you. If you're happy and satisfied, then fuck what anyone else has to say. You think me and Saint would be where we are if we gave two shits about what anyone else thought?"

"No."

Hybrid Collection

"Exactly. You have to live for yourself. And if anyone does have enough guts to call you that, you let Saint and me know. We'll squash that shit right away. They'll be lucky if they can ever speak again. Never let what you assume people may think rule your life. It's not worth it."

She nods, keeping her thoughts to herself. Hopefully, she hears me and listens about this. It's too important that she doesn't feel guilty for what makes her happy. She deserves to enjoy life, just as everyone else in the world does.

We get inside the room and Jude's uncharacteristically quiet, especially after our serious chat in the hallway and elevator.

"Talk to me, Jude," I half-ask-half-demand, as I sit on the bed beside her, fighting myself to keep from touching her everywhere.

Saint's still in the bathroom, sink water on. I suppose brushing his teeth or shaving. *Fucking pretty boy.*

"I wanted to ask you something."

"Shoot."

She draws in a deep breath. Whatever she's thinking, must be serious. "Do you kill people like Saint?" She asks it so innocuously.

It has me swallowing, as my throat's grown a bit tighter than usual. *Fucking shit.* I wasn't expecting her to ask that, of all things.

I stall, racking my brain for what the hell I should say. How truthful should I be with her? "What the...I mean, where's this coming from?"

She shrugs. "I just want to know you."

"Yeah, you sure about that, sweetheart? You might not like what you find out. Especially asking questions like that one in particular," I reply, tucking her hair behind her ear. I like being able to see her whole face when I talk to her. She's too beautiful not to look at as much as possible.

"So far, you don't seem so bad."

I shoot her a mock glare, and she grins. She's straight fucking perfection, even with the smattering of light freckles over her nose. I think they make her even more stunning, if possible. How did I not notice it sooner? I don't know how I was able to hold back from her for this long.

"Thanks, I think, anyway. You want the truth?"

"Yes, please."

Picking up her hand, I cover it with both of mine needing to make sure she doesn't take off running and screaming. With a sigh, I admit one of my worst sins. "Yes, if necessary, I will." I have many sins, but I don't want her knowing them all.

She swallows, so silent; the air thickens as I wait for her to say something—*any*thing. Even that she hates me, just say something and put me on the chopping block already. I'm not sure what to think, and I hate that feeling.

"Do you hate me now?"

"No, Sinner; I don't think that's possible."

If she only knew. Sinner really is the best name for me, even after all these years.

The truth about where her mother ended up would say otherwise I'm sure. I can't imagine she'd ever forgive me for being the one who snuffed her mother's life out. That's why I have to do everything in my power to make sure it remains buried. She can never know, no matter what. I won't let her hate me.

"Oh, baby," Saint groans, breaking the heavy moment as he comes out of the bathroom and discovers the goddess waiting on the bed.

Her lilac bra and panties are see-through after her dip in the hot tub, her hair damp and wavy with eyelashes so dark and long they're deceiving, appearing as if she were blessed with a permanent coat of mascara. I was tormented by her beauty the entire time she floated around in that damn water. I was ready to fuck her on one of the damn motel tables if needed. The possessive side of me made me wait, however, not wanting any assholes to see her like that.

Hybrid Collection

"You have no idea brother; you should've seen her in the goddamn water."

"I can imagine." He blinks with a nod.

"Shit was exotic," I comment further, and he swallows, his hand falling to grip his thickening cock. He's in a basic white hotel towel, and there's no hiding how he's feeling at the moment.

Glancing at Jude, her cheeks are flushed all over again, eyes pinned on a freshly-showered Saint.

"See something you want, baby girl?" He flicks his tongue over his bottom lip, taking her in from top to bottom and she lets out a pent-up breath. She bites her lip, scooting back a bit on the bed for him.

"You don't know what you're asking for, Jude," I warn, garnering her attention back in my direction.

"I think I do," she whispers, and I shoot her a devious grin. She can think all she'd like, but she has no fucking idea what we'll do to her over and over. Because once surely won't be enough to satisfy either of us.

"Saint, you get her warmed up, yeah? I'm going to hop in the shower and rinse the day off."

"Sounds good to me," he easily agrees as I pass him on my way to the shower. "That pussy is mine, Saint. Make your cock behave."

He grunts, not making any promises as he prowls toward the bed.

Shutting the door, I inhale a calming breath and attempt to mentally prepare myself for stealing this young woman's virginity. Removing my clothes, I turn the shower on and step under the icy spray. I need to clear the fog from my mind, so I can think clearly enough to remember to scrub my damn nuts. She has me so distracted, it's hard to focus on anything but her and Saint.

One night alone with her isn't going to be enough. I have to ruin her for all others, and Saint will help me accomplish that. I'll make sure she never looks at another man the way she does me. Ever again.

Saint

My feet carry me to Jude, her skin radiating after a dip in the steamy water. The biggest dilemma on my mind right now is where do I touch her first? My hands want to be everywhere and nowhere all at once while I stare and take my fill of her with my eyes first.

"Baby." The pet name I have reserved only for her leaves me in a quiet rasp; my body's screaming for her but my mouth can't quite form the words to say so just yet. "You're so damn beautiful."

Her lashes flutter, pulling me in even further. "Thank you," she replies softly, and I take the final step, stopping directly in front of her. Lifting her chin with two of my fingers, I bring her eyes back to mine.

I can understand why Sinner is so easily taken with her. She's enticing, even for me, a man who's had his fair share of women. The more I'm around her, the more I find my appetite unsatisfied and hungry for a taste. "You're perfection, Jude."

That compliment earns me a smile, and I dip in, claiming her lips with mine. I have her back lying against the king-sized bed with my body hovering over hers almost immediately. Her mouth's so sweet, like candy. I could kiss her for hours and not be sated. Sinner's the only other person who can make me feel that way like I could never have enough.

My eager fingers find her thin bra straps, swiping them off her shoulders. The newly freed area of pale flesh begs for my attention. She still has a bruise and the teeth indentions from my bite. I caused her a touch of pain, but fuck me, I love the sight of the aftermath. There's a piece of me that's already marked her; I wonder if she realizes it.

Leaving her mouth, I'm drawn to the bare skin, my mark taunting me to make more. Pressing kisses along the sensitive area, I suck and nibble, leaving behind hickeys in my wake. Her blunt nails rake along my biceps, her quiet hum of approval spurring me on further. I want inside her, to feel her everywhere, to own a piece of her.

Hooking my thumbs on each bra cup, I free her breasts for me to devour next. Paying equal attention to the round mounds, I draw her nipples in between my lips. Switching back and forth, busily suckling the stiff peaks and then soothing them with swirls from my tongue. She's teased me with these by wearing no bra under that T-shirt, and I'm getting my fill before she attempts to cover them once again.

The sensation has her writhing and drawing my face into her chest even more. Not that I mind one bit. I'll spend an hour playing with her tits alone if she wants me to. I'll even make her come like this. I should anyway as pay back for them bouncing and provoking me so much.

"*Saint*." My name leaves her breathily, the sound making my cock stiffer, and in return causing the towel draped around my hips to break free. It slides from my waist, and her breath hitches as she tilts her head down to stare her fill.

I've never been the bashful type, so I sit back, resting my ass on the heels of my feet. It earns me a wide-eyed stare from Jude and nothing could please me more. In this position, she can see just how big my cock really is, and I get to commit her nakedness to memory.

"What is it?" A cocky grin naturally takes its place on my mouth with the question. I already know, but I want to hear her admit it out loud.

"I uh, had no idea." She gestures toward my groin.

"About the size or the piercings?"

Did I mention my dick's pierced several times? I have five bars in a row down the girth in a neat row. My barbells are shiny silver and ready to give her some pleasure.

"Can I touch them?" She bites her lip outright staring and I growl in response. Can she touch me? Fucking right she can, any time she wants to—especially there.

Grabbing her hand, I lead her to the spot in question. She runs a fingertip up and down the neat row a few times making my abs constrict. "More," I demand, enjoying every second and her gaze flicks to mine then back to my thick cock. Each time she stares at it, I want to fill her up until she breaks.

Her fingers run up and down them several times and then I draw her up to her knees as well. "Now with your tongue," I order, and she swallows, leaning forward to appease me.

She doesn't put the whole length in her mouth as I'd expect, rather she runs her tongue up and down the piercings, and the sensation I'm rewarded with is insane. Chicks are always quick to throw the dick in their mouth without any outside tongue action. I'd forgotten what innocence was like. It's fucking bliss.

"Holy shit, baby girl, that feels so damn good." With my approval she does it several more times, licking my dick all over like it's a lollipop. I'm in heaven. I thought it'd be good sinking inside her pussy, but this definitely works too.

The bathroom door opens a few beats later with Sinner filling the space, a cloud of steam escaping around his body. He's naked and hot, just the way I like to see him the most. "Come here," I command, turning my attention back to the stunning woman who's busily working me over.

My back grows warm with his heat behind me, his body near enough to feel the temperature change. His mouth presses to the back of my neck. the place he knows makes me wild. He bites, scraping his teeth lightly against my flesh. I love a little pain with my pleasure.

There's no confusion as to what we're going to do, or why we're here. The three of us want each other, and there's nothing standing in our way from having it. I plan to sample them both as many times as my body will allow me to. Saint wants to keep Jude, so I say we fuck her into submission. Her pussy will be so sore riding on the back of my bike tomorrow, she'll never want another man in her bed.

"Jude," he calls over my shoulder, making her stop her divine torment. Her swollen lips beckon me to push her on further, not wanting her to quit. "I'm going to fuck you tonight sweetheart," he tells her bluntly. "We both are."

The best damn thing I've heard him say all day. "You good with that, baby?" I question, tilting her chin, so she peers up at me again. Or I could always stick my dick back between her lips. That was working mighty fine for me.

She nods, agreeing immediately. She wants it as bad as we do; she has since the first time she lay in her bed with me.

"Answer me, now."

"Yes, daddy." The term falls free, reminding me that I'm in control and it's so goddamn sexy.

"Jesus, that fucking mouth," I utter, holding her in place so I can kiss her again and delicately bite her lips. After a moment, I pull Sinner around in front of me as well.

"You gonna boss me too?" he mumbles playfully.

He's well aware that I will if I feel he needs it, but tonight, we're both alpha for her. I won't attempt to overshadow him in any way. We can both possess what we desire.

"You have her first," I offer, and his smile widens, dipping in to kiss me. His tongue tangles with mine, completely different from the soft woman beside us. He's hard everywhere, just as I like it. The differences are magnificent, fulfilling everything I need in a mate, or, in this case, multiple lovers.

His strong hand grips my neck as he makes love to my mouth and fills me with promises for the future. He's happy, and he's satisfied. It's what I want for him, to give love and feel the love in return. He's never felt worthy of such a gift, and he's done more than his share to receive it.

When he's finished taking my lips with his, I give them some space. He'll be gentle enough with her, so she'll enjoy it. I don't have that type of self-control. I didn't when I was with him the first time, and I want her experience to be different. Besides, I can always corrupt her with sweet torture, once she's been broken in a bit.

Jude

Sinner lies back, easily pulling me over his body to straddle his lap. He's aroused and more than prepared to have me. I can't stop my eyes from skating over him entirely; his muscles are exquisite. The angle of his jaw, that inky scruff, all of it calls to me, inviting me to do what I've dreamed of.

Leaning forward, I run my tongue along his sharp jaw and nip at his strong chin. Sinner's arms strain and begin to shake before he wrenches me away.

His eyes are angry and full of need. His mouth falls open, his lips parting to let loose his heavy breaths as he stares at me, attempting to restrain himself. "You ready for me, Jude?" He grasps my biceps tightly, holding my core directly over his length.

"Wait," Saint interrupts, moving to position his body behind me.

His palm slides over the curve of my hip at the same time that his mouth lands on my neck. My back meets his solid chest, and his fingers find a spot between my legs that's full of pleasure. It's the same place I've touched before, the one I'd fantasized Sinner rubbing as well. Saint's tongue laps and swirls, his teeth nip, and he sucks with his lips pressed against my throat. The sensation paired with his hand between my legs has me panting, my eyes rolling heavenward.

Sinner reaches between us, his finger finding my entrance, grazing lightly at first, and then pushing through the tight entry. My hips begin to rock back and forth as my mind imagines it's me riding him into oblivion. I may have felt my nub many times, but I'd never ventured as far as putting my fingers inside my core. He doesn't hesitate though, driving his in me as far as he can.

"Christ," he utters as Saint groans against me. "Fuck, I'm a bad man for doing this. She's like a vice, brother; her pussy's so damn needy and tight."

My eyes shoot open, shit when did they close? My gaze meets his as I admit, "I don't want a good man. I want one who'll do all the filthy, wonderful things to my body that I could ever imagine."

His nostrils flare, a serious nearly unwound look overtakes his face at my admission. It's true, though; I want these two men, not anyone else. Saint's hands move to my breasts as he adjusts to the side again, his cock grazing my ass cheek and Sinner's fingers leave me. The sudden lack of attention has me moving to squeeze my legs closed.

Sinner grins with amusement, watching me seek out more pleasure. "Oh no, sweetheart, I'll give you just what you want," he promises and sinks me down over his thick girth.

The breath escapes my lungs as my mouth falls open in a silent scream, laced with a moan. The feeling is pain and pleasure mixed in the most enchanting way, kind of like hot fudge mating with whipped marshmallow. The shit is delicious but too much, and it's a bit too sugary, enough so it'll give you a tooth ache.

"Talk to me, baby," Saint murmurs while Sinner groans and moves to drive in again. "You all right?"

"Yes." The word comes out as a hiss followed up with a small cry, the barrier of my innocence stretched wide and no more.

Sinner hums in pleasure, seating me down on him fully. "Good girl, now you move your hips however it feels right for you." His fingers grip my thighs, spanning nearly the entire width. I always thought they were on the bigger side, but Sinner's hands make me feel so small in comparison.

"But will it feel good for you, too, if you don't move me how you want to?"

"Jude, you just sitting there feels fucking amazing," he admits, and it strikes a bit more confidence in me. "You're so damn tight baby, my cock is in fucking shock. Normally it takes me awhile to reach my end, but you may do me in quicker."

The uncomfortable pinch of pain remains, but so does the need to finish out my budding orgasm they'd started to give me. Starting slowly, I get a rhythm going. By the way Sinner responds, I'd say I'm doing something right for him as well.

The pain begins to fade away the more that the two of them touch me. My speed increases, chasing my pleasure, shifting and sliding my hips in different motions. My skin grows slick no longer from the hot tub, but from having them so close and it feels amazing.

My center milks his cock, pulling and begging for him to release as my climax thunders over my body. Sinner follows his own right behind me. Our voices mingle, mimicking our bodies as we cry out in satisfaction when the time finally arrives.

For losing my virginity, I couldn't imagine it being any better. I let out a sigh, content and a bit sleepy. I can't help but think that with the two of them beside me; it was everything and so much more.

Sinner lays me back on the bed to go clean himself in the bathroom, offering the perfect view of his backside. Never thought about men having nice butts, but his is just the right size to grab a handful of. They're turning me into a shameless wanton version of myself.

Motioning to follow, Saint stops me by pushing me back against the pillows again. The spot is still warm and welcoming from Sinner laying there before me.

He tsks, wearing a naughty grin. "My turn baby. And be prepared, the orgasm I'm fixing to give you will have you screaming for everyone to hear."

And shout I did, along with declaring them both sex gods by the end of our time together. To say they were amused by my rambling is an understatement.

Closing my eyes my body searches for sleep, exhausted but happy. I can't help but feel that nothing's the same as it was yesterday. I'm forever changed, made for the two of them and completely ruined, just as they had promised.

CHAPTER 11

Sinner

The call finally comes in to the clubhouse that the NOMADS are getting close enough for us to leave and meet up with them. I haven't been on any runs since the compound was attacked and our brothers died trying to protect Princess, Bethany, and Nightmare's son. This isn't what Saint had been hoping for, but any ride that's over two hours' time sounds good, especially not up north. We should make it to the spot Spider picked in around four and a half hours or so. The other brothers will chill for the night there after riding twelve hours, and we'll continue back home.

It has all of us a bit on edge, knowing our club's stretched thin right now. At least with Viking at the compound, he has a better chance of protecting them if anything does pop off. We're supposedly at peace with the Iron Fists, but as far as they're concerned, I don't buy it. Nightmare's counting down the days until something goes wrong and he's able to burn the skin from Puppet's body.

This trip isn't about the Fists though. We're on the road to meet up and collect a new brother. It's been years since we've had anyone new around besides club sluts. The ones before them were the hybrids and prior to that was the NOMADS.

Most of us met Mercenary back when we went to Chicago to help the other club get set up. Other than that, I don't know much about him. Supposedly, he's a badass and will fit in better down here with our club. We seem to be the group of Oath Keeper delinquents in a sense, so that may be true, but only time will tell. We're not the type to trust easily, so he'll have to prove himself.

Saint may butt heads with him at first, but I hope not. He comes off as a bit of a dick to some guys; it's just how he is. Now around females, that's an entirely different story; they take one look at him and go all dreamy. His playful grin and a few raspy words have their panties dropping in no time. However, you notice he's never hung onto one; he's never found any he wanted to in the past.

The ride out there passes by smoothly, just as we were expecting, thankfully. In no time it seems, we're pulling up alongside our other brothers. I think the run we did from Mexico years back was one of the worst we've been on. Most of us were injured in some way and completely exhausted. Not to mention the stress of not being sure if the cartel was following us. I'll take a four-hour trip over that shitshow any day.

"Ex." Nightmare greets our former NOMAD leader, Exterminator, first out of everyone else. He's been close to the brother and our current Prez, Viking, for as long as I can remember. "Any issues?"

"Nah. Ride went by easy, nothing, not even the law around," Exterminator confirms, appearing pleased with the quick trip. He's always off riding somewhere whether it be just to feel the wind against his skin or to help run a new shipment of guns and collect a payout.

We've had so much drama these past few years it's made some of us a little more cautious and observant when it comes to the longer rides. We definitely don't want to return to California; it seems we have way too many enemies out that way. Shooting while riding and being shot at is not fun, especially in a state you don't know jack shit about.

We all nod at Mercenary, welcoming him from our bikes. "Ready to get on the road, to your new club?" I speak up.

Normally I couldn't give a shit how long we're away from the clubhouse. Saint and I enjoy hitting up bars all over the place along with a variety of pussy, but there's only one pussy on my mind at the moment. Jude has me in a rush to return and spend more time with her.

"Baby girl?" Saint questions while meeting my gaze, and I agree. He must be thinking of her too. Hell I can't get her off my mind, no matter how hard I try. "Me too," he concedes, confirming my suspicions. The bitch has both of us sprung apparently.

"Ready when you are," Mercenary grumbles, the inky scruff along his chiseled jaw not doing much to hide the small cluster of alabaster scars skirting along the curve.

He's partaken in his share of drama, no doubt. The man appears pissed off at the world, most likely exhausted from the ride and no break. He's a beast, reminds me a lot of the other club's Prez, Ares. This should be entertaining if he decides to be a dick to anyone. Half the club is testosterone-filled brutes and adding another could be a good thing or a bad thing.

Not that I give a shit what the brother looks like, I have Saint, after all, and now, Jude as well. to warm my bed. However, I can tell he's the type that women will flock to, and Saint won't be too keen on that. He may have Jude and me to preoccupy him, but he enjoys the attention he gets from his appearance. Not to be the best looking one in the club will do nothing but piss him off, and a bad-tempered Saint isn't very pleasant.

With that thought, I glance Saint's way and find him glaring in my direction. No doubt he saw me taking our new brother in and wasn't amused by it. He's territorial; he always has been. Not outright jealous, but just enough that you know his feelings about it. Next thing we know, Saint will be putting a curse or some shit on the brother during one of his sacrifices.

The last thing we need is a beef between brothers because I find them both good-looking. I would never let anyone know that. I don't want to make them feel uncomfortable. Most of them I couldn't look at like that anyhow; they're too much like family to me. But Mercenary, well, he's new...

"Nightmare? We good then?"

"Yeah, B will be waiting for me, no doubt. Fists are near here as far as we know, and the last thing I need is for my ol' lady to slit their throats 'cause they started shit with us again. I plan to kill the motherfuckers, but patience is our best bet right now, no matter how much I hate it." He cracks his knuckles, with a menacing glower toward the road.

It never crossed my mind before, but I wonder if he's having flashbacks of the whole situation. He was near here when he found out his son had been kidnapped and his ol' lady was beaten to shit. I couldn't imagine seeing Jude hurt like that. I'd want to rip the person that's responsible apart too. I wish we'd been at the club that day to protect them.

We say our good-byes to the NOMADS, planning to see them in a few days when we have our get-together to welcome our new brother. In the meantime, they're on their way to Alabama to pick up some more bottles of moonshine from Chaos' son-in-law's family ranch. I'll admit I do miss the life of a NOMAD. I was considering possibly going back on the road with them if Saint agreed. But that was before a certain woman came into our lives and threw us off balance.

Nightmare, Saint, and I have no reason to delay our trip home any longer. We all have someone waiting for us, and the sooner we get back, the better, as far as I'm concerned.

Jude

They're gone for half the day, but it seems like forever sitting around the clubhouse waiting. Thankfully Princess has put me to work with helping her prepare some food. I also assisted with getting the new guy's room cleaned and ready for him as well. It was nice to be needed and to be included in stuff that has to do with Saint and Sinner's club. The people here are like a giant family, something I've never had.

My stomach is full of butterflies too; I'm kind of excited and nervous to meet the new guy. I'm the newbie around here, too, so I hope he's nice. The others around here are friendly or else ignore me altogether. The women are catty bitches, besides the ol' ladies. The club whores have been busy whispering all day about how he's supposedly insanely good-looking. Who knows if they're telling the truth though.

Not that it matters. Besides have they not seen Saint and Sinner? Those two are hard to pass up, and I'm perfectly content to stick with them.

Life has changed so much in the matter of a few days, and it's hard for me to believe it. Saint and Sinner, along with their motorcycle club, are to thank for that fact, I suppose. One thing weighing on me, though, is not getting my online classwork completed this week yet. I don't want to fall behind because in some classes it's nearly impossible to catch up. I need to find someone around here with a laptop that I can borrow.

If I can do my assignments, then I won't worry about them. Or about the possibility of losing my degree that I've been working so hard toward. It's the one guarantee I have in life that I'll be able to stand on my own two feet and get out of my mom's trailer for good. Even if my relationship does continue with these men, then at least I'd have done something for myself. I can pat myself on the back because I went further than my mother ever did.

Saint told me to relax, and that's exactly what I've been trying to do. It's a relief if I'm honest with myself, not having to worry about everything like I was in the trailer. It's refreshing to have someone around all the time too. I haven't felt lonely or sad ever since coming here. Or hungry. These guys have so much food around this place, it's insane.

That's the scary part as well. What happens when I have to leave? Will going back home be harder than it was before? Especially now that I've had a taste of life outside the tiny town I call home that's smack dab in the middle of nowhere?

Truth be told, I don't want to find out. I wish deep down these guys will keep me here for as long as possible. And I want to live my life with them as crazy as that may seem. Then I'd like to forget about the absence of my mother and about the slimy men she paraded in and out of my life. I've heard that saying a time or two about wishing in one hand...hopefully, it's not the same in this case.

I'm aware of how out of character it is for me, but I can't find it in myself to care. Sinner was right about not caring what others think. It's never been that big of a deal to me before, but even less so now. The feeling is freeing; I can finally live for myself here and not worry about anyone else. Being around Saint and Sinner is liberating. I've learned so much from them just in the time here alone, I can imagine what the future will hold with them at my side.

The deep rumble from multiple pipes grows louder, and Princess comes barreling into the kitchen. "They're here! Hurry!"

You'd think her ol' man Viking had left as well with the guys, but he stayed behind. She's all pumped up to meet the new brother. According to her, you can never have too much family. I practically have zero family members, so I'll take her word for it. I know one thing for sure, I want to see the guys so much, it's probably unhealthy at this point.

"We could hide Jude in my room," Odin suggests to Princess. His eyebrows wiggle and his grin's full of mischief.

Her mouth falls open. "Hell to the no! The plan is to keep you alive, Odin. Those two would try to skin you if they thought you touched Jude while they were on a run. Plus, you don't want to piss in anyone's Cheerios before you get that VP patch you pant over so much."

"It was worth a shot." His playful gaze meets mine.

I wonder how much truth there is in what she says. Would Saint and Sinner care enough to go after another man like that? They claim to be killers, but it's one thing to hear someone say it versus seeing it with your own eyes.

And for me, to boot. Am I worth that much to them already? I'd like to think so. However, I doubt it, even though they mean a great deal to me already.

Odin's cute and pure trouble to some, I'm sure, and I doubt the guys would hurt him too badly. "I may be your age, but that doesn't mean anything. Sorry, kid," I reply with a touch of good-natured sass and draw an entertained snort from Princess.

Hybrid Collection

Chuckling, he shakes his head. "Nah sugar, it's not like that." He winks. "I just enjoy fuckin' with old men. Apparently, I'm not the only one..." His retort shuts me up quick.

It wasn't unkind, just true and it's a little unnerving that everyone around here has any inclination I've slept with Saint and Sinner. I don't have any reason to be embarrassed as some of the women around here throw themselves at the men all while being practically naked. Still, I like my business being my own. And I didn't just have sex with one guy, it was two. And another thing, it wasn't just random, either. It meant something to me.

Princess notices the smile fall from my lips and comes to my rescue, "Anyone in their right mind would pick a man over a boy." She pulls me into her, hugging me. "You're just lucky enough to have a few of them chasing after you."

Nodding, I brush the uncertainty off and let her lead me out to the main room. Odin follows along, tasked as Princess' permanent bodyguard. He may be Viking's younger brother, but there's nothing small about him. I can understand why Viking trusts him so much. I wonder who will protect her once he does become the Vice President of the club. Maybe Blaze, Viking's cousin would step up?

The other person I've come to associate with Princess is her best friend. They're a hoot when they're together too. "Where's Bethany?" I'm yet to run into her today or her son Maverick.

"She wasn't feeling well, so she's waiting for Night at their house."

"Oh, that sucks. Hopefully, she's better soon." I wonder what's wrong. I'm sure if she were really sick, Princess would be sending stuff over and getting Maverick for her. She probably just misses her man, and I know exactly what that feels like.

"I hope so too. If I drag you into being my drinking partner, she may get a little jealous."

"There's no reason to be. I like both of you," I admit, and her kind smile turns my way.

"You're sweet, Jude. I'm glad those two troublemakers brought you home to us."

"Me too." She has no idea, I think to myself as those two troublemakers she just mentioned pile through the door. Home at last.

A massive man shadows their wake, appearing irritated with something. I wonder if anything happened on their trip. He tugs his leather gloves free, stuffing them into his back jeans pocket and fist bumps the men standing around, acknowledging each of them. They welcome him like an old friend, but through each greeting, his mouth never cracks into the resemblance of a smile.

Mercenary's gaze eventually falls on me, and there's pure ice in his irises. Through his penetrating stare, his feet carry him directly to my path, blocking my view of the other guys. He's freaking massive compared to me. What is it with giant men around here? You'd think they were a football team or something.

He comes to a standstill peering down at what I'm wearing, making me question my lack of wardrobe. I know it's nothing special, but it's not like I've gotten to go shopping or anything. Maybe I should've asked Princess for something else to wear today. I'm not sure why I care in the first place. Maybe it's just the thought of making a decent first impression. Saint and Sinner don't seem to mind when I wear this though.

"Hi?" Staring up at him, I notice his chin dotted with small scars. I won't lie; the ragged appearance is pretty sexy. I seem to have a thing for hard-looking men.

Are they from fighting or a crash maybe? They add to his "don't fuck with me" attitude for sure. I wouldn't want to come face-to-face with him in a dark alley. I can see why he'd come here; he has a certain appeal that fits in well with the other men around here.

"This the best you got?" he rumbles, waving his hand at me. "Guess it doesn't matter since you'll be naked soon enough." He shrugs and his huge paw of a hand lands on my shoulder, "I'mma grab a beer, then you can show me my digs and welcome me properly."

Pretty sure the sound I make is a squeak at his touch. Or maybe a gasp, like a tire going flat? How in the hell do I respond to something like that? I can't, so I stand there like a fish out of water, moving my mouth. I'm sure I really look ridiculous, not forming an actual sentence in response.

Princess notices my discomfort and interrupts. "Uh, hi Mercenary, I'm Princess." She's not intimidated by the big guy one bit. Her hand shoots out, ready to shake his. "Yeah, so Jude's not really here for that sort of thing."

He ignores it, his mammoth paw still on my shoulder while the other fists at his side. "My bad; she property?"

My nose screws up, and my forehead wrinkles in confusion from his question. What the hell is he talking about? Last I checked, I owned myself. And it is his bad; he shouldn't have assumed I'd be welcoming him in his room in any way. Especially after him being so rude about my clothes. Good luck with the women, guy; you're going to need it.

"Well, not really." Princess chews the inside of her cheek and drops her hand, then glances around for I'm guessing her ol' man.

This whole situation has grown uncomfortable. I just want to greet the guys and get a glass of lemonade from Blaze. Maybe have him add some vodka, so I forget this ever happened. Mercenary doesn't seem as convinced of everything, though, and this could be a problem.

"Then let me make myself clear," he states, his voice a deep, commanding timbre. "I'm getting a beer." He points to my boobs. "And then I'm fucking her. Maybe if she's good at giving head, I'll let her stick around and suck me off in the morning too."

Princess snorts. Apparently this is his first run-in with the Ice Queen. She's sweet, but she doesn't take one ounce of shit from any of the guys. She tells it how it is, regardless. And I love her for it.

I have no freaking idea how to react. Sinner warned me that the club has certain rules that you follow around here. I just stand still and swallow, dumbstruck. This ginormous, gorgeous man just demanded that I let him fuck me, and frankly, I'm at a loss for words. He reminds me of a caveman, and it wouldn't surprise me if his next line is, "Me man, you woman."

"Brother, that bitch is on mine and Saint's cocks; no one else's." Sinner steps to my side, crossing his arms over his chest.

It's vulgar, but surprisingly, it offers me a touch of comfort having him beside me, defending my honor. If anyone around here wasn't one hundred percent sure we're sleeping together, well, now it's been announced. There's no room for speculation as he's proclaimed quite clearly that I'm indeed not just having sex with one, but both of them. I'm sure my face is flaming as it's suddenly way too warm in this room for me.

Saint appears on the other side and flings Mercenary's hand off my shoulder. "She's not a fucking club whore," he declares with a scowl pointed in the new brother's direction.

"I don't see a motherfuckin' property patch anywhere on her back. Is this how you do things down in Texas? Stake claim on bitches without putting your patch on 'em?"

Sinner's jaw tightens and flexes as he grits his teeth. His irises change to an obsidian hue, reflecting his annoyance. "We do things however the fuck we wanna around here. This is Texas."

His hand lands on my shoulder in the same spot the other guy was just touching. "In saying that, it means don't touch what doesn't belong to you. I don't offer second warnings," he finishes, leaning over and plants a kiss on my temple. It's more of a Saint move, but I enjoy it nonetheless.

He and Saint are in such a serious stare down with Mercenary, I'm a little concerned that I'll be peed on next to stake a further claim. I wish this guy would get the drift and just back off. No such luck; this battle of testosterone means whipping out your dick to see whose is bigger at the moment, it seems.

"So, you two share with each other, but not anyone else, huh? Sounds like some stingy motherfuckers, but all right. I'm not that hard up for some pussy, Chi town gave it up easily. Besides, she'll eventually come my way. If I'll have her at that point, is another story."

Saint straight up snarls, his body on edge with anticipation for a fight.

Viking makes his way over, noticing Princess' shocked expression. He strategically places himself between the puffed-up chests about to throw down. "What's the fucking issue over here?" he gripes, clearly not in the mood for anyone to argue.

"Not a fuckin' thing." Mercenary shrugs, meeting the Prez eye for eye. The guy has balls; Viking's kind of scary, in my opinion. He has that craziness about him you don't want to push, but it doesn't seem to faze Mercenary.

Sinner addresses Viking. "Prez, let this pup know that Jude is mine and Sinner's."

I nearly snort at his request. I'm theirs? I like the sound of that, but at the same time, it almost leaves him in a gruff whine. I'd never imagined Sinner being someone to ask for something. He's always struck me as the type to take and do as he pleases.

I guess Viking really is the boss around here.

"I'm not your goddamn babysitter," he huffs glancing from Sinner to Saint and then turns back to Mercenary's gaze. "In saying that, you have any clue who you're pissing off right now? You know we were all NOMADS at one point, right?"

"I've heard."

"Nightmare will light your ass on fire for a laugh. Saint and Sinner? Those crazy fuckers will string you up and Sinner will fuck with your head while Saint pokes holes in your flesh."

Saint leans over, kissing my forehead kindly, making it hard for me to believe he's capable of the things their president claims. Sure, he's rough around the edges, but poke holes in the guy? I'm not one hundred percent sure I'd go that far.

Viking continues. "Torch," he grunts. "That brother's name tells all. Blaze, well, let's just say my club has a thing for fire and sharp objects as well as our fists. I'm not getting in your shit, but don't show up at my club, stirring the pot with the veteran members. Trust me when I say these fuckers are just as crazy as your ass is, or even more so." he finishes, then tucks Princess under his arm and walks toward the bar, Odin hot on their heels.

Sinner's brow rises, waiting for Mercenary to make the next move.

"Don't take too long you two," he mutters. "'Cause she's just my type." He flicks one last glance at me from top to bottom and then follows Viking to the bar to get that beer he spoke of.

Sinner meets Saint's serious gaze and grumbles under his breath, just loud enough for me to make out his threat. "And you have a fuckin' death wish if you think I'm going to let you have her."

CHAPTER 12

Saint

"He's perfect," I murmur, garnering Sinner's attention.

"You can't sacrifice a brother, Saint."

"The hell I can't. He fucks up, I'll bleed him dry." The words leave me on a deadly promise; Jude's stunned expression, shaking me from my thoughts. I press another kiss to her forehead, making her blink. "I won't hurt you, baby girl," I vow, tugging her to my chest and wrap my arms around her tightly.

"I know," she mumbles into my shirt. "But I don't want you to hurt him either." With her admission, I thrust her back, so I can take in her face.

"Why? You want him? Think hard, baby, before you answer; there will be consequences."

Sinner huffs my name and a curse. He gets a glare from me and then I'm waiting for her to respond. The last thing I can handle is her wanting someone besides Sinner and me. I'll share with him, but no one else.

"No, I...no, of course not!" she stammers. "I said that because I don't want you hurting anyone."

Sinner tucks her into his arms next. "You should tell her about your heritage, Saint."

"No." That's the worst idea. She'd hate me in a heartbeat, and whatever headway we've achieved would be gone immediately.

"She needs to understand you; it's the only way."

"Not happening."

"How do you expect her to appreciate and trust you if you're not straight with her about why you are the way you are?"

"I'm not ready to go there, to see her look at me like I'm some kind of freak or monster. Just...no."

I already have a bad habit of scaring her; I highly doubt she'd fully understand the meaning behind my family's traditions.

"Fine, but you're going to have to open up at some point."

She turns in his arms to face him. "Please stop speaking about me as if I'm not here. And tell me what? I won't judge anyone."

"I know, sweetheart," he practically purrs and kisses her.

I don't know if it's him agreeing or the fact he has no problem sticking his tongue in her mouth in front of damn near the entire club that irritates me. I wish I could be openly affectionate with him the same way. Instead, I pretty much have to wait until we're going to fuck to make a move and touch him how I want to.

"You couldn't handle it, baby," I mutter, giving her a dose of truth, even if it does sound a bit rude.

She wrenches away from him to argue, but I cut her off, taking her mouth with mine. I kiss her roughly, Sinner's taste on her tongue, spurring me on. Taking it a step further, my hands go under her shirt, one sliding under her ass to lift her on my hips. I kiss her like she's sin herself, making a statement to the man beside me. I can sample her in front of everyone as well. She belongs to me too.

"Let's go to the room, Saint," he suggests from my left, but I ignore him, kissing her until she's breathless. "Saint!" he calls, resting his hand on my bicep.

Jude pants and leans back attempting to catch her breath, her lips puffy and rosy from my scruff, and I finally offer him some attention with a grunt but nothing more.

Hybrid Collection

"I'm not trying to be a dick, Saint, but everyone's looking, and I don't want her uneasy. You saw how she dealt with the attention from Merc just now."

"Stop fucking coddling her. She's not so innocent anymore, brother. We made sure of that." At that, I carry her over to the bar, laying her on the top.

"Saint? What are you doing?" She jerks upward to escape, and I lay my hand on her sternum, holding her in place.

I'm making my point right here in front of everyone. She needs to learn to be comfortable messing around anywhere because that's how we are in this life when it comes to women. "Stop moving, baby girl. I'm gonna order a drink, and I want you right in front of me, so I have something pretty to look at."

Her face warms, flushing a delicious shade of rouge. I don't know if it's because the bar's full and I'm making her ass lay on the countertop like it's a damn cot, or if it's from my praise. "So stunning babe. Your blush reminds me of a slice of watermelon. Just want to eat you up," I murmur, flashing a flirty grin.

With a flick of my hand, I grab my brother's attention. "Blaze, let me have a crown and coke and a shot of Ice 101 for my baby here."

"Sure, brother." He swiftly returns with our drinks, and I slam nearly all of mine in one hefty gulp. The ride may have been four hours, but it felt longer. Strange since it's usually the opposite, but I wanted to be here with her today. Instead, I had to go on a ride to pick up a new ungrateful member.

"Thirsty?" Jude whispers as she peers at me.

"You have no idea, baby." With a devious smirk, I pick up her shot. "Let daddy feed you this shot and make my boring day fade away."

Her tongue flicks over her lips, and she nods, eagerly watching the shot glass. "Okay."

"Good girl, now open wide. I wanna see how much of my cock will fit." I catch her off guard with my remark causing her to hesitate, her eyes flicking to the brothers around us. She has to move past the gut reaction to give a shit about what anyone may hear or think. She's not here for any of them; she's here for Sin and me.

"Now." At my command, she listens, opening wide. We catch the attention of a few brothers, but they keep their comments to themselves, aware I'll flip out on anyone that pushes the wrong button.

With an amused grin, I take the liquor in my mouth first and then lean over, meeting her lips with my own. Carefully, I open, letting the liquid leave my tongue into her mouth. She swallows, and I follow up, licking and sucking her lips where little droplets tried to leak free. "Mmm, babe."

"Holy shit!" she gasps.

Ice 101 does have a tendency to burn sometimes. I wanted to make sure all her senses got a little attention, plus I wanted to taste the liquor from her lips. Everything from her seems a bit sweeter.

At that, I flick my gaze in Mercenary's direction. His eyebrow rises, along with his beer. A silent toast saying he sees me. I don't fuck around. I may not have my patch on her, but he's lost his fucking mind if he thinks he stands a chance.

Sinner jerks a stool over next to mine "Blaze, brother, can I get a vodka and orange juice please."

"No problem." Blaze grabs a clean glass, adding ice and mixing the beverage.

"Having fun, Jude?" Sin asks, looking her over, and she smiles wide.

"Yes," she admits and sits up, her legs dangling in the space between us. She's adorable.

"Good." He tugs her in for another kiss. Part of me wonders if this is turning into a competition of sorts. Or if he's doing this on purpose to annoy me.

"Another shot, Blaze. This time give me three Patrons with orange slices." I wasn't planning on getting fucked up tonight, but maybe I will after all. If the shoe fits may as well wear the fucker. Besides, Jude's fun when she unwinds; she laughs at everything, and I love it.

"Bet." He sets Sinner's drink down and snatches the short bottle of tequila. Moments later, three full shot glasses are placed down on the bar top in front of us.

"Baby girl," I call, shaking her, so she breaks free from the lip lock. Her dazed gaze lands on me, and fuck if she doesn't look sexy as all hell. "Drink, now." I point in the direction of the liquor.

She licks her lips again and picks up the clear glass. Her doing so does nothing but entice me in wanting to lick them as well. Fuck! She has my mind all twisted up.

"What do you say?" Growling, I grab my shot and scoot Sinner's over in his direction. It'll fuck him up; he likes the fruity shit, not hard liquor.

Sinner's a freak when he's had just the right amount of alcohol in his system too. That's how I got him to cut loose enough to admit he wanted me the very first time we were together. Once he let me touch his cock, I knew he was mine.

"Okay, daddy," she replies breathily, enjoying the attention from both of us.

"Goddamn." My groin tightens in response. "That makes me wanna fuck you so badly. Now, down the hatch."

We throw the shots back and follow them by biting into the oranges. The tang hits my tongue mixing with my frustration toward Sinner. Before he has a chance to move or protest, I clutch the front of his shirt, jerking him to me. Then I plant my lips on his.

I've never kissed him in front of our brothers before. *Ever*. They speculate, but they've never actually seen it. When I touch him, there's always fire, a feeling no one can match. Until Jude.

With force he wrenches back, blinking, face full of shock. He scans the other bodies at the bar and is met with knowing grins from our brothers. They talk so much shit about us being together behind closed doors, but we haven't admitted anything out loud prior. I think he's been too scared...of what, I have no idea.

"Oh, fuck it," he groans a beat later and bends toward me again, securing his lips to mine. His hand grasps my jaw with force, his tongue attempting to punish me as well. I don't mind it one bit; in fact, I fucking bask in it.

Standing, I seize his throat in my grip, squeezing until he moans and lets me take control of the kiss. My own tongue's primed and ready to return what it just received; prepared to reprimand him with my own force. My anger fizzles with each twist and caress from him, the dual of sorts finally offering up something I've always craved from him.

When the kiss eventually slows to a few lax strokes, I break free. I'm left further in love with Sin than I've been in the past. He finally pushed past the final barrier between us. And it was more than the mating of lips; it was a statement made loud and clear in front of everyone. *He's mine.*

"Another round," we rasp in unison, winded from releasing a bit of our pent-up frustration.

Blaze sets them in front of us moments later, no comment on what he just witnessed. He does, however, wear a pleased grin the entire time. I guess we weren't fooling any of them.

"I'll take one too, Blaze." The gruff request comes from over my shoulder, the sound unfamiliar, not being from one of the usual brothers.

Whirling around, I come face-to-face with none other than Mercenary. He's no longer sitting in his place a few seats over, but here, expecting to join us in shots. I'm not sure that's the best idea though—tequila and Jude and his comments...I may end up punching him.

"So, it's like that, huh?" He probes before I have a chance to issue a warning threat. He flicks his gaze between the three of us as Blaze hands over the extra shot.

Hybrid Collection

"Sure the fuck is," Sinner retorts before I reply and Mercenary grins for the first time since we've come in contact. It's not fake either; he's sincere.

"'Bout time I got to a club that had some fucking balls. I have nothing but respect for the fact you don't give two fucks what anyone thinks." He holds the shot up, and we each lift ours in return, saluting, then drinking the harsh liquor down.

We place them back on the counter, and he holds his fist out for each of us to fist bump him. "I'm out." He turns and shouts the same at the other brothers as well and then heads to his new room. A few club sluts anxiously follow along in his wake.

Jude kisses the tip of my nose. "See, grouch, no need to slice and dice." She giggles, and I can't help but chuckle. Baby is feeling the liquor, and it's cute.

"Did she really just say that?" Sinner questions with his own smirk present.

"Maybe she'll fit in better than I thought," I reason with a shrug, and he nods.

"Another round?" Jude suggests, clearly enjoying the Patron and we agree.

This time she orders us shots along with requesting a margarita for herself. We have Princess to thank for that, I'm guessing. Not that I mind. Jude's too hard on herself for being young. I want her to relax and have some fun.

"You're going to need that drink; I've got plans."

At my promise, she giggles again. "And just what are these plans? Will you both be naked? Will I be spanked when I call you daddy this time around?"

Odin snorts from beside Sinner, hearing her. He's been around Viking's ol' lady too much.

Ignoring him, I kiss her forehead and sit back on my stool. Turning to Sin, I ask, "You gonna' be naked Sinner?"

He rolls his eyes, not responding to me and throws back the latest shot. He may not be ready to admit that much outright, but he'll get there. It took nineteen years for that kiss; I'm not afraid to wait a little longer for him to stop holding back on the rest.

"Yep, he'll be naked and so will you." I wink, finishing my drink before I cart them off for some playtime.

Sinner

There's a boisterous knock, waking me way too early once again. "Sinner?" An agitated voice calls after me, and I have to untangle my limbs from Jude and Saint. We sleep like a tumbleweed, all intertwined. It's been just like this over the past week too.

"Yeah, just a sec," I holler, my voice laced with fatigue from a night full of crazy sex with Saint and Jude. They never seem to have enough, going until the hours close to dawn.

Jude stirs. "Everything okay?"

Placing a peck on her forehead, I mutter against her skin, "Go back to sleep, sweetheart. It's fine." I cover her and then swing my legs over the side of the bed to answer the door.

"Yeah?"

The Prez grunts in reply, his gaze flicking over my naked body. I hold up a finger and backtrack.

Yanking on a pair of Saint's pajama bottoms, I shuffle to the hall and close the door behind me. "Better?"

"Yep. Saint in there with you?"

Hybrid Collection

"He's passed the hell out. What's up?"

"Sheriff came a knockin' at my house this morning."

My brows shoot up.

"Turns out a Lamborghini was stolen, and someone reported a man looking like Saint driving it."

"Fuck." My hand rakes through my short, dark hair. "I don't know who the fuck would do that. Saint hasn't left my sight, and we were on the run yesterday so it couldn't have been him."

"Thought so. Just found it kinda ironic since he jacked that car last week, and the police are just now showing up."

"Was it local or someone from Jude's town?"

"Didn't say, but it may be time for you to decide what you're gonna do with your newest play toy."

"It's not like that with her. You know that. I wouldn't have been riding up to see her whenever I could if it wasn't more."

"Thought so. That's why you need to have a chat with her and your boy. Find out if the bitch has anyone that'd be looking for her. She got any family?"

I nearly choked on the question, shaking my head.

"Oh, right. Good thing the cops weren't at my door because of that."

"No shit," I agree, and he sighs.

"You two going to shack up with her permanently or what?"

Shrugging, I run my hand down my face. It's too early to think about this shit. I want to.

"Figure it out; I don't like the police showing up at my house first thing."

"I will, Prez."

"And the chick's mom?"

"Will never be found," I promise, and I mean it. Not even by Jude.

CHAPTER 13

Saint pulls up next to me, killing the engine of his bike. "Where the hell are we?" He squints against the bright sunlight, looking all around, taking in the heavy brush and trees in a random spot along the highway.

"We're close to Jude's trailer." I'm surprised he didn't catch on to that already. Although he was in a car last time, so maybe that's why it looks a bit different.

"Why are we here?"

"I need your help with something," I reply ominously, toeing the kickstand down. I climb from my bike and take off in a quick stride.

"Jesus man, wait a sec," he huffs, copying me. We walk for about five minutes as I retrace my steps before he interrupts again. "The fuck, Sin? You want to share with me what's going on?"

"You said you didn't want me to lie to you or omit shit anymore, right?" I stammer, buying myself more time before I have to bite the bullet and have the serious conversation with him. One that I know will most likely piss him off by bringing up a past fight.

"Shit, what now?" he groans, placing his hands on his hips as ideas already start to run through his mind. I can only imagine what he's thinking after the recent events.

I halt at a specific, strange shaped rock, staring down at it and tune him out momentarily.

"What, brother?" He follows my gaze, seeing nothing but regular scatterings of yellow-green grass, packed dirt, and some random rocks. It's nothing special to the untrained eye, and that's one reason why I'm so good at what I do.

Wiping the sweat from my brow, I mutter, "I need you to do something for me, Saint."

"All right, but you have to stop being so evasive about it."

Gesturing to the peculiar rock, I kick an X in the dirt with my heavy leather boot. "I have to destroy evidence." My eyes flick up to meet his confused stare and give him the final bit of information I'd been holding out on. "This is her mom."

He blows free a deep breath, caught off guard. "You're sure about this?"

"I don't have another choice. If anyone finds it and discovers a lick of evidence, then I'm going away for a hot minute. Prez was pissed, telling me to make sure it doesn't come back to haunt us down the road. I can't let this possibly fall back on the club or us." He'll understand that, I'm sure.

"That's not it," he comments, calling me out, "You don't want her to find out it was you." It's true, and he knows it as well as I do. That's the last thing I want her to discover; she'd hate me for the rest of my life.

"She can never know." Agreeing, I chew on the inside of my cheek, wondering if I'll eventually wear a hole in it. What kind of man kills his woman's mother? A bad one, obviously.

"Look, you keep it straight with me until I'm done living my life, and I swear to you, she'll never hear it from me."

I nod, grateful for his promise. The only others that are aware of what went down are my brothers. I can trust them with this secret, I know that much. We all have skeletons in our closets that we keep for each other; it's part of the brotherhood.

"You bring anything to dig with?" He moves on, cracking his knuckles, ready to get to work. This isn't the first time we've had to do this, and I'm confident it won't be the last, either.

"Yeah, I snatched a few of the foldable camping shovels. They're in my saddlebags. I'll grab 'em."

"Bet. You bring along anything else or are we having a campfire to fix this problem too?"

"The smoke might tip someone off, so I took a page from Viking's book." I've definitely gotten more careful and creative with time; we all have.

His brow raises, intrigued.

"I brought some of the acid Spider had around so we could skip any uninvited visitors showing up. I didn't want to chance it with the highway so close."

"Ugh, that shit smells fuckin' rank."

"How do you think she's going to smell when we dig her up? Not like roses, brother; that I can assure you. The bitch didn't even wear any good perfume."

"Jesus," Saint gripes, shaking his head. He tugs his bandana free and ties it over his face, covering his nose and mouth while I jog back to my bike and grab the foldable shovels. It's going to be a pain in the ass uprooting this bitch with these, but they'll have to do.

We get a few inches of dirt shoveled off, and he mutters, "Next time you kill someone, just call so we can come pick them up with the truck. I fucking hate digging." We're sweaty and dirty already and have only just begun.

"I will. I hate this shit too."

"You need to persuade baby girl to give up that shit hole town. Ain't a thing for her there," he adds while shoveling like a man possessed. I don't know how he does it. The movements hurt my back. I end up getting on my knees, copying him and find it goes by quicker.

"I wanted to discuss it with you first."

He keeps shoveling, listening.

"I've had a chance to be around her for a while now; I don't expect you to feel the same way after knowing her for a little over a week. I'm not an idiot; I know you can't fall for her the same way I have in that short of time."

He grunts, not admitting anything.

"We've been riding together a long time—had each other's back for as long as I can remember. We've even shared women ever since I first started fucking...There were the times between us too..." I trail off, not sure which direction to go. It'd help if he'd at least reply more than a grunt.

He nods, listening, but keeps quiet still, digging through the packed dirt.

"I don't really know what the fuck to say here; at least, not the right thing," I admit. I'm a man; we don't discuss feelings like this all the time, if ever. He could be thinking that I'm an idiot right now. Who knows?

Saint pauses, his irises nearly clear as they look over at me, evidently thinking. At least I know he's calm. If he wasn't they'd be nearly the same dark shade as my own. "Just tell me what you want in all this."

Like that's easy to explain? How in the fuck do I say this without coming off sounding like a selfish prick? I am one, but I don't need him thinking of me in that sense.

"What I want? Her and you to keep it simple," I say, being as honest and raw as I can. It's the truth, right down to the basics of it all. Sure, I know it's more complicated than just that one sentence.

Scrubbing my hand over my face, I continue. "We're getting older, and as much as I love pussy, it's getting old doing the shit we do. I don't want to be scouring different bars for another chick that may end up being mediocre for the two of us. She fits us—both of us. I want it to be permanent between us three."

"So, what's the problem then?" He probes as we push more dirt away and uncover flesh. "Ugh, fuck!" He shields his face with his arm and jumps back.

The smell hits me, and I climb to my feet, stumbling backward as well. It's disgusting, like a rotted animal.

"I'll be right back." Jogging to my bike, I grab the container with the acid in it. I'll pour it over the body, and it'll be like it never happened in the first place. She'll disappear, and I'll be free once more. They may find a tooth or something, but I doubt anyone will ever look here, to begin with.

"The problem? Keep going," he repeats when I get close enough to finish our discussion.

Shrugging, I carefully open the container and then pour it, covering as much of the body as possible with the liquid death. "Last thing I want is for it to cause shit between you and me. But I don't want to give her up, either."

"Tell me, Sinner, would she be ours or just yours to claim?"

My mouth falls open at his question. I can't believe he would even consider me being alone without him, an option. "Of course, she'd be both of ours. If I wanted her for myself, I'd have cut you free when you pulled your blade on me."

"That again? You have to bring it up now when I'm helping you dispose of a body? I thought we were past it already. I was angry, but I was wrong. I fuckin' own it okay?"

"Case in point, you fucking owe me for spilling my blood!" I complain, gesturing to my ribs, irritated at the painful memory. My side is finally feeling better. It's not completely healed up, but the gash isn't so bad anymore. I can ride again without feeling as if I'm getting mini stabs ripping through my skin.

"You survived," he replies deadpan, not wanting the reminder. This is a prime example of why I need a woman in my life too. I crave just an ounce of compassion and worry that Saint can't provide, but Jude does so without skipping a beat.

After a tense moment, I whisper, "Do you even want to be with me Saint?" The words come out nearly broken with their implication.

"How the fuck can you even ask me that shit, Sinner?" He shakes his head. "I've always wanted you, from the moment I witnessed you broken and bloody. I made you mine. There was no other option at that moment, and I'd never go back to change it."

He pulls a flask free from his pocket, yanks the bandana down and takes a swig. Wiping his lips, he sighs, using the same hand to run through his wild hair. The man bun thing he wears came loose on the ride. "You're the only thing I've wanted for most of my life," he finishes and puts the alcohol away. "I know you need her too."

"And it won't bother you if I have you both?"

He shakes his head again. "No. I want you to be happy, and with her in the mix, I know you will be."

"But will you be happy, too, Saint?"

"I'll have you, right?"

"Yes."

"Then you don't have to worry about me, Sinner."

"And what about Jude?"

He shrugs. "She's already getting under my skin. Give her a little more time, and you won't be able to peel the bitch out of my hands." His retort makes me grin. I know what he means; she finds your soft spot and plants her ass right next to it.

We wait awhile, and I feel more at peace than when we arrived. I clean up everything, and then we head home to our woman.

Jude

Hybrid Collection

The guys disappeared yesterday without so much as a clue as to where they were going or when they'd be back. I asked Odin about it when I saw him, but he gave me nothing either. These guys are hard to get information out of if you're not one of their MC brothers.

Sinner came back eventually, and it was like a weight had been lifted from his shoulders. He wouldn't tell me anything though when I asked. This part of their life is frustrating. I guess I don't really understand the point of being secretive about so much. I wouldn't say anything about it anyhow.

"You still won't tell me where you and Saint went yesterday?"

"No. You need to drop it, Jude."

They came home hot and sweaty and went straight to the shower. What am I supposed to think about that? TV may not be my thing, but it doesn't mean I haven't watched plenty of it before. I've seen an ample amount of movies and shows where men go off to be with other women. Not to mention the way my mom would go off the deep end when she thought one of her creeps had been with another woman.

Not that I have any claim on him or Saint, but it still hurts my heart imagining them going out to be with other women. The club whores like to whisper about how the men are never satisfied and comment about Saint and Sinner going through women like they go through blow jobs. In the short time I've been here, I've discovered that's a shit ton of blow jobs. Princess tells me not to pay them any attention, but there has to be some truth to what they say, right? This is why them being secretive is making me overthink things all of a sudden.

"Is this back to the 'club business' stuff like that ride you guys went on to get your brother? Or something else?"

He sighs, drinking from his vodka cranberry before responding. "I told you when we left, that shit isn't something I can share. A lot of what we do around here, I can't. You've known this from when I first started visiting you."

"I get that, even if I don't see the purpose, that's why I'm asking if this is like that or if it's something different?" I probably sound like a nut job, but I don't know how else to ask him without sounding jealous. I want to just come out and grill him about any other woman being intimate with him.

I'm not jealous; I can't be. This has to be about safety or honesty or something. I will not act like my mother when it comes to other women. These men either want me or they don't. I just want to know where I stand. Each day here in their presence makes it harder to face the fact that I'll have to leave one day.

"Where's this coming from? Are you okay?" he grumbles, trying to turn this around and question me instead. He's smooth, but I catch it.

He reaches to pull me close to him, but we're interrupted as screeching comes from the parking lot. The noise instantly sets everyone on edge. "Go to my room and lock the door. Don't answer it unless it's Saint or me."

He's dead serious. Shaken from what? I don't know...there's so much to this life they won't share with me. Which was exactly my point from a moment ago!

"Where's Saint?" I can't help but ask as I glance around the room for him. I haven't seen him for a few hours; I just assumed he was in his room. Shouldn't I go in there with him, instead of waiting alone in Sinner's room?

A huff leaves him as it registers that he's been gone and that he's most likely responsible for whatever's going on outside. "Damn it. Stay with me at least until we figure out what's going on," he relents, and I fall in step behind him, holding the back of his cut, so he knows I'm doing as he's asked.

Sinner's only trying to protect me and knowing he values my safety and well-being, makes me fall a bit farther down the rabbit hole for him. I've liked him since day one. My body's craved his since the first time the word *daddy* fell from my lips, mocking him, and now my heart beats for his as well. He's finally begun to show me the softer, less brash side of him, and I've enjoyed it immensely.

Saint's coming in as a close second, and if it weren't for them both being open to the idea of me having feelings for the two of them. If I'm honest with myself, this entire thing has been confusing from the beginning. I've never considered the option of wanting two men. I hadn't considered it'd be a possible scenario in my future at any time. I mean, when has it ever been acceptable for someone to have that sort of a relationship?

Not that I should care about anyone else's standards, but I can't stop it from crossing my mind at times. If I mentioned it to the guys, they'd both tell me not to worry about it and to go by how I feel inside. That's one of the main things I admire about them, they want me to do whatever makes me happy. They're the same way toward each other to a certain extent as well.

"It's him," Sinner declares after sticking his head out the main door to look. He doesn't seem too amused with the outcome either, so I can only imagine. Stepping away, he opens the solid metal barrier, holding it so I can go outside with him.

Saint's back and in another sports car. Hopefully, this doesn't end up like the last time. That was a big mess. I wonder if this is a normal thing for him, stealing other people's cars. And how am I so relaxed about it? I guess stealing a car doesn't even compare to say…murder.

"The fuck, Saint?" Sinner roars, storming toward the car. "You trying to get us all killed? Tell me this doesn't belong to Mafiya too?"

The door opens, and Saint pops his head out, wearing a devilish smile. "Come on."

"Who's is it?" Sinner asks with caution. I can't blame him; supposedly, the last car that Saint took joy riding belonged to some mob member or something. I really don't want him getting hurt from poking the wrong bear—or us either, for that matter.

"Some rich fuck; nobody special. I'm heading to Oscar's chop shop." He shrugs. "Make a quick buck off this ugly monster."

"Jesus." Sinner shakes his head, chancing a quick glance at me. He doesn't seem too surprised, a little irritated if anything. "It's all right, Jude."

I can't help but laugh at Saint's animated reaction over his latest thrill. Shrugging my own shoulders, I make my way toward the shiny, dark purple vehicle. It's pretty, but nothing I could imagine driving; it's way too flashy.

"You comin' baby girl?" His wolfish smile beckons as his eyes sparkle with mischief.

I love it when he's like this; the adventurous side of me gets to come out. "Yes, daddy." The last ride he took me on, I was thrilled and frightened all at once. This time, though, I'm more confident in hopping in the car with him, and I know to hold on.

"Fuck yeah. Come on, Sin."

"How are we getting back?" He's always the one to voice reason and throws in a touch of caution I'm learning.

"I have to pick up Scot's truck; guess Nightmare pissed his ol' lady off again, 'cause she went to town on the paint job."

"B's fucking crazy." He shakes his head again, coming to stand next to me.

His hand falls on my hip, squeezing as he peers down into my eager gaze, "You're gonna have to sit on my lap. Think you can manage not to squirm or get scared?" His lips curl up just enough, giving away his front of being angry about Saint coming home with yet another vehicle.

"Maybe, if you're lucky I'll sit with you. I may want on Saint's lap instead. And I'm not scared. What kind of car is this anyhow?"

"I'm guessing some rich bitch's custom Ferrari, and you're on me, not him," Sinner rasps, drawing me down onto his lap after he's situated.

He spreads his legs, positioning me against his groin with the seat belt wrapped around both of us. With the way Saint drives, I doubt the belt would do much if we were to crash, so part of me thinks it's pointless. With those thoughts, I immediately hold on and with both hands.

Hybrid Collection

The doors shut and Saint revs the engine a few times, the tires making a cloud of smoke surrounding us. "She's got some powerrrr," he sings gleefully. "Come on sugar, you can do better than that Lamborghini," With a chuckle, he lets up on the brake and we shoot forward.

I wonder how the rest of the members feel about Saint taking off with cars and then making the tires burn out in front of the clubhouse. Last time Viking was furious. You'd think Saint would learn. He doesn't seem to have a care in the world about it though. I can't find it in myself either. I think it's awesome. My heartbeat skyrockets and a smile a mile wide fills my face.

Within seconds it seems, we're on the main road with my back pressed against Sinner like we're glued together. "I'm sorry if I'm hurting you," I call over my shoulder, while wide-eyeing everything as we speed past it. Trees shrink and quickly disappear, the compound far behind us within minutes as Saint presses down the gas pedal.

Gripping the door, I attempt to peel my body forward just a bit. It doesn't move an inch, so I give up and hold on for dear life. How does this man never get pulled over? Won't police officers be driving around and see him speeding? Hell, they probably couldn't catch him even if they did want to give him a citation.

Sinner's mouth meets my neck, his teeth lightly biting down on the soft flesh as the inky scruff from his five o'clock shadow tickles my skin. "I want you right where you are, Jude." His hand falls between my thighs, his fingers finding the spot that drives me wild for him.

Saint grins manically as the speed steadily climbs higher and higher. It reminds me of riding with him in the Lamborghini. "Redbone" by Childish Gambino thrums through the expensive sound system, and somehow the song fits Saint so well. He's utterly crazy, and I love him for it. "Pull her shorts down, brother."

Sinner follows his order, ridding me of the thin barrier and begins to play my body like a piano. He has my core singing in sweet surrender while I pant with need. His other hand circles my breast. His fingers find my nipple and pinch. It's absolute bliss.

"Oh God!" Moaning, they both chuckle in delight. "So close," I mutter, breathlessly.

"Cut lose, baby," Saint orders, staring my way a little too long for my own comfort, watching Sinner tease me in the best ways. It makes the threat of danger greater and in return has my body spiraling out of control. "Answer me!" he demands.

"Yes, daddy," falls from my lips automatically and Sinner's fingers apply just a touch more pressure in the juncture between my legs. This is craziness, having both their attention trained on me, racing down the highway, my hips moving to the beat of the music.

"I don't want you holding back. Come for us; I want to see you, here, like this."

"You bein' bad, baby?" Sinner growls.

Just hearing him call me baby like Saint so often does has my head flying back and my eyes rolling toward the sky. His mouth locks onto the spot where my throat and shoulder meet. He draws the skin in, sucking deeply. No doubt that'll leave a mark behind. All the sensations mixed together along with the adrenaline has my climax coming harder than ever before.

It hits me with so much force that my mouth falls open, a pleased moan drowning out the stereo. I do it for both of them, coming completely unglued and give into my own desire. With Sinner's skillful fingers and Saint's blazing gaze all trained on me at once, I let go. My body feels enraptured, adored, and satisfied when I finally peel my eyelids back open.

"Good girl." Saint nods, pleased to see me explode so effortlessly from their delicious torment.

The evidence of his own longing is easy to notice. He's turned on as well, with his cock straining against his pants. Sinner's length rests heavy against my ass. Is it from the speed, the excitement of stealing someone's ridiculously expensive car or from me falling apart I wonder. It could be the delicious thrill of it all.

"Will you pull over?" I request a few beats later and his forehead wrinkles.

Hybrid Collection

"Huh?"

"What's the matter?" Sinner asks nearly the same time as Saint.

"I...uh, well, I wanted to satisfy you both too." My face is already hot, but I swear it grows even warmer with me stating my intentions out loud. It's the truth though; I want them to pull over, so we can finish what Sinner just started.

Sinner lets out a deep growl, his sturdy chest, rumbling against my back. Saint hums, squeezing and adjusting his cock in his jeans. "Can't," he grumbles after a moment, not fond of the fact and shakes his head to drive the point home. Or maybe he's arguing with himself. Who knows?

"Why not?"

Sinner's nose trails over the back of my neck and goosebumps appear in response. "'Cause he boosted this car, Jude. We can't stop now. We have to get it to the shop before it's called in stolen by the owner or we're spotted by the cops. Most of them around here know us and are aware we don't own a Ferrari."

"Oh." That makes sense, so they do worry about the cops after all.

"Yeah, baby girl, can't get locked up." He winks.

I've barely escaped my podunk town; I definitely don't want to spend my freedom locked away in a jail cell. I wonder if I did if my mom would show up for me. I guess she wouldn't know unless Sinner was able to get ahold of her. I doubt he can, though. When she goes off with guys she's impossible to reach it seems. If she saw me here with these two, she'd be furious.

"I should go home," I utter quietly. I don't know why I even say it, maybe because it's how I ought to feel, even if I don't want to. Going home is the furthest on my list of things to do, but I should regardless.

"No." Sinner grounds out. "We can discuss this shit later."

I don't know what I was expecting, but it definitely wasn't that. I figured they'd be getting tired of having me tagging around all the time. Sure, we have sex and laugh and drink, but they must be missing their freedom by now.

"If my mom finds out, she'll be furious."

"Fuck her," Saint comments, his gaze trained on the road ahead.

"He's right, sweetheart. We'll talk about this when we get back to the club. But most of all, fuck anyone's feelings."

We can discuss it all we want to, but the fact remains true. If my mom catches wind of me with them, there's a chance she may leave and not come back for good. Do I want that? Could I live with knowing I angered her to the point of no return? I should be allowed to be happy, though, and being stuck in that trailer is far from it.

With a sigh, I let the thoughts float from my mind and attempt to enjoy the ride. It may be coming to an end soon, and I want to make the most of it. God knows I want every moment I can get with these men before it's too late. Eventually, Sinner lets up enough so I can wiggle around and get my boxer shorts back in place. Perfect timing too as we get closer to various buildings and Saint downshifts.

"You quit your job yet?"

"No, but she'll probably fire me," I admit, and Saint's frown warps into a smirk.

"Concentrate on your school work, sweetheart. We like it that you're smart," Sinner admits, and my chest feels like it could burst with pride. They think I'm smart and I love that.

The car slows as Saint presses the brakes, coming to a stop in front of a tall, chain-link fenced lot. There's a shack of a building up front made up of old gray siding and behind it a giant white shop looking structure with five bays. Each door's closed, and there are about ten unsavory looking men walking around the yard. There's a variety of vehicles on the parking lot, waiting for what, I have no idea.

Hybrid Collection

His smirk drops as he presses a button and the driver side window lowers. A young kid about sixteen or so pokes his head in. "'Sup?" He's fortunate Saint doesn't punch him doing that sort of thing; he must know him already, or I think he probably would have.

"Here to pick up my brother's truck. Oscar around?"

"He's out back." He gestures and steps away, then lets out a whistle. "Some set of wheels you got yourself this time."

Saint grins. "You have no idea." At that, the kid quickly rounds the front of the vehicle and shoves one side of the gate open so we can drive through.

If it weren't for Saint's MC cut and chunky silver arrowhead ring, he could pass for actually owning the car. Sinner said the cops know them, but one glance at a man as good-looking as Saint, you wouldn't second guess it seeing him with the luxury vehicle. I was dumb enough to think the green Lamborghini he initially showed up in was his. Now that I know him, I also know that I was far off. Saint is definitely a biker, not a rich, snobby hot guy.

He parks the car behind the shack. "All right, Sin, you get the truck. I'm going to go get paid for this purple monster."

"Bet." Sinner opens the door, shifting his leg outside and grips my arm, steadying me so I can climb out of the super low beauty. "You good?" He probes getting to his feet.

"Yeah, I'm great." I flash a smile and peer up into his irises. They resemble the color of gravel today, speckled with different shades of gray. It's one of my favorite things about him—how their hue alters with his moods. "Why?"

He leans in, his breath tickling my lobe. "'Cause we just made you an accessory." When he pulls away, he's wearing a pleased grin. "Ought to start calling you little lawbreaker instead of sweetheart."

Rather than shying away as he'd expect, I tug him into my body. Pushing to my tiptoes, my breasts rub up against his solid chest, and I whisper, my lips nearly touching his mouth. "I like it. Tell me, Sinner, does it make you want to fuck me, knowing I broke the law with you?"

A primal growl rumbles his chest at my reply, and his hands tangle in my hair. He closes the distance, planting a blistering kiss on my lips, showing me just how true my observation is.

"You have no fuckin' idea," he finishes, breathing heavily, and snatches my wrist. He tugs me after him toward the main office, on a mission.

Oh, but I do.

Who knew stealing cars could be so much fun? I guess I'm more like my mother than I thought because apparently, I have a thing for bad boys as well. Only I don't want just one...I want two, and if I have my way, I'll be keeping them both.

CHAPTER 14

Saint

"You need to talk to her..." His words trail off like a goddamn echo that I don't want to hear. Every chance we're alone, and he's bringing up the dynamics of our relationship. Before he wanted to keep her from me. Now he's worried that I'll be the one to lose her for the both of us.

I need to talk to Jude, I get that, but I don't want to. Once I share that part of myself with her, I can never take it back. She flipped the fuck out when I told her I was a killer. I can only imagine how she'd act if she knew everything else. She's green to this life, and while it's sexy as fuck, it doesn't mean she'll be okay with the way things are done. Or the way I do things anyhow.

Sinner believes once I open up to her that everything will be rainbows and sunshine. Maybe the brother's a little further gone then I originally thought. I wish he'd understand, but he can't. She looks at him as if he's the best thing since Cherry Coke. She's never seen him when he's truly pissed off and is fucking with someone.

I may cut fuckers up, but Sin...he filets their minds. I let them bleed dry, while he makes you question why you're even alive in the first place. I wonder if Jude saw us both in action, which of us would be eviler in her eyes?

"Not now," I argue while wiping down my handlebars with my shammy towel. It seems that no matter how many times I clean the chrome on my bike, there's always a damn water spot or fingerprint. Or blood. It never fails, I always leave some behind and not on purpose.

A rumble from pipes garners our attention as the sound of a bike grows near. We both watch as Ruger pulls into the clubhouse parking lot. I figured it may have been someone from the other club stopping by, but this is even better. With Mercenary around, it's good to have another familiar face in the club; I'm still not sure what to think of the new member.

Using my shirt, I wipe the sweat from my brow and chest. "The fuck you been?" I holler when his bike quiets, and he climbs off looking a bit weary. It must've been a long ride to have him showing up like this.

"Prez had me watching the piece of shit Fists," he replies with a wave and heads for the club.

"Damn, the brother looks exhausted. And I wasn't aware we had one spot pinned down for those asshats."

"I haven't seen him in a while," Sinner mumbles, running his hand through his dark onyx hair. He's got it combed back out of his way, but it doesn't stop the motion he's used to making when he's frustrated. "As for the Iron Fists, they haven't been at the front of my mind."

"Why's this so important to you all of a sudden that I tell her about my shit?"

"Because, Saint, I can't get her to stay here without you opening up to her."

I let out a grunt of disagreement. She'll more than likely head for the hills if I open up to her.

"I mean it, she has to know everything. No half-truthing it."

With a snort, I roll my eyes. "Really, that's rich. How fuckin' convenient that she knows fuck all about you, yet the bitch needs to know all of my shit?"

"You don't love her..."

"Jesus." Tossing the towel into the detail bucket, I meet his gaze. "It's been easy, just fucking and chilling. Why do you have to complicate it? You know how I feel about you without me even saying it, so why is it so important that I'm different with her?"

"Because, I want more, and I was under the impression that you do too. I'm not getting any younger, and I'm ready to have a bitch on the back of my bike. As for why you need to speak up with her? Because, she's a woman; she's different. You of all people should understand that with the articles and shit you read on chicks."

"Fine, Sin, then go put her back there; don't let me stand in your way."

All the questions have me wound up. It's been too long since I've made a sacrifice and talking about it, only reminds me. I haven't been keeping my promise to my father, to my family, and now I'm trying to ask the world to give me more. Maybe she does need to see this, and in doing so, I can ask for my ancestors' blessing with Jude.

The questions and emotions have me taking my anger out on him and then storming off. Thankfully, he doesn't follow; I might've ended up saying something I'd regret. Although, he's used to me getting antsy like this. With Jude in the mix, it just adds more pressure. I'm allowed to get overwhelmed at some point, though. This is a change for all of us, not just him.

"Prez," I call as soon as I find him. He's working on a bike in one of the garages next to the clubhouse.

"Brother?"

"I-I need to go."

"Excuse me?" he grumbles, standing to his full height. He's got grease smeared on his chin and three empty beer bottles around him. He obviously has his own shit he's been thinking about. At least he doesn't have to worry about scaring off his woman; she's already married to his ass.

"It's been too long since I've had business to handle." I get straight to the point. He knows me well enough to understand exactly what I mean.

"Ah, I see. Let me check somethin' real quick."

I nod, and he pulls his phone out, dialing someone. I eavesdrop as expected and figure out he's talking to Ares. I guess someone owes his club money and a lot of it. Not only that, but Viking gets super pissed when he finds out the rat bastard hurt a child. Well, it sounds like it's going to be my day after all.

Prez ends the call, sighing as he meets my eager stare. "Looks like I got something for you to handle, brother."

A grin overtakes my mouth for the first time today...shit's about to get real. Sinner wants Jude to know who I am? I'll show her first hand, and send her screaming in the process, I'm sure.

"Are you going to tell me what we're doing yet?" Jude glances from me to Nightmare's solemn face as we climb off the bikes later that afternoon. He's not a talker, so she's assed out asking him anything. I'm usually the one with a big mouth when it comes to the brothers.

"Sure baby, we're here to shake someone down real quick." Gripping her waist, I help her hop off the bike as well, careful to keep her gorgeous legs away from the pipes. "We gotta get you some more clothes, boxers are not good riding wear. You did good, though, gettin' used to being on the bike."

She glances down at her clothes and then back at me, nodding. "A shakedown because it's the first of the month?"

Her question is so innocent it even has Night's lip turning up in amusement. We don't go around collecting money on the first of the month from fuckers like this normally. We aren't drug dealers or some shit. This is much more serious than a petty loan.

Chuckling, I grab her hand, tugging her along. "Nah, where'd you come up with that?"

Hybrid Collection

She shrugs. "I don't know, just figured maybe someone owed you guys money or something and when payday rolls around..." She trails off, clearly having watched too many movies.

"More like a life," Night lets slip, and I nod in agreement. For the shit he's done, he owes blood in the least.

"A life?" she echoes with a gasp.

"You just stay out of the way, and you'll be fine, baby. Sinner wants you to learn about the other side of things with me. You may not care for it, but then you'll know just the sort of bad man you're getting into bed with."

"But I already know enough." Her eyes begin to fill with tears. "I accept you both for who you are."

Her proclamation has me leaning over to press a chaste peck on her forehead. To hear her say it and so genuinely has her making my empty soul not feel so hollow with her around. "You're a good girl, but this is our life. You need to see firsthand how ugly we really are."

The tears break free, falling like mini rain drops.

"Shh, you'll be all right, little darlin'," Nightmare murmurs, not comfortable with her upset. He's a complete hardass except when it comes to women I've discovered. He'll toss someone into a dumpster and light it on fire without a second thought, but if his ol' lady so much as pouts, he's out buying her flowers.

"Wha-what's going to happen?"

We ignore her question, not wanting to put it into words. She'd be hightailing it for the cop shop if I attempted to explain it.

"Murphy?" I holler, trampling over garbage and who knows what as we head behind the burnt down trailer. "You around?" We get no response, so we continue our trek, searching out the lowlife druggie. Prez said he'd be out here somewhere.

Trailing over the various piles of debris, we eventually find him hiding on the side of an old stripped down, weathered car. He's raggedy as all hell, clothes and face filthy, visibly shaking. He obviously was able to scrounge up some cash to get whatever drugs he's on but was too stupid to not pay up to the Oath Keepers. Bad decision on his part, that's for sure.

"Jesus," Nightmare mutters staring down at the shell of a man before us. The brother could probably break him in two if he just stepped on him with his giant leather boot. I'm not going to let him have all the fun though.

"Judgment day, fucker," I warn, a bit giddy with anticipation and his head shakes back and forth so much, it damn near looks as if he'll knock himself out if he's not careful. This guy's a freaking wacko.

"Nope, nope, nope." He continues to swing his head back and forth.

"You're nice and doped up, huh? That'll make what I have to do less painful for you. Too bad. You deserve to feel every ounce of it." I wish there was a way to sober his ass up some so he could experience just a smidge of the pain he deserves to be compensated with.

"What did he do?" Jude whispers, her hand gripping the back of my cut as she hides behind me. I'm glad she's back there, I'd never let the man die if he were to hurt her, accidently or on purpose. I'd torture the fucker for the rest of his life.

"An entire laundry list of shit, baby."

Peeking over my arm, she mumbles into the back of my bicep. "So why are you here?"

"To give the little girl he hurt some real-life justice."

"Oh God," she gasps.

Nodding, I give her just a slight bit of backstory. "He fucked her up pretty bad. Her momma came to the Oath Keepers for help since the law didn't come through for her. Anyhow, we're doing a favor for the other club. You keep that to yourself; I'm not supposed to share club business. I'm making an exception right now, so you understand why I'm doing what I am."

"What *are* you doing?" she quietly asks, repeating her earlier question and meets my stern gaze. She already knows, but clearly, she wants to hear me say it aloud.

"I'm going to kill him, Jude, and you're going to watch. Not only will I take his life, but I'll let him bleed dry. The blood will soak into the soil and be offered as a tribute to my ancestors for their sacrifices they've given to offer my family life."

More tears tumble down her face, coming quicker now, but her weeping remains silent. She's scared, and she has every right to be. In doing this, she'll also discover that I can protect her if need be, that I'm not just a soulless monster to be feared.

"Night." I signal toward Jude, and he steps forward. His hands land on her biceps securing her against his chest firmly, so she can't turn away.

Is it wrong to make her watch this? Probably, but she has too. Nightmare's the type that he'll do it because I've asked him to, even if he's not too crazy about having her here. He'd never do this to the woman he loves, but she already knew the type of person he was when they met.

I've never felt guilty about my decisions and my heritage, but right now my stomach churns for her. I'm stripping her innocence away one step at a time. Sinner was already broken, but this sweet creature isn't. For that, I'm truly sorry to be the one to do this to her.

Sinner's right though; if she ever randomly witnesses me doing a sacrifice, she'll freak out. It's better to snuff that option out now. She'll have a chance to swish the idea around in her mind and hopefully come to terms and eventually accept me once again.

"Times up, Murph." With my solemn threat, I unclip the machete that's secured to my hip.

"No!" Protesting, he scrambles to my left. He's too out of it to argue much or put up a fight. It's amazing my words register with him at all. Who knows if they really do or if it's something from the heroin or meth trip he's on right now? Regardless, half the people I kill are doped up on something, so this isn't out of the ordinary.

"Get him!" Nightmare growls, his feet planted in one spot as Jude attempts to pull away.

Murphy hops back to the right, and I slam the machete blade down across the back of his neck. "Ahh!" His pathetic wail's laced with pain and shock.

His back springs up, and I time his reaction to turn perfectly. A second quick slash across his neck has blood spraying free, and Jude letting lose a shaken scream. As much as I want to comfort her, I can't at the moment. I have to finish this.

Her voice is abruptly silenced as I imagine Nightmare slamming his hand over her mouth. I can't chance a look at her just yet. If I do, I know I won't like what I see in her eyes, and I may stop when I need to keep going.

Murphy face-plants, his blood hydrating the earth with each drop. Placing my knee in the middle, right along his spine, I yank his head back. Using my machete, I make a deeper slice across his flesh. It's an awkward position, but I make it work. The blood pours out, just as I want.

Cupping my hand under the wound, I let the blood fill my palm and begin to chant to myself. *Sacrifice to bring this man peace. Sacrifice to keep my sins quiet. Sacrifice for my ancestors no longer here. I offer this token of evil to you.*

I lay my blade beside us, and with my palm full of the crimson syrup, I transfer some to my other hand. Lifting up both, I present it to the sun, the god of light and warmth, the god of life.

For you, this I offer. Sacrifice for life.

Bringing one hand to my lips, I drink. The blood trails from my chin, dotting over the man's shirt. With my other hand, I transfer the liquid, evenly between the two and rub it into my skin, coating my arms with the wine of the gods.

"Please stop!" Jude eventually breaks free enough to cry out.

Hybrid Collection

My gaze trains on hers. "This is my heritage, baby girl. My ancestors took the evil, black souls and used them as a tribute. It's a sacrifice in our names. This blood is spilt to gain safety for you."

She sobs. "It's crazy...how can you be called Saint?"

"I killed the man I discovered torturing Sinner. He named me, I didn't choose it," I mutter solemnly, remembering that day as if it were yesterday. Nightmare's never heard this story before, none of the brothers have, but he knows now as well. No one is aware of just how long Sinner's been in my life; they know it's been years, but it's been nearly my entire life.

There isn't anything I can do about this, it's just who I am. Grabbing my knife, I slice long straight cuts on each of his limbs and one across his stomach. Sitting patiently, I wait, hoping the offering will replenish the land after he's stolen so much from it.

Sheathing my knife, I approach her, still covered in the sticky, ruby liquid. "Tell me, do you love me, baby?"

Her lip trembles. She's clearly unsure of what to say or do. I only want the truth from her and letting a bit of rage out on a piece of filth has me relaxed and bold. It's time we talk as Sinner asked me to do.

"There's no right or wrong answer, my sweet. Either you accept me for who I am as I have done you, or you don't." She said she did earlier, but that was before all this.

Tears fall, creating wet trails in their wake and she nods just enough for me to see it, her mouth opens, a whisper breaking free. "I do...I do love you, Saint. I don't know how, because it's so soon and things are crazy, but my life is fuller with you in it."

My mouth turns up into a smirk. "Time means nothing to me. I could've met you an hour ago; that wouldn't be the point. It's how you feel and how I feel that counts," I reply with my heart at peace from her answer and reach forward. My fingers trail over her face as I quietly chant, *"My sacrifice for her, to keep her safe, to give her life."* Then lean in and kiss her, blood coating my mouth as the copper taste remains on my tongue.

Her lips tremble underneath mine, but she doesn't turn away. She offers me everything at that moment—her heart and her freedom—because she'll never be the same afterward. She'll be mine too.

CHAPTER 15

Sinner

They return to the compound, both covered in blood, and I know it went well. As well as it could've, that is. He takes her straight for the room. Downing my rum and pineapple juice, I jump off the barstool, about to trail behind.

I'm torn on what to do, though. Should I give them time alone? Part of me wants to check on her: touch her, look in her eyes, that sort of shit. The other piece of me wonders if it'd be better to let him have her to himself to comfort after what she just witnessed. That's how it was after I first witnessed him doing a ritual. I needed his comfort. I've never cared so much before, and it's driving me a little crazy inside.

"Brother." Nightmare interrupts my conflicted pursuit before I have a chance to take a step in the direction of our rooms.

"Hey. How'd it go?" Fuck, I sound like an idiot. I shouldn't be concerned so much; they're grown-ass adults, and Saint's, not in jail. That has to mean something.

He lets out a sigh, his gaze hitting the roof before coming back to mine. "Truth?"

I nod. Of course, I want him to tell me how it is. No sugarcoating shit around here with me. Ever.

He gestures to the bar, and I take my spot again as Blaze sets a longneck in front of my brother. "She cried the entire time," he admits with a sigh. It had to be difficult to be a part of it as well, caring so much for his woman.

"Fuck."

"Yeah, but what did you expect? Saint doesn't do shit halfway; you're more aware of that than me."

My gaze scans over him sitting next to me, noticing he's free of any blood splatter. He must've held Jude far enough away that the blood she wears came from Saint's hands only. It offers a tiny bit of peace, if anything. I'm sure the outcome would've been worse had it been sprayed on her directly. I can only imagine—she'd probably lose her lunch and pass out at that sight.

"I was worried she'd flip her shit and head for the cop shop." My shoulders drop with the admission.

"Nah, she freaked, don't get me wrong. But once she kissed Saint with blood all over him, I knew she was straight. She's down with an entirely different level of crazy, brother. You don't find women that'll watch you kill somebody and not break. She stood strong, if not a bit scared. One thing's for certain, she's damn sure loyal to him."

A relieved breath breaks free. "He kissed her like that?" I saw the dried blood on her face but hoped that was the extent of it.

"He did his usual shit with the blood and then painted her with it as well. She's a sweet one. I was surprised she didn't fall the fuck out at that. Especially after witnessing him slice into the shitbag...She sucked it up though and admitted she loves him. Hell, it wouldn't faze me if she helped right beside him if he were to ask her at this point."

My brows drop, my worry warping into something else entirely. That sounds a lot like blind devotion to me. It took years before I was able to stand with Saint and not let the blood taint me. I was convinced I was committing a sin, even if the men he killed were bad.

Now, I don't get the feeling quite as strongly. There's still the piece that nags in the back of my head though. That's one of the main reasons why I attempt to be the voice of reason or put whoever he's bleeding dry, out of their misery quickly. We've come across a couple really bad seeds that Saint's sliced open and just let them drip out while they remain alive for days.

Hybrid Collection

"What is it, brother?" His concerned gaze rakes over me, witnessing my expression change.

"Nothing," I huff and shake my head.

Drinking from the fresh drink Blaze made me, I eventually stammer the truth out. "It's just...she hasn't even said that shit to me yet. And I've known her far longer now. I guess I believed she cared for me more." Can't believe I'm admitting it out loud; it sounds pathetic to my own ears.

"You're overthinking it, Sin; he put her on the spot and asked her straight up."

"Should I ask her like that, too, then?"

He shrugs. "Fuck if I know; chicks are confusing. I've never really understood them. One thing I have learned though, you get a chick that far gone for you, you hold on to her."

"That's the truth, and I'm trying to. That was the point of today anyhow. I'm ready for her to be on the back of my bike for good."

"Look, do you love her?"

Unable to answer him aloud, I nod.

I don't know when it happened—maybe a month ago, maybe two days ago. Who knows? But it happened. When I think of who has my heart, Saint's not the only one filling that spot anymore. Jude has quite a big chunk of it, and I don't want to lose her. It's part of why she needed to find out about Saint.

"Maybe you ought to tell her how you feel. B was a stubborn bitch; I had to pretty much spell it out to get her locked down. You remember me packing her belongings up and moving her in the house. I didn't give her a choice, even when she fought me on it. Our situation was a little different with my son involved, but you get the point I'm making."

I remember him falling for Bethany; she had his nuts in a vice every time she was around. It's surprising that one of them didn't end up shooting the other with how much they were at each other's throats at first. Now you'd look at them and not be able to imagine how they were ever apart, to begin with. Unless his ol' lady's pissed, then you hope to God she doesn't scratch up your bike on accident attempting to get to Nightmare's.

Same with Viking and Princess. Their relationship was out of the ordinary in the beginning, and yet they're fully devoted to each other. I don't think devoted is a strong enough word when it comes to them—more like obsessed. Viking wanted her from the moment he laid his eyes on her, and now they're married.

Jude was a little different for me because I fought myself over her. And there's also the complication of me being married to her mother. Which also reminds me; I need to call the club lawyer and find out what's going on with the recent paperwork he's filed with the court. We're claiming she up and left right after we were married and hope that the judge grants an annulment.

"Did he say it back when she admitted how she felt?" I can't let it go. I want every detail he has. Now I understand why Viking was such a dick when he was trying to lock it down with Princess.

"No, he went on chanting some stuff then kissed her. It was trippy," he admits reluctantly, taking a long pull from his beer.

"I'm going to sit here awhile and let him take some time alone with her I think. Maybe he has some stuff he needs to say to her now."

"This doesn't fuck with you? Him wanting her and all?"

Shaking my head, I swallow another gulp and let the alcohol calm me. "If it were anyone else, it would, but not him." I can't let it, I don't want there to be anything tearing us apart from each other or away from Jude.

"You love him too," he states, and I agree. He tips his bottle my way, and I tap my glass to his. "Whatever makes you happy, brother," he replies genuinely.

The acceptance from the brothers has been alarming, to say the least. Most I've known in the past would turn their noses up at our decision to have each other along with a woman. I don't know why I ever worried about judgment being cast by my brothers on mine and Saint's relationship. I should've known, they'd always have my back in whatever's going down. Same as I'd have theirs.

When it comes down to it, Oath Keepers are more than just a brotherhood. They're a family.

Jude

Saint tugs me along, and eventually, we end up in his room, alone. We passed Sinner by. I wanted to say something but never spoke up. I think my mind's in shock at the moment over what just happened. Like it shouldn't be real, but I know it is.

I just watched a man I care about kill someone and then drink their blood. That changes things in so many ways. He forewarned me, but I was dumb and brushed it aside. I should've listened. Next time, I will.

This means that Sinner is a killer too. No longer can I hide behind my naiveté about the things they've said. This whole time they were honest with me, and I disregarded it as over exaggeration. I was a fool not to see what was right in front of me.

These men are bad...yet I've fallen for them—both of them. Saint asked me if I love him, and despite the gruesome scene, I spoke the truth. I do. I love them both.

The part that has my mind so confused is where do we go from here? Does he kill me now because I know his secret? He said Sinner wanted me to see the other side of him. Does this mean I'm more to him than just another woman to warm his bed? It has to.

"Saint?" His name falls from my lips sounding a bit rough. My throat's sore from trying to scream through Nightmare's hand. What a mess.

"Shhh, baby. I'll take care of you."

He heads for the bathroom and turns the shower on full blast then steps back in front of me. Carefully he peels my now ruined shirt free, following with my shorts and underwear, throwing them toward his over-filled hamper. "Beautiful." His compliment's like a tender kiss after a long day.

Linking our fingers together he leads me to the shower. The room's already filling with steam, embracing me in its warm cocoon. "Let's clean you up." He holds me steady; helping me as I climb over the threshold then tosses his own clothes away. Naked Saint is one of my favorite things to see; he's breathtaking—even completely dirty.

"Why are you doing this?" The words scratch as I utter them, attempting to understand what everything means and where we go from here.

"'Cause I'm gonna take care of you, same as our boy, Sinner. I won't let anything bad happen to either of you."

"Is that why you showed me?"

The hot jets of water tumble over my hair as he climbs in behind me. He pulls me into his body, securing me to him with his strength. His embrace is full of comfort; I want to bask in it forever. He's not massively built like some of the other members, but he's definitely solid with his own striking set of muscles.

"Part of it. The sacrifice is an important part of my Indian heritage. Killing that scum was to show you that I can protect you when needed. I always fight for what I think is right. Sometimes the cost is blood. I also wanted to see how far your acceptance ran."

"You killed for Sinner." It's not a question; I already know the answer deep down.

"I did, and I would again without a second thought. I will kill for you if it comes to it," he states, moving my body to face him. My breasts press into his chest as he hugs me tightly, helping mend the pieces I feel are so scattered.

Hybrid Collection

Meeting his gaze as the water beats down on my back, I lean up on my tiptoes. He easily reads my intentions, dipping his head so I can reach his lips. "I meant it, Saint," I promise and push my lips to his.

The kiss is different from those in the past. It's loving and full of compassion. His lips move unhurriedly, allowing his tongue to love my mouth. It's everything that means so much, wrapped up into the mating of mouths.

He's feeling guilty for putting me through that ordeal; it's pouring off him. One hand holds me to him tightly as if he's scared to let me go, while his other cradles my face in his palm. We stand there kissing for what must be minutes even though it feels like longer. All I know is he sweetly coaxes my tongue with his until the waters washed away any remnant of the dried blood from them.

It could be an eternity, and yet, suddenly that doesn't feel like enough. I'm going to need this man in my life long after any word such as forever can encompass. He's shared his darker side with me, yes…but he's also opened his soul and made a place for me.

Pulling away enough so I can speak, I rest my forehead against his scruffy cheek. "I want you."

"You have me." He promises and grabs a bar of soap. Lathering it up, he spreads bubbles all over the two of us until the water begins to turn cold. With goosebumps covering our skin, we quickly rinse the soap and turn the water off.

He leads me to his bed, pushing me down. Our wet bodies get the covers wet. My hair fans out around me, and he gazes at me with such lust and heat, unlike he's ever looked at me before. Sure, I knew he wanted me, but nothing like this. It's as if he's seeing me for the first time.

His hands trail up over my knees. The callused palms follow over my thighs and spread my legs as he nears the juncture encasing my core. Planting his knees between them, he stares down at me, taking every inch of me in. His disheveled appearance—wet hair going in every direction and his unshaved face—makes him even more enticing.

"Saint?" Sighing his name, I bite down on my bottom lip unsure what he wants me to do. I'm his to use up as much as he desires.

"You're getting what you want," he mutters scooting down until his face is so freaking close to the spot where I've been craving his touch. His palms graze my flesh, stopping on each side to push my legs apart even more. Saint's presented with an up close and personal view of my pink center.

It takes everything not to squirm away. I want him there, but at the same time, I'm bashful about it. "Baby, if I'm going to lick it, I damn sure plan to look my fill." The tip of his nose softly runs over the delicate skin, as he inhales my scent. Shallow breaths escape my lips in anticipation.

He dives in with a pleased grumble along the way. "Fuckin' perfection." His blissful assault begins with long strokes, making his tongue flat. The movements of his skilled mouth cause me to gasp in response, silently wishing for him to never stop.

"Oh God." The moan leaves me breathlessly, my eyes rolling heavenward.

"Nope, just me," he groans, planting his lips on my clit where he begins to suck. The sensations have my hips jumping, and in return he plants his hand in the middle of my stomach, gripping me to the mattress.

"Yes!" The words escape on a hiss as my arms fly up, my own hands tangling in my wet hair. I don't know what to do with them, so I tug on the locks, the zing of pain adding to my pleasure.

He uses his free hand to take turns filling me with his tongue and fingers, my climax storming ahead full steam. My minds' in a blissful haze, distracted so much that I don't hear when Sinner comes into the room with us. One minute Saint's tongue's inside me, and the next, he's sitting back with lust coating his gaze, my wetness on his chin.

"You joining us?" he rasps and Sinner nods, eyes pinned on me as he strips clothes off. "How do you want it?"

"I'll lay down, Saint; let me have a turn at tasting Jude," he replies, never breaking his stare. "You hear me, Jude? I want your pussy on my lips, sweetheart."

Hybrid Collection

Clearing my throat, I scramble on to my knees and scoot over for him, my core still throbbing with need. He tosses his clothes and lies down as Saint grabs a bottle of lube from the dresser. He tugs me over, having me straddle his mouth and face Saint. These men aren't intimidated whatsoever to be up close and personal with every inch of me; if anything, the closer, the better.

Sinner lets lose a gruff sounding growl, vibrating my sensitive parts as Saint coats him in lube, wetting his cock and his ass. My eyes are wide as I watch, enraptured as Saint pushes the lube inside Sinner, eventually positioning his cock to enter him. At the same time Saint carefully drives forward, he pumps Sinner's dick with his free hand, abs constricting in response.

This is new to me too; they haven't been so open together like this. I'd wondered if they'd been together at all more than kissing and touching. Clearly, they have, and it's beyond sexy.

Saint gets a rhythm going as Sinner eats my pussy like a man possessed and eventually leans in, his kiss erotic against my lips. Pleased moans leave me between gasps for breath and teasing tangles with his tongue. I never could've imagined anything so freaky in my life. This is the type of thing that happens in dreams, and here I am in real life, living it.

Saint's drives turn hasty as he chases his orgasm, becoming lost in the feelings of his blissful reward, and Sinner's groans get buried in my pussy as he continues his assault, not stopping until I climax. "Saint!" I sing their names with a satisfied moan. "Sinner, yes!" He holds me down, not letting up as my high spikes and plummets, my body on its own private roller coaster.

With a deep groan, Sinner's come coats his muscular stomach, jets shooting in every direction. It pushes Saint over the edge as he palms my breast in one hand and watches Sinner finish. "Fuck!" Saint shouts, his eyes slamming closed as he fills Sinner with his own pleasure.

As my body hits the mattress, the thoughts pour through my mind of what today has shown me. I love these two men, and I can only hope they eventually grow to love me back. I can't imagine going back to my old life and not having them around to constantly keep my body on edge. Or to not feel the warmth surrounding my heart each time one of them kisses me.

I'm way past wanting them...I need them. *They're mine.*

CHAPTER 16

"We need to have a talk," Sinner mutters as I roll over the next morning, sunshine warming the bedroom along with the body heat radiating from Saint and Sinner. It's the last thing I'm expecting from him this early and has my heartrate spiking.

A yawn escapes as I agree. "Okay. Just us or..." I point over my shoulder in Saint's general direction. I know he's back there somewhere; I feel his presence next to me.

"I've already discussed it with him, but you can wake him if you want to."

"Ermmm," Saint grumbles. "I'm here, just sleeping."

A quiet giggle escapes as I smile at Sinner. He returns it with a sleepy grin.

"Have you been up a while?"

He shakes his head. "Not too long, just enough to do some thinking."

My stomach starts to sink. I have a feeling this is the talk I don't want to have. I thought I was becoming closer to them, but in doing so, perhaps they've finally grown tired of having me here.

"You know I care about you, right?" he continues, and I swallow.

This isn't sounding so promising. "I like to think you do."

"And Saint, too."

"Mmhmm," is groaned in agreement. Saint's not a morning person even when it comes to talks between us about feelings apparently.

My smile dims even though I fight against it. I don't want him to know our talk is going to upset me. It will though. Going home away from them will break my heart. I'll put on a strong face for them though because I can't let them see me crumble.

"You love Saint?"

"I do," I admit and I'm proud that my voice doesn't crack with the admission.

"Good." He takes a deep breath, his charcoal irises meeting mine, full of so much, but I don't know what exactly. "You love me too?"

My throat grows dry as my heart beats faster and faster, just from thinking of how much I love this man beside me. "Yes."

He nods, his gaze skirting over every inch of my face, eventually coming back to my anxious stare.

"I love you, too, Jude," he confesses softly and leans in to kiss me tenderly.

Tears crest and break free, emotions bubbling up even stronger than a moment ago. I could've handled them telling me to leave without wearing my heart on my sleeve, but to hear him acknowledge his feelings outright...I just can't. They mean so much, fulfilling something I've so desperately craved to hear him say.

Pulling free from the kiss, he says, "Saint?"

A strong grip lands on my shoulder, pulling me to face the man behind me. Meeting his ashy gaze, he's not as out of it as I'd believed as he peers down at me, clarity in his irises.

The pad of his thumb trails gently over my bottom lip, his voice a bit gruff. "I love you, too, baby."

More tears...but they're happy. My eyes shine with warmth as I look at him, and he pulls me in for a soft kiss as well. It's perfect, the way they both break their feelings to me at once. It's like having Boston Cream Pie Yogurt whenever I want it, only so much better.

Eventually, he pulls away, and they both show me with their bodies just how much they really do love me.

"So, this is your home now?" Princess asks and takes a sip from her margarita.

"Yep, they admitted they don't want me to go home—ever."

"Wow." She giggles. "I know what happens next, but the question is when?"

"What do you mean?"

"You have to be claimed by them. It happens to all the ol' ladies around here when a brother gets serious about his woman. "

"I remember Mercenary bringing this up."

She nods. "Yeah. Trust me; it's a good thing. Something you'll remember for the rest of your life."

A bright smile overtakes my face. "Oh, then I'm excited about it."

"Speaking of, here comes the grouchy man."

"Mercenary?"

"Yep, coming up hot, behind you."

"Oh God," I breathe and take a healthy gulp of my own margarita.

"Club full of half-naked women and yet you two stick out like diamonds in the rough."

Princess shrugs. She's model worthy, so she definitely stands out amongst any woman here.

"It's the boxer shorts and plain white T-shirts," I comment and copy Princess with a shrug.

"You may be on to something," he agrees, setting his fresh beer on the table and takes a seat between us. He's not invited, but apparently, he doesn't require an invitation.

My back grows stiff with his presence, but I keep quiet, sipping my drink, making it a bit awkward for him.

A few beats of quiet passes before he tries again. "What's up with that anyhow?"

"With what?" Princess cocks her head, peering over him like he's an annoying younger brother.

His stormy irises find mine. "You dressing like that."

"Oh, when I came to the club with the guys I didn't stop to grab any of my clothes. I haven't been home since, so I've been borrowing what I can."

He nods, his gaze still full of curiosity and need as he eats me up with his stare. "You're not married?"

I shake my head and catch Princess rolling her eyes.

"Look, it's not my place to say anything since you're a brother and I respect my ol' man's club a lot, but that won't keep me muzzled about this. You have too much interest in someone's woman. It won't go over well with the other brothers."

He flicks a glare in her direction. "I don't need your warnings. You're the Prez's ol' lady, I get that, but who I fuck and decide to check out, isn't any of your business."

Her hands shoot up, palms out as a smirk overcomes her. "Oh I know, I was only offering up a friendly warning. Heed it or not, it's your funeral." She ends with a wink, and a giggle bubbles up from me.

At the sound, he shoots me an amused grin. "Why do I get the notion you two are trouble in the making?"

Hybrid Collection

"I'm not trouble!" I protest with a smile.

P shrugs. "I've always walked to my own beat."

"You come off as bitchy, but I think I like you, Princess."

"Good," she replies. "Make sure you don't like me too much though, 'cause my man really will scalp you."

He chuckles, tipping his beer to her and takes a gulp.

I don't know if the guys would actually do anything to him in my honor, but I sure don't want to test the theory.

Our conversation's broken up with a shout from Viking. "Church! Get the fuck to the chapel!"

At that, Mercenary leaves us without a word, and I'm finally able to relax with my friend.

✞

Saint

"Church, brother."

"Yeah, I heard."

"When do you want to make it official with Baby in front of the club?"

He rakes his hand through his hair, wincing before glancing back at me. "She's going to freak, having to claim her in front of the club. I was thinking maybe the barbeque this coming weekend, but there will be too many people."

He's torn, no doubt. Even I'm not completely sure of how to do this, the right way anyhow if there is one. The other brothers were so unplanned, more of a spur-of-the-moment thing. Should we be arranging a specific time? It seems to be going against the dynamics of the moment; it's more intense when it happens naturally.

"What about later that night when it's members only, along with the ol' ladies and club sluts?"

He sighs, his fingers scratching through the scruffy growth of his five o'clock shadow. "Think about her, Saint. She witnessed you kill a man in front of her, and she accepted you for your true self. She put up with me being moody to her for months...not to mention losing her mother. She can never know about that, either. I want the most important thing to be for her, not us or anyone else."

"I get it."

"I want to do this for her more than the club," he repeats. "We don't technically have to do it in front of that many people, only the members, right?"

I nod. That's the deal we all agreed on after Nightmare claimed Bethany in front of us in the bar. It only seemed fair after two brothers took their women in front of the members to make it official that the rest of us follow suit. It was voted on and made into club law.

A smirk appears on his lips, his enrapturing eyes sparkling with an idea.

"What?" I grunt as we head in the direction of the chapel.

"What if we took her to church with us?"

"Fuck. It's a good idea, but bitches aren't allowed."

"So, we ask for an exception. Give the brothers a heads-up on what we have planned and see if they agree. They've had a chance to witness her naiveté for themselves."

Shrugging, we both flash her a smile as we cross through the bar, and I reply quietly, "Then let's make it happen."

"Bet." He bumps my fist with his, and it's on like Donkey Kong.

Hybrid Collection

Sinner

We take our seats around the table in each of our respectful spots.

"Oath Keepers, church is in session," Viking declares with a slam of the gavel. "First bit of business is Mercenary." His gaze hits the brother at the end of the table. "Welcome home."

"Appreciate it," the new brother acknowledges, and the Prez continues.

"We'll be havin' a barbecue this weekend to welcome you properly. Brothers, make sure you're around to join us."

We all nod, agreeing to his unspoken order. We need to be here to show support and welcome him into our brotherhood.

"Next, Ruger, will you share where you've been with the brothers?"

"Of course." He lights a smoke and passes his pack to Smokey. "Vike had me up checking out a possible spot for the Fists."

Half of the table either sighs or hisses in hearing the name of our rival club. I think every one of us wants to skin the fuckers live for how they've hit us in the past. We have too much unresolved business with them to move forward.

He continues, his normal easy-going personality nonexistent on this subject. "Spider had a general idea of the area for me to keep an eye on and other than that, I had a whole lot of nothing to go off of. But, I was able to hook up with a stripper eventually."

Blaze snorts and Ruger shoots him a glare.

"She ended up being more helpful then you'd expect," he huffs. "I found them, at least some of them."

"What'd you do?" Nightmare interrupts, leaning forward, his stare a bit wild as his fists clench.

"Nothing, Night. I watched, just like Viking asked me to. But by lying low, they have no idea that I know where they are, that we've found them."

"Vike?" Nightmare's heavy gaze falls on him. "What's the plan of action, brother?"

The Prez releases a breath. "Nothing, Night. I know it's not what you want to hear, but there's a reason. Like Ruger pointed out, he didn't find them all. I'm going to get with Ares about this, so he knows what we do as well. We're going to keep searching. Rest assured brother, when we peg the lot of them down, they will burn."

Nightmare's hands unclench and then retighten into fists, his glower toward the table so harsh you'd think it'd blow the damn thing up. "I understand, but I have a debt to settle still." He growls.

"We know brother," Viking nods. "It will be collected; you have my word."

Ruger finishes. "I'll go wherever you need me to."

"Appreciate it." He drinks from his bourbon, "Does anyone have anything to add?"

Saint's finger shoots up. I'm a bit surprised; I figured he'd want me to ask about Jude.

"Saint?"

"As an officer of this club, I'd like to put in a nomination."

Wow, really not what I was expecting. Everyone's brows furrow as well, clearly thinking the same thing as me.

"A nomination? What do you have in mind, brother?"

Hybrid Collection

Saint gets to his feet, glancing around the table before finally landing on Odin. "I think it's time we vote on our VP. Odin's paid his dues. We know his loyalty lies with the club and having you so close, he'll learn from the best."

Viking glances around the table next, noticing no protesting from the other brothers. "Well, to say I wasn't expecting this would be an understatement. However, I have to agree with you, brother. Odin has shown his loyalty, and I have it in good faith that he's racked up enough favors from each of you by now."

The brothers chuckle, and some nod—the statement very true.

"It's settled, then. Everyone think long and hard on it. It's a serious patch for him to fill and the next session, we'll hold a vote."

Odin shoots a surprised grin at Saint, and I can't help but be proud of my brother for being the one to speak up about it. We all know the kid deserves it. He's had one hell of a life and would do us all proud if shit hit the fan.

"All right, any other business?"

It's my turn to raise my fingers for attention.

"Sinner?"

"I, uh, have a personal request."

"Shoot." He tips his drink back, and I glance to Saint. He nods, ready.

"All right then, me an' Saint want to claim Jude as ours."

Mercenary grunts, and I shoot him a glower.

"I'm not asking for permission to make the bitch mine; she already belongs to me," I stress, glaring at him the entire time I grit the words out. Flicking my stare back to Prez, I explain, "I'm bringing this up because of the public claiming.

He nods.

"You've gotten to see how our girl is in the time she's been here. I'm bringing this up because Saint and I are ready to stake a claim, here and now. It'll be members only, so she doesn't have a panic attack or some shit."

"Ah, I get what you mean, Sin." He meets Odin's gaze and waves him on.

Odin sits up. "All in favor of Sinner bringing his woman into the chapel?"

We're met with a chorus of "ayes." Even Mercenary gives his approval all be it sounding a little bitter.

"We'll wait on you, brother," Viking grumbles, pouring him another two fingers of bourbon before passing the bottle off to Blaze.

"Saint?" I call and stand.

"I'm coming. Give us five."

With a few strides, we're out of the chapel and in the bar, facing a pleasantly buzzed Jude sitting with Princess.

"Hey, P." I shoot her a grin, "We need to borrow our woman."

"Sure, is church out?"

"Nah, not yet," Saint answers and Princess' eyes grow wide.

"Oh! Okay, yaay!" She beams a bright smile causing us to chuckle. Jude has no idea what's going on, so she just grins, happy to see us.

"Lemme see your bandanna, Saint." I hold my palm up, and he hands it over. "Jude, I'm going to cover your eyes, 'cause we can't show you what we're doing just yet."

Her brow furrows for a moment, but then she nods, the liquor making her relaxed. I tie the material over her eyes, securing the knot at the back of her head.

"Saint's going to carry you, okay?"

"I can't walk? I'm fine to walk, not much tequila. I promise." We both chuckle.

Hybrid Collection

"Let me just pick you up, baby."

"All right, but no complaining about my booty being heavy."

He snorts and scoops her up. "Hush up, woman," he grumbles, amused. I hurry ahead of them and open the door leading to church. I chance a quick glance at the bar and find Princess jumping up and down, smiling. She's thrilled that Jude's about to officially become an ol' lady and be a part of the club.

"Where are we going?" she asks, and a few brothers chuckle seeing her blindfolded. "Oh, sounds like the boys are here. Hi, guys!"

"She's been drinking with my sister again?" Odin asks, and I nod. It's when Jude is more likely to be more open to talking to the brothers. When she's sober, she sticks to Saint and me like glue. Which is good, I like it that she's that way.

A few brothers move their chairs back, away from the table and Saint lays her down, so she's on display for every brother. The best part is she has no idea about it.

"Geez, that's cold! Am-am I on a table or something?" she asks aloud, and I swear every brother in the place is grinning. She's so fucking adorable.

"Yeah, Jude, we laid you on a table. You have to stay there."

"Don't move at all and keep that blindfold on," Saint orders, and she remains quiet. He raises his voice. "What do you say?"

"Yes, daddy," she answers, her face growing more serious. Most of the brothers' grins grow to full smiles hearing her reply. I'm sure they find this very entertaining. Hell, we did when it was happening to Princess and Bethany. We watched and smiled the entire time, so I expect nothing less from them.

"Hold her hands." I gesture to Saint, and he grips each wrist, having her body spread out across the table so she can't move away. "I'm going to touch you now, Jude. I'm going to fuck you."

"Okay, are we...are we alone?" Her words are nearly a whisper, not that it helps keep anyone from overhearing her.

I want to tell her the truth, but I can't yet, or she won't relax the way we need her too. She has to lose it in front of them all, so they can understand there's no doubt that she belongs to Saint and me. Mercenary especially needs to see he doesn't stand a chance.

"I want you to trust me, sweetheart. You trust Saint and me?"

"Yes, I do."

"Good. You love Saint and me?"

"Of course."

"Good girl," Saint mutters, and I stop hesitating. Gripping the neck of the plain white T-shirt, I rip the material down the middle, exposing her breasts.

Odin draws in a quick breath, and Mercenary licks his lips, his stare heated looking at my property. The other brothers take it in stride, not reacting quite yet.

I place my hand on her chest, running my palm over the fair skin and over the mounds of her breasts, stopping to tweak each nipple until they're stiff enough for every brother to notice. She lets out a quiet hum of approval, her hips beginning to twist already building with need.

"So gorgeous baby," Saint comments.

"You ready for us, Jude?"

"Always," she confesses, her teeth sinking into her bottom lip with anticipation.

"I hope so, sweetheart, 'cause once I start, I won't be stopping," I promise, trailing my hand over her smooth stomach and grab onto her boxer shorts.

Tugging them down her curvy hips, I free her from the material, showing she's bare underneath. "Open those thighs and let me see that pretty pussy." Lightly pressing against the inside of her thighs, they drop to each side, and the brothers's eyes suddenly grow wider.

Sure, they have to fuck in front of the club to claim their women, but none of them has been put on display for everyone to look their fill. I can't hold back from running my finger down her tender folds.

"Oh, please!" She groans, and my lips curl up.

"Hungry pussy babe. You want my cock?"

"Yes," she hisses, and I chuckle.

"Patience, Jude," I reply and glance around the room. "Copy me," I say to my brothers, though Jude has no idea.

I run my finger through her wet lips again then bring the digit to my mouth to suck her taste from my finger. Stepping back, I wave my hand toward her spread legs. I think the brothers are shocked at my offering, but with me doing this, it'll be the only chance they ever get to touch what's mine.

Saint leans over, dipping his finger into her core, rubbing around her entrance a few times before bringing his pointer finger to his mouth, groaning as he sucks the flavor off. Odin's next, his pants unbelievably tight the entire time. Mercenary follows, staring into my eyes the entire time, full of challenge. One by one the brothers touch her once, skipping over Viking and Nightmare. They're both completely committed to their women, and I have a great deal of respect for that.

I figured letting this happen, standing back and watching my brothers touch her so intimately would bother me, but it's the opposite. It turns me on like no other because, through the entire thing, Jude believes it's me teasing her. She has no idea it was all of them, and it's something she'll never know because what happens in this room, stays here. It's MC Law so her experience will be safe from even her own knowledge.

After they finish, I go back, priming her for me. I make sure she's so turned on, she's dripping onto the table underneath her ass. "Saint?"

He nods and flicks his button loose on his jeans, "I'mma fuck your perfect mouth, baby, just like I taught you before."

She clears her throat, beginning to pant from my assault on getting her ready for me. "Okay, daddy." She licks her lips, and Saint lets loose an eager growl.

I unclasp my own button, dropping trow, so my cock bobs free. Saint stares at my cock as he frees his, running his fingers up and down over his piercings a few times. His dick's hard and eager to get started as he lines up the tip to her lips.

"Open up and let daddy in, baby."

Her lips part and I drive into her core at the same time. She's tight and perfect, pulling at my cock with need. My gaze flicks between my cock thrusting inside her heat and watching Saint's sink into her mouth. I love fucking them both; there's nothing like it. We've been with many women over the years, but somehow, Jude just seems to fit us both the best.

She moans around his cock as I use one hand to grip her thigh in place, the other playing with her clit. "Christ, sweetheart, you feel so good."

"Fuck yeah she does," Saint agrees. His hand's tightly wound in her hair to move her where he wants while his fingers on his other pinch her nipple, rewarding her for sucking him off like a damn vacuum. "You almost ready?"

I nod, pumping into her, driving her near her climax. "Do it!" I growl, and he rips the blindfold off. Not giving her a chance to react at finally being able to see the brothers sitting around the table watching us like live entertainment, I declare as my chest grows tight with emotions. "My bitch. She belongs to me."

Saint pumps into her mouth, grating out, "My fuckin' property. I'll kill any motherfucker that touches her, or him." He points at me, and I swallow roughly. I wasn't expecting him to make our love for each other so clear as well.

"My property," I repeat thrusting into her to the hilt and feeling the declaration all the way down to my toes. Jude is everything to us; she always will be. She cries out with her release, and I follow immediately.

Hybrid Collection

Saint pulls free from her mouth, her eyes going wild as Jude realizes it's all the brothers in here, surrounding us and not just a few. He doesn't skip a beat, filling my place at her core and with a few powerful drives is hoarsely calling out with his own release.

By the time I come out of my haze, every brother in the damn room has a cigarette lit—even those that don't usually smoke.

"What just happened?" Jude peers over at Saint and me. She's innocent, not stupid; she knows there was a big significance in what just went down. What exactly, however, she doesn't know.

"You are officially club property, young lady," Viking replies as Saint and me attempt to catch our breath and get our wits back. "It means these two are your ol' men and no one here can touch you but them. Or any other man, for that matter. It also means if you ever find yourself in trouble, the club has your back. Welcome to the family, Jude."

A few tears find their way down her cheeks as she sends him a small smile, her irises full of gratitude. "Thank you," she acknowledges softly.

"Don't thank me; it was them." Viking nods to us, and we both shoot her goofy grins, so in love with her and happy that we just made it official in the eyes of the club.

"Can I have a shirt, please?" she eventually mutters, and the brothers chuckle. Her face flames red, but she's good.

Yanking mine free, I hand it over. "I'm proud of you, sweetheart."

My compliment has her blushing even fiercer.

"Thank you. I love you, Sin." She tugs the shirt on, covering what's ours.

Pressing a kiss to her temple, I draw her to my chest. "I love you."

Her gaze finds Saint behind me. "I love you, Saint."

"Love you, baby," he smirks, popping a kiss on her forehead.

Viking interrupts by slamming the gavel down, making Jude jump and everyone laughs again. "Get the fuck out. Church is over," he grumbles, and we clear the room.

As we follow Jude over the threshold, she's met with a wide, knowing smile from Princess. She doesn't say anything so as not to embarrass my woman, but she does hold her hand out, collecting a high-five from the three of us.

In a flash, Jude's in the bedroom, yanking on boxers, her others forgotten in the chapel.

Jude

Glowing. Is it possible for your skin to actually glow? That's how I feel at the moment. Surprising since I essentially just had sex in front of a room full of men.

"How you doin' baby?" Saint checks me over, lightly giving my wrist a squeeze.

"I'm fantastic."

At my reply, Sinner chuckles. "Yeah? What are you up to now?"

Flashing them both a pleased smile, I pull on a pair of socks next. "You two just made me yours."

"Yep," Saint rasps and they both nod.

"I'm freaking celebrating!"

Both of their amused grins warp to full-on smiles.

"All right, sweetheart, but after that, we're getting your ass some real clothes."

"Clothes?"

Hybrid Collection

"Yeah, your ass isn't ever going back to that shithole trailer. You're ours to keep."

Saint fist bumps him. "Hell yeah. Forever, baby. Welcome home."

Home...finally.

Sapphire Knight

EPILOGUE

She's proof that you can walk through hell

and still be an angel.

-R.H. Sin

Two and a half years later...

"Great Job, sweetheart."

"So damn proud of you, baby."

My smile's so wide, it feels like my face might crack at some point. Both of my ol' men lean in and kiss opposite temples, their approval making me want to burst inside. I couldn't have done this without their support.

"You're officially smarter than all of us and you have the paper to prove it." Princess winks, beaming a smile.

"Ha! You have a degree, too, the last I checked." Shaking my head, she's next to pull me in.

"Yeah, but you just got a college degree in business. That's the real deal, and we're all happy for you."

"Thanks, guys." My happiness shines, directed at Saint, Sinner, Princess, and Bethany. They all showed up to my graduation, and I was ecstatic to see their faces in the crowd.

"Now if only you'd have gotten a degree at UT rather than in San Marcos..." She trails off, and my eyes roll.

Hybrid Collection

"Oh, whatever! I did it, so you owe me a pitcher of your famous margaritas."

Saint smirks. "You promised, P. My baby gets her favorite drink, which means you're stuck bartending all night."

"Ugh. Blaze is going to be thrilled having me take over his space," she mutters as we follow her out of the auditorium where we've just received our diplomas. "We'll see you guys at home." She and B wave as they head for Bethany's car.

"Okay, see you!" I blow a kiss in their direction, and the guys nod.

"How am I supposed to ride like this?" I ask, turning to find Sinner's gaze.

He's clearly amused as his eyes skirt over me from top to bottom. "I remember a time when you didn't have enough clothes to ride," he chuckles. "Now you have that moo-moo cape looking thing on, and it's so fluffy you may get blown away."

Saint laughs alongside him. The two think they're so hilarious, teasing me nonstop over this gown. They may hoot and holler, but when I wear it later with nothing on underneath, they'll be rethinking their comments. There's no doubt in my mind.

Sinner grabs my hand and presses a quick peck on the top. "You got a dress on under that, right?"

I nod.

"Then hike that skirt up and scoot in tight." He pulls me to a stop next to his motorcycle.

"What are you..." I trail off as he bends over and scoops the gown over me without hesitating long enough to make sure my other dress doesn't get stuck along the way. "Shit, you have to warn me," I call, with a laugh.

He hums, taking in my fitted graphite colored dress. Saint lets loose a loud, appreciative whistle, and his hands are on my back in no time, his lips on my neck. "Fucking gorgeous," he rasps.

"Thank you." I pull them both to me, a hand hooking around each of their hips. "I picked this color specifically for you guys," I admit, gazing at them both

Sinner's inky brow jumps, intrigued, and Saint smirks. "Oh yeah?"

"Yep, you know why?"

They shake their heads, peering at me like anything I may say is made of gold.

"Because it's the only color that I've found that at some point in time, matches both of your eyes. Never at the same time but it was the closest I could find that was the same as you both."

"Baby," Saint mumbles and kisses me softly.

Pulling away from him, Sinner leans in and gruffly whispers against my lips. "I love it and you, sweetheart."

"I love you both." My regard flutters over them both. "So much. Thank you for giving me this life."

They remain silent, all of us a little choked up with emotions. These past few years have been a long road. We've learned a lot, but the most important thing was that we love each other unconditionally.

"I couldn't have done it without you guys," I admit quietly, my proclamation full of sincerity.

Sinner tucks my hair behind my ear, his finger trailing along my jaw. "You did this. We just watched you grow into this strong woman."

Tears escape. "You rented an apartment here, so we could stay here the nights I had classes, and you took turns each week driving me up here and staying with me. Not only that, but you spent so many days and nights helping me study, so I could pass my classes. None of this would be possible without you two."

"Baby." Saint gives my hip a squeeze. "What did you expect us to do? You are everything to us."

A sob leaves me at the deepness of his words, of the love and patience they've shown me over the past few years, "You are both my everything, *forever*."

Hybrid Collection

They press a kiss to each of my temples, their eyes on me, full of love and tenderness. "Forever," their gruff voices echo and pull me in to embrace me in their warmth.

I never imagined I'd find my home, one full of love and acceptance with two men. They've been the backbone when I've needed it along with the shoulder I've cried on. They started out as my adventure but became my forever.

Saint

"What are you doing?" Her amused gaze meets mine.

Shrugging, I round the car. "You earned it," I reply and lean in to take her mouth. With a swift, heated kiss, I draw back, pulling her bottom lip between mine.

She hums with the enticing kiss, and I damn near press her over the hood to have my fun with her. "Earned what, daddy?" she whispers as I stare at her, entranced with her beauty.

"You get to drive this one."

She squeals. "No! It's an Ashton Martin; I really get to drive it?"

I nod, my lips tilted up at her excitement. "See, you even know what type it is; you've earned it."

She lets out a laugh that sounds like freedom against my chest and races around to the driver seat. "How far?"

"To Oscars. You should know the way by now." Sliding into the passenger seat, I buckle the safety belt.

"Oh my God, this is the best day ever." She closes her door and presses the start button, the engine roaring to life. It's a rumble that sounds like caviar and money, screaming luxury.

"Not the claiming, huh?"

Her flushed cheeks rise with her smile. "Oh no, that was definitely the best, but this...this is awesome!"

With a chuckle, I gesture forward, and she guns it. "This is me loving you, Jude."

"Never stop, Saint," she breathily responds, taking the curve like a madwoman, making me proud.

"Not on your life, baby. You're my forever."

Sinner

She smiles, and I feel it in my heart. I'd give her everything that I have to keep her happy. I'd walk to the edge of the earth if that's what took.

It still haunts me that I was the one to kill her mother. Thankfully, she hasn't found out. I don't think I could live with myself if she did. Instead of punishing myself for the sin, I do what I can every day of my life to make it up to her.

I'm the one who started driving her to school each week for her classes. I'm the one who got that apartment for her while she needed to study. I'm the one who trips over my own two feet to keep her smiling. I'll do it for the rest of my life too.

"Sinner? You okay? You look lost in your thoughts?" Her kind gaze finds mine, pulling me out of my head.

"Yeah, sweetheart, just thinking about you."

"Oh really? Anything that you feel like sharing?"

"Just that I love you and that I'd do anything I can to keep that smile in place."

Hybrid Collection

Her eyes grow soft and her palm lands on my forearm. "Sin," she whispers.

"It's true Jude, you own me."

"I know." She leans in and kisses my cheek.

"It's coming on three years here soon, and I've been trying to figure out a way to show you how much you mean to me...to us."

"You already show me, all the time. I have no doubt in my mind how you feel. You've been so loving and giving since you made me yours."

I nod, glad she feels that way. "You've changed our lives; you've given us a future."

"You are my future, you both are. You're my home."

Her words choke me up, and I gesture for Saint to join us and press a soft kiss to her perfect lips.

"I love you, sweetheart." It comes out gruff with the emotions taking over my throat.

"I love you too, Baby." Saint smiles and takes her hand in his.

"I love you, Sinner." She kisses my cheek again and turns to Saint. "And I love you, Saint."

He peers my way and tilts his head, waiting for me. Clearing my throat, I pull the box from my pocket and flip it open for her.

Her mouth pops open, her hand shooting up to cover it as her eyes tear up, "For me?" She chokes, surprised.

"Yes, my love."

"A-a gray diamond?"

"To match that pretty dress you bought for us." Saint grins.

"To show every person out there that you're taken," I add.

"Forever," she whispers, and we echo the same.

Forever...

THE END

Thank you for reading...

I hope you enjoyed Saint, Sinner, and Jude's story! I had an idea of where their story would go, but then Jude started talking to me, and I realized she was nothing like I first imagined. The epilogue was made for Jude. If you're asking yourself why not the other two...well, they're Oath Keepers, so you'll still get to see them throughout the others' stories, and I thought that was the fairest way to end it. Jude was the perfect downfall for them, as she was not what either of them was expecting and I absolutely loved that!

Please let me know if you loved them and leave a review—even a few words, is amazing. Thank you for being a part of my world and until next time!

#SaintAndSinnersDownfall

#PropertyOfOathKeepersMC

Hybrid Collection

ALPHA MEETS ALPHA

Chevelle
OATH KEEPERS MC

INTERNATIONAL BESTSELLING AUTHOR
SAPPHIRE KNIGHT

Sapphire Knight

Chevelle

Copyright © 2018 by Sapphire Knight

Cover Design by CT Cover Creations

Editing by Mitzi Carroll

This book is a work of fiction. The names, characters, places, and incidents are products of the writer's imagination or have been used fictitiously and are not to be construed as real. Any resemblance to persons, living or dead, actual events, locales or organizations is entirely coincidental.

All rights reserved. With the exception of quotes used in reviews, this book may not be reproduced or used in whole or in part by any means existing without written permission from the author.

The author acknowledges the trademarked status and trademark owners of various products referenced in this work of fiction, which have been used without permission. The publication/use of these trademarks is not authorized, associated with, or sponsored by the trademark owners.

Hybrid Collection

DEDICATION

To the haters.

May they get crotch rot and their dicks fall off.

1. She is built for a savage.
- M.A.

MERCENARY

"Mercenary." My new Prez flicks his hard gaze over me as he takes the seat beside me.

My eyebrow hikes, but that's all. I owe fuck all to him or anybody else. You get my respect by earning it, even if everyone around this place claims you're a bad motherfucker.

"Pretty sure the perfect job for you just fell in my lap."

I grunt. If he asks me to mow out front, I'm going to have to tell him to fuck off. I doubt it since he's not a pussy. Whatever he offers, I hope it's not out in the middle of this Texas sun. I came from Chicago; I'm not used to this heat. It's like being stuck in the depths of hell outside. The others don't mind it too much, but the shit makes my skin want to shrivel up and fall off.

"Heard you know your way around a few muscle cars."

Hybrid Collection

"Then you heard right." I turn my head to the side, my neck cracking with the movement.

"I've got some built up interest in a few, you could say. The bitch down at The Pit owes me a favor, and I've caught wind that a few Iron Fists have been nosin' around. This is my fuckin' turf, even where The Pit lies. I'm not trying to go to war, but I need any bit of information on these motherfuckers I can come up with."

My tongue rakes across the front of my teeth, savoring any leftover liquor before I open my mouth to think. "The fuck's The Pit?" I've already been briefed about the Iron Fists, a rival club up to no good where our colors and lives are concerned.

He smirks as his cousin Blaze sets a fresh beer down in front of him. "It's a racetrack."

"No shit?" I spent my teenage years racing old muscle cars with my father; it was the main thing we bonded over when I was growing up. Racing is in my blood the same as riding is. I can never get enough of the adrenaline, the speed, and the wind on my skin.

I'll admit, he's right about it being the perfect job for me if he wants me to drive for the club. "I don't have a car."

"Like I said, they owe me a few favors over there. They'll let you use a car, just try not to fuck it up too badly. Supposedly a few pricks wearing Fists' colors have been showing up lately to place bets. They should keep their distance from you, but if you're around Chevelle, you may hear something useful."

"All right, I can do that."

"Bet. I'll call down there, so they expect you. Ask for Chevelle. And keep your guard up; they're not the welcoming type to new faces. They'll try to ass rape you the moment they hear you can race too. I sure as fuck hope you know what you're doin' and aren't dumb enough to place high bets."

"I do. I'll keep my ears open and win some money to boot."

An amused smirk plays on his lips as if he knows something I don't. However, I know how well I drive. They don't have a fucking clue.

"How do I get there?"

"Hit the main road, hang a left. It's about thirty minutes down on your left side if you run about eighty miles an hour. I'm assuming that's not too fast for you."

I shrug and get to my feet. Obviously, he's trying to give me some shit being the new member around here, but I was in the Chicago charter since they put that bitch together. This isn't my first rodeo; they'll learn soon enough around here.

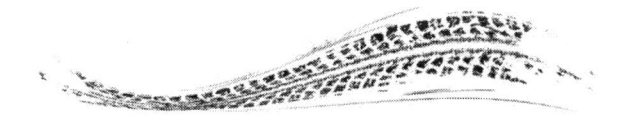

The Pit was easy enough to find. I thought it'd be some run-down dirt track off the side of the road. That's not the case though. This place is a fully enclosed old stadium. It's called The Pit because, at one time, it was a football field, and rather than having a field below, it's been replaced with a large race track. And I'm guessing with a set up like this, these aren't your backyard sports cars being raced.

Striding through the massive entry, I glance around for whoever is expecting me. There are a few guys walking around wearing blue and green STAFF shirts, but no one looking like they know who the hell I am.

"Hey, you know a Chevelle?" I holler at the dude closest to me.

His eyebrows raise, his curious gaze skirting over me from top to bottom. I get it; I look scary as fuck—been told that for years now. I think the only one not frightened when they see me is my parents. They've had years to get used to my ominous appearance.

"Thought I knew all the Oath Keepers," he comments after a second, staring at the patch with my road name.

"I just got here," I say in case he attempts to fill me full of some bullshit. Not being familiar with me, it wouldn't surprise me if he thought I was an imposter. It damn

Hybrid Collection

sure wouldn't be the first time randoms pop up dressed like rival club members. Normally I'd just tell him to fuck off, but the Prez needs me here, and I don't want to return from already screwing shit up. Being the black sheep of my last club was bad enough. I'm not aiming to be the same here.

"Ah." He nods. "You can find Chevelle down in the middle of The Pit, head tucked under a hood." He gestures to the opening leading to a tunnel on his right.

"Appreciate it," I reply, trekking in that direction. The building's pretty bare. It's like any other stadium with concrete and block walls. Various vendor carts not yet open for business pepper each side of the walkway. I bet this place makes a ton of money set up like this.

The cool tunnel opens up to stadium stacked seating, and I'm about halfway up. Glancing down, I take in multiple levels of stairs, all leading to the outside of the track. There's a fence surrounding it at the bottom and a few doors to enter. Off to the far right in the back corner is an opening the size of a car bay. I'm guessing that's how the drivers get in and out.

Pretty sweet set up, but how do they filter the exhaust out in the enclosed space? Glancing up, the very middle of the dome has various mechanisms attached to it, and it hits me. Race nights, they open the damn roof. Pretty fucking awesome. Not only do you get racing, bets, and food, but also the comforts of being inside and outside all at once. Whoever Chevelle is, they're a genius turning the stadium into this.

In the very center of the circle track is a row of five classic muscle cars, so cherry they make my dick hard. They range from bright yellow, midnight, navy, ivory, maroon, and crimson—their flawless paint covered in a clear glossy topcoat that makes them look as if they were just sprayed. Whoever owns these babies doesn't fuck around and sinks a pretty penny into keeping them top-notch. I can only imagine what's under the hoods; they're a grown man's wet dream.

Skirting down each row of stairs, my calves burn from the lack of support that my broken-in black leather steel toed riding boots offer. Eventually, I wrench open a door made up of chain-link fence and head toward the vehicles. Each car has its hood raised, and I can make out someone underneath one of them.

I'm greeted with a gorgeous ass poking out from under a waxed red hood; the rest of her body's buried under the metal. "I'm looking for Chevelle," I grumble loud enough for the female to hear me. Hopefully, she knows where I can find him.

Her body stiffens before she replies, "Who?"

"Chevelle. I was told he was down here. Is he somewhere else?"

She curses but doesn't say anything else.

I watch her wiggle around, doing who knows what under there. I'm not good at being patient, and it wears thin quickly. "You know where I can find him, sweet cheeks? It's important."

Another moment passes before she scoots back and stands to her full height, meeting my gaze. She's got grease smudged above her eyebrow, and it's pretty fucking hot to see a chick not scared to get a little grease on her.

"You a cop?"

I snort. "Do I look like a cop to you?"

Her eyes land on my Oath Keeper patch and she lets out a small sigh.

"I'm not here to cause any trouble." I hold my hands up and attempt to look friendly. I'm sure my lips moving look more like a grimace than a smile, but I'm not here to make friends, so it's the best I've got at the moment.

She licks her lips. "Chevelle." She throws her hand out, eyeing me from my boots to the spikey locks on my head resembling the color of ink.

Not what I was expecting—not one fucking bit. I thought Chevelle was a nickname for a man, but the person in front of me with curves resembling the lines of the sleekest sports car is far from a man.

My paw engulfs her dainty hand, swallowing her tanned flesh up with mine, and my signature cocky smirk plays along my mouth. This bitch will be in my bed, no doubt. Shall I wager how long it'll take me to make it happen? Nah, we'll leave that up to my talents not many have the strength to resist. Women love me, and I couldn't be more grateful for having that touch bestowed upon me.

My own gaze takes her in, looking my fill before she replaces her curiosity with a snarl. A fuckin' angry kitten is what she reminds me of, and I have to bite my tongue from laughing and infuriating her further. "I was told to find you."

"Yeah?" Shutters come over her bored gaze, and she turns, striding away without giving me so much as a second to finish speaking.

"Hey, I'm talkin' to you." The growl leaves me as I storm after her, the sway of her ass is a welcome site that's for sure.

Her head dips under the hood of an ebony muscle car, wrist twisting away at a wrench.

"Want me to fix it for you?" I offer, hoping the olive branch will get her to cool her jets.

"Cute," she scowls.

"Look, I got your name from my Prez. Like I said earlier, I'm not here to cause any shit."

She finishes tightening whatever she's been working on, standing back to her full height. I'd peg her around five feet six or so. A full foot shorter than myself, yet she doesn't even blink, looking me over as if I'm another tool she doesn't need to worry her pretty little head over. She's mistaken.

I watch as she pulls a set of keys out of her pocket, flinging them in my direction. It takes me a moment to catch on but snatch the keys before they collide with my face. This kitten likes to scratch it seems.

My own smirk mirrors on her face. "You wanna talk?" Her brow raises, hands propped on her perfect birthing hips. "Then race me for it." She nods to the car parked behind me, and I let loose a loud, devious chuckle.

"Fuck yes. Don't get too wet watching me smoke your ass on that track." I close the hood and hop in the awaiting vehicle before she can respond.

Slamming the hood of what I now see is a Chevelle, she slides in the driver seat. She winks my way as she turns the engine over and a rumble erupts so fucking loud it vibrates my feet. Gulping down, it hits me that clearly this isn't her first race either, and from the sound of that car, she knows her shit.

She romps on it as I crank my own car's engine over and follow her to the starting line on the track in The Pit. She's stuck me in a classic Camaro. Little does she know, but it's one of my favorite models and years. She has good taste—not that I'd freely admit that to her.

I'm about to roll the passenger window up when a shrill whistle comes from my left. Glancing over, her smile's purely wicked as she holds her finger up. Swinging from that finger is her tank top, leaving her clad in a black lacey bra. My mouth drops open, and so does her shirt. With that clear message, she hits the gas, and I'm easily left in her wake.

She has fucking balls—more than many of the men I've met who gather to race like they own the track. This is her house, and she's making it clear from the start just who runs it. I've raced many times, beginning when I was damn near a kid. Having the experience, the grease and gas in your blood is almost like a disease. You can fight it, but the need is overwhelming to capture that sense of adrenaline, of dangerous peace you get when driving a car so fast you feel as if you're flying.

No matter how much experience I have, her taillights mock me. I could easily hear the power her engine thundered with, feel its very breath like a hot caress against my neck. There was no way in hell I'd win this one; she'd taunted me like a dog with a bone. Making me believe I'd have her, catch her, and show her just how big my cock was. Not today, though. She has this one in the bag, and all I can do is lick my wounds at having my ass handed to me at the one place I'm most confident—the track.

She's sitting on her hood by the time I pull up next to her. Shirt back in place, covering the gorgeous exposed flesh that I'd only gotten a brief glance of. Even more fucking beautiful than I'd initially thought. It's rare in my case that you meet

Hybrid Collection

an alpha female that can truly capture your attention. I like them meek and willing usually, but this chick...well, she lights a fire under my ass so hot it burns inside, and we've barely even spoken to one another.

Climbing out, I come to stand in front of her. Legs spread shoulder width apart, arms firmly crossed over my chest, brow cocked. I know she has something to say after that show of dominance. That thought has me snorting, wondering what she'd do if I bent her ass over that hood and fucked her until she begged to know my name? Doubt she's had a man in her life or bed wild enough to stand up to her, but she'll learn.

"That lap took me one minute, fourteen seconds."

I don't ask how she knows, only swallow and remain quiet, because that time is damn good.

"That's how long you have my attention," she finishes, and I breathe deeply to keep my temper under control. It's not often that I'm not the one bending people to my will. I don't like it, but I need her to hear me out. I'll take the minute.

"Viking said you have some Iron Fists around here. I want in. He wants me in."

She scoffs. "I see you know where the gas pedal is in *my* car. Do *you* have anything besides that two-wheeled machine you rode in on?"

How does she know I rode my bike? I could've driven...maybe because of the vest.

"He said you owe him."

"He said a lot, apparently. Where is he?"

"With his woman at his club, as he should be. We do his bidding. You damn well know that."

She smirks again, and I don't know if it needs to be kissed off her or smacked off at this point. She's arrogant, more so than even possibly myself. I don't know how to deal with bitches like this. I prefer it when they crave my touch, wallow in my protection. Clearly, Chevelle doesn't think she needs either. She's wrong, however.

If the Fists are around, then she needs me here whether she wants to admit it or not.

"Fine." She breathes the word after a beat. "Keep the Camaro, but listen closely cupcake. You fuck up my car, I'll bust your goddamn knee caps so badly you'll never walk straight again. This is my pit. Learn the rules and play by them or get the hell out. Tell your President that my debt is paid. And you get one race, and then you pay entry fees like every other snake in this place." She slides off the hood, landing on her feet.

Cupcake...she called me a fucking cupcake.

"My name is Mercenary." It sounds positively feral, more animal than man.

"I heard you the first time," she smarts off, and before she can blink, I have her hair in my fist, her head wrenched back as I lean in.

Scenting her neck, my hard gaze set intently on hers. "Then you'd be smart to remember it." I rasp, and she cackles. With a grip on my wrist, she twists, bends, and sends me flying.

My back lands on the packed dirt and rocks knock the breath from lungs. Not often does someone get the beat on me. I'm blinking up at the sky, getting my thoughts together, willing myself not to kill her when her head pops over me. She blocks out the brightness of the industrial size lights, her hair draped around her enough to make out every single feature of her face.

"I wasn't kidding about busting out your knees. First race is Saturday night. Oh, and cupcake? Keep your hands to yourself, for your own safety."

I can't speak. I'm positively livid, and my growl gives it away easily enough. She smiles and then trots off without another word. Climbing to my feet, I glance around, thankful for the small mercy of being alone. I'd have to kill someone if they witnessed what just happened.

Instantly I seek her out, watching as she walks away. Her ass is beyond perfect, her hair nearly touching the juicy globes. Her attitude makes me want to rip someone's

Hybrid Collection

head off. Her smirk makes me want to implant my fist into a wall, and that body, fuck me, do I want to do things to that body.

> 2. Having a loud exhaust is like eating chips in church. Everyone looks at you in disgust, but secretly they want some too.
> - Funny Meme

MERCENARY

"How'd it go?" Odin, our clubs newest patched Vice President asks as I shut off the engine and climb off my bike. He's outside with a shiny black Doberman.

I shrug. "Fine, I guess." If a chick calling me cupcake and handing me my ass can be even called fine. "Whose dog?" I change the subject.

"This beauty belongs to Nightmare's son. I'm dog sitting while Night takes his kid and ol' lady out of town for a few days."

"Does it bite?"

"You'll be fine; just stick your hand out first. The thing about Dobermans is you have to approach them with respect. If you do, most of them won't harm you. People have the wrong impression of them."

Hybrid Collection

I nod and do what he suggests, letting the dog smell me before I attempt to touch it.

"Did Chevelle give you any shit?" His smirk is telling.

"I take it you know her?" I rake a hand through my hair, frustrated with my first impression.

He nods, "Yeah, she's not one to take any shit."

"She have a man?"

He snorts. "Brother, no one can get close enough. She's more likely to punch you than kiss you. A few around here think she may prefer women."

"Nah, she definitely likes men."

His brow hikes. "No shit? You went over there once, and you already found that out?" He switches the dog leash to his other hand, following the dog's leisurely lead.

"I may have gotten in her face a bit." I shrug and scratch the dog behind its cropped ear as we walk.

He tucks his blond hair behind his ears, glancing around the compound. "Damn, I'm surprised she didn't throw a punch. The last guy I saw grab her ass at a race was drug out of there with a broken nose." His face lights up with an amused grin at the memory.

Jesus and no one thought to warn me about her beforehand? I was on good behavior; I can only imagine what she'd been like if I'd had a few beers before seeing her. I have a feeling my "me Tarzan, you Jane" usual rationale would've landed me with a broken nose as well if I'd have attempted to hike her over my shoulder. Chicks normally love that shit, but apparently, Chevelle isn't like most chicks. Sounds like she went a bit easy on me when I grabbed her hair and she body slammed me. No wonder she's the one running The Pit. She can obviously handle herself.

"She ever have anyone around in case she needs help?"

"Chevelle's not the type to be caught needing help from anyone. She's smart and cutthroat."

"Well, she owed Viking apparently."

He nods. "That happened by chance. Viking had just killed his father and taken over the Widow Makers. Being new to the area and the Oath Keepers he rode with, he wanted us to do something other than drink at the bar."

"Nothing wrong with the bar," I grumble, and he continues.

"Anyhow, we rode out to The Pit. People didn't know what to think when they saw us, two different patches rolling up together, our bikes sounding like angry thunder."

"What was the big deal?"

"Widow Makers were notorious in the south like the Iron Fists are in the west; they didn't get along with anyone. Naturally, The Pit calls to a lot of us, the speed and engines, not to mention the fresh pussy floating around and open bets."

"That'd definitely be somewhere I'd enjoy."

He nods. "Well, when you have different folks from about sixty different clubs seeing the two together, they band together to challenge you, being that most Austin clubs are on a truce with one another."

"Oh shit."

"Viking got them all to chill the fuck out. Saved The Pit from a shit ton of damage. Chevelle was called in since she runs the place. She witnessed everything, and in the end, told Viking thanks and that she owed him. Don't know what she planned on owing him since he'd had Princess at the time. Hell, half of us thought maybe he was alpha enough that she wanted to actually fuck him."

"Did he?"

Hybrid Collection

He shakes his head. "Nope, nothing ever came of it. I'm guessing he waited until now to call her on it. And he wouldn't ever fuck her. He was obsessed with Princess from the moment he saw her from what I've heard. He had it bad enough that he chopped a guy's head clean off for talking negatively about Princess." We stop walking, and the dog lays in the grass, rolling to expose its belly to Odin.

"Hmm."

I know I'm plenty alpha to give her what she needs. The real trouble is breaking her just enough to get my chance. I've always been up for a challenge, though, and it'll be a good distraction.

My brothers Saint and Sinner just claimed their woman, and I've been a bit taken with her ever since I showed up from Chicago. I was set on getting my chance to fuck her, but club law says I can no longer touch her since she's property. As much as I don't want to respect that rule, I have to, or those two could skin me up and bleed me dry in retaliation if they wanted to.

"Anyone break club law around here?" I ask absently, lost in the thought of my brothers' ol' lady.

He pauses from scratching the Doberman's belly to glance up at me. "What did you do?"

"Nothing." I clear my throat. "Just curious what the club did as punishment."

"I've heard you were a bit rough around the edges, we all have," Odin admits. "But that's why we believed you'd fit in with us. The last thing you want to do is cross my brother or any others, in any way."

"Is that coming from the man's blood brother or the VP of my club?"

"Both. No one knows him better than me. Well, maybe his ol' lady, but when it comes to club business, I know what makes Viking tick. He values his club and woman."

"Good to know," I reply, and he stands from his haunches.

"I won't pretend to know what you're goin' through man but trust me when I say Texas is the best place for you. Especially if you don't fit in between the lines anywhere else. We're all fucked up; every single one of us, in some way."

I've never really fit. I don't let anyone know that though. I've gotten used to being alone when it boils down to it. I'm surprised Odin picked up on that so easily. Maybe he *does* know what it's like to stand outside of the lines.

"I appreciate that, O." He may be the youngest brother around here, but he's the easiest to talk to. I'm the newest member in this chapter, so I suppose it helps to have the VP at my back too.

"Were any of the Fists around when you were at The Pit?" The dog gets back up, nose pushing through the grass, searching for bugs, I suppose.

"No, just a few employees. Looked like they were cleaning up. Chevelle was down on the track working on a handful of cars."

"Those are all hers."

"No fucking way." My eyes widen, hands resting on my hips as the dog covers its nose with soil.

He nods. "She's dead serious on that track, and she's rarely beaten." We head back toward the club, dog in tow. After a beat, he asks, "Did you challenge her?"

"You could say that."

He stops, turning to face me again. "What did you do? Viking will be pissed if you fucked up their truce."

"I should say she challenged me. I had to race her to get a chance to speak to her."

His lips turn into a grin. "Yeah? How'd that turn out for you?"

"Well, she threw her time in my face, told me I had the same amount to speak. I couldn't put up much of a fight since I rode her taillights the entire time."

Odin laughs loudly, not trying to save my pride in the slightest. "Can't say I'm surprised. Like I already said, she's serious," he declares and continues toward the door.

"Wish I'd known that prior to riding over."

He nods. "You want her attention, then you need to at least *almost* beat her on the track."

"We'll see. I have a feeling she's used to dickless pricks."

"This is going to be fun to watch. You whither her resolve down so I can tap that ass after you do all of the work."

I snort in reply, and he chuckles again crossing the threshold to the bar.

CHURCH

"Brothers, church is in session," Viking declares, slamming the gavel to the table.

It's silent enough you could hear a cricket chirp as we all await to hear what he has to say. I'm at the farthest end of the long stretch of table, being that I'm the newest here. I'm not a prospect at least. I'm a fully patched member, but as far as this club's concerned, I'm fresh meat.

He draws a deep breath in and begins, his blond brows furrowed. "As you're aware, Ruger was sent on another scouting mission. He rode out with the NOMADS yesterday and is instructed to call me the first chance he gets if he comes across any Fists. We're this close..." He holds his hand up, pinching his fingers an inch apart. "To figuring out these assholes' location."

Our Nordic-looking Prez stares hard at Nightmare's empty seat. He's missing this since he's out of town with his family. "We have to get Night some retribution for what the Iron Fists have put his family through. This wait is driving me crazy; I can only imagine what our brother is dealin' with."

Several brothers around the table second his statement and hum in agreement.

Torch sits forward. "Prez."

Viking's gaze lands on the fierce man to his right. "Go ahead, Torch." The brother's built tall and menacingly. He reminds me of the Terminator with the way his sharp glower can easily make a man uncomfortable. He gives you a dark glare, and you automatically know you're going to meet the reaper by his hand.

"My buddy came through on the explosives we wanted. We'll be ready for whenever we do discover the Fists' hiding spots. No more half-assed fire; we'll blow that bitch sky high."

"Good and the guns?"

His cousin, Blaze, covered in colorful fire tattoos with ears full of multiple small black gauges pipes up. "The Russians delivered as promised, and we have plenty at the ready. Odin helped me unload them, and they're secure in the basement bunker."

That's some of the craziest shit I've ever seen too. Viking had a bunker put in under the club's basement. Unless you know where to look, you won't find it. Any weapons that come in are stored under there in case a bomb goes off, or we're raided by the cops. He's a smart fucker.

Smokey, our club treasurer, takes a long drag of his cigarette. He speaks while exhaling a hazy cloud of smoke. "Club bank is straight. Bills are paid, brothers have money in their pockets, shit's ordered, and there's still plenty for a rainy day should the need arise."

Viking nods. "I saw the books. Good work, all of you. The runs have been paying off, and we've climbed out of owing anyone anything. We need to keep the whores happy and safe. They've been handing us a steady flow of cash."

Blaze smirks. "Whores are content. We've been keeping an eye on the johns coming through, and in return, they've all remained unharmed on our watch. Girls have been tipping us more lately too, so they must be making good money."

"Bet. Any of them mention they want out of whoring yet?"

"Nope." His cousin shakes his head. He has hair the same cornfield color as Viking and Odin, only he styles his in a faux hawk whereas the other two keep theirs long.

"Even better. Remember they always have the option to leave safely. We're security, not pimps."

We all nod. He says the same thing about it at every church session I've been to. And Blaze doesn't even work the girls anymore. Once Odin took over as VP, Blaze got tasked as Viking's ol' lady's personal security.

"Mercenary." Prez's penetrating stare lands on me next.

"Prez." I nod in acknowledgement and meet his hard stare across the table. The man never eases up, always serious and concerned with club business.

"Everything straight at The Pit?

"Yep, didn't know Chevelle was a goddamn sex kitten, though," I rasp, thinking of her tight body, and a few brothers chuckle around me. *Bastards could've warned me.*

"She's something all right," he agrees, his lips turned up just a touch in amusement. "Don't fuck it up over there. We need you in the middle of it all for recon. I want to know why the Fists are coming into our territory. They think no one's paying any attention when they couldn't be more wrong. There are too many bikers in central Texas for no one not to notice unwelcome colors riding in. They're straight-up shitbags."

"She has me racing on Saturday. Were you aware of that happening?"

One side of his mouth hikes up a bit more at the new turn of events. It's sort of a part scowl, part smirk and his gaze turns thoughtful. "Hope you didn't place any bets." He said nearly the same thing before I went, and I wrote it off as nothing, now I understand why. Chevelle plays to win.

"No bets, I raced her for her time."

"Did you even get a chance to speak then?"

Odin snorts beside him. Saint snickers and I blow out a pent-up breath. "I had a minute and fourteen seconds," I admit and the brothers all chuckle.

"Fuck." The Prez actually grins and then shakes his head. "You gotta stay on your toes with that one; watch yourself."

"I plan to." I nod, and he moves on.

"Okay, you heard Merc. So, if any of you are free Saturday, head out with him and keep an eye on the crowd since he'll be behind the wheel for a bit."

"I can go," Odin offers.

"Me too, brother," Torch offers.

"Bet," Viking approves and flicks his eyes to Blaze. "Cousin, I need you to stick close to Princess now that Odin has been patched to Vice President. I know we briefly discussed it and all."

"I promised you before I'd protect her with my life."

Prez exhales and rubs his hand over his face. "I remember. I think she's had enough time to move past any hard feelings she may have carried toward you too. It's time to be a permanent move, and she knew it would be coming soon after Odin's new patch."

"You still want me manning the bar too?"

"No, my ol' lady takes priority. She's been through enough and Odin has offered her a sense of safety when I'm not around."

He turns to Chaos. "I need you to take over handling the bar. I can ask Nightmare's ol' lady to bartend a few days a week to give you a break and also when you're sent out on a run."

"Chaos' eyebrow shoots up. "I can open beers just fine, but I don't know how to mix drinks and shit. I drank my fair share during my football days at parties and what not, but never made any of them."

"Most of us know how to fix our own; I just need you back there until I can find someone else full time. Especially cause you're the first line of defense through the main door. An enemy comes in, you take that shotgun behind the bar to their chest and ask questions later. I won't fuck around after the club was stormed once before."

"No problem, boss."

"Good, anyone else have anything to add?"

We remain quiet, and he slams the gavel again. "Do your jobs and get the fuck out of my chapel!"

3. I stopped waiting for the light at the end of
the tunnel, and lit that bitch myself.
- BossBabe

CHEVELLE

Another Saturday has rolled around and another race in its place. The adrenaline and exhaust while racing around the track is the best type of escape I've ever found. I can just tune out and focus on driving and nothing else. It seems like whenever I'm not in my car, then someone is trying to talk to me and bother me with something. I swear it drives all these men mad around here to have a woman running The Pit.

But how can they complain if they can't even beat me? It's the way I've gotten all of my cars after all. I went into this with a busted up Chevelle. I started from the bottom and with each race, built my car up along with winning the others racing for pink slips and tuning them up as well. Yet it still doesn't seem to be enough for some of these guys to stop trying to take my place around here. They're dumb enough to realize that the only way they get my spot is if I fail to pay my loan and they take over payments with the owner.

The Pit was a shit hole the first time I showed up here. It's not the Taj Mahal by any means, but you no longer race and bust up your whip for twenty bucks. Now,

Hybrid Collection

buy-in alone is a cool grand, and the winner of each race walks away with five k. Some weekends we have four different races, breaking them up between Friday and Saturday, it's grown so popular.

As luck would have it, I come out with five grand nearly every Saturday. It's hard to complain when you pull in that kind of money. Sure, I dump a ton of it into buying this place, my rent's fourteen thousand a month and I have to repair my rides, but I still have enough left to live on. I have a small place here back by the offices that I use as a studio apartment, so that saves me from trying to pay for a place to sleep as well.

"Hey Chevy, you got everything set for tonight?" Ace, one of the floor guys, tilts his head with the question. He's one of the few around here who get away with calling me by that nickname. He's proved himself to be a good guy, someone I can rely on when it comes to working The Pit and doesn't give me any grief.

"As much as I can, I suppose." I shrug, polishing the hood of my fire engine red Nova I'm racing tonight. She's stacked with a badass engine to leave some amateurs in my rearview mirror. The best way to see them, in my opinion.

"I've got a hundred on you taking first tonight."

"Well then, at least your girlfriend won't be pissed at you losing money again."

He snorts and gives me the finger.

"Right back atcha, buddy!" I call as he strides away. He knows it's true. His woman was livid the last time he bet on a race and went home a few hundred dollars poorer. At least he's learned to bet on me and not some random rich asshole with a pretty sports car.

"Chevy?" A rasp like a thick warm caress comes from behind me.

I twirl around so quickly I nearly get whiplash. "It's Chevelle." I correct, and he grunts. I'm surprised to see biker boy came back. "And if I remember correctly, you're cupcake."

The side of his mouth tilts up in a cross between grimace and smirk. The man is broody as hell, and I don't even know him. Not to mention hot in that *bad boy don't fuck with me* sort of way. He's the exact type that I can't afford to get involved with either because their kind always hurts the girl in the end.

"I've knocked out teeth for less than that," he admits, and I roll my eyes. A threat from him comes off sounding more like foreplay than something to fear.

"I'm sure. Well, you're not knocking out shit here if you want a chance to stick around."

"You're taking me home tonight then?" he suggests.

"Nice try buddy, but it's not fucking happening. Ever."

He takes one step forward, and it's enough to place us nearly chest to chest. He's massive but moves like a damn cat. He licks his lips and bends closer. I swear to Christ if he touches me I'll put him on his ass again.

"Keep telling yourself that," he rasps and stands up fully. With a wink, he finishes with a growl, "Chevy."

My name on his lips has my flesh breaking out in goosebumps. The man is alpha to the fullest degree, and it calls to me like a fresh set of staggered tires on a fast car. You want to put them to work, tear them up a little and make them scream for you. I could have that man on his knees, pleading with me to let him come.

With quick strides, he heads to the end of the track where my Camaro's parked. He has Viking to thank for having a tuned car for him at the ready. I wouldn't have let just anyone borrow one of my babies, but Viking's good for his word.

Colored lights flicker across the stands as everyone rushes to their seats. I slide into the Nova and crank her over just as the speakers through The Pit blare to life. "Hands Up" by NF pours through them, signaling a race is about to begin, and people cheer.

My girl purrs toward the start line. I always get the first race. That way I can work the rest of the night. *Breathe in and out, in and out.* I chant silently to myself,

Hybrid Collection

watching as the three other vehicles come into line beside me. None of them are Mercenary though. He must've selected the second race. Smart move on his part too. He might actually have a fighting chance not going up against me. My Camaro's quick, but she's heavy. You have to know just how to push her to get her to respond to you.

One foot on the brake, my other presses down on the gas, smoking out my opponents as my tires squeal. The track is dry, but it's still good practice to clean your tires and warm up your engine. The rice burner beside me spins his tires, but it's nothing compared to the roar of my engine. I ease off the gas, and my eyes flick to the side just in time to catch Mercenary standing ominously, arms crossed over his chest, glare pointed in my direction.

A horn blares, and I drop it into first, my feet working the clutch and gas like my life depends on it. It does though; the money helps me survive. Without the wins, I'd be out on my ass again. The cash The Pit brings in only covers enough to pay the people working here and to maintain upkeep.

The front end jumps, the engine pushing out so much power it brings the front end off the ground for a split second. The trunks weighed down enough, so my ass end doesn't slide all over the place as I take off, but my gaze is still trained on Mercenary all the way up until I pass him by. The man doesn't blink the entire time either. It's like he's trying to get into my head, but for what? He needed to come in for his Prez, but I have nothing to do with whatever they're involved in.

And for his sake, I hope he's not trying to get me to fold. I'm one person who won't let him win on this track. There've been plenty of others who've come through with a pretty face, thinking they'd bed me and I'd let them win. Not hardly. They didn't get in my pants and they damn sure didn't get my money. I learned growing up that being soft gets you nowhere.

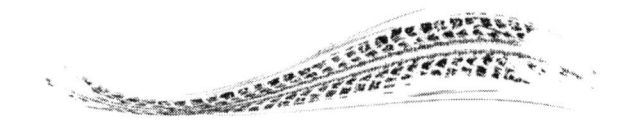

"How 'bout I take you to dinner?" A gravelly voice suggests coming into my office. I'm sitting behind the old oak desk—feet propped up, Converse sneakers resting on the edge.

"Hmm, how about no?" I reply smoothly, acting unruffled although his voice causes my lady parts to tingle with desire.

"I won't make you pay, little one. I won tonight, after all." He winks, and I scowl.

"You want a trophy to help stroke that ego too? The cash not enough for you?"

Mercenary grins and the change in his features is striking enough to make me draw in a stunned breath. He's gorgeous when he's not busy glaring at everything. "If stroking is on your mind, I have something big to put in your hands. Fill you right up and quench that need."

"Cute," I huff, and he plants his ass in the seat in front of me. "What do you really want?"

His ice blue gaze flicks over me. "You couldn't handle it if I was honest, so we'll settle for dinner for now."

"Not happening unless it doesn't include me, cupcake."

"You're not gonna drop that anytime soon, huh?"

"Not planning on it, no. Why, does it bother you?" I ask and smile sweetly. I love fucking with him already, and I've barely met the dude.

"Hmph," he grumbles as Ace stumbles in, wide-eyed.

"What's wrong?"

"A few guys claiming they need a word with you."

"So, what's the problem?"

His eyes flick to Mercenary, and he tilts his head toward him. "His club doesn't get along with them."

Hybrid Collection

"The Oath Keepers?"

At that, Mercenary turns to face Ace, finally giving him some attention. "Who is it?"

"The Iron Fists," Ace replies in nearly a whisper.

"The fuck you got to talk to them about?" The broody biker questions me next with a glare.

I shrug. I really have no idea why they'd be demanding to speak to me. Unless maybe they bet some cash and lost it. A lot of trouble comes from that shit around here, but we need the extra money too badly to stop taking bets.

"You have to go," I tell him, and he flashes his teeth, the man's feral.

"Fuck no. They're bad news. I'm not going anywhere."

"I don't need a keeper; I got you on your back, didn't I?"

"That was different."

"Um Chevy, these guys aren't the type who wait for long," Ace interrupts.

"Goddamn it," the alpha gripes impatiently.

"Fine, if you insist on staying, cupcake, you'll have to stand in my bathroom. I don't want them seeing you in here before I even know what the hell they want. You have to be quiet. I don't want to die because of whatever beef you have between clubs."

"I'm spanking your ass for this," he grumbles as his chair slings back a bit with his quick movement to stand.

"Do us both a favor while you wait in there and hold your breath."

He shoots me one last glare before disappearing into my bathroom. He leaves the door open. I'm assuming he's behind it in case these Iron Fists poke their head in to search.

"Okay, Ace, let's get this over with. Send them in."

He nods, and I sit back, relaxed. Most of these guys will back down if they think they can't intimidate you easily. I can kick ass if needed but it's better if I conserve that fact for when I really require it. I'll admit the Iron Fists make me uneasy and having an Oath Keeper in my bathroom does bring me a touch of peace of mind. Viking and his club are good allies to have around here.

Anyone in the life dealing with gambling, racing, motorcycles, etc. knows the Iron Fists aren't good news. They're a sick and twisted outlaw motorcycle club that loves terrorizing people. I would've been just fine if they overlooked The Pit. Their money is some that I actually don't want. Wouldn't surprise me if it came with conditions or blood splatter.

Ace comes back into my office, two dudes in tow. One's burly but short, kind of what I'd think of with a modern-day gnome. He's just missing a pointy hat to cover his long, unruly, cinnamon-colored hair. The other is thinner, not too hard on the eyes, with sandy locks coming to his chin, but his club colors syphon away any attraction I might conjure up immediately.

"This is Chevelle." Ace's hand flies forward, gesturing to me still kicked back behind the desk like I deal with their type daily. I do to an extent, but not quite as notorious—usually just druggies hurting for cash or pissed off racers who lost. From what I've heard in rumors floating around, the Iron Fists are an MC that you want to stay off their radar.

Blondie's stare turns heated taking me in while the other seems bored. "Get me a beer," Auburn hair gnome orders Ace.

"You're not staying long enough for a beer," I interrupt. "Now, why are you taking up my time? I have shit to do."

That gets his attention but his buddy butts in first. "Fuck, the things I'll do to that mouth. Didn't know you were running this place or my Prez would've sent us sooner."

Hybrid Collection

"Again, why are you here?" I repeat, sounding monotone and ignore his previous comment.

"Watch how you talk to us, bitch," the grouch chastises, and it takes everything inside me to remain calm. I want to kick the idiot in the balls and wash his mouth out with soap.

"You came to me, not the other way around."

"Right." The good-looking one nods and steps closer to my right side, almost around the desk. It's an intimidation tactic. In a second, the other guy will go to my left. They'll think they can box me in. "We came to you," he agrees, and I drum my fingers on my thigh, keeping my face void of emotion but my body ready to leap whenever needed.

"You could start with your names and then move to why you're standing in my office."

"That's easy." He shrugs. "Me and my brother came because our boss wants a cut."

A chuckle breaks free and they both glare, probably growing more pissed by the minute with my flippant attitude. "Why should I give you anything?" It doesn't escape my notice that they blow off the other question and skip over the names. Greedy bastards, that's for sure.

"Because we'll be taking over soon enough and anyone in business not wanting problems will pay up."

"Is that what you think? That we'll all just roll over and cough up cash for you? That this area is up for grabs?" Everyone knows who Viking and Ares are, the two motorcycle club presidents in this area and there's no way in hell they'd let someone just come right in and take over. I've heard enough employees spill rumors about the two as well as watching them with my own eyes squash down any issues when they first popped up together in The Pit.

"Stupid mouthy bitch." The one on the left nearly rounds my desk, and I stand to my feet. He seems to have a problem with his vocabulary. I should fix it for him.

Ace grows ashen. "Guys, you shouldn't get that close to Chevelle. How about you talk another time?"

"Isn't that fuckin' perfect, door boy's trying to stand up for this mouthy piece." Walnut locks nods to me and snickers. This isn't the first time someone's spoken to me with such disrespect; in fact, it happens quite often. I've learned to let the majority of it roll off because when it all boils down to it, men with small penises are not worth going to jail for.

My bathroom door widens, opening enough for a large man to fit through and out strolls Mercenary sans cut, with his chin high and sharp, eyes curious and unnervingly calm. I can't believe he thought to take it off. I'm not sure whether to be relieved or irritated with his presence. I haven't quite figured the guy out just yet. At any rate, these two jackoffs here attempting to push me around will be dumb enough to believe I have backup muscle to help me out.

"Who the fuck are you?" Burly biker gnome grumbles as Mercenary stalks around my desk to plant himself firmly between me and the asshat full of attitude.

He stands tall and imposing, arms crossed on his chest in his confident stance only making him appear bigger than before. "Boyfriend," he replies, and it takes folding my hands into fists and squeezing them harshly not to argue. Now's not the time and place to tell him to stuff his boyfriend fantasy up his ass and that it'll never happen with us.

"Tell your bitch to pay up or else we'll be the ones taking turns with her pussy."

The blond dude agrees, checking me out. "I'll take her first and then pass her around amongst my brothers." So much for him kind of being good-looking. I'd rather kick his teeth in.

"Over my dead body," Mercenary declares, and I swallow. He just threw down the gauntlet to guys like these. And with a claim like that, they'll no doubt believe he's my man now, and a stupid one at that for coming to my defense against an entire club of bikers. A regular man wouldn't stand a chance. Luckily, he has the Oath Keepers on his side.

Hybrid Collection

They both lunge at the same time, and I concentrate on goldilocks while Mercenary bloody ups the other guy. We move in sync like we'd practiced it time and time again only I barely know cupcake, how can this be possible? He throws a punch, and I head-butt the biker before he registers the move. With each punch, we remain back to back until I'm able to flip my guy and get his stomach to the ground.

Mercenary must've called someone before this all began because moments later two Oath Keepers rush in. I have homeboy planted facedown on the ground, straddling his back with his arms pinned behind his back. He's spitting mad too, promising to do all types of nasty things to me when he's free. I'll sit here until my limbs give out if I have to. I learned the hard way, growing up on the streets, alone, for the most part, you don't get up too quickly.

"You all right?" Mercenary peers down at me after driving a swift kick to gnome guy's face. He's completely knocked out, bleeding all over my office floor. I nod, and his gaze remains trained on me for longer than I care for. We kicked ass together. It doesn't mean I'll be sharing a wedding cake or anything with the man.

"Hey, Chevelle." Odin grins. "I see you're still bringing men to the ground."

I smile and shrug. "Same shit, different day."

"I'm glad my brother was here in case you needed some backup."

The guy under me twists his hips. "You're so fucking dead, cunt."

"Wow, that clearly took some brain cells to come up with." I use my free hand to flick his ear. It's petty, but I get some brief joy out of pissing him off further.

"I'll cut your tongue out," he shouts, and I flick an annoyed glare at the Oath Keepers making them laugh. These idiots like to hear themselves talk way too much.

"Torch, grab this Fist for Chevelle. We need them for questioning." He casts a strange look at the guys, but I keep my mouth shut. I don't want to know what they really plan to do with them as long as they leave here and never return.

"Can you make sure they don't come back?" I chew on my cheek and ask. I hate requesting anything, but if these two return, they'll rape me or kill me—that much I can tell.

Mercenary growls, "You'll never see them again. They won't touch you."

I swallow and inhale deeply. "Thanks, cupcake." I flash him a genuine smile. I may not need a man, but it's a relief to have one around right now to deal with these two.

Torch and Odin both cast him amused glances but remain quiet. Torch draws out some thick zip ties from his back pocket and proceeds to secure the Iron Fists' wrists behind their backs, so they can only wiggle if they move. Mercenary disappears into the bathroom and returns moments later clad in his club colors looking the part of angry biker once more.

"That was smart," I comment and gesture to his vest as I get to my feet and step away from my latest victim.

"I'm big, not dumb," he comments, and I smirk, trying to smother down my smile. Clearly, I underestimated him when we met, not something that I usually let happen.

"Thank you, Odin. Give my gratitude to Viking, please."

He nods, and Mercenary's brow furrows. "I was the one who knocked the other guy out for you."

Hmm, is that a hint of jealousy? The man pouts as if I stole his candy.

"And your club has my gratitude, big guy." I flick my eyes over him and his chest puffs in response. These damn alpha males always walking around peacocking. "Besides, I submitted the other one. I would've taken down both if you weren't in my way," I finish with a cocky grin.

He growls, and Odin chuckles. "Come on, we need to get these scum in the truck before anyone notices them gone. I called Nightmare as soon as I got your text."

Hybrid Collection

"This disagreement will have to wait until later," Mercenary declares in my direction. "You have a back door we can use?"

"Yeah, I'll take you to the delivery entrance. There are stairs though."

"Even better," Torch grumbles with a mischievous tilt of his lips. He grabs the burly guy by the leg and drags him behind us. Mercenary does the same with Blondie cussing up a storm, and I understand why they don't mind. These idiots will be hurting after being dragged down the stairs *and* receiving an ass whooping.

I lead with Odin, and the rest follow behind. We head down four flights of stairs before I unlock a heavy steel door. From there, the long, wide hallway takes us to the delivery entry. It's like a garage door that you open by pulling thick chains. Ace and I each grab a side, yanking the chains until the track pulls the bay door high enough for the tall bikers to easily exit. Nightmare waits with a pickup truck, and they throw the Iron Fists in the bed.

"I'll be back to check on you tomorrow," Mercenary promises. "You're here the rest of the day?" he asks Ace, and my friend nods, still quietly stunned from witnessing what went down in my office.

"Thanks, but I'll be fine."

"Fine," he copies. "Then I'll be back to check over the Camaro for next week."

I nod. "And thanks for the help up there." I gesture up in the direction of my office.

"It was better than dinner." He grins, and I roll my eyes then signal to Ace. We lower the door with all of the bikers wearing a smirk or grin pointed at me. *Nosey damn bikers.*

4. Money may not buy happiness,
but it's better to cry in a Lamborghini.
- PictureQuotes.com

MERCENARY

"You'll talk one way or another," Torch promises as his knuckles crunch into the man tied before us. His skull flies back with the impact, and an unpleasant groan escapes his lips yet again. He put up a good fight in the beginning, remaining silent, but Torch obviously got his death dealer patch for a reason.

"I could hit him a few times," I offer with a shrug.

"I don't want him knocked out, which seems to be your MO if we go by the scene in Chevelle's office. I need him to flip and tell me anything that has worth."

"Well, your easy hits over the past hour have barely gotten a groan out of him."

"I have other methods." He smirks with an evil glint in his eyes. "Watch them for a sec."

Hybrid Collection

I nod as he leaves the club basement. It's just me and these two dipshits that attempted to rough Chevelle up. I can't believe they lunged at her. What the fuck were they planning on doing? Beat her up? Rape her? She's a woman for fuck's sake. She'd have given them hell, no doubt, but just the thought of them harming her has me biting down hard in an angry snarl.

I'm up and out of my chair in no time, sending a swift kick to the gut of the man tied up on the floor. He immediately wretches off to the side, spilling the little bile he has left in his gut. "Piece of shit, I can't wait to take your life for trying to hurt her." I kick him in his nuts next to drive my point across.

Torch returns shaking his head at me. "Hey brother, calm down. I need him alive right now. You can beat him to death soon enough if that's what you want. I don't mind sharing when it comes to killing filth."

With a huff, I take my seat again and watch as he pulls a lighter free from his jeans pocket and lights a small torch. He must've gone and retrieved it from his room. The torch flares to life, the yellow and blue flames hot and ready to do some damage. I'm beginning to understand exactly how he got his road name.

"Can you see the flame, Fist?" Torch hisses, holding the colorful flame up eye level with the biker tied to the chair.

He remains quiet. His eyes are nearly swollen closed, and you'd think if he had any type of self-preservation he'd start giving information up.

Torch's gaze briefly lands on me. "Roll his shirt sleeve up."

I do as he asks, an Iron Fist tattoo coming into view on the exposed skin.

"They all have them," he mutters to me and scoots in closer. "Speak Fist or burn."

The guy grunts but says nothing.

"Have it your way." Torch scowls and brings the flame to flesh. The skin sizzles black and smokes, it fades away to angry meat underneath as the man wails in pain. This is not your back road, high school car lighter burn dare that a ton of us experienced when we were growing up. This is just plain torture, and it smells horrendous.

My brother pulls it away as the man begins to sweat profusely, gibberish pouring from his mouth. None of it makes any sense though; it's the pleas of a man being severely burned and nothing else.

"You will tell us what we want to know, or I'll continue to burn this shitty tat off your arm. You can't ever be an Iron Fist again if there's no skin here to tat their mark where it belongs."

With a cry, the man shakes his head.

Glancing at Torch, my brow hikes. "Repercussions must be worse than this if he refuses to speak up."

"Probably." He nods and leans in, continuing to burn the entire tattoo completely off. The smell reminds me of burnt hair, the thick air making my stomach grow nauseous.

"Okay!" The injured biker finally gasps as the pain finally grows to a high enough level to get him to talk.

"It's too late for this tat," Torch responds. "But I'm sure you have a bigger one someplace else we can move on to next if needed."

He wheezes and then gags with his mutilated arm full of twisted crimson flesh. It's a burn too, so you know that shit hurts worse than a simple slice from a knife.

"Pull it the fuck together and talk or I keep going. Let's begin with your road name. Your patch says T and homeboy over there says Shaggy."

"Y-yes that's us."

"What were you doing at The Pit?"

He breathes heavily for a moment, a nasally sound coming from his busted nose. "W-went for money."

Hybrid Collection

"No shit. Now, tell me why."

"'Cause we knew it was a bitch running it and we could make her pay up easily."

With a growl and a few quick movements, I plant my fist into his rib. T groans in pain and Torch sends me a frown. "She ain't a bitch," I grumble and sit back in my seat.

"Why are you in our territory?" Torch continues his list of questions.

T draws in a shaky breath, hesitating and my brother grazes T's lower arm with the heat. The man screams, "Okay, okay, okay! Fuck that hurts!" The wound oozes, and I have to glance away.

"Talk, motherfucker," I gripe, sick of smelling the charred skin. I have a feeling Torch is merely getting started, so this process needs to hurry along.

"We were sent by our Prez to scope the area out at first. See where your members hung out."

"Why?"

"Because," T hisses in pain, his jaw trembling to get the words out, "he wants you gone. His grandson is here...he wants him back...and he thinks if your club is gone...it'll be easier for him to take the other club down as well."

Torch flicks his gaze to me. I know that look. Pulling my burner cell free I send a text to Viking letting him know what T just shared with us. No one would have any idea what my text means who aren't a part of our club.

Nobody knows what we're dealing with and the Prez wants it to stay like that. Well, minus the other Oath Keeper charter down the road. I guess they're the reason this war between clubs began in the first place. We need these two Iron Fists to give us everything they've got on their club, or we'll be exactly where we started off before finding these two—nowhere.

T continues through broken gasps and wheezes, his forehead and body covered in sweat. The raunchy onion smell only adds to the disgusting stench of burnt skin. "They'll keep coming."

"To look for us or to The Pit?"

"Both."

Torch glances at me again. "Check on her. See if anyone's shown up and watch your six."

Nodding, I get to my feet, eager to make sure that Chevelle's safe.

"Send Sinner down."

"Bet," I reply and take quick strides to get some fresh air. The reprieve couldn't have come soon enough. I can handle blood, but the scent of torched flesh is fucking disgusting. How Torch came up with his method is a little nerve-wracking, but I understand how he got his road name and his death dealer patch, there's no doubt in my mind.

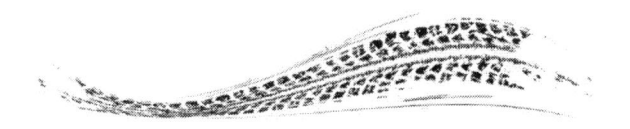

"I figured those two would've kept you busier for longer," Chevelle mutters, rolling out from under one of her cars. I didn't think I'd made enough noise for her to know I was even here.

Her eyes meet mine, brow raised, and she has grease speckles on her forehead that reminds me of dark freckles. "Anybody else been by looking for them?"

"I thought we bonded last night, cupcake. You can answer my question."

"You know my name, brat. Has anyone else paid you a visit?"

"No, but should I tell you since you don't like to share things with me?"

"I'm a man, I don't share."

Hybrid Collection

"You'd be surprised," she replies with a cocky smirk and stands. "You don't have anything better to do?"

"You owe me dinner."

"The hell I do," Chevelle huffs and closes the hood of the car. She shoots an annoyed glare in my direction before striding away, her ass swaying deliciously with each step. The woman is going to drive me insane either with that ass or her mouth.

I'm able to easily catch up to her since my legs are longer. And damn do I want to snatch her elbow and make her listen, but I learned my lesson the first time about touching her like that. She'd lay me out all over again, and that shit pisses me the fuck off if it's not foreplay. I may let her flip me if I can bring her down to the ground with me and fuck her...otherwise, not happening.

"Hmph," I grumble. "You're lucky I'm even interested."

She whips around so fast I nearly collide with her sassy mouth. "Excuse me? Look here, cupcake, you may push others around, but not me, buddy. I don't work like everyone else. I bite back."

With an exhale, I lean close enough to touch my nose to hers, my groin tightens at the irritation in her features, and with a choppy deep grumble I ask, "The real question is *where* do you bite?"

"Ugh!" She yells, hands flying up in the air and she stomps off. Knowing I'm getting under her skin has me chuckling. There are so many things I want to do to her, maybe spank that ass to punish her for that mouth.

"I like you speechless," I call out and follow her toward her office.

"Fuck off, biker boy." She flashes me her middle finger in her wake.

"No boy here. I can whip my cock out and show you if you'd like." She's silent, but I'm able to make out another quiet huff from her, and my shoulders shake with a silent chuckle.

We get to her office, and she plops down behind her desk. She's crazy if she thinks that hunk of wood will put any distance between us. I round the large piece of furniture and prop my ass on the edge of the desk right beside her.

"What are you doing? Sit in the chair!" she orders, and I don't budge.

"I'm good right here unless you want to sit with me on my lap."

"Whatever, cupcake. Now, why are you here in my face?"

"Just stopping by to make sure no other Fists came by."

"No, it's been quiet since last night."

"Mmm." My icy gaze flicks over her, taking in the cleavage from her fitted, cotton tank. It's white and smudged with various specks of grease. This woman is a full-on gear head, and it's sexy as fuck. "Fuck, why do you have to be so stubborn? Especially looking like that."

"Me? You're the one who keeps coming around to bug me."

"I just want to fuck you and then maybe I'll leave you alone."

"Oh, I know your type, and that won't be happening."

"How about I take you for a ride?"

"We both know I drive faster, so no."

"Dinner?"

"I already ate."

"Fine." The word leaves me with a growl, and I frown. Chevelle's much more difficult than most women I deal with. You'd think it'd be a deterrent, but it just makes me want her more. This is bullshit.

"See, you can go back to your club now."

"Nah, I think I'll stick around." She wants me gone it seems, so naturally, I won't be going anywhere.

"Excuse me? And do what exactly?"

"Stare at you all day?"

"Not likely. These cheesy lines leave me as dry as the Sahara."

"Doubtful. I bet that pussy's clenching and begging to feel my fingers, then my tongue, and last but far from least, my cock."

"In that order, huh? You've thought of this?"

"Every damn day since I've laid eyes on you."

"Wow, so an entire week. Excuse me if I don't feel so special."

"You're infuriating."

"And you're welcome to leave," she argues, and I have to tuck my hands across my chest. I can feel them beginning to shake, and I just want to make her submit while I bend her ass over this desk and fuck her until she apologizes for her snarky retorts.

"Fine, if we aren't going to dinner, then do you have anything to eat?"

"Seriously? I paid up my favor to your Prez; I don't need to feed you."

"And we saved your ass last night."

"You did not, I was fine."

"The least you can do is cook me dinner."

"Keep dreaming, cupcake. I'm not a domesticated chick."

"The Pit sells food, right?"

She gazes up at me curiously. "Yeah...why? I'm not paying for my employees to come in and cook for you."

"Is the kitchen unlocked?"

She nods, biting the inside of her cheek.

"You gonna be here when I'm done?"

"Oh, no, biker boy, I'm coming with you. I'm not going to let you destroy The Pit kitchen."

With a snort, I leave her behind, heading for the main level where I'm sure the kitchen's located. She may not be domesticated, but I like to eat, and I actually do know how to cook. So what if I pretty much only know how to make pancakes and steak? It has to count for something. Not that I give two fucks what anyone thinks. Even though I've never cooked for a chick before, she doesn't need to know that small detail.

Hybrid Collection

5. I can't remember your name, but you've got the red and black '67 Chevelle with the supercharged big block right?
- Future Wife

CHEVELLE

This gorilla-sized man is thundering around The Pit's kitchen, and he appears to be making about twenty pancakes on the flat grill. I never pegged him for the Suzy homemaker type, but even *I* have to admit it's pretty damn sexy watching a man cook breakfast for dinner.

"Fuck, this heat has me wanting to stroke out," he grumbles, wiping his brow on the sleeve of his plain black T-shirt.

"Welcome to Texas," I mutter, swinging my legs as I sit on the shiny metal prep table, watching him mix a bunch of shit and then pour circles on the enormous restaurant size cooker. "You're really going to be able to eat all of that?"

He grunts and next thing I know, he's shedding his shirt, draping it over his shoulder giving me a full view of his wide, muscular back. Only one thing shapes muscles like that. I'd bet the man can do pull-ups for days. No wonder he knocked ol' gnome out yesterday when he hit him. The man has the strength to easily dole out some punishment. Plus, he's like six feet six or somewhere around there.

"How tall are you, anyhow?"

He turns to glance at me, eyebrow cocked. "Why?"

"Uh, I was just thinking about how you knocked that guy out last night. I was trying to figure out how many pull-ups you can do and was factoring in your height."

His brow furrows. "You come off hostile, but I think it's because you're too damn smart up there in that pretty little head of yours." He uses the spatula to gesture toward my skull.

"And you're the size of an ogre. Should I assume you're all brawn and no brains?"

He shrugs, turning back to flip the flapjacks over, and mutters, "Wouldn't be the first time."

Staring at him with that comment, I realize I don't exactly hate him at this moment. He annoys me, but I think it's because he's so freaking attractive and he pushes me. Most men don't have enough balls to really take me for what I am. They scare easily. This ogre, though, not so much. Maybe because he's used to being the one who does the tormenting.

"So, how many can you do?"

"Pull-ups?"

"Yeah."

He shrugs then steps to me. "Watch the hotcakes."

"Uh, 'kay, but don't be pissed if I burn them."

"Won't be the first time I had them like that either." He shrugs and leaves me with a wink.

He stops in the doorway.

"What are you doing?" My gaze remains trapped on his every move. I can't seem to break away from staring.

"You're the one who wanted to know." He drops his shirt, turning to face me and seconds later jumps up.

There's a bar above the door, secured to the frame. It's so we can slide a top lock in place if needed. I never really understood why the previous owner had it like that.

He makes it to fifty when the pancakes are cooked, and I have them on paper plates. He's not even winded, chest coated in a light sheen of sweat. Fuck me, do I want to lick his freaking pecs. The man is ripped and just put me in my curious place pumping out fifty pull-ups without another thought. The sex we could have would be insane! Not that I plan to fuck him, but holy hell, I have to scrape my jaw off the floor at this rate.

"Not bad," I mutter and hand him his plate.

"Mm-hmm, could keep going, but I'm hungry," he grumbles, grabbing a plastic spork and the jar of peanut butter. There wasn't any syrup around, but he swore the peanut butter would be just as good if not better. I've never had it like that, so we'll see.

We sit side by side on the prep table and oh baby Jesus H. Christ do I want to lean over and just sniff him. The man's pheromones are blanketing me with his little impromptu workout and cooking session. Not only that, but he can drive. The bastard won his race last night. I almost don't know how to act around him.

He smears the peanut butter with his finger on each cake and holds it up.

"What?"

"Lick it."

"Fuck you."

"I'd offer that too, but I know you'll fight me about it."

"Jerk."

"Lick my finger."

"Not happening."

"You asked about the pull-ups, and I cooked your dinner. Now lick the peanut butter off my finger."

My stomach twists and heat pulls between my thighs at his demand. The man is sinful and infuriating all in one. He's expecting me to argue, poking at me for a fight, so to keep him guessing, I lean over, close my lips around his finger and suck. Yes, I said suck...the peanut butter off.

Sitting back up, I lick my lips and peer up at him through my lashes. His nostrils flare as he takes deep breaths, his cheeks flushed, eyes blazing with desire.

"Yummy," leaves me in a breath, and he clears his throat.

With a jerky nod, he takes a big bite and chews, staying silent. It worked and shook him off balance, just as I wanted. I dig into my own plate full of pancakes, using my finger to spread the peanut butter the same way I watched him.

When I'm finished, I go to take a bite, but he tugs my hand. I watch with bated breath as he lifts my finger to his mouth. He gently scrapes his teeth along my finger and follows it up by sucking the rest of the thick peanut spread off.

Oh, my.

I see now why his cheeks tinted. I feel my own grow warm, my nipples stiffening in response to his wet tongue on my flesh. "Delicious," he confesses, his voice choppy and gruff with need. I know because my own voice thickened after having a taste from him.

"It's really good," I admit after another bite.

He smirks and continues to chew. I should've bitten my tongue. Now he'll claim I owe him for cooking us dinner.

"So, were you guys able to get what you needed from those Iron Fists?"

He grows serious, his eyes guarded. "You need to forget about them."

"They tried to jump me; I can't just swipe it under the rug."

"You can, and you will," he orders, finishing his last pancake. He hops off and tosses his empty plate in the trash. I finish my food, and he takes my plate from me, throwing it away as well.

"Thanks."

He holds his hand out, palm up. I raise my eyebrow and hop down myself. "I haven't needed a man to help me down before, so I won't start now. We shared pancakes and got into a fight together. We aren't exchanging vows or anything."

"You can't handle letting a man be in control, can you?"

"Of me?" I scan his gorgeous body from top to bottom. His old jeans fit him in the perfect way, his heavy leather boots complementing the look nicely. "No. I don't have a problem with a man being in control as long as it's not with me. I'd end up breaking him."

He snorts. "Then you haven't had a real man."

I flick my gaze to his and admit, "Probably not. Doesn't mean I'll give you a shot though."

He grumbles, and I grin.

"Thanks for dinner, cupcake, but I have to get back to work."

"Strip. I'll work your body."

"Ha, nice try, big guy. Don't you have stuff to do for your Prez?"

Don't they ride their motorcycles around and glare at children for fun or something?

"I'm doing it."

"What?"

"Hanging around here and keeping my eye out for various people."

"I see. Well since you're not going away, how about you change the oil in the Camaro?"

"I can do that," he easily agrees, and it makes him even more attractive in my eyes.

He's a man's man. You don't come across many of those now that know how to fix cars, drive them like they stole them, grill food, ride motorcycles, and fight. His type goes all the way back to the cavemen. He's a provider and a predator, and that's fucking hot.

Most of the guys I come across are hipsters, growing a beard because it looks cool. They may as well have a vagina between their legs. They wouldn't know how to change a tire or defend themselves if you paid them to. It gets old for me, being more capable than the men I attempt to date. After a while, I just gave in, fucked them to scratch an itch, but gave up on the idea of ever finding something remotely close to love. In this life, it's thrive or perish, and I'm a fighter.

I watch as Mercenary heads in one direction and I make my way to my Nova. I raced her last night, so I was in the middle of changing out her oil and checking everything else over when Merc decided to interrupt me. My gaze on him only breaks when I slide underneath the door. I seal up the thick black plastic drip pan I used to catch the oil and push it off to the side. Then I go to work replacing the filter and twist the plug back in to the oil pan. She's good as new and ready to kick some ass again.

Now if I can shake this biker, I'll be the same.

Hybrid Collection

6. Prius - I get 50 mpg, what do *you* get?
Camaro - Laid.

MERCENARY

"How's the girl?" Torch asks as I take a seat in the clubhouse. Rock music plays quietly in the background, drifting in from the bar.

We're sprawled out on leather ebony couches positioned in a square around a low, polished wood table. Nearly everyone's chilling over here, so I figured what the hell. I'm already the newest member of this charter—practically an outsider and I need to break through that label. Chicago was my home, but I can never go back unless I want to find my head cut off by the damn mob.

I'm determined to make Texas a place for me; otherwise, I'll have to go out on my own. You know what it's like to be a lone rider? It sucks because you have fuck all to watch your back and shit to make money on. Most lone riders don't survive unless they're a paid killer. I don't have any strife with killing; I just want to have the decision on who I'm killing, so the paid hitman option isn't for me either.

I grunt in response to Torch's question.

"Any more Iron Fists show up or sniff around?" Viking's gaze falls to me.

"None that I've come across, Prez. It's pretty quiet around there when there aren't any races going on."

He nods and sips his whiskey.

"Chevelle let you take her out yet?" Odin asks with an amused grin.

I answer with a glower, and he hoots out a loud laugh. "Told you, brother. She's got that pussy locked up *tight*." The resemblance between him and Viking is a bit unnerving. You'd almost think O is the Prez's son rather than his younger brother. Both of them are tall with blond hair and Nordic tattoos covering them in various spots. Odin has less, but I'm sure it won't be that way for much longer.

Saint snickers, always looking to stir up a little drama from what I've seen so far. "How about we place a few bets if our new brother can even get into her pants."

"I've got fifty bucks on two months," Chaos calls from the bar. We must be loud for him to hear us over the low music and being in another room. He's the oldest brother around here and an ex pro football player. I couldn't believe it when he rolled up to get me in Chicago, and I came face to face with an NFL star clad in an Oath Keepers vest. I'm sure he has one hell of a story to bring him to an MC.

Sinner scoffs, his charcoal eyes staring down Saint. The two of them are near opposites, one with dark features, black hair, and stormy irises; the other one light, with ashy-blond hair and gray irises that appear nearly clear. "No way in hell he's that patient. I give him three weeks or else I say he gives up. I'd put fifty on it."

Hearing him and Saint on this is like sandpaper. Those two recently laid claim to the first woman I was interested in when I got here. Jude's beautiful, young, and somewhat innocent; she's a man's wet dream. Chevelle catching my attention is a good thing to distract me from Jude alone, or it could stir up shit with the brothers.

Odin pipes up again. "I don't know. He's persistent, more than any of you fuckers. I've got fifty on a week."

Hybrid Collection

"No fucking way," Viking grumbles. "Chevelle is stubborn as hell. I say five weeks."

I scoff as Prez's woman, Princess, comes up to sit on his lap. "Chevelle?" she asks, smitten and territorial staring at the Nordic Viking looking man she has wrapped around her finger.

"She runs The Pit," I supply.

"Oh." She nods and beams a perfect bright white smile in my direction. "Yeah, she's a tough cookie; I've got fifty it takes you four weeks."

I nearly sputter in surprise. I can't believe she's betting with these assholes.

"I'll take three weeks," Blaze cuts in.

"What the hell? You have no faith in a brother?" I grumble and a few chuckle.

The Prez shakes his head. "Just be glad Ruger isn't here, or you'd have some competition. You got a bet, Night?" He turns to Nightmare, back from his mini vacation with his ol' lady and son. He helped pick up the Fists from The Pit, but I haven't seen him since then.

"Daydream?" He flicks his dark gaze to his woman, seeking her input. Not only is she his ol' lady, but she's Princess' best friend as well.

"We don't know if she even likes him." She winks. I've heard about how Nightmare had to fight with his Daydream, also known as Bethany, to get her to finally admit she wanted him.

He hums in agreement. "We've got fifty on it never happens." He smirks, and brothers around him grin.

"I'll prove you all wrong, and when it happens, I get fifty bucks from each of you."

"Done." Prez agrees, and Blaze shakes his head at us, catching snippets of our conversation as he carries various cases, helping Chaos restock the bar.

It's just another day belonging to an MC. People hear all the crazy horror stories about us because we're a bit rougher around the edges than most, but what they tend to leave out is days like today. We're normal people who like to razz each other and talk shit. In that same respect, I won't think twice to help them bury a body. Does that make us better friends to have? I'd like to think so.

"What time frame are you thinking, brother?" Odin asks.

"It can happen any day." I shrug nonchalantly, and the guys holler in disagreement. Our ribbing is broken up by the club phone ringing. We quiet down once we catch wind of Chaos telling the caller on the other end to calm down, make sure the doors are locked, and that someone would be right over.

He pops his head into the room we're in and gestures for Prez. Each of us stares as Viking listens to him, huffing at parts and eventually heads back over to us.

"Prez?" Torch's brow furrows.

"You're not going to believe this shit," he begins, running his hand over his face exasperated and meets my gaze. "Mercenary, you need to head back to The Pit. You were there yesterday, right?"

I nod.

"Well someone must be watching you because Chevelle said when she looked outside a biker was sitting out front, looking like he's waiting for something."

"That was her?"

He nods.

"Is she all right?"

He nods again. "Yeah, but apparently the dipshit hasn't left his post since she first saw him out there. It's been hours according to her. She didn't want to call but recognized the familiar colors on his vest as Iron Fist."

"Fuck! They're like cockroaches," Odin grumbles and shakes his head.

"Mercenary, I want you to head back over and stay the night. I need to know first thing if anymore pop up. Torch and O, you two ride with him in case anyone's paying attention. Take the back road and go inside through the loading dock. Chevelle will be waiting for you there, and you can hide your bike inside. Odin and Torch, you two can come back to wait for word from Merc. I don't want Chevelle there alone in case this asshole tries to break in. She's a feisty bitch who knows her shit, but it only takes a second for a gunshot to hit someone and change everything."

I couldn't agree more. She can defend herself, but if someone shoots her ass, she won't be strong enough to subdue them like she normally would. She's tiny and uses momentum to make her moves, where as if one of us gets shot first it takes more to knock us down since we're huge and built differently.

"She won't like me being there to protect her."

"I know that, but Chevelle is also aware that I don't give a shit what anyone else thinks. She'll let you stick around because she cares about The Pit too much to let the Fists take it from her."

"And if more show up?"

"You call or text us immediately, and I'll send backup."

"Bet," I agree and down the rest of the cold beer in my hand. I'll sweat the one beer out before I get ten minutes down the road, so I'm not worried. Hell, as shitty as it is to drive drunk, if Chevelle needed me and I'd had ten beers, I'd still go. I'd have to drive a hell of a lot slower, but I'd make it eventually. I won't let any of these assholes harm her.

I don't know when that feeling of protectiveness planted itself in me so deep, but it's there now, and it has my insides twisting with the need for me to get there and make sure she's okay. If I had to guess when it happened, I'd say probably when those Fists lunged at her in her office; it was like a barrier for me was crossed. I've seen someone want to actually hurt her and that's a hard limit for me. She's a bitch to most, but no one deserves to be physically harmed because they have a damn attitude and they appear weaker than you. The woman's going to end up being the death of me, I can sense it.

"You have everything you need?" Vike asks as I get to my feet, Torch and Odin mirroring my movements.

"I'm going to grab my Glock and an extra clip; otherwise I'm good to roll."

"Ride safe, brothers," he replies, and fist bumps the three of us. The others repeat his words, and then I'm hurrying to get my shit and load up.

Chevelle barely tolerated me in her space yesterday, and that was with me helping her perform maintenance on her cars. Not that I enjoy doing free labor, but if it keeps her calm and I can help her out, then hopefully she has something else to keep us busy with today as well.

I'm throwing my leg over my seat loading up on my bike when Odin rolls his over to mine. "We ride for ten then hang a left on old road one-nineteen. It swings right behind The Pit. Homeboy out front will hear our bikes, but hopefully, he won't realize they're coming from the back side since the dome's so damn big."

"Got it."

"We'll wait until you're in the bay and then pop smoke back to the compound."

"Appreciate it."

He nods and walks his motorcycle a few steps then cranks her on. Torch and I follow suit, our engines purring to life and then we're on our way, the wind and road calling to us like an old friend.

Chevelle's waiting for me as promised, and when I arrive, she pulls the bay door up, closing and locking it after I've walked my motorcycle inside. "'Sup Chevy," I greet with a wink.

She snorts and rolls her eyes. "Real nice, cupcake, and you haven't earned the right to call me that."

Hybrid Collection

"But Ace has?" I ask and kick my kickstand in place, letting my bike rest on the stand as I follow her down the hallway to the staircase. It pisses me off inside that she lets him give her a nickname and I can't use it as well. I've been a bit of the jealous type in the past when it comes to women. Not obsessive, but I like to know the whys and facts when it comes to a chick I'm interested in. If they can't give me answers, then it raises red flags.

"Ace has stuck around through my shit since I took over here."

"And you haven't fucked him?"

She sends me a pissed off glare. "Not that it's any of your business, but no."

"Not your type?"

"What's with all of the questions?"

I shrug. "Just figuring out what makes you tick and weed out any possible competition."

"How do you know I'd give you a chance if there wasn't anyone else in the picture?"

The craving to touch her is too great, that when she opens the door leading out of the hall, I cage her in with my arms on each side of her body. I don't come in contact with her skin though. I learned the first time if you don't give her any warning, she'll flip you.

With a gruff rasp, my gaze lands on her mouth. "You forget I had that mouth around my finger yesterday." I'd like to have it on my cock next.

"And?"

"If there wasn't a trace of attraction to me, you never would've done it. You're not used to dealing with men on your level. I'm right up there with you, and I know what I'm doing. If I want something, I get it."

"And that's why you don't have a chance, biker. I'm not a thing to possess." With that, she ducks under my arm and continues on.

I grab her hand, light enough to get her to spin my way, eyebrow cocked, and I get to finish my thought. "Trust me; I know you're not a thing. You're a woman—one who should be worshiped."

She swallows, her eyes widening for a moment before she brushes it off with a laugh. She turns away, and I let go of her hand to keep following. She a strong woman no doubt, but she reminds me a lot of a scared animal, attacking when she's cornered. With every fiber of my being, I want to take control of her, own her, but she won't let me if I go full steam ahead, so I'll be smart about it. I'll make her believe that she's coming to me all on her own, but every move I make will be put in place to get her exactly where I want her.

Owned. By me.

7. Women are like tea bags.
You never know how strong they
are until they're in hot water.
- Eleanor Roosevelt

CHEVELLE

The week flew by in no time it seemed with Mercenary here to keep me company, and not that I would admit it to him, but having him around made me feel a little safer after the run-in last weekend. It's Saturday once again and normally the night I'm most excited for, but part of me is wondering if more Iron Fists will show up again. I shouldn't be concentrating on the bikers but on racing. I can't help the nag at the back of my mind though.

The Oath Keepers sent Torch and Odin again to watch from the stands while Mercenary races. I don't think any of the other drivers realize who Mercenary is which is exactly what Viking wants from what I understand. I doubt Mercenary will find out anything from the other drivers, but if he's racing, then no one will think twice about him being around and down in the race area. They seem to have random ears placed everywhere.

"There's still time for you to change to my race." I goad him on, looking to get a rise out of the big beautiful man as I head for my car.

"I'd hate to beat you and take your spot."

"Keep telling yourself that," I argue, and he grins. That small smile has had my core soaked for him all week—aching to feel his touch. I tell him to get a life and attempt to play it cool, but in reality, he has my head spinning for him. Sexually charged atmosphere would be an understatement how my apartment feels having him in my space and so close.

"You can have the first race, I'll take the second. It can be our thing each week." He winks, and I roll my eyes. "Kind of like peanut butter on our fingers."

I wave him off. Folding into my seat, I close the door, encompassing me in brief silence. The car drowns out the music blaring through The Pit's speakers. Everyone knows that, and the flashing lights mean it's nearly race time.

Running my hand lovingly across the old Nova's dash, I turn the ignition, and she flares to life with a sexy rumble. I line up, getting ready to race and wait for the other three to follow suit. I'm minding my business, taking deep breaths when another engine roars to life. A winding, high-pitched squeal briefly takes its place. The distraction has everyone's attention, and then right before my eyes, the car in question blows up. There's a massive boom and then screaming as people in the stands rush toward the exits. It's chaotic, and instantly my heart is thrumming so quickly, it feels as if it's going to leap out of my chest. My stomach twists with worry, my throat constricting as people rush everywhere.

I scan the entire arena and watch as Mercenary sprints for me. I'm the only one who's made it to the line so far, and I turn my car off quickly to hop out.

"You okay?" he thunders, gaze filled with uneasiness. He stops in front of me, his hands falling on my shoulders as he looks me over—concerned.

I nod, my heart still beating a million miles per hour. "I'm fine; so is the Nova." I gesture to the shiny vehicle, and his brow furrows more, glancing behind at the vehicle.

"I didn't ask about the car, Chevelle. I want to know if you're okay—*you*."

Hybrid Collection

"I know, I meant when I started it, it sounded fine too. There was that squeal then the bomb and, well, mine was fine." I'm rambling, my brain scrambled on what I should be doing—pulling me in a hundred directions all at once.

"Good."

"What do we do? Call the fire department? How did this happen?"

"We just stay here and wait for my brothers to make it to us. They've already texted the club, so they know what's going down if we need some backup."

"I have to check on the other driver. The hood blew off with the explosion. I can't believe it blew up like that...that could've been me."

"I know, I saw it all happen. The other driver got out. I watched him run to the side and then I was coming to make sure you were safe."

"Thank God." I pant, my hand still on my chest, feeling as if I'm going to have a heart attack. "You could've been hurt, what if it was me?"

"I'm fine; I had to get to you in case your car went off next. You're okay, you got out, he got out, everyone is fine."

My fist flies into his chest. "You idiot! You could've been killed if my car had blown!" His gaze grows tense, and he yanks me into his chest, wrapping his arms around me. I should fight him. I don't need him to comfort me. I don't need a man for anything. Ignoring those thoughts, I stay rooted, leaning into him until Torch and Odin find us. I don't know what I'm more freaked out about, that I could've just exploded in my car or the fact that he could've been killed coming after me like that.

"You two all right?" Odin asks, and I feel Mercenary move as he nods and replies.

"Yeah, brother." His voice is gruffer than usual, his muscles tense. "The fuck was that?"

"We don't know. Scared the shit out of us too. Viking is calling the sheriff to give him a heads-up that we're here."

"Should I be worried about getting arrested? Will The Pit get shut down?"

He shakes his head. "Nah, Vike is cool with him. The sheriff will bring a few deputies with him that he has under his thumb. Not that any of this is our fault, but it's always a plus to have the cops with you instead of against you."

I step out of Mercenary's hold, my body stiff as the guys stare me down as if I'm going to break. I may be caught off guard and worried, but I can still take care of myself. "I need to check on all the employees, make sure no one was injured."

Mercenary huffs and his hands fold over his chest causing his biceps to bulge massively. "Have Ace do it. I want you close in case this was only the first bomb of many."

"You think because you're big and hot and bossy that you can just come in here and take control of things?"

He nods. He freaking admits it! "You think I'm hot?" he asks, and I snort.

"Cocky ass," I grumble and shake my head, then pull my cell free, sending a text to Ace.

Me: Check on the employees and lock the business doors. Once everyone is out, leave only one front entry open.

Ace: Okay, boss.

Me: And Ace?

Ace: Yeah?

Me: Be careful.

Ace: Will do. You too, Chevy.

"He's checking it out and locking the business doors. I told him to leave one business entry open for the police."

"Good, also let the cops check over the other cars before you let the drivers go."

Hybrid Collection

I nod. It's sound advice even if I'm not the one calling all the shots at the moment. I'm glad Mercenary's here to do it though. I'm feeling scatterbrained, and he's a calm force if not bossy like myself.

"Uh, Chevelle?" Another racer treks toward us carrying a paper in one hand.

"Are you guys okay?" I ask, peering behind him at the others waiting off to the side, away from the cars. I can't believe this happened and that any of them could've been seriously injured. We have rules in place to keep them safe on the track, and then something like this happens.

"We're fine, but I found this tucked into the passenger window of the car that blew up. I don't know if it was for the driver or you or..." He trails off, and I take the paper, flipping it open so Mercenary can read it over my shoulder.

Pay up, get out or die, bitch.

"Are you fucking kidding me with this shit?" The massive man behind me thunders as he reads the note. "O, Torch, check this shit out."

I hand the note to Odin. He gives it to Torch nearly immediately and pulls his phone out. I overhear him talk to Viking, telling him in detail what happened and what the note says.

"Thank you, Jake." I acknowledge him by name, grateful. "Once the cops come and clear the cars, everyone can leave. I'm sorry about this. Everyone will have a credit for whenever they're ready to race again."

"I'm just glad no one got hurt. This isn't your fault. We know you'd never let someone do this intentionally." He waves me off and heads for his girlfriend standing with the other drivers.

Mercenary draws me back into his arms, his finger going under my chin and lifting it until I meet his intense stare. "I'll figure this out, I promise. I won't let you get hurt."

I swallow a bit roughly at his intensity. "It's not your responsibility," I argue. "The Pit is mine; it's my fault we didn't inspect prior to lining up."

"Bullshit. You shouldn't have to worry about this shit. I should've stayed last night, so I was here this morning. I would've known if someone got to the cars had I been here to watch."

"You think that's when whoever was here?"

"I think it was when the drivers pulled their cars in and went to lunch most likely. It was the only time the vehicles were in here unmonitored by someone."

He has a good point. The drivers have an option to come in early. They can park their vehicles to do prerace maintenance and use The Pit tools for free. It's become more popular these last few months as the tools have gotten better and better thanks to the increase in sales over the past six months.

"I'll figure this out," he promises, and I lick my lips, unsure how to respond. Men have made me false promises before, but I want to believe this one coming from him.

"It's okay, really." My life is easier when men aren't involved.

"I don't want you to feel unsafe," he growls.

I swear he's more stubborn than I am.

"I'm fine."

"You will be, I'm not going anywhere from now on. Those Fists think they can threaten you, they'll have to get through me first."

"What are you talking about?"

"I'm staying from now on."

"The night?"

"Yep."

"No." I shake my head, and the cops finally show up with a group of firemen in tow.

"You relax; we'll speak to the police." He plants a kiss on my forehead, and I'm so shocked with his bossiness and the arrival of the police that I let him without any complaint.

He leads me to a metal folding chair next to the other racers. "Jake, bring her a bottled water," he orders, and I swallow, crossing my arms over my chest. "Sit, sweetie, and catch your breath, let me handle this for you. Let me take care of you."

And then he walks away. I sit in the hard metal chair watching his ass, damn near smitten at how he's trying to handle everything without ruffling my feathers. A piece of me wants to jump up and argue with him until I'm blue in the face, but I have no idea what to even say to the cops. They'll run my name and social security number and come back with my record. Hell, I could even have a warrant I'd forgotten about from when I was on the streets, so having Mercenary here as a buffer is kind of nice if I'm honest with myself Not sure how I feel about him planning to stick around and stay the night though. I might have to fight with him on that.

MERCENARY

To say I'm stunned is an understatement. I was expecting her to knock my ass out and tell me to fuck off when I had her sit down so I could speak to the cops with my brothers. She doesn't need to worry her pretty little head with shit, especially when it comes to the Iron Fists. That's our problem to deal with. I'll probably get some lip from her later, not that I'll mind any. Arguing with her is like foreplay between us. I can't seem to get enough of her sassy mouth and strong will.

"Have you found anything else?" the cop in front of me asks Odin. He must be familiar with the way the club works as he didn't even attempt to speak to me or ask Torch questions but went straight to Odin. He's the VP so naturally, he'd be the one to handle whatever information the club wants to share with the local law enforcement.

"No, we'd appreciate it if your guys or the firefighters would check out the other vehicles, so the drivers can head on home."

"Yeah, I'd like to do a search of the premises as well."

"The Pit owner has the employees checking out the building. The owner would prefer to pass on a formal search. Unless you have a warrant with you, that is."

"Fine, fine, Odin. I know your older brother will have his own ideas on how to handle this. I'll step back for now, but if any other buildings begin to blow up or bodies surface, I'll be jumping in with both feet."

"We appreciate that, sir." Odin complies, and the two men shake hands. The cop nods to Torch and then rakes his gaze over every inch of me. It feels damn near like a caress, and I have to wonder if the cop has a thing for men or bikers in general.

"New member?" His stare meets Odin's.

"Yeah, transfer. He's a quiet one."

"Good, we like the quiet bikers." He gazes back at me. "They know how to please us."

Torch clears his throat and the cop strides toward the waiting group of firefighters.

Odin grins. "Looks like you have an admirer. Maybe you should give up on Chevelle."

"Fuck you," I grumble and sigh. "That cop would shit his pants if he ran my license and caught wind of the trouble I've stirred up."

"I'm sure he'd find a way to punish you." He snickers, and I glower at his and Torch's grinning faces.

"That's not my idea of a good time. Now, what are we going to do about that note? You didn't want the cop to see it?" Odin had stuffed it in his back pocket and never mentioned anything about it.

Hybrid Collection

"No, Vike said to keep details to us, so we have time to use it to our advantage. We don't want the law hot on our heels if we're hunting."

"Understandable."

Torch speaks up. "You need to bring some shit here, so you can stay with her."

"I figured that. I already told her I wasn't going to leave."

His brow hikes. "Oh yeah? I didn't see her throw any blows."

"I know, I think she's still in shock, so it didn't even register all the way. I was expecting her to fight me tooth and nail. I'm sure she'll let me have it when this place clears out."

"One of us can come switch with you tomorrow for a few hours so you can get some of your shit."

"Appreciate it. You think this has to do with the biker that was hanging around here yesterday that she called us about?"

Odin agrees. "Hell yes. I'd bet money on it too. They clearly have Chevelle in their sights. It sucks for her. If we weren't here, she'd most likely end up dead or kidnapped. Luckily, we caught it before things escalated to that."

I draw in a quick breath, picturing those stupid fucks taking her and knowing just a few of the things they'd do to her. "I can't let her get hurt."

"We agree with you. Trust me, this is Viking and Ares' prayers getting answered. They've been sitting on the sidelines waiting to find these guys and have a reason to take them out. They've fucked with our club enough. Now it's just about finding their locations. Each one of these fucks that comes around, we snatch them and question as much as possible."

"Good. I'll keep my eyes peeled."

"You'll need to, they tend to be sneaky," Odin supplies.

"Then we should set up a trap." A menacing grin overtakes my lips as I begin to think of what I need to make sure we have our chance to extract information out of every Fist that comes snooping around. "I need horse tranquilizer," I say seriously, and Odin smiles.

"This is going to be fun."

"I'm going to use them as target practice from four floors up. Make sure you have a truck at the ready."

"You got it," he agrees, and I fist bump them both.

Hybrid Collection

> 8. She was just another broken doll,
> dreaming of a boy with glue.
> - Atticus

MERCENARY

"I agreed to you sticking around here. I never said you could stay in my apartment." Chevelle continues to argue with me. Ever since I followed her to her apartment, she's been giving me hell.

"You keep talking as if I'm asking you. I'm not asking shit, woman. I need this window, and it happens to be in your apartment."

"It's my bedroom window, where I sleep!"

"I can take a break from hunting these assholes to fuck you if that's what you're asking for. Seems like you may need a good hard fuck to get you to chill the fuck out."

"Jesus, you're hardheaded."

"I was just thinking the exact same thing about you."

"Fine, I'll sleep on the couch."

I glance around, noticing she doesn't even have a couch. There's a bathroom and a small kitchen area. The only real furniture she has here is a big chair and her bed. "Scared?"

"Excuse me?" she hisses, her tone turning deadly. She can't handle being challenged; she likes to win far too much. It makes her a badass, but it's also a weakness if she doesn't know when to back down.

"I asked if you were scared. You're acting like a chickenshit over sleeping in the same room as a man."

"Oh, that's rich. You know damn well I can kick your ass if need be. I'm *not* scared of you."

I snort but keep quiet. It's enough of a response to make her cheeks flush. Fucking shit it makes her even sexier watching her get all wound up. Is this how she'd look riding my cock? I don't have to worry about falling asleep tonight if she does actually sleep in here. My stiff dick is way too uncomfortable to get any rest around her.

I lay my arm across my lap and glance out to the parking lot. Her mouthy replies and tight figure are too much to take. I want to toss her across the bed, pin her with my body and make her give in to all of my desires. She could just lay there naked and let me stare at her all night. I can wait to fuck her if she lets me drink in her curves and pink folds for hours on end.

I need to fuck someone before this gets out of control. Sure, I've chased pussy, but they've always given in nearly right away. Chevelle though, she's a tough bitch, acting like I don't affect her in any way. I know her pussy's wet though. she can pretend all she wants that she doesn't eat up the attention I give her, but I can smell her sex. Mix it in with her resolve, and she's like the forbidden fruit just taunting me to take a bite. I'd bite in a fucking heartbeat too. She just needs to bend a little more and admit that she wants me to fuck her.

Hybrid Collection

"And what was that shit down there? I should've spoken to the cops, this is my business." She glares at me, scrambling for something to fight with me about to change the subject away from my previous challenge.

My brow raises, ready to put this woman across my knee. "You can't say thank you, can you?"

"You expect me to thank you? For what? Having me sit back like some meek little woman? I don't think so, biker boy."

"You need your ass spanked," I growl, and she shoots off the bed.

"Try it," she hisses, coming to stand in front of me. She's way too close for us to be arguing like this. With the amount of untapped sexual tension between us, I may snap.

I get to my feet, leaning away from the wall I was propped against and tower over her smaller frame. I made the mistake of underestimating her the first time. I'll never do that again. Being slammed on my back once was too many times for me. "Be careful what you wish for, you might just get it."

Her eyes flare. "You're not man enough," she breathes.

It was the wrong thing to say. I'd have kept going back and forth with her all night if she'd persisted, but that comment, nope. She's used to weak men; I'm not one of them. My hand flies to her throat, grip tight enough to hold her in place and my arm span keeps her far enough away to retaliate.

"You've mistaken," I growl. "You caught me off guard before, but sweetie, you've met your match." At that, I hook a leg behind hers, twisting her in the process, so we hit the floor with me over her back. I do my best to not squish her beneath me, but she's got too many moves that I have to focus on subduing her more. My other hand takes over, clamping the back of her neck and I release the front, keeping her face to the ground.

I reach back and smack her ass through her jeans and lean forward, breathing against her throat. "Want another?"

"I hate you!" she screams furiously. She's so pissed it's hard for me to hold back my pleased chuckle.

I smack her ass again, and she makes a feline growl sound that I find deliciously toxic. It's her being completely livid, but it turns me on further.

Leaning back down, I rub my nose behind her ear, taking in her scent. She smells like sugary vanilla. I wonder if she tastes like it too. "Another?"

"Fuck you," she hisses, and I chuckle.

My warm breath flutters over her flesh. "I wish," I admit with a grumble and draw her lobe between my teeth. "But not tonight, I have to work." I finish and sit up then spank her again.

She does this angry scream thing in the back of her throat. I'm pretty sure if I let her up now she'll attempt to kill me.

"Be a good girl, or I'll keep going."

"You better pray you never sleep!"

My palm rests on her ass, and I laugh again. "I could sleep with you under me...naked." My hand spans enough to barely caress her between her thighs. Her folds are probably swollen and red, begging to be fucked. God how I'd love to see them right now and lick her clean.

"Let me up."

I spank her ass again, and her breathing becomes labored, morphing into more of a pant. She's turned on—she likes it as much as I do.

"Say please."

"Please, fuck off."

"You won't get rid of me that easily. Now, you gonna play nice, or should I keep spanking you?"

"I don't play nice," she admits and wiggles her hips.

"I know; that's why I can't get enough of you. Tell me Chevelle, are you wet right now?"

"Shut up."

My palm smacks down as I deliver another spanking, "You were doing well for a minute."

She takes a deep breath, exhaling, and she mumbles, "Will you please get off of me?"

Bending back over, my tongue trails along her lobe, my excited breath warming her ear as I demand, "Tell me if you're wet."

I wait with bated breath, not expecting her to answer honestly. I'm surprised she hasn't bucked me off by now.

"Soaked."

"Your panties or pussy?"

"Both."

"You've made me a happy man," I confess, rubbing my nose against her gently one last time before climbing to my feet. I head straight to the bathroom to take care of my hard on. My dick's so stiff right now if I don't get some type of relief I'll puke later from the serious case of blue balls. I've never needed to feel a woman wrapped around my shaft so badly before in my life.

CHEVELLE

He storms to the bathroom, and I couldn't be more thankful for the small reprieve. My cheeks are flushed and burning from admitting the truth to him. I'm mortified over what just happened—that I let him gain the upper hand—and the fact that I enjoyed every second of it.

He's infuriating, always arguing with everything I have to say and being so damn good-looking while doing it. I was ready to hand him an ass kicking, and then his hand just shot out of nowhere catching me by surprise. I'm going to have to store that move. Not that I'm big enough to use it myself, but I'll be damned if another man gets the jump on me like that again.

Climbing to my feet, I step to the window he was busily peering out of before I tried to pick a fight with him. I'm not used to having anyone in this space, especially at nighttime. If I want to sleep with a man, I go elsewhere—never in my home.

Mercenary just strolls in and takes over everything like he owns the place. How can he be so blasé about sticking around here so much? People have come and gone throughout my life. I learned at a young age to not expect them to stick around and having him here like this feels as if it's crossing a barrier or something. I know it's for my protection, even if I don't want to admit out loud that I need it. It's all nerve-wracking. I'm used to taking care of myself.

I blink and register the figure across the street propped up against the light post. Shit. I wonder if Mercenary saw him too.

With a few quick hops, I bang on the bathroom door and receive a grunt in response.

"Cupcake?"

"In a minute," he grumbles.

"There's someone outside."

"Fuck!" He swears and follows it up with a groan. I hear the sink turn on and jump back. I don't want him to think I was standing here listening to him do whatever he was doing. Although I have a good guess he was in there stroking his cock. I wonder if he's hung long and hard or if he's more blunt and wide?

Hybrid Collection

Damn it. He has my mind constantly in the freaking gutter around him. He's pure sex on two legs, and I can't seem to help myself when I'm in his presence. It's already bad enough I needed to put on a new pair of underwear and got zero relief from him taunting my pussy earlier.

The door opens, and he steps through, cheeks still pink with his breaths coming heavy.

"Have a good time?" I ask with an amused grin. I'm such a bitch sometimes, I laugh to myself.

"Would've been better if it was your mouth," he responds gruffly and strides to the window. "Where did you see them?"

"Him. I saw one man. He's across the street, by the light post."

His head tilts for a brief second before straightening and reaching for the CO_2 fed gun. "Son of a bitch. I think he's too far away."

"I could create a distraction, maybe get him to come closer?"

"How do you figure?"

"I can go outside; maybe he'll cross the street."

He snorts and mimics my voice, not sounding even remotely close. "And maybe he'll put a bullet in you the first chance he gets."

"Okay smartass. I just figured he'd want my money, not my life."

"Because the bomb earlier didn't clue you in enough?"

"You're a dick, you know that?"

"Maybe if I had some relief I wouldn't be so dickish."

"Dickish? Did you just make that up?"

He shrugs.

"You're just pissed because he's too far away. It's not my fault you don't know how to shoot."

With a growl, his glare lands on me. "Woman…"

The word's enough of a threat to shut me up. Clearly, he doesn't find me distracting him right now very amusing. Instead of arguing further, I whisper, "I'm making some tea then." Not sure why I whisper since we're inside this giant building and the guy's across the street, but I do.

He nods, silent and I tiptoe toward my shoebox sized kitchen. I need to do something to get my mind distracted and making tea seems to be the easiest option to put a little distance between us. I don't know how I plan on getting any sleep with him here like this. My place is a studio, which means the only real room that has any privacy is the bathroom. Even now when I'm busily digging through my cabinet to hunt down lemon and chamomile tea bags, I can easily watch him from across the room.

I find the gray box and pull two bags free and heat the water. Once it's hot enough, I pour two cups with a tea bag in each, grab some spoons and a bottle of honey. With light feet, I make my way until I'm beside him and can set the cups on the small table off to the side of us.

"Did he move?" I whisper and peer through the pane of glass.

"Nah." He swallows, and my gaze lands on the same man as before. He's still there in the same position.

I peer up at Mercenary, taking in his relaxed stance. You'd think he'd be uptight since he's planning on shooting the guy, even if it is with a tranquilizer. He's not though. You'd think it was just another day on the job for him. Maybe it is. "Is this sorta thing normal for you?"

With a huff, he flicks his gaze to mine. "Do you need attention or something? I already spanked your ass once tonight."

With a glower, I spin around and busy myself by removing my tea bag and stirring in some honey. I was going to be nice, but he can take his tea bitter. I smirk to myself and bring my cup along with the bottle of honey with me to sit in my favorite overstuffed chair.

9. Girls that like fast cars and racing
aren't weird, they're a rare gift from God.
- Carmemes.com

MERCENARY

"Where's Chevelle?" Odin asks as he and Nightmare help me load the comatose Iron Fist into the back of the pickup truck.

"She fell asleep watching me wait to shoot this asshole."

He chuckles. "Guess you can go have some fun with her now."

"I wish. The bitch is dead set on me living my life with blue balls. I didn't even enjoy tranqing this guy, my dick hurt too badly."

They both laugh. *Fuckers.*

"It's true. I had to spank her ass earlier to get her to simmer down. Probably would've lost my shit if she hadn't fallen asleep eventually."

Hybrid Collection

"She never would've gone for that," he argues and Night nods his agreement.

"I didn't give her a choice, brother. I spanked her several times." With a shrug, I grumble. "She'll learn I won't allow her to push me around."

"Jesus, brother." Nightmare shakes his head. "Be careful. Before you know it, you'll be putting your name on her back."

"I'm not looking to add a property patch to her, although can't say I'd mind too much if it ended in that."

"Damn," Odin grins. "It's only been a week Merc."

A sigh leaves me, thinking how tight she's already wound me up. "You think I don't know that? Shit, Saint and Sinner must be thrilled. At this rate, I have no time to fuck with Jude. And someone's going to win that damn bet."

'That's a positive on your part," he says and Night grunts in agreement. "Having a thing for their woman would've ended in them killing you."

"We'll have to agree to disagree."

Nightmare snorts. "Give it time, you just got here. Wait until you see them play with their food. My name may be Nightmare, but they're the shit nightmares are made of."

I've yet to see this craziness that multiple brothers have warned me of, and part of me wonders if it's mostly just hype. Viking's the brother that strikes me as the one not to cross out of all of them. Any man who carries around an axe like it's an everyday utensil should be taken into consideration. Just like Torch—the brother fucking torches people. I wouldn't fuck with him, that's for sure.

He slams the tailgate shut, and I step back. "You want me to keep shooting them and calling you if any others show up?"

O nods. "Yeah as long as it's just onesies and twosies. Any more than that call for reinforcements 'cause it'll mean they want to do more than just keep an eye on The Pit."

"All right, brother," I agree, and fist bump them before pulling the metal bay door down and locking it. I hope no others decide to show up tonight, but so far, they've been fairly resilient. I'd like to get some kind of sleep tonight, especially if Chevelle plans to keep me on my toes.

Arriving back to her place, I find her still curled up in the chair fast asleep. She's so sweet and innocent looking when she's like this. It's when she's awake that her mouth has a sharp sting to it.

I scoop her into my arms, her body tilting and curling into me like a sleepy cat. I could get used to having her in my arms, all pliant and safe but I won't hold my breath on it happening. Pushing the covers away, I lay her down, tugging her free of her tight jeans. She stirs but lets me remove them, leaving her in her tank and panties. I snuggle her under the fluffy blanket before crawling into the spot beside her.

I'm on my back, staring at the ceiling when she shifts toward me. Her arm goes around my waist, her nose tucking into my bicep. She's fucking adorable, a goddamn wildcat and having her close to naked has me wanting her fiercely. She's asleep, and it's probably the only chance I'll get to really stare my fill.

I watch her for a moment before leaning over and pressing a kiss to her temple. She doesn't say anything, but I feel her hand pull me to her, tightening around my hip a bit more and I can't help but wonder if she's faking sleep. That's fine if she is, if she feels the need to pretend to be asleep in order to touch me, I'll roll with it. After all, it's just one more step in the direction I want her to go.

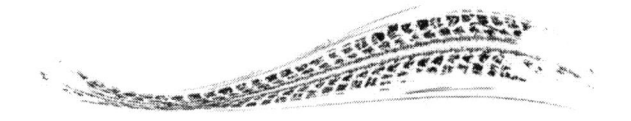

I wake to an empty bed and glance around to discover I'm alone in the apartment as well. What did I expect? Waking up to breakfast in bed or some shit? Chevelle made it clear she doesn't cook, so my mind shouldn't even be going there. Shit, I should've woken up early and done that for her. It would've caught her off guard even more. Stubborn female.

Hybrid Collection

With a stretch and a massive yawn, I head for the window to see if dumbass has been replaced.

"Motherfucker," I grumble and grab my burner from the jeans pocket on the floor.

"Odin," the VP answers.

"You won't fucking believe this."

"What?"

"There's someone hanging from the pole out front."

"Wait, what?"

"That damn light pole...it looks like a giant bolt has been screwed into it. There's a body hanging from it, rope around their neck. From here it definitely looks like they're dead."

"Fuck, fuck, fuck! Viking is going to be pissed. I'll send Torch and Nightmare to go collect the body."

"Did you get anything out of the guy from last night?"

"He hasn't woken up yet, those horse tranquilizers are strong."

"Apparently. He's not dead, right?"

"Not yet, anyhow."

I grunt. "You want me to go out there and get the body down?"

"No, stay inside with Chevelle, just in case they're waiting for you to leave her vulnerable."

"Shit, I haven't even seen her yet. I just woke up."

"Go find her and make sure she's okay."

"I will."

"Later."

"Later," I reply and end the call then yank on my pants and boots and head out of the studio.

CHEVELLE

"You weren't there when I woke up." Mercenary comes up on the other side of the hood. I was just checking the plugs before clocking my time.

"I thought you'd be tired from being up all night." I tiptoed around, not wanting to wake him. He looked dead to the world with how hard he was sleeping.

"I was. What are you doing?" His cool blue irises run over me like he's famished and I'm breakfast.

"Checking plugs then I planned to run this pretty lady to get my latest track time. I put new tires on her a week ago, and I'm not quite used to them."

He nods. "You probably shouldn't drive right now."

My back stiffens as I stand to my full height and sputter, "Excuse me?" The man has a lot of nerve; I have no doubt about that.

"A bomb went off yesterday," he emphasis slowly, tilting his head like I'm nuts. "It's smart to not drive your cars right now."

"But it's what I do," I argue. He's lost his mind telling me not to drive. It's like having your favorite toy and not being able to touch it. That doesn't sit well for me. I learned at a young age that if I want something to go for it, to take it. Waiting around gets you nowhere and nothing to show for it.

"You'll be safer if you take a short break, just a week or two."

Hybrid Collection

"Yeah, that's not happening." Not to mention that's asking me to take a ten thousand dollar cut to my monthly pay. It definitely won't be going down while I have anything to say about it.

He throws his hands up dramatically, and I hold back my smirk. "Fuck, woman, why do you have to be so damn difficult?"

I stomp around the front of the car coming face to face with the grouchy male who's decided to rudely interrupt my quiet morning time. "Listen here, cupcake, go eat a fucking banana or whatever it is you need to take it down a notch. Racing is my job, it's my life. I won't stop just because it gets a little dangerous. Racing is not safe, that's partly why it's so damn fun."

"I know," he admits, catching me off guard.

"You know?"

He nods. "I get it. I wouldn't stop if someone told me to either. At least let me check your car over before you go cranking the engine and taking off."

I release a breath through my clenched teeth, unaware I was even holding it. He wants to check my car over to see if it has a bomb in it. That's pretty freaking sweet. Why can't he always be like this? "Yeah, sure, I can deal with that. Thanks."

He tilts his head toward me slightly and then crouches to slide under the car. On the way down he gripes, "By the way, it's eat a Snickers bar, not a banana."

"Ugh, did you just correct me?"

"Well, the commercial isn't about bananas." He calls from the ground.

"Un-freaking-believable! You just can't help yourself from correcting me and being in control, can you?"

He rolls out, opening the trunk to snoop around there next. "Oh, I'm the difficult one?"

"Yes, you are. I do not remember this much stress in my life before you showed up."

He pokes his head out, meeting my stare. "All this over a banana?"

"Holy shit," I hiss and stomp away.

I go straight to one of the concession stands. They're all locked up, but the benefits of owning the place is I have a key to everything. I grab a king-sized Snickers bar and also a banana from the walk-in cooler. I knew we'd have them because one thing we offer is banana splits with hand scooped ice cream. Surprisingly they're one of the concessions top sellers.

I'm still stomping around when I make my way back down the stairs to the center and find Mercenary leaning up against my car. He's propped against the shiny paint all nonchalant, arms crossed over his chest, muscles bulging while wearing a cocky smirk. He looks every ounce of a badass, and so help me God, do I want to jump his bones.

"All done. Your car's safe for you to drive in circles now." He winks, and I toss the candy and fruit in his direction. Surprisingly he has reflexes like a cat and snatches them in midair.

"Two hands?" I gape.

"I'm ambidextrous," he shrugs and opens his fingers to see what I threw.

"You went to get me one of each?" His wide eyes meet mine.

I nod, biting the inside of my cheek.

He drops them to the ground and with a few powerful strides, stops in front of me. I'm about to rip into him for being ungrateful when his hands cup my cheeks and his lips meet mine. My world seems to stop as his mouth roots me in place. My mind and body fight each other, one tells me to fuck him while the other screams for me to thrash against him. What is it with this man that has me teetering on the edge of control?

He coaxes my mouth open, parting my lips to dip inside with his tongue. It twists with mine, caressing me, forcing my resolve to weaken. We fight each other for control, teeth clashing, and tongues sparring to gain control. I feel like I'm falling, but it's only Mercenary pushing me to the ground. His heat encompasses around me, warming like an electric blanket. His knee parts my thighs, wedging his way where I've craved him to be since I first laid eyes on him.

Rocking my hips, I flip him to the side, climbing over to straddle his groin without breaking our kiss. His hands land on my upper thighs, pulling me to him and grinding into my core. Groans escape from both of us at the delicious friction, and our kiss takes a turn to become more dirty than angry.

The craving to have this man underneath me, naked, while I bounce on his cock has my skin breaking out in cold chills like an icy wind just came out of nowhere. My nipples grow hard under my tank top, and a whimper breaks free as our tongues tangle with each other. I want to tie him up and fuck him until his dick no longer stands up.

"Uh, Chevy?" Ace's curious voice in the distance breaks through my Mercenary induced foggy brain.

He continues yammering on. "Sorry to uh, bother you guys, but the truck's here and the driver needs you to sign before he can start unloading."

"Shit," leaves me in a breathy huff as I pull back. My lustful gaze locking on Mercenary's lowered lashes as he stares back, lazily, irises portraying he wants to fuck me just as badly.

"I love Snickers," he rumbles after a second of our trance, and I smirk.

"Good, cupcake, eat up." With that, I stand and follow Ace toward the loading bay.

10. If anyone can have it,
I don't want it...
- Smart women

MERCENARY

I'm eating the banana Chevelle gave me when my brothers stroll into The Pit, finding me on my ass, stuffing my face. Odin's blond brow hikes, his stony expression reminding me of his older brother, Viking. "We interrupting your breakfast?"

Swallowing, I shake my head. "I have a feeling this is going to be breakfast and lunch. You guys get the body?"

"Yeah, I can't believe the stupid fuckers strung him up out in the open," Torch gripes and Nightmare grunts in agreement.

"Me either. Is it just you guys or did the other brothers ride over with you?"

Nightmare tucks his dark, shoulder-length hair behind his ears. "Just us. The rest were too hung over."

Hybrid Collection

I nod. The lucky asses getting to drink and relax last night. I was here keeping watch for Iron Fists to pop up all night. My eyes feel like they've been pricked by needles from the little sleep I was able to get.

"They got the Fist to talk; we found one of their locations too."

"No shit?" I ask O, and he confirms. No wonder they were celebrating. I've heard a few times how they've been waiting for years to lock down this rival club.

"Vike doesn't believe it all, of course. He thinks there's another spot they're either hiding, maybe more or something else we don't know about."

"Possibly three spots? You think they'd be that organized to have the club spread out in three locations?"

"Probably," Torch says and leans against Chevelle's Nova.

"Careful brother, if the bitch sees you on her car she'll flip."

He snorts. "I'm not so easily intimidated."

Odin scoffs. "If you had any sense of self-preservation you would be when it comes to her."

Rather than argue, I open the Snickers and take a big bite. She even got me the king-sized bar. It's the best one. I get done chewing and ask, "What'd you do with the body?"

Nightmare grins. "It's rolled in a tarp and loaded in the truck. I'm gonna let Saint feed it to the pigs at the farm. Looks like it was one of their prospects. I think they got nervous that someone ratted them out or whatever, so they killed one of their own."

A shiver overcomes me imagining the hogs eating the body. I'm a hardened biker, but that shit's gross—even for me. "You guys had good timing. The delivery truck showed up, must have been right after you got the body down or I'm sure we'd be hearing sirens about now."

"The last thing we need is the cops catching wind of this," Odin gripes and we all nod, agreeing. None of us want to end up in jail, especially for crimes we didn't commit. "Prez wants you at the club for church tomorrow. He said to bring Chevelle with you, so she's not left here alone."

"Bet, text me the time, and we'll be there."

"Yeah, good luck with getting her to go with you."

"I'll probably talk her into going for food and then just stop at the club. She won't have a choice."

Odin snorts. "You think she'll actually let you drive? Keep dreaming, brother."

"I'm going to stick her on my bike. She won't have a say in the matter."

"How you going to manage that?"

"It'll be her idea." I grin, and they chuckle.

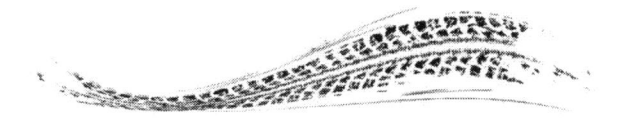

"You ever been on a motorcycle before mine?" I ask as she bites into her taco.

She chews a few times and then replies. "A Ducati but not a bike like yours, no."

Who the fuck had a Ducati for her to ride? My Harley is nice, but probably not as smooth of a ride as an expensive ass Ducati. Wonder who the lucky prick was that had her and was too stupid not to hold on to her? What a dumbass. I never would've let her go had it been me. Rather than demand a name and social security number to hunt him down, I take a swig from my beer and move on.

"What did you think of the ride?"

"Surprisingly, I enjoyed it. I can see why you guys like it so much, kind of reminds me of when I race."

Hybrid Collection

"That's because I was hauling ass with you, figured you'd appreciate the speed and adrenaline."

She nods and licks her lips. She misses some salsa just under her bottom lip, and I reach forward. Swiping my finger to catch the salsa, I bring it to my mouth and her eyes flair.

"Salsa," I rasp.

She grabs the finger I just had between my lips and brings it to her mouth, sucking it. Her tongue swipes the tip, and the stroke instantly has my imagination running wild, wanting my cock to be in its place. A growl escapes as my groin tightens, wanting to yank her across the table at the fucking taco shack. She's lucky she's not mine, or I'd take her out back and have her sucking my cock off and fucking her across my bike in a heartbeat.

"Maybe I didn't want to share," she taunts after releasing my hand.

"We need to go." I manage to choke out, staring her down.

"But I'm not done."

"I have church to get to and any more time watching that mouth, I'm gonna be fucking it."

Her cheeks heat as her breaths increase in speed. Her chest moves with her heavy breathing and her lids lower, irises dilating at my proclamation. She wants me to fuck her. She wants me to take her decision away so when she fights me on it, she can pretend she doesn't want it as badly as I do.

"You're pretty damn bossy, biker."

"And you're sexy as fuck. You want to suck my cock or head to the clubhouse? This is the only time I'm going to ask before I make the decision for you." It's enough of a threat to piss her off. She doesn't like to be bossed, and I love having control. We're like fire and fire, both burning hot and demanding, both vying for full control.

She stands with a huff. "I'll get a to go bag." She stomps off to the counter, and I watch her swing her plump ass with each step. The young cabana looking guy smiles, and turns on the charm, thinking he can flirt with her, probably planning to ask for her number. I should knock his damn teeth out looking at my woman like that.

Gritting my teeth, I chug the remaining beer to cool off my temper. I don't need to get arrested at the damn taco joint for a kid merely getting through puberty. I'd really appear like a damn jackoff to Chevelle then. Witnessing her smile for him has me wanting to lock her in my room back at the compound. None of my brothers would give two shits if I kept her as mine. Fuck, she'd be pissed if I did. She'd probably slit my throat the first chance she got. *Stubborn female.*

"A little friendly, huh? You like 'em young?" I grumble once she comes back and begins loading the rest of our food into a paper bag to take with us. I ordered like twenty tacos, so I'd have some for dinner too. Chevelle wasn't screwing around when she said she doesn't cook.

She glowers my way. "I like them when they aren't assholes, not that it's any of your business."

"Too bad." I get to my feet and don't tip, cause fuck that guy getting my money.

"Hmm?" Chevelle hums with a frown. She's a badass, but she's way too curious. It's her downfall and has been the way to get her to let her wall down with me.

"'Cause I'm an asshole," I shrug and strut toward the door, shooting a glare at the guy behind the counter. He stares at Chevy for a moment, but it's quickly broken when he catches my look. His eyes suddenly find the counter in front of him pretty damn interesting. Smart move on his part. I don't start a lot of shit, but I do tend to be territorial when it comes to a woman I'm interested in.

She follows me to my bike. "Why were you looking at him like that?" she asks, catching up to me.

"He was interested in you."

"So? I'm here like three times a week, sometimes four. He's used to me."

Hybrid Collection

"No," I hiss. "He *likes* you."

She shrugs, and I snatch the bag, securing it in my saddlebag and throw my leg over to take my seat. "It's not really a big deal." She places her palm on my shoulder and climbs on behind me. She adjusts until she's snug up to my back.

"The hell it isn't. The kid won't be able to speak if I catch him looking at you like that again." I promise and start my engine, drowning out any argument she may have. I'm being obnoxious, but after the kiss we shared, she's overtaken that possessiveness I have inside. She hasn't smiled at me like that yet, and I have a feeling that's what pisses me off the most out of the entire situation.

"Just take me back."

"I wanted you at the club with me."

"I'll go another time. I have an order coming in."

"You just had one."

"I get deliveries nearly every day. I don't want to argue about it."

"But you'll be alone."

"I'm a grown-ass woman, and I'm not alone. I have employees there."

"I don't like it."

"You can drop me off, or I can walk."

I crank the engine and take off. She jerks to hold on to me tightly, and I smirk. She deserved that jolt, arguing with me over this shit. I drop her off without exchanging a single word. Leaving her there has a bad taste in my mouth growing stronger and stronger. It's pointless to try and talk her out of it though; she's the type that really would walk back, cursing me the entire time.

The ride passes quickly, with the air hot and dry. It's another summer day in Texas, and my body hasn't adjusted to the temperature change yet. In Chicago, we'd all bitch it was too warm, but I had no idea what real heat was until coming here. The weather may say ninety-five degrees, but it has a goddamn heat index of a hundred and ten. That shit just makes me want to stay inside, kind of like Chicago winters.

I'm the last one to sit down, and it's not my favorite thing in the world to have everyone's attention on me all at once.

11. Here's to strong women.

May we know them.

May we be them.

May we raise them.

MERCENARY

"Nice of you to join us," Prez grumbles as I get comfortable and set my beer down on the large table. "In session," he states and slams the gavel down. The wood landing on the table is loud enough that the sound bounces off the walls and I have to hold myself still not to cringe. The brothers would give me a ton of shit if they witnessed me jump from the damn gavel.

"The three Fists we brought in have been talking. Leisurely, unfortunately, but at least we're getting some kind of information from them. We have two confirmed locations for their compounds so far, and until we get any others out of them, Ruger is actively searching between the areas."

Viking's cousin, Blaze, speaks up. "So you believe they'll all be close together."

He nods. "Yeah, it makes sense. It'd be easy enough for them to get to each other but safer to be spread out."

Prez has a point. The other Oath Keepers charter is about twenty minutes away from here; it's convenient for the brothers to go back and forth. It's also just far enough away from each other to deter a rival club trying to take us all out at once. The Iron Fists tried at one time but most of the club was gone and missed the hit, so in the end, the Fists failed.

"Once we find the locations and know for sure there are no others close enough to dole out immediate retaliation on us, we'll hit. We have to be certain though. This is us calling for war once we hit them, and I, for one, have breathed a bit easier having this supposed truce."

Nightmare's fist slams on the table. "Fuck the truce. I want their lives. Puppet's death is mine for the taking, and I want to see the motherfucker filleted and burned to ash for touching my family."

Viking winces at the outburst and agrees. "Yes brother, I gave you my word you'd have your revenge. When it's time, we'll coordinate with Ares' club."

"How will we get close enough to them?" Odin asks.

"Ares will split up his brothers and set one of the Fists' compounds on fire then hold back to catch any remaining stragglers that may make it out alive. We'll take whatever necessary precautions and storm the main clubhouse. Unless we can get ahold of Puppet, the Iron Fists' head president, another way. If that happens, then we just sit back and blow the third clubhouse sky high somehow."

Torch grunts. "And the cops?" He's always the one thinking about repercussions from the law.

"The sheriff will look the other way if it's in his jurisdiction. He wants the Fists gone. They've caused too many problems, and he's been friends with my ol' lady's pops for far too long. His loyalty lies with the club if it gets rid of one of his problems."

Torch shakes his head. "You can never trust the cops."

Prez sighs. "Relax, T, I've taken care of it." He turns to the brothers across from me. "Saint and Sinner, I want you both to ride up to meet with Ruger. He's caught wind of someone following him, and he may need some backup."

"Bet," Sinner agrees.

"About time we get to have some fun," Saint grins manically.

Prez turns to Smokey. "Make sure to send them with some extra cash for the hotels and shit. Keep me posted on the books."

Smokey nods, taking a drag of his cigarette.

"Odin and Torch, you both need to hit The Pit tonight." They agree, and he continues. "Anything else?"

We stay quiet.

"Do your fucking job and get the hell out of here. Church is over." He slams the gavel down, and we all rise. "Mercenary." The Prez calls my name before I take a step.

"Yeah?"

"Hold back a sec; I need to have a chat with you."

This can't be good. We're bikers, we don't 'chat.' "What's up?" I sit back in my spot at the other end of the table. I'm the newest here, so I sit the farthest away from him.

"You need to sit tight tonight."

"Excuse me? I have a race." I'm not staying at the club; I have to protect Chevelle.

He shakes his head. "I'm sending Torch in your place."

My throat nearly closes up thinking of him with Chevelle. I choke out, "Excuse me?"

With a shrug, he lets out a sigh. "I spoke to Chevelle earlier."

"And?" When was this? It had to be when I dropped her off. That was the only time she was out of my sight besides when she showered.

"Well, she wants you out of The Pit tonight."

"You have to be fucking kidding me."

"I'm not."

"Did she say why?"

"You told her you didn't want her to race?"

I nod. "Of course, I did, it's too dangerous. She could be in the next car that explodes."

"Can't do that brother." He chuckles and takes a sip from the tumbler in front of him.

"The hell I can't." He may be the President of this club, but he's no one to tell me who I can and cannot fuck. I'll decide that on my own.

He waits for a few beats, thinking over what he wants to say before speaking again. "You don't tame a wild bitch by holding her down. You set her free and give her strength. You try to snuff out her passion for living, and she'll never stick around. You take control and show her you have her back and she flourishes, standing beside you."

That's probably the most poetic shit I've ever heard come from the Prez's mouth. "I won't let her kill herself because of stupid arrogance. The woman is bullheaded and is going to be the death of both of us."

"She probably thinks you're acting the same way."

Huffing, I get to my feet.

"I mean it, Mercenary. Torch goes in your place tonight." He points, and I bristle.

Hybrid Collection

"No disrespect Prez, but this is between her and me, not Torch. I can't believe she called you. I'd just had my damn tongue in her mouth yesterday."

"You're wrong. This is about my club dealing with their enemy. You have one thing on your mind, which is fine, but you need to take your blinders off. This is bigger than your cock wanting some forbidden pussy."

"I've gotten you the Fists to question so far, not anyone else."

"And I'm grateful for it, but what happens if ten of them showed up? Could you make the right moves and think long enough to call in your brothers and also protect yourself? They could fuck you up and demand information out of you. Can you honestly say you can do what is needed or will she have you so distracted you risk your neck for her first?"

Fuck. He has a point.

"So, have Torch and Odin in the stands again like last week. I'll be down on the track to protect Chevelle. Then it all works out, and everyone's straight."

"She doesn't want you there at all. You'll step in and attempt to stop her from racing and you can't. That's her damn track; she's the one letting us be there in the first place."

"I'm not one to usually go against orders, but I'm at least having a conversation with her ass about this. I won't let her hide behind a phone because I'm not there in person to talk some sense into her stubborn head."

"Don't fuck this up, Mercenary. We need to have a spot there to get our info, and if you screw with that, you'll have me on your ass."

"Noted," I mutter with a huff and head for the door. My muscles are coiled extra tight with irritation. I have to see Chevelle; she needs to realize she can't call the Prez every time we disagree on something. I can't believe she took it that far rather than fighting with me about it. She must've realized I was serious when I told her I didn't want her in those damn cars tonight.

I pay no attention to any of my brothers as I storm through the bar for my motorcycle. The machine can't carry me fast enough it seems, and my anger only grows with the longer it takes me to reach her. The woman fights me at every turn, and now she believes she can get her way by going through my Prez.

I've never met a female who didn't give into me by now. Normally I'd have fucked them, and they'd be doing whatever I asked until I got tired of them. I've barely kissed this bitch, and she's put me on my ass. It's gotten to the point where I even spanked her, and she didn't fully submit. She's going to be the death of me one way or another.

I shake my head, pushing my bike's speed up higher. The scenery off on each side of the road passes in a blur. I don't pay any attention to it anyhow. I'm too distracted, thinking of only Chevelle and how I can get her to finally listen. The Pit comes up on my left, and I lower my speed, pulling into the parking lot and going around to the backside.

I'm met at the large silver bay door as I roll it up. My gaze instantly falls to the man lying at Chevelle's feet, draining any irritation I was harboring on the ride over. "Where'd he come from?" I nod to the unconscious man on the floor.

His leather cut gives him away as being another Iron Fist. Odin was right; they're like damn cockroaches never going away. It makes me wonder just how large their club really is. Odin said most likely fifty to a hundred members, and that's just in this general area. That's a lot of damn bikers for any club.

She shrugs, tucking her dark hair behind her ears all innocent like. "When you left they just showed up."

"They?"

"There's another knocked out over by the front. He was too fat for me to drag him to this door."

"Damn it." I flick my eyes over her. "You fight them? They hurt you?"

"No." She shakes her head, and I let out a relived breath. I'm very aware that she's tough, but they could've ended up hurting her. Thinking of these fuck faces

Hybrid Collection

showing up to do who knows what to her, has my chest swelling, wanting to dole out punishing blows to keep her safe. "I shot them with the tranq darts. I was looking out the window in my place when I first noticed them walking toward the front."

A wide grin grows on my face, despite the danger. "You shot them both?" I didn't know she could shoot. Jesus, can this woman not do anything? If my cock wasn't so enormous, she'd have me questioning my manhood. She makes everything seem easy. It's hard being so tempted by a woman who knows how to do everything you do and do some of it even better than you can.

She nods, a sheepish smile taking over. "You had that damn gun, and I wanted to shoot it. They finally gave me a good enough reason to use it without ruffling your feathers."

A loud laugh escapes me, and I pull her to me. "You know somethin'?"

"Hmm?" She hikes an eyebrow up and tilts her head to meet my eyes.

"You're a bad bitch, Chevy. I've never met another like you," I admit and a blush steals over her cheeks.

She lets the nickname slide with my compliment. "I hope that's a good thing?" she whispers, and I lean in, so my lips nearly touch hers.

"It's a damn good thing, sweetie." With my hands on her shoulders, I pull her the last step to me and plant my mouth on hers. She meets me with so much fervor in return that my body screams for more. I walk her backward to the wall, my hands reaching down and sliding up the backs of her thighs, never breaking our kiss.

My palms lift her, spreading her legs and her arms clutch onto my neck as I rest my cock against her center. Holding her up against the cement wall, I kiss her roughly. My body's beyond turned on, knowing she knocked these guys out and drug them inside and she didn't even freak out about it at all. Chevelle really is a badass, and that's so damn sexy.

Grinding into her core, my palms slide from under her ass up along her thighs and under her tank top. They glide along her ribs, my thumbs only pausing when they can rub across her breasts and play with her nipples. My fingers move back and forth, caressing and squeezing her breasts until she moans in pleasure and arches her back, pushing into my hands even more.

"I want you. I need in this pussy," I confess with a gruff voice, thick with desire. My heavy cock pushes against her, grinding in circles. I love having her like this, panting and needy. She wants me as badly as I want her. I have to make her give in to me.

With another groan into my mouth, her hands push my chest with enough force, I break away, blinking a few times to clear my lustful haze she's drowning me in. "What is it, Chevelle?"

She clears her throat and licks her lips. The action has me growling with longing, yearning to sink into her heat and not stop until I've had my fill and my cock can no longer stand firm. I lean in to nibble on her bottom lip, coaxing her to let me have more of her. I want to taste her needy pussy so badly it makes my mouth water thinking about it.

"The other guy is still up front, and the employees will be here soon. They can't see him knocked out."

"Damn it," I grumble, and she nods, agreeing with my frustration of having to stop. The other time I had her like this we were interrupted by Ace. Now it's these stupid Iron Fists. I push another kiss to her lips and promise, "This isn't over."

She hums, with a teasing smirk. "Bossy biker, I'm not that easy." Her hand trails down my abs to brush over the hardness in my pants making its presence clearly known.

"You want it just as badly. Admit it," I murmur and adjust my dick after her teasing graze against my shaft.

Her gaze watches my every move full of longing. "You're right, I do." I groan, and she continues. "Doesn't mean I'm giving it up in a hallway with a knocked-out shithead at our feet."

Hybrid Collection

With a huff, I openly admit, "I don't do romance." Ever the romantic, I should shut my fucking mouth if I want any semblance of a chance with this woman. I just can't seem to do it whether it makes shit harder for me or not.

She shrugs. "Neither do I, although I'm not one to turn down chocolate syrup, or in your case, some peanut butter. If that's your version of romance, anyway."

"Fuck," I breathe the curse. She had to bring up the peanut butter, and that makes me think of her fucking tongue and how it swirled around my finger when we had those pancakes. I want her head bobbing below me as she works peanut butter clean from my cock. God, the thought of it has me groaning low in my throat.

"Come on, cupcake. Time to grab this idiot from the front. You should probably call your MC brothers."

"I can shoot them a text. now show me where this other guy's at." The sooner they're out of my way, the sooner I can get back to touching her.

12. Buckle Up, Buttercup.
-Pinterest Meme

CHEVELLE

The Oath Keepers got here just in time to get the other bikers out of the way before my employees, and the other racers showed up. That would've been a big mess had any of them noticed an unconscious man lying around. Hopefully, no other trouble comes our way. I can't be up front to keep any other Iron Fists from getting in tonight since I plan on racing.

I can, however, warn my crew to keep a look out for them, but I won't have them turn the Iron Fists away. I'd be too afraid for their safety. Those one-percenters don't mix well with being told no, and I refuse to be the cause of them getting hurt, or worse, killed. My own safety is one thing; I'm more than capable of defending myself. My employees, however, are just normal everyday people with families at home.

The only way I knew to wait at the back door with the other biker for help was because Viking sent me a text letting me know Mercenary was on his way. I can't believe the stubborn man didn't listen to his president. I told that guy to take control of his brother. I won't let a man dictate whether I race or not. I know

Hybrid Collection

Mercenary will put up a fuss when he sees me line up on the track tonight. I don't need the distraction or any of the other racers witnessing me allow a man to have a say around here. They have to know I run this show.

On the plus side of these idiots scoping out The Pit or whatever they were doing, it was a decent distraction. Viking said Mercenary was not pleased hearing I'd called, so the unconscious guys took his focus off me for the time being. I have no idea what the Oath Keepers are doing with all these unwanted bikers they're taking off my hands, and I want it to stay that way. The less I know, the better. I've never been a snitch, but like I said, the less I'm aware of, the easier not to slip up.

Ace steps up beside me. "All drivers are ready. They listened to your suggestion and didn't bring their race vehicle on the property until thirty minutes ago, and I've had someone watching them all in case one of the drivers needs to leave for a minute or whatever."

"Good, thank you."

"I didn't like the last race any more than you. I don't want you hurt, Chevy."

Smiling gratefully, I nudge his shoulder like I would if he were an older brother. He's always reminded me of what it'd be like to have one. "All right, let's get started. The sooner we can erase the last race from their minds, the better." I nod toward the stands, and he agrees.

"I'll signal the music."

"And I'll line up."

I quickly peer around and hightail it to my ivory painted nineteen sixty-eight Dodge Charger RT. It's been a few weeks since I drove him and it's his turn to have a little fun on the track. Mercenary's distracted and hasn't had a chance to dig into me again about racing tonight. Not that I'd listen to him if he tried—he doesn't own me and never will. The man will learn that I do whatever the fuck I want to.

"Flower" by Moby begins to play through The Pit speakers, and a smile takes over. I haven't heard this song in forever, and I love to race to it. There's something about the beat; it's made to be listened to in a fast car.

I slide into the matching buttery soft leather seats—the beautiful chiffon color complementing the beast of a car and slide the key in the ignition. My stomach flutters excitedly as I twist the key and he thunders to life. He sounds like a grouchy old bastard pissed off for being woken up. No worries, he'll be purring like a kitten once I give him a little gas.

Pushing the link'd button, the stereo inside syncs to the speakers blaring through the dome. At the roar of my engine, Mercenary's gaze pins on me, and boy does he look furious. I send him a little wave with my fingers and romp on the gas. The car fishtails before straightening for the line. It's been too long since I drove him. He seems a bit angry with me.

"It's okay, baby," I soothe and rub my hand along the ebony dash. Yes, I talk to my vehicles. Anyone in their right mind who loves their cars speaks to them.

The other three vehicles I'll be going against roll up, lining up around my spot. My car rumbles, just waiting to be set free to whip some ass. The song changes, and right on cue, the passenger door swings open, a large body sliding in. I'm so focused on the sound of my engine and exhaust, gearing up for my race that it takes a moment to grasp that he's right next to me.

My mouth drops open. "What the hell? You can't be in here!" I yell as the engines around me drown out the music. I'm racing against some experienced fuckers, and I don't need Mercenary distracting me right now.

He whips the belt across his chest. "Bullshit. You want to race when it's not fucking safe, then I'm riding with you."

"You're like two hundred fucking pounds, man, get out!" I yell, pissed and glare at his stone cold blue eyes. The smoke slowly creeps up, surrounding the vehicles and cocooning us as various racers smoke out their tires.

My foot presses on the gas, my engine roaring in response as the car shakes, wanting to be let loose. It's to warm the engine up, and it also helps play a part in psyching out my opponents. They know I race to win, no matter what I drive, but Mercenary is adding unnecessary weight to my ride. It's one of the reasons I don't

Hybrid Collection

have a massive sound system in my car. I do without big speakers, and in return, my car weighs less than the others.

"I'm not moving, so if you want to win, I suggest you pay attention."

"I'm so kicking your ass for this shit," I swear as the song changes to 'Zombies' by The Cranberries and the race begins.

I let up the brake, and the car's so powerful the front end lifts off the ground. All of my cars do, and I freaking love the feeling of immense horsepower at my fingertips. Mercenary's arms shoot out with a curse, one holding the dash, the other gripping the oh shit handle like it's life or death for him. An evil smile takes over as we slam back to the ground and the Charger shoots forward as if the devil's nipping at its heels.

My rear tires squeal even though I already ran the set of rubber earlier and Mercenary shouts, "How is this legal?"

I scream at the distraction. "Shut the fuck up, cupcake!" I shift gears and swerve to the right, blocking the clown coming up behind me. I have to concentrate. It's the main reason I always win—not the car, but because I pay attention, I don't get sidetracked. I'm sure he growls in response, but I shut everything out and race. There's five grand on the line, and I don't plan on losing it.

We head around the last turn, and one of the cars bumps my rear end. I swerve, nearly losing control, but keep my cool as I sail over the finish line. As we pull to a stop, I leap out of my car and fly for the other driver.

He's just climbing out when I lay into him. My fist flies at his face in spite of his carelessness. We have rules in place to keep drivers as safe as possible. It's already dangerous enough driving at that speed on an enclosed track around so many people, but this asshole wants to rub me? "You hit my damn car!" I yell and throw another punch.

He reciprocates with a punch of his own. He has enough muscle behind it, I see stars for a moment, and then I hear a roar. I'm thrown to the side as two hundred pounds of pissed off alpha makes ground beef of the dude's face that just hit me. I stand there, shocked as I witness why the guy I've come to push around without a second thought is called Mercenary. The man wails into the other guy with such speed and strength the asshole's knocked out within moments of it even beginning.

Odin and Torch hurry to him, each grabbing for the mammoth of a man, taking hits in the midst of pulling him off the unconscious body below him. They eventually wrestle him off, but it's no easy feat. Breathing deeply, I stare, wide-eyed. Mercenary could've easily killed the other driver.

I lost my temper, and he fed off of it, going ballistic. The man is raw power, ready to dole out punishment. It makes me think that when I flipped him before, that he touched me with kid gloves. The animal in front of me could've killed me that day if he'd wanted to. Instead, he pulled my hair and stared at me like he wanted to fuck me. Jesus Holy Wow Christ.

Ace is by my side the next time I blink. "You okay?"

I swallow and nod. "My cheek is throbbing, but it won't hurt too badly until my adrenaline wears off."

"You could've wrecked, had that asshole hit you off to the side, and you spun out."

"I know. I was so pissed I couldn't stop myself."

He nods. "I figured." Our gazes lock on the rear of my Charger. "At least the car's good." He's right, there's paint on the bumper, but it'll buff off.

"I love old cars," I sigh in relief. I would've been even madder had it been dented up.

"Me too," he agrees. "What are you going to do with him?" He gestures to the guy on the ground.

"Someone drag him out back and drive his car out too."

"You want him banned?"

Hybrid Collection

I nod. Whoever drives his car outside will spray paint "banned" across both sides of his car. He'll be pissed, but he's lucky I let him keep his car after breaking the rules. I should be a real bitch and send it to a chop shop.

I make my way to a panting Mercenary. My palm finds his cheek, his crazed gaze finding mine. "You okay, big guy?" I swear he grows an extra foot taller and wider when he gets into a fight. He was massive the last time the Iron Fists came to my office too.

"I'd be better if you'd listened to me and parked the damn car."

I roll my eyes and Odin interrupts us. "Prez wants you at the club, right now."

"I'm racing next," Mercenary argues.

Odin shakes his head. "Forget the race. Head back before more shit hits the fan."

"You told him I was in the car with Chevelle?" His brow furrows.

"I had to; he told me if you tried to stop her from racing to call him immediately."

"Fuck!"

We've caused a big enough scene; I can't do more drama without losing business. Last week it was a bomb, this week a near wreck, and then an all-out brawl. We need to get out of here so the others can race.

"Hey, Titus," I call to one of the workers on the track. "Park my Charger in his spot, please."

"Okay, boss." The kid nods and hops into my car eagerly.

"Let's go to the club, Mercenary."

"No, I'm racing and staying here to keep you safe."

"Fine." I shrug and start walking to my other cars. "Then I'll go by myself and tell Viking all about tonight," I threaten and quicken my steps.

"You're a fucking tattle tale now? Is that how you're going to play this?" I hear him behind me, his voice getting closer. I know he's chasing me down, his fast stride easily catching up.

I hop in my Chevelle and push my door lock down. He watches me on my side and with a huff, rounds to the passenger side, sliding in and slamming my door.

"I hit that fucker back there because he touched you! None of it would've happened if you'd listened to me, damn it!" he grumbles, and I start the Chevelle, heading for the bay in the back. Ace will take care of everything here for the time being.

Hybrid Collection

13. A king only bows down to his queen.
- 100XSUCCESS

MERCENARY

I can't believe she went against everything I warned her about and decided to race. She's so damn stubborn. The woman has me vibrating with anger. I can't believe she hit that fucker rather than letting me take care of it for her. I would've killed him had my brothers not wrestled me off.

"You're infuriating, the most difficult damn woman I've come across."

"You're no spring picnic yourself, you know. You come into my life, demanding to take over. It won't happen with me, I don't need to be smothered."

"If I want to take over, you'd know it, and it'd fucking happen." Smothered my fucking ass, I've stayed so far back when it comes to being all up in her shit. She thinks this is bad, she hasn't seen smothered yet. Once this bitch is mine, she won't be able to walk five feet away without me knowing about it.

"Oh really? Is that what you think?" she huffs, her cheeks turning a sweet shade of pink with her frustration. "Clearly you didn't catch my drift when we first met or every day since then!"

"I caught it, trust me. You need me to spank your ass and fuck you until you break."

Chevelle's gaze flashes to me. "I *let* you spank me." Her eyes train back on the road in front of us. She's driving way too fast, still pumped up from the race and the fight no doubt.

Arguing with her only increases my heart and turns me on. "And you were soaked from it. You need to be fucked, Chevelle, and hard. You need to feel what it's like to have a real man between those thighs and in your life."

She snorts and my face flushes, not being able to show her right this second. My cock wants to be buried in her so badly it's on my damn mind constantly. Prez was right about me not being able to focus. Especially when she gets like this, all wound up and gorgeous and shit. *Fuck.*

"You won't break me, Mercenary," she declares, and I respond with a smug smirk, watching her breasts heave with each heavy breath she draws in and exhales.

"The hell I won't. When this is over and done with, you'll be begging me for more. I'll have my cock in you so deep you won't be able to speak, and when I finally *let* you, it'll be *my name* on that tongue."

"Does your ego have no bounds?" She shakes her head.

If she only had a clue—my ego's bigger than this damn car. I've had way too many women to not be confident when it comes to my cock and the female anatomy. Women love me when I'm eight inches deep. I may not be able to bend her to my will right this moment, but I can tease her a bit.

Turning in my seat, I reach across with my right hand, tweaking her nipple.

She sputters, her mouth dropping open as a deeper blush spreads across her cheeks and chest. "What are you doing? I'm driving!"

"Exactly...and I'm doing whatever the hell I want to," I grumble, and my left hand takes over, plucking her now erect nipple. My right hand lands on her thigh and the gas falters momentarily as I catch her by surprise. My palm slides up her thigh, closer to her core and her neck moves as she swallows, trying to remain unaffected.

"Mercenary?" It leaves her with a breath, the sound making my shaft grow.

"Right here, sweetie."

"You have to stop, I'm driving."

"Nah, don't think so." My palm stops at her juncture. I move my fingers and palm against her core, her back arching her chest against my other hand.

"Oh!" Chevelle moans. "I'm not fucking you. When I park this car, this stops," she threatens, and I continue to rub her until she's a turned on, whimpering mess. "You should've trusted me back there," she mumbles, her thoughts jumping back to earlier and then back to the present.

"If you want my trust, Chevelle, you'll have to give some first. And this body is aching; it needs me to fuck it. You want me just as much, whether you admit it or not."

"That's not how this works, Mercenary."

We arrive at the club far too soon in my opinion. I was enjoying being in the position to drive her crazy and her not being able to stop it without pulling the car over. She brings the vehicle to a stop, and we both hop out, rounding the front until we meet in the middle. Chevelle believes she's in control. She's the most infuriating woman when she attempts to fight me for dominance.

"I'm the fucking alpha, Chevelle. I run this shit," I declare with a harsh growl, glowering down into her horny stare. Those eyes of hers are swirling with emotion. She's pissed and turned on all at once, and boy is she the sexiest fucking woman I've ever seen when she gets like this.

"Others may put up with your Neanderthal ways, but I don't. I'm in control," she hisses. "That back there was bullshit. You weren't being fair!"

Another growl rumbles my chest. "In control?" I ask with a deadly undertone lacing my voice as I lean in, my nose a hair's breadth away from touching hers. "Fuck control! I take it. I own it. You want control, pet? Too fucking bad, 'cause I bend it to my fucking will. *You* will bend."

My hand flies to her toned bicep, yanking her to me like a rag doll; my other grabs her high ponytail and wrenches her head back. She moans at my dominant behavior, wanting to possess every ounce of the control she *thinks* she has. "You're mine," I declare and slam my mouth to hers.

I take the kiss. Stealing whatever bit she'll offer me of herself. I have to own her. I need this woman on my cock too fucking badly to be gentle with her. Our teeth clash, both of us strung so tightly and wanting to dominate the other.

I hold her so tightly to me that she can barely move. Her breath's come out ragged as she attempts to catch her breath in the midst of me owning her mouth with mine. Nails that she's bitten down to the skin try to rake over my chest, dragging me to her and pushing me away all at the same time. Chevelle fights the desire we're both so desperately filled with. She calls to my body like none other—it's the type of craving that'll make a man lie, cheat, and kill to possess it.

Wrenching back from her blissful lips, I draw in a few deep breaths, and in the next blink I'm grabbing her other arm and slamming her back down onto the hood of her car.

"I'm not yours," she chokes out, glaring daggers at my mouth. The mouth that just stole a kiss from hers, that branded her until her lips reddened and swelled to a delicious pout.

"Keep telling yourself that. I've already decided you're mine and I take whatever the fuck I want."

She burns for me; I can see it. Her nipples are hard through the thin tank top material, her cheeks flushed. My nostrils flare as her scent hits me. Her pussy is wet and ready, and I've barely even begun to touch her. It's enough to cloud my vision as I jump forward, taking over every ounce of her space. Shoving her up farther on the hood, her body's sprawled against the warm metal. She's angry, needy, and absolutely beautiful.

Without another thought, my hands yank her tank top, ripping the thin cotton in half. Flinging the barrier to the side, her tits left exposed. Her breasts heave as she draws in a stunned breath at my so-called Neanderthal ways.

"You tore my fucking shirt!" Her hands fly toward my chest, shoving me hard once and then grabbing my shirt to yank me closer. I bet her panties are soaked from me taking over and I can't wait to find out if I'm right.

My mouth laps at her breasts as soon as I see them. My lips switch from one to the other, wanting to have them both at the same time. I squeeze the melons together to my delight. She has the perfect set of tits, just big enough if I squeeze them a bit she has a sexy line of cleavage. My cock's so fucking hard, if I'm not careful I may dent the hood of the car.

I make her wither and groan in delight as I suck and nip at her divine chest, before beginning my trail lower. Her hands find my spikey hair, gripping the locks between her fingers to tug. My tongue skirts along her tummy, dipping into her navel. She shudders at the movement, enlisting a primal growl from me. *I must have her. Own. Conquer.*

My fingers find the button and zipper of her shorts, plucking and tugging until the obstacle's free. I can't move fast enough when it comes to Chevelle. I have the insatiable need clawing through my veins to pound into her pussy until she gives in to me and swears to obey me in every way.

"That feels so good, Mercenary. You better stop. I'm not some cheap whore you pick up whenever you want. We fuck when I say so."

"You better shut that fucking mouth, Chevelle," I grumble. "I'm fucking you. Now." At that, my hands close around the waist of her shorts, tugging them over her muscular thighs. She can pretend to fight me, but I know the truth. I can feel her practically vibrating with desire under me. Her scent is all around, utterly intoxicating.

I pop the button on my jeans and shove them down enough for my cock to spring free, eager to feel her.

"You couldn't keep up with me," she claims, and my fingers claw at the scrap of material she wears as panties. She's constantly challenging me, seeing how far she can push. She'll learn I'm not breakable; she can shove me, but I always push right back.

I'm too far gone. My cock strains, craving her as she enrages and goads me on. My hands shred her underwear into pieces, leaving behind red marks on her skin in my impatience. "Keep up?" I ask as I lick my lips, my gaze trained on her glistening folds. "You are so goddamn wet. Your juices are dripping on the fucking car."

At that, I wrap my arm around her lower back and slide her to me, impaling my cock into her at the same time. She cries out at the surprise intrusion. "Fuck! you're huge!" Her shocked irises find mine.

"You thought I was playing? I told you I would own you, pound this pussy until you've surrendered."

Her mouth falls open as I jerk my hips back and drive into her even deeper this time. "Oh shit. You were telling the truth about the eight inches."

"That's right, Chevelle. I'm the fucking alpha. I have the cock filling your pussy. Tonight, you succumb to me, sweetie."

"You're the alpha?" She gasps on another thrust. "Fuck me for it then. Show me." She leans up, pinning me with her burning gaze.

At that, all I can do is drive into her harder and roar. It feels like all I do is growl around this bitch. She drives me crazy inside, makes me want to pound my fist to my chest and own every piece of her.

"Faster," she orders.

Hybrid Collection

At her command, I slam her back against the hood again. She starts to lean up, but I hold her still by wrapping my free hand around her throat. She wants to move then she'll stop breathing. Chevelle will learn I'm in control even if I have to break her to do it.

My other hand holds tightly onto her hip as I thrust forward, attempting to shove my cock so deep into her she feels it in her throat. With each pop of my hips, her tits shake, my gaze trained on each bounce. "Why do you have to be so difficult? I swear to Christ if you don't learn, I'm going to start shoving my cock in that pretty mouth every time you fuckin' speak!"

"You want pliant? Go find some timid bitch who's scared of you," she yells back, as my hand squeezes her delicate throat at her words.

"If you were smart, you'd be scared." My mouth descends on her nipple again, biting until she whimpers.

"Fuck. You."

"You are," I rasp, driving deep enough that her next cry has her hands flying to my chest, grabbing for anything she can reach.

"Hurt?" I ask cockily as I continue to take her body with wild abandon. There's nothing like the whimpers and moans from a woman as I fuck her to stroke my ego. This chick just so happens to be as crazy as I am, which is a first. I've come across plenty of women who claim to be alpha, but none of them hold up to that title. Chevelle is an entirely different breed. She was made for me.

She's the type that has you going back to the beginning, back when it was important to seek out the strongest mate to breed. You searched to find the one that could bare your children that would be healthy and strong—someone to compliment your own attributes. A male was supposed to hunt, to provide for his family and to keep them safe. It was his job to protect and provide and the woman's to have his children, to continue his blood line...to worship him.

Chevelle has me wanting to prove to her that I'm the strongest mate she'll ever come across. That I can offer her what she needs, to claim her and make her mine.

What is it with men and wanting to own pretty things? To possess them so another can't have it? I want to lay my claim on Chevelle, so no one even dares to fucking look at her.

"Please," she begins to beg, her pussy squeezing my cock harder and harder as her climax builds. I love hearing the surrender in her voice as she gets closer to bliss.

"You mine?" The question escapes before I can push the thought back down and what it means exactly. I don't care about the technicalities; I care about her pussy wrapped so tightly around my cock that it wants to explode.

"Oh, please," she whimpers.

"Say it, now." I squeeze her throat, stealing her air as I stole her kiss earlier. Her pussy pulses in response and I loosen my grip.

"Yes," she croaks on the verge of spiraling into bliss, but it's still not good enough.

"Are. You. Mine." My demanding voice rises with every word and each plunge into her core.

"Fuck! Yes, I'm yours, you selfish bastard!" she finally admits on a lurid exclamation, and a raging desire unlike any I've ever felt before shoots through me. My hips pound so deftly into her that the sound of our flesh meeting echoes into the night.

"Say my fucking name."

"Mercenary," she chants loudly. "I'm yours, Mercenary. Please let me come." I release her throat completely, my hand falling to pinch and pull her nipple and it sets her off like fireworks on the Fourth of July.

She screams through her orgasm, into the black night. My own mounting pressure erupts at her declaration, and my cock pumps my come into her waiting heat. A few easy thrusts and I'm spent for the moment. I'll want her again in a few minutes, I know it. She's like a drug, and one hit is not going to be enough to satiate my desire.

Hybrid Collection

Holding still in her, my dick throbs, pumping every last drop I have. She remains laying on the hood, covered in her sweat, panting and staring up at the sky. I think it's the most beautiful look I've seen on her. Like this, covered in my scent and utterly content from me giving her a good fucking.

Cheering and clapping comes from off to the side, and we both turn to find my club brothers lined up against the front of the clubhouse. They just got one hell of a show. I wonder how long they were watching us and if Chevelle's going to lose her shit? However long, it must've been for a while as they continue to wolf whistle and make brash comments.

14.

MERCENARY

"Damn Merc! I'd say the bitch is yours!" Saint calls, a shit eating grin plastered on his pretty boy model face. I'm sure he loves this since he knows I think his ol' lady is fine as fuck. I figured he and Sinner would've left to find Ruger already, but apparently not.

The brothers make their way to us, and I pull my dick free from Chevelle's tight center, tucking it back into my pants. She stays rooted in place, my come dripping from her slit, breasts still heaving as she sits up. "Fuck," Chevy whispers for my ears only. Her irises flick over the approaching men. She remains calm though thanks to her orgasm and natural confidence.

She may not care if these guys see her naked, pussy still full of my come, but I'm not thrilled with it. She's hot as hell with clothes on, naked is even more of a reason for them to try and get in her pants. I set my cut down on the hood and tug my shirt off then pull it over Chevelle's head. Every bit of me wants my cut over the bitch too, showing the world she belongs to me and no one else.

Hybrid Collection

Chevelle catches on to my movements, covering her up and sticks her arms through the holes, pulling the fabric over her. When she stands, the material comes all the way down to her knees. The sight causes my dick to harden all over again, seeing her in my shit, knowing she's naked underneath it.

Putting my cut on, I fist bump each of my brothers as they step up, standing around the car. They each wear various amused smirks and grins. Viking flicks his sturdy gaze over Chevelle and then it lands on me. "Quite a show you two put on," he observes.

I shrug.

"Want to fill me in on what went down tonight?" he asks, and Chevelle stares at me, biting her bottom lip, looking all cute and shit.

"She decided to race and then punch the other driver."

My brothers snicker and give her props.

I continue, unfazed. "The guy hit her back, so of course I beat him into a coma. And then she had the audacity to get pissed at me over it. We were arguing, so I had to show her who the fuck was in control."

She snorts, and my arctic gaze turns stormy, landing on her. She quiets with wide eyes. I doubt she's scared. I'm confident she knows I'd never hurt her. That doesn't mean I won't hold her down and fuck her in front of the club again until she admits that I'm right.

The guys all nod, their faces in agreement. Viking shrugs. "Makes sense. You two finished out here?" He gestures to the car and Chevelle's cheeks redden. I doubt she'll ever be able to look at that car again without remembering us on that hood.

"For now," I agree and grab her hand in mine. She pauses to swipe her shorts, and we walk hand in hand behind the Prez to the clubhouse. The brothers trail us as we enter the bar. "I'll show you the bathroom." I tug her off to the side.

We cross the dark bar. The light's at a low, comfortable level and various TVs all turned on to sports channels but muted, and rock music drifts throughout the room. Once we get to the hallway leading to our personal rooms, I open a door off to the right that has the public bathroom. She flashes me a grateful smile and hurries inside. I head back to swipe a clean shirt from my room and then back to pull out a stool at the bar next to Viking. He needed to talk to me; hopefully, it's not too serious, and it can be handled right here.

"O said you wanted to speak with me."

"Yeah, he'd told me what went down and then hung up when you started fighting. I wanted to get you out of there before you were arrested and ended up in jail. I heard you liked to knock some skulls around from your old Prez, not that you were always about to get locked up for your temper."

I shrug and signal for Chaos to get me a beer. "Same thing."

"Hardly. What's up with you and Chevelle? Is shit getting serious?"

"Well, it wasn't before, but after that fight and fuck, I suppose so."

"We take claiming in front of the club serious. If it's not a club whore, then we're expecting to be welcoming a new ol' lady. You know the club laws here."

I agree. "I do." I had to know them and take an oath before they'd even vote on me transferring to this charter. Chicago's laws were similar but no public claiming was ever mentioned. I guess these Texans like to watch their brothers fuck their women. I can see the attraction to it after witnessing Saint and Sinner fuck Jude in church. Holy hell, that was hot.

"So, we treat her as an ol' lady then. She'll get your property patch, but listen carefully..." He trails off, and I give him my full attention.

"If you plan to keep fucking the club sluts around here, you keep Chevelle away. We don't do drama; I'll boot her out on her ass if she comes in here kicking all the club sluts' asses and stirring up trouble with the brothers."

"I won't be fucking any of the whores again. Chevelle's all I want."

He nods. "Good. Most of us prefer to take the faithful route. That being said, though, the club sluts will come on even stronger at first. They seem to think when we put a property patch on our bitch that they have a chance. They don't ever realize that they never had a chance in the first place."

"I'll keep it in mind. Maybe if Chevy sees them like that it'll get her to come to her senses quicker."

"Another thing...when we claim the women, well..."

I stare, waiting, wondering what the hell has the Prez at a loss for words. He's not much of a talker, but he has me thinking that what he has to say must be top secret or something of that nature. Do they grow tails or something? I mean, what the fuck?

"I've been told they go, ah, a little cum crazy."

I nearly choke. That was the last thing I was expecting to hear from him. "Excuse me?" He has to be fucking with me.

Viking's tongue flicks against one of his canines before grunting and taking a gulp of his drink. He sets the tumbler on the bar, a smirk taking over as he thinks over something. "When I claimed my ol' lady, I pinned the bitch down and fucked her in the middle of a bar for taunting me."

My eyes grow wide. It's hard to imagine, Princess, his woman, seems too feisty to let that go over smoothly. "And Princess?"

"Oh, she was fucking pissed being claimed out in the open. I'd barely spoken a handful of words to her beforehand."

My eyebrows must be to my hairline at this point hearing all of this come out. "You started the public claiming?"

He nods. "She slapped the shit out of me in front of the entire bar too."

A grin breaks free as I attempt to hold back a laugh from spilling. Her slapping him is something I can definitely see happening. My Prez is a brute, though; I don't see him putting up with it.

"Anyhow, that's not where I'm going with this. My point is, after the slapping incident, she went a little nuts. She basically jumped on my cock, and I fucked her for four days relentlessly. The only break I had was to eat and shower."

"Damn, sounds like you locked her down."

He snorts. "I was dumb enough to think that at the time, but no."

"No?"

"No brother, I didn't lock her down. She locked me down. I was fucking hooked. I've taken her and planted my seed in that woman every damn day since."

"Doesn't sound so bad to me." I shrug.

He shakes his head, gesturing for Chaos to refill his glass before turning back to me. "It's not—at all. It's part of the reason why my loyalty has never wavered from her. I'm her king, and she's my queen. This doesn't have to do with me though. The way I saw you and Chevelle act and fuck, it just reminded me of myself when I first met my woman. Don't be surprised if Chevelle acts a little crazy and possessive for a while. It's all part of the effects of being owned properly."

"I can't believe I've never heard of this before." The concept is a touch crazy in itself. However, it would explain why my presence around Jude didn't do anything. Usually, I can have a woman eating from my palm if I wanted to, but she couldn't see past Saint and Sinner. I'm glad too. Clearly, I wasn't meant to have her. I just didn't know I'd be meeting Chevelle at the time. "I appreciate the info. I'll do what I need to."

"Good. Now we need to discuss those Fists that popped up earlier. What the fuck happened?"

Hybrid Collection

I let him know everything Chevelle told me all the way up until Torch and Odin showed up to collect the unconscious men. When I finish disclosing what I know, she's making her way to us.

CHEVELLE

"Chevelle." Viking greets with a nod as I sit on the other side of Mercenary at the bar. Every man in this place looks like a goddamn tank. I'm not normally very nervous around men since I can usually kick their asses, but this place has me off balance. There's so much testosterone floating around, I swear you can taste it. Not only are the bikers in the Oath Keepers the size of mountains and full of muscles, but they're all gorgeous in their own unique way.

"Hello, Viking," I greet, feeling a bit more confident now that I've had a chance to clean up and put my shorts back on.

The MC brother behind the bar approaches me. He's built like a linebacker and fits in here with the rest of them. I grin reading over his name patch—*Chaos*. If I was a biker, I'd definitely want a road name like that.

"Cool name." I nod to the right side of his cut, and he offers me a grin in return. He's older than the rest of the guys around this place but super good-looking. I don't know what they put in the water or beer here, but it's a club full of ridiculously hot, broody, outlaw bikers. I wonder if you have to be hot in order to wear the Oath Keeper patch. It wouldn't surprise me, at this point.

"Thanks, peach, can I get you something to drink?"

"Sure, I'll take a seven-seven if you have it."

"That's vodka and seven up, mixed with ice, right?"

My grin drops as my eyes scan over the bar, checking if they have the liquor for the drink in stock. "It's Seagram's with 7 Up." You'd think he'd know how to make the simple drink; he's the only one back there.

"Okay, no problem," he mutters and turns away to mix it.

"Thanks," I say, but I don't think he hears me; he seems to be in his own zone, concentrating on pouring the Seagram's.

Viking leans in. "He just started tending bar for us this week."

"Oh." I nod. Not that it matters to me. It was nice of him to ask if I wanted something since Mercenary didn't think to.

"Now, Chevelle, would you mind explaining to me your side of what all happened today? I need to know from you shooting those two guys all the way down to my brother here getting into a fight over you."

"Well, it wasn't over me, per se. I sort of jumped out of my car and threw the first hit. It wasn't until the guy punched me back that Mercenary lost it on him."

"The guy hit you?" Viking grumbles, stunned, his face turning from friendly to grim.

"Yeah. In his defense, I punched him first. The dick ran into my rear end when we were racing, and it's prohibited at The Pit, for safety. Needless to say, I was pissed."

"I understand." His stare lands back on Mercenary. "I thought you just popped off, being a loose cannon. My mistake brother. I would've done the same thing had I seen it."

Mercenary waves it off as no big deal and Chaos sets my drink down.

"Thank you," I repeat and take a long gulp through the straw. I'm suddenly thirstier than I'd originally thought, and the mixed beverage goes down smooth and refreshing. The racing, fucking, heat, and not to mention everything with the rival MC, has really been a lot to take in.

"You had the Iron Fists knocked out before you drug them inside, right? They didn't have a chance to touch you or talk to you?" Viking presses on, switching subjects quickly and I shake my head, reassuring him. "Good. I think it's probably safer if you two start staying here at night."

"But who will watch The Pit?" I sputter, caught off guard by his suggestion. He wants to protect me? What is it with these guys thinking I can't handle my own problems? Where were they when I was a ten-year-old living on the streets? I guess they were kids, but still, it would've been nice to have someone back then.

"I'll have my guys ride by randomly, and I'll also have a chat with the sheriff. See if he and his deputies are willing to drive by a couple times a night when he patrols as well. It won't be left abandoned or anything."

"You're friends with the sheriff? Aren't cops and bikers supposed to hate each other?"

"In most cases yes, but not in ours. Our alliance benefits the community, and the people's safety around here is important to all of us."

I turn to the silent man beside me; he's usually not this quiet. "And what do you think of all this?" He's normally first to voice his displeasure about anything to me, it seems.

"Viking's suggestion makes sense." His beefy arm falls across the back of my barstool. The heat coming off him so close it makes me shudder as the air conditioning kicks on, and the two temperatures clash against my skin at the same time. "The guys today make five Iron Fists disappearing, all while watching you."

His thumb trails over my spine, his sky-blue irises full of scorching heat as he gazes at me. "That's a large enough group to be noticed and to take out retaliation. If they decide to hit back, they'll rape and kill you, if you're lucky."

My mouth drops open. "If I'm lucky?" That's not my idea of luck, nor should it be anyone's.

He nods. "They could keep you alive and torture you for who knows how long, along with continued rape throughout the club members. Maybe after so much, they decide to sell you off so some twisted fuck can continue doing the same sort of abuse."

"Holy shit," I gasp and swallow the sudden lump in my throat. "How did I get in the middle of this and how can they get away with that?" The fingers on my right hand float toward him, eventually landing on his thigh, unconsciously seeking out his strength.

Viking interrupts. "You started making money. In our world when it comes to gambling, racing, drugs, that sort...if you make enough money, you get noticed. It was their fuck up believing that you're an easy target without someone watching your back."

"This is bad. All I wanted to do was run a clean track where people could relax, place some bets, drink a few beers, and watch races. I don't need these assholes coming and screwing it all up for me. And I damn sure don't like having my place bombed for their sick entertainment."

"Well, it may take some time, but we're working on getting rid of this problem. Luckily you'll be able to benefit from it as well."

"By staying here, do you mean with cupcake?" I tilt my head toward the broody biker at my side.

"Cupcake?" Viking snorts out a chuckle and Mercenary grumbles while shooting me an unamused side-eye.

I nod, glancing at the both of them. Mercenary's the only man I call cupcake. At first, I did it to piss him the hell off, and it worked flawlessly. It quickly morphed into me calling him cupcake 'cause he was pretty sweet to me when he wanted to be. And now, well...it's because his cocks as thick as a damn cupcake. The fucker's got a massive sized dick. I could stuff myself with it all the damn time and be peachy keen.

"Listen, doll, Merc here," he gestures to the man in question, "claimed you out front. He essentially made you his ol' lady since he fucked you in front of the entire club and then made you admit that you're his."

I blow out a breath, pretty confident I know enough biker lingo to understand what he's getting at. I ask anyway, just to be certain. "What does that mean?"

"You belong to him; you're a part of this club."

Hybrid Collection

I jump to my feet, my thoughts confirmed and my fist slams into Mercenary's rock-hard bicep. "You ass!"

He stands, towering over me. "Woman, don't make me take you over my knee."

I sputter, my cheeks growing warm with my irritation at this bossy-ass man. "You're off your damn rocker if you think I'll put up with your macho shit!" I yell, and he moves like a freaking ninja, catching me off guard. I'm good at defending myself when I'm expecting it, but Mercenary whips me up in his solid arms, hiking me to hang over his wide shoulder. I curse him loudly, and his brothers throughout the bar snicker. His hand lands on my ass—hard.

"Shut the fuck up, Chevelle!" he commands, and his MC brothers laugh even louder at his disgruntled boom. He grumbles, "I'll catch you later Vike, obviously this bitch has been without my cock for too long. She gets mouthy; I have to go fix it."

"Remember what I said," Viking responds ominously, and I flash my middle finger at Mercenary's back. He can't see me, but it still counts.

I let out my own growl, hanging upside down but I have a feeling that with all the noise in the bar, that I sound more like a pissed off kitten as Mercenary stomps away, taking us to his room.

15. Happiness is an inside job.
Don't assign anyone else that
much power over your life.
- HPLYRIKZ.COM

MERCENARY

I feel the woman at my side stir, rousing me further from my deep, sated sleep. We're both still naked from a long night of me proving just how much she really is mine. Pulling her closer, I line my cock up and sink into her from behind.

I'll never have enough of her or her body; the woman keeps me on my toes. I'm quickly learning the only way to keep her temper from lashing out at me is to keep her satisfied with my cock. Not that I mind in the slightest. I'm getting to know every inch of her delectable body, and a pleased Chevelle is even sexier than a pissed off Chevelle.

"Mmm, again?" she mumbles sleepily, and I push farther, sinking deeply into her warm sheath.

Hybrid Collection

"As much as possible," I groan against the back of her neck, pushing her hair out of my face, and breathe her in. "You smell so damn good. Like rain and springtime."

With a quiet laugh, she replies huskily, "I smell like your soap."

"I know, and I like how my soap smells."

She snickers, and I find myself grinning like an idiot against her skin. She asks, "No more fucking this morning?"

"I'm tired. Besides you said you were sore the last time," I rumble and slowly plunge into her again, my hand skirting over her ribs, stopping to cup her full, heavy breasts.

"Mmm, I should've believed you about the eight inches thing. I thought you were full of it. Turns out I'm full of it."

"You're still chirping about that?" I groan as my cock throbs, encased in her welcoming core.

"It's impressive."

"You needed to be fucked badly, sweetie. Your pussy belongs on my cock." I nip at her neck, pulling my hips back to sink into her again, driving my pleasure on. "Fuck, you're good for my ego." Reaching down I seek out her clit. We're old friends by now with how well I know that part of her body after merely one night.

Her head turns, burying her mouth in my pillow as she moans loudly and bites down. I've discovered just the way to touch her to make her beg me for more. I had her shooting off like the Fourth of July all night long. I'm not going to let her forget who's in control of her pleasure. I'll give it again and again until it's seared into her memory.

"You're gonna give it to me easily today then?"

Her bite on my pillow releases as she turns toward me as much as she can. "You got it easily last night too," she replies huskily, her voice laced with desire and sleep. Her leg hikes behind her, hooking over my thigh so I can go in deeper.

Bullshit. She fought me at every turn, making me work for her orgasms. She's stubborn, but I love a good challenge. "What can I say, your tight pussy likes me. It can't seem to get enough of my cock making it come."

Tucking my arm around her chest, I pick us up until I'm on my knees with her back pressed firmly against my chest. My free arm wraps around her, my palm landing on her core, grinding against her clit. My other plays with her breasts, squeezing and caressing her nipples with my fingertips. Her head falls back, resting on my shoulder. Her eyes stay closed with her mouth open, whimpering and moaning with my caresses.

My hips rock hers, my shaft thrusting into its own rhythm drawing a soft whimper from her. Her head turns to watch my face. "See, you shouldn't be able to move like that without breaking contact." The vixen smiles as she adds, "Eight inches *really* makes a difference."

"Nah," I rasp, turning to meet her lips. "You haven't been fucked properly before, that's all. Now you know that no motherfucker can do what I can." I take her mouth—morning breath be damned. I want to feel her tongue against mine. I was just kissing her hours ago, but it feels like it's been too long since we've had that contact. Her center tightens around me, already starting to milk my length as her climax draws near.

Breaking my hold on her breast, I use my arm for balance and lean us back until I'm lying flat on my back, impaling my cock into her heat in another position. Our mouths break apart in the move, and the change draws a deeper whimper from her. It's the perfect spot for me to play with her sensitive nub.

Her legs fall open, spread completely apart for me. Each leg rests across each of my thick, muscular thighs. Her long locks fall off the side of my shoulder, and I catch the scent of my shampoo as well. I like this, having my smell everywhere when it comes to Chevelle.

"Yes, oh yes," she cries deliciously.

I tilt her head farther off to the side and draw her skin between my lips to suck. She starts to shoot off me, but I hold her to me tightly. One hand continues to rub her pussy ruthlessly, the other wraps securely around her chest. My hand reaches up, gripping her neck in place, bracing her body to mine.

My moves coax the orgasm from her while I mark her so severely, the delicate tanned skin bruises with a deep purple hue. She'll wear it for the next few weeks to come before it fully disappears. Hell, something buried down wants me to bite her and draw blood. I've never had the feeling like that before, but I have this insatiable need for everyone to know she's taken. And to know death will follow them if they touch her.

Chevelle screams my name loudly, as the pleasure fully blooms over her body. I'm slowly wearing down her resolve toward me. Her tight, wet core squeezes my thickness so tightly, I follow her, pumping my own pleasure into her. Not only am I wearing her down, but I'm falling farther down the rabbit hole when it comes to her.

I hold her to me as I inhale and exhale a few times deeply, catching my breath and come down from the intense climax. The woman steals a piece of my soul each time I take her. Morning sex is one of my favorite things with her, no doubt. It's passionate, the pleasure reached easily, and so damn fulfilling.

When my arms finally fall away, she rolls off me to the side. Her hand flies to the spot showing the world that she's taken. "You marked me!" She hisses and glares. She can try to be pissed, but her eyes are still glazed over from how much she enjoyed it. The look makes me want to fuck her—hard this time.

"And?" My brow lifts, and I shrug, not fazed in the slightest bit at her irritation.

"I don't enjoy going around with hickeys on my neck. I have a business to run, and I'll look cheap."

"You're wrong," I argue. "You look like a woman who's been thoroughly enjoyed. A woman that's been claimed and has a man. A woman not to be fucked with by anyone with a cock in their pants."

She throws her arms up and huffs. "Men won't take me seriously, especially when it comes to cars. They'll see this mark and then look for a man, instead of taking me seriously."

"Then they'll find me right next to you, and I'll tell them you run The Pit."

"You don't understand, Mercenary. I don't want them to look for a man at all. They should see me in charge."

"Excuse me? Too fucking bad, because I'll be there and if any of them disrespect you, I'll knock their fucking teeth out."

"Some woman may fall at your feet hearing you proclaim that Tarzan crap, but I can take care of myself. I happen to enjoy doing the knocking out with my own two fists."

"Fucking shit, you're a pain in the ass."

She climbs out of bed and searches out her shorts and one of my shirts.

"What are you doing?"

"Going home." Chevelle sulks acting every bit of the flustered woman she was just claiming she isn't. She busily pulls her clothes on and covers up that beautiful body that I was lucky enough to get very acquainted with last night.

I jump out of bed and pull on a clean pair of jeans, garnering her attention.

"What are you doing?"

"Going with you." I shrug, gearing myself up for an argument. She'll no doubt have something to say especially right after I put a dark purple, huge hickey on her throat.

"Uh, no..." Chevelle trails off and shakes her head. She continues searching under random objects for her other shoe.

"You're not going back there alone. We don't know if there are Iron Fists waiting for you to return, and my bike's still there. We came in your car, remember?"

Hybrid Collection

She sighs. "Fine, but we're stopping to get breakfast on the way, and since you want to be all manly, you're buying," she grumbles, and I yank on my shirt.

"Hard deal, but I think I can manage being forced to eat and pay." I tug on my boots, ignoring what I'm sure is an eye-roll directed my way.

We ended up going back to the taco shack to pick up breakfast burritos and thankfully the dumbass from yesterday wasn't working again. I don't think I could've handled seeing him eye my woman right after I've claimed her. I'd probably break his frail little beta male neck.

"Does it bother you that I don't cook?" Chevelle peers at me curiously. We're in the middle of eating after doing a search of The Pit. It was all clear, so now I'm enjoying nearly cold eggs, bacon, and cheese wrapped in a freshly made tortilla.

I shake my head. "Nah, why would I give a shit if you can cook?"

"Because I'm a woman." Her gaze flicks to the ground, and it has my own curiosity flickering to life. Is she actually nervous about what I think and over something so insignificant?

"That's pretty damn sexist," I mutter around my mouthful.

"I know, but most of the men I've come across tend to think something's wrong with me."

I swallow. "Well, for one, I'm not most men. And for another thing, they're fucking stupid. I'm used to eating out or my own cooking. I don't give a fuck if it's got to stay that way either. If I get too hungry, I could always just feast on your pussy."

She bites her bottom lip, her neck flushing at my suggestion and her gaze grows thoughtful. "What's your story, cupcake?"

I nearly choke on the new bite I've taken. "Uh, what?" It's so out of the blue that my mind spins over her question.

"What happened to make you decide to become a hard-ass biker? Don't take this the wrong way, but you're nothing like I'd expected when you first came to The Pit."

I swallow and offer her a smile. "Believe it or not, nothing."

"I'm not buying it," she admits, biting off her own mouthful of burrito.

"You don't have to, but it's true. I grew up with both of my parents, they're good people. I had a fun childhood, well, besides normal hormones and teenage shit. My family had enough money to get by, and I have an older brother who's a doctor."

"You're shitting me!" She stares at me, chewing slowly.

"Nope, I was fortunate in that department."

"Are you the black sheep or something, at least?"

I snort. "Why, because I ride a motorcycle, enjoy a good fist fight, like my liquor, and enjoy pussy more than the average feeble male?"

She nods, being completely honest with me.

"No, sweetie, my family loves me, rough and wild and all."

"You're lucky."

I nod. "I am. Got my first motorcycle in high school. I had a part-time job, and the bike was the first transportation I could afford. The rest is history. What about you?"

"Why do you want to know?"

"Well, besides the fact that you just bombarded me with all those questions? Because I want to know more about you than just your attitude and tight pussy."

Hybrid Collection

Her cheeks tint, and I grin again. It's hard not to smile when she's sitting here all quiet and sweet, eating her breakfast and has made me come all night long. Usually, she tough as nails closed off Chevelle. I like her like this.

She tucks a long dark lock behind her ear and shrugs. "Not much to tell. I grew up on the streets."

"On the streets? Here?"

"No, in Houston. I ended up here by accident."

I nod, wanting to hear more. I want her to tell me everything there is to know when it comes to her. "And your family?"

"I have none." She shrugs, and I find it hard to believe that she's so unaffected. I may be a dick and all, but I still love my parents and sibling.

"Wait, you're an orphan." It's more of a statement than a question as the thought hits me.

She swallows. "Yes."

"Weren't you in foster care or something?" The thought of her alone all this time has my stomach in knots. No wonder she can easily be so closed off and cynical. It's how she's learned to protect herself on the inside.

"They tried, but I ran away."

"And no one caught you?" *My sneaky girl.* Can't say that surprises me. Chevelle likes to prove to everyone and herself that she needs nor wants anyone.

She clears her throat, growing tense. "No, I adapted." I can feel her closing off, so I drop it for now, but I still want to know.

"Damn, those burritos were good." I rub my hands over my stomach drawing her eyes to the taut, muscular area.

Her shoulders relax as she takes the subject change with ease. "I love that place. Eighty percent of their monthly sales probably comes from me."

"That's a lot of tacos, Chevy."

She smiles with a nod then stands and takes our trash, throwing it away. My eyes remain glued to her form as she sways in her own erotic strut she seems oblivious to. We were eating in the middle of the track. Random spot but this is where we ended up after searching the place, and with both of us starving decided to just sit and eat right on the track.

"So how did you get into racing?" I ask as she comes back, and I stand up. I don't know where we'll end up next, but I start walking beside her. Taking her hand in mine, she doesn't pull away, and like a fucking chick, I get all excited inside. Her pussy already has me whipped after only one night being buried in her wet warmth.

"I met this older man." My hard gaze finds hers, and she smiles. Shaking her head, she backtracks. "Think of him as a grandpa in a sense. He had a shop and fixed cars. He caught me begging near his place one night and told me if I helped clean up his shop, he'd buy me dinner. Being young and the promise of a full stomach, I jumped on the offer."

She takes a drink of her soda and continues. "His shop was trashed, but regardless, I cleaned it. The job ended up taking me nearly a week to complete, but each day as promised, he'd order a bunch of food. I'd eat until I was in a food coma and clean my ass off in return. He never asked me where I'd go at night, and before he'd have a chance to forget about me, I'd be out in front of the shop, first thing."

"Where *did* you go at night?" I interrupt to ask.

She sighs. "I was sleeping under a bridge near his business."

I make a sound in my throat, a cross between sadness and anger on her behalf. "Oh wow, you were serious about being on the streets." I didn't realize how much truth those words had held when she'd originally said them. No wonder she has it in her head that she has to do everything all on her own.

"Yes, anyway, he kept coming up with things for me to do. I was about twelve at that time, and eventually, his tasks switched to me helping him work on the cars that came in needing repairs. He taught me everything he knew about mechanics. After about two years of helping him, he started letting me work on cars by myself. Turned out, I could fix them faster than he could."

"I'm not surprised," I comment, and she smiles.

"Not only did he feed me, but he began paying me as well. A year before that, he'd let me start sleeping in the office at his tiny shop. It had a bathroom and a roof, so I was beyond grateful."

"You were fortunate he didn't take advantage of you."

"Trust me, I know."

That thought alone is enough to make me want to rip someone's head off. I'd kill them without a second thought if they touched her wrong in any way.

We get to her apartment, and she sits in the overstuffed chair. I take the edge of her bed. "He also owned a dirt track on the outskirts of Houston in this town called Katy. When I got old enough to drive, he taught me how in a race car around that track. A lot of the other drivers brought their car into the shop for mods, so I was already familiar with how a race car ran, how it ticked."

"Jesus, I bet you were a natural."

She nods with a wide smile in place. I've never seen her smile so bright; the beauty makes me swallow roughly.

"I started winning money racing one of his cars along with being paid to work in his shop. I was finally doing something real with my life. I had a purpose after so long of being filled with emptiness."

"So, what happened? Why'd you leave?"

The smile drops, her bottom lip trembles for a beat before she hides it. "He died."

"Sweetie, I'm sorry."

She nods, a sad smile taking the place of the tremble she wore moments prior. "His shop was sold by his lawyer as instructed in his will. I had some money to survive on at the time, but nothing to keep me afloat in Houston. Then his lawyer got ahold of me one day when things were looking down, and I found out the crazy old man had left everything to me."

"No shit?"

She nods. "He had a son somewhere that he knew nothing about and a bitter ex-wife that wouldn't speak to him. He'd told me I was like a daughter to him. I just never realized that he was serious, I guess. Anyhow, I immediately started looking for something…a small shop or whatever I could buy to make money and live a quiet life. I found The Pit. I bought my Chevelle and put the rest of the money I had as a down payment to the previous owner, and I've been racing to pay it off and fix it up each week since."

"Damn, Chevelle. I'm impressed. The man would be proud of you, no doubt."

"You are?" Is that hope in her eyes? She's like a kitten that scratches and hisses at first but then basks in attention shown to her by her owner.

"Hell yeah. You're a fighter in all senses. I suppose you learned to defend yourself from growing up like that then?" I can't believe this beautiful woman had such a hard life. I really am lucky with my family.

She nods. "You fight and adapt, or you die."

"You really are a badass," I mumble, and she pulls me down to the bed.

"Mmm, then it's my turn to have my way with you. Badasses get what they want." She smirks and pushes me against the comforter. She climbs over me, straddling my waist, giving me a perfect view of her beauty. She doesn't have to tell me twice. I'll gladly let her have her way with me.

16. If you're sad, add more
lipstick and attack.
- Coco Chanel

CHEVELLE

The sounds of multiple motorcycles draw Mercenary's attention the next morning. He hops from the bed, nearly tripping in my sheet on his way to the window. We were supposed to go back to the club but wasted the day away talking about anything and everything. Then the night was spent filled with passion, wrapped in each other's bodies between the sheets on my bed.

"Shit, are you okay? What's going on?"

"I'm fine," he waves me off and mutters dismissively but not rude as he stares out the window to the parking lot below. "Fuck!" He curses as his eyes go wide at the scene. He flips around, scanning over every surface, not saying a word.

"What is it? You're freaking me out over here!"

"The fucking Iron Fists."

"So, shoot them!" I point to the tranq gun, my voice a higher note than normal.

"There's too many. Fuck!" Both hands rake through his spiked, inky hair in frustration. His stomach muscles clench as he paces, the movements offering up a delicious view of every toned inch. He's all strength and corded steel, strung tight at the impending fight the Fists will no doubt bring to The Pit.

"Can you shoot any of them or something?"

He tosses me his phone. "First number listed," he orders. "Dial it and tell them we need backup—quick—and to bring a fuck ton of it."

Fumbling with the phone, I do exactly as he says, watching as he points the tranquilizer gun and curses with each shot.

"O," a gruff voice answers the phone.

"Uh, Odin?"

"Yep, who's this?"

"It's Chevelle."

"Chevelle? You okay, chick?"

"Yes, there's no time to explain, but Mercenary says to bring a lot of backup to The Pit."

Merc hisses, a curse drawing my attention. He's fumbling with the gun. "What is it?" I ask, forgetting about Odin momentarily.

He flicks his gaze to me, not stopping his fingers from jiggling the metal. "I hit three, missed two and then this jammed." He briefly holds the gun up before turning his concentration back to it.

Odin yells through the phone, and I scramble to get it back to my ear. "What the fuck did he say? He shot three?"

"Yes, with the tranquilizer gun," I reply, not taking my gaze from Mercenary.

He grumbles. "Fucking shit, how many are there?"

Hybrid Collection

I call to Mercenary, "How many are there?"

"I didn't stop and count the fuckers, tell him at least a dozen."

"Holy shit," Odin murmurs, yelling to people in the background. "Tell my brother to take you somewhere safe and wait us out. There's too many for you two to fight off. Your lives are too important to waste trying to stop the Fists. They're dangerous. If I thought you two could take them all without getting hurt, I'd say differently."

"Okay," I whisper, and he hangs up.

Mercenary pulls his Glock off the side table and checks to make sure it's fully loaded. I highly doubt his weapons aren't ever unloaded or not cleaned. He's too meticulous for any of that.

"He said for us to hide until they get here, cupcake."

He nods, yanking up his pants and tucking his feet into his boots. "Get dressed Chevy, quickly."

A loud boom shakes us, drawing my breath. I fall over my feet, hurrying out of bed toward my dresser and yank on the first thing I find. "What the hell was that?"

I want to scream but refrain. I'm not a screamer but whatever they blew up downstairs has me jittery. Mercenary's mood change has me a bit fidgety as well. I'm not used to him on edge except for when it comes to arguing with me. Even then, he's not as solemn as now.

"My guess is they couldn't get in, so they made a new door."

"Ugh!" The exclamation leaves me in a furious, unladylike growl. "I'm going to wrap each of their nuts around their throats and make them chew on them like fucking bubble gum!"

He smirks and tosses me the tranq gun after I slide my feet into a pair of Toms slip-on shoes. "Damn sweetie, you're mesmerizing when you're pissed." He gestures to the metal contraption. "Use that on any fucker who comes at you."

"I'd rather fight."

"If you want to make it safely out of here, you're going to have to trust me on this, Chevelle. I know you can fight, but what if there are three coming for you? Take out whoever you can safely, and then use your fists."

I huff but refrain from arguing with him. He knows this type of life better than I do. I got through the streets as a kid; I'll make it through a pack of rabid bikers.

"You'll wear yourself out too fast, and we may need to fight at some point to get out of here. If we can take some of the threat out with weapons, then let's use it to our advantage. I couldn't handle it if one of them hurt you. It'd be a bloodbath as I tore them limb from limb for it."

"I get it."

"Good, now where can we hide for the next twenty minutes or so where no one will think to look for us? We need to wait for backup to get here. I won't do anything to jeopardize your safety."

"Follow me." I gesture toward the door with him in tow. I lock it on our way out, and we walk down the hall between my office and my apartment, stopping in front of the maintenance door in the middle. "I need to lock my office."

"No, we don't."

"It'll be a distraction if they think we're locked in one of these rooms."

He has an 'ah-ha' moment and takes off jogging to my office. He opens the door and quickly locks it before closing it silently. "Locked." He tilts his head to me, coming to stand at my side.

I nod, remaining silent and open the janitor closet door. He rakes a hand through his spikey dark hair and then massages the back of his neck. "Locking three doors wasn't my idea of hiding out, sweetie."

"Shh!" I shoot him a glare and lock the thick metal maintenance door behind us.

He huffs, not so patiently watching me with a raised eyebrow. I head for the corner in the back right of the small ten-by-ten-foot room, lined with metal shelves and various cleaning supplies. I wave him to come near and point at the small square cut in the roof covered by thin wood. It's painted to match the ceiling, so you don't notice it right away when coming in the room.

"An attic?" he guesses.

I whisper, replying, "No, it's access for an electrician or to fix the dome, that sort of thing."

"Ah." He nods again, concentrating on listening for anyone coming up to this level.

"I'm too short; you have to pull the lip down."

He pulls me behind him and hops, easily touching the ceiling. His fingers skirt over the lip, missing. Taking a deep breath, he jumps again, this time finding purchase when his middle finger sinks into the one-inch-sized slot. He pulls the door all the way open, so it hangs toward us.

"I'll lift you." His hands go out to grip my waist, hefting me up. The man is definitely stronger than any other I've been with. He lifts me with such ease, and I can't help but think of what else he could do with my body like this if we were naked and not being hunted down by an irate MC club.

My hands reach for the opening, and I help to pull myself into the small entry area. Turning over, I sit on my butt and slide backward to give him some room. My hands come away covered in dust, and I quietly clap them together to remove the scratchy feeling. The area's a bit musty, the air stale like a closed-up attic. Good thing I don't have asthma—this would be an attack waiting to happen.

Good thing he enjoys pull-ups so much; a weaker man wouldn't make it. A few beats pass, and I'm about to pop my head back over when his hands appear, grasping the sides. He easily pulls himself up, high enough to readjust and get his elbows planted on the beams running along each side of the opening. This is just another randomly placed work out for him I suppose. Who needs a gym when you have ceiling beams to keep you fit?

He finds me. His brows jump, and I see he has a flashlight gripped in his mouth between his teeth. I go to reach for him to try and help pull him in, but he shakes his head. I reach for the flashlight and free it from his clenched teeth. He blows out a breath, his muscles bulging as he finishes lifting himself up. Once he makes it, he flips around, lies on his stomach, and reaches for the door, securing it to the ceiling before scooting back beside me.

"Good thinking," I praise, holding up the flashlight.

He nods, drawing in a deep, shaky breath. Sweat dots his brow as he peeks around me. "Now what?"

"We should probably move farther away in case any of them find the ceiling entry and pop their heads up to look for us."

He agrees, and I click on the flashlight, crawling on my hands and knees under the low roof until we make it next to the air conditioning unit. I edge around it until I'm safely hidden from sight, and he does the same.

"It's hot up here," he releases a breath, as more sweat droplets drip down his brow.

"There are roof fans around the dome. Otherwise, the only cool air is what escapes right here." I thumb toward the big machine and the leak in a huge tube leading off of it. The tube's been patched twice since I took over The Pit, but the air's so strong that the patches keep bursting. The tube needs to be replaced, but I can't afford it yet. "Switch me spots, so you're closer to it."

His head cocks to the side, his lips tucked into a thoughtful grin. I smile in return and his dusty palms land on my cheeks, pulling me to him. His kiss is sweeter this time rather than all-consuming. It's different than we've shared before like he's rewarding me for being thoughtful. His tongue tangles with mine before he draws away, taking my bottom lip with him. He sucks it in his mouth, making me groan with pleasure.

We switch spots, and he pulls me to sit next to him. "I'm sweaty, but I prefer you close."

My shoulders bounce in a shrug. "I don't mind you sweaty. You forget we've been naked and sweaty together."

"I could never forget," he mumbles, and it could be one of the sweetest things I've heard from him yet.

MERCENARY

Having her next to me, smelling her scent and mine mingled has my groin tightening and my cock growing heavy. I just fucked her not even an hour ago, but I can't seem to get enough of being inside her. Once I started last night, I couldn't seem to stop. We're both going on barely any sleep, and I can't think of a better reason to be up all night than being with her.

"What do we do now?" she whispers.

"We could make out," I mutter, and she laughs.

"I think we're way past that point already."

"Nah, you can never be."

She grins and my lips land on hers again, only this time my kiss is far more heated. Pushing her onto her back, I brace myself over her. The massively sized air conditioning blocks our bodies to keep us out of sight from the ceiling door. The cool air blows over both of our bodies in this position, rewarding us for our lust.

I take her mouth with a fervor closely matching the first time I wrapped her tightness around my cock in front of the clubhouse. Pushing her shirt up to bare her breasts, my mouth leaves hers to suck each of her nipples into my mouth. She's delicious with creamy skin that reminds me of silk. I could touch her for hours and never have my fill of her.

"Mmm..." She hums in her chest, the sound drawn out as her hips twist side to side. Her nipples are a direct link to her core. I learned that if you want to get

Chevelle turned on immediately, go for her tits. She loves when I play with her pussy too, but her breasts are hypersensitive.

"You should pierce these succulent tits, with just a flick of my tongue, your panties would be drenched."

"They already are."

"Damn, I love it that your pussy gets so wet for me."

My tongue trails over her tummy, licking at the soft, smooth flesh, tasting a bit salty. It's hot up here, and we're both sweating. Rather than it turning me off, it does the opposite. I want to see her drip with it, all because my body drives her completely wild.

Her chewed-down fingernails rake through my spikey hair that's the color of freshly poured asphalt. Our features closely match, both of our flesh is dotted with a light tan. Her hair and mine are nearly the same—the only big difference is our irises; mine are like ice—blue, cold, and ruthless. Hers, on the other hand, are like embers—the light tawny color full of warmth and honey.

"Oh yes. God your mouth is perfect," she whimpers with desire. Her hips rise until she can create some type of friction for her pussy against my arousal.

My teeth clamp down, biting into the only fleshy part of her tummy. The move elicits another enticing moan from her. The sound makes me feral inside, wanting to rip her jeans away and take her with a force some would deem unsafe. She belongs to me, and with every breath, I want to mark her so deeply that another wouldn't dare attempt to take her from me.

Is this love? No. Not yet, anyhow. This is passion so fierce with each thrust, claiming another's body so desperately that when you do finally fall in love with them, it consumes your soul entirely.

When I give Chevelle all of me, she'll have the power to take my life if she desires. That's the amount of devotion she'll gain from me. At that point, I will no longer be able to survive without her. I'd simply cease to exist if I loved her as she deserves, without knowing she's enraptured the same way in return.

Hybrid Collection

My fingers land on her pants button and in my haste, yank the material apart. The zipper protests but then relinquishes its hold as well. Chevelle's palms land on each of my cheeks, wrenching my head up to meet her fiery gaze. On a wispy breath, she demands, "Take me, Mercenary, please."

I'll take her all right. I'll fucking keep her too. My hands fly back on course, and I sit back on my haunches. Stripping the tight jeans free from her, I toss them to the side. She's bare. In our hurry, she never stopped to put on panties, and at her exposed pink folds I groan with desire.

Leaning in, I plant my nose to her pussy and inhale deeply. She smells sweet with her need. The scent mingles with my come from earlier, and the knowledge has me wanting to roar in pleasure. She's pure sex, and it calls to everything inside me to slam my cock into her deep, to keep my scent on her.

"You're so goddamn enthralling," I murmur, tilting my head to lick up the inside of her thigh. "I knew you needed to be fucked when I first laid eyes on you. This pussy needed to be owned and now look at it, soaked for me."

She moans, and I in turn to do the same. My tongue caresses her other thigh, lapping at the wetness from her excited core. I want more. I want to bury myself in her and never come up for air.

"You want me to lick your wet pussy, sweetie, or you want me to fuck it?" I've never given her a decision before, but I'm feeling generous after she's taken my cock so wantonly all night.

"I want you inside," Chevelle admits. She meets my eyes as I trail my gaze from her pretty pink center to over her flat tummy. I take in every inch of her curvy hips and full, round breasts. She's utterly sensational. Her body's made for a man's pleasure—*for mine*.

"Mine," I let out a growl as my tongue trails upward again. It moves over her stomach, through the valley of her tits and stops with me tenderly biting her chin. My lips find hers soon after, a kiss overtaking her mouth as I line up the head of my dick to her blissful center.

She breaks away from my lips to heave in a deep breath and firmly proclaims, "Mine."

Her dainty hands grab my ass cheeks, yanking me to her, my cock impaling her pussy. Rather than scream at my huge size plunging inside her fully, she moans against my throat. Her little mouth finds my flesh with her teeth, biting as I adjust to go deeper and draw a whimper from her. She wants all of my length in her, even if it brings a touch of pain laced with the pleasure.

"You know my cock's big, sweetie. Why'd you hurt yourself with it?"

"Mmm," she hums, sucking my skin between her lips.

She releases me, and I move again as her tongue licks along my neck to draw my lobe into her mouth next. Her palms apply more pressure to my ass, and I grind against her in response. Breathily she orders, "I want to be fucked biker boy. I have so much adrenaline inside, I could tear you up right now. If I didn't have to be quiet, I'd scream the walls down right now with how badly my body craves yours. *Make me come*."

"Careful with your words, little woman, or I'll be the one tearing this pussy up. I don't want to hurt you, but I will if you provoke me. I fuck to own, Chevy."

"Please?" she begs, moving her hips to create more friction between us and it's my undoing.

Grabbing her hands from my ass, I pin them both in one of mine above her head. My free hand wraps around her throat, holding her in place as I gain my bearings and start to pummel into her. She's frightened but doesn't want to admit it. I can feel it in my gut. She needs me to take the control from her. She craves this more than anything, to keep her distracted from the danger literally underneath us.

Her mouth falls open as near silent moans and whimpers escape her as I continue my assault. Mere moments pass before her cunt grips me like a vise, squeezing and pulling. The hungry muscles attempt to force the come from my cock with its needy little sucks. Her pussy wants me to claim it.

"You're mine, Chevelle."

Hybrid Collection

Her mouth closes to swallow as her climax begins to fade away, and I squeeze her throat in my grasp, stealing the air from her. "Say it," I demand, never pausing in my assault. My nuts grow heavy, full of my seed wanting to mark her in ways others won't be able to see.

She gasps, and I squeeze tighter. I don't stop until her other hand pushes against my hand, as she attempts to break free. She fights with my fingers stealing her oxygen.

Thrusting into her hard, I offer an ultimatum. "You'll say it, or else I'll squeeze your fucking throat until you pass out." My dick expands, my come nearly about to burst as I take her as she desired but also demand her to admit my ownership. There's a price for her pleasure, my own pleasure.

"Yes," she mouths, and I briefly release my hold. My hand rubs against the bruised flesh in soft massaging circles to get the blood flowing again.

"What was that?" I order and again squeeze her sensitive flesh. This time my grips tighter than before, but only for a beat. I want to cut off her oxygen quick enough to immediately spike her adrenaline.

She throws her head back, a deep moan braking free as an even stronger orgasm overtakes her body. I move my hand, resting the palm in the middle of her breasts. Her eyes meet mine, and she breathes, mid climax, "I'm so fucking yours."

The way she proclaims the words makes them powerful. I roar out my own release. The come bursts from my tip, coating her insides with my dense essence. I brace over her until I'm fully spent. My face drips with sweat. It trails over my bare back and chest. My breaths come deep, as I try to regain my bearings.

Chevelle's so utterly divine right now—lying below me sated and thoroughly fucked after she's admitted to being mine. "Beautiful," I whisper. Her body flushes for an entirely different reason than the heat and spontaneous bought of sex.

She's like a flower. Soft and colorful with breathtaking beauty on the outside, full of thorns to protect herself with, and resilient on the inside, always seeking out the sources to keep her alive. She's strong, stubborn, and motivated. Those three on a woman make up such a magnificent creature.

And she's *mine*. I think that's the part that fills me the most. Being in her presence and knowing that I'm lucky enough to have her in my life. She could have chosen anyone and yet she's let me in. Not anybody else.

"Did I break you?" I mumble, and she giggles. Chevelle actually giggles, and I find myself wishing I could wrap the tinkling sound around me always. "And what is the sweet smell on your throat?"

"Oh, it's Calvin Klein Eternity Air for women."

How fitting, I think with a pleased grin. *Air.* It definitely suits her when I think of being without her—not being able to breathe properly. She's my own air.

"I like it."

"I'm glad," she replies and reaches for her shirt. I grab it before she can and shake out the dust, and then help work it over her head. "I can do it." She takes over.

"I know," I mutter, even though I didn't want her to. I was enjoying dressing her after undressing her. Rather than sulk like a child giving up his most precious belonging, I go about pulling my jeans over my ass and buckling them.

I was so consumed with her I don't recall even unbuttoning them or shoving them free from my cock. One minute we're sitting here, she's asking me to fuck her and then I was. That sums it up in my mind. Once her tits were bared, everything else just faded away.

She attempts to stand, but the ceiling's too low. When she starts to fall, losing her balance, I reach out, steadying her so she can finish getting her pants on. "Thanks."

"Of course. I'm the one that took them off, after all."

She grins about to respond when an even louder boom than before shakes the building.

Her eyes grow wide, her mouth dropping in surprise. "Shit! What was that?"

Hybrid Collection

I shake my head. "I have no clue."

I'm a lying bastard too because I'm pretty sure that was another bomb and those fucks down there just blew something big up.

17. Give me 6 hours to chop down
a tree and I'll spend the first 4
sharpening the axe.
- Abraham Lincoln

CHEVELLE

"They're ripping apart my race track. I have to get down there and stop them!"

He shakes his head, placing his hand on my arm. "There are too many, sweetie."

"I don't care if there are twenty of them. I can't afford to fix the damage they're inflicting on my home. I won't let them demolish what I've worked so hard for."

"I get it, but we have to wait, just a little longer."

I'm ready to argue my case more when sirens wail off in the distance. "Is that?" I gesture with my thumb toward the sound.

"Sounds like it," he agrees.

"Thank God. Never thought I'd be this excited to see the cops before." I release a breath and crawl toward the way we came in. Pressing my head against the thin panel, I try to listen for anything that'll clue me in on anyone nearby. After a few tense moments, I don't hear anything coming from the other side, so I lightly push the panel.

"Be careful," Mercenary scowls from behind me.

"I am," I mumble. Leaning my head out of the hole in the ceiling, I peer around the maintenance room. I pause a few more seconds to listen for talking or footsteps in the hallway. It's hard to concentrate with my heart beating so loudly in my chest; it feels like it could burst out at any moment. "All clear," I say, leaning back up.

"Let me lower myself first. You can jump down into my arms."

I agree, backing away a bit more. His thoughtfulness doesn't go unnoticed on my part. He's willing to jump down and risk his neck. He could easily let me go by myself, but he doesn't. Instead, he's going to catch me in his arms like some fairytale prince. I doubt princes wear leather and ride Harleys, but clearly, mine does.

He eases through the hole, dropping lithely like a ninja and holds his arms up for me, just as he'd offered. His muscles bulge from all the exertion he's putting on them, and it has me wanting to lick his biceps. "Ease your legs down first, babe. I'll be able to reach them and work your body down without you getting hurt."

He acts like I'm a china doll, but yet he forgets I flipped him flat on his ass the first time we met. Regardless, I find myself following his instructions, even though I don't need them. But for some reason, I want to please him, I want him to think I need his guidance, and that I value it. It's pretty damn sexy having a man that acts like a real fucking man doing man shit. He's nothing like these weak beta males floating all over the covers of magazines right now. I don't know what ever made them suddenly interesting, but I take pleasure in making those betas my bitches.

His thick arms wrap around my legs, carefully sliding me downward along his body. I'm breathing heavy when I come in line with his face and it's not from nerves. It's from his touch. He presses a tiny kiss to the tip of my nose and keeps lowering me until my feet hit the ugly scratched tile floor.

"Stay behind me." He pulls the tranquilizer gun from his back pocket and hands it to me. I'd completely forgotten about it in my rush and then with the sex. He yanks his Glock from his holster attached to his jeans, and opens the door a crack, peeking out into the hall.

The siren outside stops and then a shout comes from the lower level. I race around Mercenary, passing my office door and around the corner. It's reckless, but I have to see what the hell is going on below. Keeping my body pressed against the wall, I lean my head forward just a smidge until I can make out the men at the very bottom. There's a group in the center, all their weapons pointed toward a lone cop walking into the main area.

"Put your weapons down!" The officer shouts sternly, and before I can blink, a random gun discharges a bullet. It slams into the cop, and he immediately hits the ground.

I utter a whispered, "Fuck," just as Mercenary steps beside me.

"What is it?" he murmurs quietly.

"They just shot a freaking cop! He's on the ground."

"Fuck, this is bad."

"Surely there are more police with him?"

He shrugs. "Not if it was one that's in Viking's pocket. He could've been closer than the guys and stopped in to be a distraction."

"Damn it. More like a dead distraction, the poor guy. What if he has a family?"

"Viking will help take care of them; he'd never leave them on their own."

A roar combined of various engines comes from outside, the sound echoing in the dome shaped building.

"Hopefully that's our backup and not theirs."

Hybrid Collection

I nod, holding my breath as moments after the engines quiet, a few bikers edge their way inside, weapons drawn. The guys below automatically begin popping off bullets like it's the goddamn Wild West and the Oath Keepers all dodge in several directions to take cover behind rows of seats. They exchange fire as another group of Oath Keepers silently enter The Pit from the back entrance we use for deliveries.

I watch with rapt fascination. The drama below unfolds so quickly right before my eyes. I can't seem to look away no matter the danger.

The door down the hall next to my apartment creaks opens, and Mercenary pokes his head back around the corner, Glock ready to shoot. He relaxes his gun filled hand, pointing it toward the floor to click the safety in place and leans back next to me with a deep exhale.

"What was it?"

"It's Odin. I texted him when I pushed you up in the ceiling again, so he'd know where we were. I didn't want to take them by surprise and have a brother shoot us by mistake."

So that's what had taken him so long to get in the ceiling with me, besides searching out the flashlight.

As soon as he's finished filling me in, Odin's head appears around the corner. "You both okay?" he asks, and we nod, our faces quickly turning to watch the scene unfold below.

"Give me the tranq gun." He holds his hand out to me.

"What, why?" I place it in his palm.

"I'm going to see if I can help my brothers and keep a few of these fuckers alive to torture later."

I draw in a harsh breath, knowing how true his words are. I know they won't hesitate to hurt the rival biker club members, but I prefer to pretend to be ignorant to it all. Odin and I watch as Mercenary picks off two more guys before a few turn their heads up, looking for us. It's enough of a distraction that the Oath Keepers have time to riddle the remaining threats with bullets.

With the cease of weapons, we're drenched in silence. It's so stark, it's nearly louder than the shooting was, it seems. My shoulders drop, the muscles in my back starting to unwind from the tightness leaving my body, knowing we're finally safe. I'm going to be sore from being strung so damn tight during this whole thing rather than from fighting.

A loud boom rattles everything in the building pulling a harsh curse from me. Mercenary yanks me to his chest, his arms wrapped around me tightly to protect me. Holding onto the railing beside us, I lean over to see a few Oath Keepers had fallen with the blast, but no one looks injured from it.

"We need to get down there."

"The fuck was that?" Odin sputters. His mouth's slack with shock from the explosion.

"Bombs," Mercenary grits. "The motherfuckers have set off three since they showed up.

"Holy shit," he curses, and we both nod our agreement. "We found the guys out front that you knocked out earlier."

"Good." Mercenary reloads the tranquilizer gun and hands it back over to me. I grip it tightly, afraid I may accidentally shoot someone and knock them out. I don't say it aloud, but the thought does bother me. He grabs my hand as we head for the stairs to join the others.

Odin keeps talking as we travel down the steps in a rush that lead to the delivery hall and back entry to The Pit. They take a few stairs two at a time, but my legs are too short, and I nearly have to jog to keep pace. "Torch has them tied up and waiting in the back of the truck."

"A cop showed up; he was shot dead upon entry."

Hybrid Collection

I listen idly, concentrating on not falling and busting my ass. With one hand firmly planted to the banister, the other remains secure in Mercenary's firm grip.

"Son of a bitch. This is going to be a big fucking mess."

"Prez here?"

"Yeah, he's down there." Odin doesn't even sound winded. What the hell do these guys do to stay in such good shape? Yeah, I can fight, but shit, it's not like I do cardio or anything.

On the next break between levels, I run my hand through my dusty hair. Using the band around my wrist, I twist my long locks up into a topknot. This seriousness definitely calls for it.

"You okay, Chevelle?" Mercenary flicks his gaze over me as we make our way down the next flight of stairs and my hand shoots out to keep my balance.

"Honestly, I have no idea how to answer that," I mutter, thinking over the carnage I just witnessed in the middle of my beloved race track. He gives my hand a squeeze, and both of them stay quiet after that until we make it to the main level.

"Is it clear?" Odin calls out and gets a few yesses in return.

We enter in the middle of a heated debate. Nightmare scowls, his voice raised as he drills in his point. "We need to hit these fuckers now! Enough waiting. They were here to kill more of ours, and with a big hit like this, they won't be able to react to us right now."

"We have to wait, brother," Viking argues. His right hand tugs at his beard in frustration.

Nightmare flings his arms out. "Fuck waiting! I've been patient enough, we attack now."

Odin interrupts, "And walk into the unknown? They could end up killing us all."

Nightmare shakes his head, exasperated. "Man the fuck up, O. You're the new VP. Time to see just how savage you are, brother." He lays down the challenge, but rather than jumping on it, Odin just shakes his head.

"If it was the right move, I'd be all for it, but it's not. We've left them alone for this long, and it's throwing them off. We've been patient and have just picked off...how many?" He glances around, his fingers moving as he counts the bodies littering the floor. "Fifteen, at least?"

Viking agrees, confirming the count at sixteen Iron Fists total. The thought of killing sixteen people, even if they were evil, makes me feel sick to my stomach.

Odin carries on. "That's blowback we've inflicted on them without them even being aware it was us doing it. They may suspect, but they have no way of proving it. Unless they were to all just show up right now or have spies in place."

He glances at his fellow club members and then looks back to Nightmare, continuing. "You telling me that you can pull the same off by showing up at one of their clubs to get retaliation? You may cut the snake, but it won't be the head brother. I don't know about everyone else, but if we're going after a snake, I want it dead. I'd rather plan to cut the entire fucking head off and not worry about it coming back around to sink its teeth into me."

Brothers around the room murmur their agreement, and Viking gazes at his younger sibling, more like a proud poppa than a blood brother. "He's right, Night." The Prez agrees.

Mercenary cuts in. "What are we going to do with all these bodies? Anyone can walk in right now. I'm sure the first fucking bomb was them blowing a hole in the entry."

Viking grunts. "You're right, a big fucking hole's there." He glances at me, empathy in his gaze. He knows this place is my life. "O and Torch look for something to block the front from curious visitors. See if you can find some plywood or similar for the time being."

Hybrid Collection

They both stride off toward the front and Viking continues barking orders. "Saint and Sinner, make sure they're all dead in here and anyone still breathing, tie them up." He holds out some thick zip ties. The guys snatch them and take off to do as ordered.

"Nightmare, back the pickup to the loading bay door. We'll get these bodies loaded that way." He turns to an older man. "Smokey check supplies for the largest black trash bags you can find. We need something to wrap these bodies in. Oh, and some duct tape."

"You got it, boss," the old timer rasps.

"Mercenary, take your woman to her apartment to gather whatever belongings she needs. No more bullshitting around. She stays at the club until this is sorted. I knew I should've sent someone out here last night to get you guys to come back."

I don't have anything in me to fight him about it right now. My mind and body are still in shock over what just transpired here. Part of me is glad they're here. Obviously, they have a better idea of what to do to take care of everything. I wouldn't have a clue where to begin.

He gestures toward the back entry. "Chaos, start carrying the dead bodies to the bay door. They need to be wrapped and loaded. I'm going to find some mops and bleach buckets to get this shit show of evidence cleaned up."

I listen to Viking still barking off orders as Mercenary leads me back to the stairs, ears still ringing from the blasts.

18. Here's to chasing your dreams in
the cutest pair of shoes you own.
- BossBabe

MERCENARY

Now that I'm coming off of the spike in my adrenaline, thinking there was a chance I wouldn't be able to protect Chevelle in a room full of that many men, I'm livid. She never should've been put in that position in the first place. Who the fuck do these jokers think they are, coming heavy at her like that? She's one fucking woman for heaven's sake!

I see the Prez's point, not wanting to attack right this minute to retaliate. At the same time, I'm with Nightmare. I never want Chevelle to be frightened again. She may have put up a brave front, but I felt her trembling next to me on those stairs when we watched those filthy dicks shoot the cop. I know she thinks she's strong, and to a point she is, but this is too much for her. She's a rough woman, trying to make a good life for herself, and if it wasn't for these fuckers, she'd be doing just that.

Hybrid Collection

Her hold on my ribs loosens as I pull my Harley to a stop at the compound. Dropping the kickstand, I swing my leg over my seat and then grip her waist to help her off too. She's more than able to do it on her own, but I can't stop myself from touching her. Placing my arm over her shoulder, I tuck her into my larger frame, and we walk together inside. "You okay, sweetie?"

She sighs, her dark hair floating out of her face as the air conditioner hits us crossing the threshold. "There's no way I can fix the track in time for Saturday, and I have to race. I don't like leaving my cars there without me, either."

"No, you don't. Besides, it's not safe right now. As for your cars, I already told you, the brothers will bring them here for you."

Golden embers burn in her irises as they meet mine. She's wound tight, ready to argue with me. "Yes, I do. I told you that's how I pay the mortgage for The Pit. I can't afford to miss a chance to win, but I also don't have the cash for what it'll take to fix everything in time. I'm screwed."

Releasing her, she turns her body my direction. My hand reaches up, and my thumb trails over her bottom lip then along the curve of her jaw. She's upset, and I don't know what to do with a woman who's melancholy. Pissed off, yes...turned on, yes...hungry, yes...but not like this.

"I'll fix it," I promise before thinking it through.

"Thank you, cupcake, but you're already letting me take over your space and time to help keep me safe."

I shrug. "It's no big deal."

When my hand drops away, she leans forward, placing a tender, chaste kiss on my mouth. It's so insignificant that it means way more than any touch she's shown me since we've met. It's tender. Nothing is coaxed or heated about it. It's full of real feelings.

"It is to me. Not many men come around who give a shit; they all want something in return."

"I'll fix it," I repeat. This time I know exactly what I'm saying, and I mean it one hundred percent.

She offers a sweet smile, so non-Chevelle like. I think the craziness has her a bit shaken up. Whatever it is, I have to keep my guard up because kisses and smiles like those will have a man falling all over his own two feet. They're the type that'll have a man planning his future out.

We're interrupted by Blaze. He's back behind the bar, polishing the top until each bit shines. "Merc, everyone okay?"

"Hey, brother. Yes, they made it through okay."

"Thank God." He releases a heavy breath, and I tug Chevelle with me to sit on the stools in front of him.

"You here with Princess?" He's Vikings cousin and the Prez's ol' lady's personal guard. After the stories I've heard about what she's gone through, can't say I blame him for putting a steady man with her all the time.

"Yeah, you know with their past, Viking told her what was going down. Prez doesn't keep anything from her anymore to keep her safe. Anyhow, she gets worried about shit like this and she starts cooking like crazy."

"Cooking?" I cock an eyebrow as he gestures to his beer. Chevelle and I both nod, wanting a cold drink.

He grabs two longnecks, pops the tops and places them in front of us on coasters. "The first time shit went down with her, she'd been making a bunch of food to welcome the brothers home off a run. She and Vike were barely fucking back then. Anyhow, shit hit the fan, and it's been a way to ease her anxiety since then."

"Hard to imagine P having any sort of anxiety."

He nods. "She does and pretty badly when shit like this goes down. Probably a bit of PTSD mixed in with it too. She's really good at bluffing. We better drop it. If Viking catches any of this convo, we'll be missing skin for it."

Hybrid Collection

With a chuckle, I throw back a hefty gulp. "You hungry, Chevy?"

"I could go help," she offers.

"You don't cook," I reply, puzzled.

Blaze smiles at her warmly. "Go on back there, darlin'. Princess will be happy for the company. Take your beer, and I'll fix a pitcher of frozen Margaritas."

"Margaritas?"

He nods, his smile growing. "Yeah, trust me, it's a P thing."

I press a kiss to her temple and point in the direction of the kitchen.

"She ever meet Princess before?" He turns back to me.

"I don't think so unless Viking took her to The Pit or something. You sure she won't care about Chevelle going back there?"

He shakes his head, refilling the plastic square container off to the right of me with a stack of bar napkins. "No, she needs the distraction."

"It doesn't piss the Prez off that you know his ol' lady so well?"

His gaze grows weary; he rakes his hand over his face. "In that first attack when I met her, I nearly killed her."

My eyes grow wide. That was definitely not what I was expecting from him. I know he was part of the group that came for Viking and Princess was attacked, but everyone left out the part of Blaze being one of the attackers. "Fuck."

He blows out another breath, busying his hands further by filling a container with straws. "I'll do whatever I can to make her happy and keep her safe. She's become a little sister to me, and the thoughts of what I was planning to do to her will haunt me for the rest of my life. If making her pitchers of margaritas, helping her cook, and keeping her safe makes her forgive me in some small way, well then it's all worth it."

"I get it. I'm trying to keep Chevelle safe too, but these dicks just won't stop."

"That's the Iron Fists for you. Those motherfuckers nearly killed me. I can't wait until the club snuffs the life from every single one of them."

"They trashed The Pit. I need to figure out how to fix it for her. She can't afford to hire anyone, and I don't want her there in case they show back up and try killing her again."

"What exactly needs to be done?"

"Mostly asphalt and concrete work, I think. The main entry has to be redone too." I finish off my beer while he blends the tequila mixture.

He pours the frozen strawberry tequila concoction into a plastic pitcher and grabs a few of the colorful plastic cups we've used in the past for barbecues. "Odin has an in with the City," he mentions, moving around the bar to grab everything he needs. "He may know someone who can help with the asphalt. Torch knows how to pour concrete. I think Nightmare might, too. If you give them a hand, I'm sure they wouldn't mind helping you."

"No shit? Appreciate it, Blaze."

He taps the bar top with one of the plastic cups. "Bartending isn't just making drinks...you hear everything. You ever want to learn about the brothers around here, jump back behind the bar and mix shit up for a night."

"I'll stick to racing and motorcycles." I shrug, and he nods, heading for the kitchen.

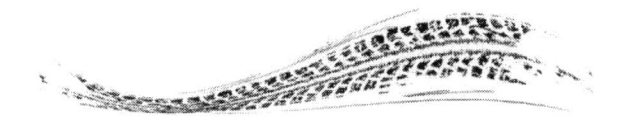

A week passes quicker than I'd like it to. A few of the brothers and I have been keeping busy at The Pit. Blaze was right about Odin knowing someone with the City. Turns out it's the manager who owed Odin a favor. My brother called it in, and one evening a handful of workers showed up to patch the asphalt that one of the bombs had blown to shit.

Hybrid Collection

Torch knew how to pour concrete like it'd been his profession in another life. Nightmare helped, grumbling the entire time that it'd get one more thing out of the way, so he could have his revenge. Saint showed up one day with an old gate. He'd found it out at the pig farm by the compound. Viking welded some hinges on it, and a brother named Spin from the other charter sanded the metal and painted it. Once we repaired the concrete up front, we turned the gate sideways, so it was long enough to cover the open space and secured it. Chevelle now has a steel barrier to help keep unsavory folks from breaking in the front entry.

Over the week together, Chevelle and I fell into an easy routine. It was like she was an extension of myself. She has no clue about anything we've done to fix up The Pit. I got ahold of Ace, and he's been handling everything as far as the races and business deliveries go. I've led Chevelle to believe we've been watching her business, but it's too dangerous for her to be there right now. Surprisingly, she's listened, and I'm guessing her seeing the Fists in action up close has put the severity of the situation in better perspective for her.

I think the only thing that's kept her sane through the time away is that we brought her cars to the compound with us. She's had full use of Viking's garage and the tools he has in there is no joke. It's a mechanic's wet dream and Chevelle has been tinkering with her own vehicles and any other that's been near the garage. It's kept her busy and distracted enough not to notice my lack of presence.

The nights, however, I walk in filthy, covered in sweat, while she treks in full of grease. It's hotter than hell seeing her all dirtied up from working on vehicles. We shower, and she lets me wash her body until every speck is clean. In return, she does the same for me, and it's become my favorite part of the day.

Being around her like this is almost too easy, and it's a bit disconcerting. Of course, I want a woman. Every man with half a brain wants one, especially a female like Chevelle. Doesn't mean I was expecting to start imagining her on the back of my bike every day or keeping her things here or staying with her permanently at The Pit. When I came across her lithe body the first day, those thoughts were the furthest from my mind. I wanted to fuck her, to make that smartass mouth of hers scream my name while I made her climax. Now I'm finding out that I don't want to stop.

"Ready, sweetie?" I grumble watching her pull on her jeans. They're so tight the damn things mold to every curve from the waist down. She needs a pair with my name across the ass so fuckers won't stare.

I'm doing a man pout thing right now because she told me we have to eat food before I can be inside her again. I offered to grab the peanut butter, but she said no. My babe wants tacos so, of course, she's getting them. Little does she know we're actually going to The Pit. It's Saturday. We've fixed everything, and the brothers have done a full sweep of the property.

I don't have to worry about her cars because they've been parked at the club under our watch. She's been so busy spending time under their hoods that I know she has them all race ready, just waiting for the chance. I feel like a fucking chick, excited inside because she's going to get to race, and rather than being a bitch or pain in the ass thinking she wasn't going to, she's taken it in stride. I can't wait to see her face when she realizes what's happening tonight. Not only that, but Ace has rounded up three sets of racers tonight. The Pit will make more money than it usually does on an average weekend.

"The weather's starting to change; it'll be a nice night on your bike." She smiles at me in the parking lot, and I lean in to kiss her.

"Which is your favorite car?"

She snorts. "Please cupcake, you don't ask a girl that sort of thing."

Jesus, I love this woman and the way she thinks—she's so different.

"Okay fine," I throw my hands up wearing a grin. "Not favorite, but if you had to pick one just for tonight, which would it be?"

She turns, gazing at her classic beasts all parked in a row. They're nice and shiny from the fresh washes she's given them the past two days. "I'm going with the Chevelle."

I grunt.

Hybrid Collection

"Not because of why you'd think." She backtracks, and I stride toward the vehicle in question.

"Then why?"

She follows. "Not because it's my name, either. Although that's one of the reasons, it's always been my favorite."

"You're such a girl," I mutter, and she laughs.

"Not because she's the fastest..." She trails off, and I spin around, pulling her into me.

"So, tell me why."

"Because of the hood." Her face flushes and my gaze flicks to the hood. I was so far gone with her that night, furious at her for racing and also the guy hitting her and then burying my cock in her for the first time. The car escaped my mind.

"This is the car?" I stare at her, catching the way her breathing comes in little pants, her flushed skin and how her breasts suddenly seem too heavy for the bra she has on.

She rolls her eyes and copies me. "You're such a man."

With a cocky smirk, I yank her into my body, my cock ready for action. "A fact you can't deny." I take her mouth with mine again, this time turning her and laying her on the hood as my tongue makes love to hers. Her stomach grumbling breaks the spell, and I pull away, leaving her breathless.

"You're hungry babe, and I'm going to drive your favorite car."

"We're not taking the bike?" she asks after gazing at me for a few beats.

"No, you've been a good sport about riding it all week; we can take this pretty lady." I stroke the smooth, buffed paint. She no doubt waxed it this morning when I took off. It doesn't have any small flecks of dust like the others.

"I'll drive."

"Nope."

You know that saying you catch more bees with honey? The alpha in me hasn't quite figured that out yet, and I still find myself arguing and barking orders like she's a submissive.

"It's my car," she hisses.

Swallowing my pride to get her to let me drive so I can surprise her by going to The Pit, I momentarily tuck away the bossy attitude. "Please, sweetie? I haven't driven this one yet." I trail my fingers along the column of her neck, attempting to distract her from kicking my ass. I need to learn to just open up with words like this rather than demands. But she likes my bossiness in some shit, I can tell.

"Ugh," she groans. "Fine. But once you drive her, that's it. You're not keeping her, and I drive after that."

I chuckle. "Sure slugger. If that's what it takes right now to get you to give up the keys, I'll agree. Not saying I'll agree in the future, but one day at a time."

She rolls her eyes, her lips breaking out into an amused grin. "So charming." She tosses me her keys. It's a plain silver ring with a key for each vehicle.

"Hey," I point in her direction, rounding the car to the driver side. "You're welcome," I reply sarcastically with a pleased smirk.

"Oh lord," she sighs and climbs in to the passenger seat.

"That's what you were calling me earlier." I snicker with a wink and crank the engine.

Hybrid Collection

19. Date a car guy.
We break parts not hearts.

CHEVELLE

Mercenary flies by the turnoff for the Taco Shack. I think nothing of it, writing it off as him joy riding in my Chevelle. Down the road a ways, he pulls my baby into The Pit and circles around the building to the back by the loading bay.

"What's going on?" I ask, shooting my gaze around. "Why are there cars here? I thought you told Ace to make sure everyone knew not to come in." The last thing we need are people in the building when they could get hurt, or worse, killed.

"They're here working," he replies absently, busily texting someone with one hand.

"You fixed the front? There wasn't any plywood or anything when we passed it. Was that a gate I saw at the entry?"

What have they been doing since I've been away? I thought they were just here to make sure no one tried to break in or blow up the place more than it already had been. I didn't know they were fixing anything. That's surprisingly thoughtful on the bikers' part.

He nods. "Yeah, we had to repair it, so no one would try breaking in."

Well, that makes sense. I'm still pleased to see it. It was hard enough leaving this place to begin with. I'm grateful for The Oath Keepers providing me with their protection, but The Pit is not only my business. It's my home as well.

"These people need to go home. The Pit won't make any money tonight to pay them to be here." And I won't be able to afford to pay for this place if I have employees around and no income coming in.

He shrugs. "We can talk about it inside."

I reach for the door handle, but when his palm lands on my other arm, I pause. Flicking my gaze back to him, he shakes his head.

"Wait." He tilts his chin toward the bay, and it rolls open.

I sit back as the bay door raises and Mercenary pulls in through the race and delivery entry. "At least no one's bothered with the back doors. I have to find something in this mess to be positive about."

"Relax, Chevy. We've had plenty of people here night and day to keep the Iron Fists away."

"It didn't stop them from setting up a car bomb the last time though," I mutter. My stomach squeezes at the not so distant memory. I've had a few random dreams about it all, and with each one, I've awakened covered in sweat. Thankfully Mercenary has been out like a light and hasn't witnessed me being a scared fruitcake in the middle of the night.

"They did that shit when no one was paying attention. Your employees know what to look out for."

"Oh yeah?"

He clears his throat and nods. "Odin filled them all in. Each one has my number to text if something's suspicious."

"They should be messaging me," I grumble as we drive past Sinner.

I wave, watching his dark gaze sparkle with amusement. He's been around a few times this week when I've argued with Mercenary over something random. The brothers find it highly entertaining to see me give cupcake shit as well as he dishes back to me. He'll learn eventually, though, that I'm not some meek woman. I'll stand up to him again and again until it sinks in. No man will ever push me around unless I ask him to.

The main door off the hallway is spread wide open, so we can drive right through. Usually, I keep it locked unless cars are loading and unloading to race. I don't like anyone snooping around the entry hall since the stairway off it leads to my apartment and office. You can never be too careful when it comes to creepers—especially now, I'm learning.

As soon as we get inside The Pit, Mercenary takes off, hauling ass around the track. Normally I'd be all for it, but the other club set off bombs and blew the track up along with various seating areas with a second bomb. His safety and mine, has me shouting to warn him, "What are you doing? We'll wreck!"

He shoots a confident smile at me and twists the volume to the radio up. He completely ignores me while we sail around the room in my favorite muscle car. This is the first time I've ridden with him driving a vehicle that's not a motorcycle; it reminds me a lot of myself. He's relaxed and appears to be completely in control. I swear if he wrecks my car, he'll never see that motorcycle of his again. I'll have it in a chop shop before he can blink and say *Chevy*.

The destroyed area comes into view and my stomach twists with nerves—my chest tightening until it feels like I can barely squeeze out a breath. If he doesn't slow down, we're going to crash and most likely roll. "Stop being reckless!" I yell over the stereo, nearly panicking as I scowl at him like he's nuts.

Swallowing roughly, it takes me a moment to realize we've actually passed the area completely. I try to spin around and get a decent look, to make sure I'm not losing my mind, but he's going way too fast, and we've sped right by it all while I was distracted trying to warn him.

With a deep breath, I sit back and attempt to coax my muscles into relaxing once again. Mercenary acts like this is just another day in the park, so maybe they laid concrete down or something. Watching everything as we speed over the track, he finally begins to slow down and eventually comes to a stop.

I nearly jump from the car before he shifts into park. Curious, I spin in a circle, searching for the damage caused by the rival bikers. It's completely gone. The place even appears better than it had when I initially bought it. The only way to tell something happened in this area is the lighter gray from the renewed concrete and the darker shade of black on the freshly paved road. It even smells of chemical cleaners and asphalt, another clue pointing toward the work that's been completed recently.

"No way," I comment to myself as I stand there staring, taking it in. A car door closes behind me, and Mercenary comes to stand beside me. On a whisper, I ask, "You did this?" My eyes flick to his.

With a small smile, he nods. "With help from everyone."

"I didn't know."

"I wanted to surprise you," he admits, and I swallow thickly at the gesture.

His thoughtfulness has me choking on emotions I'm not used to feeling. "I can't believe you did this. I will pay you back. I promise. Every single cent." And I will. It may take me five years, but I always settle my debts. I don't like owing anyone anything.

He grunts. "That's not what this is about."

"No?" I swallow roughly again with my voice higher and water swimming in my eyes. I need to keep these emotions locked up. I don't want him witnessing me so vulnerable. He's used to seeing me strong and capable, the way I prefer.

Hybrid Collection

His finger tilts my chin up, gazing at me full of tenderness as I lick my lips. "Are you happy?" he asks, and it's said softly, not like the Mercenary I've grown used to full of rough edges and grouchy tendencies.

"So much," I admit with a grateful smile.

He beams, his bright white teeth on display, making me want to mimic him. "Well then, it was all worth it."

I can't hold back from leaping at him. He turns me all upside down with myself. It's like my body doesn't know what's up or down when it's near him and then he goes off and does something so kind and thoughtful like this making it even harder not to be sucked in even further with him. My arms wrap around his neck, and my lips find his. With a searing kiss, I attempt to show him just how much his actions really do mean to me.

The kindness reminds me of when I was younger and met the old man who stepped up to help me. It takes a special kind of guy to care for someone like that. Breaking away, I rain kisses all over his cheeks and chin. "Thank you."

He chuckles, setting me back on my feet. The man is as tall as a mountain. "You're welcome."

"I mean it; I'll pay you back."

"Don't worry about it. The guy who repaved that portion of the track owed Odin a favor. And Torch knew how to lay concrete and form up everything for the stairs. With everyone else helping as well, the only thing I came out of pocket for was the concrete." He shrugs, waving it off.

"Then the concrete—"

He interrupts. "No. You lent me your car to race in the beginning without batting an eye. If it wasn't for that, I wouldn't have been able to even win a race here. You helped put that cheddar in my pocket. Not that it would matter; I did this because I wanted you to be pleased, not so you'd pay me back."

Biting my lip, I go up on my toes to kiss him again. He's a giant dick, but when it comes to me, he's a big softy. Who'd have thought? "That explains everyone here too." I gesture around, taking in the employees carrying out various tasks.

He smirks, pulling my bottom lip in between his. Releasing it, he rasps, "No, sweetie. Everyone's here because Ace set up three races tonight, and you've got the first run. We've got plenty of Oath Keepers around to help with security as well so you can enjoy yourself tonight."

I'm stunned. The man has made me speechless with the degree of his thoughtfulness. Did he...plan this? Not only is the front fixed, but the track and the seating too, and he did it all without me having the slightest clue about any of it. I never would've thought *sweet* would be an appropriate word for him, but that's exactly what he's being.

"You all right?" he questions after a beat.

"We need to go to my place." And right the fuck now.

"I thought you were hungry. Tacos, remember?"

"Oh, I am, cupcake, but my hunger's for something else entirely." I don't think I've ever wanted to jump a man so damn badly as I do now.

"Yeah?"

I nod. "I'm thinking eight inches long, and three inches wide will fill me up quite perfectly."

"It sure the fuck will," Mercenary agrees, yanking me against his body.

In the next breath, he's trekking across the track toward the hallway, carrying me right along. My legs wrap securely around his waist and my arms around his neck to hold on while he strides like a man possessed. Leaning in closer, I draw his lobe between my teeth, applying enough pressure to make his chest rumble with need. I should've given him one hell of a blow job before we left. He definitely deserved it. Instead, he was thinking of what would make me happy again. I wanted food to eat, and he didn't even blink at my request. Then he brought me here to surprise me and fill me with even more good news.

What kind of a man puts a woman's happiness before his own?

A good one.

20.

MERCENARY

We eventually make it to her apartment upstairs after what feels like takes forever. I'll say one thing: those fucking steps suck. They're almost enough to put a damper on my aching cock, but I'm not one to skimp on a decent workout, so I decide to consider it my warm-up. I can fuck all night—what's a few stairs thrown in, carrying a woman up the entire way? With how she's been kissing and sucking on my neck, I'd almost consider the trek foreplay at this point.

"I can't believe you did all this," she says again, regarding me as if I've hung the moon. I'm used to attitude from Chevelle—hostility, even heat—but this wanton, tender gaze she's shooting me now is something entirely new.

"I had help, it wasn't all me."

"But it's you who came up with this…don't attempt to deny it. Admit it. You have a soft spot for me, cupcake." She smirks, and I grumble to myself something not making much sense, cause she's so fucking cute all happy and turned on.

Hybrid Collection

Rather than egging her further, I pull her shorts and undies free then sit on the edge of the bed. I push her over to the side and position her so that her ass is up, front and center on my lap. The rest of her hangs to the side, her hands on the floor and her head hanging. I have her just where I want her. Flushed and ready for me has her looking beyond stunning.

"So fucking sexy," I mumble, holding her in place with one hand. My fingers on my free hand trail through her slit, relishing in the wetness. "You're so ready, sweetie…fucking drenched. You're craving my cock, huh?"

"Yes," she confesses. "Are you going to let me up, so I can have it?"

"Not yet. I will when I'm ready."

"So bossy."

I shrug, but she can't see me. Not that it matters, because it's true. I am bossy, and I don't care in the slightest bit either. "Mmm…but would I be bossy still if I was to sink my fingers into this pretty pink wet hole and make you feel good?"

"Maybe not quite as bossy, then," she replies, her tone heavy with her pent-up desire.

One digit trails through her slit and I draw in a breath with anticipation. The wait is always the hardest. I want to bury myself in her and never come up for air. So far, she's been pretty good with me taking her body when I want it. The first few times she made me work for it, but now all I have to do is stroke her the right way, and she's damn near purring with need for my cock.

I wonder how she'd feel if I really did keep her? She may be my ol' lady in the club's eyes, but we haven't established anything else between us as far as our relationship goes. I should do that before she has a chance to slip through my fingers. I have a feeling if she were to walk out of my life right now that I'd survive, but I'd damn sure miss her, and that's something I don't want to experience.

"Tell me, Chevelle," I murmur, petting her pussy without pausing. "What do you think this is between us?"

The muscles in her thighs tense, along with her back but she doesn't tell me to stop touching her. "Aren't I your ol' lady?" Her voice is small, almost unsure. My Chevelle has really let her guard down with me today, and I couldn't be any more pleased with it.

"You are, but do you know what that really means?"

"I have a good idea." She releases a breath as I push a finger into her heat.

"You're my property. You belong to me, and I always take care of what's mine."

"I'm no one's property; I've already told you this." She huffs as I draw my finger free.

Rather than inserting it again, I cup my hand and smack her drenched core. The wetness rolls down her thighs, and fuck me, every bit of me wants to bend over and lick it all clean.

"Wrong answer. That mouth is what got you in this situation in the first place. Had you been quiet, I'd have left you alone. Instead, you popped off, and I had to claim you to show you who's alpha. You craved my cock, and you got every fucking inch of it. Now, I get you in return."

She snorts, and I smack her pussy again. The air hits her in the right places but with my hand cupped, she gets no real contact, only the skin surrounding her core. It must be so frustrating to seek your pleasure and have it right there yet not be able to reach out and take it. Now she knows how I feel when it comes to her giving in to being my property.

"You can argue with me all you want, but it's the truth. You're mine, and I'll fight back even harder, sweetie. I have the cock, Chevelle. Dick runs this house, not pussy."

She pants as I smack her core again but offer her no relief.

"You are such an asshole." She squirms in my lap, her thighs beginning to vibrate with more pent-up desire.

Hybrid Collection

"Never claimed to be anything different." I straighten my palm and lightly slap her pussy—once, twice, three times in a row. A loud moan breaks free and then pain spikes up my leg as she bites into my calf. Even with the jeans, her sharp teeth clamp down hard enough to cause me to draw in a quick breath.

Her mouth releases and I use my arm in a curl motion to pull her ass closer to my face. "Fuck," I breathe, my breath blowing over her glistening folds. She's so fucking turned on and ready for me, it nearly possesses me with want. Leaning forward, I bury my tongue in her core, licking and sucking at her center until she finally breaks and comes over my tongue.

Licking my fill, I rasp, "So sweet, Chevelle. You're a goddamn peach, ripe and aching to be bitten. I want your come all over my tongue and my cock...I want you everywhere."

Her hand fumbles to hold onto me, as she wiggles to get to me. She's still breathing hard, but eventually, I let her crawl over my lap. With eyes wild, hair a mess and so utterly beautiful, I can't help but gaze at her.

"I love peaches," she confesses and then plants her lips to mine, sweeping me up in a blistering kiss. Once she's had her fill of her taste in my mouth, she climbs down off my thighs.

Gazing up at me, her fingers move to my waist, tugging and working on my belt. Easing her struggle, I stand and yank the leather free. She plucks the button and pulls the zipper down. My cock falls forward, heavy with length and girth, finally free from being tucked up against my stomach.

"You have the biggest cock I've ever seen, ever felt...ever sucked," Chevelle admits, and my chest puffs a bit at the immense compliment.

Her small hands take my shaft, one working up and down, while with her other she lightly scores her nails along the tender flesh. Eventually, she stops at my full nuts. She caresses them and then grazes her nails in a motion that has my gut tightening.

"Fuck!" I gasp, ready to surrender my body to her. "You're good at that." My gaze meets hers, and I see power reflecting in her irises. She's the type of woman to let me *think* that I have all of the control when in reality it's hers.

"I haven't even put your cock in my mouth yet." She licks her lips, and I groan. I'm a cocky fool to have teased her earlier; now it's her turn to return the sweet torment.

Pushing my length up, she holds it against my groin with one hand and continues her assault on my balls with her other. Leaning forward, she draws one in her mouth and then switches, sucking the other in as well, swirling her tongue as her nails continue to caress the opposite.

"Fuck a damn peach; you're a goddess, babe."

She lifts my heavy sac off to the side and her tongue trails just on the underside of them. The action has me searching for something to grab on to. The sensations are insane. No one—and I mean no one—out of the many women I've been with have licked me there. *Holy shit!*

She sits back and swirls her tongue around the tip of my head. "Beg me," she orders.

I nearly choke at her command. "W-what?" I stumble like a fucking schoolboy.

She runs her finger under my nuts in the same spot she'd been licking and swirls her tongue around the head again. Shit feels so good, I may black out if she keeps it up.

"I said…" She nips at the tip of my cock, and I nearly come right there. "Beg. Me."

"Put it in your mouth, please?"

"Hmm," she hums with a tease and repeats the previous action again.

Precum coats the top of my dick in anticipation, and if she's this good, I'll say anything she wants to hear. I may just end up blowing my load all over her face if she keeps toying with me, and I'd rather it be inside her somewhere.

She swipes the head, lapping at the precum and scores her nails under my sac. It's the breaking point for me. "Please baby, please, just put my cock in your mouth or pussy...somewhere. Let me sink into that tight, wet pussy again."

Her mouth closes over me, and it's like being touched by a sex god. The woman swirls her tongue over me repeatedly. One hand works the bottom of my shaft side to side, and her other hand continues to pull and caress my balls.

"Holy shit, Chevelle!" My labored breaths speed up. "If you don't stop, I don't think I can hold myself back from coming," I admit, nearly purring from the sensations in my cock. She's had my dick in her mouth all of two minutes, and I'm ready to explode.

She doesn't even hesitate at my words, so I grab two handfuls of her hair and sink down as far as she'll let me go. Each thrust has her gagging, her throat attempting to close around the head of my shaft. Tears trail over her cheeks, but I don't break my rhythm. There's no turning back now. The bitch wanted it, well, she's getting it.

This is her fault, teasing me to the point of bursting; it makes a man nearly uncontrollable. I'm no different. If anything, I have even less control. My testosterone spirals through me, telling me to own every crevice of her flesh with my essence. *She's mine.*

One last pump and I'm shooting off. With a mighty roar that echoes through the room, my come coats the back of her throat. My seed's thick and warm as she swallows everything I offer. She takes control yet offers me submission all at the same time, and it has me nearly falling to my knees to worship at her feet.

Eventually, my throbbing resides, and I release the beautiful woman waiting patiently on her knees. She sits back, licking her lips like the cat that got the cream. She's no doubt pleased with her performance. Hell, I am!

"Feeling better?" She hikes a brow.

I yank her to her feet and return her blistering kiss from earlier. There are no words to fully explain to her how I'm feeling at the moment. Overwhelmed would be one of them, sated, insatiable, hungry, yet full. There are so many conflicting thoughts running rampant in my mind to voice them properly.

"Mmm," she sighs in my mouth as we part. My lips follow the path of her jaw and down over her throat. I nip and suck, not having enough of her taste. "I should do that more often."

"I won't mind, I promise."

Her laugh's husky with our passion. "I'll keep that in mind. Now, should we see what we can find to eat?"

"I'm not done with you yet," I promise and yank her shirt free.

"But you just...you can get it back up that quickly?"

My gaze flicks down, and she follows my stare. My cock hasn't even budged. I may have just come, but you'd never be able to tell by looking at my length. I grab her around the ribs, under her tits and easily toss her onto the bed. Chevelle's face flushes with surprise, and I hop in after her.

21. If you don't look back
at your car after you park it,
you own the wrong car.
- Truth

CHURCH

Everyone's tense as we pile into church, claiming our usual seats. Viking sent a massive text calling us here immediately.

Blaze shuffles in behind Chaos, the brothers' hands loaded with various cups and two bottles, one of whiskey, another of moonshine. They sit and pass the cups to the sides, so everyone will have one. We all hurried rather than stopping for a drink like we normally do. I've only been here about four months now, but I'm quickly catching on to how things are run around here.

Nightmare lights a smoke and then puts his pack and zippo in the middle of the table. Various brothers reach for it. Smokey grabs it first, taking one, lighting it, and passing it on. Odin's busily filling his tumbler half full of moonshine when Viking slams the gavel down.

"I called you all here for a reason," the Prez grumbles, pulling us from the various distractions. "Torch was able to break one of the Iron Fists we collected from The Pit a couple of weeks back."

We're so silent, waiting with anticipation that you could hear a pin drop.

"We got a final location. I called up Ruger, and he was able to do a little recon. He confirmed the Fists' location."

Nightmare's fist lands on the table. "Fuck, finally! It's been three goddamn weeks since they blew up The Pit and I'm sick of fucking waiting."

Viking nods. "I know brother, I know."

Saint sits forward, eager. "What's the plan, Vike?"

He lifts his hands up, conveying we need to chill the fuck out so he can finish speaking. "That's exactly why I called you in here. We need to all agree on how we want to handle this. Their attacks were personal. Not only have they tormented the other charter, but they targeted you specifically, Night. You're ol' lady and your son, Maverick. They hurt my Cinderella, and you all know I will scalp a motherfucker that touches my ol' lady. I want blood, as I'm sure all of you do. Blaze, they nearly killed you. Hell, they did kill Scot and Bronx. I say we make every last one of those motherfuckers bleed."

Everyone nods their agreeance, and I speak up. "They targeted Chevelle too, for over a month now. She's my ol' lady, and I'll do whatever I can to make them hurt."

A few brothers cast surprised glances at me, but I see something only a few had offered me already—respect. Viking meets my gaze. "We can use all the help we can get."

I take a swallow of the moonshine one of the brothers passed to me and then nod. He sets a phone on the table drawing everyone's attention back to him. We're forbidden to bring phones in this room, so this'll be good, I'm sure.

Hybrid Collection

"Spidey wants us to put him on speakerphone when we discuss what our plan is. He and Ruger have been working together on the recon of the Fists for us." He hits a button and puts it on speaker.

"Yeah?" Spider barks into the phone.

"Spidey," Viking speaks loudly. "We're making plans, brother."

"Bet, I've been thinking up scenarios since we last spoke on how to go about hitting all three of their clubs at once. I'm putting you guys on speaker as well. I have Exterminator beside me."

"All right, what do you have for us?"

"From the cameras Ruger's set up and Google satellites, I've been able to pick up fairly decent images of the buildings and the surrounding areas. When we hang up, I'll send you an encrypted email with photos. Open it in my room on the blue laptop. It's secure."

Viking gestures to Torch, and he nods in agreement. "All right, I'll have Torch go over it with me when we get out of Church."

"So, we have a few options, but I'll bring up the one I think will be the most successful. Oh, first of all, is Ares' charter going to help out?"

"As far as I know, they are," Viking mutters. I've learned that the Prez is decent friends with the Prez of the other charter about thirty minutes away. I've met the brothers from there on a few occasions. They seem like good guys.

"Perfect. So, the Fists have a smaller building that has around ten guys there at any given time. I'm certain this is where they keep the drugs they distribute. I think it would be smartest to have Ares clean up that mess when we hit the others. I'll hack into one of the military's drones and use that to take out the other building that houses their weapons. They keep another ten or fifteen guys at that one. I think these spots are more like warehouses that they always keep guarded."

We all stare at the phone, eyes wide after hearing Spider declare he can hack into military grade weapons. The brothers have told me the guy is smart, but damn, that's an entirely different level of genius.

He continues. "That'll leave the main club open for you. The property is surrounded by an electric chain-link fence as the first line of defense. Odin should use his contact at the City and get a dump truck. You can ram through the fence, and a handful of the brothers can safely ride in the back. I'd bring a van to help haul the guys back home or something. If you go with this option, you need to come heavily armed and prepare for a fight. Even taking out the twenty or twenty-five at the other buildings, it leaves behind a good twenty or so at the main club."

"Christ," Viking gripes. "That plan actually sounds doable, and we have a chance at minimum injuries or blowback on our members."

"Exactly," Spider agrees.

It all sounds a bit nuts to me, but it's one hell of a plan, that's for sure.

Nightmare huffs. "I'm having flashbacks of our Mexico trip. Anything inside that fence we need to worry about besides a group of pissed off cunts posed as an MC club?"

I have no idea what he's talking about, but it must've been bad by the ashen tone of his face.

Viking's mouth drops open, a look I'm not used to seeing from him. Ever. "Fuck, good point, Night."

Spider speaks up. "No, no, nothing like that. Ruger has been watching the grounds himself and has reported back that there are no animals."

"Pretty sure I can't run from another lion again," Nightmare mutters, and I draw in a quick breath between my teeth. Fucking shit, a lion? No wonder Chicago sent me down here. They obviously think I'm just as wild as these fuckers.

Viking shoots his gaze around the room, landing on each of us. "Anyone else have anything to say?"

Everyone remains quiet.

"Good, then let's vote and work out the fine details."

Odin cracks his knuckles and begins. "Everyone in favor of Spider's plan vote aye. Any nays, offer up an explanation after voting is complete so we can look at other options."

Each of us agrees, ending with Odin commenting "aye" as well. There's not much to discuss when a member of the NOMADS talks about blowing up an entire clubhouse with military grade weapons.

"It's settled then. We'll go with Spider's plan unless something comes up and then we'll improvise. Do not show mercy to any of them. They will all be armed and ready to kill. I suggest you do the same."

"When will we ride out?" Odin questions and then drinks from his tumbler of whiskey.

"Spider? How much time do you need?" The Prez holds his gavel as he asks.

"An hour, maybe two."

"I'll call Ares and we'll get organized," he informs us. "Prepare to ride in three days if nothing spooks the Iron Fists." At that, he slams the gavel down, officially dismissing us.

I think most of us are in shock as we leave the room quietly and head straight for the bar. I'd left Chevelle in my room, asleep. It's been over a month already since the MC tried blowing up The Pit. She's remained here with me each night.

We've fallen into our own routine of sorts. I usually help her during the day with things at The Pit, and as the evening approaches, we make our way back here. Every night I come in here like a man possessed and tell her she's mine. I think she's finally beginning to realize that I mean it, and in return, I'm falling for her a little more each day.

When this is all over with the Iron Fists, I can't help but hope she'll stay. I want her safe, but I want her with me even more. I'm selfish, no doubt. And most of all, I'm not ready to give her up. I meant it when I said I want to keep her.

CHEVELLE

"How was church?" I greet the distracted biker as he enters our room. It was only his before all this began, but I've been staying here long enough to claim at least a quarter, if not half of it, as mine.

"Surprisingly productive." His mouth hikes up into a sexy grin.

"Nice. Anything about The Pit yet?"

His eyebrow skyrockets. He's already warned me about how he can't share any biker business with me. "No. But, if all goes right, you'll have less to worry about."

I'm surprised he's admitted as much so easily. I was expecting him to tell me to mind my own business. "So, you'll finally have me out of your hair, then."

His grin falls, his forehead wrinkling as his brows furrow. "Uh, no."

"No?"

He steps closer, pulling me to stand on the bed, so we're nearly the same height. The man is a freaking tower. I rest my palms on his wide, sturdy shoulders and his hands come to grip my waist. "You think once this is all over with, I'll up and pop smoke?"

I shrug, my throat growing tight. When did I catch a case of the feelings for this brute?

"Not happenin', sweetie. I'll still be there every Saturday night, racing your Camaro and taking home my winnings. Perhaps one day you'll even get the nerve to race me."

The snort escapes before I can smother it down. "You won't win."

Hybrid Collection

"How do you figure?" His icy irises sparkle at my confidence.

"I don't lose." I shrug again, this time feeling a bit cocky.

"Babe..." His voice leaves him in a rasp as he leans in, his whiskey flavored breath warming my lips. "I've already won."

My breaths increase, my chest brushing his deliciously from the movements. I swear when he's near, I can feel everything. "How do you figure?" I copy him, licking my lips, wanting to close the distance between us, yet I hesitate.

He steps back, and I teeter to catch my balance. He reaches to the chair beside his door and lifts a leather jacket that's far too small to fit him. Stepping back from me, he twists the jacket around and stretches it, so I can easily read the patch on the back.

"For me?"

He nods, suddenly appearing a little nervous. Not like my alpha biker at all.

"No one's ever gotten me anything like this before," I admit. Bringing my hand up to his face, my thumb brushes over his lips. "This kinda makes it official, huh?"

He nods again. "I told you, I've already won."

"You would rather win me?"

"Of course. Nothing could ever compare," he replies quietly.

"Oh, biker..." I pull him to me, finally planting my mouth on his. I lose myself in the kiss, reveling in the knowledge that to him, nothing compares to me. That knowledge is consuming, knowing that you mean something to that extent to another.

He pulls away to set the jacket beside us, then strips me of my clothes. Leaving me in only my thong, he lifts the jacket again, and I slide my arms in the soft black leather. I've seen his jacket hanging up, and it's the same as mine, only much bigger.

His desire filled gaze flicks over me. "If I wouldn't end up killing someone, I'd tell you to stay like that forever." He rumbles. "I didn't think you could get any sexier until now."

His blazing stare has me feeling every bit of it too. He doesn't want some frilly lingerie, but a scrap of underwear and a jacket with his name on it. Men are so strange and yet easy to please. "You like your name on my back, cupcake?" I ask, coyly.

He straightens up and growls. There are no words involved. Just some primal sound that has him sounding more inhuman than the average male. With one hand he jerks me against his vast chest, my arms flying forward to hold onto him. His lips come back to mine, impatient and needy. His tongue thrusts inside as the fingers on his free hand push my panties aside, finding my pussy in a rush.

He's nearly frenzied like the first time he took me on the hood of my car. Two fingers fill my center, and I gasp into our kiss as he plunges them deeply into my core. He doesn't allow me to pull away either, owning every whimper and moan that tries to escape between our lips. His other massive hand grips my ass cheek, keeping me firmly against him.

His fingers pump, going in deep and quick until my climax thunders through me. The pleasure soaks my entrance from his touch alone. I never want him to stop this madness—it's addicting. He coaxes my pleasure so easily, my body wanting to bend to his touch to please him.

His fingers leave me, and I'm so close to begging him to keep touching me. His fingertips rub over my stiff nipples drawing another moan from me. He pulls back, and I ask breathily, "What..." I trail off as he draws his fingers in his mouth next, sucking them clean. Soft pants leave me, witnessing him so savage when it comes to me is a huge turn on.

"I want to taste you when I fuck you, and it'll be even better if I'm sucking on your tits while I'm buried inside you." His free hand falls to my thigh, hiking it around his hip so he can sink his length in with one firm thrust.

"Oh, fuck," I moan as he fills me so completely. "Your cock…it's so fucking big…so good."

"Mmm, I love hearing that come from your mouth." His palm on my ass moves to my thigh to lift my other leg around his waist. When he has me completely wrapped around him, one hand palms my ass cheek while the other grips the back of my neck. I couldn't go anywhere even if I wanted to. This man and his big-ass muscles have me surrounded by him.

He kisses me deep and wild, his lips punishing my mouth as he takes more and more. This level of fucking is so powerful, so damn primal, I feel like we could bring down the clubhouse if he wished. He's deep enough that I could swallow and feel the tip of his cock in the back of my throat.

A cry bursts free from me and his mouth moves to my throat, his five o' clock shadow scratching along the way. The stubble against my skin burns in a delicious reminder that Mercenary is ravishing me. A few jerks of his hip, drawing moans from me isn't enough. He slams us to the bed. He rarely takes me on my back, but right now, he hikes my legs up farther, resting my ankles on his shoulders as he buries himself to the hilt.

I scream his name, and he revels in it. His gaze is full of possession and promises. I'm falling in love with this man. I know it. I can see it in the way he looks at me, how it hits me straight in my heart. I care for him.

His mouth moves lower, sucking and biting along the way until he pushes my breasts against each other. "I love tasting your pussy juice on your tits, straight fucking perfection."

They're big enough that my nipples nearly touch, and he sucks and laps at them with such unrestrained eagerness that I shoot off like a rocket again. My climax is so strong, my body feels like it's floating through space. He groans into my heated flesh as I cry out in bliss, my body shuddering with satisfaction.

His gravelly voice whispers my name over and over like a chant, and my insides squeeze his cock, rewarding his plea. "You taste so damn good. You smell so damn good. Fuck, I just can't get enough of you," he admits and sucks the top of my breast marking me in purple and maroon once again.

I'm not going to be the only one this time. My tongue whispers over his sweat slickened flesh, the salt is tangy and addictive. Reaching the middle, I breathe his scent in deeply, letting the leather and hint of cologne eclipse me like a heated blanket. This may be Texas, but I love it when he makes me burn when he makes me sweat.

My teeth clamp down, and his back stiffens in response. He's bitten me before, but this motherfucker is mine. It's time I claim him just the same. My tongue swirls the area, and I draw the flesh into my mouth until I've left a mark. I continue my task, peppering half a dozen hickeys over his neck. Releasing the skin, I breathe against his throat, claiming him with a ferocious purr, "Mine."

"Fucking right," he rasps and slams into me, pouring his come deep. The throbbing of his thick cock has me exploding all over his dick, gripping and releasing again and again. Both of our centers fight each other as we come together, skyrocketing with our pleasure. He kisses me once more, soundly, ending his passion perfectly. The man can fuck like no other.

Once we catch our breath, he climbs off me, holding a hand out to pull me to my feet. "I love the jacket, thank you."

He nods, tugging me toward the shower. "Good. I spoke to Princess before she ordered the patch. I told her you're always in tank tops." He heads for the bathroom, and I trail along.

"They're easier to work in, especially since it's so damn hot here most of the year."

"She figured. Said she's going to order you some with my patch on the back, so you always have my name on you."

"If it were anyone other than Princess, I'd be pissed over this."

He flips on the shower. "I know, babe. I'm glad you two hit it off, even if you burned half the shit she was cooking."

I burst out laughing. That was definitely one way for me to leave an impression on the queen of the club. She doesn't fuck around though, and I liked her instantly for it. He rids me of my jacket and underwear before tugging me into the water with him. His hands already stirring up my fire inside for another round.

22. Women who say "I want a bad boy" are clueless. What you need is a man who will break someone's face for you but also make you breakfast in bed.
- #ZKK

MERCENARY

Three days pass in no time, and before I can blink, we're pulling our bikes to a stop not far from one of the Fists' clubhouses. Odin remains on his motorcycle beside me. "Now we wait for the sign from Spider," he says, repeating the plan we've gone over each day, so everyone remains on track. His cobalt irises glance around at everyone minus Viking, the NOMADS, and Saint. Viking and the NOMADS are all with Spider, and Saint is driving the dump truck, on his way to us.

Odin speaks louder over the cars passing us on the highway. "When Spider blows the other club up, Ares' charter and ours will storm the Iron Fists clubs at the same time. That way it all happens at once, and there's less chance of reinforcements getting to other clubs to fuck us up. Saint will be right behind us. Half of you load up in the back, and everyone be ready to fuck shit up. The NOMADS and the Prez will be meeting up with us coming from the other direction."

Speaking of Saint, the beefy dump truck comes into view with his crazy ass hanging halfway out the window, flipping us the bird. The vehicle eventually pulls off the side of the road ten feet in front of us, and multiple kickstands hit the dirt. We're tucked right behind a group of bushes alongside the road. It'll be easy for us to get the hell out of here but also keep the waiting motorcycles hidden.

We decided that our bikes may be quicker and easier to hide if the cops show up. With a van, we risk a group of us getting popped and snatched up by the police. None of us want to have a shoot-out with the law or end up in jail. Another downfall of driving the van is if the Fists happen to muster up some backup, they could easily catch and kill us in one van.

Patting my chest, I reassure myself my vest is securely strapped on. I can feel the warmth but smoothing my fingers over it helps my mind catch on that shit's about to get real. We've spoken about it over the past few days, working out times and places, all the fine details, that sort of shit. This type of thing always seems surreal until it's actually happening.

Nightmare, Odin, and I remain on our bikes as Sinner, Blaze, Chaos, and Torch dismount. Blaze and Torch each take out a small glass vile filled with white powder and put it to their nostrils. Snorting up a deep inhale of powder, their eyes slam closed with the impact. A few beats pass as the drug hits them then they're all piling into the back of the massive truck.

I guess we all have our own ways of dealing with what's about to go down. Various brothers took a few shots of moonshine before we left as well. I, on the other hand, strapped on my bulletproof vest. I need to be clearheaded for this; I don't intend to die today.

The three of us riding are the biggest here other than the NOMADS, so it'll be easier if we approach the compound on our bikes. The smaller guys need more of the protection of the vehicle. Not saying they can't hold their own, but Nightmare, Odin, and I could probably take down a small army just the three of us. Viking tried to make Odin stay back in case anything happened to him. He'd need to step up as the new Prez, but O wasn't hearing it.

"Here we go." Odin blows out a breath, eyes trained to the sky.

"We've waited long enough," Nightmare growls and flicks open a purple switchblade. "I have a promise to keep."

An explosion rattles the ground, a smoke cloud rising toward the clouds, and the truck ahead of us lurches forward. The guys in the back are most likely holding on for dear life, so they don't show up with broken bones before the fight begins. Rocks spew in their wake and our engines thunder to life. The three of us move quickly to tuck in behind the brothers.

We get one chance to make our surprise entrance; it has to go off without a hitch. The other club will already be wondering what the hell's going on with the loud noise. With any luck, they'll think it was weather related, but I'm not holding my breath on that one. Our bikes lurch forward as we attempt to keep speed with Saint. The fucker has a lead foot, even in a heavy-ass truck.

I take up the rear. On a mission, we still don't break formation. I can't help but send up a prayer that God be on my side today. Chevelle's become too important to me. I don't want to leave her so quickly. I need more time in this life with her.

As we approach the electric chain-link fence, I brush the thoughts away. My mind chides myself for being a pussy. I need to harness my anger and get some payback for these assholes trying to hurt Chevy. I have to make it safer for her so she can do what she loves.

Hopefully the massive tires we stuck in the back of the truck work, and none of the brothers get toasted from the fence. Saint picks up more speed, and as we get closer, we fall back. Just in case the fence flies toward us with the impending impact, we don't want to be prematurely injured. My gaze skirts around the surroundings in the moments we have before shit hits the fan.

An Iron Fist attempts to leap out of the way but Saint slams on the gas, mowing the guy over and flying through the locked gate. We swerve around a bloody, detached leg and I decide right then to keep my eyes on the target and nowhere else. Some of the rival MC members out in the yard take off in different directions. Saint runs anyone over in his path.

Hybrid Collection

Odin yanks a Glock from his boot, lacing the men still running away with bullets. They fall to the ground in motionless heaps. O doesn't even falter with the deaths, and I can't help but wonder what kind of life he had to make him so hard inside. He's too young to be so damn jaded. The kid's like nineteen. Regardless, he carries out orders, killing on sight.

This isn't payback. No, this is an extermination.

Viking said he only allows someone to fuck with him so much before he makes an example of them. He's setting the bar really fucking high, so bigger clubs won't attempt to fuck with us in the future. He said we knock out a huge, ruthless outlaw club and word will travel fast and far. One thing is for certain, this damn sure isn't Chicago. Texas is an entirely different type of beast.

Saint veers off to the side, the brothers spilling from the back. We pull to a stop on the other side of the truck for protection, weapons in hand as Viking and the NOMADS roar in from behind. They dismount their bikes beside us, so Odin and Spider can defend the vehicles and get anyone who may try to escape.

The brothers and NOMADS storm the club. Viking's first in, clad with an AK-47. He pops rounds off clearing a path through the men already shooting at us. Nightmare takes off past me toward a hallway. Exterminator's hot on his heels tossing smoke cans in his wake. The clubhouse is bigger than ours, with rooms and hallways veering off in every direction it seems.

I split off with Torch, having his back as he works to clear various rooms. We come across multiple bikers and return fire. Whores scream frantically, running in all directions. It's pure chaos; the magnitude of this job didn't fully hit me until now. No wonder the Iron Fists were able to keep coming at the Oath Keepers over the years. They're fucking everywhere!

We leave the whores be, as they're most likely not here of their own free will. The members we caught from The Pit were tortured extensively and admitted to all types of sordid shit going on at this club. The President, Puppet, has been around for far too long. He's had free reign from his high number of members and secret compounds spread from Texas to California.

Someone comes at me from behind, catching me off guard. A forearm wraps around my throat, and I rear back, stumbling backward until I slam him into the wall. It dazes him enough to shake his arm lose, and I spin around. He lands a blow to my jaw. Good thing the fucker's practically made of concrete; the hit against my jaw doesn't even rock me. He gets another in close to my temple, and I see red.

I counter with a right straight into his gut and then stun him with a head-butt to his nose. *Stupid motherfucker.* The bones crunch and blood pours free like a faucet. His arms flail, looking for purpose and I take a step back, with my left foot forward as I land a solid uppercut with my right. He wavers for a second then drops to our feet like a sack of flour. I land a kick to his temple for good measure.

"That's for sneaking up on me, motherfucker."

"Come on." Torch nods with an amused eyebrow lift. We keep to our path before a shrill whistle rings through the air. My gaze meets Torch's, and he holds a fist to his chest telling me to stay in place and remain quiet. He listens for a minute, then when a series of three sharp whistles follow, he nods for us to go back the way we came.

We make our way there quietly, waiting for any other clues. Back in the main entry, we're met with a scattering of dead bodies everywhere and Nightmare holding a bloodied older man. He's been beaten, and Night has the dark purple switchblade pressed firmly in place.

"Brothers," Viking thunders. "This is the root of our problems."

"Fuck off Oath scum," the broken man spits. Prez presses his finger into the man's temple so hard, I'm afraid he's going to stab through his skin and into the guy's brain. I have pent-up anger inside and enjoy a good ass kicking, but I'm not much for torture.

Blaze steps forward, his hunting knife in one hand and Glock in the other. The knife is already bloodied, I notice. "No, fuck you," he snarls and stabs Puppet in the gut. The older man hisses in pain but remains standing.

"I should've put a bullet in your skull," Puppet coughs.

Hybrid Collection

In response, Nightmare flicks the blade up swiftly. He slices a gash into one side of Puppet's mouth. With that move, his eyes widen in shock from the jolt of pain.

Torch yanks his blade free from his holster, approaching Nightmare and the prisoner. He drives the blade into Puppet's upper thigh. "For Bronx, cunt."

The man groans, his head swaying side to side and I can't help but wonder how he's even still alive. Viking approaches them next, and I swallow roughly. He grabs the man's shirt collar with both hands and rips it completely open. Blood sops out from the gash Blaze already inflicted.

"For Scot—may our road father rest in peace—and for Princess, my ol' lady." He draws a small axe free, and with one harsh swing, hacks into the injury free side. That's the hit that hurts, as Puppet wails in pain.

Scowling, Nightmare growls, "The fun's only begun. When I'm finished with you, that hatchet will be child's play. You kidnapped my son, you beat my ol' lady, you *will* suffer."

With a nod to the brothers still beside me, I make my way outside before I puke my guts up.

23. Bikes are like ol' ladies,
if it ain't yours don't touch!

CHEVELLE

Princess wears a pleased smirk as I tromp into the kitchen clad in leather. "Well, he was right about the fit, but you're not burning up in that jacket?"

"In here, no. The guys keep this place like an icebox." I gesture around at nothing in particular. "There's no way I can wear it outside though. Mercenary said you were ordering me some tanks also?"

She nods, opening the oven to pull a casserole out and check the temp in the middle.

"I appreciate it."

She waves me off. "It's nothing girl. I practically live in them too. You know how this summer heat gets the end of August."

"Miserable," I mutter, and she hums in agreement.

"So, what's up? The guys say you usually only cook when something's going on." We discussed this briefly the last time I was here too. I, in turn, burned her food, but not on purpose.

"What did Merc say before he left?"

"That he was going to help the club make it safer for me to be at The Pit."

"Did he tell you anything else?"

I shake my head. "No, and come to think of it, he distracted me before I could get anything else out of him."

"Sounds about right. Let's just say it has potential to be really dangerous. I'm trying to keep myself busy so I can pretend that they're fine and the cooking is keeping my mind occupied."

"But the cooking's really not?"

"No, not really."

"I get it; I can lose myself in an engine and drown any outside shit out."

"My best friend's out in the bar with Jude; they're getting drunk. That's her way of drowning it out."

"You don't want to be with them?"

"When my ol' man's on a run? No. We all cope differently. This is my way."

"That's Nightmare's ol' lady, right?"

"Yeah, Bethany. Their son's Maverick."

"I saw him running around the other day when Nightmare brought him to the club with him. Cute kid."

She smiles wide. "I know. I love that little boy as if he were my own."

"What about you and Viking?"

She wraps foil over the casserole and sets it aside on a hot pad. "What about us?"

"No kids for you guys?"

She places something else that resembles lasagna into the oven and turns to me. "Not yet."

I grow quiet, not sure what else there is to say about it. I don't want to push her on it. Usually, when you bring this stuff up, chicks chat your ear off. I keep to myself a lot besides when I'm in "Pit Master mode," so I'm not very good talking to women. They normally don't care for me much.

She leans against the counter across from where I stand and breaks the silence. "I have a feeling I'm going to be seeing a lot of you around here, Chevelle, so I'll share some back story with you."

"You do?"

Princess nods. "Mercenary did put his patch on you," she says, staring at me thoughtfully. I'm sure too many write her off as a pretty face and not realize she's wise beyond her years. "The club that the brothers went after beat me up badly when they stormed our compound. They did the same to Bethany as well and stole Maverick. The bastards nearly killed Blaze and succeeded in killing two of the other members."

My eyes widen. I knew they were dangerous, but goddamn, that is way beyond what I thought they were capable of. No wonder the Oath Keepers have been all over their asses when it comes to The Pit. "Holy shit," I whisper.

The skin around her eyes tightens as if she's remembering everything from that time. "That's not even everything. They hurt my father's old club too—the one Ares is President of now. They're with our guys now, helping. The Iron Fists club is massive, so the brothers had to sit back and wait for the perfect timing. I'm praying that they're right and that the time for retribution is now."

I swallow, my throat feeling dry with the sad story. "How do you deal with knowing about it all and having to stay here?"

Hybrid Collection

"I deal because I couldn't imagine my life without Viking or the brothers of this club. They're my family, and they're doing what they feel is right, what will keep us safe. I'd do the same thing if I had the chance to offer them that protection."

She gestures to my leather jacket that I've worn since Mercenary left with the others. "You're a part of that family now too. We may not be in the club, but these men are my brothers. You're special enough to Mercenary for him to make you his ol' lady, and that makes you my sister."

"Thank you," leaves me on a breath and she flashes me a small smile.

"Now get your sexy ass on over here. I'm going to teach you how to make my mom's macaroni casserole. It's the best comfort food."

I hop off the stool and say a silent prayer that I don't ruin more of her food.

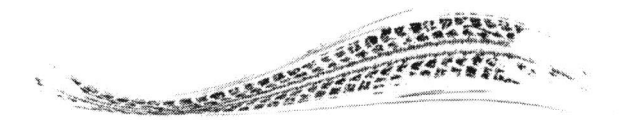

The thunderous roars outside from various motorcycles are loud enough to feel as if the compound is shaking from a small earthquake. The Oath Keepers all ride in together as one big group and park in front of the clubhouse. The tension in the air is thick. We wait with bated breath to see if they'll all return to us through that door. Anyone could've been injured or worse, killed. I may not know the other brothers like I do Mercenary, but I can only imagine how their loved ones feel, worrying about their men's safety.

The door to the main entry flies open and one after another, massive men enter. Their presence quickly fills up the space of the bar. The room's large but they almost make the area seem too small to fit them all at one time. Each one of them is splattered with blood, and one of the meanest looking guys of them all helps a smaller man through the door.

As soon as I find Mercenary, I jog to him. "What happened?" Thank God he's in one piece, and I don't think the blood he's wearing is his as most of it's dark from drying.

He glances at the two hobbling past us. "Exterminator's fine. Ruger was shot in the leg, so he's helping him."

"Shot? Shouldn't he be at a hospital?"

He shakes his head. "Nah, he'll be fine." The movement lets me catch the side of his face. A dark bruise is already forming near his temple.

"Shit, your face! Are you hurt badly?"

He pulls me into his arms, burying his face in the top of my hair. Princess did a good job of keeping me busy, but now that I have this big man in my arms, I realize just how worried I was for him. "I'm fine, I got jumped from behind. The fucker got a cheap shot in, catching me by surprise but I got the better of him."

Releasing a breath, I pull him to me, holding his muscular frame a bit tighter. Relief fills my chest as I take in his scent. "Thank God."

His fingers go under my chin, tipping my head up to meet his gaze. "Careful sweetie almost sounds like you care." His voice is gravelly, still laced with a dangerous edge. His body vibrates with adrenaline, and I know he needs to release some of it with me.

My bottom lip trembles and fuck if I don't want to kick my own ass for wearing my feelings so openly. It's been close to two months since he first showed up at The Pit demanding my attention. Now I don't want to think of a life without him in it. "I do care, cupcake; I'd miss kicking your ass at everything if something happened to you."

His lips turn up at the edges into an amused smirk and then *finally* his mouth falls to mine. With a swift kiss, he holds me firmly against him, warming me from within. "You remembered your jacket," he mutters when he eventually breaks free from my lips.

"Wouldn't forget it for the world," I admit softly, and he swallows.

"You make it really easy for a brother to fall for you, sassy-ass mouth and all."

Hybrid Collection

"So charming." I roll my eyes, and his grin makes me smile in return.

"Tell me, Chevy. I want to hear you say it back."

Rather than correct him on my name, I give in and go a little further than his statement. With my mouth still close enough for my lips to brush his, I whisper, confessing the one thing I've never felt for another man. "I love you, Mercenary."

Mercs grin blooms into a full-blown, wide smile, white teeth showing and everything. He scoops me into his arms and my legs wrap around his waist to hold on. Embracing his neck, I press a quick peck on his lips, and he rasps, "I love you, Chevelle." Then he's walking us to the bar, joining his brothers in a shot to celebrate.

Whatever happened with the Iron Fists, it must've been a win for the Oath Keepers. While they celebrate together, I bask in the warmth of being wrapped in Mercenary's arms, knowing he loves me.

With a pleased gaze in my direction, he draws everyone's attention. "A toast! Here's to keeping our women and club safe. The Iron Fists breathe no longer, and we breathe easier without them."

"To our women," Viking echoes.

"The ol' ladies," Nightmare joins in.

"And to us," Saint interrupts. "Because God help anyone who attempts to take or hurt what belongs to us!" His stare locks on Sinner, and he nods his agreement.

"To kicking ass." Odin holds up his full shot glass.

"And family," I speak up. "With it, we have everything." I receive soft looks from the boulders of men and prideful glances from the woman beside them.

"Yes, we do," Mercenary mumbles in my ear. "With you, I have everything."

EPILOGUE

*If someone tells you that your car
doesn't need that much power,
stop talking to them. You don't need that
kind of negativity in your life.
- Pinterest Meme*

CHEVELLE

Twenty years later...

"Damn it, Chevelle, get her out of the driver's seat." Mercenary grumbles in my direction.

Nova giggles at her father's frustrated shout, and I smile wickedly. "Go ahead, Nova; crank her over before your daddy catches us."

"He's going to be so pissed. You heard him last week when he said my first car wouldn't be a race car."

I shrug. "Your father knows damn well that I do what I want to. Now let's hear how she purrs." I also remember when he swore Nova wouldn't go to prom either, yet she went to both her junior and senior proms. Or how he yelled the house down about her not being allowed to date, yet she did that too. He may huff and puff, but she has him wrapped around her finger.

I know what you're thinking, and no, we didn't teach her how to drive in a race car. Mercenary would've stroked out and spanked my pussy until I couldn't walk for a week if I had. However, with The Pit booming business wise, I had to treat my girl for her eighteenth birthday. I handed over the keys to my Chevy Nova, the car that her name originated from. Our daughter's about to graduate next month, and she's already been accepted into Baylor to study psychology, so she's earned it.

"That is *so* not fair, Daddy! Why does Nova get a car and I don't?" Our sixteen-year-old daughter shouts and runs to catch up with Merc as he storms in our direction.

My eyes meet Novas, excitement sparking in our matching irises. "Shit. Shelby's with Dad. You better drive this beast, baby girl."

With a calming breath, Nova puts the car into gear and then peels out as she slams on the gas.

Nova's definitely my daughter, one hundred percent. She doesn't get that lead foot from cupcake. Not that he's given me a chance to ever race him, the bastard. I think he's too chicken to get beat by his woman, but he swears it's because he doesn't want to see me lose to him. And we all know the stubborn man would never throw the race, even if it came to me. Not that I'd want him to. I'm perfectly capable of winning on my own.

"Where's Hemi?" I ask over the rumbling engine and stereo.

"Last I saw him he was talking to some girl on his cell."

I'm pretty certain Nova's twin brother's going to be hitting me up for a car next, or worse, asking Mercenary for a damn Harley.

"Who? Do you know her?"

She shrugs. "The last thing I want to overhear is his phone sex conversations."

"Ugh, Nova! That's my son!"

"He's my brother, I feel the same way." She makes a quick bleh face at me before concentrating on the road again.

Jesus, when did these kids grow up? I blinked, and they were no longer my babies but young adults.

We lasted two years before I threw the birth control out the window and demanded my stud give me a baby. The club was in a good place with possible enemies, and I had an abundance of his attention. I grew up alone nearly my entire youth. I wanted family and a lot of it.

What are the odds we'd get pregnant with twins on the first go? I was absolutely terrified when we found out. I had no parents, so how could I be a decent mother? Especially to two crying, pooping babies at the same time? Thankfully Mercenary's mother and father stepped in to offer advice and a compassionate ear to listen when we were feeling overwhelmed.

Being first time parents wasn't easy by any means but loving the twins and each other was effortless. Having Mercenary around all the time to demand random sex and spoil me, definitely helped get us through the rougher times. It seemed like once we finally caught our stride with the twins, that Shelby decided to surprise us. She's completely rotten too, every bit of the sixteen-year-old princess, but I'd have her no other way. I never had that freedom to be carefree, and I relish in seeing her so innocent and happy in life.

Hemi is another story all together. He's so much like his father it drives me crazy some days. I thought men grew into the broodiness, but hell no, that's not true. I have a broody-ass eighteen-year-old alpha who thinks he's God's gift to women. Hemi seems to believe that he has a chance with any female under the age of thirty, and cupcake eggs him on without a thought. Betty, Mercenary's mom, tells me that he was the exact same way at that age too.

And I'm in love—complete mind-blowing, soul shattering, heartwarming love with my ol' man. If I could go back and do it all over again, would I flip him like I did? Damn right. The stubborn biker needed to know he'd met his match, and I'm pretty sure that move hooked him from the start. He's been good to me all this time. I couldn't ask for a better man in my life. He loves me as if every day is his last and he's been a damn good father to our children.

With them, I'll grow old feeling loved, knowing what it is to love, and never be alone again.

MERCENARY

"I thought Nova wasn't getting a race car, Daddy?" Shelby's bottom lip trembles as she stares at me with a look like I killed a kitten.

"I had nothing to do with that." I point toward the car as we watch the ass end lurch forward with Nova driving like a maniac. "You know your mom does whatever she thinks is right."

Tears crest in her eyes and I swallow roughly. I don't do so well when my girls cry—any of them. Seeing them sad makes me feel like I've been stabbed in the chest. "But…" she whispers, trailing off as a tear breaks free, wetting her cheek as it runs down the creamy skin.

"What, baby? What is it?" I question softly and pull her to my chest where more of her tears break free.

"Mom always drives with Nova."

"Yeah? Why does that upset you so much?"

"Because she believes that Nova is so much like her."

"They have a lot in common, that's all." I attempt to reason as she hiccups.

"Nova's going off to college…but, *I'm* like mom."

"Well, you're all stubborn like your momma." A chuckle breaks free, as I think of my headstrong ol' lady.

"No, Dad," she pulls away, meeting my gaze with a new fire burning in her irises I've never seen before. "I want to race." She hisses and at that moment she's right, she's every bit Chevelle twenty years ago.

Sweet Jesus, I feel for the kid who falls in love with her. He'll have his hands full. Not that it'll happen before she's at least thirty.

"If you're serious, Shelby, I'll talk it over with your mom." I give in, not wanting her to be upset. I'd rather we know what she's doing versus her attempting to hide it from us. I'm an asshole to nearly everyone else, but one tear from my little girl and I'm bending over backward without blinking to make her happy.

She pops up, suddenly full of pep, and pecks my cheek. "Thanks, Daddy, love you!" And miraculously the tears instantly disappear, and she runs off toward the house.

Brat...she's spoiled like her mom! I wouldn't change them for the world though. I've never loved someone so much in my life.

HEMI

"Bro, you're not going to fuck her." My buddy Maverick chides through the phone. He's a couple years older than me, and he recently got his patch. His dad let him start prospecting for the Oath Keepers MC back when he turned eighteen. He thinks he's a total badass now because of it.

"I'm giving it two weeks at the most."

"Hmm, two weeks? You want to bet on it?"

"I've got fifty saying I hit it."

"All right, if it doesn't happen by the beginning of week three, you owe me fifty bucks."

"Done," I state firmly, knowing I'll wear her guard down by then.

Hybrid Collection

He laughs. "You need to hurry up and come prospect for the club. The brothers would get in on this bet in a heartbeat and then you'd really lose some money."

I snort. "Because losing money should make me want to join up even faster?"

"No, because you'd have the entire club behind you. Think of the cash you'd get if you won."

"You have a point Mav; maybe I should talk to my dad about joining..."

THE END

STAY UP TO DATE WITH SAPPHIRE

Email
authorsapphireknight@yahoo.com

Website
www.authorsapphireknight.com

Facebook
www.facebook.com/AuthorSapphireKnight

Sapphire Knight

Also By Sapphire:

Oath Keepers MC Series
Secrets
Exposed
Relinquish
Forsaken Control
Friction
Princess
Sweet Surrender – free short story
Love and Obey – free short story
Daydream
Baby
Chevelle
Cherry

Russkaya Mafiya Series
Secrets
Corrupted
Corrupted Counterparts – free short story
Unwanted Sacrifices
Undercover Intentions

Dirty Down South Series
1st Time Love
3 Times the Heat

Standalones
Gangster
Unexpected Forfeit
The Main Event – free short story
Oath Keepers MC Collection
Russian Roulette
Tease – Short Story Collection
Oath Keepers MC Hybrid Collection

Capo Dei Capi Vendetti
The Vendetti Empire - part 1
The Vendetti Queen - part 2

Printed in Great Britain
by Amazon